Although this book was ☑ **W9-BID-889** speaks of today's politics and problems. Read and reflect.

the President

a novel

PARKER HUDSON

MULTNOMAH PUBLISHERS | SISTERS, OREGON

THE PRESIDENT
© 1995 F. Parker Hudson

Published by Multnomah Publishers, Inc.

Edited by Rodney L. Morris
and Danelle McCafferty

Cover design by Kirk DouPonce

Printed in the United States of America.

International Standard Book Number: 1-57673-457-9

For information:
Multnomah Publishers, Inc.
Post Office Box 1720
Sisters, Oregon 97759

98 99 00 01 02 03 04 05 — 11 10 9 8 7 6 5 4 3 2 1

FOR OUR CHILDREN

Chanler, Parker, Marshall, William, and Michael

That we Americans may reverse our ways and
pass on to the next generation a nation
better than our parents gave us.

Foreword

Like most authors who have found themselves immersed in such a project, I could write a short book about writing this book. Instead I'll summarize the process by stating that watching this manuscript evolve has been one of the most uplifting experiences of my life.

Acknowledging the critical technical help on this novel is best saved for the end, where the final word can be of thanks to those who helped so much. I do want to acknowledge that the historical quotations cited herein are found in the works of Dave Barton (*The Myth of Separation*) and Gary DeMar (*American Christian History: The Untold Story* and *You've Heard It Said*), both of whom helped me greatly.

I also want to thank Michael Youssef, Gene and Ruth Williams, Bill Roper, Bradley and Susan Fulkerson, John and Laura Wise, Van Hudson, Roy and Nell Ludwig, Jim and Sally Wilson, Gil and Bonnie Meredith, Mike McDevitt, Roy Jones, Page Aiken, Mark Stiles, Sergey Riabokobylko, Terry Parker, Chip Traynor, Bick Cardwell, Currell and Margot Berry, Charles Wilmer, Hank McCammish, and Lori Wells, all of whom made significant contributions to the final text or gave crucial encouragement. Their prayers, and those of many others, are particularly appreciated. Special thanks goes to Jan Dennis for his constructive criticism and to Ted Baehr for his prayers, suggestions, and encouragement. Of course any mistakes or oversights are my responsibility alone.

It's hard to imagine a better editor than Rod Morris or a more encouraging publishing team than the good people with Don Jacobson at Questar. And a last special thank you is saved for Danelle McCafferty, who showed me how to write ten words in only eight.

This is a novel begun and ended with thanks for all those who added so much to what you now hold in your hands. I sincerely hope it touches, entertains, and challenges you as much as it did me in writing it.

Prologue

UKRAINE On a windy and unseasonably cold late October evening, Yuri Kazminov drove his small Lada automobile along the nearly deserted highway, leaving behind the relative brightness of downtown Kiev and heading south into the dark Ukrainian countryside. Soon he would meet the truck at the appointed crossroad and lead it to the location that only he and his best friend, Peter, had known about for several years.

Unlike most Ukrainians, Yuri hated all Russians. Ever since Chernobyl had opened his eyes to the truth, he had been consumed with seeking revenge on their "fraternal brothers" to the north. And he thanked God, if there was a God, that he and Peter had been given this chance to avenge the death and destruction the Russians had inflicted on his people. As he sped along the highway, he thought about the circumstances that had led to this night's meeting...

When the Soviet Union split apart in the last months of 1991, after the August coup in Moscow, Yuri's position in the Soviet Missile Force stationed in his native Ukraine had given him a unique opportunity. During those months of confusion, Russia and Ukraine were disputing control of the Black Sea Fleet and all other Soviet military assets in the second largest republic.

Yuri Kazminov was a nuclear transport sergeant stationed in southern Ukraine, near Perzomaisk. While many of their friends had mixed loyalties, Yuri and Peter knew they were Ukrainians first and Soviets last. That belief had grown stronger when they read the first clandestine pamphlets about the horrors of the Red Army's expulsion of Poles and White Russians from Ukraine in 1921 and of the forced collectivization of the rich Ukrainian farms that followed. That process, culminating in the man-made "famine" of 1933 ordered by Stalin, resulted in the death or departure of virtually everyone who owned land, who was educated, or who understood simple commerce.

Then came Chernobyl in 1986. In Yuri's mind it was a terrible tragedy made worse by Russia's callous disregard for human life: they built unsafe nuclear plants in Ukraine and elsewhere to provide electricity for themselves.

In November 1991, on what would turn out to be one of their last missions in the Soviet Missile Force, Yuri and Peter by a stroke of luck drew an assignment together transporting nine nuclear warheads for their SS-19 missiles from the division's train depot to its hardened storage site, located thirty kilometers away for protection from missile attack. It was normal to make such moves at night to avoid the American satellites overhead. Usually a three-man team was assigned to the task, but the Russian sergeant who normally accompanied them was ill, and as the Soviet system ground on by inertia, it was not out of the ordinary for the job to be done by two. That meant, however, that in this case two Ukrainian nationalists were alone with nine Soviet warheads.

Using the excuse of changing a tire to explain the time delay and altering the nine on the transport manifest to an eight, Yuri and Peter executed their well-thought-out plan of stealing a warhead. They spent two hours burying it in a location concealed from the main military road by a small hill, an equipment shed, and trees—a place they had chosen for just such an opportunity two months earlier.

As Yuri had expected, the Soviet Missile Force split the following week, and he was dumped onto the streets of Kiev without a job. He and Peter waited for the opportunity to sell their "Russian gift" to someone who would help make the Russians pay for all they had done, in Yuri's and Peter's minds, to their native land.

Eventually they were hired as drivers for one of the newly privatized trucking firms. But the trucking business and the open markets attracted the "mafia." In the vacuum created by the turmoil in their society, when making a profit was still technically a crime and laws were only partially enforced, various groups "protected" those in legitimate enterprises for a "fee," with true criminals focusing on the trades with the greatest cash turnover.

One dark morning while he was waiting for his truck to be loaded in Kiev, Yuri overheard two drivers who were apparently from a small republic still trying to break away from Russia's domination. They were talking about a rumored offer of $1 million in cash for a nuclear warhead to be used in threatening the destruction of a Russian city, thereby either forcing independence or creating a large number of dead Russians.

Yuri had joined in the conversation, encouraging the men in their hope for independence and eventually asking them about the rumor. One of the drivers replied he had heard it the day before in the Kiev market, reportedly from a mafia type named Poznikov.

A few days of listening and asking questions had finally culminated in a meeting with Poznikov at the back of Yuri's truck. An obtuse question brought confirmation of what Yuri had heard from the drivers, including the $1 million reward, and the intended use of the warhead for independence from Russia. Yuri said he might know of someone who could help, and he asked for a meeting with whomever would be providing the reward.

It had taken two weeks, but eventually Yuri and Peter were invited to dinner in a quiet corner of the Castle Restaurant, located in the Passage off Kreshatik in downtown Kiev. It was a feast like neither of them had seen in many years. Their host, who appeared to be a leader in one branch of the Ukrainian mafia, paid with hard currency.

By the end of that evening a deal had been struck. Yuri would meet a truck with the necessary equipment for loading a heavy crate and be shown two suitcases with $500,000 each. If he was satisfied, he would then lead the truck to a site in southern Ukraine, where Peter would be waiting with a nuclear device that the two partners guaranteed would meet their host's requirements. Their host, plus an expert to verify their claim, were invited to come on the appointed night.

That dinner had been three nights before, and now Yuri glanced in his rear-view mirror at the lights from the Mercedes and the truck that followed his humble Lada to the spot where the warhead was buried. An hour before, when they had met at the appointed crossroad, he had run his hands across the American $100 bills in the two large briefcases, satisfied after a quick inspection that the bills were real and that they were all there. His mind raced, imagining what he and his wife could do with so much money. Those images made the long trip seem much shorter.

It was a little after one in the morning when the three vehicles turned into the same dirt road that Yuri and Peter had traversed in late 1991. Soon they pulled up next to the equipment shed where Peter was waiting, shovel in hand, having unearthed the crate and also dug channels around its sides.

From the Mercedes three men emerged. The shortest one headed for the hole next to Peter, where Yuri joined them. The other two stayed by the car. Yuri recognized their host from the dinner. He assumed the other, darker man was the mafia's client from the breakaway republic, although it was hard to distinguish his features in the dark. There were also three large men who had driven in the truck. They stood off to the side in respectful silence while the small man and Peter pried off the top of the crate.

Once the contents were revealed, the visitor knelt down and worked for about ten minutes with some special tools he had brought. When finished he returned to the Mercedes, nodded, and spoke softly to the two men standing in the cold. Then their dinner host advanced, smiling, shook Yuri's and Peter's hands, and motioned for the three large men to finish dislodging the crate and load it onto the truck.

Peter and Yuri stood watching as the three men did as directed. Once the crate was hoisted onto the truckbed and covered with a tarp, the guest by the car nodded his approval to the mafia host. He opened the door of the Mercedes, extracted the two briefcases, then walked over to Peter and Yuri, who were smiling nervously.

He placed both briefcases on the ground in front of him, knelt down and opened the latches on one. The top popped open, hiding its contents from the two friends. The mafia boss reached inside and pulled out a large automatic pistol with a silencer already attached. Yuri just had time to raise one hand in stunned disbelief before the bullet split his head; Peter's futile attempt to turn and run only meant it took two shots to end his life instead of one.

The briefcases were retrieved, and the three large men silently set about burying the two bodies in the grave Peter had unknowingly dug for Yuri and himself. Soon the convoy departed with one of the large men driving each of the two cars. Hours later these were dumped into deep lakes more than a hundred kilometers apart.

The Mercedes headed back toward Kiev, following the truck with its prize. The short nuclear weapons expert rode in the front seat of the Mercedes with the driver, while the mafia boss and his guest exchanged pleasantries in the back. Anyone hearing the accent of the guest would have known that he was not from any small Soviet republic, but rather from the Middle East.

For one rule the Ukrainian mafia had already learned about their nation's emerging free enterprise system: the finest goods go to the highest bidder.

BOOK ONE

I have lived, Sir, a long time, and the longer I live, the more convincing proofs I see of this truth—that God Governs in the affairs of men. And if a sparrow cannot fall to the ground without his notice, is it probable that an empire can rise without his aid? We have been assured, Sir, in the sacred writings, that "except the Lord build the House, they labor in vain that build it." I firmly believe this; and I also believe that without his concurring aid we shall succeed in this political building no better, than the Builders of Babel: We shall be divided by our partial local interests; our projects will be confounded, and we ourselves shall become a reproach and bye word down to future ages. And what is worse, mankind may hereafter from this unfortunate instance, despair of establishing Governments by Human wisdom and leave it to chance, war and conquest.

I therefore beg leave to move—that henceforth prayers imploring the assistance of Heaven, and its blessings on our deliberations, be held in this Assembly every morning before we proceed to business, and that one or more of the clergy of this city be requested to officiate in that service.

BENJAMIN FRANKLIN
THE CONSTITUTIONAL CONVENTION, JUNE 28, 1787

I

Several Years from Now
Tuesday, April 3

WASHINGTON It was six o'clock and still dark that early April morning when the Secret Service agent made his quick call on the telephone outside the living quarters in the White House. He then opened the door for the National Security briefing officer who had arrived minutes before, and escorted him into the living room. In the bedroom, President William Harrison, who had just received the call, turned on the bedside lamp and said to his half-sleeping wife, "I'll be right back." He got out of bed, put on his robe, then walked out into the living room.

"Excuse me, sir," the officer said, always a little embarrassed, despite the nature of his job. "This is not all that momentous, but it is unusual. And we knew it was almost time for you to wake up."

The president replied, "That's fine. Whenever you folks think I should know something, by all means bring it on."

The officer handed the president a summary page and waited respectfully for a few moments while he read it. Then the younger man added, "The unusual thing, besides the note on his body, is that nothing like this has happened since the end of the cold war. Thompson was one of our best agents. He was working in Odessa with the Ukrainian government's approval, following up on the longstanding rumor about the missing warhead. He was too good and too experienced to have been killed by one man. And, as you can read, he had been dead for only a few hours when he was found in that deserted warehouse. At the regular intelligence briefing this morning CIA will ask for permission to flood the area with agents and cash to pick up useful information before the trail goes cold. We thought you might want to get a jump on the situation early, since you will probably want to call the Ukrainian president, if the CIA's request is granted."

"Yes, yes. Thanks a lot," the president said, reading again the last paragraph which described the note found on Thompson's corpse. The note read, "The first of millions of Americans who will die by our hands. The Council." He did not recognize the organization or even its country of origin. The president frowned and returned the briefing paper to the officer, who turned and left.

The president returned to his bedroom, took off his robe, and got back into bed. He put his arm loosely around the waist of his wife, who was lying on her side, with her back to him. He sighed into her hair.

Carrie Harrison half-turned and asked sleepily, "What was that about?"

After William had explained the situation, Carrie asked, "Do you think there could really be any connection with that missing warhead? Or was that just a coincidence?"

"I wish I could tell you. I wish I could tell *them.*" He sighed again. "A junior year abroad at a German University and I'm supposed to be a foreign policy expert!"

"Well, you've learned a lot about it already during these first months. After all, it's quite a jump from the governor of North Carolina to the White House."

He paused in the semidarkness as he considered her encouragement. "But I told them during the campaign that I'm a foreign policy expert," he whispered, "so I can't very well go back now and say, 'Stop the world for six months while I catch up and figure out what's really going on.'"

"Well," she said, rolling on her side again and taking his hand in hers, "all of the men who've lived here have had to learn a lot. You'll do just fine. You're *already* doing just fine."

"You know, during these first few months of sleeping here I've sometimes wondered what I could learn if only these walls could talk."

"And I've often wondered," she said, snuggling backward into him, "whether these walls might listen and watch, rather than talk. When the Secret Service says they guard you twenty-four hours a day, William, do you think they check on your breathing in here?"

"That's an interesting thought," he agreed. He started to say, "Let's find out." But the words wouldn't come. At an earlier time in their marriage the two of them would have given any potential eavesdropper something to listen to. *What, twenty-five years ago? Even twenty?* he thought as the new day outside their windows began to brighten. *But not now. Not for a long time.* He sighed quietly, but didn't make a move.

He and Carrie just didn't do such things, not spontaneously. They hadn't for years. He seldom thought about it except just for brief moments at rare times such as this, when the crush of being the president of the United States—or previously the governor of North Carolina or a busy lawyer—stopped long enough for him to consider their relationship.

It was pleasant enough, he thought. What word could he use? *Familiar? Comfortable? Set? Convenient? Friendly? Just There?* They knew each other like two old friends. He had his habits, she had hers. She was loyal, concerned, and helpful. He was pleasant, friendly, and successful. They even occasionally made love on a sort of infrequent unspoken schedule. They went through life as a matched set, living together and trying to raise two children in difficult circumstances.

But real love? Early morning passion? No, he thought, *those emotions faded away years ago. Or rather, I stopped them.* Not that he cheated on her. At least not recently. Several years ago when he was a busy, aspiring attorney flying from city to city he'd had a few brief flings. And then one serious affair with a beautiful, smart young attorney from their Charlotte office. Diana Johnson. She had wanted him to divorce Carrie and to marry her. He had considered it for months. She broke off their relationship when it was finally obvious that William wanted to stay conveniently married to Carrie and living with his children.

No, he didn't cheat on Carrie. Not now; not with AIDS out there and a political career. Except he cheated on her every day by withholding his innermost feelings and his most difficult decisions. Somewhere along the years they had lost the total sharing which they had experienced in the early days. Slowly and imperceptibly—then more quickly while he was spending so much time in Charlotte with Diana—he had built a wall between them. An invisible wall. Not of overt hostility. Just of constant and incredible busyness, every waking hour of the day. A wall of not sharing, and of not loving.

During just the past few months he had come to realize how much Carrie was hurt by his years of withdrawal, but pride and habit kept him from reaching out. He was so busy! *I don't have time to share things she won't understand anyway.*

They had been married in a firestorm of passion after his first year of law school. But after the kids were born and his legal practice grew, William found it harder and harder to relate to Carrie. She stayed at home; he was surrounded by equally intelligent, dynamic women in his business life. Diana had captured him with her youthful intelligence, her business sense, and her wit as well. He began sharing his aspirations and his problems with Diana when they met for weekend "company retreats." Carrie didn't know she was competing in a contest, but she lost nevertheless. Finally, completely he gave up trying to relate his world to hers, and he relegated Carrie to a second class position. Carrie became less of a partner and more of a fixture. The passion left their marriage, and Carrie couldn't understand why.

When Diana left him William's exclusion of Carrie turned hostile for a few months. She couldn't comprehend his constant putdowns. Then he seemed to mellow, and the hostility stopped, but so did all other feelings as well. He was neither hot nor cold toward her. Just completely aloof; it was like the door to his soul slammed shut, leaving her alone in the cold and the dark.

As his first gubernatorial campaign picked up steam he concentrated totally on politics. She thought their relationship would return to normal after the election, but it never did. She tried for years to figure out what had happened, what she could do to be his wife and lover and soulmate again; but after a few years his aloofness became so well defined, and he seemed so uninterested in changing, that she finally accepted the way things were and made the best of it, hoping that someday, somehow, he would let her inside again.

She ached when she thought about it, so she tried to avoid the subject by making herself busy and helpful. Always hoping. Always knowing that she was excluded, but not knowing why. For several years she had consoled herself with the bottle; but finally her own pride pulled her out of that pit, at least on most days. When they "made love" she sometimes had to bite her lip to keep from crying. *Where did you go, William? And why? What did I do? Please share with me. Please let me inside. Please love me again!*

For his part, since the end of the presidential campaign William had reflected on several occasions how awful he had behaved toward Carrie over the years. At times there seemed to be a battle going on inside him, one force telling him to continue to ignore her, that he didn't have time to relate to her given the incredible responsibilities his team felt to implement their programs for improving the nation. But occasionally another voice reminded him of their early days together and urged him to restore their relationship. He felt that tension this April morning, but did nothing, not wanting to open a potential cauldron of emotions when it was almost time to start another important day as president of the United States.

So the president and first lady lay together in their private bedroom in the White House for another ten minutes without speaking. He kept his arm around her but was careful not to squeeze too tightly. His mind quickly turned from their relationship to the more immediate events of his day. She held his hand loosely, her head turned away from him. She, too, tried to think about all she had to do that day; but for once in a long while the pain and the emptiness of their lost love crashed through into her emotions, and, unseen to him, a single tear ran down her cheek.

NORFOLK, VIRGINIA Thomas Dobbs, a bachelor and a lieutenant commander in the United States Navy, could hardly bear the sound of his alarm clock through his hangover. Why had he done this to himself on a weeknight, knowing he had to report to his duty station early the next morning?

Well, it was a great celebration, he thought, as he slowly lifted his still sleeping date's arm from his chest and swung his feet to the floor of his tastefully decorated Virginia Beach apartment. But now he was paying the price for last night's liquor and late-night transgressions. And what was this young thing's name, whom he had picked up at the bar? *Oh, yes. Pat,* he remembered.

Too bad his steady of two years had been transferred to a Mediterranean base three months earlier. What a joy it would have been to share yesterday's news that he had finally received orders to be the operations officer on a guided missile cruiser. Not the newest warship in the navy, but still an excellent assignment. He had not known which to do first: write the new president a letter of thanks or celebrate with his friends at the bar. Unfortunately for his pounding head this morning, the bar had come first.

Fifteen minutes later he had shaved, dressed, and taken several aspirins with strong coffee. He decided to leave a note and some money for Pat. He hoped this pick-up would not steal him blind later in the morning. Gathering his things, he placed a note on the bedside table where Pat couldn't miss it on awakening.

Thomas unlatched his apartment door and thought how nice it would be to come home to Pat after a hard day in the navy. That pleasant thought was the best medicine for his hangover. Yes, he would call the apartment in a few hours and invite Pat to stay with him for at least one more night.

RALEIGH, NORTH CAROLINA At about that same time, Mary Prescott finished her usual morning quiet time. She rose from the comfortable seat in the nook of her bedroom by the large picture window. The first light of dawn was backlighting the early buds of spring in the heavy foliage around their home in suburban Raleigh.

Mary walked quietly to the kitchen for another cup of coffee and fixed one for her husband, Graham, who would momentarily awaken to his alarm clock.

She heard the shower running upstairs in her daughter Sarah's bathroom. The stereo beat on the ceiling of their dining room meant Sarah's younger brother, Tim, was also awake, "gearing up" for the ninth grade.

Her husband had been right. Even with the recent addition of a grandson from Jonathan and his wife, having Sarah and Tim several years behind Jonathan had kept her feeling young for an "old woman" of fifty-two.

Thirty minutes later, with everyone dressed, the Prescotts were sharing a large breakfast that was still their tradition, despite the health warnings about most of its contents. Her husband, a loving man from a large family, had insisted as their schedules became crazier that they at least share breakfast together during the week as a touchpoint. And the two children, now a junior and a freshman in high school, had been sharing it for so long that they, too, missed this family time together on those rare occasions when one of them had a conflict.

Graham Prescott was an engineer, like his wife's retired father, Thomas, who was still going strong at seventy-eight. Raised on a farm, Graham had met Mary Harrison at a college fraternity party. They had fallen in love, and as was the custom at that time, they had been married in the summer after their graduation. Their first son, Jonathan, had been born ten months later. He was now married and a father himself, giving them a grandson, Peter. It seemed to Mary only yesterday that her two younger children, Sarah and Tim, had been born. How the generations ran together!

She smiled across the table at her two children as they discussed the most recent developments at school. "Hey," Tim asked Sarah, "isn't today the day they're going to tell us about that new computer?"

"Yeah," Sarah said. "It's supposed to be something amazing."

Their father, who enjoyed computers, looked up from his breakfast. "Tim, do you know anything about it yet?"

"Not much. But some bio-tech firm in the Research Triangle supposedly bought this really advanced computer just last year. Only now they've had to buy an even newer one. So they're donating their 'old' computer to our school, I guess because so many of the kids' parents work in the Triangle."

"Sounds interesting," Graham said.

"This thing is supposed to be just awesome!" Tim went on excitedly. "It's like a hundred thousand times faster than anything available until just a few years ago. They're going to run terminals to most of the classrooms, and we'll be able to use it to solve all sorts of problems."

"And someone even said it can do virtual reality," Sarah said. "I guess that means," she added, "we'll be able to put on headsets during breaks and travel anywhere we want to go or see anything we want to see."

"It all sounds wild to me," Mary interjected, as she finished her coffee. "I just hope you can spell and do math when you graduate without having to turn on some black box to do it."

"Oh, Mom," Sarah said, finishing her breakfast and rising, "you know we can do that. This computer is just going to make school a lot more interesting."

Glancing at the clock, Mary said to Sarah, "Well, you and Tim had better get going, or you're going to miss that special assembly."

After another thirty minutes Graham also left for work, and Mary quietly dressed for a busy day of appointments as one of Raleigh's most successful real estate agents.

ATLANTA, GEORGIA Rebecca Harrison, Mary's younger sister, did not have to wake up so early that morning. Her only child, Courtney, the product of a short and tempestuous marriage while Rebecca was still in college, had graduated from the University of Georgia and was a management trainee with a large bank in Denver.

Rebecca, who had never remarried, had thrown herself into her nursing career to provide for herself and for her young daughter. But that had been more than twenty years ago. Now, at age forty-four, Rebecca was a senior Ob/Gyn nurse at Peachtree North Hospital, one of Atlanta's largest and most prestigious private hospitals. Or, that is to say, semi-private. Since passage of the National Health Plan a few years earlier, there was virtually no truly private health care available in America. Every hospital, including Rebecca's, had to participate in the plan and follow the guidelines if it wanted to survive financially. So there was now a much greater mix of client types than in previous years.

Because Rebecca was working on the afternoon/evening shift at the hospital that week, there was no reason for her to wake up so early. Except for Bruce Tinsley. Six years younger than Rebecca and originally from Boston, Bruce was the first man in years she had allowed herself to become seriously involved with. They had first met at the Buckhead Health Club where Rebecca worked hard to make her body look half as old as its forty-four years. She had believed him, three weeks later, when he told her he thought she was thirty-two. She had fallen for him almost immediately. He had moved into her apartment in January.

On almost every morning for the three months they had lived together, Rebecca got up, even when she didn't have to, in order to fix her younger lover's breakfast. Their relationship and his doting over her had picked her up immeasurably, and there was now a bounce to her step and a lilt to her voice that had long been buried by single-parent responsibilities and the demands of her profession.

When Bruce finished his shower and came into the kitchen, clad only in a towel, he found Rebecca still in her nightgown and robe. She was humming a tune and stirring their oatmeal on the stove. "So, how is Ms. Harrison this beautiful morning?" he asked, as he came up behind her and kissed her gently on the neck. She shivered and laughed. "Not bad for an old broad with two jobs: nursing a floor of patients by day and keeping a younger man by night." She turned and smiled up at him.

"Well, if I haven't told you before, I *really* appreciate how you do both," he said, returning her smile.

"The *night* job I understand why you appreciate," she said, running her finger down his chest. "But what do you know about the day job?"

"Well, I don't want to turn too serious this early in the morning, but I do read the newspaper and watch television. I know what all of you at the hospital have to go through. Just to get to your jobs some days, you have to run the gauntlet of those crazy abortion protestors. And now the medical board is gearing up to fight your patients' right to die when they want to."

Rebecca knew that Bruce's younger brother had died tragically of AIDS several years before. Bruce was quick to blame the government's lack of research and intervention for his brother's early death. He had become an activist where medical care was concerned, belittling those who protested any part of the activist agenda, including abortion, euthanasia, or AIDS research.

"So that's why I appreciate so much what you do," he concluded with a smile, putting his arms around her.

"Well, you'd better not let my sister, Mary, hear you. Though you and brother William should get along famously!"

"How can two people from the same family be so different?" he asked.

"Beats me. As we've all grown older, Mary has become even more set in the ways of her faith, and William has perfected Mom's liberal agenda while moving to the top of the political ladder."

Bruce shook his head and chuckled, "When your family gets together there must be some real explosions!"

"Sometimes there are," she admitted. "But at least little brother Hugh and I are not as outspoken, so we try to keep peace between the older two. You'll see for yourself when we get together at Camp David for Easter."

"Are you sure you really want me to come? Do you think your extended family's ready for the new perks of presidential living *and* a live-in boyfriend for the little sister?"

"Absolutely. It'll do them good!" She grinned. "After all, my brother promised to change the country for the better. And I figure having you move in right after his inauguration was my own personal contribution to making life better, at least for one overworked and underpaid nurse!"

"Well, I definitely want to come. But just remember I warned you," he finished, still smiling and pulling her closer to him.

"Noted," she said, then gave him a gentle push. "Now please sit down and let me finish cooking this oatmeal before it all boils away."

ATLANTIC OCEAN ON BOARD THE USS *FORTSON* Hugh Harrison, the youngest of the four siblings in the president's family, began that same April morning two hundred miles out in the Atlantic ocean as his guided missile cruiser steamed westward at an economic speed, expecting to make their homeport of Norfolk, Virginia, the next day. Hugh, as the weapons officer on the *Fortson,* had been invited with the executive officer and the other four department heads to Captain Robertson's cabin for breakfast, a first for Hugh during his two months on board.

To the untrained eye the *Fortson* looked like the most modern of fighting warships, with an anti-aircraft missile launcher forward, anti-ship missiles and torpedoes in canisters amidships, a helicopter platform and five-inch gun aft. Her modern radar and communications equipment was in every way state-of-the-art, and they had scored several kills in Operation Desert Storm, belying her thirty-nine years of age. But belowdecks the *Fortson* was a dinosaur, the last capital ship in the navy to operate on high pressure steam, rather than on the jet engines that powered all of her younger cousins.

No one knew why the *Fortson* was still steaming. The logical answer was that she had been completely overhauled and upgraded in the early nineties, so there was no economic reason to discard her. But all the other ships of her class had met that fate. Many sailors believed that the admirals running the navy kept her around as a visible link back to the days when steam drove all the navy's ships, and jet engines were found only on airplanes. But whatever the reason, there was a great sense of pride on the *Fortson,* and her clean decks and sparkling spaces looked newer than most others in the fleet.

Once the seven men had seated themselves around the large table in the captain's office and breakfast had been served from the adjoining small galley, the steward closed the door to leave the officers alone, and the captain cleared his voice.

"Please dig in while it's hot," he said with his "take charge" manner and a characteristic wave of his hand. "We've got a lot to talk about, but let's grab some chow first."

While they ate, the conversation did not stray from normal shipboard small talk. Hugh Harrison certainly had no idea why the captain had called this unusual meeting, and being relatively new on board despite his many years of naval experience, he was prepared to listen rather than lead the conversation.

The executive officer, or second-in-command, was Commander Richard Anglin. Commander Anglin was the perfect XO: he was a detail-oriented, serious-but-fair administrator who made an excellent match for the more gregarious Captain Robertson. "We're going to hate to lose you, Jimmy," Commander Anglin said, addressing Lieutenant Commander Jim McKnight, as the steward returned to pour coffee at the end of their meal. "But I'm sure you're ready for some shore duty to be with your family."

"Yes, sir, you're right. Shirley and the girls are looking forward to me being home, and I'm ready to start XO school myself next month."

Captain Robertson turned to Hugh Harrison. "Hugh, does the Secret Service watch your wife and kids, now that your brother is the president?"

"Not really, sir. Just his wife and kids. They called on us once and checked out our living situation and gave us some advice. But since we live in the naval community near the Norfolk base, they don't seem too concerned about us."

"Well, be careful. Even with the cold war over there's still a bunch of crazy people running around with all sorts of causes to promote. I'd hate to see your kids, or your wife, mixed up in anything like that."

"Thank you, sir. Having my older brother in the White House has, of course, made me think about a lot of things, and we're staying alert to any potential problems."

When the dishes had been cleared, except for seven cups of coffee, the captain leaned forward on the white tablecloth and signaled that it was time to start the real agenda.

"Gentlemen, the conversation we're about to have will undoubtedly prove to be one of the most difficult in my almost thirty years in the navy. I'm going to assume that, like me, you will not personally agree with everything you're about to hear. But I also assume that, like me, you're a committed officer, prepared to take orders from our commander in chief, even when you do not personally believe in them, so long as they don't violate our Constitution. So please bear with me on this, and try to think how we can make what I'm about to describe to you work, rather than fretting about why it's happening. Because, gentlemen, trying to buck this order will apparently do us no good whatsoever."

He sat for a moment and slowly looked around the table, meeting each man's eyes for a moment, letting his words sink in before proceeding.

"You may remember that before we left for this missile firing exercise last week I went to Washington for a day. I was called to a series of meetings in the Pentagon, and what I'm about to tell you is the result of those meetings. I've waited until after our training exercise to talk with all of you together so we could concentrate on the missile shots that had to be accomplished over the past several days. But now, as we head back to Norfolk, we have this new issue that will require our full attention, although it's of a completely different nature." There was another pause, then Robertson leaned even further forward, looked down at his hands momentarily, exhaled slowly, and began again.

"As you certainly know, each of the armed services has been trying to deal with the two issues of women and gays serving on active duty status ever since the broad guideline of inclusion was handed down several years ago. It appears the measures which the navy has taken to date have not been adequate, at least not for the more militant advocates, nor for our president." Robertson paused, and Hugh Harrison noted a few glances in his direction.

"So, our new president has signed another executive order mandating affirmative action. We have been given twenty-four months to implement it in every phase of military life.

"Our meeting in Washington was with the chief of Naval Operations to discuss the navy's two new experiments, one on the East Coast and one on the West, on how best to implement the president's order in the real world of manning and fighting a U.S. naval warship.

"On the West Coast our sister ship, the USS *Pierce,* is the ship that has been chosen for the experiment. Gentlemen, we are the ship chosen on the East Coast."

Again he paused and looked around but was met by neutral stares. "Here are our orders. Hugh, your weapons department is going to get a new section in Fourth Division: all women who have been selected from shore stations, training commands, and missile ranges around the world. Our new missile fire control officer will be Ms. Teri Slocum. She's an Annapolis graduate. These ladies—or women, I guess it is—will berth as a group in somewhat modified Fourth Division spaces. By the way, Hugh, all of your current fire-control technicians will be reassigned to shore duty unless they specifically request a ship, so there should be some relatively happy families there."

Another pause and a glance at his hands. This time Captain Robertson spoke more slowly.

"After we return to Norfolk we're going to slip over to the yard for two weeks to receive some modifications to our living quarters." Looking at Lieutenant Henry Early, the administrative officer, the captain continued, "Henry, you're going to have some admin personnel replacements in the ship's office. All seven of them are lesbians. And, Bill," he addressed Lieutenant Commander William Hatcher, the supply officer, "Supply Division will receive twelve homosexual men."

There was a general stirring in the captain's cabin as the officers responsible for operating the ship cleared their throats, looked down at their hands, or shifted in their seats. *What has William done now?* Hugh thought.

"I'm told by those who supposedly know more than we ever will about this subject that the only way women, gays, and lesbians can be assured a fair chance at both numerical equality and non-discrimination in advancement is by creating divisions made up of people with similar characteristics, and putting them on board fighting ships like ours. I offer you that wisdom, and I hope you'll keep it in mind when and if some problems ever arise, which I certainly hope will not happen.

"Finally, to insure that the leadership on this ship is sensitive to all of these new needs, we will not only have Lieutenant Teri Slocum in the wardroom, but Jimmy McKnight's relief as operations officer will be Lieutenant Commander Thomas Dobbs, who is a homosexual."

There was more stirring and looking around by all of the men seated in the captain's stateroom.

"Please remember that this is an experiment. CNO is going to want an accurate report and evaluation from us after three months and again after six months. By the way, if you find our experiment interesting, on the USS *Pierce* there will be the same numerical quotas of women, gays, and lesbians, but these individuals will simply be sprinkled all around the *Pierce* in virtually every division. For berthing purposes, 'changing areas' will be installed in all of their sleeping quarters and *everyone* will be required to change behind these partitions, so as not to offend anyone else. Their experiment is apparently based on some other group of experts who believe the best policy is anonymity. I'm sure we'll all be interested to see how these two experiments turn out. Now, are there any questions?" the captain ended with a curious smile.

Silence greeted his question. Most of the men studied the tabletop. Hugh Harrison could not imagine how this plan could work, but he knew he was in no position to speak. Finally, Lieutenant Commander McKnight spoke up. "Captain, since I'm leaving, I guess I can say something. Has the navy lost its mind? This 'melting pot' of eighteen and nineteen-year-olds that we call the navy has just barely survived the combination of different ethnic backgrounds and races within our country. We throw young men together on a combat ship and immediately expect them to work as a team. Going to sea for six months with that already volatile mixture plus women, lesbians, and homosexuals is just asking for trouble. Don't they think there won't be fights? And there's not much room to separate two guys or two girls fighting over someone when the ship is only five hundred feet long, and we're stuck together for six months."

"And, Captain, what about our wives?" asked Lieutenant Commander Perry Colangelo, the engineering officer. "Forgetting about the possible consequences for these new groups, what will our wives say when they find out we're putting to sea with a whole division of women? The navy already has enough marital problems caused by long separation. How is this going to help?"

"You gentlemen just took the words out of my mouth. I said the same thing when we met in Washington last week; as did most of the squadron captains at the meeting. But those concerns carried no weight because the *political* decision had been made." Captain Robertson looked again at Hugh Harrison, who had not looked up from the table in some time. "I'm afraid we're going to have to make a go of it, do our best, and report up the chain of command what we see, hear, and experience. That's the policy. Now do any of you have any practical questions on actual implementation that we can talk about?"

The department heads stayed with the captain and executive officer for another twenty minutes talking about the details of transferring in and out such a large number of sailors at one time. At the end of their session the captain concluded, "By the end of today I want each of you to have a meeting similar to this one with your junior officers, chiefs, and leading petty officers. Please be enthusiastic and upbeat, no matter how you might actually feel. We simply have no choice but to give this experiment a chance, and the chiefs and petty officers will be the ones on whom much of the implementation responsibility will fall. They're going to have to be extra sensitive and extra helpful. Once we get these new people on board we'll be starting a regular training cycle, leading up to our scheduled deployment to the Mediterranean later this year. Coming back from Washington, it occurred to me that if the navy has to go through this, then I'm at least proud they've chosen our team to try to make it work. Let's give it our best."

ODESSA, UKRAINE, ONBOARD THE *BRIGHT STAR* It was already afternoon in the northern part of the Black Sea. There another ship, a freighter, prepared to depart the major Ukrainian port of Odessa to return to its home port in the Mediterranean Sea, further to the south. The captain of the *Bright Star* stood on the port bridge wing giving orders, as the nondescript freighter, similar to hundreds of others plying those waters, let go its last tie to the former Soviet republic and edged its way toward the mouth of the harbor. Watching these routine events from inside the shade of the wheelhouse was a tall, sunburned man with jet black hair and dark glasses. Although Sadim Muhmood was not the captain of the ship, he was nevertheless the leader of everyone and everything on the *Bright Star*, including the captain himself.

Once they were far enough from the docks to prevent his recognition by anyone who happened to be following the movements of the freighters in the harbor, Sadim joined the captain on the bridge wing and allowed the fresh breeze to revive his mind, which was slightly numbed from twenty-four hours without sleep.

"Allah has granted us good weather for the beginning of our voyage," said the captain in Arabic, speaking toward the sea, but loud enough for Sadim, who was standing behind him, to hear.

"Yes, we are grateful," responded Sadim in a low whisper, "but it is almost always so," he added, referring to their practice of leaving port only after a front passed to insure the smoothest possible transit, given the nature of their work.

"It's too bad about the American," the captain said.

Squinting his eyes behind the dark glasses as he remembered the previous evening's execution, Sadim responded, "He asked too many questions and was spending too much time at the docks. Besides, he was an infidel. Think of it this way: He had the privilege of being the first of what will be many, many Americans before we are finished." He smiled in satisfaction as he touched the captain on the shoulder. Then he headed into the wheelhouse and down the ladder that led belowdecks.

The *Bright Star* was of a traditional design for a dry goods freighter, with a raised four-story superstructure for the crews' quarters and command bridge located approximately one-third of the way back from the bow of the ship. There was a single hold forward of the bridge and three holds aft. Sadim descended the stairs through the working and living spaces in the freighter's superstructure until he came to a doorway that led out onto the afterdeck.

He did not exit, but instead placed his hand on a special sensor on the bulkhead at the landing. Three seconds later, after the computer matched his handprint with its entry authorization, Sadim passed through a door that was not part of the freighter's original design. He descended another ladder which was newer, cleaner, and better lit than the one coming down from the bridge.

These stairs took him down inside a void that had been created between the number one forward hold and the number four hold aft. In reality the number two and three holds, in the middle of the ship, were now only ten feet deep below the deck. Anyone opening a hatch from the deck and peering down for an inspection would see whatever goods the manifest declared they were carrying. But they always carried considerably less than the manifest stated, which mattered not to Sadim, so long as the papers were legitimate and no one on either end cared, which was always the case, thanks to the money that was paid.

At the bottom of this newer stairwell Sadim again placed his hand on a sensor in the bulkhead, and again a door opened, this time into the top floor of a three-level laboratory carved from the inside of the freighter. While the *Bright Star* had its normal share of dirt and rust, the laboratory was spotlessly clean, air-conditioned, and very bright. Sadim looked through the thick glass of the protective airlock and waved to a short man wearing white surgical-type clothing inside the lab. As the man walked toward the intercom on his side of the double door, Sadim reflected again how incredible it was to have such a complex facility inside such an ordinary-looking freighter. The facility had taken several years to build, while the special treasure from the Ukrainian countryside he and his colleague had purchased that singular night had remained hidden. But now the warhead was on board—it had been on board for three months—and his small team was well into its eighteen-month program of carefully refurbishing and slightly modifying the device. What a long journey it had been since the night when he and the man now approaching the thick glass, Andrei Kolikov, had first seen Allah's gift in the rich Ukrainian soil.

"We are underway for Tripoli, my friend. Is everything in order here?" Sadim asked, using the intercom built into the wall.

"Yes, everything is in order," came the reply from behind the white surgical mask. "We were able to find everything we needed in the usual ways, and we can now proceed to the next stage of our work."

"Well, we will be at sea for the next few days, but then we will tie up securely again for at least two weeks. May Allah speed your success. I will see you at dinner."

The man inside nodded and turned back toward his colleagues and their work.

Sadim retraced his steps up two ladders to his own spacious cabin, where he expected to be a voluntary prisoner for the next eighteen months. As he ascended the stairs he thought again how brilliant had been the Council's plan to use this freighter as their mobile work station, allowing them to spend most of their time in a very friendly and sympathetic port, yet giving them the mobility they needed to tap into the former Soviet supply system when parts or information were needed for their highly specialized work. This had been their second trip to Odessa in three months, and in each case they had been able to find exactly what they needed for the right amount of hard currency.

After the difficult events of the last twenty-four hours, Sadim was exhausted and ready to sleep. He considered again that they finally had a plan of revenge for the desecration of Palestine which no man, and certainly not this new American president, could stop.

Wait until the pictures start arriving at the White House and the Pentagon, Sadim smiled. *Will they do as we demand?* he wondered. *Or give us the pleasure of killing millions of their countrymen in one instant? Hopefully our pictures and threats will cause their leaders to worry for their very lives, and to suffer daily, as our people have suffered...*

ATLANTA Later that day Eunice Porter sat somewhat nervously in the Ob-Gyn waiting room at Peachtree North Hospital, one of Atlanta's largest and most prestigious hospitals. She was not nervous over the prospect of bearing a child, since she already had two young boys, although neither father lived with them. Nor was she particularly nervous over being at Peachtree North, even though it was a hospital she could never have frequented before the new National Health Plan made excellent health care more available to persons like her, who could not afford to pay.

She was nervous because she had taken one of the new "morning after" birth-control pills almost three months ago, but a drugstore pregnancy test and her own body suggested she was pregnant nevertheless. She had sworn that she would bring no more children into her life; she could barely make ends meet as a waitress. Yet now she nervously waited to learn whether or not she was really pregnant.

"Eunice Porter!" a familiar voice called. She turned to the next row of chairs and saw a friend from her high school days, Sally Kramer. Eunice smiled and moved over next to her acquaintance.

"Are you pregnant again?" Sally asked.

"I'm afraid I may be, despite a pill my boyfriend gave me. That's what I'm here to find out," Eunice replied. It was obvious she was not pleased at the prospect.

"Hmm," said Sally, glancing down at her magazine. "I found out I was pregnant a few weeks ago." There was a pause, and Sally quickly glanced around their seats. "Listen," she continued, lowering her voice, "if you *are,* would you like to learn how to make a quick five thousand dollars?"

"What do you mean?" asked Eunice.

"I mean instead of a pregnancy costing you money and messing up your life, would you like to earn five thousand dollars, like I'm doing?"

There was another pause as Eunice tried to imagine what her friend was talking about. Then she said, "Sure, I guess. How?"

WASHINGTON That afternoon President William Harrison and his closest advisors were gathered in the Oval Office in the West Wing of the White House. The first press conference of Harrison's new presidency was scheduled for the following week. They would have a full dress rehearsal on the day before the press conference, but for now they were reviewing subjects that would probably come up, talking through with Harrison how to field the reporters' questions. The best questions they hoped to turn to their own advantage; the hardest ones they hoped would at least do them no harm.

Seated in an imperfect circle around a large coffee table, with William Harrison at one end in a comfortable stuffed chair, were seven of Harrison's nine closest advisors. Jerome Richardson, his chief of staff, one of the few top advisors who had not also been intimately involved in their political campaign, chaired the meeting and would try to keep the agenda on track, even though the subject was relatively free form. A tall, Harvard-educated African-American who had been the CEO of a major New York securities firm, Richardson gave no doubt whenever he was in any room that he was in charge, except when he was in a room with President Harrison.

Ted Braxton, one of Harrison's oldest and closest friends from North Carolina, had been a young, brilliant economist based in Charlotte. His focused reports had led him to become a syndicated columnist, and he was now the president's domestic policy advisor. He and Harrison attended high school together in Raleigh but had drifted apart until Braxton had been one of the earliest supporters of Harrison's liberal/activist campaign for the North Carolina governorship eight years earlier. The two men had grown close again during that first gubernatorial campaign when Braxton only occasionally chided Harrison publicly, primarily when he hesitated to implement an activist, bigger government approach to solving their state's problems.

Harrison had chosen Sandra Van Huyck to head his foreign policy advisory team. About Harrison's age, Van Huyck had moved over the years between jobs in the State Department, several major educational institutions, and two foundations. She had always been a voracious reader, and she prided herself on her analytical and problem-solving abilities. Bored with her last academic post, she had walked in off the street to the Harrison campaign eighteen months earlier. She had not only tutored him in many important areas outside the natural domain of a state governor, but she had also written several excellent one-liners which he had used continually during the campaign.

The president's press secretary, Chris Wright, was pulled up to the circle in his wheelchair. Chris had lost the use of his legs thirty years earlier at age fourteen, as the result of a boating accident. The settlement of his parents' subsequent lawsuit against the boat manufacturer for failing to install adequate seatbelts and warning labels had allowed Chris to attend college and to pursue his love of writing and journalism. In the early nineties, in addition to his job as an anchorperson for a Seattle television station, Chris had become a gifted spokesperson for the handicapped citizens of the nation. He volunteered to join Harrison's campaign in its first month and had handled the press very well during the entire campaign, making him the natural candidate for White House press secretary.

Bob Horan, Harrison's chief speechwriter, had also been a journalism student when he and the future president first met at the University of North Carolina in the late 1960s. Horan had enjoyed a multifaceted journalism career, including long stints as a reporter with several major dailies and a wire service, and he had written two books on how to write books. When William Harrison first needed a speechwriter for his early presidential aspirations he had called Bob Horan; the man known for his "velvet hammer" phrases had been a member of the inner circle ever since. And Bob Horan was a homosexual, with strong ties to the gay rights movement.

A newcomer to the inner circle was Patricia Barton-North, the vice president of the United States. Mrs. Barton-North had been a very liberal, pro-government-intervention congresswoman from southern California who had been appointed to fulfill the unexpired term of the junior senator from her state when he had collapsed and died on a basketball court. Senator Barton-North had done well during those two years and had then been reelected in her own right. A strong feminist, she had been chosen to balance the presidential ticket both geographically and by gender.

William Harrison considered himself to be a liberal humanist in the enlightened tradition of North Carolina politics. He believed that human intellect, education, and government intervention could eventually overcome almost any problem. But during their successful campaign of the previous year he had been surprised to learn that his running mate from California seemed to begin each day as if she were preparing for battle with almost everyone. Patricia Barton-North was a strong force who got things done for her constituents, worked hard, and pushed even harder for the causes she believed in, centering on women's, children's, and minority rights. Her husband, Frank North, a general contractor in Los Angeles, kept their home there, although their one daughter was away at college. Patricia lived in the official vice president's residence at the Naval Observatory and commuted home to California as often as possible. She obviously revelled in her role as the nation's first female Vice President, and her strong personality guaranteed her a say on those issues in which she was interested.

Barbara Morton had been William Harrison's personal secretary since the days he had been a lawyer and North Carolina state senator before running for governor. Because she had worked with him for so long, Harrison valued her input, which she rarely volunteered but gave freely when asked. At meetings like this one she always took extensive notes and then gave well-prepared summaries to her boss in a matter of hours.

William Harrison looked around at the closely knit team he had selected to advise him. The only two people missing were Lanier Parks, secretary of state, and Robert Valdez, secretary of the treasury. Both men were out of town that day.

With the exception of Jerry Richardson, the chief of staff, who had been a young officer in the army right after college, none of those seated around the coffee table, including the president himself, had ever served in the armed forces.

As President Harrison surveyed his inner circle of policy advisors, it once again occurred to him that he had successfully outdone even his predecessor in choosing a group that was above reproach for its balance. *Men and women, black, white and Hispanic, straight and gay, even physically challenged,* he thought. *How can anyone beat this group?* He had indeed been praised by the press for selecting such a diverse team.

President Harrison cleared his throat and said, "Let's be efficient with our time. This is important, but the mayors from our five largest cities will be here in ninety minutes, and I need ten minutes to prepare for them." He then nodded to Jerry Richardson, who opened a three-ring binder on his lap and began the meeting.

"All right, let's focus first on the likely domestic issues the press will ask about next week. Then we'll move to foreign. Remember, we'll practice how to field specific questions on Monday and have a dress rehearsal in the family theater on Tuesday afternoon. For now we want to familiarize ourselves with probable question areas, particularly those that might create some tension, and consider ways to handle them. Let's just freewheel for a while on domestic issues, and Barbara please take good notes, as always."

"Well then, I'll start," Ted Braxton led off, leaning forward in his chair, his own binder propped on the edge of the coffee table. "I think this equal-but-separate movement that started on several university campuses a few years ago is a real hot potato and should produce one or more questions at the press conference."

"Can we just duck it for now, saying that we're studying it?" asked Bob Horan.

"I have to tell you," said the president, slightly shaking his head, "I'm not comfortable with this issue yet. If there are any old Ku Klux Klan members left from the fifties and sixties, they must be laughing at this one. Here we've spent well over forty years trying to integrate all our minorities into one mainstream, with equal opportunities for all, and now the minorities themselves want to be segregated in the name of equality."

"But, Mr. President, that's just the point," said the vice president, tapping a fingernail on the arm of her chair. "Minorities can't really be free to be equal as long as they're overpowered by the majority in every walk of life. And this is *voluntary* separation. I think if African-Americans, women, homosexuals, or other minorities want to have their own separate dormitories in college, or units in the armed services, or even schools, then I think this is how they will finally reach their full potential. I think we should get behind it, after an appropriate period for the press to educate the public, and push for this legislation. This press conference will be a great opportunity for you to plant those seeds so the legislation can be written early next year."

"But, like the president, I'm still not sure," interjected Jerry Richardson. "It might have made me feel great for about a week to be in a black dorm in college, studying about the history of Africa, but I don't think I would have learned what I needed to learn, or made the relationships I needed to make, to wind up as the CEO of a Wall Street securities firm by living for four years in an African-American dorm. Whatever you call it, aren't you really creating new plantations and dividing our nation into many, many sub-categories, sort of like the former Yugoslavia, where everyone eventually despised everyone in a different sub-group? And what if white males, who I guess are now arguably a minority, wanted to form their own equal-but-separate living quarters in school?"

"No way," said Vice President Barton-North, her voice rising a bit. "This is affirmative action we're talking about. It's the way for individuals in our various minorities to realize their own self-fulfillment. White males, who are the majority, no matter their numbers, could not set up such a group by definition, because this legislation would only be for the minorities who have been persecuted for so long by previous laws and policies. I repeat that it's a good idea, and we should support it."

"Well, I'm not there quite yet," said the president, leaning back in his chair. "It's a very complex issue, and I'm just not sure the folks with the loudest microphones really represent the true wishes of the minorities involved, much less of the nation as a whole. But I hear your concern, Patricia, and I'll think about it over the weekend. Barbara, let's ask the staff to research as many angles as we can on this one. For now Bob may have the best thought for the press conference: we can legitimately say we're studying it."

The vice president started to speak, but the president raised his hand, and she stopped.

"Now, Ted," the president continued, "Let's talk for a minute about the church tax proposal. We'll probably have some greater agreement there."

"Yes, sir. That legislation should pass the House shortly, and it might even have a good chance in the Senate. As you know, it'll repeal the non-profit tax status of any religious organization, including churches and synagogues of course, which practice any sort of discrimination, or which get involved in political activities. We may pick up some swing votes from the other side in the Senate because of its tax-raising benefits, to help fight the deficit. The legislation will stop bigots from hiding behind the facades of churches. If an organization won't allow women or homosexuals, for example, into all positions, including that of priests, then there's no reason for that organization to enjoy the benefits of tax-free status. 'Separation of church and state' means that the state should not help any church with its rightful tax bill when that church does not abide by the laws of the land, like non-discrimination. And the same goes for those 'churches' that try to tell people how to think and how to vote. They can continue to do so, if they want, but not on the government's nickel."

"I like that last line, Barbara. Please make a note of it for the press conference. Does anybody have a problem with this one or see any potential traps at the press conference?" asked the president.

There was silence around the circle. Everyone believed it was high time for this legislation to pass, and with a majority of the press also in favor, they doubted any questions would be too difficult.

"What about abortion?" asked Bob Horan. "In the past that's always been a killer." He smiled slightly at his own pun.

"Surely that one's dying down now that we've got a real morning-after pill," said Patricia Barton-North. "I mean, is anyone much even doing the old-style abortions these days?"

"Yes, unfortunately they are," answered Ted Braxton. "Unfortunate in the sense that we have to continue to protect the abortion clinics from the fanatics."

"I feel strongly on this one," said the president. "The Supreme Court has clearly said that abortion is the law of the land, and years ago under the Health Reform Act abortions were made available through government assistance. An abortion is certainly preferable to another child on welfare! That's why I signed the executive order during our first week allowing full-term abortions in any facility that receives federal funds under health reform. After all, a fetus of any age is not a living, breathing baby. I hope someone does ask a question on it because I'd love to have the opportunity early in our administration to send a loud and clear message that we're not going to tolerate any type of disturbances at licensed abortion clinics. We'll arrest and prosecute to the fullest extent of the law."

"Remember what you said and how you said it just then," said Bob Horan, smiling, "and you'll come across just great on the cameras, as you did during the campaign. Get some of that same fire in your belly, and the people will love it. And I guess you should be prepared for a possible question on how you feel about already appointing two Supreme Court justices in just three months."

"Well, the retirement everyone foresaw; but the tragic death of Justice Miller was completely unexpected. For public consumption, that's it. But between us, I hope our nominees have a lasting effect on this nation for progressive thinking long after we've all moved on to other things. Jerry, how are the confirmations looking?"

"Very good, Mr. President. Even though we don't control the Senate there's still enough of the honeymoon feeling around to help in the hearings. No one should ask too many questions, so in that sense we're lucky on the timing."

The group continued to discuss other domestic issues for thirty more minutes before turning to foreign policy matters.

"Well, Sandra, what sort of questions are likely on problems overseas?" asked Jerry Richardson.

Sandra Van Huyck adjusted her glasses and began. "Of course the foreign policy question that is also very much a domestic issue is Free Cuba. Now that Castro is gone and the boats from Cuba have been pouring into south Florida for almost six months, all of the social service delivery systems in the Miami area are terribly overloaded. The question is how can we stop the boats?"

"Surely the free entry of Cubans can't go on forever," said Richardson. "Even Cuban-American leaders must realize there has to be a reasonable end to this policy. Isn't it better to provide services there than to continue to flood south Florida?"

"I agree with Jerry," said the president. "Let's pick an end date—something reasonable, say sixty days from now. And we'll tell everyone about it, let as many come as want to before that date, and then enforce the same rules that we've been using for the Haitians for many years now." *Fair is fair, and where will we put all those people anyway?*

"All right. We'll look at it and have a date set by our meeting next week," agreed Van Huyck. "Next issue: we haven't said anything publicly about the small political party in Kuwait 'inviting' Saddam Hussein to come and 'rescue' the country from the totalitarian Kuwaiti royal family."

"That's absolutely absurd," said the president.

"I know, sir. And that's the point. You should use any opening at the press conference to label that invitation and the entire Kuwaiti Nationalist Party as what they are: puppet fronts for Saddam Hussein. But you should also, by the way, call for reasonably early and fair elections there as well, which will undermine the growing audience in Kuwait for groups like the KNP. Vince Harley at the Joint Chiefs of Staff doesn't want to have to remobilize in the Persian Gulf now."

"Okay. Good, Sandra," said the president. "What else?"

"I'm certain someone will ask a question about the referendum vote that the new British Socialist government is going to have next month on the future of their monarchy. Since we need the British government's help in so many areas right now, I suggest you divide your answer into an official part, affirming the right of one of our oldest allies to decide such issues on their own, and a personal part, reiterating how much most Americans cherish British traditions, especially the monarchy."

"I agree," said the president, starting to appear restless, as he usually did after an hour of sitting. "What else?"

"Well, there's usually an inevitable question or two about Russia. There I think you can point to the stability and successes of the past several years, especially in Russia and Ukraine, as a testimony to their human spirit and to their love of freedom, even in times of great economic difficulty."

"Sandy, what about the agent killed in Odessa? The rest of you probably haven't heard, but it happened sometime yesterday in the Black Sea port. We want to keep the lid on this while we investigate, but by the press conference some facts may have leaked out. And for your ears only there was a note attached to the body vaguely threatening to kill millions of Americans"—everyone looked toward the president—"which we *definitely* don't want to mention while we're investigating. We assume it's the result of an overly imaginative zealot. At any rate, we might get a question inquiring about whether the cold war is starting over again."

"Yes, I was getting to that," said Van Huyck. "We obviously won't bring it up, but if you are asked, the official response from the Ukrainian government so far has been very positive and very helpful. They appear to be as shocked as we are, and they're permitting us to send a special team to the Odessa area to ask more questions around Old Towne, near the waterfront, where the agent was killed. So I think you can truthfully sidestep the question, if it comes, as an isolated event without any known connections to any specific government or organized group."

"Kill millions of Americans?" Richardson asked for all the others. "How could anyone do that?"

"I don't know," William Harrison lied, not wanting to leak even to his own advisors the remote possibility that the agent's death was somehow connected to the old rumor of a missing Soviet warhead.

As his chief of staff looked back to his notebook, the president moved on. "Okay, fine. What else have you got?"

The session lasted another twenty minutes. By then it was almost time for the president's meeting in the Cabinet Room with the delegation of big-city mayors from the Mayors' Conference. Harrison needed a few minutes to read his brief on their names, backgrounds, and a family fact he could "remember" about each one.

As their session broke up and President Harrison opened the door of the Oval Office to receive his briefing memo, he found his seventeen-year-old daughter, Katherine, waiting for him in the reception area. She did not look happy. She obviously wanted to see him, despite the fact he was late. *Oh, no, what now?* he thought. *Where's Carrie?*

"Hi, honey." He stopped just outside the door as the other participants from the meeting filed past on either side. "How was school today?" he asked, regretting the words as he spoke them, remembering the disappointment he had caused her by not attending the annual father-daughter luncheon at her school.

Tall like her mother, her reddish-blond hair giving a hint of the fire in her personality, Katherine crossed her arms and looked at him with a scowl. "Well, as you know, I had a lot of free time during lunch today."

"Katherine, you know I wanted to come to that luncheon, but I had a meeting that had been scheduled for a month."

"Yeah, I know, just like always."

William, sensing others nearby in the reception area were beginning to feel uneasy about this exchange and were turning away, said, "Again, I'm sorry. Is there something I can do for you now? Where's your mother?" He wished that his wife was there to handle whatever was on his daughter's mind.

"She told me to come see you, that there's nothing she can do."

Oh great! Thanks a lot, Carrie. "Look, honey, I'm late for a very important meeting. Can't this wait?"

"No, it can't! It's about these stupid Secret Service people who treat me like a two-year-old and try to run my life. I'm sick of it," she said, her voice rising.

Glancing up, the president took his daughter by the arm and said in a low and calm voice, "All right, let's find a private place to talk for a minute and you can tell me what's the matter."

The president and his daughter stepped out into the hallway and walked around to the Roosevelt Room. William closed the door. He took a deep breath, trying to focus on his daughter. *Carrie is supposed to handle this stuff, not me..*

"Now, please Katherine, tell me as calmly as you can what the problem is."

"The problem, which is the same problem I've been having for the last three months, is that I no longer have a life. Being the president of the United States is obviously fantastic for you, but being the daughter of the president of the United States sucks," she said angrily. "After you missed the luncheon today, Susan Thompson invited me over to her house to do our science project homework together. I mean, is that a big deal? But the Secret Service agents said no. They said neither the Thompsons' home nor the route there had been approved for me, and their orders were to bring me back here, to this giant prison.

"So basically I'm locked up in this cage without a life of my own. I'm seventeen years old, and I've been sentenced to at least four years in prison with a mother who's almost always unhappy and a father who's usually home, but who I can *never* see, because he's too busy running the world. At least Robert has escaped to college and has some *freedom.* I'm just *here.* How would *you* feel? Do you ever even think about me?" she asked. By now the tears were running down her cheeks.

William realized he was into a conversation that had been building in his daughter for weeks, if not months. He tried to reason with her.

"Katherine, you're right. I haven't thought enough about your situation. I guess I thought you were happy, but obviously I was wrong. The Secret Service people are just doing their jobs."

"But Robert's not locked in like I am. He's told me he can decide to go places on the spur of the moment and the Secret Service people let him do it. Why can't I?"

"Sweetheart, he's four years older than you, living in Chapel Hill, a small college town, and he's a boy—a man really. And he does have Secret Service protection, though you're right, it's not as structured as yours."

"So there it is again. He's a boy, so he gets special treatment."

"No, Katherine. It's not that. It's just that—well, more can happen to you. I mean, imagine if some terrorist group grabbed you. Think of what they might do. And the public might demand some type of retaliation."

"So all this just has to do with public relations and politics, and not me, right?"

Despite his best efforts, William was becoming exasperated. He took a deep breath, then put a hand on his daughter's shoulder and looked into her eyes. "Katherine, I hear you. Like I said, I probably haven't paid enough attention to you, or to your mother, since the last three months of the campaign—that's almost nine months now. I tell you what. I can't change it all overnight. And I may not want to change much. But I promise you that I *will meet* with the head of the Secret Service. Okay, *we'll* meet with him," he corrected himself, as she started to speak, "to see what we can arrange about them being more flexible.

"And I also promise you that while we're at Camp David for Easter weekend, you and I—with Mom if you want—will take some special time together and play tennis, go for walks, or whatever you want. I'm sorry this is such a mess. But I hope that's a good enough answer for now. And I've just got to go, because people are waiting for me."

Katherine lowered her head and folded her arms across her chest, a tear hitting her right forearm when she did so. William handed her his handkerchief.

"Okay," she said as she wiped her eyes with his handkerchief. "If that's all we can do today. I guess it's a start. I just want you to know that unless things change, this job may be wonderful for you, but I hate it. And I hate what it's doing to our family. I hate my life. I hope whatever you accomplish as president is worth all the pain you're causing us." She handed him back his handkerchief and walked out the door without saying good-bye.

The staff members who were gathered outside the door of the Roosevelt Room made way for Katherine as she walked back toward the family's private quarters in the main building. William noticed they looked somewhat embarrassed as he also came out of the room, looking for Barbara Morton. When he found her, he asked her to set up a meeting before the Easter break with his wife, daughter, and the Secret Service chief. With that issue temporarily settled, he walked quickly toward the Cabinet Room, reading his briefing report as best he could, to meet the delegation from the Mayors' Conference.

THE RESEARCH TRIANGLE, NORTH CAROLINA *This is incredible!* Ed Cheatham was in the middle of the most enjoyable fantasy he had ever imagined. He found himself alone with three of the most beautiful young women he had ever seen, and they were taking turns making him very happy.

I can't believe this! For another fifteen minutes all of his senses were in complete overload, building to a crescendo that left him exhausted.

When the fantasy ended he had to wait a few minutes for his heart rate to slow down to normal. Overwhelmed by how wonderful he felt, he slowly removed all the special equipment that was connected by wires to the computer in the adjoining room.

He got up from the comfortable reclining chair in which he had actually been sitting alone during the entire experience, walked across the room, and opened the door into the control room.

"Well?" his colleague, Carl Hess, asked with a smile.

"You folks have *really* leapt light years during the past six months!" Ed exclaimed. "That was simply incredible. It was exactly like I was really there, though I can't say I've ever experienced anything even close to that in real life."

"And that's the whole point," Carl added, obviously pleased that his boss appreciated the improved version his hard-working software team had created. He continued, "How much do you think an organization like Pet Girl International will pay us for the exclusive rights to distribute this product in the adult entertainment market?"

"I can't even imagine. They should go crazy over this. But," Ed paused for a few moments to consider, "we'll need the still unavailable PC-ZT with the 986 chip to mass produce a portable system. That'll take over a year. But the board and I have already started the wheels rolling on a potentially even more profitable market—one that should be available right now."

Carl frowned slightly and asked, "What could be bigger than Pet Girl International?"

Ed shrugged his shoulders and then smiled. "My girlfriend, Jean Bowers, teaches sex education in a Research Triangle high school. She's always complaining about how rigid and unrealistic it is. We think we can ride the current wave of revulsion over AIDS and teenage pregnancy and offer a totally realistic but *completely safe* method of sex education for our public high schools."

"You mean put this equipment in a *high school?*"

"I mean," Ed's smile broadened, "we've already won approval to test the concept in her school. Then we'll obtain a government grant to put this equipment in *every* high school in America!"

WASHINGTON   That evening the president and first lady were the official hosts at the Kennedy Center for the annual black tie Distinguished American Artists ceremony. It was late when they returned to the White House, and, after saying good night to the last Secret Service agent, they boarded the elevator to their private quarters and were alone for the first time since breakfast.

On the elevator William turned to his wife, his arms stiffly at his side, his anger obvious. "Don't *ever* suggest to Katherine that she come to see me during my work day, unless it's a real emergency, or you at least call first. I was late and I was unprepared for a meeting with five of the most important men in the country, because *you* told her to bring her complaints to me." As the elevator door opened he let her out first but continued his lecture to her back as they walked down the hallway to their bedroom. "I'm trying to cope with problems you can't even imagine, and you send our daughter to whine about how she's being protected!"

At the door to their room, Carrie wheeled around and looked up at her husband. "Maybe I can't 'imagine' your problems, William, because you never tell me about them. You used to, but you don't now. Yes, I sent Katherine to see you—she's our daughter and she had a problem that was *important to her*. Since it involved you, I thought you should deal with it. Maybe the timing was bad, but William I *don't* have a clue about your day—or your problems. You keep both of us out of your life. Do you have any idea how that hurts me, William? And Katherine, too? She and I might as well move back to Raleigh. We'd both probably be happier, and I imagine you would, too. Would you, William? Think how much you could get done without us to cut into your day! Think of all the phone calls you could make and all the meetings you could attend and all the programs you could implement without a wife who just wants to love you and help you…"

Her anger peaked, and she sighed heavily. Her shoulders slumped. "I'm not the enemy, William," she added. "You may have more problems than I can imagine, but I love you more than you can imagine. I just want us to be in love again, William. You can be the president of the United States or a ditch digger, I don't care. But I just want us to be a *family* again, sharing and trusting and loving. The rest doesn't matter one bit to me any more."

She turned and walked into their large bedroom, leaving him standing at the door.

William watched her starting to unzip her evening gown, but he didn't move or say anything. *She hasn't talked to me like that in…years. First Katherine this afternoon and now Carrie tonight.* He opened his mouth, about to give her an angry response. But he stopped himself. He felt terrible. Carrie had finally verbalized what he knew to be true but had only recently expressed to himself—that he *had* stopped communicating with her. *What have I done to our family? Am I really this bad?*

For the first time in a long time William admitted that his wife of almost thirty years was right. She was still facing away from him, and he looked at her, really looked at her, as though it were the first time in…years? He couldn't help being moved by her beauty. *This woman must really love me to put up with so much from me.*

Carrie, having unzipped the long zipper on her gown, turned her head to look back at William. He could see the tears streaking her make-up. Her words had pierced him. Finally he walked toward her, and she turned to face him.

He stopped a few inches from her. For a long time he was silent. Then he said, slowly, "I...you're...I'm sorry, Carrie. I *don't* know why...but you're...you're both—you and Katherine—are right. Why has it been like this? I'm...sorry. I'm going to try to be better—to communicate." He gave her a smile tinged with sadness. "Please for..." He started over, unable to say the word *forgive*. "Please help me. I've been less than—I've been too busy. I'm sorry. Help me again be the husband you want. Be persistent, like tonight. I'll try to be better—really!" He smiled again.

She moved toward him, put her arms around him, and lay her head on his shoulder. It was her turn to be silent, thinking about what he had said. "I'll try, William," she said softly, "if you will. I tried years ago, but I finally gave up. You may not even remember. But, yes, I'll gladly try again. All I want is—I hope you mean it, William, because all I want is us. And I don't want to be locked out anymore. Can you open up again and let me know what your thoughts are?"

He returned her hug and felt closer to her than he had in a very long time. "I'll try, Carrie. I really will. I'm sorry. Yes, I'll try."

She pulled back from him and looked into his eyes. Then he leaned down and kissed her. She opened her mouth and kissed him back, moving her arms up around his neck. He pressed against the small of her back and pulled her closer to him.

It had been a long day, but the next hour was by far the best. They finally lay quietly in each other's arms, having made love with the excitement of newlyweds, but with the intimacy of old lovers reunited after years of separation. Neither of them could believe how surprisingly intense it had been. But as William turned out the light, each of them silently wondered whether it could really last.

And can the liberties of a nation be thought secure when we have removed their only firm basis, a conviction in the minds of the people that these liberties are of the gift of God? That they are not to be violated but with His wrath? Indeed I tremble for my country when I reflect that God is just; that His justice cannot sleep forever.

THOMAS JEFFERSON

2

Wednesday, April 11
One Week Later

RALEIGH Mary Prescott stirred grated cheese into the grits simmering on the stove that morning and mentally checked off the things she had to do in order to leave for Washington on Friday morning for the long Easter weekend at Camp David.

Mary still had a problem thinking of her younger brother as the president of the United States. Knowing his human faults better than most people, she had been praying daily after the election that the demands of the office would quickly bring out his many strengths, which she also knew so well. But as she moved to the refrigerator to take out the milk, she could not help thinking once again about how much she disagreed with him on so many issues. She believed that God had created everyone and everything, that he ultimately rules, and that good and evil are real forces competing for men's souls. Governments should therefore, in her mind, only adopt systems with checks and balances that recognize man's imperfect state, and laws that mirror God's commandments and truly punish wrongdoing so that the majority can live in safety and peace.

But William believed, she knew from their many discussions, just as their mother believed: People weren't innately evil. They were just uneducated, impoverished, or in need of a better government program to train or to improve them. So it followed, according to William, that by themselves men could educate and reason their way to a better life, particularly if the right "enlightened" people were in charge. He believed it was the government's responsibility to implement programs that make men and women better, more equal, and more productive.

Mary had tried to tell him that simple sin, in the form of greed, dishonesty, and jealousy, had always and would always ultimately destroy every family, business, and government that denied sin's existence and didn't provide for ways to deal with it, since it was the constant human state. But William had followed his beliefs with great success while he had been governor of North Carolina, setting up one program after another designed to improve the state and its citizens.

They had discussed their differences again on two occasions during the presidential campaign, but he had not been able to see her side. Ultimately she had to be content with the possibility that she might have at least planted some seeds. But she doubted whether these seeds would ever grow in the environment she assumed pervaded the White House. *I wonder how often the topic of good and evil comes up in their discussions?*

In two days she would have a chance to experience that environment herself. *It should really be interesting.* Just then Sarah and Tim came into the kitchen, followed by a shout from their father, Graham, that he was right behind them.

Sitting down for breakfast, the teenagers' excitement over their departure for Washington was obvious. "Do you think Aunt Carrie fixes breakfast every morning for Uncle William and Katherine?" Sarah asked, passing some toast to her father.

"I don't know," her mother said and smiled, "but I sort of doubt it. Anyway, you can ask her on Friday. I'm sure she won't be cooking for all of us at Camp David!"

"Will there be guards everywhere?" asked Tim. "Like if we want to play tennis, will there be guards all around the court?"

His father chuckled. "I doubt it. Camp David ought to be a pretty secure spot. Now if your cousins Robert and Katherine visited us here and you played tennis down at the park, there probably would be a few Secret Service people around."

"Wow! I bet it's cool being driven everywhere by the Secret Service," Tim concluded.

"Well, again, I don't know," said his mother. "But while Sarah finds out about Aunt Carrie's breakfast, you can ask Katherine about the Secret Service. Please pass the strawberry preserves."

There was a brief silence as everyone ate, and then Sarah said, "It was nice of Uncle William to invite us to Camp David for the weekend. I'm sure there were lots of other important people he could have asked."

"It *was* nice," agreed her mother. "When your Aunt Carrie called me a month ago, she figured he could probably use a little rest, away from the newsmen and the politicians and all that. She said it would be good for the family to get together again, to sort of help him recharge his batteries. Since we don't have a 'family retreat' like some of the other presidents, it's wonderful that we can use Camp David. By the way, are you guys pretty well packed? Do you need me to do anything? I've got two closings tomorrow, so this is my last day to handle any details."

"Oh, I forgot something!" Sarah said, getting up and walking toward the den for her bookbag. "Last night when we came in so late from Tim's baseball game, I was supposed to give you this paper for you to sign from health class. I'm supposed to tell you about this thing the school is thinking about doing next year, if the PTA approves it."

Sarah returned to the breakfast room and handed the paper to her mother, who began reading it while Sarah sat down again and continued. "It's about a meeting in three weeks—Thursday I think—on one of the capabilities of this huge new computer we've got. Ms. Bowers, our health instructor, is all excited about it, and she wants to explain it to the parents." Sarah noticed the surprise registering on her mother's face as she neared the end of the letter.

Suddenly serious, Mary handed the letter back to Sarah. "Please pass it to your father. Graham, take a look at this. Sarah, exactly what did Ms. Bowers tell you?"

"Now don't freak out," Sarah said, glancing back and forth between her parents. "I think this is pretty wacko, too. I'm just like telling you what she said. I don't necessarily agree with it, okay?" Both her parents nodded as Tim reached for the last bit of cheese grits in the bowl.

"You know about virtual reality, right, Mom?" Sarah asked.

"Yes. It's when they use a computer to set up these arcade games where you wear a helmet and pretend to have a shootout with an imaginary gunman, or something like that."

"One of its original uses was in training a fighter pilot in extremely life-like emergency situations while he was safely strapped into a simulator," her father added.

"Well, apparently this computer," continued Sarah, "is like a thousand times more powerful than even those airplane simulators, and one of the things it can do is realistically stimulate human senses. So, apparently—and please don't freak out—the computer company says they can set it up to teach what Ms. Bowers calls 'no-risk sex education.'

"They've devised some way for a student to go into a room by himself or herself, put on this helmet, special gloves, and some sort of pants that you wear, like football pants—one designed for boys and one for girls—and then using virtual reality, supposedly the computer can create a completely real sexual experience for whoever's wearing this stuff."

"You've got to be kidding!" Mary exclaimed, looking across the breakfast room table at her husband. "That's absurd. What's our high school doing, giving our children realistic sexual experiences?"

"Mom, I asked you not to freak out. Ms. Bowers said it's a way to teach sexual responses in class without anyone getting pregnant, or catching a disease, or anything like that....She's really excited about it and wants to tell the parents about it at this meeting next week."

"I can't believe it," Graham said.

With a little pleading in her voice, Sarah continued, "I don't know the details, Dad. That's what this meeting's about. I think the parents have to approve it first. Please just go to the meeting and hear about it yourselves. I can tell you that a lot of the senior boys are upset that they're going to graduate before all of this gets going next fall." Sarah tried to smile.

"I bet they are," said her mother, not smiling at all. "Graham, I think we've both got to go to this meeting."

"That's fine, honey," he said. "Of course we'll go. But please, I know how you get sometimes. Maybe we don't understand it all yet, and it's not as crazy as it sounds." He smiled. "Please just relax and enjoy this weekend with the family in Washington, and don't let this computer thing spoil it. We'll find out about it in a couple of weeks."

Mary took a deep breath. "You're right. I'll try not to think about it this weekend, though it's the sort of thing that drives me crazy. The social experimenters just keep chipping away at the few values we've still got left. I know, I know," she smiled, and raised both hands to her family before anyone could protest. "I'll quit. Thanks for the uplifting information, Sarah. Now you and Tim better get going if you plan to make it to school today."

WASHINGTON That morning the president and his domestic policy advisor, Ted Braxton, invited the formal congressional leadership—the top senator and congressman elected by each party caucus—to meet in the Cabinet Room at the White House. After some polite talk, the six men shifted to business.

We really need this meeting to go well, William thought, stopping himself from nervously tapping his pen on the table. "Again, thank you all for coming," he began. "As you may know, we have our first press conference later this afternoon. While that may receive the media's attention today, I consider this meeting to be far more important. We want to move our domestic program forward as quickly as possible, and we've asked you here as a bipartisan group to seek your input on how to accommodate as many constituencies as possible. John, do you want to start?"

John Dempsey, the senior senator from the president's party, who had been a Washington fixture for almost forty years, cleared his throat. "Mr. President, you obviously have our full support for your programs. We completely agree that the way to get this nation back to work is more job training, plus more public-sector-funded jobs, like road construction and environmental clean-up. Once the spending authorizations are introduced in the House, we'll drive hard for approval in the Senate."

"And we should be ready to introduce the spending authorizations contained in your budget right after the Easter recess," said Trenton Patterson, the majority whip in the House. "We've taken a little longer than usual on the budget, to run all the possible scenarios with OMB and Treasury, including various interest rate assumptions so we can speak decisively about the deficit implications."

"And what is the consensus?" asked the president, turning to Ted Braxton.

"Taking mid-range figures for the projections and including the proposed tax increases on cigarettes, liquor, and some church incomes, the deficit should only be about $350 billion this year," Braxton replied.

"And that's where you'll lose us," interrupted Warner Watts, the opposition's majority leader in the Senate. "Besides this church tax business, which many of us feel is unconstitutional, your spending program is just off the charts. What about the national debt? We don't have the votes to stop you in the House"—he glanced at Bill Phillips, his party's counterpart in the lower chamber—"but I think we can at least hold you up for a good long time in the Senate."

"Warner, you know I hate the deficit and the national debt as much as you do," William replied. "But we've lived with it for years, and somehow we've survived. You also know I campaigned on the pledge to spend whatever it took to get everyone who is now on welfare trained, to get thousands of units of public housing built, and to get hundreds of thousands of jobs created over the next four years, *then* cut back the spending, once and for all, after those goals have been reached. That's how we'll finally get rid of the deficit. When everyone is self-sufficient and everyone has a decent home."

"Mr. President," Senator Watts responded, "that plan sounds noble as all get out, but it won't work. Creating all those new bureaucracies to train people and to build houses and to make jobs—the bureaucracies never go away. They become permanent, costing us more and more. And the deficit also includes all these entitlement programs, from health care to military pensions. I understand you also plan to increase those benefits. How are you going to pay for all of this, sir?"

"First, we're writing 'sunset' provisions into all of our new programs, just as we did in North Carolina, where it worked perfectly. A program came on line, did its job, and then shut down."

"This is Washington, Mr. President, not Raleigh," Congressman Phillips offered.

Annoyed by the interruption and the implied put-down, the president continued, "And we're only increasing benefits by a small amount to make up for years of neglect. People are ultimately more important than any budget. And, to pay for it, all of these new jobs will create new taxpayers and new tax payments. Our projections show the deficit will be large this year and the first half of next year. But as new jobs create new taxes, the deficit will come down quickly."

"You hope," said Watts, obviously skeptical.

Hold your temper, the president thought, *but be firm. We need his support for this legislation to pass.* "Warner, we've got to give this program a chance. It's what I campaigned for, and it's what the American people elected me to do. I'm asking for your help."

"With all due respect, Mr. President, the majority of Americans split their votes last November, and they weren't for you. Despite what most of the press says, we don't feel you have any mandate to push through these spending increases when the nation is obviously broke."

His anger rising despite himself, Harrison sidestepped the last remark and said, "So it's going to be politics as usual for another four years? We propose realistic and innovative ways to move our nation out of stagnation and malaise, and you thwart us at every step; so that nothing gets done? Is that what the American people deserve?"

"I wouldn't want to speculate on what they deserve, sir," Watts replied. "But as long as they keep splitting their votes between different parties in the House, Senate, and presidency, so that no party or philosophy has a clear majority or mandate to lead, I guess that's what we'll have." He smiled. "Maybe you'll get lucky and win a huge majority in next year's congressional elections. Many senators from our party are up for reelection, too."

"Maybe," the president said, refusing to return the smile. "But that's over eighteen months from now. Our nation needs to create new jobs and housing today, not tomorrow. Will you help us?"

"Not if it means the spending increases we hear you're about to propose."

"Even if they'll help the hardest hit in our society and they're guaranteed to last only four years?"

"Mr. President, pardon my bluntness," Watts said, "but your guarantee isn't worth much in this town. We've heard it all before. Most of us figure that in four years there's a good chance that you'll be gone. But we and the nation will have to live with the increased interest payments on the national debt you're proposing for years and years to come. We just can't saddle future generations with that, and we won't help you do it."

"Mr. President, I think it's pretty obvious that the opposition's leaders are doing their usual best to be obstructionists," volunteered Congressman Patterson. Ted Braxton frowned.

"And I think it's pretty obvious that these programs are the epitome of the tax-and-spend approach that has kept us in this mess for almost forty years," retorted Senator Watts.

It's slipping away from us, William thought. *What's the answer?* Trying to sound more conciliatory, the president tried again. "Warner, Bill. More than anything, the country is sick and tired of gridlock. I was elected to move us forward again. We can't have four more years of stagnation; not even two. Stopping all federal programs might end the deficit, but it will hurt too many people. I'm asking you to trust me that we can build up programs, accomplish our goals, and then reduce spending way below where it is today."

Senator Watts paused and looked at Phillips before replying. "Mr. President, we know you're a good man and that *you* believe that's possible. But we've been here a long time, and all we've ever seen is programs grow, costing more taxpayer money, with fewer results; they never go away. So we can't in good conscience help create more of them. You send your folks back and see where they can cut, not just spend, and we'll be happy to talk again, any time. But we're firm on opposing these spending increases."

"Then it's politics as usual," said the president, obviously unhappy. He paused and seemed to relent. "We'll try, Senator. We'll try. Ted, let's get our team together next Tuesday morning, right after the Easter recess, and see where we can cut." Standing up to signal the end of the meeting, the president forced a cool smile, then shook hands all around. "Thank you for coming," he said, as they walked to the door.

NORFOLK, VIRGINIA The USS *Fortson* was tied up at Pier 24 undergoing modifications to the crews' quarters. She was not scheduled to depart again for six weeks, giving the crew a much needed rest while some significant personnel changes were made. After lunch that same Wednesday afternoon the ship's executive officer, Commander Richard Anglin, convened a department heads meeting in the wardroom. The attendees were the ship's six senior officers, the same ones who had met the previous week in the captain's cabin, absent the captain himself. Two days earlier, Lieutenant Commander Jimmy McKnight had departed the ship, finishing two years as the operations officer. His replacement, Lieutenant Commander Thomas Dobbs, had arrived on the Friday before to conduct the turnover of the operations department before McKnight's departure. He and the other department heads, including Lieutenant Commander Hugh Harrison, the weapons officer, followed the executive officer's suggestion that they be seated. He chaired the meeting from the head of the wardroom table.

Commander Anglin surveyed the five other men seated around the long table, then said, "Let's get started. I think you've all had a chance to meet Thomas Dobbs, and I've waited a few days to hold this meeting until he could at least get his bags unpacked. I'd like to stick to one subject: the two new divisions we're getting and the berthing changes the shipyard is making now.

"Starting at the top, Thomas, with you, you'll be berthing in the admiral's cabin, since we don't have a flag officer on board now. That'll give you your own stateroom and head, and obviously the accommodations are the best on the ship."

"Thank you, Commander, but that's really not necessary. I've felt out of place there for the last five days. I'm happy just to have a normal department head's stateroom," said Dobbs.

"Well, the instructions we received from the admiral were that to the greatest extent possible the women and homosexuals were to have separate berthing and heads, and I think this makes the most sense, so just enjoy the accommodations."

He turned to the weapons officer. "Now, Hugh, let's talk about your new missile fire controlmen—uh, women. Your ten new FTM's will be arriving next week, since the Fourth Division berthing spaces were easy to divide and there were two heads nearby. And of course we've had to install a bulkhead to separate Third Division from the passageway, so the women can walk back and forth to the ladder without viewing a naked torpedo man.

"But the new fire control officer, Lieutenant Slocum, arrived on board this morning. She'll live up in forward officers country, by herself, in one of the three staterooms. And shipyard has installed a little three-way sliding indicator on the outside of the small head, marked 'Vacant,' 'Men,' and 'Women.' She should probably go ahead and meet with you and the FT chiefs before they depart next week, to go over the equipment and the departmental procedures. Any questions?"

"No, sir," said the president's younger brother. "I met Lieutenant Slocum this morning, and she and I are set to meet again right after we break here. She's had quite a bit of experience at shore-based facilities and a missile range, but of course she's never served on a warship before. She seems ready to go, and she wears her uniform really well, by the way," he added.

"Thank you, Hugh," said Commander Anglin, "but please watch comments like that from now on. We've all got to learn not to make remarks about how anyone looks, so we don't offend anyone."

"Sure, sure," said Hugh, obviously embarrassed. "I'm sorry. But I can assure you that a lot of the men are going to share that opinion."

"Opinions we can have. Expressions we've got to watch. Especially the officers and chiefs. Now let's talk about our new dual department, the Admin and Ship's Store personnel.

"Thomas, Bill, and Henry, as you've probably already seen, we've taken the old Admin berthing space and part of First Division to wind up with two spaces and two separate heads for the homosexuals and lesbians. As I understand it we've got twelve homosexuals, seven lesbians, and a homosexual chief, right?"

"Yes, sir. They're due here in two weeks," replied Henry Early, the administrative officer.

"I think the work'll be finished by then," Commander Anglin said. "We've bumped two ensigns out of a stateroom in after officers country so the chief will have an officer's stateroom very near to the homosexual head."

"Why can't Chief Osborn just use the chief's head right behind officers country?" asked Dobbs.

"Again, because we've got sixteen chiefs sharing that head, and I don't think they want a homosexual mixed in with them."

"Oh, come on, sir. Chief Osborn is just like everybody else. We've had homosexuals in the navy for years and years. Chief Osborn isn't going to bite them, and for that matter, neither am I."

"Lieutenant Commander Dobbs, I'm doing the best I can with what I consider to be a difficult situation. When things get tough, I've found the best policy is to follow orders. And that's what I'm doing. I'm supposed to give all the homosexuals, heterosexual women, and lesbians their own heads whenever possible, and that's what I'm doing. And I would frankly ask you, except in an emergency, to use them exclusively, for the sake of the other men on the ship and for your own sake as well.

"Now, as to the new Admin personnel themselves, my only concern is that they're berthed so close to First Division, where traditionally some of our youngest and least experienced men start out. I just hope there won't be any problems.

"We're all going to do our best to 'sensitize' the crew, but we've occasionally had problems in the past just mixing white country boys and black guys from the big cities. We're going to try hard to work through this transition. Thomas, yesterday we all reviewed the affirmative action video you brought with you, and I'm not sure it will really help. In fact, it might hurt."

"I'm surprised you would say that," said Dobbs, still smarting from the executive officer's earlier words. "It's been used for many years in college dormitories to sensitize residence hall counselors on how homosexual love is really quite normal."

"But I'm not sure that showing videos to the crew—many of whom are still boys—of men engaging in homosexual acts is very helpful, either for them or for what we're trying to accomplish here."

"Why not?" asked Dobbs. "It's been proven to be a completely normal lifestyle. What's the problem?"

Hugh, thinking about his last mistake with Commander Anglin, refrained from saying he found the video repulsive.

The executive officer thought for a few moments and appeared to be choosing his words carefully. "Well, for starters, many of the crew will think it's perverse and grotesque. On top of that, I'm not sure that showing any type of erotic material helps any of us when we have five hundred people crammed into a ship less than five hundred feet long. And there might just be some jealousy, thinking that the guys in that division are having a great time together, while the rest of us suffer on a six-month deployment. I guess those are the first three reasons that pop into my head. I could probably think of others if you gave me more time."

"I'd like to ask you a question, please," interrupted Lieutenant Commander Perry Colangelo, the engineering officer. "I've already had two of my young men who grew up in the Bible Belt, and one young man from an Italian family like mine in New York, ask me about these changes and why we're bringing men and women on board who openly violate the laws of most states, not to mention God's laws as well."

"Oh, come on," said Dobbs.

"No, please, tell me what you think I should say," continued Colangelo, "when a young man reminds me that the Bible says homosexuality is wrong, and here we are promoting it in the United States Navy?"

"Just tell him the truth," replied Dobbs. "Tell him the Bible was written thousands of years ago and contains many myths that are obviously untrue and/or irrelevant to today's life."

"So as an officer in the United States Navy, I'm supposed to tell a young Christian man that he is not supposed to believe the Bible?"

"I'm not going to get into this kind of argument with you," Dobbs said. "Congress and the president have acted, and whatever some backward states or the outdated Bible may say, the law of the land is clear. Homosexuality is a natural and normal lifestyle, and not to be discriminated against. So tell those men whatever you want, but be sure you also tell them to keep their opinions—and particularly their actions—to themselves." Turning to Commander Anglin at the end of the table, he asked, "Do you really think there may be some problems, particular with First Division?"

Anglin again paused and appeared to weigh his words. "I certainly hope not. But these young men are from very diverse backgrounds and very diverse beliefs. I guess that's why CNO is running these two experiments: to find out what may or may not happen. You can bet there's going to be a lot of attention. And a lot of wives at home worried about their men off on a ship for six months with women and homosexuals."

"You mean they'll be afraid that the ship's homosexual barber might seduce their husbands?" Dobbs laughed.

"Not really. I think they'll be more concerned about the women on board. But I would imagine there are some parents who are worried about their eighteen-and nineteen-year-old boys."

"Look," Dobbs said, straightening up in his chair, "I have to submit a report about this 'experiment' as you call it, plus reports on all of the department heads on the ship. Frankly, I'm disappointed by this first meeting, and I don't appreciate many of the remarks. So I'm telling you all right now in no uncertain terms that I don't appreciate bigots, and I'll be on the lookout for bigoted remarks, particularly from the senior officers."

"I'm sorry," said Hugh. "Is this the U.S. Navy or the old Soviet Navy? I don't remember studying political correctness or mind control in my four years at Annapolis."

"And that's just the kind of remark I don't appreciate," retorted the operations officer, his face turning red. "You *obviously* are a bigot!"

Hugh leaned forward, his disgust obvious. But before he could speak, he was interrupted.

"Hold on a minute," said Anglin, his voice also rising. "Whatever else you may be, Thomas, you're first and foremost a naval officer. You asked a question, and I answered it as best I could. I didn't make a bigoted remark, and Hugh has a point, although he might have chosen different words. *All* of us will be writing reports on this 'experiment'—and that's exactly what the CNO himself calls it. So please, Thomas, don't threaten us with statements like that. I can assure you we're all going to do our best to make this situation work. We've got our orders and will carry them out." Looking around at the other department heads, the executive officer concluded, "And I assure you that you'll have one hundred percent cooperation from us. But I'm simply predicting that it won't be easy."

Dobbs started to say something, his face still red, but stopped, apparently thinking better of it. He simply nodded, but it was obvious to everyone that he was not pleased.

Thirty minutes later there was a knock on Hugh Harrison's stateroom door. "Come in," he said loud enough to be heard over the background noise that was always present on the ship, even when tied to the pier. The door opened and Lieutenant Teri Slocum came in. Without thinking, Hugh stood up, then quickly swallowed the smile that started to form. Embarrassed by his own good manners and natural reaction to a beautiful younger woman now sharing a very small space with him, he motioned for her to be seated in the second chair, turned ninety degrees to his, and they sat down together, only a foot apart.

"Are you getting everything unpacked?" he asked. As unprofessional as he knew it was, he could not help noticing her eyes, which seemed to sparkle, her short-cropped brunette hair, and her shapely legs, which were almost touching his knees. *Whoa!* he said to himself. *You're a happily married man with three kids. This is just the new fire control officer. Take it easy.*

She smiled, and her eyes seemed to sparkle even more. "Yes, that's a nice stateroom. I've met William Hatcher, the supply officer, and Henry Early, the...uh...Admin Officer, who are berthing in the stateroom next to me. The other two guys are on leave, but I'm sure the five of us will get along just fine. I'll try not to take too much time in the head!" She laughed.

He laughed, too. "Well, good. I'm glad. If you have any questions or problems, of course, just ask. I know you must feel this is quite a responsibility, being the missile fire control officer on your first time at sea. I recommend you spend as much time as you can with our two chiefs before they leave. I think we've arranged it so your chiefs and the outgoing chiefs will have a three-day overlap to go through the turn-over procedure."

Slocum turned slightly in her chair and crossed her legs. "That'll be very helpful. Thanks."

Hugh stood and walked over to a shelf, where he picked up several books. He handed them to her. "Here are our weapons department manuals." Then he sat down again. "I'd like to spend some time now briefing you on all the changes that we're going through, not just with your new personnel but with everything else as well. I suspect the next eighteen months are going to require some patience, tolerance, and flexibility from all of us."

Lieutenant Slocum leaned forward to put the weapons department manuals on the deck by her chair, almost brushing him with her hair and affording him a glance at her cleavage, since her shirt was unbuttoned at the collar. *And maybe we should only allow cold water in the showers,* Hugh thought. *Very cold. What on earth are we getting ourselves into?*

Teri opened her notepad, took out her pen, smiled, recrossed her legs, and said, "Okay. Shoot."

ATLANTA That same April afternoon had been one of the first really warm ones of the year in Atlanta. Rebecca and her boyfriend, Bruce Tinsley, decided to share a bottle of white wine on the balcony of her apartment overlooking the city. It was her day off, since she had worked the previous Sunday. One of the first Atlanta Braves games of the new season was on television, playing quietly behind them in the living room.

"I always feel better during the half of the year when baseball is being played," Rebecca said, taking a sip of her wine and looking out at the skyline that seemed to jut into the darkening sky. "It's such a great sport. You can either concentrate and watch every move, nuance, and shift, or you can just let it be there in the background for three hours, drifting in and out as things happen. I've always loved baseball."

"I would never have guessed that," said Bruce, reaching for the chilled bottle to refill both their glasses. "How did you get into baseball?"

"I guess from being in the middle between two brothers. There was always a game going on somewhere. I watched William play when he was in high school, and I remember teaching Hugh how to bat from a tee. You know, I'm thankful to have Courtney, my daughter; but I always wanted a boy, too. At forty-four, though, I've about run out of time." She sighed and looked off in the distance.

Bruce didn't know what to say. He enjoyed his relationship with Rebecca, particularly since she was the president's younger sister. As a securities broker he had already felt the benefits from being able to tell his clients brief anecdotes about the president, even though they had not yet met. But he was not ready to consider marriage to Rebecca, and her occasional talk about wanting another child worried him. He could hear her biological clock ticking, and he decided to change the subject.

"Well, I'm really looking forward to meeting your brothers and the rest of your family this weekend." He took another sip of his wine. "But are you really sure I should go to Camp David? I mean, this will be your family, with husbands, wives, and children. Won't I sort of be the fifth wheel?"

Rebecca seemed to come back from wherever she had been, turned, smiled, and reached for his hand. "No, no. Believe me, you'll be welcome. Yes, I imagine nearly everyone will be there, but I want to show you off!" She smiled even more and squeezed his hand.

"I'll try to be on my best behavior," he said and grinned. "But from what you tell me about Mary, I may not be able to stomach all of her Christian fundamentalism."

"Oh, she's actually very sweet and has always been sort of like a second mom for Hugh and me. She and Graham have raised three great kids, and now thanks to my nephew Jonathan, she's even a grandmother. She just 'got religion' as a teenager, I guess, and it's stuck. And, whatever else you might say, she certainly 'walks her talk.' She'll always let you know what she thinks—or I guess what she thinks God thinks—but she's nice. I promise you she'll be okay."

"Well, I just can't stand these in-your-face Christians who're always pushing their beliefs on the rest of us." Bruce took another sip from his wineglass and continued, "I mean, anybody with two cells in their brain knows that abortion is a woman's right; that someone in terminal pain should be able to decide to end his or her life; and that homosexuality is an acceptable way of life, just like it was for my brother. I mean, where were his Christian 'friends' when he got sick? They deserted him. His church voted to expel him. Can you imagine how that crushed him? I saw it. But these people just keep talking about 'sin' and 'evil' and all that garbage. If your sister starts with any of that stuff, I don't know if I can take it. I just get so angry when these fundamentalists hold back progress."

"Look," Rebecca said, rubbing her hand up and down Bruce's forearm, "the last thing I want to do is defend any of Mary's more farfetched ideas, but I must say that the 'progress' you're espousing is not always what it's cracked up to be."

"What do you mean?" he asked, turning toward her.

"I mean it's not." She withdrew her hand. "Whether or not you believe what Mary believes, just look around. Life is not as simple as you sometimes make it, Bruce. I can't explain it like Mary does, but I see it every day at the hospital."

"What do you mean?"

"Well, take, for example, the supposedly safe, improved morning-after abortion pill. It was finally approved for general use almost three years ago, and it was supposed to end the need for abortion clinics and all that confrontation stuff on the sidewalks."

He nodded.

"Despite what you might have read in the newspapers, the reality is not so wonderful."

"Why not?"

"Well, unlike the first French abortion pill, this one, as you know, doesn't have to be taken under a doctor's direct supervision. You only have to have a prescription, so everyone who can afford to has these pills. I mean men and women. For a while it was fashionable for women to carry condoms in their purses. Now men carry morning-after pills in their wallets." She raised an eyebrow and looked at him. "Do you have one?"

He sheepishly nodded.

She continued. "The result is that everybody's having *unprotected* sex. Women who were afraid of the side effects of the birth-control pill have stopped taking them. Condoms are no longer 'cool.' And so the net result overall—seemingly much to the experts' surprise—is a lot more drug-induced abortions, a huge increase in venereal disease, and a spike in AIDS again in the heterosexual population, just when it had appeared to be leveling off."

She took another sip of wine, and Bruce avoided direct eye contact, turning instead toward the city. She waited for him to reply. When he was silent, she added, "And on top of all that, there are rip-off, bootleg drug companies putting cheap lookalike pills on the street for unsuspecting lower income families. So we're seeing a sharp increase in what I'd call unexpected pregnancies. Women think they're taking a morning-after pill, but it doesn't work as advertised, so the number of women going to abortion clinics now that the new national health system will pay for abortions has actually increased, not decreased."

She paused again and then concluded, "So that's what I mean by saying that progress is not always what it's cracked up to be."

Bruce turned back to her, obviously annoyed. "Rebecca, I've never heard you talk like this before. If *you* think that way, I can't imagine what Mary is like. Thank God William is interested in real progress, not just peripheral issues."

"Look, I'm not trying to pick a fight," Rebecca said. "It's a beautiful evening, and I want us to have a great weekend together. But I don't consider what I just described to you as 'peripheral.' In fact, I think the consequences of the morning-after pill are getting worse and worse. And you've got to realize that for me this is not a sterile political issue. This is a real life problem that I have to deal with every day at the hospital. With real people going through real pain, and suffering real loss."

Bruce raised his hand in mock surrender. "Okay, I understand you're 'in the trenches.' You probably deal with it too closely to be able to have the perspective. I appreciate that. I call a truce. Let's go see how the Braves are doing and put the steaks on, if you think the baked potatoes are about ready." Standing up with him, Rebecca took his hand and said, "Your truce is accepted and, by the way, if Mary gets a hold of you, you'll probably wish you were still talking to me." She laughed.

WASHINGTON Leslie Sloane stood with the White House behind her in one of the spots designated for the network press corps to file evening news reports, going over her notes one final time. Ryan Denning, the network anchorperson in New York, would soon cut to her as the lead reporter for the first story that night. She had already taped a piece with clips from the president's press conference that afternoon, to which she would now add a live introduction and a live close.

Leslie had been the U.S. Network's White House correspondent for almost a year, and she was thankful for the spring warmth and the recent switch to Daylight Savings Time so that she was no longer doing these reports in the dark and cold of winter. But still the television required a bank of artificial lights.

The director gave the cue in her earpiece, and on the monitor by the minicamera she saw Ryan Denning beginning to speak on the set in New York. Then she was on.

"Yes, Ryan, President William Harrison held the first press conference of his new administration this afternoon, and by all accounts he did very well, answering virtually every question with precision and occasionally with some wit as well." On cue, the prerecorded tape rolled, showing short segments from three of the president's answers, in all cases portraying him as firmly in control, gracious, and smiling.

At the end of the tape the camera cut back live to Ryan Denning in New York, who looked very serious as he asked their preplanned question. "Leslie, were there any surprises at today's conference?"

"Not really, Ryan. Other than perhaps the especially strong tone in which the president defended the legal rights of abortion clinics against those who have recently stepped up their scare tactics on women trying to get help. The president sent a clear message that his administration will not tolerate those tactics and will prosecute violators to the full extent of the law."

"Thank you, Leslie," Ryan continued. "Now from Kiev, Sam Rollins has the latest on that American embassy employee who was found dead in Odessa last week."

Leslie Sloane put down her microphone and removed her earpiece. She was done for another day. "Thanks, guys," she said to her regular crew behind the camera. "A good report. See you tomorrow." And she headed toward Pennsylvania Avenue to catch a taxi back to her apartment.

She felt good about her report. The president had by no means been perfect, but she had decided even before the news conference began that unless he really blew something wide open, she would put a good "spin" on his performance.

It had been an open secret during the campaign that Leslie, like many in the press, agreed with William Harrison's stands on most issues, and she particularly admired his choice of Patricia Barton-North as his vice presidential running mate. Now that Harrison had been elected, Leslie hoped his administration would get off to a good start and quickly pass many of his campaign promises into law, despite opposition from the other party. She never said so to anyone, but she felt a part of her job was to help him. His policies were too important to leave to chance. And she had appreciated being chosen by the White House to do his first interview right after the election. She smiled, thinking that the two of them made a pretty good team.

What a day, William Harrison thought as he hung his suit jacket in his closet and loosened his tie. *Besides all the work we're doing on policy and legislation, like this morning's frustrating meeting, we had all of those high school kids before lunch and then the press conference this afternoon. Finally the state dinner for the French president. Sometimes I wonder how one human being is supposed to do all this! As much as Abraham Lincoln supposedly complained, I wonder if he would trade places with me now, or figure that fighting the Civil War was maybe a better deal than he knew.*

Carrie looked up from the mirror at her dressing table where she was seated and noticed his silence and his frown. Trying to continue the new communication her husband had seemed to encourage, she smiled and said, "It's been particularly rough these last couple of weeks, hasn't it? I'm afraid we didn't win any points tonight with Katherine by suggesting she attend the state dinner."

"But she looked lovely in that new dress, and she's been studying French all these years. I thought she would have *wanted* to practice on the French president. Sometimes I feel like I can't win with her, no matter what I do."

"I know, sweetheart. I know. We just happened to catch her on a night when she wanted to wear jeans and eat popcorn and study for her history exam. Anyway, she *did* look lovely, and you *did* score some points yesterday by having that meeting with the chief of the Secret Service detail. I think she feels a little more in control of that situation now. And the loosening of the procedures a bit will give her some much needed freedom. Thanks."

"Well, I don't want her to suffer, for heaven's sake," William said, walking into the bathroom. Carrie followed him a few minutes later and saw him leaning on the sink, a hand on each side, lost in thought, looking down at the running water.

"William, what's the matter?" she asked, coming up behind him and gently putting a hand on his shoulder.

He began to speak slowly, almost in a whisper. "Sometimes I wonder if being president of the United States is really all it's cracked up to be, Carrie. Here we worked so hard and sacrificed so much, and now I hardly see our children, one of whom lives right here with us. We almost never have any time to ourselves. Every member of our family is studied like a rat in a laboratory. The press is always taking shots at us. And, worst of all, everyone from the man on the street in Des Moines to the president of Russia thinks I somehow have an answer for every problem facing the world today."

He looked up into the mirror and met Carrie's eyes. "I know it's more than just Katherine tonight, William," she said softly. "Please don't worry. You're doing a great job. You're the best man for the job. No one expects perfection, and you're doing great. We'll get through it."

A month ago he would have just grunted and turned away, but he had to admit that his first attempts at communicating again with Carrie had not been all bad. He still found it awkward, but she'd even helped him with some unusual insights once or twice this week. So he turned to face her and responded. "Carrie, we both know the majority of the voters wanted someone else. The press says I have a 'mandate' for change, and I certainly would never deny that publicly. But you and I know that if there had not been a split-away conservative third party, we wouldn't be in this room tonight. And the problems and programs that seemed big but manageable in North Carolina just defy understanding here in Washington. Without one party in control there is constant gridlock. Everyone protects his or her own turf. I knew foreign policy would be difficult, but now I'm worried our important domestic policy will never get off the ground." He paused and looked away. He had not shared feelings like these with her in a very long time. "Frankly, Carrie, our domestic program's in trouble, and I'm running out of answers."

"Well, maybe there *was* a majority for the others. But we're here nonetheless. Answers will come," Carrie said calmly. "Maybe God has a reason for you being here. I certainly feel that way."

"You've been talking to Mary again," William said, a faint smile momentarily replacing his frown.

"Mary's not the only one who believes in God," Carrie smiled back, trying to be open with him. "I guess I just don't know whether he has time to control every little detail of every day, like she apparently believes. But on the big issues, yes, I believe in him. And I don't think we would be here if there were not some reason."

"Hmm." He leaned against the sink, crossed his arms, and said with a note of sarcasm, "Now on top of everything else, you think I should be listening for God's purpose? What if I miss his signal? Will he sound a trumpet?"

Carrie felt the moment slipping. *He opens up just a little bit and I have to talk about God! Why did I do that?* "Please, William. Don't worry so much. Look at today's press conference. I watched you on television and you were magnificent. I understand why everyone thinks you have all the answers. You certainly seemed to have them today. I was so proud of you."

"Thanks, Carrie, for that completely unbiased assessment. I'll tell Jerry to think about firing Chris and hiring you as my press secretary." She couldn't really tell if he meant it as a compliment or as a put-down. She hated not being able to read her own husband, but she decided to let it pass; he *had* been trying, she knew.

"Really, William, you *were* very good today, and I *was* quite proud. Sometimes you get down on yourself, but no one is perfect. I still say that there must be a reason why we're here."

William turned and walked past her toward his closet, unbuttoning his shirt. "Well, maybe so," he said. "But I tell you, if they want to see real commitment and confidence, they ought to let our vice president hold a press conference! She never seems to doubt one single thing. It sure would be nice to know how to approach every issue with such single-minded certainty. I mean, give her an issue, and she'll tell you the answer!"

"I know, William," Carrie said, sitting down at the dressing table again and picking up her brush. "Sometimes I worry that Patricia sees everything from only one perspective."

"Well she's right, of course. Our nation *has* got to change and be more progressive. That's obvious. But unlike Patricia, I feel we have to do a little educating of our people as well. I'm not sure we can just cram all these changes down everyone's throats in a matter of months, even with congressional help. In fact, if I'm honest with myself, I worry that the majority of this country doesn't really want our domestic program at all, even though it's best for them."

Carrie turned on the dressing table bench to face him. "Please don't get down on yourself and your programs again, or you won't be able to sleep. It has been a very difficult few weeks, and it's been hard on you. I'm worried that you haven't been sleeping well. I'm so glad we've got this weekend with your family at Camp David. William, you need to rest and relax with your family."

William paused and said, "You're right. It *will* be good to relax and see everyone again. Also, I want the family to see a little bit of what our new life is like. I really hope they enjoy it. It's wonderful that Graham and Mary can bring Mom and Dad from Raleigh. By the way, do you know exactly how many of us will be there?"

"I think the total count is twenty-one, including Robert and the Russian friend he wants to bring from Chapel Hill; plus Rebecca's new boyfriend, whose name, I think, is Bruce."

"Well, I hope you've left plenty of free time for us just to 'be,'" he said. "I promised Katherine. And you're right that we need a rest. I'd like to have a few days together without a whole lot of scheduling."

"I agree," Carrie confirmed, continuing to brush her hair. "And William, please leave your papers here. You need a real change for a few days, not just a move of the White House to Maryland." He returned her smile and saluted in agreement as he headed for the shower.

She had done her best to reinforce her husband's confidence. But she was quietly worried. In their more than twenty years of politics together, she had never seen him so down on himself. *I want to help you, William. Please, just let me,* she thought. But she was glad for their small exchanges over the past week. *Well,* she thought, *maybe he does just need to recharge his batteries. Some time with the family will be good for all of us. Hopefully he'll come back refreshed and relaxed.*

ON BOARD THE *BRIGHT STAR* It was still dark in the early morning hours in the Eastern Mediterranean. Sadim Muhmood lay in his bunk on the *Bright Star,* having passed another sleepless night. But Sadim's sleeplessness was not due to worry or self-doubt; those were two emotions Sadim never allowed himself. Rather, he had been awake all night because of a fire that burned inside him. A fire that burned more intensely the closer he came to his goal. And a fire that increasingly would not let him sleep.

One did not grow up in the Palestinian refugee camps and become at an early age one of the acknowledged leaders of the Movement by doubting one's abilities. As a young street lieutenant he had been singled out by the elite, very secret, and totally committed Free Palestine Movement. He had learned a great deal in the twenty-year period from the early seventies to the early nineties. He had learned how to steal and how to kill. He had learned how to organize men so that secrets would be kept. But because of his special abilities, which were recognized early by the Movement's leadership, Sadim also learned how to move transparently in international circles, how to blend into the highest circles of power in the world, whether in the Mafia leadership or in the most conservative governments, and how to play the shifting winds of the cold war to secure the greatest material and political benefits for his comrades.

The end of the cold war and the isolation caused by the Persian Gulf War had cut the Movement off from its primary sources of funds and support in the Eastern Bloc countries. But by then the Movement had amassed enough financial wealth to be self-supporting, and the end of the cold war had created another very beneficial effect: a period of three years in which the former Soviet Union was essentially without order or discipline. During this period Sadim and the Movement had acquired the nuclear bomb that now rode safely in the modified cargo hold of the *Bright Star*, less than two hundred feet from his stateroom.

Despite this great victory, or rather because of it, Sadim occasionally could not sleep. The Council's plan, of which he was the partial author and now the single leader, was running like clockwork. But the clock was running too slowly for Sadim's internal fire. This fire had been kindled in the camps of his youth, as he watched his parents humiliated and driven from their land, his teenage friends punished, and his faith belittled by callous politicians and the necessities of 'world order.' He wanted the clock to run faster so the end they planned would come sooner. And on those nights when he heard the clock ticking too slowly he sometimes could not sleep.

He rubbed his temples, trying to relieve a mild headache. Nevertheless he smiled, considering how all of the events had played into their hands, from the acquisition of the warhead to the availability of the parts and expertise they needed, even to the obvious weakness of the current American president. It would be eighteen more months before they attacked the United States, but he doubted whether William Harrison would be a worthy adversary, given the weak and indecisive president he appeared to be.

Sadim had never met President Harrison, but he had watched him many times on television. The eyes. He had studied Harrison's eyes and seen a politician, not a warrior. And of course an infidel who did not believe in the Prophet Mohammed. *What will he do when the pictures start arriving? Feel helpless and confused, as we have done for three generations?* He smiled again. That morning as he began his prayers, Sadim thanked Allah for giving him William Harrison. Sadim even prayed for the president's continued good health, at least for another eighteen months.

Religion in America... must nevertheless be regarded as the foremost of the political institutions of that country.... I do not know whether all the Americans have a sincere faith in their religion; for who can search the human heart? But I am certain that they hold it to be indispensable to the maintenance of republican institutions. This opinion is not peculiar to a class of citizens or to a party, but it belongs to the whole nation, and to every rank of society... Christianity, therefore, reigns without any obstacle, by universal consent.

ALEXIS DE TOCQUEVILLE

3

Easter Weekend
Two Days Later

WASHINGTON A cold front blew across the East Coast on Thursday, replacing the first really warm weather of April with a reminder of the winter just passed. It rained in Washington on Thursday, but Friday morning dawned clear, cool, and windy, with the promise of a beautiful Easter weekend ahead. Congress had already adjourned for the Easter recess, and Washington assumed the slightly slower pace that was possible when the House and Senate were not in session.

The previous evening the president's son, Robert, had arrived from Chapel Hill, North Carolina, along with Alexander Piminov, an exchange student from Kiev. Robert met Sasha, as he was called, through his Russian language studies, and they happened to live in the same dorm.

The extended Harrison family gathered at the White House at noon. They came from as nearby as Norfolk, home for Hugh, Jennifer, and their three children, and as far away as Denver, where Rebecca's daughter Courtney lived. Carrie and her daughter, Katherine, conducted the family's tour of the White House, for which there had been no time at the inauguration, and the president walked along with them, listening to his wife and daughter describe the national monument in which he hoped to live for eight years. He was pleased to see that Katherine appeared to be enjoying herself. But on three occasions he was called away to phone calls.

Will they leave him alone at Camp David? Carrie wondered.

The first lady designed the luncheon to be casual yet with enough ceremony to give her husband's family a taste of what White House formality could be like.

The luncheon over, the family moved to the West Wing, where the adults had coffee in the Oval Office and the youngest children played outside on the lawn. Exactly at 2:30 Hugh heard the familiar beat of what he knew would be three Sea Knight helicopters, painted green, descending on the South Lawn.

When the family members arrived at the White House earlier that day they had given their luggage to a member of the staff. Now they were to be ferried by helicopters to Camp David for the weekend. The customary three helicopters, deployed as a group to confuse anyone trying to do harm to the president, would be more than adequate to transport even their large family. Only the president's parents had elected to be driven to the Maryland hilltop retreat.

Once the helicopters had landed and disengaged their rotors, the family assembled in the sunshine for a group picture on the South Lawn steps. Then with waves and smiles toward the small army of reporters and photographers who covered the president's every step, the Harrison family moved toward the waiting helicopters. Within five minutes the rotors were again engaged, and the three craft took off one at a time for the low-level, exhilarating ride to Camp David. For Hugh a ride in a helicopter was nothing new, but even he enjoyed the view of Washington and the Maryland countryside. And for the other family guests it was a thrilling kickoff to what they hoped would be an exceptional weekend together.

Thirty minutes later Leslie Sloane was devouring a pita pocket sandwich at the U.S. Network's Washington bureau when the telephone on her desk rang. She removed the large earring from her right ear and answered.

"Hi, Leslie. It's Ryan. How are you?"

"I'm fine, Ryan. Sorry, you caught me with my mouth full of a very late lunch after covering the president's getaway to Camp David."

"That's actually why I'm calling. Is there a story there? Is he really just going off with his family for Easter Weekend, or is something else going on we don't know about?"

"I don't think so, Ryan. I know Chris Wright pretty well now, and he swears it's just what it appears. I even asked Bob Horan which staff members are going, and he said *no one,* not even Jerry Richardson. Bob said the president basically gave everyone the weekend off and told them to go home, that he was going to spend some time with his family. There's a rumor that his wife put her foot down and even made him leave all his files here. Other than the military aide who carries the codes, the communications personnel, and the Marines who guard Camp David, and his family, of course, I think he really is alone."

"Well," Ryan pressed, "is *that* a story? I mean, is he tired? Does he already need to recharge his batteries? Is the job getting to him?"

"Hey, let's give him some slack." She took a sip of her soft drink, then continued. "He's the best chance we've got to make a real difference in this country. Remember what happened last time when we lambasted the president after only a few months? We made him a lame duck for almost four years. Let's not shoot ourselves in the collective foot again and kill one of our own before he even gets started. I assure you I'm on top of this, and let's just play it like it is: a restful weekend with his family, showing them what it's like to be the first family."

"Okay. But don't be blinded and miss a story when it's right in front of you."

"Ryan," Leslie said, her tone conveying her irritation, "how long have I been at this? If anything, I'm becoming *more* of an insider. These people are really beginning to open up to me. Just this morning Patricia Barton-North's domestic policy advisor gave me some unreported examples of how some new equal-but-separate arrangements are working at colleges and public schools, and she asked me to help with a story on them. I'll pass them to Julia Porter there in New York. If she does the story, the VP will owe us one."

"Sounds good. I know you're doing a great job. I'm sorry if I came on too strong."

"Apology accepted," Leslie responded.

"Listen, when are you coming up to the Big Apple?"

Leslie smiled. The gossip columns had speculated for months that she and Ryan Denning were an item, but so far there was no truth to it, other than that they worked closely together, and they were both recently divorced. His had been messy, involving two teenage children. She, at thirty-five, had no children, given her clear commitment to a career. *Too bad we work for the same network,* she thought for the hundredth time. *Daddy always said not to mix work and romance.*

But to Ryan she answered, "Next Friday, I think. Don't we have that planning conference?"

"Yeah, we do. How about if you and I have dinner on Friday?"

She paused for a moment. "Sure, Ryan. That sounds great. Have a good weekend."

The presidential helicopters were spaciously outfitted. William and Carrie sat facing each other in aisle seats, giving the window view to Mary and Graham. As they flew across the countryside William was drawn back, as usually happened when he was with Mary, to thoughts of growing up, and particularly to that Sunday in their high school days thirty-five years before.

William Harrison came of age in the early sixties, when the intoxicating idea first convinced Americans that they themselves, and particularly their government, could solve virtually any problem with enough thought and enough of the nation's plentiful resources.

The Missile Race, the Space Race, the War on Poverty, the Peace Corps, the Bomb, the Civil Rights Movement, the Pill, the Great Society, Vista, Head Start: these and other endeavors all proclaimed to William's generation, particularly as citizens of the world's most powerful nation, that their future, whether for success or for failure, was totally in their own hands. William Harrison, then a young teenager, believed.

It was easy to believe. Almost everyone did. Especially in William's family. His father, Tom, was an engineer with a company that had secured one of the first communications contracts from NASA, as the nation's concern about Sputnik turned into a race to place a man on the moon. His father's education had been interrupted by World War II, and when he had returned from the Pacific and graduated from North Carolina State University he had stayed in Raleigh and taken a job with an electronics firm.

If William inherited an ability to think through and then solve problems from his father, he inherited from his mother an activist value system that encouraged him to find problems to solve. A graduate of Duke University in the heady days during World War II, Elizabeth Harrison imbued her family with an intellectual curiosity and a willingness to challenge the status quo, which she had learned in her early "firebrand" days at lectures and rallies for socialism and justice, both at Duke and at neighboring Chapel Hill.

Although she had never worked outside the home, William's mother was always challenging their local politicians and writing letters, believing that opportunities were available every day to make the world a better, more just, more rational place.

Their family had belonged to a large, mainline church in the northwest suburb of Raleigh. Architecturally beautiful with its classic red brick facade and bells that were famous in the community, the church was a gathering place for those who wanted to attend church in a manner that reflected their intelligence and their position in the community. These were definitely not "holy rollers." The members of St. Stephen's Church represented the New South, and they appreciated that their worship service reflected the same inclusive, liberal concerns that characterized the other aspects of their lives. Above all, they were comfortable with their pastor, with his calls for action on the many social ills of the day and with his lack of demands for anything to do with their spiritual lives, a concept most of them would have found to be old-fashioned and beneath them, anyway.

In William's sophomore year their popular pastor was called to a larger congregation, leaving the members to search for a new minister. They had gone about that task in a characteristically organized way and had narrowed the candidates to three by that spring. Each of these men had been asked to preside over the worship service and to preach on two consecutive Sundays. It was on the second Sunday for Rev. Gene Wilson, the youngest of the three candidates, that the remarkable event occurred.

After his first week some said the search committee had invited Rev. Wilson only as a contrast to the two older, more traditional men. For in his first of two sermons Rev. Wilson had talked almost exclusively about spiritual matters, including the state of their souls and their prospects for spending eternity with God in heaven, not even mentioning a single one of the many social problems that needed their members' attention. He did criticize the Supreme Court's decision to bar prayer in public schools, but no one cared much for that issue. And few of the members of St. Stephen's had ever questioned their own fitness for heaven. After all, they attended church regularly and did good things, didn't they?

His mind snapped back to the present when Mary turned from the window and noticed him deep in thought. He smiled and said in a low voice, "I was just thinking again about your Rev. Wilson."

She leaned a little closer, and her surprise was obvious. "What made you think of that?"

"Oh, I often think about all of us growing up. Different things. And about that day, strange as it may seem."

"I didn't know you remembered it."

"Of course I do. Particularly how Mom and Dad didn't want to go to church that morning, after Rev. Wilson's sermon the week before. I thought we were going to skip it."

"Yes, I remember them debating about it. Thank goodness habit won out," Mary added.

Both of them reflected silently on what had happened that morning. They had dutifully dressed for church, including the usual search for young Hugh's shoes, then deposited Rebecca and Hugh in Sunday school. After a special class for the high school students, Mary and William joined their parents in the main sanctuary during the offertory, in time for the sermon.

Young Rev. Wilson—he was only in his early thirties—began by acknowledging the "constructive criticism" that several of the church members had expressed to him during the week after his first sermon, but he looked down from the pulpit with a mixture of compassion and concern and told them that he nevertheless had a responsibility to convey what he felt God had called him to preach, whether or not he would be chosen to be their pastor, and he would therefore submit to God's will.

To the sound of much rustling in the pews and some coughing, Rev.

Wilson described to the members of St. Stephen's how the power of God had changed his life, how Jesus described salvation as a conscious act of being born again through belief in him, and how both salvation and God's power, in the being of the Holy Spirit, were available to each one of them that day, if they believed in and confessed Jesus as Lord.

William, seated between his mother and sister in the polished wooden pew, noticed that his mother's back stiffened on several occasions during the sermon and that his parents exchanged glances more than once. But he also noticed that Mary seemed to be listening intently and hanging onto every word. The one time he actually looked at her, there was an expression of concentration and of what could only be described as joy on her face. William, focusing as best he could at fifteen, was mostly curious.

Rev. Wilson had built a logical and impassioned case, quoting scripture throughout, that the most important choice any of them could make was not which cause to support, but whether they would submit to God and let him run their lives. The rest could follow, but that day they needed to choose whom they would serve: man or God. And then he did something no preacher had ever done at St. Stephen's: he asked all those who wanted to confess their sins and to inherit eternity that day by accepting Jesus as the Lord of their lives to come forward so that they could pray together.

The event William would always remember was that his sister Mary immediately stood up, the first in the congregation, and moved toward the aisle, trying to pass in front of him and his parents. And he would also always remember the look of shock, disbelief, and embarrassment on his mother's face, as Mary waited to pass and the two women's eyes met. His parents finally made room, and Mary walked forward, joined in the front of the church by about fifteen other members.

The young minister, smiling warmly, walked down from the pulpit and prayed with and for the members who had come forward. As William listened to his sister and the others confess their sins and ask Jesus to take over their lives, the hair on the back of his neck stood up, and he felt a distinct chill, almost as if an invisible wind had blown through the crowded, warm church. And when Mary turned around to walk back to her seat, William saw that she had been crying. Yet the joy he had noticed earlier now seemed to radiate from her. When she sat down next to him again, she quietly asked him for his handkerchief.

Brought back to the present, he again leaned over and asked, "Did you know how angry Mom and Dad were with you that day?"

"Oh, yes." Mary nodded her head at the window, then turned to face him. "I think I really embarrassed them. Mom said I must have been crazy to get caught up in such a blatantly emotional appeal, 'as if we were at a tent revival, for heaven's sake!' she said."

"I didn't know."

"Yes, she was pretty hard on me. But unlike what she thought, it was just so simple for me. I felt God's real presence in my life for the first time those two Sundays, and I decided then and there that I wanted to accept his offer of salvation. I felt a new power in my life after that."

"I've never understood why that event had such an impression on me," William said, "especially since I didn't really share it with you, but only watched. I guess it was just a stage in my life—or maybe the fact that you so spontaneously did something that Mom and Dad didn't like." He grinned. "But you sure got good at expressing your faith!"

"Well, thanks, little brother. You know I still enjoy doing so—in fact, it's about the most important thing any of us can do."

Raising his hand, he said, "I know, I know. And remember, I've heard it *plenty* of times. I don't need another lecture. I just wanted you to know that even at my old age I can still remember some of the special times in our family."

"Okay, no lecture. But I make no promises for Camp David, once I find out what those advisors of yours have been filling your mind with."

William laughed. "Truce. We can lecture each other hourly, and Mom will be there to fill in if we miss anything. But for now, don't miss this wonderful view."

CAMP DAVID, MARYLAND   Camp David, with its rustic, wooded charm, dated back to the Roosevelt Administration, when it was originally carved out of Catoctin Mountain in the Maryland countryside. Called Shangri-La by Franklin Roosevelt and renamed by President Eisenhower for his grandson, Camp David had undergone minor transformations by each succeeding president. But the basic layout of small cabins spaced around Laurel Lodge, the "main house" for the compound, had remained unchanged. The only exception was the home used by the president himself, Aspen Lodge, which had been enlarged several years before and contained an office with modern communications equipment. Circling the entire perimeter was a tall, electronically monitored fence. The whole facility was guarded by a detachment of Marines.

When the helicopters landed, William Harrison realized he was out of the presidential fishbowl for the first time since taking office. He actually smiled and thought of a remark Carrie had made: *The world and its problems would probably still be there on Tuesday.* He helped his wife and daughter down the stairs of their helicopter and pointed Robert and Sasha toward the superintendent, who was waiting with members of the staff by the landing site. He met all of the president's family and gave them their cabin assignments.

As Carrie Harrison had promised her husband, the weekend was purposely unstructured, with the exception of one event a day. There would be an ongoing round-robin tennis tournament with trophies to be awarded at lunch on Monday. There was an intergenerational softball game scheduled for Saturday afternoon between, roughly defined, the Public Sector and the Private Sector, the teams selected by household employment. And there was an Easter morning service planned for the chapel, followed by an Easter egg hunt for the children. Since William and Carrie did not regularly attend church, the first lady had asked Mary if she knew someone in the Washington area who would be appropriate to officiate. "Not too wild, now," Carrie had warned good-naturedly but quite seriously. Mary had assured her that she knew a pastor in Baltimore who would be appropriate, and the arrangements had been made.

Other than those events, the weekend was to be free, allowing plenty of time for rest, conversations, walks, and playing with children.

Rebecca's daughter Courtney, at twenty-four the second oldest of the "children" after Mary and Graham's first son Jonathan, pulled her cousin Robert aside as they walked from the landing site toward Laurel Lodge. "Your Russian friend, Sasha, is kind of cute. Does he play tennis?"

Robert smiled. "He's Ukrainian, not Russian, and, yes, he's pretty good."

"How about if we warm up for the tournament together? I'll ask Katherine or Sarah to join us. In about thirty minutes?"

"Sure. Sounds good. If they both want to play, ask Tim, too, and we'll all play around," Robert suggested, and moved off to find Sasha.

Rebecca was wearing a long-sleeved, flower-printed dress and a large straw hat. She and Bruce were holding hands, taking their time walking toward their cabin, enjoying the sunshine together now that the strong breeze of the morning was dying down.

Katherine and Sarah, the only two cousins who were almost exactly the same age, had always been close. They had grown up in Raleigh together, though they had attended different high schools and Katherine had lived most recently in the governor's mansion. "I can't wait to get into some jeans!" Katherine exclaimed, as they walked together up the gentle slope toward the main house nestled in the trees. "And I think we can walk almost anywhere around this place without being followed! Please, Sarah, tell me what's going on in the real world. Is it still there?" she asked, her bubbly personality returning now that she was out of her "prison" and together again with her favorite cousin.

"Yes, it's still there. And Matthew is still *it.* Too bad he couldn't come this weekend. He says hi."

William and Carrie, having helped the superintendent give everyone their cabin assignments, walked along with Graham and Mary in the warm afternoon sun. "It was wonderful of you both to arrange this weekend for all of us," Mary said, smiling at her brother and sister-in-law. "Obviously it will mean a lot to all of us, and especially to Mom and Dad."

"It's our pleasure," William answered sincerely, genuinely glad to be among his family. "We need it, too," he added, taking Carrie's hand. "I can't think of a better way to spend a little of the taxpayers' money to recharge the old president!"

"Fifty is not exactly so old, dear." His wife returned his smile and squeezed his hand. "It's a nice, distinguished age. But even young presidents like you can use some rest and relaxation."

Graham asked his brother-in-law, "Didn't President Eisenhower add a short course to this place? Would you like to play pitch and putt?" They had played many rounds of golf together in earlier years.

"I can't think of anything I'd like better," the president replied. "That is, if it's on the schedule." He glanced at Carrie.

"I told you, there's almost no schedule. Yes, you and Graham go on and play before your parents arrive. And you might ask Hugh, too. Jennifer says he's learning golf when he's not at sea."

The two men accepted the suggestion and moved off to change into their golf clothes, leaving Carrie and Mary together on the path just short of the main house.

"How is he, Carrie?" Mary asked, as they walked slowly along the path.

"Oh, he's fine." She gave a half-smile, then added, "Parts of the job are glorious and parts are really grueling. We're all glad to be away this weekend with the family. And I'm especially glad our Katherine and Sarah are together again; the White House is no place to be seventeen, at least in this day and age."

"It sounds awfully glamorous on the surface," Mary said, "but I guess the reality could grate on a high school junior. Maybe this summer Katherine could spend some time with us. I know Sarah and Tim would be glad to have her, and it would probably do her good just to knock around Raleigh again with them. Sarah's going to work part time at a sandwich shop owned by Graham's nephew. Would the president's daughter like to fix sandwiches and scoop ice cream?"

"I'm sure she'd love it," Carrie said with enthusiasm. "Let's talk to them this weekend. And it would be one less thing for William to worry about."

"Are the bad guys getting him down?" Mary asked seriously.

"No, not really. He just worries a lot. His domestic program is not moving as quickly as he wants, and it seems like there's a new international problem every other day."

"Does he get good advice?"

Carrie paused. "Yes…I think so. I guess it's just that the world has become so complex, and the president of the United States is supposed to be…well, omniscient, I guess. He feels a burden to know everything about every subject. It's hard on him, frankly. He spends a lot of time studying."

"We find it almost impossible to raise a family using just our own strength, so I can't imagine trying to be the president of the United States on my own."

Carrie stopped and looked at her sister-in-law. "What do you mean?"

"I mean without God's help," Mary replied. "I don't see how *anyone* makes it today without him. And I can imagine William is finding his hands full, trying to master everything, all by himself; trying always to be the best and the brightest. He's been like that for a long time," Mary said, "but he may have met his match in this job!"

Carrie was momentarily flustered. She started to speak, stopped, then said, "That reminds me. Tell me about the pastor coming on Sunday." She and Mary continued along the path.

"Michael Tate. He's bringing his wife, Elizabeth. He's a great guy, and she's pretty special, too. He's in his mid-forties and is the CEO of the International Training Institute in Baltimore. It's a large, interdenominational organization that trains Christian political leaders in their home countries. He's been there about ten years and travels all over the world. It's a big job, and he has a real heart for the Lord."

"How do you know him?"

"We met at a conference several years ago, and he stays with us whenever he's visiting the Research Triangle on business or on a speaking engagement. The great thing about Michael is that besides his job, he's an ordained minister. He serves as an assistant pastor at a large suburban Baltimore church. He's a great speaker. I thought William and the rest of the family would enjoy meeting him because he knows what's really happening in so many countries."

"He sounds interesting. I hope he and his wife can stay for lunch on Sunday," Carrie said.

"Oh, I'm sure that won't be a problem."

"Good. Well, we'd better get unpacked before the afternoon is over. Your mother and father should be here soon."

"Thanks. Unfortunately William's not the only one with too much to do. I've got two home closings which were looking shaky when I left, and I've got to check on them one last time before the weekend."

"Then we'll see you in the Great Room at Laurel Lodge. It's wonderful that everyone could come," Carrie concluded, as she moved up the path that led to Aspen Lodge. Mary nodded as Carrie left, feeling that her sister-in-law was actually more worried about William than she had been willing to acknowledge.

The cabins at Camp David turned out to be one, two, and three bedroom cottages, each with a living room and porch. Mary Prescott had just emerged from the shower in their cabin and wrapped a towel around her when she heard the rest of her family coming in from tennis and golf.

"First for the shower," she heard Tim say through her bedroom door, as he clomped down the hall on feet that still seemed too big for his body.

As Graham opened their bedroom door, Mary had a glimpse of Sarah. "How was tennis, dear?" she asked.

"Fine, Mom. Robert and his friend Sasha are really good. We split up and played teams. It was fun. But I'm starved."

"Well, we're invited up to the porch of Laurel Lodge at six-thirty for cocktails and lemonade, and dinner is at seven. You'll probably need the time to shower and change. And how was golf?" she asked, turning to Graham as he closed the bedroom door.

"The golf was fine. William shot pretty well after three months in the White House. But, boy, did he and Hugh get into an argument," Graham replied, as he unbuttoned his golf shirt.

"Over what?" Mary asked, starting to comb her wet hair in front of the mirror over their dresser.

"William made the mistake of asking Hugh how the new policy on women, gays, and lesbians in the armed forces is coming along. Hugh gave William an earful on what they're going through. Mary, you wouldn't believe what they're having to do in order to implement these new policies. It sounds crazy to me. Hugh's concern is that the results will inevitably be disastrous. He actually told William that a combat ship is no place to be trying out half-baked social experiments! It was wonderful. William missed a two-foot putt."

"What did William say?"

"He argued at first how it was not right to discriminate against a legitimate alternative lifestyle—"

"I wonder if he's read the Bible on that subject lately, or even applied common sense?" Mary interrupted.

"I doubt it. But, anyway, as we played on, Hugh really wore him down. I don't think William, since he never served in the military, ever really thought through what it means to put so many young people so close together in those living conditions."

"What about Hugh? What is he having to do?"

"Well, he's doing his best to follow orders. He told William his captain and all the senior people are on top of the changes and trying to implement them smoothly. I don't think Hugh had thought very much about the subject until he wound up in the middle of it. But the other day he had to watch a homosexual 'sensitizing' video. I think that may have planted some real doubts about this 'alternative life style' business. He seems genuinely concerned for his men, and I think he's also worried because he's suddenly going to be responsible for twenty young women in his department. On top of all that, he hasn't figured out how to tell Jennifer that his new fire control officer is a twenty-eight-year-old single woman, and apparently very good looking."

"Poor baby brother Hugh. It's kind of ironic he's on the receiving end of his own brother's policies. But I guess we couldn't ask for any better feedback than his. William certainly can't accuse Hugh of being a Christian fundamentalist!"

The family assembled before supper that evening on the large porch at Laurel Lodge, where conversations begun earlier at the White House were continued and everyone had a chance to catch up on family news. The senior Harrisons, Tom and Elizabeth, arrived by car.

The first lady had given instructions to the superintendent not to create one long banquet table for their meals, but instead to break up the tables into seatings of six and eight. As she walked around the porch greeting everyone again before dinner, she made it clear that they were supposed to sit at different tables for each meal over the weekend so that all of the family members would have several opportunities to spend time with one another.

For their first meal William and Carrie were joined by his parents and their own two children. Sasha sat next to Robert, and Katherine invited her cousin Sarah. Three other tables were arranged around the president's central table.

"You're looking great, Mom," the president said to his mother, after they were seated.

"I've got to. Someone from our generation has to be ready to explain your policies when the press asks. Your father won't give them the time of day, so it's left for me to be your ambassador to the old folks. So far I'm holding up okay, but the pay is really lousy for the long hours involved." She finished with a smile and a flourish of her knife, which had been on its way to the butter.

"Well, we appreciate it. And please don't stop explaining what the government should do next. You've been at this for at least fifty years that I know of, personally."

"And if they'd have listened to me all those years ago, you wouldn't have such a mess to clean up now, William. But we're glad it's you who's trying!" The uncharacteristic moment of pride was pleasantly obvious to everyone at the table.

"Please pass the potatoes," Robert asked after a moment's pause.

The conversation at the president's table continued in a light-hearted vein throughout the meal, and Carrie could see her husband unwinding. Those at the three other tables seemed to be enjoying themselves just as much. Carrie was pleased that the special weekend was off to such a good start.

As dessert was served, the president turned to Sasha and said, "Robert has told us a lot about you. It's wonderful you're here. Tell us about conditions in Ukraine now."

Their guest spent several minutes telling his hosts about the improving conditions in his country. The situation had begun to change about three years after Russia's reforms and had gathered speed once large amounts of real estate had been privatized and businesses were sold to local entrepreneurs at fair prices.

"Looking back on that process from the perspective of a few years," the president continued after Sasha had finished, "what would you say were the principal causes for this change? Has it been the spirit of your people, or their hope for material improvement, or technical assistance from the West? What's been behind this success, which seemed so impossible only a few years ago?"

Sasha did not hesitate a moment. "That's easy. It has been God."

The president stopped stirring his coffee. Everyone else seated at the table looked at the young Ukrainian.

"God?" the president asked. "Why do you say that?"

"It's obvious. I've seen his power. First in our people. Then through them in our government."

"You've seen God's power?" Elizabeth Harrison asked, her voice carrying a hint of skepticism.

"Yes, ma'am. Of course." The young Ukrainian spoke slowly, searching for the right words. "How else can you explain the fall of the—how do you call it in English?—Iron Curtain...and the disappearance of the largest empire on earth at the time? Almost overnight. No shooting. As if it had never been there?

"Men tried for decades to destroy it. Or to contain it. But then it just...just disappeared! Only God could have done that. No man could have planned it. Nor would anyone have believed it, do you think, if they hadn't seen it. In the Bible, they call that a miracle. It must have been God's work. Who else?"

There was an embarrassed silence at the table. William smiled and started to speak, but Sasha continued. "You must realize...we lived for generations in a society that denied God's existence. Men were supposed to improve everything themselves. But they completely failed. Tens of millions of people were killed instead. Then into this vacuum suddenly came the Word of God. Perhaps it has more strength there, because it's such a difference; and people really believe, once they've seen God's power at work. I've seen drunk men healed overnight. Women who...who sold their bodies stopped after praying for God's help. Men who beat their wives and families have been cured." Several of the Harrison family members exchanged glances.

"My own father—" Sasha was visibly moved. "My own father changed after hearing God's Word. Several years ago my uncle Yuri went away one night from our apartment. He told my father that when he came back, everything we had ever dreamed about would come true for our family. He never came back. Neither he nor his car was ever seen again. He and my father were mixed up with the mafia, I think, which was just starting in our country.

"For a week my father was very upset. He drank heavily, swearing that my uncle would return. When he was drunk…he hit my mother. Then that Sunday my mother convinced him—I do not know how—to go to a church that had been started in our apartment block by a young man who had been trained for a year by a team from America, one of the first such groups in our country."

He paused again. "That Sunday our family heard about a new way of living for God…who made us. No matter what the consequences. The minister told about how his own life had been changed, and he read several passages from the Bible about how God had changed other people. And at the end of the service, my father was changed, too. He has never been the same since that day. On Monday he quit his job with the truck company and asked to help the minister at the Christian Center in downtown Kiev, as a way to learn more about God.

"He did little jobs around Kiev for three months, but always helped at the center, doing whatever had to be done, without pay. Through them he met a Ukrainian-American woman, the local representative of Delta Freight, who opened their office in Kiev, and who had a strong Christian faith. The center recommended my father to be their first driver because he was hard working, faithful, and honest—you would never have described him like that only a year before. Now he is the dispatcher for the company and I am at college because of a corporate scholarship. And, above all, my father is changed on the inside. He loves my mother and sister, and he reads the Bible every day. He helps other people. That is the power of God. Yes, I've seen it."

No one spoke. Several studied their coffee. Sasha was silent for a moment. Finally he said, "Those same kinds of stories have happened over and over again in our country, thanks to God and to the hard work of many people who are spreading his Word.

"And one by one, changed people have come into our government. And *that* is what has made so much difference in these three years. Men and women who believe in God and try to do his will every day have taken over from four generations of leaders who…who tried to pretend that God does not exist. The difference is amazing and very real. That is what has happened to our country."

The three tables around the president's had also fallen quiet as Sasha had begun speaking again. As he concluded, the entire room was silent, including the staff. He looked around, embarrassed. Sarah looked across the table at her uncle, who was staring at the young Ukrainian.

Finally the first lady cleared her throat, smiled, and said, "Thank you, Sasha. You, your family, and your country have been through a lot. We've enjoyed hearing about it firsthand. Haven't we, William?"

"Yes…Yes, thank you, Sasha. It's great having you here. Now, let's all not get *too* serious," the president continued, raising his voice slightly to address the whole room and smiling. "It's a beautiful evening. Some of us may want to walk off dinner or relax here in the lodge. Please just enjoy yourselves and feel at home."

As Rebecca and Bruce entered the dining room the next morning, the president and first lady were just leaving, having finished their breakfast early.

"I didn't get a chance to tell you yesterday, little sister, but you look great," William said, as they paused in the doorway. Glancing at Bruce, he continued, "Something must be having a positive effect on you."

Rebecca smiled and hugged Bruce's arm. "You're right. I feel great. Wanna hit some balls later to get ready for the softball game? I bet I can hit 'em farther than you."

"No contest." The president returned her smile. "I just hope I don't make too big a fool of myself at the game. Look, I see you two are already in your tennis gear, but would you like to walk with us after your breakfast? We didn't get much of a chance to talk yesterday."

"Sure, that'll be great. We'll come over to your cabin—is it Aspen?—as soon as we've finished breakfast."

Thirty minutes later the two couples set out on one of the several trails that crisscrossed the forested presidential retreat.

After some small talk on the beauty of their surroundings, Bruce said, "I for one am sure glad to be here. And particularly with Rebecca." He squeezed her hand and she smiled at him.

"You do seem to have a medicinal effect on our nurse," William laughed, noting the bounce in her step.

"I've got a long prescription, big brother."

They walked a little farther in silence.

"That was some story the Russian—uh, Ukrainian—boy told last night, wasn't it?" the president asked as they turned a corner in the trail.

"We only heard the last part," Bruce replied, "but it sounded a bit much to me. Things just happen. There doesn't have to be a God at work every second of the day to make a few things go right for a change. He sure had his story straight, though. He sounded like he'd practiced it, almost."

"I don't know," Carrie said. "I felt like he just got more excited as he went along. I think he was really sincere. And his English is exceptional. I felt he made some good points, especially about changing people."

"Well, thank goodness we've got an administration that doesn't wait for God to get around to doing something about all the problems that need fixing in *this* country!" Bruce complimented William. "If there *is* a God, maybe he's focusing too much on Ukraine or Africa or somewhere else, because we've got problems here like AIDS and crime and social injustice that need to be addressed. Until you were elected, Mr. President, no one was doing one thing about them. I just hope you can really pick up support and get your campaign programs passed."

"Me, too, Bruce," William replied.

Carrie noticed William frowning slightly, and to change the subject, she said, "So, Rebecca, we see your social life seems to be just fine. Tell us about your work. How is it going?"

"Fine, I guess. With health reform everyone is of course very cost conscious. Sometimes I feel we do everything now by committee, which is time consuming but not all bad. I *am* worried about this new, 'improved' morning-after abortion pill. Not because I'm opposed to abortion when necessary, but because of its other effects."

"I haven't heard about any negative effects at all," William said. "I thought the results were all positive."

"I wish they were. The empirical data may not be available yet, if anyone even has the guts to print it. But as someone in the trenches, I can tell you that there are some unpleasant side effects when you make everyone think they're immune to getting pregnant no matter what they do."

"How so?" the president asked.

Rebecca gave him roughly the same information she had shared with Bruce several days earlier about unexpected pregnancies, a spike in venereal disease and AIDS, and increased clinical abortions.

"I hadn't heard any of that," Carrie said, when Rebecca had finished. "Had you, William?"

"No. Just the opposite, really. But, like Rebecca said, maybe the figures haven't caught up with what she's seeing."

"Or maybe it's just one woman's experience in one hospital in one city," Bruce said. "Maybe there should be a few additional warnings with the pill. But the main thing is that many women *are* protected from unwanted pregnancies, which gives them choices about how they want to lead their lives. That's progress, and we've got to keep doing research and pushing the envelope of what's possible, to help people."

"But what if the negative effects exceed any possible good results?" Rebecca asked. "And don't forget, this morning-after pill doesn't really protect a woman from pregnancy; it ends pregnancy."

"Now please don't start sounding like Mary," William chided his sister good-naturedly. "Don't tell me that a bunch of cells twelve hours old makes a baby."

"I don't know, William. I'm sorry. That's not really even what I'm concerned about," she said, as they rounded a curve in the trail and looked out on a small mountain field. "It's all the other things I see happening to the people involved. Anyway, it's real to me, and I'm worried about it."

"And my brother's death was real to me," Bruce added icily. "I think our government could have done much more on AIDS research, and I just get tired of all these worrywarts who want to go slow with everything new. And there's usually some moralist like your sister Mary behind them, telling us we're all going to hell if we do this or that. It drives me crazy. If they had their way, we'd all be back in the Dark Ages!"

"Well, I agree we have to do research," Rebecca said. "But you know, Bruce, maybe part of what Mary and Graham believe *is* right. Maybe there are *some* things we shouldn't be doing, even though they're possible. I don't know. I wouldn't have said that a few years ago. But I live with the *consequences* of what we do—and what our government does—every day. I see the messed up lives and the pain and the fear. Mary would say it's the result of us violating God's law; I can't say that. To me it's just common sense, based on what I see."

"This stuff is really getting to you, isn't it?" Bruce said, taking her hand.

There was silence as they walked several more paces. "Yes, I guess so. I'm sorry," she said to Carrie and William. "I didn't mean to sound like I was on a soapbox or anything."

"You didn't, Rebecca," Carrie said, taking William's hand. "We all need to catch up with each other; and if this is what's happening in your life, then we want to hear about it. William apparently got an earful from Hugh on another subject yesterday. That's what family is for!"

"What did Hugh have to say?" Rebecca asked, curious.

"Oh, nothing," William answered, looking down at the path as they walked, wishing Carrie hadn't mentioned it. "Just some military policies. Anyway, I sure hope the situation with that pill gets straightened out. Next week I'll see if I can get some more information about it. Now, enough about all of that. Tell us about Courtney. Then I want to hear about what you do, Bruce."

They walked on for almost an hour, returning to the cabins about ten. "It's a few minutes past time for our tennis," Bruce reminded Rebecca. "But I really enjoyed the walk. You're a good man, Mr. President. The nation is lucky to have you. Hang in there."

"We'll see you both at lunch." William waved as Rebecca and Bruce left for their cabin to get their rackets.

As Carrie and William turned and walked toward his office in Aspen Lodge to check the morning communications, he remarked to her, "It's strange how both Hugh and Rebecca seem to be on the receiving end of policies started here in Washington. I guess it's rare to hear firsthand what happens at the other end of the line when someone here throws a particular switch." He was silent a moment, thinking. Then he said, "The result, apparently, is not always what we think it will be."

"The nation *is* lucky to have you," Carrie responded, "and you're lucky to have such a family. They certainly aren't afraid to share their thoughts with the president!"

"No, to them I'm just their politician brother. I guess that's good, really. And we haven't even heard from Mary yet!" he laughed.

NORFOLK The only crew members on board the USS *Fortson* that Saturday were the one-sixth who pulled that day as their normal duty assignment in rotation, and the single ones who lived on the ship full-time. Lieutenant Commander Thomas Dobbs and Lieutenant Teri Slocum fit the latter category. They were using the weekend to read the ship's operations manuals and the personnel files on their key men and women.

There were only eight of the ship's twenty-four officers in the wardroom for lunch that day. As they concluded the meal, Thomas Dobbs said to Teri Slocum, "If you've got a minute, how about stopping by my stateroom so we can talk."

"Sure. You're in the admiral's cabin aren't you?"

"Yeah," he said, with an expression that communicated his dislike for his special quarters.

"I'll be right there," Slocum answered.

Both of them left through the port wardroom door. She stopped by her stateroom in forward officers country, then ascended the ladder to the next deck and knocked on the door of the flag cabin.

Dobbs let her into the spacious accommodations and motioned for her to take a chair under one of the few portholes built into the ship's hull.

"Here, please have a seat."

"Thanks," she said and looked around the room in appreciation. "This is quite a cabin."

"Yes, but it's too much, as I've tried to tell the XO. Anyway, since we're the senior officers in two minorities stationed on a warship for the first time, I thought we should get to know each other," he began. "Have you always been in missiles?"

She laughed. "Yes, ever since Annapolis. As a range missile officer, at a training command, and on an admiral's staff."

They then described to each other their naval backgrounds and touched on their personal lives.

"I came out of the closet three years ago, thank God," Dobbs said, tapping his pen on his note pad and pursing his lips slightly. "My partner was in the Supply Corps here in Norfolk, but he was transferred to Spain three months ago. How about you? Are you married or engaged?" He smiled.

"Actually I've been dating a civilian guy off and on in town. He's an architect I met at a friend's house. But it's tough with our schedule."

"I can imagine. Listen, are you planning any sort of women's rights awareness programs for the crew?"

"Uh…no…I hadn't really thought about it," she said, looking a bit puzzled and running a hand through her hair. "Why?"

"Well, you need to plan some awareness programs. Otherwise, these guys will chew you up and spit you out. I know. I've seen it. Look how long African-Americans have been on active duty on warships, and we still need Affirmative Action Officers and Black Awareness Week. The navy is designing some similar programs for women and gays, but for the time being it's up to us to lead the way, particularly with this crew."

"I'm still not sure what you mean. I just figured my division would come aboard, keep a low profile, stay out of trouble, and do our jobs well. What else is there?"

"Oh, come on. You'll play right into their hands. Soon they'll be treating you like second-class citizens, telling jokes behind your backs and not respecting you."

"Hey, I've got two brothers. Guys have been telling jokes about girls and vice versa since time began. I'm going to tell my crew to concentrate on their jobs, not to mix romance with duty, to hold their heads high no matter what happens, and above all to keep a sense of humor about this whole thing."

"No. You've got to do much more! You're a leader of a minority that's been denied its rights for years and years. Now you have the chance to create new respect for women. It's not enough just to do your job!"

"But that's what this opportunity is all about: doing a good job. I don't feel oppressed. Just the opposite. I feel like we've been given an opportunity," she interrupted.

"That's the beginning," he agreed. "But there's so much more if you want women to be respected and taken seriously."

"Like what?" she asked.

"Just like the affirmative action programs for African-Americans on Black History, Black scientists, African culture. All that. I'm already planning a Gay and Lesbian Awareness week—we'll call it GALA. We'll show movies by and about gays, emphasizing the naturalness of homosexual love. We'll invite in some speakers; I have a gay friend who is a minister, for example, who can perform the Sunday service that week. We'll also review for the crew about AIDS awareness in the gay community, showing how the disease can be transmitted. All of those kinds of things, to raise the awareness and the respect for gays within the crew."

"Well," Teri said, smiling, "the last thing we probably need to show the crew is movies on the total naturalness of *heterosexual* love! I think they already know that pretty well, and it could produce just the opposite result after a few weeks at sea, I'd imagine. And I'm not sure your homosexual awareness movies are very helpful either." She hesitated, then said, "I have to be honest with you. I came away pretty disgusted from the one you had us preview the other day."

"What do you mean, Lieutenant?" Dobbs's tone was suddenly formal.

"I mean it was disgusting to me, what those homosexuals and lesbians were doing in that movie, if you want to know the truth."

"Are you prejudiced against gays and lesbians?" Dobbs asked.

"I try not to be prejudiced against anyone."

"If you had watched a movie featuring African-Americans, would you be disgusted? Or do you limit your prejudices to the gay community?"

"Look, I just told you I try not to be prejudiced against anyone, either professionally or personally. But if you showed me two African-American men or two African-American women doing what those gays were doing in your 'sensitizing' movie, I have to tell you I'd be equally disgusted. I think the movie is gross—it's pornography. And it shouldn't be shown on a ship where we're trying to keep emotions under control, not arouse and enflame them."

Dobbs crossed his arms in front of his chest and glared at Teri. "Lieutenant, that movie was made by a team of leading psychologists from four of our best universities. It's designed to bring an irrational taboo out into the open and to deal with it openly and rationally. I don't appreciate your remarks. I hope you'll keep them to yourself and not infect other crew members with your irrational prejudices. I'm disappointed that someone in your position of exceptionally important minority leadership could be so backward in her thinking. It's very disturbing, and I'll have to make note of it if you continue. And I again suggest that whether you personally want to or not, you should be thinking about a program to raise the level of respect for women on this ship, if you want your crew to survive."

Slocum stood up, her face turning red but her voice under control. "I don't appreciate your logic, your insinuations, or your threats, Lieutenant Commander Dobbs. I'm here to do one job well: control the missiles on this ship. If my crew does that, we'll have carved out all the respect I or they need or want. And I'm also worried about the welfare of my women; I want them to have a low profile, not a zealous mission. You may think that sounds like I'm chicken. I'm not. But I'll have twenty women on a ship with over four hundred red-blooded American men, and we'll be thousands of miles from home. I don't want to be shoving my women in their faces every day with a cause. I just want us to survive."

"I'm trying to tell you how to do just that, but you won't listen to me,"

Dobbs said, his own anger rising. "You've got to win their respect and guard it daily."

"Well, if there's a black lesbian among the new admin personnel, send her to me, and we'll make her the "Everything Awareness Person"—women, African-American, homosexual, everything. She can just go from division to division, telling the guys how to be politically correct. I'm sure she'll be very popular, and it'll free everyone else to do their real jobs," Slocum said, walking over to the door and opening it.

"I don't appreciate that kind of remark," Dobbs fumed. "And I'm noting it."

"Oh, lighten up, Lieutenant Commander. You may be gay, but you're certainly not very happy." With that, she closed the door behind her.

CAMP DAVID   When Mary and Graham entered the Great Room that evening at Camp David for dinner, almost everyone else was already seated. By agreement at lunch that day the four siblings and their spouses, or "significant other" in Rebecca's case, were sitting together at the big table for dinner, while the older children and the grandparents helped with the younger children at the smaller tables.

"Here we are, finally," Mary said happily.

"Please" Bruce said, smiling and offering Mary one of the two remaining chairs.

Graham and Mary had gotten to know Bruce and shared several pleasant conversations together when seated with him and Rebecca the previous evening. Then at the softball game that afternoon the four of them had been assigned to the same Private Sector team, based on their employment. The first lady had designated the teams, as well as the coaches, who were Rebecca and Hugh. Rebecca had made all the field assignments for the Private Sector team, which included herself at second, Bruce at shortstop, Graham in left field, Mary in short field, Courtney pitching, and young Tim Prescott at first.

Both teams had special T-shirts that commemorated the day and the event, and virtually everyone who was old enough to walk was on a team. It was a beautiful afternoon as they began playing at one end of the same field the helicopters had used the day before. Those on the team at bat sat along a grassy slope along the first base side enjoying the sun, talking, and cheering on their team.

In the bottom of the third inning the Private Sector was at bat, behind by five runs, and Bruce was sitting on the knoll when Mary and Graham walked over to sit by him. Rebecca was coaching from near first base. Bruce was not in a particularly good mood, given the earlier conversation with

Rebecca. *What's gotten into her?* he thought. *She's losing her sense of what's right. Oh, no. Here come Mary and Graham!*

"Hi, Bruce," Graham said, sitting down with Mary on the grass. "That was a great throw you made at the start of the inning."

"Yeah, thanks. But we're not doing so well." He said jokingly, "If you two pray as much as Rebecca says you do, you'd better pray for our team to win!"

Mary wrapped her arms around her knees. She smiled and turned her head to Bruce. "So Rebecca says we pray a lot?"

"She says you can't get enough of it. Praying about everything and everybody. Praying all day. I've always wondered: does God actually answer you? I mean, do you hear a deep voice telling you what to do, and what will happen?"

Graham ignored Bruce's veiled sarcasm. "Not a voice," he answered. "At least I've never heard a separate voice. But I think he does answer our prayers. I hear my own inner voice speaking, sometimes saying things that I couldn't know or hadn't focused on. And events happen, or don't happen, that are clearly answers to our prayers. That's how we've felt the response of God in our lives." Graham smiled.

"Well, I can't imagine that God sits and answers the prayers of individual men or women," Bruce responded, looking to his left at both of the Prescotts. "How could he? Do you know how many people there are in the world? It's impossible. I tried once, but he obviously didn't hear my prayers for my brother—so I'm never going to make a fool of myself again! Whether some god made us originally, and we're now running along on our own, or whether we're all just some great cosmic mistake, the result is the same. We've got to work for ourselves, to make our lives and our world better. If there is a God, surely he wants us to do that."

"He does want us to do the best we can," Mary agreed, "but in submission to his will and his laws for our lives."

"Submission? Come on! Submit to what? The stories in the Bible?" Bruce's voice rose, and Rebecca turned from behind first base. "I don't know how people like you can still believe that stuff. This is the twenty-first century, you know."

"Bruce, if you haven't felt God's power in your life, it's almost impossible for us to explain it to you; and it says *that* in the Bible, too. But we'd be happy to tell you more about what he's done in our lives, as a way to start," Mary offered. "We think it's kind of interesting."

"Thanks, but save your breath. Or go tell it to all the supposed Christians like you who deserted my brother once they found out he had AIDS. Where were all of you when he was dying? Off at a prayer meeting, probably, thinking how much better off than him you are. I'm real big on Christians and prayer. You're a lot of help. Well, that's the third out. Time to hit the field again."

The Private Sector picked up their gloves and headed for their positions. The Public Sector's leadoff batter that inning was Hugh's wife, Jennifer. Soon they had the bases loaded with two outs, and William Harrison came to the plate.

Bruce, assuming the ready position at shortstop, thought, *What a great thing it would be to tell my clients I personally threw out the president of the United States!* To the plate he yelled, "Come on batter, try to hit it. Give him your floater, Courtney."

On the second pitch the president hit a high fly ball to short left field, where Mary Prescott would only have to take a few steps to catch it. But Bruce came running back fast from his shortstop position. He was looking up, intent on catching the ball and putting the president out. Mary heard him coming, as she, too, focused on the ball and yelled, "Mine." But Bruce kept coming.

Travelling backward Bruce tripped just as he caught the ball and then ran into Mary. Mary, her arms outstretched for the catch, took a heavy blow, and they fell down together. The ball flew from Bruce's glove. Just before it hit the ground, Mary, on her back, made a lunge and caught it. The Private Sector cheered wildly. Rebecca ran over from second base to separate Mary and Bruce, who were tangled together on the ground. Mary got up, unhurt, and beaming. Bruce was smiling sheepishly and said, "Nice catch."

The rest of the afternoon had turned out to be a lot of fun for everyone, including Bruce. He now stood at dinner and pulled out a chair for Mary. In a contrite voice he said, "I'm really sorry, again, about what happened this afternoon. I didn't mean to clobber you. What a catch you made."

Mary smiled as she moved in front of the chair. "I'm fine. Don't worry. And miracles *do* happen."

"I guess I'd have to admit in this case that you're right," Bruce replied.

"So!" William Harrison poured the Prescotts some champagne as they took their seats. "You missed the Public Sector's victory celebration at cocktail hour, but we saved you some champagne. There's already talk of a rematch next year, but I'm afraid you Private Sector people had better practice a bit."

"It's just that you government types with the nine-to-five jobs," Rebecca added, tipping her glass at her older brother, "have plenty of time to practice. Those of us who really work for a living don't have that luxury."

"Well, invite us back to this wonderful place next year," Graham suggested, "and we'll arrive a day early to warm up."

"If the House, Senate, and world crises permit, consider it done," concluded the president, laughing with his family.

"And here's hoping," Bruce added, raising his glass, "that all of your campaign promises are enacted by then."

"Thank you, Bruce," William acknowledged. "But if *all* of them were enacted, I'm not sure that Mary or Graham would ever be seen with Carrie and me again."

"Oh, we'd be here," Mary continued the good-natured ribbing, "but we'd probably spend the whole time in our cabin, praying that God wouldn't strike this place with lightning."

Bruce started to say something, but a glance from Rebecca made him think better of it.

The conversation continued in a happy and upbeat mood throughout the dinner, with the Harrisons sharing stories about their years growing up together. Carrie was delighted. She hadn't seen William so cheerful in. months. But then an aide approached and whispered in the president's ear. He seemed to frown for an instant, then nodded. As the dinner plates were being cleared, William turned to Mary. "Tell us about the minister who's coming tomorrow for the Easter service. He's from Baltimore, isn't he?"

"Yes, that's right."

"And is he a fire-and-brimstone preacher, like your Reverend Wilson when we were kids?" William asked teasingly.

"Well, Reverend Wilson really wasn't 'fire and brimstone' as you call him, and neither is Michael. But both of them do zero in on one's relationship with God. I think you'll like him. He's intelligent and articulate. And he's felt the hand of God on him from the beginning of his life."

"Oh? How so?" William asked.

"His mother had five children and was getting older. She unexpectedly became pregnant again, and their doctor advised both her and her husband that it would be dangerous to go through childbirth. He told them— remember this was almost fifty years ago—that she should have an abortion because otherwise she might die giving birth. They reluctantly agreed, and the doctor wrote the necessary paperwork.

"Then, I think it was the night before the scheduled abortion, their minister was awakened at two in the morning and couldn't go back to sleep. He kept hearing a message in his mind, and he couldn't shake it. Finally, exhausted, at seven in the morning, he drove over to Michael's parents' home.

"They were obviously surprised to see him. I think he was still standing outside their door when he told them that God had awakened him with a message, that despite the possible risks, she was not supposed to have the abortion.

"They went inside and the three of them prayed for quite a while. When they finished, Michael's mother said she was at peace and that she agreed with their minister. Her husband also felt the same. So they cancelled the abortion. Michael is the baby who was born seven months later, and there were no complications. One other thing: the minister had also told them that their baby was going to serve the Lord in a special way.

"So we've always felt that Michael approaches life and his ministry with an enthusiasm I think you'll find to be infectious and refreshing. He knows from the bottom of his heart that he was singled out to do the Lord's work."

After a few moments of silence, Bruce looked around the table, pausing for an extra glance at Rebecca, and finally said, "Come on, Mary. You don't believe that, do you? Were you there?"

"No, of course not."

"He probably just made that story up to impress people."

"Actually Michael has never mentioned it. I heard it from his mother, several years ago, when she visited us. There were tears in her eyes, all those years later. I can't imagine why an eighty-year-old woman would make up a story and lie to me about her son. Can you?" Mary asked.

"Well, maybe the minister just had indigestion and couldn't sleep. God doesn't wake people up in the middle of the night and talk to them about abortions, or about anything else, for that matter. If there even is a God, he has too much else to worry about than one unborn child," Bruce said, obviously flustered.

Graham smiled and said, "There most definitely *is* a God, because he's wakened *us* up in the night and answered our prayers in other ways. And the incredible thing about God is that even though he holds the stars on their courses and causes the sun to shine, he also bends down and listens to each person, each sinner, who asks for forgiveness. He cares about each one of us that much."

"I just can't believe you two," Bruce retorted. "You think God intervenes in people's lives through prayer? That what is going to happen is changed by people praying? Come on. How did he miss my brother? If he *is* so powerful, surely he knows everything that's going to happen, whether you pray or not."

"That *is* a mystery, I admit," Mary said. "But yes, he knows everything that will happen, yet he has told us to pray. Even his own Son, who was also God, prayed constantly to his Father. It's sort of like he knows what will happen, good or bad, but he wants us to pray because of the important relationship it builds between us and him and because it is the prayer that causes the good to happen."

"What circular reasoning," Bruce said, leaning back in his chair, confident that he had scored a victory.

"Reasoning won't usually get you to God," Graham said, "although some people have found him by reasoning that there can be no other explanation for our universe than God Almighty. But most people come to him by faith, seeking forgiveness for their sins, or experiencing a particularly difficult time, or suddenly feeling his power in their lives, or seeing it in someone else's life. Now faith *is* real, and it produces amazing results. Look at what Sasha told us last night about his family, for example. But you can't 'reason' it, by definition. It's faith, not reason. But once you've surrendered to it, the power of faith is incredible."

"There you go again," Bruce said, ignoring Rebecca's warning glance. "Surrender. Submission. This isn't the old days. We don't have to submit to anyone! What about you, Mr. President? Do you think God wakes people up in the middle of the night and tells them what to do?"

The other five people at the table had listened quietly while Bruce, Mary, and Graham debated. Now they all turned to hear William's answer. The president was obviously embarrassed to be put on the spot. He looked down at his bowl of ice cream, which had just been served.

"I...I honestly don't know, Bruce. I haven't thought much about God for the past thirty years or so. I think I had a faith as a child and a teenager. Not as strong as Mary's, perhaps. But a faith. Then at college I decided, sort of like you're saying, that God must want us to make the world better. So I decided I could do his will and help other people at the same time by trying to make the world a better place. That's the philosophy I've been following for a long time now. And God certainly hasn't awakened me in the night." He grinned. Bruce nodded.

"But I have to say that God can and probably does do that," William continued. Bruce frowned. "And he does intervene in lives, I also have to admit." Carrie couldn't believe what she was hearing. "I saw Mary changed while she was sitting next to me in church that day, as teenagers. She's never been the same. And that, I have to admit, is the one thing my own philosophy of the last thirty years has not included: a personal relationship with God. I haven't needed it, really. I feel that in my own way I've been doing what he's wanted me to do anyway. I've been at peace. But I also realize now, as I've grown older, that I haven't experienced the kind of personal relationship with God that Mary and Graham and Sasha have described. And I probably never will," he concluded.

Everyone was silent again. Bruce sensed that he had just heard a bit of the president's innermost thoughts and it would not be wise to argue. After a moment the president smiled again and said, "Anyway, we got off on all of this as the result of a simple question about tomorrow's service. Mary, when is it?"

"You're right. I'm sorry," Mary said. "Michael and Elizabeth are joining us for breakfast and then the service will be in the chapel at ten. Obviously everyone is invited, including the staff."

"Great. Thanks again for setting it up. Now everyone, let's finish up our dessert so we can have that awards ceremony that Carrie's organized." William reached for his wife's hand and squeezed it affectionately.

As coffee was served, Carrie announced the various winners. Amid much clapping and cheering, Mary and Bruce jointly won the award for the best play of the game.

Ninety minutes later, while the family was enjoying a movie, William heard the distant sound of a helicopter and excused himself. Carrie frowned, but he whispered to her, "This is what the note at dinner was about. I'll just be a few minutes." He left and walked quickly over to Aspen Lodge.

The single helicopter landed in the brightly lit field. Shortly thereafter the chairman of the Joint Chiefs of Staff, General Vince Harley, and two of his aides were escorted to the president's cabin.

"Vince, it's good to see you." William extended his hand as the two men and one woman, all in impeccable uniform, came in from the porch.

"Thank you, Mr. President," the older man replied. "I'm sorry to bother you on this special weekend, but we received something late this afternoon that I believe you need to see."

"Fine. Here, please sit down."

"Thanks. We don't plan to stay long. I just wanted you to be aware of this message, which is addressed to you through me, and arrived on the special coded fax machine just outside my private office this afternoon." He handed his commander in chief two sheets of paper.

As William looked at the written message and the picture, he asked, "How could anyone do that?"

"I'm not sure, sir, but you can believe we're checking."

The message was short and read:

> Greetings. We have an operational .6 megaton Soviet warhead. We are modifying it for our own use and will detonate it in a major American city within eighteen months unless you change your policies. We send you this message so that you can die a little every day before it happens, as we have died every day at your hands over so many years. We will communicate again shortly.
>
> The Council

On the second page was a picture, slightly distorted by the faxing process but clearly showing what appeared to be the exterior of a nuclear warhead and the crate that had presumably housed it. The serial numbers had been obliterated.

William looked up at General Harley. "Is this real?"

"It appears that it may be, sir. We believe it may be the warhead the Russians feared was lost several years ago. The one the CIA agent was investigating in Odessa when he was murdered. But we're not sure. We've sent a copy of the picture to our counterparts in Moscow and Kiev, but for now we've got to assume that it's real."

"And can they detonate it?"

"With the right expertise to modify it and the right equipment to initiate the firing sequence, I'm afraid so. A whole lot of Americans and Russians know how to do it."

"Americans?"

"Yes, sir. Since Oklahoma City in '95 and the three copycat bombings since then, we can't discount any possibility. The fax even came from Omaha. The FBI is checking right now and the police are questioning the staff at the copy shop it was sent from."

William was silent for a long time, studying the pages. He was suddenly very warm and felt his hands growing moist. The visual image was burned into his memory of the the the federal office building in Oklahoma City. *That was one truck with some fuel and fertilizer. What would a nuclear warhead do if exploded without warning?*

"Do you have any idea who this 'Council' is or even what policies they're talking about?" he finally asked.

"Right now we have no idea. They could be a renegade militia group or terrorists from the Middle East, Bosnia, Ireland—we just don't know."

William was again silent. "What do you suggest we do, general?"

Vince Harley moved to the edge of his chair. He looked first at his aides, then spoke. "Offensively, our military intelligence and CIA assets will be alerted to the threat and will redouble their efforts to turn up a lead or an association, with the emphasis being on Russia, Ukraine, U.S. militia cells, and the Middle East. Defensively, we'll assign a special team to update earlier studies done on a nuclear threat to our twenty largest metropolitan areas. Here are summaries of those studies for you to review. We'll war-game how to neutralize the threat, reviewing various scenarios in each city. Assuming, of course, that we're even told where it's located *before* it's detonated."

The general's professional but sterile manner sent a chill down William's spine. He was again silent.

Finally he spoke, almost in a whisper. "It must be more than revenge, or they'd just detonate it and claim responsibility later. The note sounds more like blackmail. But we don't know what they want."

One of the aides spoke. "No, sir. But we imagine they'll be communicating their demands pretty soon."

"Maybe. Or maybe they'll just wait and give us a very short time to react. General, please do get your offense and your defense cracking. Coordinate the military effort closely with the FBI, ATF, and CIA. Given the military nature of the warhead, I'd like you to set up a special task force under your command. Give the other agencies free rein in their own areas of expertise, but for now ask them to report and coordinate through you. The main thing right now is results, not who gets credit. It's hard to imagine how we'll handle this if we're not prepared. Can you give me an update at least every week?"

"Yes, sir."

Standing, William added, "And for now, at least, let's keep a very tight lid on this. The last thing we need is a panic, when we're not sure where, when, or even if this will really happen. I pray it won't."

The others rose as well. Vince Harley took back the two pages William offered him. "Of course. And, you're right, until we know more, there's little reason to scare anyone needlessly."

The four of them looked at one another. William spoke for all of them when he said, "General, you'd better plan for the worst. Better yet, find out who's behind this, so we can try to stop them. If we have to face them in an American city, it won't be easy, and I'll really need your help."

"Yes, sir," the general said as they walked to the door. Ten minutes later William heard the rotors on the helicopter turning as he sat alone in his chair, trying to imagine what he would do if the threat was actually real.

PARIS, FRANCE While the Harrison extended family slept that night, it was already Sunday morning in Paris where Sadim had just arrived on one of his rare trips away from the *Bright Star.* He had taken a circuitous and tiring route through Malta and Athens, using tickets bought from different agencies several days apart, and using different names and passports for each leg of the journey. He had taken a room in a small hotel near Montemarte using yet another name and paid for three nights in advance.

At two on Sunday morning, dressed as a waiter from the ground floor restaurant which had just closed, he left through the rear door of the hotel with his belongings in a shopping bag and headed for the Northern Train Station. There he picked up an expensive suitcase that had been left for him at the baggage storage area, changed clothes again, and arrived at the elegant Hotel Louis XIV satisfied that he had not been followed.

Sadim allowed himself the minor luxury of sleeping until eight that morning, when he rose and, after prayers, made one call from a pay phone located near the hotel. At eleven he was sharing a booth in the restaurant of a third hotel with his main contact.

"Thank you for arranging the bag at the train station," he said to his breakfast companion. "Everything went well."

"My pleasure," replied Wafik Ahmady, his fellow countryman. "It is always an honor to have you here. How goes our work?"

"Very well, my friend," Sadim said with a slight smile. "The Council's plan, of which you were of course a part, has worked very well, and we are actually ahead of schedule on the modifications. The first message went out by fax Saturday evening. I wish I could have been in Washington to see his face! We have more messages and 'leaks' planned that will lead them on blind chases all over the world and away from us. Let *them* feel what it's like to worry about your very existence with every breath! How about your work?"

"Fine, as you will see."

"When is our first meeting?" Sadim asked.

"Here, in ninety minutes. I've arranged for you to have that booth across the room, and you'll hear our conversation with this earpiece." Wafik slid the small device across the table. "The microphone is this button on my shirt."

"Do any of these men know the others are here?"

"Anything is possible, but that is highly unlikely. Each believes he and his contact are the only ones we have met with. Given the large sums of money involved, that should be believable."

Sadim felt quite comfortable with Wafik's ability to perform this part of their plan very well on his own. But as the leader, Sadim also knew it was important for him to be present at key times and to ask questions.

Wafik had turned a scholarship at Georgetown University and strong family connections in Lebanon into an international consulting firm with deep ties to the powerful elite in Washington. He had carefully watched, and participated over the years, as politicians traded favors with each other on pet projects, both foreign and domestic. He had acted as a key go-between on many occasions when a trade treaty or foreign aid package could have beneficial side effects for a particular group, either in the U.S. or overseas. And always he had noted carefully who listened to whom, because he knew that someday he would need to use those channels himself. For, despite his almost invisible work at the highest levels of international commerce and politics, Wafik never forgot the roots he shared with Sadim and with so many others.

An hour later Sadim moved to the booth nearby where he could observe each person meeting with Wafik and hear their conversation. Right on time at twelve-thirty the first man arrived and sat with Wafik.

"Francis. So glad to see you," Wafik said, as he extended his hand to the tall American in the conservative blue business suit with a red handkerchief in his lapel pocket.

"April in Paris. How could I refuse your invitation?" Francis Palmer replied as he slid into the booth across from his host.

"Would you like a coffee or a glass of wine?" Wafik asked as the waiter approached. "I regret that I cannot have lunch with you, but my time is very short."

"I understand. Yes, I'll have a glass of red wine."

Wafik ordered wine for his guest and espresso for himself. The two men continued their casual conversation until their beverages were served and the waiter retired.

"So, Francis, have you had a chance to consider the proposition we discussed last month in Washington?" Wafik asked.

"Yes, and if I understand it correctly, and if you'll sweeten the pot a little, I think we can do business."

"Tell me what you understand." Wafik took a sip of his espresso.

"That along with my official duties as a registered lobbyist for the cable television industry I am to approach my good friend Congressman Trent Patterson and make him an offer it will be hard for him to refuse."

"And the offer we discussed?"

"I am to offer him three-quarters of a million dollars in cash, deposited secretly into a foreign bank account of his choice, in return for his leadership and support to make our country's approach in the Middle East more balanced. Specifically to use his influence to pass a congressional resolution endorsing the United Nations resolutions requiring Israel to give back the land it has taken since 1967. And to pass appropriations bills that cut back our aid to Israel if they don't. He will receive a special notice of when he is to move for adoption of these measures, which will happen sometime within the next two years."

"You have understood my request and my offer precisely," Wafik confirmed. "Do you think he will agree?"

"For $750,000? With his campaign debt and a wife who's suing him for divorce? A *secret* $750,000 that no one will know about? He might say no, but I think it's very unlikely."

"And what do you think needs to be 'sweetened,' as you say?"

Francis Palmer took a sip of wine before replying. "I think he needs an incentive—it's the American way. I propose he gets another $250,000 if he gets the measures passed."

"Is that the total of what you want?"

"Almost. Most importantly, I think my good services, if he says yes, are worth half a million to you, not a quarter million."

Wafik paused. There was an almost invisible nod from the single man occupying the booth across the aisle.

"Agreed, but in your case, half now and half when the resolution passes."

"Four hundred when he signs on. One hundred on passage."

Wafik paused again. "Done. When will you meet with him?"

"As soon as I get back. Late this week, or early the next."

"Excellent. And on top of everything else, he'll be doing the right thing for America and finally supporting policies that the rest of the world ratified many years ago."

"Whatever. I hope it's right, obviously. But there's certainly nothing wrong with one million dollars in cold cash!"

"Call the number I gave you in Washington when you have something to report, and we'll set up a meeting."

"He probably won't want to meet, at least not in the U.S. We may have to come back to Paris or some place similar."

"That will be a pleasure." Wafik smiled. "Just do your job well, and we'll meet wherever you like."

CAMP DAVID Michael and Elizabeth Tate arrived from Baltimore in time for breakfast with the president, first lady, and the Prescotts. The conversation never touched on politics or religion, other than when William Harrison asked Michael about his work in foreign countries. The president was impressed with the minister's grasp of geo-politics in the Middle East and in Eastern Europe.

After breakfast the superintendent showed Michael to the wooden and stone chapel, where he met briefly with young Robert Harrison and Sarah Prescott, who had volunteered to read the lessons from the Bible.

By ten o'clock the rustic chapel was filled with the weekend guests plus many young men and women from the marines and navy who were stationed at Camp David. By the time Michael Tate entered the sanctuary from the side door, all of the president's family were present, including his parents. Only Rebecca's daughter, Courtney, and Bruce were absent.

After the opening hymn of "Jesus Christ Is Risen Today" there were prayers and Scripture readings from Isaiah 53, giving the promise and purpose of Christ from seven hundred years before his birth; and from Luke 24, giving the report of his resurrection from those who were eyewitnesses. After another hymn and several prayers, Michael rose to begin his sermon.

"It goes without saying that we are here today in a political environment, but I'm not going to talk at all about politics." *Thank goodness!* William thought. "But I do feel led this glorious Easter morning to talk about what politicians must deal with every day: choices.

"There are quite a few children here this morning, and one can look upon the parenting experience as preparing our children to make the best possible choices in their lives as they naturally grow in their responsibilities. We can teach them and tell them what we believe is right; ultimately, however, our children will be on their own, and the choices they make will be theirs.

"There is almost nothing sadder than the parent whose heart is broken by the choice of a grown child to take drugs, to commit adultery, or to fail to raise their own children properly. But these are the choices that our children must make. We pray they will follow the paths we have set for them and that they will remember the foundation of spiritual truths we have taught them. But ultimately and finally, the choices are theirs alone. And the consequences for those choices are theirs alone, too.

"This Easter I want to look at several choices that come to us from the Scripture, to see how others handled them and what their consequences were. We'll go through these quickly, and I'll give you the references for your own study, because my emphasis here will be on the choices we make."

He then described Jesus' choice to submit to his Father's will on Good Friday and Peter's choice to deny that he ever knew Jesus.

"In the months and years that followed that lowest of low points in Peter's life, he went on, once he had been filled with the eternal power of the Holy Spirit forty days later, to become one of the greatest speakers, writers, and leaders of all time. This uneducated fisherman led a movement that, without newspapers, television, or books, literally turned the known world upside down. And I believe his later willingness to submit his own will to that of the Lord, to let the Lord lead him, began early that awful morning of denial when his own power failed him miserably, and he knew it. He made a choice that morning relying on his own human resources, and he realized the consequences from then on of limiting himself in that way.

"The third and fourth choices were made by the two thieves who were crucified on each side of Jesus, as described in Luke 23. Please read it yourselves. Essentially one ridiculed Jesus. The other believed in him. Which one are you? Jesus told the one who asked him for salvation that they would be together in heaven that day. Not a hundred years later. Not at the millennium. But immediately. The implication is clear that the other thief would be somewhere else.

"There are two conclusions from this encounter. First, that what we do decides where we will spend eternity. One thief ridiculed. The other believed. The believer was promised heaven by the Son of God himself. The second implication is that we *are* spiritual beings. We *will* exist throughout all eternity, somewhere. We don't have a third choice of just passing away and opting out. Like the two thieves, we *will* go somewhere, and where we spend our own eternity depends on the choices we make as individuals."

Tate then described how he had made the choice in his own life to follow God's will. And he described the difficult choice his wife, Elizabeth, had made, coming from a family that had ignored the spiritual aspect of life. Finally he recounted three moving instances of individuals whose lives had been completely changed by the choices they had made to follow the Lord: a seventeen-year-old girl dying from leukemia who went on to change hundreds of her schoolmates; a business leader workaholic who redeemed a college age son from drugs; and a couple with three small children who had saved their marriage when it had been on the brink of dissolving. Each story illustrated how the Lord breathed new spiritual life into a situation that from a human perspective had seemed hopeless.

"There is one choice that we all must face, individually. Imagine that Jesus has come here himself this Easter. He has not only announced the way to eternal life, but he has himself provided the way to salvation through his divinity and his obedience. Imagine that he is here, now. He has reported to you through his written Word the consequences, good and bad, of your choice. He is standing at the door of your heart and knocking. But only you can open that door. Only you can submit to his will in your life. Or you can reject him and the consequences he clearly describes. It is up to you. It is so simple. Yet so powerful. You must choose."

Oh no, he's not going to ask people to stand up or walk forward, is he? William thought, already embarrassed.

"If you elect to choose God today please pray with me. And then if you want to talk about your choice after the service, Elizabeth and I will be staying through lunch and will be delighted to meet with you and to share God's love with you. Let's now bow our heads in prayer.

"If you truly want to lead a new life and be part of God's kingdom forever, please pray along silently with me."

William politely bowed his head, but he was astonished to hear Carrie whispering Michael's words next to him.

Michael continued to offer a prayer of personal repentance that William could tell at least some of those in the chapel were repeating quietly.

As Michael finished his prayer, William clearly heard the sound of weeping behind him, though he could not tell if it was from one of his family members or the staff. Then Carrie, sitting next to him, turned toward him, and he saw tears running down her cheeks. She asked quietly for his handkerchief, as Mary had done thirty-five years earlier.

He felt transported back to that morning when Mary had been changed. The message was the same today, but if anything, more powerful. Or at least described in a way to which he could actually relate. But again he had not prayed. In fact, he was embarrassed that Michael had been so explicit, and he was relieved that there had not been an altar call. *This is such a personal thing!* he thought. *I'm not going to change my life based on something I hear from someone I've only known for three hours!*

Yet here was Carrie, his wife, crying as she sat next to him. *Has she, like Mary all those years ago, made that choice this morning?* He had been moved, fair enough. It all sounded so sensible. Yes, he believed there probably was a God. But not one you had to personally submit to. And certainly not like this, in front of so many people. *But has Carrie made that choice?*

They stood to sing another hymn, "Amazing Grace," and William glanced back to see both Hugh and Jennifer smiling at him. They, too, seemed filled with peace. He could see it! What exactly had happened this Easter morning?

Communion followed, and when the service was over, Michael walked to the back of the church to greet the congregation as they filed out. William shook his hand and told him how much he had enjoyed the sermon. As he started to walk away, Carrie said, "William, I want to stay and talk to Michael and Elizabeth before lunch. I'll join you at the lodge in a few minutes."

"Sure, Carrie. I'll see you there," the president responded. He moved over to walk back with his parents.

"Where did Mary find *him?*" his mother asked. "I was expecting him to tell us about the devil next. How embarrassing to ask people to pray to be born again, as if some cheap chant like that would guarantee you a place in heaven! God doesn't want prayers and chants; he wants actions and deeds. What a waste of a beautiful morning."

As they were about to round a curve in the path, William looked back at the chapel, where Carrie, Hugh, Jennifer, all four Prescotts, plus Robert, Sasha, and six or seven of the marine guards were clustered around Michael, deep in discussion. "Mom, you may be right," William heard himself saying, "but *something* happened in that chapel this morning. Even *I* felt it."

PARIS It was already late afternoon in Paris. After yet another American rose and departed from another restaurant meeting, Sadim left his nearby seat and joined Wafik in his booth.

"I have seen enough, my friend," Sadim said. "You are right, it does go well."

"But that is only six men. We have twelve more to meet over the next two days," Wafik protested.

"You will meet them, but there is no reason for me to stay. You are doing fine. American Congressmen and Senators must need money more than even we imagined. So far we are actually below budget."

"Remember, these are only the go-betweens, not the politicians themselves. We could still have a significant drop off from our original hopes."

"I think you have selected your contacts well, and I don't believe these men would have come so far and be saying what they are saying—and asking for more money—if they didn't think they could deliver. I've watched their eyes. Most of them have already spent their fees."

"Then let's hope we wind up with twelve to twenty leaders in the American House and Senate, all of whom start talking about a more balanced policy in the Middle East and who are then surprised to find they have strong support from their colleagues! They will need one another when our special surprise arrives."

"They will make a good nucleus, Wafik. You have done well."

"Thank you, Sadim. May Allah continue to bless our work."

"I am sure he will. Send a message after these men have had a few weeks to make their proposals to their politician friends. The meetings with the politicians themselves will be more difficult to arrange, but necessary. I will try to attend at least a few of them. But feel free to begin on your own. Just be sure every meeting is recorded."

And with the conclusion to this phase of their business, Sadim left the restaurant before the next American was due to arrive. He had a long and circuitous trip ahead returning to the *Bright Star*, and he was impatient to get started.

CAMP DAVID Back in Maryland on Easter Monday the president and his sister Mary strolled along the perimeter path around Camp David, walking off their breakfast. William was tired. He had not slept much that night despite the quiet surroundings. He took several hours to read the briefing book brought by Vince Harley on the nuclear bomb and its possible consequences in an American city, and then he found he couldn't sleep. Despite his headache he was genuinely glad to be with Mary, and he asked, "How's the real estate business in Raleigh?"

"Very, very busy right now. If it stays like this for another few months, Pam Wynn and I are thinking about opening our own firm."

"Really? That would be great."

"Yes. But, my dear brother," she chided good naturedly, "all the experts say you'll have to borrow so much to finance your programs that interest rates will skyrocket, killing the private housing industry again."

"Are you an official lobbyist now?"

"No. Just a bearer of common sense."

He held his hands in front of his chest in surrender. "Okay, Okay. I'll record that under 'common sense'—it's one of our smallest and least used files in Washington."

She laughed, and they walked on in silence for a few moments.

"I'm glad to have some time with you," William said. "You're really the only one in the family I haven't had a chance to talk privately with, though I feel like I've been bombarded with an 'Agenda Made by Mary' since we got here." He smiled.

"Oh, come on."

"No, really. Hugh disagrees with the new policies involving gays and women in the navy, Rebecca thinks the morning-after pill is causing all sorts of problems, and then there's Carrie's reaction to Michael Tate's sermon yesterday. To be perfectly honest, I'm just a little tired of all these conservative ideas, topped off by all this spiritual stuff."

"Well, I hope you know I didn't plan any of it, other than inviting Michael. But we *have* been praying. And so has a group at our church we call our prayer warriors. Sometimes the best and most powerful things happen when we don't try to plan or to control, but instead just let the Spirit lead."

"You're beyond me there. But I'm not really complaining. I have to admit that it's been a great weekend." *Except for Vince Harley's news,* he silently added. "In fact, just what we needed."

"It *has* been good. The Easter egg hunt after lunch yesterday was perfect for the little ones, and I truly can't remember the last time we played bridge. That was a great idea Carrie had last night."

"Yes, it's been very special. I even had a long talk one-on-one with Katherine after tennis—something we've both really needed. This hasn't been so easy for her," the president said. There was a long silence as they walked along together in the quiet morning. Then William asked, "Mary, what *really* happened to Carrie yesterday? And to you, all those years ago? I talked with her last night, and she said she felt a little bit like she was a child again, like she had discovered a Father she never knew. How could that be?"

"William, yesterday Carrie asked God to forgive her for a lifetime of sins. She committed her life to following Jesus' will, not her own. In short, she has been saved by God's grace and born again as a citizen of his kingdom. You'll see changes in her, and hopefully you'll like them. A process has been started in her that can build a personal relationship between Carrie and God if she reads her Bible, studies with other believers, prays regularly, and worships."

"Mary, is it really possible for someone to change like that? So quickly? You know nothing was really wrong with Carrie, anyway."

Mary smiled. "Perhaps only one thing, but that was the most important. She was trying to run her own life without God. And when she dies, as Michael said, even all of *her* good deeds would not measure up to God's perfection. Now she has Jesus to intercede for her. You watch. She'll begin experiencing a joy and a freedom in her spirit you'll find exciting to be around. I've seen it happen many, many times, when the Holy Spirit enters someone's life and begins to take over. His power can do anything."

William was silent again, thinking. "What about me, Mary? Can the president of the United States be 'saved,' as you call it?"

"Of course, William. And there are hundreds of thousands of people praying every day that you will be."

"Mary, it's just so personal," he said, obviously irritated. "I don't need those prayers. I feel like I've been doing what God wants me to do all of my adult life. I'm not ashamed of what I've done. I've been trying very hard to help people. I may not be a saint, but I'm not a bad guy, either. I don't need to be saved. I'm okay. I'm no worse than most people."

"You know, if I had designed the plan for salvation, I probably would have written it the way you just said it. The problem is that God wrote it, not me. And *he* says, as Michael reminded us yesterday, that all of us have fallen short of his perfection, and therefore we're not fit to inherit eternity with him. 'No worse than most people' apparently won't carry much weight in heaven. So if you want to follow *God's* plan, and not some Plan B, you *do* need to be saved, to be washed by the blood of the Savior, in order to spend eternity with him.

"And you know what else? Besides where you will spend eternity, which is clearly the most important thing, you'll also begin experiencing the life Jesus provides us on earth. It's like a preview of what heaven will be like. Not materially. But an inner peace and focus and love that help you know what's really important, and his power to accomplish it. It's a personal *relationship* with the Creator, the Source of all wisdom and understanding. I've seen it happen to so many of us 'mere mortals.' Frankly I get goose bumps just thinking what it would be like to have a president in the White House who really knows the Lord and has a relationship with him. What could that president accomplish, if he let the Lord do the work?"

Another silence as they walked. "Well, don't count on *this* president. We've already embarked on a course that will help our nation. I'm excited about what our programs will mean for our people."

"How is it all going?"

"Fine," William said.

"Hey, this is your big sister, not the Washington press corps. And we're alone. How is it *really* all going?"

"I...it's...there are a few bumps in the road, but all new administrations begin this way. We'll be fine," he said and gave her a smile.

"Well, if you ever need help, remember that God is there, and his Son, Jesus, is knocking. More than your policies or your good deeds, he simply wants *you*. He wants you in his kingdom. Then he can use you. First you've got to surrender to him, and I know that's tough enough for most people. Particularly for the man they say has the most power in the world. But you haven't experienced anything until you've felt *his* power! Call on him when you need him, William. He's amazing. If you let him in, he'll never let you down."

"All right, big sister, I'll remember that. Maybe I'll call *you* to call him." He looked up and saw they were almost back at the lodge. "Unfortunately, our long weekend is about over. It *has* been great, in so many ways. Whatever might happen to me, apparently God does have you and Carrie. Let's go say good-bye to Mom and Dad. I think their car is about to leave."

"Sure. But first let me give you a hug."

The elder Harrisons were walking down the steps of Laurel Lodge on the way to their cabin when they saw Mary and William hug.

Tom Harrison said to his wife, "Can we really have seen a half a century of Mary hugging William? Who would have imagined all those years ago that we would wind up here, with Mary hugging the president of the United States?"

Elizabeth smiled, "You're right Tom. It's sort of incredible. Sometimes I find myself wondering, 'Why us?'"

Hugh and Jennifer were placing suitcases on their porch. Jennifer stopped and said to Hugh, "I sure hope our children grow up to be as close and as open with each other as your family is. It's really remarkable."

"You're right," Hugh replied. "Several times this weekend, as I've looked around, I've thought to myself, 'Why us?'"

Graham Prescott had just finished packing and noticed his wife and brother-in-law through the living room window of their cabin. He had no way of knowing exactly what they had talked about, but he was glad to see them hugging.

Carrie was walking by herself toward the lodge, still trying to sort out what had happened to her on Sunday. She reflected that she had prayed Jesus Christ into her life that weekend, after realizing, sitting in the pew, that she could never solve all of their problems herself.

She wondered what would happen next. For the first time in her life she had prayed to God the night before in real paragraphs, not just in phrases. She felt amazingly at peace, seeing her husband and her sister-in-law hug. She said a silent prayer of thanks to God for all of these completely unexpected events.

Rebecca Harrison and Bruce Tinsley were returning from a final tennis game. "Isn't it great that Mary and William are so close after all these years?" Rebecca asked, watching Mary hug her brother.

"Frankly, I'll be glad when she leaves. I hate to see her with him. It's scary. She's nice enough, I know, but she's such a religious fanatic. If someone with her ideas ever tried to force them on the nation, we'd have a civil war on our hands."

This is a religious people. This is historically true.
From the discovery of this continent to the present hour, there is a single voice
making this affirmation.... These are not individual sayings, declarations of private
persons: they are organic utterances; they speak the voice of the entire people.... These,
and many other matters which might be noticed, add a volume of unofficial declara-
tions to the mass of organic utterances that this is a Christian nation.

U.S. SUPREME COURT
CHURCH OF THE HOLY TRINITY V. U.S., 1892

4

Thursday, May 3
Three Weeks Later

RALEIGH The Northside High School auditorium was almost full that
Thursday night three weeks later as parents gathered at the regular monthly
PTA meeting to hear, among other things, about the new Titan Computer
and its projected use in senior health class. Graham and Mary Prescott along
with a few of their friends were seated in the third row.

"Thank you for coming tonight," opened Norman Templeton, the
president of the PTA, from behind the long table at the front of the stage.
"Let's get down to business so we'll have plenty of time for the presentation
by Titan Computers."

Twenty-five minutes later President Templeton introduced Ms. Jean
Bowers, the teacher for the junior and senior health classes.

"We're privileged tonight to have with us," Ms. Bowers began, "two
experts in their fields, Ms. Debbie Vick and Mr. Ed Cheatham, who work
for the Titan Computer Company and the BioTeam Company, respectively,
here in the Research Triangle. Both have advanced degrees. As you know,
the BioTeam Company has graciously donated to the school one of its Mark
VII Titan computers, which will make a remarkable difference in almost
every subject we teach. We are here tonight to learn from our guests about
an exciting new way this computer can advance and revolutionize sex education in high school if we accept the offer these two fine companies have

made to us. Ms. Vick, do you want to begin?"

"Yes, thank you." Debbie Vick took a few minutes to give the history of the computer company and of the Mark VII in particular. "One of its planned capabilities right from the start was enhanced virtual reality, which was developed for fighter pilot training but is applicable to almost any field. The BioTeam Company, for which Mr. Cheatham works, was doing research with us to enhance the emotional capabilities of the computer displays and stimuli when this particular computer became redundant for them. So, along with their gift of the hardware to the school, they are also offering several modules of their virtual reality software, one of which harmlessly simulates sexual responses. Your school administration agrees with us that this program will be ideal for teaching no-risk sex education, so they have asked us to come tonight to show you the equipment and to answer any questions you may have."

Mr. Cheatham rose from the central table and walked over to the left corner of the stage. A computer terminal and laser disc reader were sitting on a portable stand next to a small table filled with unusual looking equipment, all connected to the computer terminal by long, thin wires.

"Thank you, Debbie. This is the equipment itself. The laser disc reader provides millions of color images, computer generated from real-life videos to be exceptionally lifelike, which are coordinated and directed by the computer, depending on the response of the student. Each session with the system is therefore completely unique. The visual images and sounds are fed into the helmet, and corresponding tactical sensations are created, if appropriate, in the other sensors.

"The student can study a natural sexual response and then with this equipment simulate it, enabling the student to compare and contrast normal types of sexual experiences on his or her own, in a low-key, nonthreatening manner with complete safety.

"This system will allow students to study lifelike sexual responses, which will arm them and prepare them for the real world, without risk of pregnancy, venereal disease, or AIDS. You parents shouldn't worry. What they'll experience is no big deal, in that most of the students will have seen or heard about all of these subjects in other, less well controlled settings. We believe this system is absolutely the state of the art, and we are pleased to make it available to Northside High School at no cost."

There was general applause, and Mary felt that a majority of the parents appeared to be in favor of the proposed gift.

"Now our guests and our own Ms. Bowers will be happy to answer any questions," Mr. Templeton announced. "Please use one of the microphones set up in front so that everyone can hear."

Several parents walked down to speak. Mary recognized Claudia Farris at the microphone.

"I'd just like to thank you and congratulate you for your gift," she began. "We so much want our daughter to understand the power of the sexual experience, so she will learn to stay away from real sex for as long as possible. This system looks like it's a godsend, and we thank you for it." More applause.

"Graham," Mary whispered to her husband, "this is awful."

"Besides the protection from pregnancy and disease," Ms. Bowers volunteered from a microphone on stage, "I'm really excited about how this equipment will allow our students, particularly our girls, to have these experiences without significantly altering their relationships with their boyfriends. Those relationships should be strengthened and deepened without the need and the pressure for sex."

Another mother came to the front. "That all sounds great. But are you talking about a one-time experience, or an ongoing way to have singular sex all during the school year?"

"Well, we'll of course expect them to experience different responses as we move through the curriculum," Ms. Bowers answered. Mary stood up and moved toward the aisle while the health teacher continued. "So, yes, there will be several opportunities for each student to use the equipment during the school year."

"About how many?" the mother asked.

There was a pause. Ms. Bowers looked over at their guests on the stage and then flipped through what was apparently a course curriculum in a binder in front of her. "Over the entire three months that a student takes the sex education section, he or she should have between fifteen and twenty completely safe experiences on the system."

There was a stir in the auditorium among the parents. One man in the back said loud enough for all to hear, "That's more than I get!" to which there was general laughter.

Mary approached the microphone on the left. "When you say 'experience different responses,' exactly what do you mean? Blonds and redheads?"

Mr. Cheatham responded, smiling. "Of course. But Ms. Bowers is also talking about the full spectrum of experiences the equipment can provide."

"Like what?" Mary asked. "Group sex?"

Mr. Cheatham paused. "Well, of course. From one to six partners at a time, male or female." There was another stir among the parents as that revelation sank in.

"You mean you can teach group sex and homosexual experiences with this equipment?" Mary asked, her voice rising.

Ms. Bowers answered. "I would have thought that would be obvious. We don't intend to limit valid experiences and lifestyles when we have a machine that can simulate almost anything you can imagine. It's not really different from today's movies or television. But it's totally scientific, it's controlled, and it's safe. The student simply enters the type of experience the curriculum calls for at the beginning, and then interacts as the equipment leads him or her in that scenario. That's the whole point. To give the students the broadest possible experiences with absolutely no risk."

"No risk?" Mary asked. "Sex has been addictive since Adam and Eve. You'll have kids hooked on your machine and then going out and looking for those same experiences on Friday nights, for real, when they can't get some action from these electrodes." There was a smattering of applause.

"Actually, we'd thought about having the classroom open on the weekends for just that reason, to give the students a private and sensible way to relieve those pressures without hurting themselves," Ms. Bowers said, looking down from the podium and obviously annoyed.

"Well, I think this is a preposterous idea, and I hope the PTA votes it down." There was a mixture of applause, boos, and calls for her to sit down.

The mother at the microphone on the other side spoke up. "I don't agree with her at all. My husband and I know our son is already, or soon will be, sexually active. We can't stop him. No one can stop their children once they're seniors. We want him to experience just as many things as he can under the controlled environment you've described so it won't hurt him. What more could we possibly all want for our children, as concerned parents? We've needed something like this for years. We strongly support your offer." There was extended applause, though not quite as loud as at first.

Mary wanted to say, "You're being deceived by the Father of Lies, who is out to destroy your children and your families," but she knew she would be branded a religious fanatic. And there were more battles to come. So instead she said, "I think this system will hurt the very people and relationships you seem to think it will help. At the very least I think it's presumptuous to vote on something so important after such a short introduction. Let's at least set up a study committee to look into it further and to make a recommendation."

"We can study things to death. It's a good system. Let's vote on it," one man shouted from the back row.

"No way. It's too much for one night," a woman said from the middle of the auditorium. The meeting was threatening to get out of control.

President Templeton spoke over the rising din. "This is a big decision, and I don't want anyone to feel railroaded either way. I think we *should* set up a committee to meet with Ms. Bowers, and with our guests if necessary, to review every aspect of this proposal. The committee should be balanced. I will appoint six parents, and we'll ask those appointed to submit a report with recommendations at our next meeting, which will be the last one of the school year. Then we'll vote. Unless anyone has a strong objection, we'll proceed in that way. Now, while they're here, does anyone have any more questions for our guests?"

WASHINGTON William closed the top secret briefing book Vince Harley had given him late that afternoon. He walked over to the safe in the corner of his upstairs study and locked it away before undressing for bed. He was frustrated that the government's best professional agencies had been so unsuccessful in turning up a single verifiable connection to the fax they'd received at Easter. The clerk at the copy shop could only remember a young man entering, using the fax machine, and paying in cash at the counter. The latest lead was through the Drug Enforcement Agency that the Columbian drug cartel had just acquired a nuclear device, and he had approved a multi-agency covert insertion which should be in-country within another week. Otherwise they had nothing, and William regretted that he had spoken so caustically to General Harley at their meeting. *But what am I supposed to do when the phone rings and five million innocent Americans are about to be vaporized? No one will remember who the chairman of the Joint Chiefs was that day, but history will always record who the president was!*

As William entered their bedroom, Carrie, who was getting undressed, asked "Is it possible the three of us could go to church on Sunday?"

Oh no, he thought, *Here we go!* William knew his wife had been reading the Bible at least once a day since their weekend at Camp David. And he knew she had had several long phone conversations with his sister Mary, ostensibly to arrange the details for Katherine to visit the Prescotts in Raleigh that summer. But he had walked in during one conversation when Carrie was flipping through a Bible open on her lap, apparently marking verses, as Mary led her. And he believed she had even talked to Michael Tate at least once. All of this he had ignored, hoping it would simply blow over and go away. But now she was asking *him* to become involved, while he was trying to deal with complex legislation and a very real threat to millions of Americans.

"Carrie, except at Christmas, Easter, and an occasional wedding or funeral, you know we haven't been to a regular church service in well over ten years. I wouldn't even know where to go to church here in Washington."

"That's no problem. I have a short list of recommended churches."

Oh great! "From whom?"

"Michael Tate. I called him the other day to say hello. He gave me a list of five churches—four different denominations—and recommended that we try them all. He said they're slightly different in the form of their services, but the five pastors all believe very strongly in the Bible and teach from it."

William paused, thinking, as he unbuttoned his shirt. Then he said wearily, "I was planning to do some work Sunday morning on the upcoming summit meeting with the Russian president." *Among other things I've got to find out exactly how many of those nuclear warheads may really be missing.* "And it's awfully late for the president to go popping in on an unsuspecting congregation. How about if we make plans to go next week?"

It was Carrie's turn to pause. "If you don't mind, I think Katherine and I will go to a church this week, just to see what it's like. And if you decide to go with us at the last minute, we'd love to have you. Okay?"

"Sure," the president said, relieved to be off the hook. "That sermon at Camp David really moved you, didn't it?"

Another pause. Carrie turned around from her dressing table and smiled with a remarkable warmth. It struck William's heart, despite his efforts to ignore it. "I know it's hard to understand—I'm only just beginning to myself. But I *know* that I belong to God now. I'm a mess. I drink too much sometimes, and I worry too much. He has a lot to clean up in me. But I know that I'm *his!* And he *can* clean me up. I know he can. Whatever happens, as Michael said that morning and Mary has shown me since then in the Bible, I know I'll be in heaven with him, forever. William, that's incredible! I never knew that before, ever. Now I do. And not because of me, but because of Jesus. God sent his Son to save *me.* Can you imagine that? *Me.* And everyone else who believes in him. And ever since I realized that truth, I've been wanting to read his Word, to find out more about him. And I really want to worship him. That's why I want to go to church on Sunday. I know it's hard, but can you imagine even some of what I feel?"

William took down his pajama top from the hook in the closet and slowly put it on. "Intellectually, I guess I can, Carrie. At least some. But you've made a commitment I *don't* feel, frankly, and apparently it's really changed you, at least for now, just like Mary. But I can't make that kind of commitment. I'm too busy. I can't get sidetracked into religion. I have too much on my plate as it is. But I hear you, and I'll try to accommodate you as best I can. Go ahead and make your plans with Katherine. I doubt I'll have time to go, but we'll see."

He started for the bathroom but then turned to face her. With a genuine note of exasperation in his voice, he concluded, "And please don't push this on me. I don't need or want to be 'saved.' And I don't know if I can survive having the two women closest to me as head-over-heels Christians." Then he added with a little sarcasm, "You'd think God was coming after me!"

NORFOLK At midmorning the next day there was another department head meeting in the wardroom of the USS *Fortson.*

"All right, let's get started," Commander Anglin began as his senior officers pulled up to the table. "Are all our berthing modifications completed to everyone's satisfaction and all our new people onboard?"

"All but one fire controlwoman who's on emergency leave from her last duty station due to her father's unexpected death. But she should arrive tomorrow," answered Lieutenant Early, the admin officer.

"And are the new people okay in their new quarters?"

"Yes sir, I think so. I haven't heard any complaints."

"What about you, Thomas?" the executive officer asked, turning to the operations officer.

"We're having the first meeting of our gays and lesbians this afternoon. But I *have* heard already about some derisive comments."

"All right, gentlemen." Anglin looked slowly around the table, then said forcefully, "If you have to repeat this *every* morning to your people, do it. We don't want any problems or any name-calling. Got it? And be sure your chiefs are onboard with this. They can often set the right tone better than officers. Hugh, what about the new Fourth Division?"

"Teri Slocum seems to have fit in fine. She knows her missile stuff cold, though she's a little rusty on shipboard procedures. But her leading chief is a crackerjack."

"Good. Then it sounds like we're ready to get underway on Monday morning for ten days of anti-submarine warfare training. After that we'll be home for six weeks and then off to lovely Guantanamo Bay for three weeks of high-pressure training in the tropical heat. It will be particularly tough on our new people. But it's the only way we can be ready to deploy in early October. If there's nothing else on personnel, let's move on to the underway replenishment training the squadron commander has scheduled while we're at sea next week."

WASHINGTON That Friday the president had a working lunch in the Roosevelt Room with Chief of Staff Jerry Richardson, Secretary of the Treasury Robert Valdez, and his domestic policy advisor, Ted Braxton. The vice president, Patricia Barton-North, was expected to arrive late from a speech at the nearby OAS. There were only two items on the agenda: their domestic program and the budget deficit.

"We met together last week after the Easter recess to go over the numbers and the complaints from the congressional leadership on the other side of the aisle. What have your teams been able to put together?" the president asked.

"I'm afraid it's not particularly good, Mr. President," Robert Valdez replied. "Under any reasonable proposal we make about the economy for the next decade, our programs increase the deficit during the early years. We can't get away from it unless we play games with the numbers, which I suspect some earlier administrations have done."

"We're only doing what we said we'd do in the campaign," Ted Braxton added. "We *told* the American people that our vision is to fix the employment and housing problems, no matter what the cost, once and for all; then count on increased employment and production to kick in the extra taxes needed to decrease the deficit."

The door opened and Patricia Barton-North came in just as Jerry Richardson said, "We just hadn't originally counted on such vehement opposition from the other side, now that we're actually trying to do it."

The president put down his sandwich and leaned forward with both of his hands on the edge of the table. "So what's the answer? Are you saying that after all the months we spent before the election on designing our programs, and all the months we've spent since the election planning to implement them, we won't be able to fulfill *any* of them! That we're impotent against a filibuster in the Senate, and therefore our programs are finished? That it's another four years of political gridlock?"

"That's unacceptable," the vice president said, sitting and leaning against the antique table, looking to her right at the president.

"Don't shoot the messenger," Braxton said. "You asked. We've always known that our programs would bust the short-term budget, but for a purpose. It's not *our* fault that the voters have elected such a conservative Senate."

"Yeah, but *we'll* be blamed. Just watch the press have a field day with us if the current stalemate goes on much longer," added Richardson.

"Again, what's the *answer?*" the president asked. *There's got to be one!* he told himself.

"Do we know anything about these obstructionists that we can use against them?" the vice president asked.

"You mean blackmail?" the chief of staff asked.

"I mean this is hardball, Jerry, for the future of America. So we play just as hard as they do. We know our nation desperately needs these programs. Lives and jobs are at stake. We can't allow a few old men to hold up everything we stand for just because of a budget that no one believes is important anymore, anyway."

"Can we compromise? Is there *any* middle ground?" William asked.

"Yes, but it's not very attractive, I'm afraid," replied Valdez. "If we water down our programs to fit a reduced budget, then they don't stand a chance of creating the real cure we need to increase jobs and incomes later. We'd just sort of muddle along, speaking the platitudes, going deeper into debt, but not really changing anything."

"And what about *their* budget proposal?"

"We still don't have it. They're waiting for ours before they issue an alternative. But I suspect it will be a rehash of the status quo. No real change, no real benefits, no real savings," offered Braxton.

"This is about the most depressing meeting I've attended since we set our course three years ago," the president said, throwing down his napkin.

"Our nation is in a mess, and sooner or later the press and the American people will figure out that their country is stuck again, going nowhere, except deeper into debt, with nothing to show for it. The greatest nation on earth can't pay its bills, can't educate its children, can't house its people, and soon may not be able to defend itself. And we're supposed to be in charge, but we can't do a thing! How's that for leadership?" *Not to mention a nuclear bomb in the hands of terrorists who say they'll kill millions of us, but we don't know when, where, or why!* he thought.

"Mr. President, you can't be worried about defense with so many other, more important problems," Patricia said.

"But I do, Patricia. We were elected by *some* of the people, but we are the leaders of *all* the people. Including the ones in the military. And including all those who will not be pleased if we strip our military of its assets and then can't respond during a crisis."

"William, I don't mean to be disrespectful, but sometimes you say some incredible things. If you worry about *everybody*, you'll never get anything done. We've got *our* programs and *our* constituency, and we have to stick to them," the vice president emphasized, indicating her unhappiness.

This woman is incredible, William thought. *Is she selfish, crazy, or brilliant?* He turned to address everyone. "Before I get angry, let me just say that I want to accomplish *so much more,* as I know you all do. We're starting to bicker among ourselves because our hopes and our dreams for a better nation are being frustrated. I'm very disappointed." The president stood up. "Robert, Jerry, please give me a synopsis of your findings so I can study them over the weekend; maybe something will jump out at me. Ted, set up some one-on-one meetings with key members of the opposition. Let's listen to them and find out if there's any common ground. Or at least some pet projects they want over which we can bargain. Not exactly blackmail; just 'compromise.' Does anyone have any other ideas to get our nation moving again?"

"My mother," Richardson said, trying to smile, "always said to pray for what was important to you and that God would bend down and listen."

The president started to smile and to say something flip in response. But then his expression grew thoughtful, and he just nodded, as if he took the statement quite seriously, to everyone's surprise.

"We'll set up the meetings for next week," Braxton said to the president's back, as the commander in chief left the room.

ATLANTA Rebecca, who had signed up for a twelve-hour shift that day, was surprised to hear herself paged. When she reached the central nurses' station, she learned that she had a phone call. *Who knew I changed my shift?* she wondered as she picked up the phone.

"Rebecca, hi. It's Bruce."

"Hi. What's up?" Bruce never called her at the hospital unless it was important.

"Nothing good. My dad called. My mom didn't want to tell me, but she's been undergoing all these tests, and they've found a brain tumor."

"Oh, Bruce, I'm so sorry."

"Thanks," Bruce said. "It's a real shock. On top of that my dad's not in good shape either. His emphysema is worse. Anyway, I need to fly up there this afternoon. I'll call you from Boston. I'm sorry, but I don't know how long I'll be gone."

"Of course. I understand. Listen, let me check around, and when you call back I'll have the names and numbers of some really good specialists in case you want a second opinion."

"Thanks. We may. From what Dad said, it doesn't sound very good."

"Well, call me tonight at the apartment. I hope she's better. I love you," Rebecca said, trying to sound as upbeat as she could.

"I love you, too," Bruce answered, obviously depressed, and hung up.

NORFOLK Hugh and Jennifer had been to an early movie at the mall and were having a casual dinner at a new restaurant that had just opened there. They were using a young baby-sitter and had to be home before eleven. Ever since they were married they had made a point of going out for dinner or doing something special just before Hugh went to sea, even if he was only going for a week. They both hated the upcoming separation, and Hugh particularly liked to feel he was doing something special for Jennifer. Like all navy wives, she would have to be both mother and father come Monday morning.

After the waitress brought their iced teas, Hugh talked about what was planned for the week he'd be away. "We'll be doing a lot of anti-submarine warfare, which will keep us busy around the clock," he said. "And on Thursday we've got a full vertical replenishment by helicopter scheduled. Most of the guys have never participated in one."

"How are all the new people working out?" Jennifer asked, a note of concern creeping into her voice.

"Fine, I guess. It's really too early to know. We haven't been out to sea with our extended family yet. The real test will come at Guantanamo Bay in a few months. I'm not real happy about it, but I'm the last one who can complain. The guy who wrote the executive order is my brother."

"Yes," Jennifer agreed. "You know, I've never understood homosexual behavior. But I do understand how men and women behave together. And I'm not crazy about you going to sea and spending twenty-four hours a day with a lot of eighteen- to twenty-five-year-old single women. And neither are most of the other wives I've talked to.

"Honey, it'll be fine. Women have been going to sea in our navy for several years, now. It seems to work out."

"But you told me yourself, before this came up on the *Fortson,* that a combat ship is different, with less space and tougher routines. And you told me there are quite a few pregnancies every year, which the navy tries to hush up. What's going to happen when men and women get thrown together for months, working in cramped spaces, away from home, even sharing some danger? I'm a woman. I know. They're going to be drawn together. It's natural. I don't like it. The other wives don't like it, either."

"I don't particularly like it either, but there's nothing I can do. I at least had the satisfaction of telling brother William all of that at Camp David. No other naval officer can say that."

"Well, you should write him regularly and tell him what's going on in the real world we live in. And what about this new female officer?" Jennifer continued, her unhappiness and concern obviously growing. "I hear she's a looker. What's she like?"

"Teri Slocum is her name," Hugh said slowly, trying to sound as clinical as possible when talking to his wife about a woman whom, he had to admit, *was* a "looker," and with whom he would be spending the next ten days. "She's an Annapolis grad and a competent officer. She seems to be real level-headed and is telling her girls—uh, women—to keep as low a profile as possible and just do their jobs. Other than that, I really don't know that much about her."

"*Is* she good looking?"

A pause. "I guess she looks okay. But *I'm* not looking. I'm happily married and very much in love with a wonderful woman who loves me." He smiled as their dinners arrived. "So please don't worry about her or about any other women. And, by the way, I hope to spend any extra moments I may have on this trip reading the Bible for a change. In fact, it's the only book I'm taking this time." Hugh desperately wanted to change the subject.

"Yes," Jennifer said, brightening a little. "Ever since Camp David I've read a few chapters from the Gospel of John every day, just like Michael suggested. It's really interesting. I haven't read the Bible since I was a kid. But *our* kids just about drive me nuts sometimes, interrupting me so much. I hope I can get into it, too, this week. I really liked his sermon, but I can't say I feel any different. Do you?"

"Not really," Hugh replied. "He made so much sense at the time. It's like I don't want to lose that feeling, but all the business of the day just tears me away from it. Maybe we can both get some time while I'm away this week to get into it.

"I tell you what," he continued. "Let's both reread John and this time take notes, to force us to think about it. Then when I get back, we'll compare our notes. How about that?" he asked, as their dinners were served.

Jennifer finally smiled. "You're on. And I promise not to cheat more than five times by calling Mary."

NEW YORK Later that same Friday evening the maitre d' at one of Manhattan's finest French restaurants led Leslie Sloane and Ryan Denning to their seats in a quiet corner. Even in New York, where celebrities were relatively commonplace, the two well-known television personalities turned heads.

"What a session," Ryan said after they had ordered their drinks, referring to the meeting that had lasted most of the day. "I hate it that we're closing yet another overseas bureau. Soon we'll have only third party sources for what's happening anywhere in the world."

"But the audience seems to want more talk shows, more entertainment 'news', and more literal ambulance chasing," Leslie answered, also miffed by the direction in which their network was headed, away from "hard" news, and toward a mix that blurred the line between news and entertainment. "No one really cares what's happening in Buenos Aires or almost anywhere else."

"But someday we may need to know what *is* really going on in another part of the world, and we won't have that capability any more," Ryan continued as their drinks arrived, and he held his up to toast her.

"And someday very soon our audience may not know, or care, if there *is* any difference between what is really happening and what we're inventing for them," Leslie completed the thought, touching his glass with hers across the table. "And that's not only scary—it also gives us an incredible responsibility."

Ryan smiled. "I tell you what. Let's try not to talk about television for fifteen minutes. Do you think we can do it?" He looked at his watch.

She returned his look. "Frankly, I doubt it, but let's try."

They actually made it for twenty minutes, through the ordering of their meal and finishing their drinks. This was their third "date," and they shared stories with each other about their college days and about their first jobs. Leslie enjoyed Ryan's company. He was not just a talking head. He worried about their industry, wanted to do a good job reporting the news, and seemed to have real concerns.

She was pleased to learn that, like her, he believed the nation should work hard to solve its many domestic problems as quickly as possible. He shared her passion for helping the downtrodden in America. And he agreed that the media, and particularly the press, had a large role in, and a big responsibility for, shaping that future.

As their appetizers were served Ryan asked, "What's your latest reading on the president?"

She took a bite out of her stuffed mushrooms, then said, "In my opinion, his ideas for rebuilding America are exactly what we need, but he may have a very hard time getting them enacted. For example, he always said his budget proposal would be out of balance at the beginning, and it is. But the other side isn't buying it, big time."

"Can they stop it?" Ryan asked, taking a spoonful of his onion soup.

"I think they probably can, Ryan. Maybe in the House, and almost certainly in the Senate. It's not just that Harrison's people are new to Washington and for the most part aren't used to wheeling and dealing. They're actually doing a pretty good job on the mechanics. It's more fundamental. The innovative fix he's proposing includes big spending, and the other side is diametrically opposed to the progress he wants to bring to the country because of the short term deficit. It drives me crazy that they can't see the beauty of the president's plan."

"How is the president reacting?"

"They'll only speak off the record, but both Ted Braxton and Bob Horan are worried that the gridlock is starting to get to him."

"Already?"

"Apparently so. They've seen—we've all seen—some days when the president seems really short tempered and almost depressed. He was like that just before he and his family went to Camp David. When he came back, he seemed to be his old confident self for a few days. But the last part of this week, from all accounts on the inside, he's been almost withdrawn."

"Anything you can report on?"

Leslie took a sip of wine. "No. It's too soon. And I don't want to go with that story unless it really becomes obvious. Remember again what we did to our man last time. Let's not add to Harrison's woes. He's the best chance we have to implement real change in the country. If we kill him off, we may not get another progressive thinker in the White House for a decade or more."

"But what if his mental state becomes news?" Ryan asked.

"Then we'll report it," Leslie answered. "But for now, it's not."

"Who says?"

"I do." Leslie returned his smile, but it was obviously forced. "Look, I know the White House. I'll report it. But there's no sense in causing some guy making minimum wage at a fast-food restaurant to worry unnecessarily about his president. Especially when that president is trying to help him."

"So *you* know better than that average man what he should hear and see on the news?" Ryan raised an eyebrow and gave her a devilish look.

Leslie paused. "Actually, yes, and you know it just as well as I do. We both make those decisions every day. So does everyone else in the news media, particularly with the networks. Don't play Grand Inquisitor with me. We have to do it. The future of this nation is too important to leave to the average man."

"Or woman?" Ryan asked. His smile broadened.

Seeing him grin, Leslie realized that he had been egging her on. She paused again. "Well, maybe the average woman *could* handle it," she answered with mock seriousness.

"Well, just let me know when you deem that the president's mental state *is* news, and those of us in New York who make the *final* decisions will let you know whether you're right or not."

"You jerk." She laughed.

For the rest of their meal they had a lively discussion about books, movies, and people they both knew. When the waiter came to their table with dessert menus, Ryan glanced at his, then looked at Leslie. "I've really enjoyed being with you tonight. You're a wonderful woman. Why don't we skip dessert here? There's a bakery near my apartment that stays open late on weekends. We can pick something up and take it to my place."

Leslie paused once again. She was torn. Finally she said, "Not tonight, Ryan. Thanks. I've got to get up early and head back to D.C. to find out what happened today. I'm substituting on 'The Week in Washington' on Sunday morning. But I've had a great time, too. I hope you'll ask me again."

Her tone and the expression on her face let him know that the next time his late-night invitation might actually be accepted. "You can count on it," he said.

ATLANTA AND BOSTON   It was late Friday night when Bruce called Rebecca at her apartment. She was sitting in bed reading, waiting for his call. "How's your mother?" she asked.

"Not good."

She could hear that his voice was cracking and very tired.

"It hasn't been a good day. She apparently *does* have a brain tumor. It's operable." He almost whispered the next sentence. "But she doesn't have enough points, Rebecca, to warrant an operation."

"Oh, Bruce, I'm so sorry."

"I never heard about 'points' before this afternoon when this sniveling little twerp of a doctor told me that my mother didn't have enough points to rate an operation. Can you believe that? My mother doesn't rate on some bureaucrat's chart, and so now she'll die. What are points, Rebecca?"

"It's...they're these points that get assigned by the government. I have to deal with them every day. Ever since they passed health reform several years ago there has to be some way to decide who gets which procedures. Theoretically everything is available to everyone, but of course, in practical terms, that's impossible. So the government has a book of points. It includes age, family responsibilities, other diseases, things like that. The doctors on the committee fill out a form, add up the points, and then look up the proposed procedure. If you have enough points, you get it; if not, you don't. It's very cut and dried."

"Well, I think it's terrible," Bruce rasped.

"It can be," Rebecca agreed, "and I have to counsel people every day who are denied operations because of it. But supposedly it insures a 'fair' distribution of the medical resources in our country. Remember, they used to be decided by how much money or how much insurance you had. Now the government insures that everyone is treated exactly the same. But of course there's still the private alternative. Does your mother have health insurance to cover the operation?"

"No. She and Dad paid for it for years, but when health reform passed, they canceled it. Of course no one ever told her she might need it! No one ever told her she wouldn't be *good* enough to rate an operation!" It sounded to Rebecca like Bruce was crying.

"I know it's hard, Bruce. And I'm so sorry."

"If anything happens to her, who's going to look after Dad?"

"Did you tell them that?"

"Yes, yes. They said if Dad were already in a facility because of his emphysema, then that would earn Mom more points, so she would qualify. But because she's been taking care of him at home to save money and to make him happier, his condition is not considered serious enough, and so she can't qualify. It's insane!"

"It's the government."

"Well, whoever or whatever it is, it's terrible."

"I know, I know. Stay up there as long as you have to, and I'll be here to help any way I can. Oh, I've got that list of specialists if you'd like to write them down."

"I do, but it'll wait till morning. I'll call you back. Good night. I'm glad you're in my life!"

"Me, too."

RESTON, VIRGINIA Saturday was warm and sunny, just right for the tennis game Francis Palmer had scheduled with Congressman Trenton Patterson at his country club in northern Virginia. Ever since the problem with Trent's secretary, when the congressman's wife had demanded that he leave their townhouse in Georgetown, Francis had been able to play tennis with his fellow Pennsylvanian and newly minted bachelor almost every week.

They were playing singles on a clay court, and when they took a break at 3-2 under the shade of a small pavilion between the courts, they found themselves alone.

Seated next to the congressman in a white outdoor chair, Francis Palmer wiped his face with a towel and asked, "Trent, hypothetically speaking, how would you like to wind up with a million untraceable, untaxable, but very spendable dollars, for not doing much of anything?"

"Sounds fantastic, Francis," Patterson grinned, "but it also sounds like a bribe."

"No, just call it a little off-shore consulting. The money would never even come here, so why report it? And all that's involved is helping to support something that the rest of the world thinks is A-okay. I wouldn't be proposing it if I didn't think it was golden."

"This isn't hypothetical, is it?" the congressman asked, looking at Francis. "You're serious."

"Very."

The congressman paused and looked around carefully. Sensing what he was thinking, Francis opened his arms to reveal a sweat-soaked tennis shirt that anyone could see through. "Hey, we've known each other a long time. This isn't a sting. I'm not wearing a wire. This is real. A million bucks, tax free, for you, and a big chunk for me. All you have to do is be generally supportive of a particular policy and vote for a single bill. No one will ever know. And you'll have a million dollars in your name in an overseas account that no one can trace. It's a once-in-a-lifetime chance."

Congressman Patterson thought again and wiped his own face and hands in the heat. "Well, tell me more about it. Just hypothetically, of course."

WASHINGTON That evening President Harrison and his daughter, Katherine, were walking down the hall of the East Wing of the White House. They were headed for the small movie theater where their guests from North Carolina were waiting for them with the first lady. After their dinner William had been called to the West Wing to read an overseas cable, and Katherine had gone with him. Now they were walking back together.

"It looks like I'm going to be able to spend at least six weeks this summer with Aunt Mary and Sarah in Raleigh. I'll hate to leave you and Mom, but I'll be *so* glad to be out of *this* place!"

"It'll be great for you to be back in Raleigh again," her father agreed. "I hope you have a wonderful time."

"I will. Sarah and I are getting jobs at a sandwich shop. Won't that be a hoot—me making sandwiches!" Katherine was known for not eating anything with fat in it, if possible. "I'll be rolling in mayonnaise! Ugh." Her father laughed.

"Dad, thanks for getting those Secret Service people to be a little more flexible. It's not great, but it's better. I know you're trying. And the summer ought to be terrific."

He reached out and gave her a hug with one arm as they walked. "I'm just sorry you had to hit me with a two-by-four to get my attention."

They walked on. "You know, Mom is *really* getting into the Bible since Camp David. She like seems to enjoy it. And you know something else? I haven't seen her drink since we got back. Have you noticed?"

"To tell you the truth, I hadn't paid much attention. Now that you mention it, though, I haven't seen her drinking at all."

"Also, Mom seems somehow more patient, too. Anyway, we're going to church tomorrow morning. I'd really like it if you'd come with us."

William could tell how much it meant to her. "We'll see, honey. Maybe I can. I've got a lot to do tomorrow, but maybe I can make it. Did your mother put you up to this?" he asked, teasingly.

"No, Dad. I just want you to come with us. Like a family. Like at Camp David."

It was Sunday night and William was working in his private study in the family quarters on the upper floor of the original part of the White House. Carrie, sitting around the corner in their bedroom, had just told Katherine good night and now picked up the telephone next to her own comfortable chair. She dialed her sister-in-law in Raleigh.

"Mary, hi. It's Carrie. Yes, we're all fine, though I haven't talked to Robert there in Chapel Hill for a few days. Listen, I want to arrange the final details for Katherine's visit with you this summer. But first I have to tell you about what happened this morning. The three of us went to church together!"

"Carrie, that's wonderful. Where did you go?" Mary asked.

"A large church downtown, not too far from the White House. Michael recommended it. It's called Church of the Good Shepherd. The pastor is a really good speaker, named Robert Ludwig. You won't believe what happened."

"Try me."

"Well, besides all the Secret Service consternation at the last-minute schedule change, and the press corps who followed us, the main thing is that Reverend Ludwig was preaching today on, of all things, a new book he's just read, called *The Foundations of America, A Study in Christian Faith*. I mean, can you believe that? What a coincidence!"

"Carrie, after you've been praying and listening to God for a while, you'll find these sort of 'coincidences' seem to happen all the time. Just remember that nothing happens by chance."

"Well, I hadn't thought of that. But, anyway, we just sat down like 'normal' folks and listened and worshiped. The sermon was wonderful. The author of this book, Gary Thornton, I think, has done years of research, and he's proven that the Founding Fathers quoted the Bible four times more often than any other source in their writings. I didn't know that most of the original state constitutions and university charters gave as their purpose the spreading of the gospel of Jesus Christ. And he said that the framers of the Constitution followed Franklin's advice and prayed daily for God's presence in their meetings. I mean, he gave example after example. He had even prepared a handout—can you believe that?—with specific references for all of these examples."

"Carrie, that does sound incredible. But God works in incredible ways."

"Yes, but the strangest part of all was at the end, when he just blew apart the myth of how the church and the state are supposed to be separated. Do you know it doesn't say that anywhere in any of our founding documents, neither the Declaration of Independence nor the Constitution? But God is mentioned four times in the Declaration. He said the whole point of the First Amendment was just to insure that no one particular federal denomination was set up, the way it was in England at that time, and the way it was in most of the original colonies. And it was supposed to protect churches from state interference. *Not* to take general Christianity out of our laws or out of our schools or out of our public places." Carrie's voice was rising as she talked.

"What did William think?" Mary asked.

"That's what you won't believe!" Carrie said, then lowered her voice. "He listened and started to get into it. He made some notes on the handout. Riding back, he said that what Reverend Ludwig had said sounded interesting, but he wanted to read it himself and have someone look up the references. You know William, always the lawyer. Anyway, I think he may actually ask someone to look up the original texts cited in the book and maybe even read the passages about good government in the Bible."

"Oh, Carrie, we should all keep praying. And don't be bashful. After a week or so, why not suggest that William meet with Robert Ludwig, or even with the man who wrote that book, if he's really interested? I bet both of those men would change their schedules in a minute to discuss the Christian foundations of our country with the president!"

"Good point. I'll keep praying. And you're right, only God could have arranged all of this. I don't know where it's heading, but I thank him for it."

"Me, too. Now, did you want to talk about the summer?"

They talked for another twenty minutes. Then Carrie said, "I'll call you tomorrow about my Bible reading, Mary. And pray that Katherine will start reading with me. She says she might."

"We've got a lot to be thankful for, and a lot to pray about," Mary concluded.

No person who shall deny the being of God, or the truth of the Protestant religion, or the divine authority of the Old or New Testaments, or who shall hold religious principles incompatible with the freedom and safety of the State, shall be capable of holding any office or place of trust or profit in the civil department within this State.

NORTH CAROLINA CONSTITUTION, 1876

5

Thursday, May 10
One Week Later

THE WESTERN ATLANTIC For three days the USS *Fortson* and two other warships had been simulating ASW attacks on two U.S. nuclear submarines and then allowing the submarines to attack them in turn in the Western Atlantic. Now the surface ships took a break from undersea concerns to practice another more basic skill: underway vertical replenishment by helicopter. Like underway refueling, it required the participation of the entire crew below the rate of first class petty officer, including those who had just come off their regular watches and those who had been up most of the night. Hugh Harrison's First Division prepared the helicopter deck for this event.

There was a huge amount of material that had to be unloaded quickly from large pallets dropped on the helo deck near the stern of the ship by a squadron of helicopters. The choppers flew back and forth like swarming bees, to and from the supply ship. Each box had to be checked and then taken to a freezer, cooler, or a temporary storage area, which was usually the mess deck where the crew ate their meals. The crew formed a human conveyer belt. As each helicopter arrived overhead from the supply ship and deposited its pallet on the helo deck, the next man or woman in line was given a box and a destination by the supply officer, with the details noted on a large preprinted order form held by the senior supply chief.

It had been over two years since the *Fortson* had participated in a vertrep, so most of the crew were new to the procedure on the ship, and the younger recruits had never seen it done on any ship.

The Vertrep Detail was called out thirty minutes before the designated time for the first helicopter that morning, and members of the supply department coached the sailors in small groups on what to do. Then the helicopters started arriving, and the boxes started moving. At times it was like an old television comedy, with the number of boxes seeming to overwhelm the capacity of the crew to move them off of the helo deck.

It was at such a hectic moment when Seaman Apprentice Raymond Tyson, one of the new men who had just reported onboard with the supply department, responding to yells to hurry up and return to the helo deck, dumped his heavy load on top of a hatch cover in a corner of the mess deck and started to move aft for another round.

Unfortunately Tyson did not notice the large sign printed on the bulkhead above the hatch cover warning that this particular hatch cover was the top of one of the escape routes from the fireroom below. Under the mess decks the ship's large boilers developed high pressure steam to drive her turbine engines, and even a pinhole leak in one of the steam pipes could fill the fireroom with scalding steam in about ten seconds. Therefore, the boiler technicians took their escape routes very seriously.

Boiler Technician First Class Wulford Higgins, a large man known to his friends as "Wolf," was just climbing up the ladder from the after fireroom when, despite all of the noise and confusion from the vertrep's deposits on the crew's tables, he saw Tyson drop his box on the escape-route hatch cover.

"Hey, you!" Wolf roared across the open space full of sailors, as he bounded toward the hapless recruit. Tyson, like most of the other men and women on the mess deck, turned toward the sound of Wolf's shout. A moment later Tyson found Petty Officer Higgins in his face, yelling.

"You stupid little faggot—can't you read? Or don't you have to worry about your shipmates, 'cause you're some kind of special prima donna? How would you like to be trapped belowdecks in a steam cauldron, trying to get out, and find the hatch stuck because some queer put a box on it, and went off to redo his makeup, while you burn to death? Huh, how would you like that, you little twerp?"

Wolf was so intent on chewing out Tyson that he didn't notice someone coming up behind him. As he finished the first part of what he planned to say and took a breath to begin again, he felt a tap on the shoulder and spun around. There, big and smiling, was Yeoman First Class Diane Davis, the senior petty officer for the lesbians who had joined the admin department, and who had herself been on duty in the ship's office, just aft of the mess deck. Yeoman Davis was almost as tall as Wolf Higgins, and she obviously worked out regularly with weights. Around her neck, now inches from Higgins's face, she wore a gold choker that was inscribed "Bull Dyke."

"Hey, big guy. Why don't you pick on somebody your own size?" She smiled tauntingly.

"What!" was all that Wolf could muster.

"So this guy made a mistake. So what? He's new. Didn't you ever make a mistake? Or are you another Mister Perfect? I've seen a *lot* of those in the navy. Tell me, are you one, too? You seem to qualify. Big, white, obviously not too bright. Yes, you *must* be another Mr. Perfect! I'll mark it in your service record. We're *so* lucky to have you on board."

Wolf raised a fist to punch her, then remembered she was a woman and realized that everyone on the mess deck—gays and straights, blacks and whites—had stopped what they were doing and were watching the three of them. It suddenly dawned on Higgins that Tyson and Davis might have other friends in the crowd, and he started to look around for his own friends, if it turned nasty. Could he count on his black, straight shipmates, or had she neutralized them? Confused and flustered, he started to explain, looking at Davis. "He put a heavy load on top of our—"

Wolf never finished. Just then Hugh Harrison pushed his way onto the mess deck. "What's going on here? The helo deck is jammed with boxes, and the helicopters are having to stand off with our loads," he yelled at no one in particular. Realizing that everyone was focused on the three people in the corner and sensing the tension, Hugh quickly looked around for the senior person there, who seemed to be Gunnersmate Chief Grimes. He repeated his question, looking at Grimes. "What's going on here?"

"A little altercation, sir," Chief Grimes said. "Nothing really happened."

"Well, you stay here with the people involved. Where's the mess deck master-at-arms? Everybody else, back to the vertrep. We've about messed up the whole thing."

Hugh stayed long enough to be sure the process began again and that Chief Grimes had moved over next to Davis, Higgins, and Tyson. Then he turned and headed back to the helo deck.

RALEIGH "This equipment is just what we've needed for years," said Claudia Farris, one of the parents appointed by PTA president Norman Templeton to the study committee for the BioTeam gift offer. The two of them plus Mary Prescott, four other parent members, and Jean Bowers, were meeting late that afternoon in Principal Lawrence Perkins's office, sitting around his conference table. "I honestly wish we'd had something like this when I was in high school. Maybe it would have settled some of my curiosity, and I wouldn't have done all the things I did after my senior year.

"Back then even the consequences, as serious as we thought they were, were nothing compared to today. I hope our daughter will learn as much as possible with this system. Then we won't have to worry about AIDS or pregnancy or the clap. My husband and I are all for it."

Tom Williams, the husband of one of Mary's best friends in Moms-In-Prayer, said, "No one can deny, of course, the need to stay away from the consequences of premarital sex. But there's a lot more involved here. Let's just start with a few. God intended sex as a great joy and a blessing for married couples, not as cheap entertainment. Now I know his design has been violated for centuries, but we shouldn't add to it. Husbands and wives are supposed to learn about 'advanced' sex, if you will, beyond the technical basics, together, not at an arcade.

"And, second, this equipment will expose our kids to possibilities and experiences far beyond what they could even imagine on their own, and some of which are apparently immoral and unnatural."

"Oh come on, Tom," said Scott Blanship, "join this century. You live in a dreamworld. *You and I* grew up in the 'feel good' generation. What do you think kids want today? Whatever God may have intended sex for in the beginning, we've progressed far beyond that now. Sex *is* entertainment. Open your eyes. But this machine is trying to channel that energy back into real learning, and it will do it in a way that won't hurt anyone. And who cares what they experience, so long as it's by themselves?"

"I do," Mary answered. "Have you ever read interviews with men who have committed all sorts of awful crimes, including murder, because they became hooked on pornography and were always seeking greater and greater thrills? Or people who were despondent or mixed-up as teenagers, who found themselves drawn into a homosexual life style which years later they claimed was 'natural'? Or a wife who is left, divorced with young children, because her husband has decided to chase a sex life based on this kind of deceptive fantasy, which no natural man or woman can hope to create or sustain? I don't want either of our children experiencing those kinds of lies about their bodies and about their future spouses. There are other ways to stop the kinds of problems you mentioned which don't make an awful situation much worse. Like virginity."

"Well, break out the hoop skirts and warm up the barbecue," chided Claudia Farris. "Miss Scarlett is back in town! Do you realize how silly you sound? Nothing you just said makes any sense today. It's not relevant. It's irrational." She turned to the PTA president. "Norman, how can people with such thoughts even have a vote on this issue?"

"Claudia, that's enough," said the PTA president sternly. "We're all parents and all equally entitled to our opinions. That's why we have this committee."

Mary smiled and looked at Claudia. Speaking quietly, she said, "The ideas I've just expressed made sense thousands of years ago, and they'll still make sense thousands of years from now, if the human race lasts that long, because they're based on the principles of the One who made us. Our problem is not those principles. Our problem is that we've ignored them."

"Have you ever thought about becoming a preacher?" Farris asked.

The committee continued talking for another hour with little progress in changing anyone's initial opinion. Finally Principal Perkins said, "I'm concerned we're never going to get beyond the tie vote we would have had when we walked in here."

"I agree," said Tom Williams. "None of us appears to be ready to bend. So let me ask you this, Jean: I assume that even if the gift was accepted and the class was instituted as you have proposed, individual parents could still request that their children not participate, couldn't they?"

Ms. Bowers looked at Mr. Perkins. She paused. "I suppose that technically they could. But I would really discourage it. It would really disrupt such a high-tech learning curriculum to have a few students not participating. How could they even learn or experience along with the others? How could we test that group? You know, sex education is mandated by the state school board."

"How do you other parents feel about that?" asked Mary.

"Well, as much as I'm in favor of this program," said Scott Blanship, "I don't think any student should be forced to participate against his or her will, or against their parents' will, if they're not eighteen, of course."

"Oh come on," Farris said impatiently. "There's nothing wrong with this. We've got some of the best minds in the world giving us something incredible, and it's free. It can't hurt anybody, only help. Jean Bowers will be in charge of the whole program. If some students don't use this gift, how will she possibly grade them with the others? I'm tired of creating special rules for old fashioned ideas. We're in a new century, folks, and we'd better get with it. I say there are no substitutes."

There followed another ten minutes of even more contentious discussion. Finally Norman Templeton called a halt. "Unfortunately, I don't think we're getting anywhere on this, either. Now is there any reason to meet again next week, or are we deadlocked on both the system itself and on making it mandatory?" There was silence.

"Then I really don't see any need to meet again. I tell you what I'd like to do. Will each 'side' write up a report—no more than two pages—with your views on the proposal? Then we'll send a fact sheet on the system, plus both reports, and a notice of our next full PTA meeting to every parent in the high school. Hopefully we can then have an enlightened discussion and a vote in three weeks. Unless someone has a better idea, or an objection, we'll proceed that way. Okay?"

ATLANTA Rebecca opened the door to the examining room and realized that her memory was correct. She smiled.

"Hey, Eunice. Didn't we just do this together last year?"

Eunice Porter, wearing a paper gown, was sitting on the examining table. She looked up but didn't return Rebecca's greeting. After a quick glance at the floor she nodded her head and said, "Yes. Yes, we did. I'm no more pleased to be here than you are to have me."

Rebecca walked over next to the young woman. "Well of course I'm glad to see you. I'm sorry if I sounded flip. I guess I just didn't think you'd be pregnant again so quickly."

"Me, neither. In fact, I took one of those morning-after pills this time, and I never thought I'd be here. What a mess, with two little ones already at home. I haven't seen my boyfriend in a month, so I guess he's gone. I just don't know what to do. I'm thinking about getting rid of this one."

Rebecca lowered her clipboard to the edge of the table and matched Eunice's seriousness. "Well, under the national health plan you certainly have the right to terminate the pregnancy at any time. But for your own sake, if you're going to do it, you should probably do it soon."

Eunice paused and looked again at the floor. Finally she said again, "Maybe...or maybe there's a different way."

"What do you mean?" asked Rebecca.

Another pause. "Oh nothing. I was just thinking. I haven't made up my mind... Say, I guess your brother is the president now, isn't he? I remember when he was running last year."

Rebecca's smile returned. "Yes, it's exciting. In fact we all got together recently."

"Well, next time you see him, you can tell him for me that this 'wonderful' morning-after pill he talked about so much last year obviously isn't worth a dime when it doesn't work."

Rebecca placed her hand on the younger woman's shoulder. "I'll do that. I promise. Now let's get a blood sample."

WASHINGTON Late that same evening the president and first lady were sitting in bed, reading. After almost an hour William lay his book on his lap. "Carrie, I don't know whether to get mad, laugh, or cry. On the one hand, everyone around me seems to have decided to talk to me about God for the past month, and I'm so tired of it I could scream. I don't need to 'accept Christ'—I'm not a bad person. I don't want you or Mary bugging me any more about it." He paused for a moment, then said, "But on the other hand, given what I'm reading, maybe there is a reason that I'm supposed to listen to all of this. Why?" He frowned and looked away through the large windows at the lights in the distance.

Carrie lowered her own book and said with genuine concern, "William, if I've upset you, I didn't mean to."

"It's not you, Carrie." He turned back to look at her. "It's everything.

This mess with our legislation. Those dingbats on the other side. My *own* team. I don't know how to break the gridlock. It's driving me crazy. Then Hugh tells me we're wrong to give gays and lesbians their rightful place on ships. Rebecca reports that the abortion pill is messing up more than it's helping, Mary has just written to me about some sex education computer at their school, and Katherine is just working out of being miserable living here. Besides all the other problems, there is still that bomb out there and someone threatening to kill millions of Americans, maybe without any warning. The military, CIA, FBI, and ATF have teams following what seem to be hundreds of leads, but so far absolutely nothing of substance has materialized. And then out of nowhere this book by Gary Thornton arrives!

"Here I've been a lawyer all my life and a politician. Yet reading this book I feel like I'm learning about a new nation I never knew existed. I've almost finished it, and I'm blown away.

"I'm the president of the United States, and *maybe* just now learning what I'm actually president of." He paused again. "I'm struck by how we've been running around all these years—both political parties—trying to 'fix' the country, but we never studied the original model to know the ultimate purpose for what we're doing. Again, I don't know whether to laugh or to cry. None of us here in Washington has had a clue; it's incredible. We've all been messing with something we haven't known anything about! I just hope this Gary Thornton has really done his homework. I asked Barbara to have one of our staff spot-check the original texts. So far, he's right on."

"What have you learned?" Carrie asked, turning to him, amazed by his willingness to talk to her about God, of all things. "Give me some examples."

Flipping back through *The Foundations of America, A Study in Christian Faith,* William said, "Well, just the fact that almost *all* the Founding Fathers were strong Christians and identified this nation with that same faith. He makes the point that we've interpreted the First Amendment all wrong for over forty years; it apparently was never interpreted the way the courts do now for the first 180 years of our nation's history!" He stopped and read briefly to himself before continuing. "The amendment was clearly meant, from reading their actual deliberations and defeated substitute wordings, which he's included, to prohibit the government from establishing an official 'religion,' meaning an organized official denomination, like the Church of England. This issue has actually come up several times over the years; we didn't just invent the debate in the sixties."

William stopped and searched through the book for a moment. "Listen to what the House Judiciary Committee reported in 1854:

> Christianity must be considered as the foundation upon which the whole structure rests. Laws will not have permanence or power without the sanction of religious sentiment, without a firm belief

that there is a Power above us that will reward our virtues and punish our vices. In this age there can be no substitute for Christianity: that, in its general principles, is the great conservative element on which we must rely for the purity and permanence of free institutions. That was the religion of the founders of the republic, and they expected it to remain the religion of their descendants. There is a great and very prevalent error on this subject in the opinion that those who organized this Government did not legislate on religion.

"I mean, who ever heard that before? If that's what our nation is supposed to be about, why haven't we heard it? Frankly, if it's true, it makes me mad to learn it at age fifty.

"And then the House passed this two months later:

The great vital and conservative element in our system is the belief of our people in the pure doctrines and divine truths of the gospel of Jesus Christ.

"Carrie, why aren't we told any of this any more?" He paused. "I guess I know why, actually. The 'separation of church and state' keeps it out of the schools, so it's a self-fulfilling cycle. We don't hear it, so we don't act upon it; if we don't act upon it, we won't hear it.

"Anyway, I turned down the corner of this page, too. Listen to what Patrick Henry said, and he was one of the champions of the First Amendment:

It cannot be emphasized too strongly or too often that this great nation was founded, not by religionists, but by Christians; not on religions, but on the gospel of Jesus Christ! For this very reason peoples of other faiths have been afforded asylum, prosperity, and freedom of worship here."

He looked down at the book in his lap, then over at his wife. "Carrie, I can hardly bring myself to say this, but if this man is right, the 'separation of church and state' we've heard so much about since we were kids is simply not true. Look: everyone points to the First Amendment as the source of this 'separation,' stating that the Founding Fathers never meant to mix faith and government. That just seems to be a figment of the recent Court's imagination, repeated enough in the media to be believed. On the day after the House passed the First Amendment, the very same elected representatives passed a resolution calling for a national day of thanksgiving and prayer to thank God for our Constitution. Does that sound like 'separation of church and state'?"

He turned over a few pages in the book. "And he points out that the same First Amendment also contains the famous clause guaranteeing the free exercise of the press. The same amendment that guarantees the free exercise of religion. *The same one!* Try to take a newspaper down from the wall of a courthouse, and there would be howls and lawsuits. But the Ten Commandments is ordered to be taken down by the Supreme Court itself! No newspaper would accept the exclusions that are placed on religion in all facets of our society, yet it's the exact same amendment guaranteeing the same freedom of expression for both.

"Carrie, I'm sorry to go on like this. I'm certainly not the world's strongest Christian—I'm not even sure I *am* a Christian. How many people in Washington are? What *is* a Christian, anyway? Am I supposed to pray every hour for divine guidance? Hire my sister Mary as our domestic policy advisor?" He laughed. "But one thing's for sure, the guys who defined our country weren't running around scared of their own shadows about 'church and state.' They were shouting their faith from the rooftops and wanted their descendants to know it and to live by it. But we obviously *don't* know. Whether they were right or full of bull, I'm just flabbergasted that all of this is unknown today. It's incredible. Like a cover-up, almost." He closed the book and looked her in the eyes.

"Did you know most of the states *required* in their constitutions that their politicians be overt Christians or else they couldn't serve? I mean, this was only a little over two hundred years ago. What—only about eight or ten generations, that's all. I've been alive a quarter of that time myself, for goodness sake! It amazes me that our ideals have apparently changed so much from what the founders fought for. We politicians have been focusing on the short term, no matter what our ideology. When was the last time any of us stopped to consider how our beliefs—or lack of them—impacted our national policies? Carrie, we don't do it; it just doesn't happen. Have we improved on their original model? Or have we lost the most important foundation of all? To say I'm confused is an understatement."

The first lady had been watching her husband while he was speaking, sharing his amazement and his bewilderment over these discoveries. "It's strange, William," she offered, after they were both silent for a while, considering his words. "Lately I've been absorbed by how God can and does affect individuals—me, in particular. And you've been absorbed since last Sunday by how God apparently established this nation through men and women who had already been changed by him. Isn't it incredible how he can work on an entire nation as well as on an individual person?"

He considered her words for a moment and frowned. "Carrie, this isn't about some personal leap of faith for me! I don't feel any closer to God. I'm just overwhelmed by how little most of us apparently know about the men who founded our country, what inspired them, what they believed, how they made decisions, and what they intended for our nation. I suddenly feel like I've been flying this plane blind and someone just told me there may be instruments I can use to find my way, if I choose to do so—and *if* the instruments *really* work, I should add. What would happen, I'm asking, if we applied the principles our founders intended to the problems we have today?"

"I don't know, sweetheart," Carrie said. "But it just gave me a chill when you said that. How would you ever know that you were really doing it?"

He paused again and spoke more slowly. "I guess I'd have to study their more personal writings and then study their faith, which certainly appears to have been Christianity. If Thornton is correct, our forefathers really lived their faith."

There was another long moment of silence, and then William said thoughtfully, "You know, most of my contemporaries have always looked at Christianity as something nice for naive people and goody-goodies, but now it looks like it was the most central force for men who were such giants that they make most of today's leaders seem pitiful by comparison. What did they know about their faith that most of us—me in particular—don't know?"

William chuckled. "Mary could never get me to read the Bible. But now I'm mad, and my curiosity's up, both as a lawyer and as the president.

"I'm obviously having problems—we're both living with them. I'm going to read some more about what these men thought and believed. Maybe I can find out how they overcame problems. It's amazing. I never really thought about it before. But think what Washington went through, from commander of the army to president of the Constitutional Convention to two-term president of the country. He must have had some problems along the way that make ours today seem pretty mild. He and his friends had to invent the whole thing as they went along! And until now I've never even thought to ask how they handled their problems. But I'm going to."

Carrie returned his smile and took his hand in hers. She was overcome, as Mary had said she would be. But she held back, uncertain of her own new beliefs and of his new questions. All she could say was, "I think it might be one of the most important things you've ever done."

*Providence has given to our people the choice of their rulers, and
it is the duty as well as the privilege and interest of our Christian nation
to select and prefer Christians for their rulers.*

JOHN JAY
FIRST CHIEF JUSTICE
U.S. SUPREME COURT

6

Tuesday, May 15
Five Days Later

ATLANTA Rebecca and Bruce were again sitting on the terrace of her high-rise apartment, sipping wine in the lingering May sunlight before their dinner. Much had changed in Bruce's life since their first such evening on the terrace earlier that spring. For several years he had coped with the early death of his brother and the steadily worsening condition of his father. But the sudden and unexpected illness of his mother and the prospect of her approaching death had almost robbed him of the youthful joy that had originally been one of the qualities that attracted Rebecca to him.

She was trying to be as supportive as possible. She had provided Bruce with the names of brain specialists in Boston. She had reviewed in detail with him the forms the hospital there used to calculate the number of points through which his mother might qualify for an operation; and she had confirmed that unfortunately his mother fell short of the minimum needed.

Now they sat on her terrace, both silently sipping their wine. Bruce appeared to be very far away. Finally he spoke. "I got a call from Mom's doctor late this afternoon at the office. She's getting worse, and he was asking me what I wanted to do about Dad." There was another long pause. He looked down at his wineglass, and Rebecca thought he was close to tears. "I didn't know what to tell him. Rebecca, I'm just not ready to deal with the deaths of my parents. What am I going to do?"

She sighed heavily, understanding his pain but feeling helpless. "I don't know, Bruce. It's really a mess. I deal with problems like this every day at work. But I'm not very good at coping with them when they hit someone I care about."

Bruce was bent over in his chair, his glass between his knees. He turned his head to look at her. "I've been thinking, Rebecca....You know Mom needs this operation desperately, and you know she doesn't have enough points to qualify. But as far as I'm concerned that's a stupid bureaucratic decision, made by bureaucrats and politicians. Your brother is the president of the United States. Don't you think a word from him could change that decision?"

"Oh, Bruce. I don't know. I've never asked him for anything like that, and I'm not sure it's even right."

Bruce looked at her in amazement. "You mean saving my mother's life isn't right? How can you say that? Your brother is the most powerful man in the world. One word from him can send fleets of ships and squadrons of aircraft scrambling in all directions. So why can't he say the one word that will save my mother's life?"

Rebecca paused. "Bruce, first of all, there is certainly no guarantee that even if she has the operation it will save her life. A brain tumor is a very tricky thing. As you saw on the points summary, the doctors think the chance of recovery is at most forty percent."

"But that's forty percent more of a chance than she has without the operation!" Bruce exclaimed.

Rebecca leaned back and glanced down briefly at her own glass. "Bruce, I don't know. The system was set up when the National Health Plan was adopted, and it's supposed to be fair. If politicians begin to override medical decisions, where will it all end?"

"I don't care in the slightest where it might end! I'm only interested in saving my mother's life. Can't you see that? How can you worry about some far off political consequences when she's about to die?"

Rebecca was silent again. Then she spoke slowly, looking directly at him. "Bruce, I know your pain. And, obviously, I want your mother to recover. I'll think about it, of course. But I just don't know if it's the right thing to do."

Bruce stood up and put his wineglass on the table in front of him, his anger obvious. "Well, don't take too long to think about it, or she'll be dead. Sometimes I just don't understand where you're coming from, Rebecca. But right now I need some time to myself. I'm going for a walk."

He left the terrace, moved quickly through the apartment, and slammed the door behind him.

AT SEA That night Lieutenant Teri Slocum had the mid-watch as the junior officer of the deck. For that four hours she was the ship's second-in-command, standing watch on the bridge while the captain and most of the crew slept. Since this was her first duty assignment on a warship, she was in a learning capacity as the J.O.O.D., taking her place in the normal one out of five watches in the daily rotation along with the other junior officers on the ship. This particular night in the western Atlantic the sea was as smooth as glass, and the lack of a moon meant that she could see more stars than she had ever imagined possible. The officer of the deck, Lieutenant Henry Early, had already demonstrated that they could see the rings around Saturn with the Big Eyes, the ship's very powerful binoculars.

Lieutenant Early was conning the ship from the center of the enclosed bridge as they headed west toward Norfolk and home. Lieutenant Slocum was standing out on the starboard bridge wing, just outside the enclosed bridge, using the binoculars slung around her neck to watch the lights of a tanker about three miles away, which they were slowly overtaking along their starboard side. The door from the combat information center at the back of the bridge opened, and Hugh Harrison walked in. After waiting a minute for his eyes to adjust to the almost total darkness on the bridge and saying hello to Henry Early, Hugh walked out onto the bridge wing, where he and Teri Slocum were alone.

"Hi. How's the mid-watch going?" he asked.

Her smile was reflected in the dim red light from inside the bridge. "Hi. Fine, I guess, but it's only twelve-thirty. I'm glad to see you, but why are you up so late?"

Hugh, who was senior enough as the weapons officer not to stand a rotating watch, replied, "I couldn't sleep. I thought some fresh air would do me good. I checked the radar back in CIC, and it looks like you don't have too many surface contacts to worry about."

"Nope. I was just keeping an eye on that tanker over there. It shouldn't be a problem for us, though. Why do you think you couldn't sleep?"

"Oh, I don't know. Maybe the natural excitement of getting home to Jenny and the kids tomorrow. And maybe a relief that this underway period is almost over. It's been difficult, to say the least."

Teri frowned. "Well it's my first time underway on a warship, so I have nothing to compare it to. But it seems fine to me."

"Oh, you and your division have done great. Of course the real test will come down at Guantanamo Bay when we actually fire some missiles. But I think your people certainly know what they're doing."

"Thanks."

He paused for a minute. "Frankly I'm finding it difficult to deal with all the new undercurrents on board, with a crew as diverse as we now have. I mean we used to have some flare-ups now and then between members of different ethnic groups or races. When it happened, which wasn't often, we dealt with it quickly. But with women, lesbians, and homosexuals added to the equation, these situations may not be as easy to deal with—or as infrequent—as the social engineers in Washington thought they would be."

"Why do you say that?"

"Well, take the Captain's Mast for Wolf Higgins. I had to attend because I was the first officer on the scene at the problem. The captain was in an impossible situation. I mean, this young guy, Tyson, had definitely done something wrong. But Higgins came on to him too strongly and then called him a 'queer.' There's not really anything in the Uniform Code for that infraction, since until just recently it was actually against the Code itself for a homosexual to be on a ship! But Captain Robertson had to do something, particularly since Thomas Dobbs insisted on being involved, even though none of the people in the altercation were in his divisions."

"How did he get into it?" Teri asked, turning slightly to check again with her binoculars on the tanker, which was maintaining its course and speed, now directly on their beam.

"He apparently told the captain he had special status as the highest ranking homosexual on board to protect the rights of all the homosexuals, no matter their divisions."

"Does she really have that status?"

"I don't know, and I doubt the captain does either. But just to be sure no one got bent out of shape, he let Dobbs attend the hearing."

"And what happened?"

"Well, the only thing that really happened on the mess decks was that Higgins yelled at Tyson and talked down to him. But Dobbs—and Davis, the lesbian petty officer who slowed Higgins down—told the captain that Tyson's rights and standing on the ship were gravely affected by Higgins's verbal attack. I really felt for the captain. He was in a no-win situation. Anyway, he gave Higgins a written reprimand in his personnel record and a three hundred dollar fine. The reprimand will hurt his future, but eventually he'll work through it. What I'm more worried about is the tension I've felt ever since that confrontation on the mess decks, which the Captain's Mast didn't help.

"The chiefs are telling me they hear the men muttering in their berthing compartments about the 'prima donnas' in the homosexual and lesbian divisions. Four guys in First Division supposedly took Polaroids of themselves in the shower and were offering to sell them to the homosexuals in the Admin Division as a joke. But it wasn't taken as such, and Tom Dobbs again complained to the captain. I just don't know where all this is going."

Both of them paused before Teri looked up at him in the dark and asked, "So what's the answer, Hugh? Should women and homosexuals serve on warships?"

Now it was his turn to smile. "I don't know, Teri. That's for others more senior than me to decide. I guess that's one of the purposes for this experiment. Maybe it'll all work out. But I already have serious doubts."

She straightened up and turned directly toward him. "Do you think we just aren't capable?"

Again he paused. "Is this for the record? Are we on tape?"

She relaxed a bit. "No, of course not. I'm just interested in *your* opinion."

She was standing very close to him. The breeze brought the light, floral scent of her perfume to him. He felt an unexpected tightness in his chest and experienced a slight rush to his head. "Well, as far as I'm concerned, the issue has never been capability. Obviously, for example, *you* are very capable. You're a good officer. But this experiment has made me think about things I hadn't much considered before. The question to me comes down to whether it makes sense to try to override what appear to have been eons of God's laws—or nature's laws—or someone's laws—to put men and women—and even now homosexuals—into such a tight working, living, and fighting situation. We all have many natural beliefs, feelings, and reactions that are hardwired into us as human beings and that are difficult or impossible to cancel simply because some professor with a new theory says we ought to. You may be perfectly capable, but even so, do the overall results make sense? Is the price we pay in other ways too high?"

Teri looked out to sea. She didn't say anything for a few moments. "It's funny. Ever since I was a teenager I've wanted to be in the navy to do exactly what I'm doing right now. I really enjoy it, and I think I'm reasonably good at it. I look forward to learning more. This underway period has been wonderful.... But I have to admit that I can also see your point. For example, there's no denying that strong attractions"—she turned her head and looked directly into his eyes, then paused for another moment—"do exist. I don't know exactly where it all might lead. I guess I don't have the answers, either."

There was a long period of silence between them as they stood close together and listened to the bow of the ship cut through the dark water. Each of them could feel the unspoken tension passing between them, even in the incongruous location of the bridge wing, as they stood close together on the warm night. Finally Hugh said, "Well, closer to home: how have your women survived their first sea duty on a warship?"

Teri smiled. "Real well, I think. They've been very busy, and though I've asked every morning, there haven't been any real complaints, except, perhaps, that the food is too good and they're all worried about gaining weight!"

"Good," her department head replied. "What about relationships?"

"I've noticed a few of what I'd say are budding, good-natured, seemingly friendly relationships between several of my women and some of the guys. But so far I don't think it's anything too serious."

"Well, good. We'll all have to keep an eye on that." He paused again, as they looked directly at each other. *I do like looking at her,* he caught himself thinking. "Anyway, now that we've answered most of the world's major geopolitical questions, maybe I can get some sleep. And I'll sleep better knowing that you're up here until 4:00 A.M. protecting me against all harm."

Teri laughed. "No question about that," she said as Hugh turned to leave. "Henry and I have it under control. I hope you get some sleep so you can greet your wife with a smile."

WASHINGTON While his younger brother discussed the immediate results of one of his administration's earliest policies, William Harrison lay awake in bed. Carrie slept soundly beside him. It now seemed that several nights every week he lay awake, unable to sleep. He was beginning to run on adrenaline during the day, and two days earlier Carrie had mentioned as gently as she could that his eyes looked terrible. He knew that if Carrie mentioned it, he must really look bad. And that realization did not help him fall asleep.

At one o'clock he rose quietly from their bed and walked out onto the Truman balcony. The lights of Washington shone brightly in the dark night. He grasped the railing of the balcony and tried to imagine what he would actually do when the telephone rang and a nuclear bomb was about to be detonated in an American city. *What will they want?* he thought. *And what will I do? I wish I could watch someone else handle this, but I'm the one in this office.*

The afternoon's meeting with Vince Harley and the agency heads of the special team tasked with finding the weapon added to William's insomnia. *Two weeks ago they thought they had it identified in the Columbian mountains. Today the general has to admit, after the deaths of eight agents and fifty Columbians, that the information must have been incorrect. Came from a satellite, with only limited corroberation on the ground! Now I'm told there is strong evidence that the bomb is either in Bosnia, Iran, a former Soviet republic, or Wyoming. I could have told them that from reading the newspapers.*

And then almost as a relief his mind turned to all the budget figures and the arguments that he and his advisors had reviewed so many times. *What are the answers?* he asked himself once more. *Anywhere we try to cut, someone immediately screams. But then we can't spend more money on our programs because the Senate won't pass them. What are we going to do? How can we break through this gridlock?*

William knew the press was already starting to hint that his leadership was ineffectual. In honor of the last two administrations, they were now starting to call his administration "Gridlock III." He hated it. He had been a reasonably effective governor in his state. He had instituted many progressive and permanent changes there. His political philosophy, which he recognized had its roots in his mother's activism, should work. He knew there was an element of experimentation behind his plan for employment and housing, but all of his advisors' figures said it would work, if the Senate would just give it a chance. But so far it appeared that those policies would never be implemented. And so, even though he had been in office less than six months, he was already being labeled as a weak and ineffective president, and he hated it.

The one consolation over the past weeks had been his readings about the problems that had beset Washington, Franklin, Madison, Lincoln, and virtually all of the early American leaders. They had apparently also had to cope with constant bickering, different political philosophies, and different proposed solutions to complex questions.

Frustrated and still unable to sleep, William decided to continue reading the early writings of the founders that his team of interns had assembled, following the outline in Gary Thornton's book. Quietly taking the briefing papers from his bedside table, he moved over to his comfortable chair by the fireplace and switched on a reading lamp. *These guys obviously had problems, too. I wonder if any of them lay awake, trying to figure out how to move the country forward, or how to save it.* He flipped open the notebook to several of the pages he had marked earlier and started to reread them.

When Carrie awoke in the morning, she found her husband asleep in his chair, the briefing book open on his lap.

*No people can be bound to acknowledge and adore the Invisible Hand which
conducts the affairs of men more than those of the United States.
Every step by which they have advanced to the character of an independent nation
seems to have been distinguished by some token of providential agency.... We ought to
be no less persuaded that the propitious smiles of Heaven can never be expected
on a nation that disregards the eternal rules of order and right
which Heaven itself has ordained.*

GEORGE WASHINGTON
INAUGURAL SPEECH TO CONGRESS, APRIL 30, 1789

7

Thursday, May 31
Two Weeks Later

ATLANTA As Rebecca pulled out from the hospital driveway at the end of
the day and headed north on Peachtree Street she saw a familiar face standing at the bus stop. She pulled over and pushed the button to roll down the
passenger side window. "Can I give you a ride, Eunice?" she asked.

Eunice bent down and recognized the nurse. She hesitated for an
instant, looked up at the time on the clock tower, and said "Yes, thank you."
She opened the door and took her seat as the car moved away from the curb.

"How are your children?" Rebecca asked, as she drove along Peachtree
Street.

"Oh, they're fine. I called my sister, and they're home from daycare. I
hate not being there—they're so young, and it's gotten so there's a shooting
almost every week—but I had to come here and then get to work."

"Where do you work?"

"At a restaurant up Peachtree—I'm a waitress, and I'd be late if you
hadn't stopped. Thanks."

"I'll drop you off. I live just up the street here, but I'm heading for the
post office to mail a letter to my brother."

"The president?"

"Yes. There's something I need to ask him." Rebecca nodded toward
Eunice's lap. "How's your next one?"

The mother-to-be hesitated, and the smile left her face. "Oh, it's okay, I guess."

"You don't seem too excited."

Another pause. "I guess I'm not. How can I be, really? What a mess. Too many kids. Anyway, I'm going to take care of this one."

"Really? Abortion? Isn't it getting a little late for that, as far along as you are, even if it's now legal right up to the end? Or do you mean adoption?"

"No, I...I guess I don't know what I mean. A friend is looking into something for me. It's kind of like adoption, I guess. I mean you help people with children. I don't know. Anyway, it'll be okay. Please tell me more about your brother and the White House. Is it beautiful?"

What's this all about? Rebecca thought for an instant. Then she began telling her passenger about her brother's new home.

RALEIGH The small group of twenty or so parents was still standing at the bottom of the front steps of the high school in the fading light of the late May evening. It was fifteen minutes after the school year's final PTA meeting had adjourned.

"In my case, I know it's because I didn't think it was possible, so I never really prayed or sought God's guidance," Tom Williams said. "I relied on my own strength and never called on his."

"Me, too," said Graham Prescott, his hands in his pockets, his head down. "We never seriously imagined it was possible. Now what?"

"Prayer, lots of prayer," said Mary, standing next to him in the circle of concerned and devastated parents.

Their PTA had just voted by an eighty percent majority to recommend that the school board accept the gift from the BioTeam Company, including the new sex education curriculum. The vote had come after a bitter, acrimonious debate. Then, by a narrower majority of just over half, the parents approved Claudia Farris's motion that the class be mandatory, with no substitute curriculum available. The only alternative for a student, if he or she declined to participate, would be a failing grade.

"I guess, despite what the Bible says," Tom added, "I still wasn't ready for the hatred. You would have thought we were planning bodily harm for the kids, the way some of the parents yelled at us."

His wife, Cynthia, said, "We just forgot that it's not our fight alone, and we forgot to call on God's help. We've lost a round, but we can still appeal to the school board."

"A lot of help they'll be," another parent said. "Judging from their previous actions, they'll probably want to clone the machine and put it in *all* the schools. When do they come up for reelection, anyway?" he added as an afterthought.

"Eighteen months from now. Next November."

"Anyway," Mary said, "lets pray now, and then meet next week—Monday or Tuesday at our home would be good—to discuss what we can do in our churches and with the school board."

"And maybe you ought to write your brother in Washington and tell him what a mess this is," Tom suggested.

"Unfortunately—or fortunately, I guess—the school board is not his responsibility. But maybe you're right, Tom. Perhaps I'll write him again. Maybe he can say or do *something*. But for now let's do what we should have been doing all along."

The group of parents moved closer, joined hands, bowed their heads, and prayed for their children.

WASHINGTON "Come in, John," William motioned with his coffee mug, as the senior senator from his party stuck his head through the door of the president's suite on Air Force One that Friday morning. "Great weather to fly out to Ohio this morning. Here, have a seat. Would you like some coffee?"

"Yes, thanks," said the older man, taking a mug from the steward and sitting in one of the spacious built-in chairs in the flying White House. "I'm glad you could make it today, Mr. President. Every six years the race gets tighter, and in eighteen months I'm up again. It'll be good to have you at the opening of this new job training facility."

"Glad to do it. And you know it's what our domestic program is all about. I hope we can get the legislative package passed and then open hundreds more just like it. But, here, we're about to take off. We'll talk more about it over breakfast once we're up."

For the next twenty minutes the two men sat alone in the cabin and caught up on Washington small talk until the large Boeing flattened its climb and the steward began serving the two men a breakfast of scrambled eggs and sausage. "I can eat like this up here," the president said, grinning, "but don't tell Carrie. I figure the high altitude dilutes the fat and the calories."

"Your secret is safe with me, Mr. President." John Dempsey returned his look knowingly.

"Thanks. Now eat your eggs while they're hot."

After the steward departed with their last used dish they were alone again, sitting across from each other at the small table with fresh mugs of coffee. "John, you've been at this a lot longer in Washington than I have. I wanted us to have this time completely alone. I hate to be a broken record, but I hope you can give me some ideas—be as candid as you wish—on how to deal with the other party, so we can move our legislation forward. And, please, this conversation is just between us."

John Dempsey paused and looked out the window at the American countryside speeding past them far below. He sighed. "Is this really just between us, Mr. President?"

"Of course," William said.

Dempsey turned back to face the president. "Well, let me tell you then—it wouldn't bother me much if your package never did pass."

"*What?*" William Harrison exclaimed, obviously stunned by the statement from his own party's senior senator.

Dempsey didn't answer immediately—he just looked at the chief executive. Slowly he began, "You're what, about fifty? I'm almost half again as old, the oldest son of a Baptist preacher. When I got back home from World War II—I was alive by a miracle—and finished school, I went into politics because I believed God wanted us to make this world a better place. As a child of the Depression I joined our party and worked hard on legislation to right wrongs and to uplift the oppressed.

"I don't know exactly how to say this, Mr. President, but somewhere, somehow in the last fifty years we've done too much, intervened too much, interfered too often. Now we create more problems than we fix. Oh, some of our programs are still okay—usually the ones where we give an incentive for someone in the private sector to do something right. But on balance, I'm afraid that *we're* the problem. We tax too much and regulate too much. For me, what started as a righteous quest by a preacher's son is now mired in bureaucracy and waste. So in my heart of hearts I privately agree with Warner Watts that your package is just too much government."

William was speechless. *Has he been quietly torpedoing our own legislation, all the while pretending to support it?*

"You see, Mr. President, what looks good and seems to work in a single state isn't the same in Washington. In your state you were *taking* programs from the federal government, trying to get your fair share of scarce resources. Here we *make* the resources, or try to. So it looks deceptively like these resources are no longer scarce. But that's a lie. They *are* scarce. We can't have it all. We try to play God, making programs to 'improve' this group or that. But we forgot to include values. And once a program gets started and the bureaucracy gets hired and the beneficiaries put on their pressure, it never ends."

There was a long, awkward pause, and finally the president said. "I...I really can't believe what I'm hearing, John. From you! I believe *our* programs will really help people, bring America to full employment and provide decent housing. And here I've been looking to you for help and support, and you're *against* them?"

"I know it sounds strange. I've supported your package in our committees and will do so on the floor of the Senate. That's my own problem I'll have to answer for someday to the Creator. I haven't much believed in these kinds of programs for ten years now, but I haven't had the courage to come out against them in public. Sad, isn't it, how things turn out sometimes? Maybe in this next election I'll find the strength with God's help to do so. But you asked for my personal opinion, and I gave it. I'll firmly support you in public and in the legislative hearings, but I won't go the extra mile and twist arms, because I think your program would be a disaster for our nation."

The president blanched, his anger rising. "Then how do we create jobs and housing?"

"It's funny, Mr. President. The more I see, the more I think my father was right. He told me that we'd never succeed in Washington because we were focused on making people better through programs. He said people only get better when they change their hearts, preferably with God's help. He said people first had to recognize the most important thing—that God is in control—and then there was hope they could change themselves. He said programs could help, but people had to change first; and that the programs by themselves would fail—and he really worried about this, all those years ago—because they ignore the only source of real change in anyone's life and instead bamboozle people into thinking that the government can fix them. Imagine his foresight! You know, Mr. President, he'd be a hundred years old this year, and *he was right!*"

The president of the United States was flabbergasted. He didn't speak for almost a minute. "So this legislation—like what we're doing today in your own hometown—you don't believe in it?"

"Like I said, not for several years. I did, once. But we've taken it too far. We've torn up families, and now you want churches—at least some of them—to pay taxes. How was this country built, anyway? Families and churches. It all seemed to make sense when we started after the war. And then the Great Society. I fought hard for it. But somehow we lost—maybe we killed—the very values that we started with, the ones that held us all together. Just one generation ago fathers stayed with their families and taught their children values; people could walk and drive without fear of being shot or raped; children didn't have to worry about being snatched or abused or killed in their schools; students respected their teachers and wanted to learn, to better themselves. But we weren't watching, and we lost those values, given by God a long time ago. Little by little. *Maybe* we can get them back. But it won't be by more government—I'm dead sure my father was right about that! In the meantime, this is what I do for a living," the Senator touched the president's knee, "so I'm glad to be with you today."

I'm glad he's staying in Ohio for the weekend so we don't have to fly back together! How is this possible? Are there any more like him? No wonder nothing works for us!

"Well, I hope you realize how disappointed I am. I guess I feel betrayed, actually. I'm going to have a hard time keeping this to myself. My team ought to know how you really feel."

Senator Dempsey frowned.

William continued, "But I'll keep my word. I'll just tell them to look elsewhere for help. Now I've got some foreign policy briefing papers I've got to read through."

For the rest of the trip to Ohio the two men sat a few feet apart without speaking to each other.

NORFOLK Hugh Harrison drove to the navy base that morning glad that Jennifer had tried a church near their home while he had been at sea. He had now been to the services himself, and the night before they had attended a small Bible study in their neighborhood built around church members. The group was halfway through the Gospel of John, which coincidentally he and Jennifer had been reading and studying themselves during the six weeks since Camp David. *Maybe this church will be a good place for us,* he thought. *They seem so committed to their faith, so sure, and happy. Is that what Michael was talking about at Camp David? I wonder if I could ever feel that certain about my beliefs? Jennifer seems to enjoy both the church and the Bible study, but I think both of us still feel like we're on the outside looking in. What is it these people have?*

And then he couldn't help thinking about Teri. It wasn't that he tried to. It just seemed to happen in the mornings as he drove to work. He left one good woman whom he loved at home, and the thought of the other good woman with whom he worked usually made him happy to be going to the ship. It was strange; he didn't mean to fantasize about her, but sometimes he did anyway. This morning he remembered how funny she had looked the day before. They had both spent an hour in the heat of the Virginia sun, drenching wet inside one of the fire control radar housings above the ship's bridge, getting briefed on a change that the shipyard wanted to make during their next overhaul. Her face was dirty, her hands covered with grease, and her khaki uniform clung to her, but she had kept right up with the guy from the yard, matching him step for step. He enjoyed her positive attitude and her intelligence. *What would it be like to be married to someone like her?* he had caught himself thinking.

Four hours later he was again in the wardroom as a mid-morning department heads meeting was ending just in time for lunch. The executive officer was speaking.

"Our departure date for refresher training at Guantanamo Bay is July fifteenth, and we'll be gone for almost three weeks. I don't have to tell you how hot it's going to be down there. Perry, let's be sure the air conditioners are in top shape, so we don't boil people or equipment. I think that's about it for today, but Tom has an announcement on an upcoming event."

"Thank you, XO," said Lieutenant Commander Dobbs, sitting up straight in his chair and clearing his throat. "I'm pleased to let you know that we're going to have our first Gay and Lesbian Awareness Week at the end of June, just before the Fourth of July. Every day we'll have one or more events designed to heighten the awareness of the crew to gay issues and to increase the sensitivity to gay problems and to prejudice. Each night that week the crew's movie will have a gay theme. For an hour each morning we'll have a mandatory seminar for petty officers on homophobic disorders and how to overcome them. And that Friday night the gay members of the crew are inviting everyone to a GALA party at the BEQ Club Room. We'll have a gay band, but of course everyone is invited, and we hope everyone will have a good time. We expect a good turnout from the local Norfolk area gay community to help celebrate this first event of its kind.

"Hopefully events such as GALA Week will help dispel any lingering doubts about the complete normalcy of the gay lifestyle and help stop the smattering of ill-will that still seems to exist on this ship."

None of the other department heads spoke. They knew, just as Dobbs did, that the tension was there, only partially diluted by their return to the naval base. Hugh thought, *Maybe this* will *work, but I don't think Dobbs will let up until we all joyfully proclaim in unison, "It's normal, Tom, it's normal!" Right here in the wardroom—around this table. Wouldn't that be great? Maybe that should be his new nickname: "Normal" Dobbs.*

"Did I say something funny?" the operations officer, who had noticed Hugh grinning, asked.

"What? Oh, no," Hugh said, forcing a serious expression. "Nothing at all."

"Well, you may be the president's brother, but I haven't appreciated your earlier remarks or your implied defense of Petty Officer Higgins, who almost destroyed that young Seaman Tyson. Oh, one last thing, Hugh. I'm sure you'll be pleased to know that during the week *before* GALA we're going to have the same seminar on homophobic disorders for all officers, right here in the wardroom, around this table. You'll have a chance to explore your prejudices and unconscious behavior patterns with a trained counsellor." Dobbs looked around the table at the other department heads. "So please mark your calendars for those mornings, first thing. Commander Anglin has confirmed that this training will be mandatory for all officers."

The department heads looked at the executive officer. He pursed his lips and nodded. "We're going to try whatever it takes to make this experiment work, gentlemen. Thomas assures me that this training has been very successful on college campuses, so we'll try it here. Please be present, and bring a positive attitude."

"I still want to know what to tell my men who ask me about what the Bible teaches," Perry Colangelo said.

"That's irrelevant and will only cause hatred," Thomas said.

"The Bible will cause hatred?" Colangelo asked.

"Perry, hold that question for the seminar. Maybe there'll be an answer for you," Anglin interjected. "Now, if that's all, let's clear out so they can set up for lunch."

This is getting beyond belief, Hugh thought, standing up. *Now I've got a disorder that has to be cured! I've got to write to William and tell him how crazy this is.*

NEW YORK "Leslie, the commentators are calling it Gridlock Three, and the other networks are starting to run it," Ryan said, putting down his sandwich. "We can't ignore the ineffectiveness of this administration any longer."

Leslie took a sip from her iced tea and looked out through the large windows of the thirty-seventh story restaurant toward Central Park in the distance. She turned back to her colleague and answered. "I know, Ryan. I don't plan to ignore it. But I'm working on the possibility of a personal interview with the president—the first for anyone since right after the inauguration—and I don't want to blow that chance."

"But how long will it have to wait?"

"I should know about the interview by Tuesday and finish it within two weeks, max."

"Do you think they'll do it? I've heard there's a bunker mentality developing at the White House."

"I've had several talks with Chris Wright, and I'm ready to help them blow the whistle on the *real* problem with their legislation: a do-nothing Congress, particularly the Senate. I certainly won't ignore his problems, but I'll ask questions with a spin that should allow the president to get in some licks on his congressional tormentors. So, yes, I think there's a chance."

"Well, try to make it happen as fast as you can."

"I'll be as fast as possible," she said with a smile and a slight turn of her head.

Ryan paused, taking in the beautiful woman sitting across from him, and returned her look. Finally he said, "Listen, after this afternoon's meeting, instead of that French restaurant why don't we just go up to my place and I'll cook you an Italian seafood dinner."

Leslie blushed slightly and leaned forward on her elbows. "Only if it doesn't take too long. This huge shoulder bag I'm lugging around today is really an overnight bag...I thought you'd never ask."

Ryan's smile broadened and his throat suddenly went dry. He reached for the water and said, "I hope they don't want too much input on network promotion this afternoon. My mind may wander a bit."

WASHINGTON The president had scheduled a tennis game early Saturday morning with Trent Patterson, his party's chief whip in the House of Representatives. Originally he had hoped to get a double-barreled shot of personal advice from his party's two top legislators on how to break the congressional logjam; but the "advice" from Senator Dempsey had been so unexpectedly negative that he had hardly slept on Friday night. And his appearance in the mirror that morning worried even *him*.

Now he and Trent, who was about the president's age, were sitting alone in new chairs at the White House tennis court after their first set, which the congressman had won easily.

"Good playing, Trent," William complimented his guest.

"You hardly got going, Mr. President. Now that you're warmed up I'm sure it'll be closer."

William smiled. "I'll try to give you more of a run this set. But listen, before we play another game, I'd like to ask you a question."

"Sure," Trent said. "Go ahead."

William wiped his face with his towel, then put it around his neck. "I'd like to know if you have any ideas on how we can get our legislative package unlocked before the next election?"

"It's tough, Mr. President. You've put together a good set of programs, and I think we have the votes to deliver in the House. But as you heard from the opposition in the Senate a few weeks ago, it's going to be tough sledding over there."

"So what's the answer, Trent? How do we get moving? You've been at this for years. I really need your advice and help—just between us."

The congressman paused. "Between us? Well, you can always go back and study the masters."

"You mean Washington and Lincoln?"

"Heavens, no. I mean someone like LBJ. Look what he got through Congress. They say he twisted arms. I hear he either knew exactly what every one of his potential opponents really wanted, or else he knew something they didn't want known. And he used that knowledge as leverage to push his programs through."

"A combination of pork barrel and blackmail?"

"I'd call it carrot and stick." Trent smiled at the chief executive.

"LBJ put in a lot of years to come by that information. I don't have that much time."

"Have your team make a list of exactly who's standing in your way and then come to some of us who've been here awhile. I think we can point you into some productive areas. I suggest you plant that idea with someone on your team whom you can trust and then step back and let our staffs work together. And if you've got some friends in the press, have your staff make quiet inquiries among them, looking for pressure points—either good news or bad news—with those particular senators."

William thought for a moment. "What if hypothetically some of those creating the problems are in our own party?"

"I doubt that'll be the case, but if it is, let it rip. You've got a government to run, and obstructionists need to be rooted out."

The president paused again. "Thanks, Trent. I appreciate the advice. I'll think about it. Will you be in town during the June recess in case we need to talk again?"

"Except for a few days next week in Paris with some friends. With my new bachelor status I've got to make hay while the sun shines."

"Sounds good to me! I'll let you know about the staff thing." The president stood. "And now let's see if I can give you a set this time."

A few hours later the three Harrisons were gathered in the dining room of their private quarters at the White House having a rare Saturday lunch together.

"I'll have the package ready to go to your aunt Mary by Monday afternoon, Katherine, so you can take it on the plane on Tuesday morning. It has lots of pictures of all of us together at Camp David," Carrie said to her daughter, as she finished her salad.

"Sure, Mom, no problem," Katherine responded, mixing the last bit of her low-fat yogurt and fresh fruit together. "Don't forget to call me just as soon as my grades arrive. Okay?"

"Sure, dear, no problem," her mother smiled. "I know you did just fine."

"I think so, but I'm kind of worried about the history exam. Math was easy—I studied too much. Boy, I wonder how Sarah did on English lit—she was really sweating it on Wednesday when I called her."

"Well, you'll have all summer to compare notes on high school—and on college, for that matter," William said. "Are you both still hoping to go to the University of North Carolina?"

"Of course. And think how good our resumés will look after a summer of working and making sandwiches! If I live past being around so much fat and cholesterol all day, every day!"

"You'll survive," her father said dryly. "And I hope you have a great time. We'll certainly miss you around here."

"I'll miss you, too," Katherine said, rising to leave, "and I really appreciate your setting up the summer for me with Sarah. I'd go crazy here for the whole summer, despite the company. Anyway, see ya after shopping. Bye." Katherine left the kitchen with a smile and a wave.

"She's almost like a new person," William remarked. "I guess a little freedom and something to look forward to can work wonders."

"It does in all of us, particularly at seventeen," Carrie replied. "How was your tennis?"

"Trent won both sets, although I gave him some competition in the second set. And I got some advice on how to move our legislative package."

"Which was?"

"It parallels Patti Barton-North's: find some reason, good or bad, why each senator should do what we want, and then use that reason to get his attention. It's not particularly original, but Trent thinks he can help us do it."

"Is that what it's going to take, William? Can't the programs stand on their own merits?" Carrie asked, obviously not happy with her husband's proposal.

He waited for a moment to answer, rubbing his hands on his forehead, his frustration with his own political impotence turning at last to anger. He had admitted to himself, in a quiet moment, that he enjoyed sharing thoughts with Carrie again, but what did she know about Washington politics? And she tended to think answers could be simple, when in fact the world was very complex. With a derisive tone he had not used for weeks, he responded, "I don't know, Carrie. They ought to. But I've tried that way and gotten nowhere. *Nowhere!* Do you understand that? I'm becoming the laughingstock of this town. So maybe programs don't get passed on their merits any more, if they ever did. Maybe we *do* have to play 'hardball,' as Patti says. At least Trent offered to help, which is more than I can say for some other members of our party! I'm fed up with being a loser, and I've about decided to try *anything* that has a good chance of winning. So don't come on with some simplistic advice about how things *ought* to be—I've got to cope with how things *are*, and right now they're a mess."

Carrie frowned and looked down. Here again was the William of the last ten years, putting her down. She was tempted to meet his anger with her own, but she sensed that his was passing, like a wave, so she waited a moment, then said. "William, I know the situation is complex. I just worry that once you start digging into people's lives, you'll create more problems than you'll solve. How deep do you dig, and who gets hurt? You believe in your programs—we know they're good. Surely they'll pass if these congressmen really look at them fairly. But, William, please don't get mad at me. I'm not the enemy—I'm truly trying to help."

The wave of anger passed, and William sat back in his chair, his hands folded in his lap. He closed his eyes, took a deep breath, and began speaking before opening them. "Carrie, I'm sorry. I'm just so frustrated. I didn't mean to get mad at you. I'm just mad at myself and this whole stupid situation. Our domestic program, the key to our campaign, is dead in the water, going nowhere. Nothing. Foreign issues right now seem controllable, but then there's that bomb threat. Every day it's there. Neither Vince Harley's people nor the CIA have been able to figure out who's behind it or what they want. When will we hear from them again? It's like an impending doom—we know it's coming, but we don't know when, or what we're supposed to do about it. Anyway, I do appreciate your advice—I just may not be able to accept it. But keep trying." He then unexpectedly said with genuine affection, "I *do* feel better after talking to you. Maybe I should let *you* go to work on those senators! Anyway, I was just trying to get advice on our domestic problems from some experienced hands."

She paused, uncertain of how much she should suggest. Finally she felt led to say, "I understand, but please be careful. It seems to me that sometimes experience, particularly in Washington, doesn't always equal good sense." He nodded, and she continued, "Oh, here are some letters the staff picked out as personal." She went over to the sideboard and brought them back to the table.

The White House staff sifted through the thousands of pieces of mail that arrived daily at the president's residence trying to spot, among other things, those letters that were genuine personal correspondence. Weekdays these were placed in a special basket for the president, but on Saturday any such letters were usually given to the first lady.

William flipped through the stack on the table. "This looks like it's from Richard Sullivan," William said, opening a white envelope.

"We haven't heard from them since we moved up here," Carrie said. "I wonder how Susan and Tommy are doing; Tommy ought to be looking at colleges this fall—he's the same age as Katherine."

The Harrisons had been good friends with Richard and Janet Sullivan when the two men were in law school. They had first met as neighbors in married student housing. After law school Richard received a good offer from an out-of-state firm and had left North Carolina. But the friendship stayed strong despite the two men's ever diverging political views. Over the years they found themselves in numerous good-natured debates, as William advocated an expanded role for government in curing his state's ills, and Richard tended to disagree.

"He's coming to Washington in three weeks for a legal conference and wonders if we can get together."

"That would be great!" Carrie said. "Is Janet coming, too?"

"It doesn't say."

"It sure would be nice if we could all get together again—have them over for dinner and a movie," Carrie said, her tone almost wistful.

Suddenly William realized that his wife must feel as isolated at times as their daughter did. "Why don't you call Janet and see if she can come, too? They could even stay here. Call her this afternoon."

Carrie smiled. "All right, I will," she said. "It would be wonderful to spend time with old friends."

The moral principles and precepts contained in the Scriptures ought to
form the basis of all our civil constitutions and laws.... All the miseries and evils
which men suffer from vice, crime, ambition, injustice, oppression, slavery, and war,
proceed from their despising or neglecting the precepts contained in the Bible.

NOAH WEBSTER
1833

8

Wednesday, June 6
One Week Later

WASHINGTON William was sitting alone at his desk in the Oval Office. It was after lunch and he was reading letters that had arrived that day from Mary, Rebecca, and Hugh. *I've never received letters from all three of them on the same day,* he thought again. *What a mess. Mary's a little off-base complaining to me about sex education, but she does make a point about moral leadership. Hugh blasts our affirmative action program for gays, as if I'm supposed to know the details of every video they make. And Rebecca beats around the bush but basically wants me to play God with Bruce's mother's life.*

What do they expect me to do? Renounce our first positive steps while our legislative package is still in limbo? That sure makes sense. Here I want to make America a better, more progressive nation, but the harder we try the worse it seems to become. We've got to get moving. Bold steps.

The door opened after a knock and Bob Horan, William's chief speech-writer, put his head through. "You wanted to see me?"

"Yes, yes, Bob, come in. I was just looking over some notes." The president put the personal letters away and motioned him to the chair at the side of his desk. "Listen, with Chris out of town today, I wanted to let you know that I've okayed that TV interview with Leslie Sloane for next week. Can you give me some quick, good lines on about ten likely subjects? Include the state of our budget package, which she's already said she wants to talk about."

"Sure. When do you need them?"

"By the weekend would be great."

Horan nodded. "Is that all?"

"There's one other thing, Bob. I've been thinking about some advice I've received from several quarters on how to recapture the momentum of our vision and break out of gridlock with Congress. I'm ready to adopt some tried and true tactics, well tested here in Washington. Do you have someone you can trust on your communications staff—man or woman, and if you do, don't tell me who—who could work with someone on Trent Patterson's staff to quietly uncover the likes and dislikes of some of our opposition?"

"You mean stuff they don't want anyone to know? Their personal lives?"

"Well, if some of that turned up, so be it. We could start in a more positive vein, looking for potential carrots instead of sticks. But frankly," the president said, "at this point I wouldn't turn down *any* news that helped us change a stubborn mind. Do you agree?"

The speechwriter thought for a moment. "Is there a tape machine in here?"

"No. You know I wouldn't do that." The president was honestly incredulous at the suggestion.

"Just checking. Yes, as a matter of fact I do have someone who could quietly work on such an assignment. He's very loyal and has no fear."

"Great. Here's the man to contact in Trent's office. And here's a list of senators and congressmen who aren't very excited about our vision for America."

Horan took the two sheets of paper from the president and scanned them. "John Dempsey? Are you sure?"

"Unfortunately, very. Bob, listen: we never had this meeting, okay? Just have your guy report directly to you. If he asks why you're doing this, tell him it's your idea, and you're checking for leaks and sources for unauthorized disclosures. If anything interesting turns up, good or bad, report it directly to me, one on one, and we'll figure out how best to use it. All right?"

"Anything to cut loose those old windbags who're screwing up what we came here to do. Of course it's all right. I'll start today." Horan stood up to leave.

"Thanks, Bob. Wait just another minute. I do have one other thing to ask you." When his guest was seated again, the president continued. "This may seem a little naive coming from me after all our years together, but is it simply equal *treatment* that gays really want, or a positive *affirmation* that the gay life style is, well...normal?"

Bob Horan was obviously surprised by the question. After a pause, he said, "There's no difference, William. Do *you* see a difference?"

William studied his advisor for a moment. *Does he really believe there's no difference, or is this his politics talking?* He replied, "It does seem to me that there is, Bob. In one case gays are simply treated like anyone else, legally and socially. No personal discrimination. In the other, gays want everyone to agree with them that their lifestyle is normal, embraceable by anyone. And basically they won't take no for an answer, forcing that opinion on everyone around them."

"But without the second, there will never be the first," Bob answered. "Look what happens with rental apartments, or Boy Scout leaders, or church ministers. You say non-discrimination, but until gays are recognized as completely normal, we'll be discriminated against in those and many other situations. It's up to all of us who know the truth to push it in front of everyone else, to force them to accept it."

William started to nod his agreement, then had a visual picture of his son ten years earlier camping overnight with two gay Scoutmasters, and his intended "Okay" became a "Mm." He thought a little longer. "Bob, is it that homosexuality is completely normal, or just that those who practice it should not be harassed?"

The younger man's eyes narrowed slightly. "Mr. President, what is this? Are you backsliding on an issue so clear and so important? Are you saying I'm not normal?"

William didn't know what to think or say. He'd asked his first question from genuine ignorance, reacting to his brother Hugh's letter; but now he was stuck. The actual truth was, he had to admit, he *didn't* think homosexuality was normal; he certainly wouldn't want either of his children to be caught up in what seemed like an unhappy and unfulfilling life style. But he'd bought into the rhetoric for so long, considering another down-trodden minority being discriminated against, that he couldn't very well reverse himself. *He* had always meant that he just wanted homosexuals to be left alone, but now it seemed he had to endorse their behavior as completely normal, which he frankly found difficult to imagine. *How did I get into still another mess?* He tried to buy time to think.

"Bob, of course you're normal. It's just that I got a letter today from my brother in the navy—he's on one of the two ships with the manning experiments, and apparently they're having some tough times with the videos and other teaching aids that push the concept of homosexuality on everyone."

"Well, they need to straighten up," Horan said forcefully. "Look, either homosexuality is normal, or it's not. Something can't be sort of normal. And if it's a normal lifestyle, then it needs to be accepted and defended in *every* situation—with churches, children, the armed forces, marriage, television, movies, legal contracts—everywhere. I've fought for years for these rights, and I don't want to hear now after we delivered ninety percent of the gay vote to you that you're waffling on us. Are you?"

Confused, afraid to lose another key support group, and wishing he'd never received the letter from Hugh, William managed to smile and reassure his speechwriter, "Oh no, Bob. I'm just as solid as I ever was. Of course you need your rights protected. And I understand about the affirmative action. I guess I'm just a little old and slow to catch on to what really has to be done for the country's best interest."

Horan waited a moment, studying his boss, then nodded, apparently satisfied, and rose again from the chair. "Good. We need your strong leadership. I know sometimes the right thing is hard, but it's got to be done. Maybe someday I can meet your brother and explain it to him. On that other subject we discussed, I'll talk to my guy and get back to you in a day or two."

William stood up and offered his hand. "Thanks, Bob. I really appreciate your help with this problem. And, again, I'm totally with you."

After his advisor left, William returned to his chair behind the big desk, picked up Hugh's letter, and swiveled around toward the light from the windows as he reread it.

What is the answer? Hugh makes it sound so gross, so bizarre. But Bob seems so normal; should he be discriminated against? How would I have felt about him as a PE instructor for Robert in junior high? Not so good, I guess, if I'm honest. Isn't that discrimination? Why can't he just be happy with quietly doing most things? I guess that's not good enough. Is homosexuality normal? How on earth do we get ourselves into these situations?

William put the letter in his lap and rubbed his temples, an excruciating headache now added to the dull pain which had been there all day from his lack of sleep.

He jotted down a note to have Barbara ask an aide to check on the questions raised by Mary and Rebecca; after failing to resolve Hugh's problem, William wasn't feeling particularly adventuresome with his two sisters' concerns.

He heard Barbara's knock on the door and then she opened it for General Vince Harley. William rose and motioned for the chairman of the Joint Chiefs of Staff to join him as they took chairs by the fireplace. "Thank you for coming on short notice, Vince," William began as they took their seats. "I wanted just the two of us to meet, without a commitee around, because I respect your military experience and your judgment, and I want your personal assessment and advice on this nuclear bomb threat."

The general glanced briefly down at his hands, which were folded in his lap, then looked up to answer his commander in chief. "Mr. President, since this threat first appeared at Easter, we've spent the last two months following up on every lead, every connection, and every informant we've got. It now looks like that mess in Columbia gained initial credibility from a tip passed on by someone who yesterday turned up dead. Something like that has happened in virtually every case."

"But in Oklahoma City they began making arrests the day after the explosion."

"Yes, sir. And we've got many of those same agents working on this one. But the operative word there is the day *after*. Then there's the chance for identifiable physical evidence. About the only way to stop a terrorist before the fact is to infiltrate his organization or the organizations that supply him. Frankly, sir, starting about thirty years ago, successive administrations have all but eliminated our resources in those kinds of covert activities. The best and brightest thought back then that satellites could do everything, so they began cutting out the people. Satellites can do an awful lot, sir, but they can't attend meetings in back alleys or listen while someone fears for his life and tells what he knows. And, in all candor, your administration's upcoming military budget will virtually eliminate our ability to field those critical assets. So in a sense, I'm afraid we're reaping what we've sown over many years."

William reflected on the general's words and then asked, "So, Vince, what do we really know?"

Harley cleared his throat. "The most substantiated lead is still the very first one, from several years ago, that a single nuclear device was somehow stolen from a depot in Ukraine and then sold through a mafia figure to a small former Soviet republic. That was the lead that Thompson was revisiting, before the fax even arrived, when he was killed. He had learned that the mafia leader supposedly involved in the sale was himself killed in a mysterious car accident a week later. Thompson went to Odessa, hoping that a shipment had been made. There the trail, weak as it was, ended completely. Just like all the rest.

"The fact is, sir, that it's as if the warhead has dropped off the earth. Unless and until whoever now has it—and it could be anyone, anywhere— tells us more or makes a mistake, we have very little chance of finding it."

William was silent for a long while, rubbing his temple. "Vince, this thing is starting to get to me. A day doesn't go by that I don't think about it. It's not exactly the best thing for a peaceful sleep."

"I know, sir. I share it with you, as do all the men and women on our team. But I guess that's exactly what whoever's doing this wants—they'd take great satisfaction in knowing that you and I are not doing whatever else we should and are instead worried about their bomb. So my advice, sir, would be to try not to give them that satisfaction."

William half smiled and looked knowingly at the professional seated across from him. "That would sound great in a novel or a movie, general, and I appreciate your advice. I wish I could do it. I hate the idea of giving those people any satisfaction. But this is real life, and that's a real bomb. If they detonate it, millions of real, innocent people will die. And that's why I can't shake it."

THE RESEARCH TRIANGLE Ed Cheatham opened the door to the large computer/video control room and walked up behind his colleague Carl Hess in the director's chair. On the monitors overhead were the virtually lifelike computer-created images of two young women and a man, as Carl manipulated the panel to simulate what the human participant in the video action might do, checking the response time and the naturalness of the motions.

Ed quietly watched the action, amazed again by how real it all looked and frankly excited by the scene playing out in front of him. Finally he said over Carl's shoulder, "I know—this is tough and dirty work, but someone has to do it. Right?"

Carl turned and smiled. "You got it. I didn't hear you come in. What do you think?"

"It just gets better every time. Haven't you changed the faces?"

"Yeah, for the high school this fall we thought we better make the participants look like teenagers, so we shot some young models and then used them to alter the computer generated images. Looks pretty good, doesn't it?"

"I'll say. That blond is awesome."

Carl nodded and then added, "And an unexpected benefit is that Pet Girl International really likes this younger look. Their marketing team was in here all day yesterday—we finally had to throw them out—they wanted to see more and more. But they flipped over these teenagers. They said they'll be calling you next week to make us a better offer. They know this will be unbelievable in the PC/video market, and they want it. Maybe they'll offer both cash and residuals."

"Sounds good, Carl. Your team is doing great. Just have it all ready in plenty of time for school to start in August so we can apply for the federal education grant as soon as we have some preliminary data. Then we'll roll out the PC version in January. I'm sure glad we've got stock options! I'll bring Jean in next week so she can see how real it is. Just keep up this great work!"

"I think Peter will adore this tractor. You can never go wrong with a tractor for a little boy," Elizabeth Harrison, the president's mother, said to her husband, Tom, as they walked slowly in the early North Carolina summer evening from the department store to their car parked near the mall's outer ring.

They had stayed in the mall to have an early dinner at the food court after selecting a birthday present for their great-grandson. They knew they could not hurry too quickly because of Tom's hip, but they wanted to be home in time to see the seven o'clock news, which they watched every evening as a ritual. So they made haste slowly, and, as usual, Elizabeth filled the time with her latest thoughts and opinions.

"I remember Jonathan's first tractor, and even William's, of course. Those wouldn't do what this one will," she said, raising and shaking the shopping bag, "but they were wonderful just the same. Can you remember William in that sandbox the summer he was four?" she asked as they walked along behind the parked cars, which were becoming fewer in number as they moved farther from the department store.

"Gosh...he had a yellow tractor, didn't he?" her husband tried to remember.

"No, that was Hugh. William's was red. Bright red, with big black tires. Made of metal—weighed a ton. But how he loved to move sand with it!"

As they neared their new sedan, purchased as a gift to themselves on their fifty-fifth wedding anniversary, Elizabeth opened her purse and removed her keys with the special activator on the key ring. She pushed a small button from ten feet away; the car's alarm was deactivated and the doors were unlocked. While she put their purchase in the trunk, Tom opened the passenger door and began the laborious job of entering the car.

Elizabeth closed the trunk and moved around to open the driver's door. Just as she did, her keys in her hand, three young men in jeans and sweatshirts suddenly appeared from where they had been hiding behind the van parked next to the Harrisons' car.

The first one, the oldest and the tallest, ran around to Tom's side and quickly pulled him out of his half-sitting position at the door. The next largest in size grabbed Elizabeth and spun her toward the rear of the vehicle, grabbing her keys as he did so and tossing them to the third one, who moved toward the driver's seat.

"Leave us *alone!*" Tom said, his voice rising, as the young tough pushed him to the side. Due to his hip Tom had to struggle to maintain his balance.

"What are you *doing?*" Elizabeth yelled in anger and indignation, bounding back toward her assailant, her hands raised, not believing what was happening. "This is *our* car."

As the engine started, the teenager on the passenger side pushed Tom again and pulled a handgun from his back pocket. He said, "Too slow, old man." Glancing quickly at Elizabeth, he added, "You shoulda run." Then he leveled the gun and shot Tom Harrison in the head.

Elizabeth screamed and put her hands to her face. Her attacker grabbed her and pushed her forcefully backward. "Shut up, old woman. He's nothing!" Then he climbed into the back seat.

Elizabeth stumbled and fell backward onto the pavement behind their car, where she saw Tom lying in a pool of blood only a few feet away.

She cried out and began to roll over, wanting to get to her husband, but the teenager driving the car revved the engine and shifted into reverse, peeling backward and running over Elizabeth with the left rear wheel. Then he roared out of the mall as the three young men laughed together at their good luck.

PARIS It was just after midnight when the limousine stopped in the gravel drive outside the front door of a small but magnificent villa thirty kilometers to the west of Paris. Even in the dark, Trenton Patterson and Francis Palmer could tell from the long entrance drive, the immaculately sculptured and lighted landscaping, and the classic French architecture that this was a very fine country residence. The driver got out and opened the right rear door for the Americans and their two female guests.

The large front door of the villa opened into a spacious two-story foyer ending in a wide staircase, with a classic Greek sculpture of a goddess standing at the middle landing. A uniformed maid took the coats from the tall, dark-haired identical twins and showed them through a door at the back of the foyer, while the butler politely led the two men to the right into a paneled drawing room, one entire wall of which was lined with books.

The man seated at the desk at the opposite end of the room was working on a personal computer. He looked up as they entered, smiled, then came around the desk to greet them.

"Trenton, Francis, so glad to see you in Paris. I hope our personnel have treated you well on your first day. This is not quite like the old dorm at Georgetown," he said, looking around at the handsome room, "but it will do, don't you agree?"

Trent shook the outstretched hand and returned the smile. "Yes, I'd say it will do, Wafik. I didn't realize business school could make such a difference."

"Perhaps not always. But in our case it corresponded with the early run-up in oil prices...and so, with a little luck and a lot of good friends from those days with whom we're still doing business, here we are. Anyway, how was your meal? I'm sorry I couldn't join you, but we had another dinner meeting that I couldn't cancel. Are the young ladies all right and to your liking? Would you care for some brandy?"

Trent laughed. "Yes, yes, yes, especially the ladies and the brandy." He lowered his voice a little. "Where are they from? They're beautiful! They're like twin goddesses. And their English is perfect." As he spoke he looked at Francis Palmer, who nodded in silent agreement and smiled.

Wafik moved over to the bar between tall windows and poured brandy into two snifters. "Marie and Paulette are French-Algerian. And, yes, they are rather nice, aren't they? Again, I'm sorry I couldn't join you, but I hope everything has gone well. Here are your brandies, and now we can sit and talk. The night is still young, and the drive back to your hotel is not too long. Or perhaps you would like to stay here with the two young women...The world will think you're at your hotel, and we have everything you need right here."

Trent suddenly saw a visual image of himself alone with Paulette. His throat when dry. He couldn't suppress a smile. Maybe they could have a *short* meeting.

The three men sat together in comfortable chairs in front of a fireplace. It was too warm for a fire, but the setting was very congenial. They talked about American and world politics in general for about ten minutes, including Patterson's guardedly optimistic prediction that the Harrison Administration would soon hit its stride.

After the natural flow of the conversation took them to the Middle East, Wafik, his hands folded in front of him while the other two men drank their brandies, said, "And of course, Trent, that's why we're here tonight. I assume that Francis has filled you in on our interest."

Trent raised one finger in warning, then reached into his coat pocket and removed a small device with a meter and several dials. He stood up and began walking slowly around the perimeter of the room, watching the instrument.

"Trent, really. Don't you trust us? Must you scan for listening devices in this room and at this hour?" Wafik asked, smiling but clearly perturbed by the congressman's caution.

"Just being careful, old friend. Another friend gave me this. He says it'll find an activated microphone or an open line at the other end of an enclosed football dome. So just give me a minute to check. Imagine if you want to that I'm doing this for all of us."

As Wafik and Francis sat in silence, Trenton continued around the room, past the large library and over to the desk. He placed the meter next to Wafik's personal computer, which was still on. Trenton noticed a small microphone imbedded just above the color monitor.

"The meter gives no indication, but I see a mike; what's this?"

"It's a voice activator for performing simple commands. If it makes you more comfortable, just turn the machine off. The switch is on the side. I've saved the letters I was writing. Go ahead," Wafik concluded with a wave of his hand.

Trent shrugged, turned off the computer, and continued his walk, closing the curtains at the windows as he went. When he was finished, he put the meter back in his pocket, smiled at his host, sat down again and said, "I'm sorry, Wafik, but you just can't be too careful these days. Everything's fine. Now, please continue."

What the congressman didn't know was that Wafik's computer was no ordinary PC. The voice activator was much more than a servant for simple commands. Even when the computer appeared to be off, it still secretly listened to and recorded everything on a special internal tape. It was always at work, except when it heard the preprogrammed words "listening devices," at which point it instantly turned itself off for two minutes, then silently turned on again, listened, and recorded. As Trent sat down, the computer's internal clock registered 120 seconds since Wafik had said the command words. So as Trent finished his apology, his voice was captured perfectly on the slowly turning tape.

"Think nothing of it," Wafik returned the smile. "I guess the world has reached the point where one never knows whom to trust. Now hopefully we can talk openly and candidly." He turned to the congressman. "I trust that Francis has explained our offer to you. I wanted to meet personally with you to answer any questions, hear your reaction, and, if you are agreeable, to set up the personal codes you will need to retrieve your money when you want it."

Francis Palmer spoke. "I've of course repeated your offer, Wafik, but I think Trent would like to hear your requests directly from you."

"Of course. We simply want at least one more balanced voice of reason in the U.S. Congress where the Middle East is concerned. We want an honest assessment of the plight of Palestine and a balanced approach to the solutions, one of which requires Israel to participate in those solutions. We don't expect anyone to sell out Israel. We just want the U.S. to blend its policies so that they conform to the body of U.N. resolutions, which include Israel returning lands to the Palestinians. You are one of the most powerful and respected men in Congress. We would like you to support this view in general, and to begin to shift public opinion with your voice. And during the next two years or so we will ask you to lead the vote for a specific resolution along those lines. That's it—pretty simple, and actually in the best interest of your country anyway."

Trenton shifted slightly in his chair. "That's all? And you'll deposit one million dollars in an untraceable account in Zurich if I simply speak a little more pro-Palestine—'balanced' as you call it—and then vote for a similar resolution?"

Wafik again smiled. "That's it."

"When?"

"We're prepared to deposit $500,000 tomorrow, an additional $250,000 when the vote is scheduled, and the same amount when it passes."

"I thought you said $750,000 would be paid now," Francis protested.

Without looking at his companion, Trent raised his hand, thinking about half a million tax-free dollars that could be available to him tomorrow, following a long night with Paulette. Still, there was his honor. "Make it six hundred now, then two hundred at each point in the future, and you've got a deal."

Wafik seemed to take a moment to think, then nodded his head, smiled, and rose, extending his hand. "All right. Done. Francis's fee will be paid in the same proportions." As he shook each man's hand in turn, he continued, "Let's take a minute to set up the account codes, and then you can both experience the unusual delight of true French-Algerian culture. I think you'll enjoy it immensely. And since we've successfully concluded our business in such good time, there's absolutely no rush in the morning. Perhaps your jet lag will be completely cured!"

Twenty minutes later, his left hand almost shaking with anticipation as he placed it on the latch to an upstairs bedroom door, Trent Patterson smiled broadly, unable to believe his good fortune at being reelected so many times from his home district. *This is the payoff for serving my people so well,* he congratulated himself. He ran his right hand through his thinning hair, pulled in his stomach, and opened the door.

WASHINGTON AND ATLANTA "Rebecca, are you by any chance alone there tonight?" William asked his younger sister over the telephone. He was seated at his desk in his White House bedroom. She was reading a nursing journal in her living room in Atlanta.

"As a matter of fact I am, William. Bruce is still working out at the sports club. Why?"

"Well, I wanted to talk to you about his mother's situation, to get your personal input."

"Oh. Okay. Shoot. But I put everything I could think of in the letter."

"I appreciate that. But I guess I just wanted to hear your thoughts first-hand, while I'm trying to decide. It sounds like it's a mess."

"It is, William, and Bruce is about to go crazy. But, William, like I wrote in the letter, I know you can't go around overruling the Surgery Suitability Board for someone you know—or really don't know, in this case. Anyway, for Bruce's sake, I had to ask, in case you knew of some way."

"It's a new subject for me, actually, so I had an aide check on her case specifically, and on the point system in general. I had no idea, by the way, but almost fifteen percent of the letters received at the White House are from people asking for the president's intervention on a health plan requirement for themselves, their children, or relatives. Can you believe that? It's a huge number of letters, every day. I've just read some of them this afternoon, and frankly they're gut-wrenching. What a mess some people are in. I don't know how you do it, Rebecca, dealing with illness all day, every day."

"And what does the White House say in response to all those letters?"

"We apparently send a pleasant form letter telling them in so many words that it's not appropriate for the executive branch to get involved in health decisions, that they should consider the established appeal process if they think there has been an oversight, and we hope they have a nice day."

"And that's what Bruce would have received if I hadn't written a letter to my big brother. I guess it's what has to be."

"I don't know, Rebecca. There is a provision for awarding extra points for cases deemed to be in the special interest of the country. I imagine I could write a letter and the points would be awarded. Actually, I've just found out that there are apparently some senators and congresspeople who write such letters on a fairly regular basis for some of their constituents. If you think about it, I guess it sort of stinks, letting politicians play God with the lives of their voters; it's really the ultimate 'favor.' But I *could* do it this once for Bruce's mother without raising too many eyebrows, I think. But some reporter *might* not agree that her life was in the national interest, so I wanted to get your input. How upset is he?"

"He's *real* upset. Between his brother dying from AIDS, his father's illness, and now this mess with his mother, Bruce feels the government hasn't lived up to its part of the 'social contract,' as he calls it, and he's really bitter. One part of me cries out for you to help them, William. The other part knows that it's probably asking too much."

"Is he close to his mother?"

"Very. Sort of like you and Mom, I think, when you were first running for governor, and she was your kitchen cabinet policy advisor. They talk all the time. He really loves her."

"That's tough. What do you think I should do?"

Just then the call-waiting feature on Rebecca's phone beeped and almost simultaneously the second line in the Harrison's bedroom rang. "Can you get that, Carrie?" William asked over his shoulder.

"Just a second, William," Rebecca said, as she clicked over to the other line.

William waited, seated at his desk, while Carrie answered the phone in the adjoining room. "Hi, Mary," he heard her say. *Is it about Katherine or Bible study or sex education?* he caught himself thinking when he heard his older sister's name. "He's on the other phone. With Rebecca, I think. Oh, no. Oh, dear God."

William half turned in his chair to ask Carrie what had happened when Rebecca came back on the line and said, "William. Oh, no..." Her voice was quavering, and she was obviously having difficulty breathing. "It was Graham. He said Mom and Dad have been killed in a parking lot. I mean murdered." Her voice cracked. "Why would?... Why would someone want to murder them?"

It is the duty of nations as well as men to own their dependence upon the overruling power of God, to confess their sins and transgressions in humble sorrow yet with assured hope that genuine repentance will lead to mercy and pardon, and to recognize the sublime truth, announced in the Holy Scriptures and proven by all history: that those nations only are blessed whose God is the Lord.

ABRAHAM LINCOLN

9

Thursday, June 28
Three Weeks Later

WASHINGTON The president of the United States sat alone in the backseat of his limousine for the ten minute ride back to the White House from the Grand Hotel. The trip would be short because there was not much traffic at this time of night, particularly in the summer. But he still found time to pour himself a shot of scotch, which he nursed as the lights of the city passed by his windows.

The Harrisons had been through a difficult three weeks, as the nation had mourned the loss of the "first grandparents" with them. William had canceled all speaking engagements and interviews—until tonight—and the family had assembled in Raleigh immediately after the murder. Their parents' car was found late the same night, abandoned behind a convenience store. The police had a vague description of three teenage boys who were seen riding off in the car after the gunshot. The double funeral had been held at St. Stephen's three days later. Mary and Graham, with help from Rebecca's daughter Courtney, volunteered to work on beginning the estate process and on boxing up the remains of Tom and Elizabeth's long life together. On the day after the funeral the president and first lady had returned to Washington.

But not to normal, William thought, taking another sip from his glass. *Why did I agree to do this tonight? It's too soon after their deaths. The rest of the world moves on. Three weeks is an eternity for a nation that consumes all its news in sound bites, but not for me. If the police ever find the scumbags who killed them...*

But that's the problem. Like tonight. It's all messed up. Am I a liberal or a conservative? What was I supposed to say to the nation's police chiefs? That I'm for tougher gun control, because it will save lives? Or against gun control because that will save lives? I've always believed that if we eliminate poverty, then crime will virtually disappear. But there was nothing economic about killing my parents and joy-riding for a few hours! What are the answers? And how am I supposed to always know them?

All I want is for all this violence to stop, but every interest group and reporter scans every word I say for some nuance or shift, supposedly signaling some new policy change on this program or that law. Just show me how to stop the senseless violence, whatever your political label...and, oh, how I wish you could bring back my parents!

Then he felt again the cold pain that had pierced him almost daily since their deaths. *They were so good, so committed to making people better. And we were so close to passing the kind of legislation they've always wanted in this country, when some joy-riding teenagers kill them! Now they'll never be able to see it.*

He had drunk more in the last three weeks than he had in the last three years. As he and Carrie had been seated alone in the funeral home on the night before the burial, he suddenly realized that his whole life had been dedicated to trying to make the world better, just as his parents, and particularly his mother, had done. It struck him like a hammer blow that he had hoped to accomplish the goals of his presidency for her, and now she had been stolen from him. She would never see or share in his victories. And for the past three weeks he had been like a ship without a rudder. Or sails, for that matter. Going nowhere slowly and not really caring, he had to admit.

I'm one impressive president, he said to himself as they neared the White House gate and he downed the rest of the drink. *Can't get any programs going. Can't spend money. Can't save money. Can't lead. I've chosen advisors who see every issue through their own narrow perspectives. Now my parents are gunned down in a parking lot, and I act like I'm five years old, not sure of what to do. I'm really great for our nation. Maybe I should just resign. Resign,* he thought again, as the long car swung through the gates and pulled up at the entrance. *And before we hear again from whoever has that nuclear bomb. Go home to Raleigh, raise Katherine, and forget about all of this garbage. Well, Richard and Janet Sullivan will be here tomorrow. Maybe I'll see what they think. Resign...*

ATLANTA The next morning in south Atlanta, Sally Kramer opened the front door to the doctor's office located in the former single-family home and motioned Eunice to go in. Once inside they signed in and took their seats in what had once been the living room of a fine old Victorian home on a busy street. There were several other women and a few children waiting to see the group of doctors who worked in the neighborhood clinic.

After a few minutes the receptionist called their names, and they were escorted down a long hall into an office. The sign on the door read Dr. Fritz Archer. Eunice was puzzled. They were to meet a Dr. Thompson. A man was seated behind the cluttered desk. On seeing the two women, he rose, smiled, and offered his hand across the desk.

"Eunice," Sally said, "I'd like you to meet Dr. Harvey Thompson. He's the one who did my procedure, and we hope you'll let him do yours, too."

"It's a pleasure to meet you Mrs. Porter. Sally's told me a lot about you, and I'm glad our schedules worked out so we could meet this morning. Please, have a seat."

Once they were all seated, Dr. Thompson, a rotund man in his mid-forties, continued, "Please don't be confused by the office. Dr. Archer is a friend and lets us hold consultations here. My office is actually in Peachtree North Hospital, where you've been having your check-ups, but we find it's usually more convenient to meet here. Now, has Sally explained the procedure to you? Do you have any questions?"

Eunice looked down at her hands folded in her lap and then fixed the doctor in the eye. "She said I could get five thousand dollars for letting you abort this baby. Is that right?"

Dr. Thompson smiled reassuringly behind the desk and straightened up in the chair a bit. "Yes, that's exactly right. And Sally will get five hundred as a finder's fee. We'll pay you one thousand now and the rest on the day of the procedure. All in cash. No checks to worry about cashing."

"I see. A thousand dollars today if I agree?"

"Precisely. In cash. Now, how far along are you, Eunice?"

"The doctor at the hospital says I'm due in mid-September."

"Fine. We've got plenty of time, of course. We'd like to schedule you for about September first. Will that be convenient?"

Eunice nodded her head in agreement, then frowned. "Let me ask you this. How come if I want an abortion now, it costs *me* money, but if I do your deal, you pay me much more?"

"That's an excellent question, Eunice. Here's the simple answer. Once you've carried the fetus almost to term it has some valuable organs and parts that people desperately need and are willing to pay for. You see, there are many children suffering from disease or needing transplants. So in a way it *is* kind of like you're providing a baby for adoption—only better. You're making it possible for many babies to live who otherwise wouldn't. It's a very good thing to do for others. And it gives us the chance to pay you for your trouble."

"I see...Well, why don't you have plenty of babies—fetuses—from miscarriages and stuff?"

"Another good question. The doctors who transplant these organs—and even eggs from the fetus's ovaries, if it's a girl—have to get them on some sort of a predictable schedule, and quickly, to be of any use to the child or the infertile woman who receives them. They need to be able to plan. So we go ahead and set up a date with you now, then alert our doctor friends who know people in need, and they get ready, based on our agreement. Does that make sense?"

Eunice thought for a minute. "Yes. I guess so. It sounds like we'll be helping others. But is any of this illegal or anything?"

Both Dr. Thompson and Sally Kramer shifted in their chairs. The doctor smiled again and leaned forward, his hands on the desk. "Yes and no, Eunice. Since the president signed the executive order permitting abortions at any time right up to natural delivery, that has removed any legal hindrance or stigma to the procedure itself. There is still an old law from the early eighties that technically makes it illegal to sell donated organs, but it's not clear whether that law even applies to fetuses, and we expect Congress to change the law shortly, anyway."

"So it's because of that technicality that we're meeting here and not in your office, right?"

Dr. Thompson looked momentarily flustered, but Sally nodded, and he regained his composure. "I guess you could say so, yes. Frankly, we think the old law discriminates against good, hard-working women like yourself whom we want to help. But there could be those who don't understand, so until the law is changed, we use this method to make these arrangements."

"Is the procedure done here?"

"Oh, no," the doctor said, regaining his composure. "Everything is done at Peachtree North with the finest personnel and equipment. And the government even pays for the procedure for someone in your financial situation."

"How is that possible?"

"You just show up 'spontaneously' at the time we'll prearrange and complain about pains and tell them that you've had second thoughts and you want an abortion. I'll be the doctor on duty at the time, with a partner as back-up in case things get unexpectedly busy. You just fill out the forms, we'll do the abortion, and you'll be on your way. The balance of the money will be delivered to you that night. It's that simple. Although we began years ago, we've expanded to do about one abortion a week for the past several months, ever since full-term abortions became legal, and we've had no problems at all. Everything works fine."

Eunice was silent again for a while. Then she asked, "And I get one thousand dollars today if I just say yes? What happens if I have a miscarriage?"

"That's our risk. But you're a perfect candidate, having already birthed two healthy children. Children, I imagine, who could use an extra five thousand dollars. Right?"

Eunice nodded and thought some more. "I guess it sounds okay. I mean an abortion now or an abortion later—what's the difference? And we help other children. All right. Do I get that money now? Do I have to sign anything?"

"Yes, I've got the money right here in this envelope," Dr. Thompson said, opening the top desk drawer. "And no, we don't sign anything. We'll look at the schedule for early September and let you know through Sally. It's her job to be sure you're there on time. I'm sure there'll be no problems," he concluded, smiling and handing the envelope to Eunice.

She opened it and looked inside. "No, I don't think there will be either."

Dr. Thompson rose. "If everything goes well, you might want to consider becoming one of our regulars, like Sally." He smiled at Eunice's friend as the three of them walked to the door. "We'll do her procedure a few weeks before yours. I think it's a great way for you to earn some regular extra money."

"I'll certainly think about it. Thanks. It sounds good. I'll wait to hear from Sally about which day you want to do it. Thank you again," she said, as she placed the envelope in her purse.

WASHINGTON "I wish I could postpone this interview again," William said to Carrie as he changed his shirt in their bedroom after lunch, "but we already delayed it for the funeral, and I promised this Sloane woman a month ago that I'd do it. I just don't feel very 'up' today."

"You'll do fine. The old inspiring William Harrison will kick in when the TV lights come on, and you'll be amazing. I know you too well," Carrie said, handing him his tie.

"I hope so." As he turned to the mirror, he reflected that he had received one piece of good news that morning. Bob Horan had squeezed briefly onto the Oval Office schedule to report that his associate and the Patterson staff had found some potentially interesting past indiscretions on the part of three key senators, including their own John Dempsey. Each one involved a woman—or women. More research needed to be done, but this was a start. *So maybe we will find the dynamite we need to break up this logjam,* William thought, as he finished tying his tie and looked to Carrie for approval.

"Very handsome. You'll be awesome, as Katherine would say. Oh, listen," she continued, as he put on his coat and headed for the elevator, "Richard and Janet Sullivan are due here in about thirty minutes. If they want, can I bring them into the back of the office during the interview?"

"Sure. It'll be great to see them. Maybe they'll bring us some good luck."

Twenty minutes later the president was seated in a comfortable chair in front of the Oval Office fireplace with Leslie Sloane in its twin on his right.

Jerry Richardson stood and Chris Wright sat in his wheelchair behind the cameras near the president's desk. Leslie had gone over several general questions she would ask on camera, but she had reserved with a smile the right to ask a couple of others, to get a "spontaneous" reaction, as she called it. He had agreed.

She led with an almost obligatory question about the brutal murder of his parents only three weeks earlier. "Mr. President, have your tragic personal experiences of the past several weeks affected your position on crime in any way?"

He took a deep breath and replied, the hurt clearly visible in his eyes, "Only to the extent that we're even more dedicated to ending violence and violent crime in America, Leslie. Even before this awful event we were already studying, and planning to introduce this fall, a comprehensive crime bill, which will include handgun registration, more police officers, increased prison construction, prison education funds, and, of course, job creation to reduce the ranks of the unemployed and the unemployable. We're convinced that it's only this type of comprehensive, multifaceted program that can have any effect where it matters."

"Could any of those investments have saved your parents, do you think, Mr. President?" She tried to ask it with the concern she actually felt so that it didn't come across as a flip question. "Can we really reduce crime in the next few years?" she added.

Although he had not planned it, he found himself slowly saying, "Leslie, the alternative is just too awful to imagine. We *have* to be successful. If the trends of the last ten years continue, our society just won't make it."

Both his presidential advisors behind the cameras frowned and looked at each other. William caught them out of the corner of his eye and noticed the confused look on Leslie's face. William hoped he didn't look as flustered as he suddenly felt.

"You paint a pretty bleak picture, Mr. President. The murder of your parents has really hurt you, hasn't it?"

William could sense her genuine concern, but his political alarm bells went off as he saw Jerry beginning to pace nervously. *Too negative—too weak—too introspective. Maybe it's genuine, but it's not supposed to be associated with the president! I've got to pull out of this,* he realized.

Just then Carrie opened the side door to the Oval Office and quietly led Richard and Janet Sullivan behind the TV crew toward a free spot in the crowded room. The Sullivans each raised a hand and smiled in William's direction. He gave a small nod while still looking at the camera, with Leslie's question hanging in the air, waiting for an answer.

"Well, yes, of course personally it has, Leslie. But leaders have to move beyond personal pain and focus clearly on what's best for the country. I was only talking about criminal trends, and even some of those have actually been improving in the last few years. It just seems that we hear so much more about crime these days. But in other areas—areas that are also very important to improving the American way of life—we've made great strides. Look at health care, gay rights, women's rights, children's rights, education—in all those areas we're far ahead of where we were only a few short years ago. And if Congress would simply act on our proposals for jobs and housing, our nation's economic progress could match our significant social progress." After hitting his stride in mid-statement, he finished with a notable burst of energy. William noticed that Leslie looked as relieved as he felt. He couldn't help a small smile of confidence.

She leaned back slightly, the moment of mutual recognition between them clearly noted, and threw him a pitch he couldn't miss. "And what do you think is the matter with Congress, Mr. President? People are dusting off the old gridlock label."

"I've heard that, too, Leslie," he agreed, turning a little fatherly, "and it galls me just as much as it must gall every thinking American. Our economic program has been designed and tested using the best computer modeling by the finest minds in economics, business, education, and housing. It's virtually foolproof, and it's ready to go. We'll prime the pump with investment dollars spent on education and job training; we'll tap the well of economic development by investing dollars in housing construction; and the healthy flow of jobs and prosperity—combined with a phasing out of these same programs once their missions are accomplished—will then produce a steady stream of new taxes that will balance the budget at near full employment.

"It's just that simple, Leslie, and that powerful! And the only reason Congress hasn't approved it yet is because some of the men over there apparently have no vision for the boldness that made America the great nation we are! *We're* not contributing to gridlock. We're *leading* with a positive new plan. If the American people are as tired of delay as we are, I urge them to write their congressmen today and to demand passage of our initiative to turn America in a new and a prosperous direction!"

Jerry Richardson had long since stopped pacing, and now he and Chris were smiling. When he finished, they simulated clapping, as did Carrie. The Sullivans stood and watched; Richard had his hands in his pockets.

Leslie Sloane went on to ask a question about the administration's proposed tax on those churches that did not adhere to federal antidiscrimination laws, and the rest of the interview went very well for William, to his relief and apparently to Leslie's as well. As they finished and stood up, the camera lights were turned off. She removed her microphone, extended her hand, and said, "Thanks for the interview, Mr. President."

He returned her smile and replied, "Any time, Leslie. Thanks for the questions—and I appreciate your concern for my parents."

She was about to turn toward her camera crew when the first lady appeared along with a couple who seemed to be about the same age as the president and his wife.

"Richard, you old conservative, you." The president beamed as the two men hugged.

"Ms. Sloane," Carrie was saying, "I'd like you to meet our oldest, dearest friends, Richard and Janet Sullivan. We all met when Richard and the president were in law school together a year or two ago."

Richard extended his hand to Leslie as the president added, "And one of us actually practices law."

Richard looked around at the Oval Office. "These digs don't look too shabby to me. What do you think, Janet?"

"I think we're all amazingly blessed. What a great day for us. It's a joy to meet you, Ms. Sloane, though I feel I know you because I'm the promotion director for one of the network's largest affiliates." Before Leslie could speak, Janet added, "And it's fantastic to be here with you two. How long has it been, Carrie? Four years and one very important election?"

"I think that's right, Janet," Carrie replied. "The twentieth law school reunion. I guess that means twenty-five is coming up."

The five of them talked together for a few minutes, and then Leslie excused herself, saying, "Here's my card, Mrs. Sullivan. If you're ever again in D.C. or I can help you in any way, please let me know."

"Thanks, Leslie. Here's mine," and Janet shook her hand.

"It's great to have you two here," William concluded after everyone else had departed, "but I've got a couple of more meetings this afternoon. Richard, do you have any meetings today yourself?"

"No, the conference ended at lunch after two full days. I'm ready for a break."

"Good. I suggest you let Carrie give you her patented tour of these 'digs,' and I'll catch up with you before dinner. We're looking forward to spending most of the weekend with you, even if I'll have to constantly remind myself how violently reactionary you are," he concluded, looking at his old law school classmate.

Richard took the kidding with aplomb. "Sounds great. Whatever the schedule of the world's most important man allows is obviously okay with us common folk."

"Now you two stop," Carrie intervened. "We'll see you upstairs, dear. And, by the way, I was right."

William was momentarily confused. "About what?"

"The interview," she said and gave him a big smile. "You *were* inspiring."

"Oh. Yeah, thanks. It felt okay."

But as the other three left the Oval Office, William Harrison was left alone with a hollow realization: he couldn't remember any specific point he'd made during the entire interview. He'd just repeated the words he'd learned in two straight years of campaigning, perhaps with some new twists, but still the same old words.

I really don't *know what will happen to taxes with my plan,* he admitted to himself. *In fact, I couldn't describe how those computer models work. It's all too complicated. The absolute truth,* he realized, as he collapsed into his big leather chair, *is that I don't understand much of this at all. I'm really a big-picture man. A vision man. Don't ask detail questions, Leslie, because I probably couldn't answer them! Details. The answers are in the details, someone suppos-edly once said. Maybe that's why the answers escape me—I don't understand the details. Does anyone? Did anyone before? Washington? Lincoln? Franklin?*

He closed his eyes and suddenly felt cold in the middle of the warm summer afternoon. *I know it looked good, Carrie.* That *I know how to do. But how to govern this huge and complex country? When you get right down to it, I guess I don't really have a clue…*

He sat staring out the window until the intercom buzzed with his next appointment.

NORFOLK "Please join us," Hugh Harrison said, rising from his seat across the table from Jennifer and motioning to Perry Colangelo and his wife, Marty. The Colangelos accepted the offer, and the two couples filled a table at the edge of the dance floor in the Bachelor Enlisted Quarters Dining Hall, converted that Friday evening into a dance hall.

"This is something else," Perry slightly yelled to the Harrisons over the din of the band, Hung Jury. "I hope you're having a gay old time!"

The two department heads and their wives were attending the final event of GALA Week, a command performance for all officers and chiefs on the ship. The normally utilitarian base mess hall had been decorated with huge interlocked male and female symbols, red AIDS awareness bows, and pink streamers. The lights were turned down and two spotlights played across the all-male band, dressed in white underpants, black leather boots, and chains. Although the entire ship had been invited, it looked to Hugh as if the crowd at this early hour was mostly homosexual and lesbian, judging from who was dancing with whom. He also noticed a large contingent of non-naval invitees from the gay community in Norfolk.

"Chief Raines told me today," Perry continued, "that a good number of closet gays are supposed to 'come out' tonight at the last intermission, some of whom have been in the navy for years."

"I can't wait," Hugh responded. "I'm more worried about the rumor that a large contingent of skinheads is going to be waiting outside when the party's over to bash heads. I hear the base commander has the entire security force on patrol tonight, and they're planning to mass here about eleven."

"I hope we're leaving by ten, then," Jennifer said, looking at her husband with obvious concern.

"You and Marty can take off together any time, but the captain wants us here to help quiet things down, given all our new sensitivity training," Hugh said, taking another sip. "It might seriously make sense for you two to leave a little early."

"What a wonderful, gala evening," Marty Colangelo said to no one in particular.

Just then two men dressed in their summer khaki uniforms slow danced right in front of the two couples, locked in a tight embrace. All over the dance floor partners, mostly of the same sex, clung together during the slow dance.

Since the noise was not as loud, Marty asked her husband, "Perry, I can't believe this. This isn't normal—or at least it isn't the navy. What's going on with this world?"

"Oh, but sweetheart," her husband turned and chided her with a smile and a glance at Hugh, "this *is* completely normal. We've been told hundreds of times in our homophobia class this week that *we* are the ones who aren't normal—we're uncaring, unloving, small-minded, and bigoted if we don't think this is just what everyone's entitled to do, anywhere, anytime. Or at least we're supposed to give it a try before we decide. Isn't that great? Telling my eighteen-year-old sailors, some of whom are struggling to read, that they should *try* homosexuality if they feel the least little bit inclined. That's sure going to help our six-month deployment. Have they announced yet whether we're also supposed to *try* intercourse with the women in your FT Division, Hugh?"

Hugh grimaced, knowing that Teri Slocum's division was still a sore subject with Jennifer, and he expected to see his junior officer at the dance any minute. Hoping to change the subject, Hugh leaned across to Perry, grabbed his hand and said, "I don't know, but while we wait to find out, can I have this dance?"

The other three laughed and Jennifer spoke up, "Actually, I guess we ought to strike a blow for heterosexuality." She took Hugh's outstretched hand and said, "Come on big guy, let's dance. But let's buck the trend here and wait till later to do anything else. At least I can close my eyes while we dance and imagine how things used to be, when the world made sense."

As they danced together in the bizarre surroundings, Hugh whispered to Jennifer, "I love you, Jen, and I'm so glad we at least have each other and our family, since the world appears to be going crazy."

"I wonder if your brother William realizes the reality of what his executive order really means, here at the level of the base BEQ?"

"I don't know," Hugh sighed. "I've told him in person and I've written him. I didn't want to mention it at the funeral. Maybe someday he'll respond in some way, and we can talk about it again."

As the slow music ended and the band announced their first intermission, Hugh recognized Thomas Dobbs right next to them, holding hands with a much younger man with bleached blond hair and an earring in each ear. The two department heads smiled politely to each other in recognition, and Hugh introduced Jennifer. "This is my friend, Phil," Thomas replied. "Phil, meet the Harrisons. Hugh is actually the brother of the president." The four spoke together for a few minutes, then separated. As the Harrisons neared their table, Hugh noticed Teri Slocum walking their way from the nearby bar, followed by two of the young women in her division.

"Teri, hi. I'd like you to meet my wife, Jennifer. Jen, this is Teri Slocum."

"Glad to meet you," Teri said, smiling and shaking Jennifer's hand. "And this is Maggie Simpson and Alice Pritchard. Maggie and I are from the same hometown. She was a few years behind me in the same high school. She's now a first-class petty officer—and Alice is a third-class."

The women shook hands and smiled. Jennifer said to all of them, "Are you with anyone tonight—dates?"

"No, not tonight. I came over with Maggie, Alice, and some of my other girls. I think we all feel a little bit like fish out of water."

"Please join us," Jennifer said. "At least for a little while if you can. We'll be fishy together." She laughed.

"Alice and I are going to get a Coke," Maggie said. "We'll see you in a little while. Nice to meet you."

"Go on ahead," Teri said to Alice and Maggie. "I'll catch up with you." Then she turned to Hugh and Jennifer. "I'll stay, but just for a few minutes. I think my group may want to leave before too long."

Hugh found an extra chair and the five of them squeezed around the table. There followed several minutes of getting acquainted small talk, mostly about the navy and the changes on the *Fortson.*

Then Teri said to Hugh, "Listen, Hugh, a lot of the junior officers really appreciated how you stood up and blew some holes in what our homophobic disorders instructor was saying all week. It was about time."

"What did you do, Hugh?" Marty asked.

Hugh paused and looked embarrassed. "Nothing, really. I just stopped by Cambridge Bookstore on Wednesday and found a copy of the book this guy's been quoting from all week, purporting to explain scientifically that homosexuality is normal and caused by something in the brain."

"And?" Jennifer asked.

"Well, I'm no expert, but I found his scientific method to be less than rigorous, and I have to question the findings on this subject of someone who writes that he is gay and that being gay is 'cool.' I mean the fact is that I *don't* know why some people are gay, and he wrote exactly the same thing, though our instructor never quoted *that* part in class. I've almost gotten to the point where I don't care *how* it happens. But look at this tonight"—he waved his hand around the room—"this *can't* be normal. This can't be what God—or nature—or whatever—intended.

"I'm not even talking about what two people do on their own—that's between them and God. I'm talking about all of *this*. People could just as easily say that it's natural for men and women to have heterosexual sex and then create adulterers rights groups, marching and showing videos and conducting classes and dissecting brains and demanding that we all say it's just wonderful for men to leave their families and to sleep with lots of other women every chance they get, because it's so normal and natural, and demanding that the government then cure them of any diseases they may catch from sleeping around. What if some guy said he chases skirts because some piece of his brain is bigger or smaller? So what? Most men probably have that precise natural impulse, but it's what we *do* that matters. I mean, come on, I'm a naval officer, not a sociologist, but you can't build a lasting society on the theory of 'follow the erotic impulse of the moment.'"

"*That's* what he said today in class," Teri laughed.

"Hugh, where did that all come from?" Marty asked in amazement. "Maybe *you* should run for president!"

"Not on your life. Jen and I enjoy visiting the White House, but we wouldn't want to live there. No, this whole situation just started me thinking, that's all," Hugh replied. "I'm sorry for becoming so serious."

"Well, anyway, Mrs. Harrison," Teri said, pushing back in her chair, "it was a real pleasure to meet you, and you've got a great thinker for a husband. He's also a good officer. You're very lucky. But I've got to round up my ladies and head for the ship. I've got duty in the morning. Good night, and try not to get too wild."

Teri nodded to the other three and turned to look for Maggie and Alice.

"She *is* nice, Hugh," Jennifer said, touching his forearm with her hand. "But I just can't imagine the two of you on a ship for six months together." Her tone turning bitter, she looked around and added, "But of course I couldn't have imagined *this* six months ago, so maybe I'll get used to you and Teri and the other women being together four thousand miles from home. When did the world turn upside down? I must not have been looking. But what you said seems to make sense. Why don't politicians listen to logic like that?"

"I don't know, Jen. I wish I did, but I simply don't know."

WASHINGTON   "So, Robert is backpacking out West. How is Katherine enjoying the summer in Raleigh with her aunt and uncle?" asked Janet Sullivan, as she passed the salad bowl to William.

The Sullivans and Harrisons were seated in the small family dining room in the White House private quarters. They had spent an hour together in the living room, catching up on the many events in each family's life over the past several years. Now they were enjoying a simple dinner together, prepared by the White House chef, with a movie scheduled in the theater afterward.

"Oh, we're afraid she won't want to come home in August," William nodded, taking the bowl from Janet. "She loves being back in Raleigh, and she and Sarah are so close. I'm sure she wishes she could just stay there for the rest of our term."

"Is the glamour of the White House too much for her?" Richard asked, cutting his steak.

"I'm afraid she views it as a not very glamorous prison," Carrie said. "Too many restrictions and limitations for a high school senior."

"It's so hard to know the right balance in our own much simpler world," Janet volunteered, "so I can imagine that it's almost impossible for you. But our Susan found just the opposite situation in her first year at college. There were absolutely no rules or restrictions. No one knew when the girls came or went from the dormitories, and they sold condoms in the girls' bathrooms, if you can believe that."

"It *is* just the opposite of when we were in school," Carrie agreed.

"But you want to hear something interesting?" Janet continued. "At the end of her freshman year, Susan and some of the other girls, many of whom are believers, banded together and petitioned the university for a girls' dorm with real rules, no men, no visitations, and a dorm mother. After about a month of negotiation the university finally agreed, but they made all the girls who wanted to live there sign a waiver releasing their 'natural rights'! What a reversal the world has taken since we were in college. Anyway, the end of the story, so far, is that there is a long waiting list for Susan's 'special' dorm, and the university is going to add another one this fall. Isn't that great?"

"It sounds like Susan is one of the pioneers in equal-but-separate education," William said, sipping his iced tea.

"No, I don't think so, at least as I understand equal-but-separate," replied Janet. "These girls want to learn in the mainstream and have classes and all other activities with boys. It's just that they want to have some privacy and some basic rules for living for which they can hold each other accountable. In fact, when you think about it, they're saying that they don't want to be 'equal' so much as they want to be safe and individually responsible."

"Whoa!" smiled William. "Maybe they've started a new unequal-but-safe movement! But I *don't* think it'll go over too well with our cabinet, and particularly not with our vice president."

"Well," Janet continued, "I'm not sure I'd use the word 'unequal,' but perhaps 'different.' And the system of 'different and protected'—but equal in rights and before God—seemed to work reasonably well for women, at least up until about thirty years ago, that is."

William wanted to change the subject. "And how is Tommy?"

"He's great," Janet said. "You know he'll be a senior this year, and he's doing really well academically."

"He went through an awkward stage at fourteen," Richard added. "But thanks to God's help and a lot of prayer he got into weight training, and six months later it was like something just clicked inside him. He found his coordination and his confidence. Now this is obviously an exaggeration, but it really seemed to happen overnight. He even got to where he could regularly hit home runs this spring, and the great day for Tommy was when the baseball coach asked him to play second base. You know what Tommy said? He told the coach 'No, thanks'—he wanted to concentrate on hitting, and the outfield was just fine for him. For Tommy, that was quite a statement."

"So how is this young man's love life?" asked the president. "Should we be reintroducing your Tommy and our Katherine?"

Richard smiled, and he and Janet shared a glance. "That would be great, William. Who knows what might happen? But for now he's got more local attention than he can handle, and one long distance love as well."

"Who's that?" Carrie asked.

"It's a girl he's seen every summer of his life on vacation in Vermont, Caroline Batten. She's even flown in for some big dances, and he visited her over spring break. They have a lot in common, and I think they're even trying to figure out how to go to the same college, or at least to schools near each other."

"Sounds pretty serious," Carrie mused. "Tommy has obviously grown a lot. Just remind him that Katherine is around in case this Caroline doesn't work out."

Richard smiled back. "It's a deal. And of course the really great thing about Tommy, just like Susan, is that he knows the Lord." Richard could see the president's eyes squint slightly and a small frown develop on his face. Richard continued, "We gave both Susan and Tommy to the Lord three years ago, after we submitted to God. It was kind of late to do it, I guess, but his grace and power are infinite, and he literally continues to change both of them. It happens before our eyes, and we give him all the credit." As he finished, William started to speak, but just then the special telephone rang in the adjoining living room.

"Please excuse me," William said, as he stood up and walked through the open archway and across the hall to the private telephone next to the sofa. "Hello." He expected to hear either a close family member or a very senior advisor.

"Mr. President, do you by any chance recognize my voice?"

The president was certain he was speaking to his party's senior senator from Ohio, John Dempsey. "Yes, sure. Hello, John. Why on earth are you calling me here, at this hour? And how did you get this number?"

There was a pause. Then the senator spoke, slowly and emphatically. "I called you on this line because I don't know which of your regular phones are tapped, and I doubt that you *really* know which ones are, despite what they may tell you. And I got this number the same way I get most things in this town. It comes naturally after being here all these years."

William was surprised by the call and by the older man's rough, disrespectful tone. "So what do you want?" he asked, trying to sound just as brusque.

"My other reason for calling you there is so you clearly understand that I have methods for discovering things. By the way, is your wife there, and those friends of yours from law school?"

"What's this about, John?"

"It's about you, you Southern hypocrite. All glad hands and, 'This conversation is just between us,' and all that other hogwash you use before you knife people in the back."

"What are you talking about?"

"You know *exactly* what I'm talking about. Give me one of your old Southerners any day, someone with whom I totally disagreed all those years ago, but someone with whom I could debate, give and take, and respect as an honorable opponent. You're of the new generation—and it's not just Southerners—who smile and say nice things, then take the first opportunity they can to blow you away in a dark alley."

"John, whatever is bothering you, you've got to be more specific. We have dinner guests, and I don't have time to play twenty questions."

"Well, you'd better *take* time to talk to me, or you could be in for a real surprise."

William sat down on the sofa. "Okay, John. I'm all yours. Again, what is it?"

"It's about telling me to open up to you for advice, and then when I did, putting out the bloodhounds to scare up anything you can to try to pressure me—blackmail me—to support all your we-know-what's-best programs. Well, you can count me out."

"I really don't know what you're talking about."

"You see, that's the problem. Once you start lying, it's hard to go back. I guess I shouldn't have expected much else from you. But I hoped for a lot more."

William turned to see Carrie standing in the open door. "Is everything all right?" she asked. William nodded his head and raised his hand to indicate that he would be rejoining them in a minute.

"Is that it, John? Is that why you called?"

"Almost. One more thing. There's a young attorney in Charlotte—not quite as young as she used to be, but still very good looking—who has some really interesting things to say about you, Mr. President. In fact, she's already said them, and I'm lucky enough to have her comments on tape, along with a signed affidavit. Does your wife know about those particular legal maneuvers, Mr. President?"

William's blood froze and his hands turned sweaty. He closed his eyes and didn't speak for almost thirty seconds, while his heart raced. "What...Who?... Who else has this information?" he finally asked in a hoarse whisper.

"I thought I lost you there for a minute," Dempsey laughed. "I was about to call 911. Glad you're still with us to savor the situation, Mr. President. Let's just say that your history in this matter is known to a select group of us, but of course we could enlarge that circle of informed Americans in just a few hours."

"So I guess we both might know about each other's pasts."

"You *might*. I *do*. And remember, my dear Mr. President, what you might find out about me happened many, many years ago; and I'm an old senator, about to go out to pasture. You, on the other hand, are a young, vigorous president with a wife and two kids. They might even make a hero out of a virile old man like me, even though now I'm very sorry for it. But they'll do the math on you and figure out that you were fooling around and lying to your wife with children at home. Those kinds of revelations don't do much for presidential credibility, much less for a marriage. So if you want to go toe-to-toe, it's your move."

William heard Carrie talking in the other room and suddenly visualized their family breaking up because he had been so stupid several years ago. He was angry, ashamed, frustrated, and powerless. All he could do was clench his fist. After another pause he said, "No, I'm not going to make the first move. Where do we go from here, John?"

"I'm glad to hear that. As to where we go from here, I guess I'm still an honorable man, even when dealing with your sort. I guess it's because I recognize my own faults. I've got a pretty strong Christian faith, despite my gruffness, and I won't blackmail you like you're trying to do to me. You go ahead and try to get your legislation past Congress any way you can, so long as you do it fair and honest, on top of the table and with words, not threats. You keep this bargain and learn to treat people by the Golden Rule, even if they disagree with you, and this little tape and affidavit will be handed to you on the day the first one of us leaves office. But if I hear about any more threats or blackmail—and I *will* hear—then I hate to think about all the tape players where this lady's song might be singing. Do you understand me, Mr. President?"

"Can you control it that well yourself?"

"I think I can. But nothing is one hundred percent. So you'd better pray that I can."

Carrie returned to the door, obviously concerned by her husband's long absence. William took a deep breath and concluded for her hearing, "Okay, we'll do it that way. Fine. I look forward to seeing you next week, and I'm glad we could work it out. Good-bye."

"Good-bye, Mr. President. And enjoy your dinner."

William returned the handset and waved at Carrie while wiping the sweat from his forehead. "Sorry. It was nothing that important. I don't know why they called me now." He suddenly felt very unclean and hollow, as if he were wearing a large sign which said "For years I cheated on you."

She rarely pushed him when he didn't offer more details, so she smiled and replied, "It's okay. Anyway, are you ready for dessert and coffee before the movie?"

When he didn't respond, she asked, "Is something wrong, dear?"

"Oh, no," he said, standing up. "Everything is, uh, fine. Good. Yeah, of course." But he made a mental note to call off Bob Horan first thing on Monday morning.

The two couples rejoined each other in the dining room for dessert and coffee. William apologized, "I'm sorry. Sometimes that happens. I guess it comes with the job. Now where were we?"

"Richard was telling us about how God had changed Susan and Tommy," Carrie said, offering the cream to her husband.

Richard noticed that William didn't frown this time, but stared at him. "So, anyway, I was just saying that it's obvious to Janet and me that God has changed our children just as much as he changed us. His power is really amazing. Giving our lives to him three years ago was, on a scale of one to ten, a fifty. Of course, we've had some real problems," Richard again looked at Janet, "but we now know that those problems are virtually nothing compared to spending eternity with him in heaven. Can you imagine what that's going to be like?" Richard asked with obvious joy and enthusiasm.

Richard looked toward his friend William, expecting an answer. But William just stared back at him, stirring his coffee almost as if he were in a trance. After a moment, Carrie touched his sleeve, "William, are you okay?"

"What? Oh, yes. I mean, no, Richard. I really don't have any idea what heaven might be like. Do you?"

"Well, I can't tell you the colors on the walls," he said, laughing, "but yes, there are many references in God's Word to heaven, so we do have some idea. The main thing is that God and Jesus will be there, and that's good enough for me."

William seemed to be thinking, then said, "And what about hell? Do you believe in hell? Does the Bible even mention hell?"

This time Janet spoke. "Yes, William, the Bible mentions hell many times. It's described as a place of pain and suffering. Can you imagine that for eternity? But like Richard said about heaven, the main thing about hell is that God and Jesus *won't be there.* Can you visualize spending eternity without God, in the hands of Satan?"

William tried to smile. "Well, when I get to that point I think I'll just check the box that says 'neither of the above' and go off to nothing."

Richard spoke again. "That's depressing enough in itself, William, when heaven is available. But unfortunately the Bible doesn't mention anything about that third option. Janet and I came to realize three years ago that we all are definitely spiritual beings. We're not just flesh and blood. Each of us certainly feels that spirit inside him. And that spirit is *eternal.* So the option you just mentioned doesn't exist. God, who made us, has mandated that our spirits will spend eternity either in heaven or in hell. That's it. And the Bible even says there's a huge gulf between them, and specifically that no spirit can go from one to the other. So where you wind up, forever, William, depends on what you do here."

A frown formed on William's face. "I know. I've heard that fundamentalist stuff many times, starting as a teenager with my sister Mary. Look, I've been reasonably good"—the memory of his conversation with John Dempsey flashed through his mind, and he suddenly missed a breath—"so if it's, uh, what I've done here that counts I feel, uh, pretty good about that," he finished, but with less enthusiasm than he would have said those same words an hour before.

Janet said, "It's not what you've done that really matters, William. None of us can possibly do well enough or be good enough on our own to make it to heaven. We're not just making this up; it's what God's Word has said over centuries. It's much simpler than *doing* anything. It's about giving up, genuinely asking for forgiveness, and submitting to God's Son as the ruler of your life. That message is so simple and so powerful that the only reason Richard and I can now imagine we didn't hear it sooner is that we must have had voices inside us, like doubt and pride and envy, blocking it out. It's hard to realize, I know, but just because something is simple doesn't mean it's not also very powerful."

William seemed to slump a bit in his chair, and he stared at his coffee. After a long silence he finally looked up at Richard and said, "I...I don't know. Can life really be as simple as you say it is? My life certainly isn't. It seems to be one problem after the other. I think your answer is too simple for the life I lead."

Richard spoke. "I didn't say, and more importantly the Bible doesn't say, that life is simple. Rather that the *solution* to living an abundant life, with all its complexity, both now and for eternity, *is* simple—it's belief in the lordship of God and his Son, Jesus Christ. Believe me, William, we wouldn't be telling you this if we hadn't felt his amazing grace and power in our own lives. It's very, very real. If nothing else, Susan and Tommy are visible, living proof of that fact."

William's gaze moved above Richard's head as if he were looking to some distant point. Finally he said, "Well, it's very, intere— I guess everybody's been telling me the same thing. Anyway, I guess it's about time for our movie." William looked at his guests, but his eyes still appeared to be glazed over. Then he shook his head, as if forcing himself back to his surroundings. "Has anybody got room left for popcorn?" he asked.

As the four of them descended in the elevator and walked down the hall to the theater, talking again about everyday matters, it occurred to Carrie that for the first time in her memory William had listened to the gospel message and then actually tried to discuss it.

ATLANTA   Later that same evening Bruce and Rebecca were sitting down to a meal of fettucine, salad, and Italian bread in the dining area of her apartment. The many lights of Atlanta stretched out below them, and the television was turned on without sound, anticipating the start of a late-night Braves game from the West Coast. They were continuing their tradition of a Friday night workout at the Sports Club followed by a quiet meal at her apartment.

"Would you like some wine?" Bruce asked, opening the refrigerator.

"Yes, I think I would tonight," Rebecca replied. "Isn't there some Chardonnay?"

He found two glasses, poured their wine, and sat down across from her. By tradition two candles on the television were the only light during their meal, emphasizing the effect of the view from her highrise. Months earlier this scene alone would have led them to make love passionately; but time and difficult events had created a routine which no longer always included passion. As they ate, each of them talked about their day at work, and then Bruce complimented Rebecca. "That trainer was really pushing tonight on the step. I was surprised you could keep up so well after taking the time off for your parents' funeral. I've got to hand it to you, Rebecca, you're tough."

Rebecca leaned back in her chair and took a sip of her wine. "It was a good workout, you're right. And I needed it. But you know, hearing you say that reminds me of how tough everyone is always saying I am. I'm supposed to be tough at work dealing with life and death every day. Everyone said how tough we were to come through our parents' murders. And I've tried for years to hold off nature with tough workouts." She looked at Bruce and shook her head slightly, a rueful smile on her face. "But you know, Bruce, right now your tough old broad isn't feeling very tough at all. In fact, I wish there was someone I could just give all of this to—the problems at the hospital, my parents' deaths, and my fear of growing old—and curl up in his arms like a little girl and just not have to be tough ever again. Can you imagine how I feel?"

The last few weeks had brought a significant change in their relationship. The sudden loss of Rebecca's parents propelled her unexpected family concerns into the middle of their relationship, whereas in the past they had focused on Bruce's problems. As for Bruce's mother, the president had instructed his surgeon general to write a letter of waiver on the requirement that Bruce's father be in an approved institution in order for his mother to receive points for looking after him, which then raised her total to just the amount required for her brain tumor operation. It was scheduled for the next Wednesday, and Bruce would be leaving Sunday night to fly to Boston to be with his parents. These developments had altered their relationship and removed Bruce's main cause for complaining.

Bruce twirled his fork in the fettucine, then looked up at her. "Yes, I guess I can. And I can tell how your parents' deaths have really affected you. But I'm not looking beyond my mother's operation right now. Maybe some day I can be that person for you, but at this moment I'm still focused on my mother, which I hope you can understand."

She leaned forward, put down her wine glass, picked up a piece of bread, and said, "I do understand, Bruce, and I certainly don't mean to sound uncaring in the least. But, you know, your mother's operation isn't the only event in our lives. Whatever happens, we'll have done all we can for her, and we have to think about the future."

Bruce looked down at his own half-finished plate, then returned her gaze. Quietly he remarked, "You're still unhappy that your brother told the surgeon general to write that letter, aren't you? I mean deep down inside. You don't think my own mother should have this operation, do you?"

She pursed her lips and looked at him with obvious concern. "Bruce, you know that I'm the one who asked my brother to do it. You're right that I feel it's wrong to bend the rules for personal gain," she held up her hand as he started to talk, "No matter how correct the motives are. I mean, the flip side is that there are only so many available brain tumor operation slots each year, and by your mother taking one, someone else is being pushed out. But it's done, we did it, and I just hope it all goes very well."

"Well, you know how I feel about all those other unnamed people. This is *my mother*, and I'll be forever grateful to your brother for helping her."

"But, you see, that's just my point. When he and other politicians do these things for people, they become grateful for a long, long time. In the old days the system was far from perfect, but people pretty well knew whether they had the resources to pay for a procedure and accepted it. But now theoretically *anyone* can persuade a politician to help, yet there still aren't enough operations to go around. So we have an underground network developing of people who can 'fix' an operation, either for money or for personal political gain. I'm not saying that your mother's not important, or that's what happened here. But if we're going to use a point system, then we should set it up and leave it alone. We've been over this before, Bruce, and I really don't feel like another fight."

"Okay. Okay. I just meant that I appreciate what your brother did, and I'll try to help him if I can in the future. Anyway, the operation is set, and I'll be leaving for Boston on Sunday night. So let's just leave it that your brother is a nice guy."

"Yes, he *is* a nice guy," she said and smiled, signalling a truce. "Sometimes he may just be too nice."

NEW YORK Following her interview with the president that afternoon, Leslie Sloane had spent two hours at the studio reviewing the segments for initial editing recommendations. Just before five she took a cab to Union Station to catch one of the new high speed Metroliners to New York. Only two and a half hours later she was at Grand Central Station where Ryan met her for the brief taxi ride to his apartment.

This was her fourth weekend in a row with Ryan in New York. Each time their routine had been similar, but this week they at least waited until they made it to his bedroom to begin their embrace. As he urged her onto his bed, she smiled, ran her fingers through his hair, and asked, "Oh, Ryan, where is this going? I love it, but we can't keep on like dogs and cats. Is there a relationship here or just weekend sex?"

Propped on one elbow, he traced patterns on her body with his free hand. "I don't know, Leslie," he honestly replied. "But can we talk about it later?"

She smiled again and took his hand in hers. After a long, deep kiss she pushed him back a few inches and said, "Okay. Later. But I'm just warning you that sometime this weekend I want to talk. Agreed?"

"Absolutely. No problem. Any time starting about an hour from now," and he kissed her again.

"How many segments do you plan in this one-hour performance?" she asked.

"I don't know," he said, laughing. "But we're definitely live, so hold on tight and we'll find out."

Ninety minutes later they were sharing food and champagne—their own Friday night tradition—in the kitchen. She was sitting on the island in the center of the room, dressed only in one of his blue cotton shirts. He sat on a stool facing her, sipping his champagne.

"So the interview with the president went pretty well?" Ryan asked.

She wrapped her arms around her knees and smiled. She turned her head slightly toward him and said, "Yeah, I think so. We'll look at the finished product on Monday, but I think we captured both his vision and his frustration...You know, Ryan, he's really a good guy...and that's not always true of career politicians."

"I've only been around him a few times, but he seems to be."

"He wants the best for the country, and I think he has the vision to do it, if people like us keep giving him chances to accomplish it, and, frankly, sort of hold his feet to the fire—build up an expectation in him and in the country that the things he wants to do are right."

Ryan, wearing a black silk robe, leaned back and put his feet up on the counter. He took another sip and then said, "Nice guys don't always finish first, Les. He seems to have some pretty tough opposition. Along with building up his goals, maybe we ought to look into what his opponents want, and portray them for what they really are."

"It's funny, Ryan. I was thinking the same thing on the way to the train station. Most of those old guys are do-nothings, and many of them are closet fundamentalists—I know from their abortion votes—more concerned with 'values' and 'salvation' than with real issues like jobs, rights, and housing. It might be interesting to do some 'Up Close and Personal' studies on them. Who could do them?"

"I think Bob Whalen would be good. He used to have your post, and he's got a little gray hair, for credibility. And he's 4.0 on the issues."

"Good. I'm sure a couple of those a month as special assignments would really help." She held out her glass for a refill from the bottle on the floor. A moment passed and then she continued, "You know, the president was kind of funny this afternoon. Just as we started he seemed sort of down, a little vulnerable. Like his parents' murder and all this opposition has really gotten to him. It flashed in my mind for an instant that he was going to smile and say, 'Leslie, I'm glad you came by today so I can announce that I resign. I'm going home to North Carolina this afternoon.'"

They both laughed. "That's a bit bizarre, Les. What were you smoking in the White House?"

"I know. But it just flashed across my mind when he started off talking about how awful things are. But then just as quickly it was like he threw a switch inside himself and recovered. From then on he was fine—inspired even. But for those few moments I felt that I was looking into his soul," she grew serious, "and he seemed really worried. Isn't that strange?"

"I guess that's even more reason to keep 'holding his feet to the fire,' as you said a minute ago, on his goals."

"Yes. And you know what else? For some reason it also made me curious about his family. I mean his sisters and brother. We see them, like at the funeral. But what are they *really* like? What do they think of his programs?

What are they like on the inside? Are they winners or quitters? I thought that along with the pieces on his opponents it might also be good to build up his family a bit."

"Sounds okay to me, at least to get started."

"And, Ryan, I don't know why, but I'd like to do those stories myself."

He rocked forward on the stool and picked up the bottle. "Oh, yeah? Well, what sort of quid pro quo can I expect for supporting that assignment?"

She turned toward him on the counter and smiled. "Oh, I think I can find a way to make it worth your while."

WASHINGTON The heat and moisture hung in the summer night until well past midnight, spawning thunderstorms into the early morning hours. William Harrison tossed and turned in bed, once again unable to sleep. Despite his physical exhaustion, his mind raced in maddening circles, back and forth between his congressional problems, the loss of his parents, John Dempsey's frightening phone call, the bomb threat, his lack of leadership, Carrie's sudden faith, Hugh's letter, his readings of the founding fathers, Bob Horan, the Sullivans' strength, and even for some reason the Ukrainian boy at Camp David. Round and round these and other thoughts swirled, as the heavens seemed to be warring right outside his window.

Once he almost stopped breathing when he thought about John Dempsey telling the press about his affairs. What if he lost Carrie, Robert, and Katherine? He actually shivered at the thought. *I really love Carrie more than I have in a long time,* he thought, *and I don't want to hurt her or lose her. I was such an idiot...Or am I now just sorry that I got caught? I wish I could go back and undo it. But I can't and it's there and the whole world might soon know. What if Dempsey can't control it? Who else already knows? Why did I do it? What a fool!* Just then a huge bolt of lightning lit the sky, and thunder crashed almost instantly. He wondered if Madison or Lincoln had ever heard the sound of artillery so close in the midst of their own wars.

Finally he rose in the dark and once again picked up the briefing book with the writings of the founders, which had remained untouched on his table since the phone call from Raleigh about his parents. As the stormclouds finally subsided in the distance, he read.

Much sooner than he wanted, he and Carrie were awakened by his alarm clock. Even though it was Saturday, he had scheduled briefings all morning on Mexico and South America, where he was headed in ten days. And since the staff was working on the weekend, he had to be on time.

William felt awful, but he reminded himself that the afternoon was free to enjoy with Carrie and the Sullivans, and he hoped that the weather would not affect their scheduled tennis game. As he shaved in the mirror he thought that there was now something different about Richard and Janet which was really unusual. He finally had to admit it was the strength of their faith. He had seen this same quiet strength and confidence earlier in Mary, Graham, Carrie, and now his oldest and dearest friends. *Where does it come from? Does it really come from God? Richard seems so different...He's so...so at peace. I wonder how he got there? Do you just ask for it, like Mary says? It sounds too simple...but look at Richard.* Something *has happened to him...just like Mary...just like Carrie. Is it possible that it's real?* He shivered again.

Three hours later he finished his last briefing in the West Wing, checked with the national security officer for an abbreviated world situation update, then returned to their private residence in the main building. He looked outside and saw that the heat from the midday sun was already turning the weather ominous, a large black cloud forming to the southwest across the Mall. He found Carrie and the Sullivans sitting in the living room.

"Oh, hello, dear," Carrie smiled as William came in. She noticed the bags under his eyes but didn't say anything. "We were just talking about lunch. It looks like another thunderstorm is brewing, so I doubt we'll play any tennis—the courts are still wet from last night. What do you want to do?"

William greeted their friends, looked out across the White House lawn, and said, "I'm not feeling one hundred percent anyway, but I think a light workout would do me good—maybe a sauna, too. Might perk me up. How about you, Richard? What about a late lunch after we work out in the gym downstairs?"

"Sounds great—I could use the exercise. Can Carrie and Janet join us?"

"You two go ahead," Carrie said. "I'll be much happier showing Janet some of the amazing old things that are stored away in nooks and crannies in this place. Is that all right?" she asked, turning to her guest.

"Absolutely. You guys go exercise, and we'll look for items for a garage sale, in case the federal budget really needs help."

"What a great idea. I bet we could raise millions," Carrie responded. "Come on, and I'll show you two huge closets you won't believe." She turned to the men and said, "We'll have lunch about two, back here. Okay?"

Ten minutes later William showed Richard the small but well-equipped gym that had been built into the basement of the White House. There were ample windows along one wall at ground level, providing plenty of natural light for the twin stationary bikes, stairclimbers, assorted weights, and the universal gym. Around a corner and out of view of the windows was a changing area with two benches, several full-length lockers, a sauna, and shower.

"Nice set-up," Richard said, noting the rich paneling, built-in televisions, and obligatory telephones.

"I'm not sure what this area once was, but we only made a couple of changes. It's all compliments of a previous 'tenant,'" William said, smiling, as he walked over to the locker area to change his clothes.

After some stretches William was soon riding one of the bikes, while Richard started slowly on the neighboring stairclimber.

"So, how's your law practice?" William asked.

"I've got no complaints. Besides the usual corporate work, the real estate market is picking up a bit, and of course there are always enough people angry at each other in our society to keep us pretty busy. We added a few young attorneys from this year's law school crop, and three older guys moved over from another firm to do medical malpractice defense. So it's fine."

"And Janet's work?"

"She's really happy. Soon after we gave our lives to the Lord, we had an interesting run-in with her network over the suitability of a particular show. It turned out all right, and Janet was asked to serve on a joint network committee on violence and family programming. With a pledge from her network that it was truly committed to the process, she agreed to serve. Now she's this year's chairperson, and she spends a lot of time in New York working to improve what we all see on TV. And of course she loves her local station. So all in all, things are going great for her."

William rode for a kilometer in silence, reflecting as he had in the early morning hours about the differences between their two families, watching as the sky outside turned dark as ink and wispy fingers of low trailing clouds swirled in the increasing turbulence, seeming to reach down for the White House roof.

"What about you, William?" Richard finally asked, his climb picking up speed. "How are you liking this fairly unique job?"

William started to say "fine" but stopped as his lips formed the word. He was just thinking for the hundredth time that week about the bomb threat and about John Dempsey's phone call the previous evening when Richard asked his question. Something seemed to shift inside him.

He slowed down his pedaling to a more comfortable pace but kept looking out the windows at the quickly gathering storm. "Richard...what a question. I'd like to answer you as my best friend, like I would have done twenty years ago. Is that possible? Can this be just between us?"

Richard noted the change in his friend's voice and said, "Of course. What's wrong?"

"Frankly, just about everything, if I take the time to admit it." He raised one hand as he noticed out of the corner of his eye that Richard was about to speak. "No, don't say something nice. I really mean it. Let's see. Where do I start? Katherine hates living with us here. My parents have been murdered by three guys from 'good' families who were apparently just bored one afternoon and out looking for a car to steal. Our domestic program, which we worked so hard on, is going nowhere in the Senate, meaning that I may preside over three more years of complete government gridlock, while we sink deeper into debt every day. Mary, Rebecca, and Hugh—all of whom you've met while visiting in Raleigh—are writing me detailed letters about how our society is a mess as a result of our policies. Foreign leaders genuinely ask us to solve all their problems, but we can't even educate our own children. There are threats to our nation I could not have imagined before we got here. And, to top it off," his voice cracked, "after being a jerk to Carrie for years, I love her more now than I have in a very long time, but some mistakes I made in the past may soon become public knowledge, which will hurt her deeply, not to mention hurting the kids, and perhaps even cause her to leave me, and for good reason."

He had stopped pedaling halfway through the list, and now he finally turned to face Richard, who had stopped exercising. "So that's why I can't sleep at night, and I read about our Founding Fathers and their faith and their strength, and I feel like a ten-year-old playing at being president, wearing some adult's shoes which are way, way too big for me. And I can already see," he wiped his eyes with his hands, then ran them over his cheeks, as if it were sweat that was making them wet, "that this is all going to be a *failure*. The whole thing, Richard. This administration, our policies, and my family. All failures. Big time. All because of me. And very soon," he concluded and turned back to face forward, again wiping his eyes with the towel on the handlebars.

Richard didn't know what to say, so he stepped off the stairs, picked up a towel, and walked over to the windows, not wanting to embarrass his friend by looking at him while he silently cried. Finally he said, watching the first bolts of lightning against the dark sky, "I'm so sorry, William. I had no idea."

The president stepped slowly off the bike and walked over to the water dispenser for a drink, taking his towel. He wadded up the paper cup, threw it away, and faced his old friend, who turned to meet his eyes. A bolt of lightning hit nearby, and both men flinched. After the thunder, Richard asked in a whisper, "The 'mistakes,' William, were they recent?"

William turned and said, "I think I need to sit down for a minute." He walked over and sat on one of the benches in the locker area, straddling it and wiping his face. Richard followed and straddled the other bench, so that their knees almost touched, and they faced each other.

"No, not really. It was about ten years ago. I say 'it'—the main one. But there were others, several others. But this woman was an attorney and I guess we thought we were in love, and I was awful to Carrie." He closed his eyes for a moment and raised his head, trying to hold back the tears, terribly embarrassed when he failed. His voice cracked again, and he said in a whisper, "I've been such a bad husband, Richard. For years I just ignored Carrie—worse, I walled her out, on purpose. She's so loving and just wants the best for me. But I slept with this young attorney and lied to Carrie and then pushed her out of my life, all the time figuring she'd always just be there. I hurt her so much. I was so selfish. But now I feel so dirty, like I can never be clean again, ever.

"It's too much, Richard. It's all crashing in. I've tried to do the right things, but I've pretty well screwed up everything, though I doubt you'd really understand, even as good a friend as you are. I'm sure you've never experienced anything like this."

Richard let him finish and waited. Then in a low but calm voice he said, "Only a few years ago, William, I was having an affair and doing the same things to Janet that you did to Carrie, including the walling out. I didn't just feel dirty, I felt like garbage, like there was no hope for me or my family because of me. But I kept on doing it! Janet should have left me."

As Richard continued, William looked up and watched him, surprise and concern on his face. "I...I came that close to personal and financial ruin, and our kids were only a few months away from being destroyed by the pressures of our society, compounded by my own ignorance and stupidity. I should have lost them, William, lost them completely, and forever...*Forever losing your own children.* Can you imagine, William? What worse thing could a father possibly do?" And now it was Richard's turn to wipe his eyes.

"I didn't know," William said. "I thought you and Janet were always pretty happy. And now you seem so in love, and it sounds like your kids are doing great. What happened?"

Richard took a deep breath and exhaled, looking straight at William while he did. "You want the truth?"

William nodded.

"Okay, here it is, man to man and friend to friend—if you're ready for it, because it isn't easy. I got down off my high horse as the macho I-know-it-all-and-can-do-it-all male, and gave up. I finally realized that in my own power I was about to crash and burn and take my wife and children with me. Some loving and patient people took a lot of time, first to get my attention by the quiet power of their lives, and then to lead me to that same power. But they couldn't do it all. *I* had to be broken. *I* had to realize that I was flying the plane into the ground on my own, and *I* had to ask for help. And I had to be ready to admit that I had been wrong and ask for forgiveness. William, those were the toughest and the happiest things I ever did. And whatever has happened to me since, it's happened because I gave up trying to do it all and submitted to God's will."

"God's?"

"Yes. The Father who wants to say 'I know you sometimes feel like a ten-year-old. But hold tightly onto my hand, and I'll give you the power to have all the wisdom you need. Because it will be *my* power.'... William, let me ask you: do you see a difference in Janet and me?"

William didn't pause. "Yes."

"Is it real?"

"Yes, it seems to be."

"Then God is real, William, because the *only* difference in us is that his Holy Spirit is living inside us, right now. And he cleaned up all that miserable garbage like you're feeling right now in one instant. We're truly new people, born again by his grace and his mercy. We can feel it, and people tell us they can see it. It's very, very real, William, and very powerful."

Something snapped inside William. All the words that had been spoken to him over the years, from Mary to Michael Tate to his reading of the Founding Fathers to Carrie, were preparation for the truth that suddenly burst upon him with Richard's explanation.

There was a bolt of lightning and a crash of thunder so close together that both men involuntarily ducked. They could hear rain starting to come down in torrents. William felt the hairs on his neck and arms standing up from the revelation that swept over him. He closed his eyes as the truth penetrated him. *Richard's right. It's obvious. They* are *different. Why haven't I understood it before? If they're real, then he must be real. And God can get rid of this awful pain I feel? Forgive me for all the terrible things I've done, especially to Carrie? O God, yes, please forgive me. I'm so sorry. Please help me. Please, please help me. O God, I give up. I don't want to run from you any more. Please, please help me and forgive me. O God, what have I done? What a fool I've been. Please forgive me. Come and help me. I'm sorry. Please...HELP ME!*

Richard watched the waves sweep over his friend and the tears stream down his cheeks. William shook and slumped slightly on the bench, broken and sobbing.

When the waves appeared to have slowed, Richard asked quietly, "My friend, do you want a new life?"

William nodded and then looked up. He wiped his tears with his towel and asked, "How, Richard? How can I have what you've got? How can I get rid of this pain?"

Richard smiled and said calmly. "You and I can't do anything, but Jesus can do everything through the power of the Holy Spirit. Let's ask him." Richard moved to the side and got down on his knees. "Let's ask him together." William joined him without hesitation, on his knees to his Lord for the first time in years.

"I'll pray to God, and if you feel the same thing in your heart, you pray to him directly from *your* heart. Okay?"

William nodded and closed his eyes.

They prayed together, with William following Richard in a prayer of repentance and faith.

After Richard stopped praying out loud, neither of them moved. Each of them continued to pray silently. Finally William looked up, smiling, his cheeks still wet but his tears no longer flowing. Unsteady, he rose to his feet. Richard followed.

"Richard, I...my sister was right, all those years ago! Where have I been? He took all those sins! From me! Richard, am I really a new person today? It's funny—I don't feel completely different or light headed. But I do feel *clean*. For the first time in a very long time. Why did I wait so long? I'm sorry, God, that I waited so long. Thank you. Thank you, Richard." William reached out to Richard, and they hugged.

"I'll tell you the same thing a younger man said to me, William: 'Welcome to God's kingdom, my friend.'"

William stepped back and asked, "Richard, what happens now? I don't feel like dancing and singing—I just feel drained and at peace."

"William, your name is now written in the Book of Life. You're God's, forever. But if you want to experience all that he can do for, with, and through you, then you need to do a few things."

"What? Tell me."

Richard smiled. "Here, let's sit down again." Richard spent ten minutes telling William about his own experiences when he first gave his life to the Lord.

When Richard finished, William said, "So read the Bible, pray, and find teachers and a good church to join. That's how I can build a relationship with God?"

"Yes."

"It seems so simple."

"It is, William, but very, very powerful. It's just amazing. You'll learn new things about yourself and about the world, especially about how God wants us to live in this world. Given your unique job, I think you'll find it very, very interesting."

William smiled. "I think he may have already been trying through the writings of earlier presidents and leaders. But I wasn't ready to hear. We'll see."

"Isn't God amazing?" Richard asked. "Imagine all of the many threads that wove together in both our lives over many years for us to be here, in this place, on this day, for you to become part of God's kingdom. He is simply awesome. That's an overused word, but not where God's concerned."

"Richard, I can't thank you enough," William said, extending his hand.

They shook hands firmly. "Don't thank me: thank God. You're his now. It's the greatest joy and a great responsibility. But work on the relationship, William, particularly for the first few months. Become grounded in his Word, and seek godly men to advise you. Pray about his will for you. Don't rush into things. He's totally faithful. He *will* answer."

"I guess we'd better go find Carrie and Janet. I don't know about Janet, but Carrie isn't going to believe what happened in this gym today!"

Richard returned his smile, and as they turned the corner into the main exercise room, they were astonished to see that the storm had blown completely away and bright sun shone in through all the windows. "Can you believe that?" Richard asked.

"Richard, after the last hour, I can believe absolutely anything, so long as God is involved."

William and Richard were early as they returned to the president's private quarters and tossed their streetclothes over a sofa on their way to the kitchen. Janet was seated at the island and Carrie was cutting a tomato for their sandwiches. The two women were talking about an old painting they had found behind a table leaf in the second closet they had searched. They looked up and saw their husbands returning in their workout clothes.

"William, lunch isn't ready yet, and you're a mess. Why didn't you get cleaned up?" Carrie chided him.

William smiled. "Carrie, I just got cleaned up more than you can imagine! I...you won't believe this. I'm a...It's even a little hard to say." He was half-laughing, half-crying. He turned momentarily to Richard, then back to his wife. Finally he said, "I'm a Christian!"

Stunned, Carrie put down the paring knife and looked back and forth between the two men. Janet stood up and moved over next to Richard, who was smiling and nodding.

"I gave up. I admitted to God that I've made a mess of our marriage and this job and just about everything because I've only thought about me, not him or you. Even that reading I've been doing was to get something out of it for me, rather than to learn about him and his will. Anyway, with Richard's help, we just cleaned me up good. God's got all that old stuff, and Richard says he'll keep it—I can start over and try to do it right this time. Starting with us, if you'll let me," and he hugged Carrie tightly in his arms. She clung to him, her face beaming.

While they were still embracing, she said softly, "Oh, William. You're right. I *can't* believe it. But it sounds wonderful! Praise God for such a miracle, and for his grace and mercy!" She leaned back and looked at him. "William, is this really you?"

"No, I guess not." He smiled, teasingly. "At least not the me who went down to the gym bemoaning his fate. I'm a new man, and I intend to make the rest of my time on earth count for something, if he wants it. But I realize I know almost nothing about the God who just saved me. I've hardly ever read the Bible. But I know today I've felt his power, so I'll try to learn more about him, as Richard has told me. Carrie, I feel clean, like a kid. Hey, I've got to call Mary."

While William took the phone from the wall, Carrie stepped over and hugged Richard, tears starting to pool in her eyes. Then she embraced Janet and sat down. William rang through to his older sister, and the instant joy on both ends of the line was obvious. A few minutes later he ended with, "Yes, I'll pray. And read the Bible. And find a church. Hey, did you and Richard write a script? That's what Rev. Wilson told *you?* Way back then? Come on! Really?"

"That's what another man told me, William," Richard interrupted. "Both the weakness and the strength of our faith is that we have to tell each other. God could tell us himself from mountain tops, but instead he's given that job exclusively to people."

"What?" William said, switching his attention back to the phone. "Oh, I was listening to Richard. Yes. Okay. Richard, Mary wants to know if we can switch it to the speaker phone, and she'll get Graham and we'll all pray together."

"Sounds great. Yes, let's do it."

William pressed the speaker button and hung the phone up. Richard motioned for the four of them to join hands in a circle, and then the six of them prayed prayers of thanksgiving and praise that Saturday afternoon, as the sun shone brightly on the Mall for the first time in days.

After they finished and said good-bye, William sat on one of the kitchen stools, and Richard took a stool across the island from him. "We'll take showers in a minute, ladies, but I was wondering while we were just praying: Do you think that studying and learning about God will change anything about how I approach this job or about our policies?"

Richard and Janet shared a quick glance, then Richard looked at William. "In my life, as I listened and read and learned from godly teachers and from the Bible, my business goals and practices changed pretty dramatically. Obviously I'm not the president of the United States, but I've frankly never known anyone who genuinely asked Christ to rule his life who didn't change. Almost by definition you have to, if you're a new person in him, and you ask the Holy Spirit to fill you afresh every day."

William was silent for a long moment, lost in thought. "Then I might learn things from his Word and teaching that could not only change me, but change how I view the world?"

"I think you can probably count on it."

William thought again. "Hey, you three, that's a little scary for a fifty-year-old politician."

Richard paused, then said seriously, "It seems scary at first for everyone who chooses Christ, William. But the blessing is that now you have him living inside you, and if you're faithful, he'll give you the power to do anything."

William shook his head. "That sounds impossible. But I'm really new at this. I hope the three of you, and particularly you, Carrie, are prepared to help this uncertain old politician."

Carrie walked over to him and put her arms around his shoulders. "Of course, sweetheart. It's all I've ever wanted. But he'll be so much more help to you than any of us. Just let him."

"I'll try...I really will try. I'll pray, just like our early leaders did." He thought for another moment, looked at the Sullivans, then turned back to his wife, his eyes wide. "Good heavens, Carrie. What's going to happen now?"

BOOK TWO

The Bible…is the one supreme source of revelation of the meaning of life, the nature of God and spiritual nature and need of men. It is the only guide of life which really leads the spirit in the way of peace and salvation.… America was born a Christian nation. America was born to exemplify that devotion to the elements of righteousness which are derived from the revelations of Holy Scripture.

WOODROW WILSON

10

CAMP DAVID "It's great to see you again, Michael." William extended his hand to the man who had given the Easter sermon three months earlier.

Michael Tate walked up the steps to the porch at Aspen Lodge and took the president's hand. With genuine concern he said, "It's wonderful to be with you again, Mr. President. But of course I can't help thinking of your parents when I'm here. Elizabeth and I were so sorry to learn of their deaths, and in such tragic circumstances. I hope Mary expressed our condolences to you."

William held the other man's grip for an extra moment. "Yes…yes, she did. Thank you. It *was* terrible. But our responsibilities don't stop, and we've got to keep going despite their deaths." After another moment his smile returned. "And Carrie and I are so glad you could join us on such short notice."

"How could anyone refuse a White House summons to lunch at Camp David the day before Independence Day? And Mary hinted at some news which sounded wonderful."

William escorted his guest into the lodge. "Yes, it is. And that's why I've asked you to join us. Your sermon meant a lot to Carrie, and Mary obviously thinks the world of you. Frankly now I need your help and advice—maybe more than I've ever needed advice in my life. Here's Carrie."

The minister and first lady exchanged greetings and a hug, then the three of them sat down in comfortable chairs near the fireplace.

"Lunch will be in a few minutes," William began, "but I hope we might go ahead and start—I have a lot of questions, and I know you want to get home to your family for the holiday."

"I'll stay as long as you need me," Michael replied.

"Thanks." William looked first at Carrie and then reiterated how Carrie had become a believer at Easter. He talked of his own ongoing readings on the faith of the Founding Fathers, and finally the events of the previous Saturday with the Sullivans. He left out his guilt and fear over his past affair but hinted that he'd had some setbacks in his private life that had perhaps acted as the spark for the change of his heart.

"At any rate, for reasons I still only partly understand, God has chosen to let this sinner be part of his kingdom, and I've given my life to him." William was leaning forward in his chair, his elbows on his legs, hands folded in front of him. He looked down, then up at Michael, genuine humility and awe clearly on his face. "I…I don't really know why. But I know that I'm his now. I've made a pretty big mess of everything on my own, and I want to stop. I want to submit to his will for me. I've only been a real Christian for four days, and I want to learn about the faith that obviously drove and guided the founders of our nation—but I don't just want to learn *about* it— I want to *know* it, to make it part of me.

"Richard said that I should pray, read the Bible, find a Bible-believing church, and be taught—discipled he called it—by godly teachers. Well," William concluded, "you're about the godliest teacher we know, so that's why we invited you to join us today."

Before Michael could respond, Carrie interrupted. "And I think lunch is ready, so let's continue in the dining room."

Seated in the small, informal dining area off the living room, with a grand view of the camp around them, they were served lunch on presidential china. Michael offered a blessing.

When he finished, William picked up his fork, grinned, and said, "North Carolina barbecue—in honor of the holiday. Hope you like it."

"It looks delicious," Michael replied. They each took a few bites before Michael continued the conversation.

"I've never met the Sullivans, but it sounds like they gave you good advice."

"I finally thought to ask Richard why he was in Washington." William almost laughed. "I knew it was for a legal conference. But it turns out that some Christian and constitutional lawyers were getting together to plan strategies for fighting our administration's proposed tax on churches which refuse to comply with federal non-discrimination laws."

William turned serious. "I want to come back to that in a minute. But on Sunday we changed our schedule around and made the Secret Service real happy by visiting the Church of the Good Shepherd—your friend Robert Ludwig. He's the one who started me reading the Founding Fathers. Anyway, he gave another great sermon on the kingdom of God versus the kingdom of man—two different worldviews. Again, it was uncanny—like I was somehow supposed to be there. I want to learn more from him."

"And the church tax?" Michael asked.

"Oh, yes. As ironic as that was—and I think it's great that Richard never mentioned it until I asked—that's exactly why I need you, and I guess Robert Ludwig, if he has time, and maybe others, to teach me what the Bible says about all these subjects. I think I'm a pretty good constitutional expert, although my recent readings have made me wonder if I *really* understand that incredible document. But I *know* that I don't know the Bible. And that was the one document the founders relied on most. So I want to understand the Bible and its meaning for me as an individual—like any other new believer. But then I also want to try to understand how its teachings might influence what we do as a nation—specific legislation, for example. Like this tax. If I'm really going to be God's servant and I'm in this office, then I want to do what he wants."

There was a long moment of silence as all of them ate and thought about what the president had just said. Finally Michael responded. "I'm a little overwhelmed, to be honest. One thing's certain: we can't accomplish any of this relying on our own strength. We'll have to pray constantly and seek his will. We could easily go off on some human tangents and agendas that are not of the Lord. So we'll keep our focus on him.

"The most important thing, it seems to me, is for godly people to teach you about our faith and about God himself—Father, Son, and Spirit. That's how you'll develop your own foundation of God's principles and begin your walk with the Lord. Then you'll have to decide, perhaps with others, how God's Spirit speaks to you on these governmental matters. Teachers can and will certainly give you principles, but the actual laws are for men like yourself to propose and to pass—maybe that's why you're here."

William looked at Carrie. "It seems you said something like that a few months ago."

"Yes, but I had no idea it would turn out this way," she said, reaching for his hand.

"How much time do you have, Mr. President, given your schedule, to devote to this teaching?"

"Please, Michael, call me William. I'll certainly try to make time. I've got to. Maybe early in the mornings and in the evenings. Who do you recommend to help?"

"I wouldn't presume to undertake such a task on my own—or limit your teaching to one man or one view of our faith. I'll be glad to call Robert Ludwig and some other teachers in the Washington area from different denominations—men and women who share a strong faith in the Bible as the foundation for their belief. Give us a few days, and we'll pull together a course, if you will, starting in 'kindergarten' on the basics and describing

God's worldview, like Robert apparently preached when you heard him."

"That sounds good, Michael. I'll talk to Barbara Morton about scheduling. Let's keep this in the private quarters and off the nightly news for now, if we can. But early and late should work. Do you really think you can find people to help?"

Michael smiled. "I think so. We Christians have been complaining for years. Now God has apparently given us the opportunity to teach his principles to the president of our nation. I think many will jump at the chance. But there's the interesting tension. What do we teach? Laws and legislation, like in a theocracy? No, I don't think so."

He paused and then continued. "This is really important, William, and I'm glad we're focusing on it early. There will be a temptation for each teacher to try to tell you his or her agenda—what that person thinks God wants you to hear, he or she would no doubt say. But I'll speak to them and emphasize that we're to treat you like any other new believer who has felt God's power and now wants to learn his wisdom. We're going to compress the process as much as we can, but not change the subject matter.

"Once you understand these principles—again, God's worldview—then it will be up to you and others to debate and decide what laws should govern our country. We can give you God's principles, but it's your job to govern. And both of those important but separate roles are established and confirmed over and over again by God in the Bible."

It was William's turn to think for a minute. "I understand," he finally replied, imagining for the first time what it really might mean to have been elected for God's purpose, as Carrie had told him months before. The thought sent a chill through him, and Carrie noticed his sudden introspection. After a few moments of silence, William asked, "When can we start?"

"I'll make some calls this afternoon, and I suspect we can have a rotating schedule of men and women you'll enjoy getting to know and learning from ready to go by Monday."

As Carrie rose to take a telephone call from her aide at the door, William said, "The sooner the better."

"In the meantime, keep reading Luke and Acts. And if you have some time this afternoon, I might build on what Robert preached and show you the foundations for God's worldview in Genesis."

"That would be great. Sure. And if you can recommend a book or two, I'd appreciate it, although I'm still fascinated with the early writings of the founders, both their letters and their laws. I'll keep reading those as well."

"Fine. I'd like to hear what you find out from that reading as we go along."

Carrie returned to the room as the two men rose from the table. "That was Rebecca. Bruce called her from Boston, and they wanted you to know that his mother's operation went well. It's too early to tell anything conclusive, but the first indications are that they were able to remove all the tumor. They wanted to thank you."

William was touched but a little embarrassed. "Thanks, Carrie. But they shouldn't thank me. I didn't do anything."

"Well, they wanted you to know, and they're thankful. Oh, and she also said that Leslie Sloane has called her and wants to fly down to Atlanta to do an interview—she's thinking about it."

"That's fine. Well, let's get our Bibles—mine's so new the pages still stick together. Michael is going to spend some time with us on Genesis."

"Great. I'll be right back. I'll have some coffee brought into the living room."

As Michael followed his host into the living room, it was his turn to feel a chill. *God, give me the words you want so that through me you can teach this leader of the most powerful nation on earth exactly what you want him to know about you and your will for our lives.*

All the good from the Saviour of the world is communicated through this Book; but
for the Book we could not know right from wrong.
All the things desirable to man are contained in it.

ABRAHAM LINCOLN

II

Monday, August 27
Eight Weeks Later

CHAPEL HILL "I've had a really great time this summer, Aunt Mary," Katherine said as she, her cousin Sarah, and Mary walked across the University of North Carolina campus after their lunch with Robert. They were headed toward the administration building, followed discreetly by one of the Secret Service teams that had been assigned to the president's daughter for her working vacation in Raleigh.

"Well, if your interviews today go well and everything else falls into place, maybe you two will be together again next fall when you start college," Mary replied, as they walked in the shade of the large oak trees for relief from the summer heat.

"And if we survive senior year in high school," Sarah added. "That new computer is affecting just about every class at school, and I'm not real crazy about computers."

"I thought computers made work easier," her mother said, "Not that I understand them."

"I guess, but not always for me. Matthew loves them, though. He's promised to help me whenever I like get bogged down."

Katherine turned to her cousin. "Sounds like a great excuse to spend lots of time with Matthew!" she said teasingly.

"Well, he really does know all about that stuff." She couldn't help laughing.

"And your new health class," Katherine continued her teasing, knowing that she was treading on thin ice and glancing at her aunt. "Will Matthew help you with computer applications there, too?"

Sarah blushed and glanced sideways at her mother, but didn't say anything.

Mary looked at her niece—they were almost the same height—and said with as much maternal authority as she could muster without ruining the mood of their day together, "I don't think Sarah will need any help there, Katherine. We've given Sarah our permission to use her own judgment on that confounded computer course. She's old enough to make her own decisions. But the last I heard, she's had the courage and the faith to say no. Is that still your decision, Sarah?"

As they walked, Sarah looked down at the brick path in front of her. "Yes…I guess so. It does sound pretty weird. But a lot of the kids, and most of my friends, are going to try it once, I think. Matthew's parents told him they don't care, that it's up to him."

Katherine regretted she had pushed so far. She knew from their many late night discussions over the summer how torn Sarah was about the health class. And she had heard her aunt and uncle discuss the situation in very vivid terms. Aunt Mary was apparently looking into some sort of group or legal action to try to stop the class, or at least to prevent it from spreading to other schools.

"I'm sorry," Katherine relented. "Those computer people have probably programmed all the guys to look like geeks anyway." She tried to atone for her choice of subjects.

"Well, whatever they look like," Mary added, smiling but obviously very serious, "I just pray Sarah has the good sense not to take a bite out of that particular apple."

Mother and daughter exchanged glances, and then Sarah looked down at the path again. "Anyway," Katherine concluded, "Here's the admin building. Let's forget about this September for a while and focus on the next. Aunt Mary, keep your fingers crossed for us during the interviews."

"I'll do much better than that, dear. I'll pray."

ATLANTA As one of the Ob-Gyn head nurses, Rebecca had stayed late that Thursday night at the hospital to catch up on the paperwork that had piled up during her recent vacation in the Pacific Northwest with Bruce. It was early in the evening as she finally closed the door to her shared office and started down the hall, hoping to get home in time for the first pitch of the Braves game, when she ran into Dr. Harvey Thompson and an anesthesiologist, Dr. Priscilla Sawyer, heading for what appeared to be a delivery.

"Someone going to ruin your dinner?" Rebecca stopped and asked Harvey as they came together in the hall. They had been on staff together for years, though they were not particularly close.

"It shouldn't be too bad," he replied, slowing a bit but appearing to be in a hurry. "An abortion. No problem. We'll be done in an hour."

"Medical complications?"

"No, I don't think so," he said, continuing down the hall but turning back to finish. "She's apparently decided it's too much of a burden. We got a call from admitting. Gotta go. See ya."

And under the new health plan, she's 'gotta' get an abortion when she wants it, or we get cut off from federal funds, Rebecca thought, as she walked to the elevator. She was torn by two conflicting forces. Her feminist friends, as well as Bruce, argued, as did her brother, that an abortion was a woman's inalienable right. And William had signed an executive order allowing full-term abortions. "A fetus is a fetus," she could remember him saying during the campaign. "And an abortion one month is the same as an abortion any other month."

But her training and her heart rebelled against that notion. She recoiled at the single full-term abortion she had witnessed, called a "D and X." The doctor had used forceps to locate the baby's feet, then pulled the almost born baby out of the womb until just the head remained in the cervix. It was when he cut open the baby's neck and then sucked out the brain with a cannula that even Rebecca's veteran stomach had turned.

After the first few full-term abortions at the hospital, many of the nurses and other staff members had requested that they not be used for *any* abortions, including some staff who had previously worked on first trimester abortions but had apparently been affected by what they witnessed.

Soon after, however, federal guidelines were issued mandating that anyone on the staff at any federally funded hospital could not discriminate against any lawful procedure by refusing to participate, because costs would be increased by the restricted labor availability. So several of Rebecca's oldest friends had quit, and others relied on their relationship with the schedulers to swap duties when necessary.

All of these thoughts were swirling through Rebecca's mind again when the elevator doors opened and Sally Kramer walked out.

"Hello, Ms. Kramer." Rebecca smiled, obviously confused. "You were just here a few weeks ago, weren't you?"

Sally looked down and then started to walk toward the double doors that opened to the ward. "Yes, hi. Uh, Ms. Harrison, right? Yes. For an abortion. I was. You're right. Hey, I'm just visiting a friend tonight. Good to see you." And she went through the doors.

GUANTANAMO BAY, CUBA   The officers club at Guantanamo Bay Naval Station occupied a prominent location on a hill overlooking both the bay and the deep blue ocean beyond. A breeze always blew through its white tropical porches. Since Castro's death and Cuba's improving relationship with Washington, there was no longer the siege mentality that had existed for over forty years. Local musicians made the club a popular place for officers to relax away from their duties on the several ships that were always at the base for training.

The USS *Fortson* had been at Gitmo—as the base had always been called in navy jargon—for three long weeks. Gitmo's instructors and inspectors prided themselves on the realism and the seriousness of their exercises—and for good reason. Lives would depend on how well a ship's crew could react to an enemy's challenge or to a natural disaster. The standard routine for the *Fortson's* crew was to awaken the off-watch sections at five every morning and be underway by six. The heat of August only added to the difficulty of the seemingly impossible combination of tasks the staff planned for each day's training.

Everyone on board was initially apprehensive about how they would perform together under pressure. But what had seemed impossible on arrival became commonplace by the third week, as the crew learned to work together, despite the difficulties. Of course the *Fortson's* crew was aware they were a source of comment for the Gitmo staff.

The outside threat of the Gitmo staff had actually acted as a catalyst for the crew, who rose to the challenge under the leadership of the ship's veteran officers and petty officers. On their fifth day a fire control party that included a large group of the ship's homosexuals received the first perfect score of the training period, and everyone on the ship shared in the pride. The younger members of the crew had never experienced the satisfaction of a life-or-death job completed successfully by a highly trained team.

Then late one night Teri Slocum's division helped shoot down three incoming drone targets in rapid succession, earning the ship another well-deserved commendation from the inspectors. Hugh and Teri, sitting side by side at two radar screens in the darkened combat information center, shared a smile, a hand squeeze, and a look of mutual accomplishment as the third missile split its drone over fifty miles away.

By the end of the training period the *Fortson's* crew was handling each exercise as well or better than the other ships at the base, and the admiration of the instructors was infectious. Pride in a job well done spread throughout the whole crew. Age, color, and sex were forgotten as individuals learned to rely on one another and to respect each other's abilities, rather than focus on each other's differences.

Any ship's last night at Guantanamo Bay was always a celebration. Captain Robertson read the *Fortson's* excellent scores and a letter of commendation from the base commander to the crew over the ship's public address system late that afternoon. The pride in his voice was obvious. Then there was general liberty call for the first time in three weeks, and the only constraint was that each crew member had to be able to function at sea detail for departure the next morning.

As the officers left the wardroom after the Gitmo staff's positive assessment of the ship's preparedness, Hugh asked Teri in the passageway, "Are you going to the O Club tonight?"

She stopped, looked up at him, and smiled. "Sounds good. Is that an invitation?"

He hesitated for a moment and then smiled back. "Sure. Let's have dinner together. I don't think we'll start too many rumors after three weeks at Gitmo, a perfect missile shoot, and a 'date' with hundreds of fellow officers, all out in the open."

"I'll try to control myself," she said laughingly, "but it *has* been three weeks, and I *do* like older men."

"Then I'll both participate and chaperon at the same time, being so old. Let's leave in about an hour."

"Fine. Will you knock at my stateroom, or shall I knock at yours?"

"I'll try to navigate the fifty feet and the one ladder between us, even at my age," he replied. "But don't keep us out too late."

That had been four hours, several drinks, a great dinner, and many dances earlier. The mood among the *Fortson's* officers was one of joy and satisfaction. As the night, the long-standing fatigue, and the alcohol took their toll, most of them departed for some much needed rest. But Hugh and Teri seemed to gain energy from each other's presence, the electricity between them obvious to both, delicious in its forbiddeness. They danced and drank and laughed like two college students on a first date.

Wet with perspiration from their dancing and needing fresh air, they left the bar and walked out onto one of the club's terraced porches, cooled by the breeze off the ocean. They looked out at the beautiful view of lights and stars.

As they reached the low stone wall at the far end of the terrace, they were alone in the dark. Teri stood so close to Hugh he could see the shine in her eyes. "Thanks, Hugh," Teri said. "What a great evening. I needed to let my hair down. It hasn't been easy at this pace. I feel like maybe we finally proved our worth, after being on board four months."

"Yes, you and your division did a great job, Teri. Everyone's noticed what you've accomplished. You really came through. I think the captain and XO are rightly impressed with your abilities."

"Thanks. But a lot of it's because of your help and guidance. You've been a big help. And you're a pretty good man yourself."

They stood looking into each others eyes, smelling the perfume from the wildflowers on the hillside mixing with the clean scent of the ocean below. Knowing he shouldn't, but believing he could control it, Hugh reached out and took Teri in his arms. Without another word he bent forward and kissed her.

She seemed to hesitate for an instant, then kissed him back, deeply and passionately, moving her arms up and around his neck.

After a long moment they broke their kiss but hardly moved as they looked again into each other's eyes. "Hmm," she whispered, cocking her head slightly. "You do that well."

"You're not so bad yourself," he murmured, feeling a lightness in his head and his heart beginning to race. He kneaded the small of her back, and she melted into him. They kissed again, even longer this time.

When they finally stopped kissing, she placed her head on his shoulder. "Where is this going, Hugh?" she whispered.

"I…I don't know," he whispered in reply. But suddenly he had a mental image of the short distance between their two staterooms on the ship. *No one would ever know.*

"Hugh, you're one of the most wonderful men I've ever known," she said, with her head still on his shoulder. "I think you're great at what we do. You're kind but firm. A real leader. I… But you're married and have kids. There's no future for us together—just a mess."

Holding Teri close, he felt as if the temperature on the terrace had risen ten degrees. His heart was pounding, and he visualized the two of them in his stateroom. It was excruciating, but her words started his return to earth.

Still holding her, he took a deep breath. She felt so good. *No one would ever know…I bet she's incredible.* He breathed deeply again, then gently pushed her back and smiled.

"Teri…Teri. This isn't easy, is it? Okay. Let's talk weapons department operating procedures."

She shared his laugh, which helped ease the tension. Still looking into his eyes, she stepped back, took his hand, and leaned toward the main building. "Come on, Lieutenant Commander. I think we've both operated enough for one evening. Morning is going to come real early."

They made their way back into the officers club and said good night to the few friends who remained there. They stuck to small talk on the walk to the ship, but Hugh kept his arm around her.

Back at the ship they stopped at the door to her stateroom and Hugh joked, "My place or yours?"

"Neither one tonight, old man." She laughed. "I don't have a headache, but my fire control computer needs checking at six. Don't get lost on the way home."

As Hugh ascended the ladder to his stateroom, he believed he heard Tom Dobbs and a vaguely familiar voice behind the door of the flag cabin. *I guess everybody's celebrating tonight.* But he blocked that mental image with another thought of Teri.

Twenty minutes later, after a very cold shower, Hugh crawled into bed, torn by feelings of both excitement and guilt. He read his Bible, then put out the light. He hadn't kissed another woman since he and Jennifer began dating, and he felt terrible. But as he was dozing off, he reflected on what had happened, and it occurred to him: *She didn't say never...just not tonight.* The mental image of their hug and long kisses flashed back into his mind, like a bolt of lightning. He started to say his prayers, then felt oddly unworthy, and stopped.

WASHINGTON The next morning President Harrison and his chief domestic advisors were gathered in the Oval Office for their first legislative strategy session in six weeks. Seated at the head of the circle of chairs around the coffee table, William led off.

"I hope everyone has enjoyed a bit of vacation with your families and a rest from the D.C. grind. Now that it's late August I'm afraid it's back to work in earnest. Jerry, Ted, has there been any response to our compromise initiative?"

"Some, Mr. President, but not enough to assure passage of a program with the kinds of initiatives we've wanted," the chief of staff replied.

"William," the vice president injected, her arms folded in front of her, "you know I've disagreed with this new approach since you first proposed it a month ago. Sending our team out, hat in hand, to grovel before power-drunk old senators who long ago stopped knowing what's best for our people is just the *opposite* of what we should be doing! It didn't make sense. Now it's accomplished nothing, as I predicted, and I say we go back to hardball right now—immediately. Take away funding for whatever projects are controlled by our administration in their states. Find out who they're sleeping with. Blow some whistles. See how they like *that* approach to move them off their duffs!"

There was silence around the table as everyone weighed the harsh tone of the vice president's words. William noticed that Chris Wright and Robert Valdez were nodding while Patricia spoke, and he wondered what the others were thinking as all heads turned in his direction. He paused and looked calmly around the table before he spoke.

"Patricia, there's no reason to be so vindictive." He noted that her eyes widened. He turned first to Jerry Richardson, then to the others on his team. "We can only work with what we have." More curious looks. "It's frustrating, but maybe there's a reason for this. I don't know. But it looks like, despite our hard work and very best efforts, our legislative package just can't be passed." Silence greeted his assessment.

He continued. "I've thought a lot about it over the last month, while we've been probing for compron.ises during the recess, and I've concluded that rather than play hardball"—and he looked directly at the vice president—"we should be openly candid about it. Instead of huffing and puffing and pointing fingers, as both parties have done for decades, let's work with our opponents to get the best package we can, as close to our goals as they'll accept, and then try to pass it.

"But then let's go one step beyond. Quietly, sanely, without throwing rocks, let's spell out for the American people why this legislation is a compromise. Let's show them clearly what we want to accomplish and why—and then, with help from the opposition, show exactly why others disagree with us." As William spoke, Ted Braxton's mouth dropped open.

"We'll show the costs, the risks, and the potentially negative effects on the budget and the debt if our estimates are wrong. And we'll show the positive effects if our estimates are right. But I want this done calmly, with help from the other side, so that we present as honest and as balanced a view as possible, without political trappings.

"When that's been done—and we ought to be able to do it in about a month, don't you think?—I'll invite the leader of the opposition in the Senate to join me for a televised session in which the two of us will again explain these differences. I'll tell the American people that as long as they continue to elect people to Congress and the White House with such differing approaches to running the country, this kind of stalemate and compromise is inevitable. Hopefully Warner Watts will concur, and we can both say that we're proposing the best legislation we can, given our different philosophies."

No one moved or spoke, and William continued. "In short, our team will tell the American people the truth, and do the best we can with what we have. Then we'll get back to running the government as efficiently and cost-consciously as we can, and concentrate on foreign policy and the things that the executive branch is supposed to do. Oh, and we'll look forward to next November's elections, when maybe, if we treat them with intelligence and respect, the American people will elect more men and women who agree with us, if that's what they want."

There was silence around the circle of advisors. No one moved. William waited. Finally, Jerry Richardson leaned forward. "Do you really think that will work, Mr. President?"

"Do I think the truth will work?"

"Uh, yes. I guess so. And not defending our program."

William's eyes narrowed slightly. "I didn't say that we're not defending our program—just the opposite, really. But I said that from now on we're going to do it in a balanced, calm, and logical way, rising to higher ground by trying to show *both* sides of the issue, like leaders should, and by not treating the opposition as the enemy, but rather as the mostly intelligent, patriotic people they are."

That was too much for the vice president. "I can't believe this. What's happened to you? If you give them an inch, they'll destroy our programs completely. We'll accomplish nothing. We've got to fight with everything we've got if there's going to be change in this country. Go on national television with Warner Watts and throw in the towel? That's crazy. Our supporters will rightly feel betrayed."

All heads turned back to William. He again paused before speaking. "Patricia, it's hard to explain, but I guess I've had a change of heart. I've been reading and thinking—even praying, as hard as that may be for you all to believe—and I just think we've been going about this all wrong. Not just us—both parties. For years. The American people aren't stupid. They can think beyond thirty-second sound bites. Let's tell them the truth and give them our best projections, pro and con, then let them decide. Maybe our program won't be enacted until after the elections fourteen months from now. Or maybe never. But perhaps we can at least move the discussion on this and other issues back to an intelligent debate, instead of a media shouting match. And ultimately it's up to them to decide anyway, not us."

"But they elected us—" the vice president started to protest, when the president raised his hand and smiled.

"Yes, and I guess if I have to pull rank, they elected me president, Patricia. You and I can discuss strategies by ourselves later, if you want. But for now, that's how I want to approach the new legislative session. Jerry, I'd like you, Ted, and Robert to put your heads together with your staffs and write up what you think can really get through Congress, based on your recent conversations. When it's ready, we'll call in Warner, and Bill Phillips from the House, and go over this strategy with them. We'll give them a week or so to improve our portrayal of the two views and the compromise, and then hopefully we can go on television together and finally pass it. Please have our part ready in a week, if you can. Is that realistic?"

"Yes sir, Mr. President," the chief of staff nodded.

"Then that should do it for today," William concluded, rising from his chair. The others rose as well. The vice president turned and left the room. The others lingered and spoke among themselves as they slowly filed out, a new level of energy apparent from their conversations.

When they were alone, Jerry Richardson stood next to the president by the open door and said, "That was amazing. So simple and unexpected. I agree. It really might work. And it'll certainly be refreshing. How did you come to it?"

William thought and then said. "I guess I just followed your mother's advice."

As Jerry left and the president turned, Barbara Morton came up behind him. "Mr. President, this is for you. I've been holding it myself for almost an hour. It came in on our private fax line."

William could tell that his oldest friend in the office was agitated. He took the manilla folder from her, opened it, read the contents, and stopped smiling.

Greetings:

Enclosed is a picture of the warhead so that you may see the progress we have made with our modifications. Everything is on schedule. Unless you want millions of Americans to die unnecessarily, you must agree to our requests as soon as you receive them. We send you these messages so that you will believe us when we make our final communication to you. The fate of your people is in your hands, which is more of a chance than you have given us. We will communicate again soon.

The Council

She looked up at him questioningly, a note of real concern on her face. "What does that mean?" she whispered, "And is that a picture of a bomb?"

He glanced at the faxed picture as he felt the blood draining from his head and his breathing became short. "What? Uh, oh yes, it is, Barbara. But it'll be all right," he managed to smile. "We know about it, and everything's under control," he reassured her. "Please get Vince Harley at the Pentagon on the secure line for me. Thanks."

He turned and took the folder with its contents into the Oval Office.

HARRISBURG, PENNSYLVANIA Congressman Trent Patterson was home in his district that Friday. He resided in a small townhouse since his former wife had taken their home in the messy divorce. But this afternoon he was in his congressional office, finishing an interview with a local newspaper reporter, Mark Aiken.

"So you think the president's domestic program will be passed soon in Congress?" Aiken asked.

"I said it ought to...it really ought to. But we're stalled, no question about that. We hope to find ways to move forward in Congress right after the summer recess."

"Okay. Turning to foreign policy for a minute, have you received any feedback on your recent call for U.S. reconsideration of the U.N. resolutions on Israel?"

"Yes, some. Both pro and con."

"We ran a story on the strong negative reaction you suffered from the leaders in the Jewish community."

"I wouldn't use the term 'suffered.' And besides, that's the 'leaders.' We've also received many letters from Jewish people in the district who support our call for realism and peace. They know it's time to move on to some sort of settlement for everyone's sake. And remember, we only called for a reconsideration. Maybe it won't pass. But at least we should discuss it and not bury our heads in the sand."

"Were you surprised by the support you received in Congress?"

Patterson nodded, picked up his pencil, and wrote several names on the legal pad in front of him. "Frankly, I was amazed. I've, uh, just written down the names of—let's see—fifteen men and women in the House and Senate, some of them key leaders, who went out of their way to thank us for bringing this subject to light again and who told us they'd support the reconsideration. To be honest, I think we've uncovered an issue that will receive strong consideration in this coming year and significant support. I'm surprised and pleased that so many of my colleagues agreed with me on this important issue."

Faith in the transcendent, sovereign God was in the public philosophy—the American consensus. America's story opens with the first words of the Bible, "In the beginning God..." We are truthfully one nation "under God" and our institutions "presuppose a Divine Being," wrote Associate Justice William O. Douglas in 1966. Only a nation founded on theistic pre-suppositions would adopt a first amendment to ensure the free exercise of all religions or of none. The government would be neutral among the many denominations and no one church would become "the state church." But America and its institutions of government could not be neutral about God.

THE CAPITOL: A PICTORIAL HISTORY
U.S. GOVERNMENT PRINTING OFFICE, 1979

12

Thursday, September 27
One Month Later

WASHINGTON   "We're almost there, Jen," Hugh said encouragingly as he turned off the interstate and headed their minivan for the White House. "If the weather holds we should get in quite a bit of tennis this weekend."

"Hmm," Jennifer replied. She never failed to enjoy the sights of Washington, but her mood was subdued by Hugh's upcoming departure for six months in the Mediterranean at the end of the week.

Hugh had tried his best to be upbeat on their drive from Norfolk—in fact he had tried to be upbeat for the past several weeks, knowing that his deployment was coming. This would be the seventh major separation of their marriage, he had calculated, but they still didn't come any easier. Leaving Jennifer with their three children was tough for a week, but he knew that a six-month separation meant she would have to be both mother and father to them. He hoped that the church they had joined would mean a new network of friends and support for her.

But this departure carried a lot of extra emotional baggage for both of them, because Hugh would be leaving with Teri and the other women in the Missile Fire Control division. Jennifer was not pleased, and despite her almost daily resolve to ignore her feelings, they nevertheless surfaced regularly. For his part, Hugh had been on an emotional roller coaster since that night a month earlier at Gitmo. There had been no repetition—nothing close—while the ship was tied to the pier in Norfolk preparing to deploy. But Hugh couldn't put that night out of his mind. And that made him feel terribly guilty, because he often reminded himself that Jen was a perfect wife and a wonderful mother to their children. He knew that he loved her. But Teri was younger, somehow more dynamic, and, well, nearby. He spent more waking hours with Teri than he did with Jennifer.

The only way he could handle the situation was to put each woman in her own compartment in his mind. The problem was that as the countdown for their departure continued, the two women's presence merged. Jennifer's unhappiness and Teri's excitement whipped him between emotional extremes several times each day.

The long weekend in Washington had been his idea as a special getaway for the two of them. William and Carrie had volunteered the White House as a base, and they'd also promised to stay out of the younger couple's way if they wanted to be alone. The trip up that Thursday afternoon had been very quiet, punctuated occasionally by Hugh's attempts at conversation. Jennifer knew she was beginning her usual withdrawal routine, which she went through to fortify herself for his coming absence. She didn't like the result any more than he did, but she always felt powerless to stop it.

Twenty minutes later they pulled up to the White House gate and were immediately passed inside. Carrie greeted them at the entrance and showed them to their room in the private quarters on the upper floor of the oldest part of the building.

"What are your plans?" she asked.

Hugh looked at Jen. She smiled and replied, "Oh, we're pretty flexible. I'd like to go to the National Gallery. If the weather's pretty, we might take the boat ride down to Mount Vernon. We're up for whatever seems interesting."

"Well, we won't get in your way. Can you have dinner with us tonight? William expects to be finished about six-thirty. And then we've got a Bible study. In fact, our teacher will be dining with us."

"Bible study?" Hugh asked Carrie. "Since when have there been Bible studies in the Harrison White House?"

"Since about the middle of July. Over two months now. We've really been blessed with some great teachers. Michael Tate—you remember him from Easter—and some other pastors have designed a three-track course for us. We're studying the gospel through Jesus' sayings as one track; key concepts woven throughout the Bible as another; and then on the third track we're studying individual books of the Bible. So far we've done Genesis, Luke, and we're almost through Acts."

"And William studies with you?" Jennifer asked, obviously surprised.

"It was his idea," Carrie said cheerfully. "We try to get in six classes a week, two from each track. Either in the morning or at night, or both, depending on his schedule. When he went to South America in late July, he took audio cassettes. It's been wonderful. We've learned so much, and frankly we can't wait for each class. Michael has arranged for some gifted men and women of God to disciple us. And what we're learning seems so relevant to today. We can't believe we never took advantage of all God's power and wisdom sitting right on the shelf in the Bible."

The younger Harrisons were speechless. Finally Hugh asked, "William has felt God's power, you said? You mean he's been saved, like Mary?"

Carrie's smile broadened. "Yes. He gave up trying to run his life about three months ago, when our friends the Sullivans were here. You remember Richard and Janet? Well it's a long story, but the result is that both of us have turned our lives over to the Lord. William is a different man. Many people see it in him, but they don't know why or what to say. Sometimes it's really amusing."

"I was going to say this hasn't exactly been on the nightly news," Hugh reflected, "though I don't guess it's really any of their business. I'm just having trouble taking it all in. You know, ever since Jen and I prayed with Michael on Easter, we've been trying to read the Bible, and we've joined a church. But with our crazy schedules and the kids and everything, we haven't gotten too far with our faith. In fact, at least in my case," and Hugh looked at Jennifer, "it's been sort of dead lately."

"Well, then join us tonight, if you want. An African-American preacher from a local church is one of our teachers—he's covering biblical themes. His name is Joe Wood, and tonight we'll be continuing with God's concept of a just and lasting government. Now that's only a coincidence tonight. We've also studied all sorts of other things—what the Bible says about marriage, the family, debt, the Holy Spirit, and lots of other subjects. We just happen to be on government now."

"Sounds fine to me," Jennifer responded. "It'll probably be interesting." She turned to her husband. "What do you think, Hugh?"

He was delighted to see the first spark of positive interest from his wife in weeks. "Sure, let's do it. Do we need Bibles?"

"I'm sure we've got a couple of extras. Now you two relax and we'll see you for dinner between six-thirty and seven."

RALEIGH   That afternoon the Northside High School varsity cheerleading team finished its last practice before Friday night's upcoming football game. Sarah Prescott and her three best friends on the cheerleading squad, all seniors, sat together in a shady section of the bleachers, cooling off after running through all their cheers twice. Sarah, an accomplished tennis player for

her school, had enjoyed gymnastics as a young girl, and she thought of cheerleading as a way to have fun with her friends while also keeping herself in
shape.

But the girls' topic of discussion that afternoon was not sports. Two of
Sarah's friends, Jessica and Maria, were in the section of senior health which
opened the year with the human sexuality curriculum. Sarah and her other
friend, Becky, were scheduled for human sexuality during the second six-
week period. Jessica and Maria had both experienced their first sessions with
the virtual reality computer that afternoon, and the other two girls were very
curious.

"So what was it like?" asked Becky, sitting one row above Jessica and
Maria and retying her long blond hair into a ponytail as she talked.

Jessica blushed slightly and looked down, but then smiled. "It seemed
kind of stupid at first—real unnatural I guess. But then, I don't know, it sort
of got interesting, and I guess I liked it."

Maria, who had announced to her friends six months earlier that she
was no longer a virgin, turned on the seat to look up at Sarah and Becky. "I
thought it was *awesome*. You wouldn't believe how realistic it is! This
guy...well, you'll see. You get to choose between six different guys. I mean,"
she blushed slightly despite her obvious bravado, "it was almost better than
the real thing...maybe because I could completely control it. I'm not scheduled for another session until Tuesday, but I'm looking forward to it."

Sarah asked, "How about you, Jessica. When's your next time?"

"On Tuesday, too. I think it's some sort of group thing. It sounds creepy
and sort of gross to me, but I guess I'll try it."

"Sounds fantastic to me," Maria interjected, almost laughing.

Becky turned to Sarah. "I can't wait till our class gets its turn. Grant and
I still haven't gone all the way, and I'm like really curious to see what it's like.
How about you?"

Sarah looked down at her hands, which were clenched into fists in her
lap, then glanced at each of her friends in turn. "I don't think I'm going to
be trying it. Mom and Dad have said it's up to me, but I agree with them
that God intends sex to be between a husband and a wife in marriage, not
with a computer in health class."

"Oh, come on," said Maria, leaning back against the bleachers. "That's
absurd. Nobody believes that old stuff any more. And besides, this isn't real
sex—it's education! And fun, too. Anyway, isn't Ms. Bowers failing kids who
don't work with the computer?"

Jessica was more sympathetic and touched Sarah's knee. "Hey, I'm still a
virgin, too. But this isn't bad. I mean, I guess it's like having sex, but nobody
gets hurt, and that computer sure won't give you AIDS or a baby. So it's not
a big deal. You really ought to try it."

Sarah looked down again, bit her lower lip, and shook her head. "I know. One part of me wants to, but the other part believes it's wrong. I mean they're going to do group sex and lesbians and all that wacko stuff."

"Yeah, won't that be cool?" said Maria. "Hey, it's just a computer. We're not *really* doing any of it. It's just thirty minutes or so in a room with a computer. Does it say anywhere in the Bible that you can't have fun with a computer?" She laughed.

The other girls had known about Sarah's faith for several years. Sarah was a respected class leader and usually no one teased her about her strong beliefs. But Sarah's opinion on the computer seemed bizarre to her friends. Nevertheless, her pain was obvious as she wrestled with the competing desires within her.

"Hey, it's okay," Maria said sympathetically. "Do whatever you want. It's *your* body and *your* mind. But I don't think it's that big a deal. And I have it on good authority from Tyler that Matthew really enjoyed his session. In fact, he's signed up for extra tutoring," she said, trying to cheer up her friend with a joke.

Sarah smiled half-heartedly. "I'll see. I'll try to figure it out." She looked up and across the football field at nothing in particular. "I guess I've got about three weeks to make up my mind. Jessica, has anybody in your section not used the computer?"

Jessica shook her head. "No, I don't think so. I heard there are maybe like eight or ten in the whole senior class who might not, but, I mean, that's out of over two hundred. But no one in our section."

Sarah rose and said, "Well, it's all very interesting. Mom told me that the big trauma of her senior year was staying out until two in the morning after their prom. Here I am, thirty something years later, trying to figure out whether to make love to a computer and some group of electronic people in health class. God help my children, if I ever have any. I wonder what they'll be dealing with?"

ATLANTA Rebecca held the telephone to her ear and was relieved when it was answered. "Is this the home of Eunice Porter please?"

"Mmm." the voice was distant, almost like a whisper. "This is Eunice Porter."

"Hi, Ms. Porter. This is Rebecca Harrison from the hospital. Remember me?"

A short pause. "Sure, Ms. Harrison. The president's sister." Her voice was still a low monotone. "What can I do for you this afternoon? I'm about to leave for work."

Rebecca tried to sound friendly. "I just hadn't seen you in quite a while and I wondered how you're doing. Have you had your baby yet?"

There was another, longer pause. "Why are you asking that? I was in your hospital and had an abortion almost a month ago, so why are you calling me now?"

Rebecca was suddenly very embarrassed. "Oh, Ms. Porter, I didn't know. I must have missed it. I'm terribly sorry. This was just a personal call because I hadn't seen you, and I wondered what had happened. You had an abortion, huh? Gee, it was pretty late in the term for that."

Now there was a trace of hostility in Eunice's voice. "That's my business, not yours. Really, why are you calling me? Don't tell me it's just because you're curious about me. You can't be opposed to abortions with that brother of yours. So tell me what this is about."

"No, really, Ms. Porter, I was just calling you on my own time because I...I'm interested in you. I don't do this very often, but once in a while I get interested in someone, and today I was thinking about you and your ba—I mean, I just wanted to find out how you're doing. Really, that's all it is."

"Well, we're fine if having too many kids and not enough money is fine."

"How long were you in the hospital?"

"I came in late one afternoon, had the abortion, and left early the next morning. That's all."

"Well, I'm really sorry I missed you. We work staggered shifts, and I must have just not seen your file. Anyway, let me know if I can help you in any way."

"Sure, Ms. Harrison, I will. Now I've got to go or I'll be late for work. Goodbye, Ms. Harrison."

"Good-bye, Ms. Porter." Rebecca put down the phone.

WASHINGTON The two Harrison couples and Pastor Joe Wood were about halfway through their dinner that same Thursday evening. So far the conversation had involved catching up on the time since the four Harrisons had been together at the funeral and on the younger couple getting to know the gregarious but obviously very intelligent Pastor Wood.

William had introduced him as being "sold out" to the Lord. The man exuded a strength that simultaneously drew others to him because of his openness and created a respect that clearly signaled "Don't tread on me." A Vietnam veteran from a tough neighborhood in Chicago, Joe Wood had accepted the Lord thanks to a prison ministry thirty years before. Then he had gone on to become a minister, biblical scholar, and author.

"But the ministry I like best, and the one that gives me the most challenge is getting men back in the ball game," Wood said, as he passed the rolls to Jennifer.

"Really? What do you mean?" asked Hugh.

"I mean reaching out to men and teaching them how to let the Lord make them servant leaders in everything they do, but particularly in their families."

"And you focus primarily on men?" Jennifer asked.

"Yes. Women and children desperately need ministering to, and the best way I can minister to them is by bringing the love of Jesus Christ and the power of the Holy Spirit into their men's lives, so those men can become the husbands and fathers God intended them to be."

The four Harrisons were silent, struck by the simple truth of Wood's statement. Finally Jennifer said, "Excuse me for asking in this way, and I hope you don't mind—is most of your ministry in the black community?"

Wood smiled broadly. He pointed a forkfull of mashed potatoes at the president and said, "Until my friend Michael Tate got me this high-paying job working strange hours in the White House, I can't say I'd ever been quite this far up the ladder. But I divide my time pretty much between corporate boardrooms and the streets. You see, this isn't a black problem or a white problem. It's a problem almost *all* men have—of pushing God, the One who created us and told us how to live, completely out of our lives.

"We've got black men having trophy children without marriage and white men having consecutive children through serial marriages, and the net result is the same: a generation of children growing up with no fathers to train or to teach them. So the cycle repeats itself and gets worse and worse."

Wood ate the mashed potatoes. Then he continued, "If you want to talk about black and white, I'll do it in a different context. Take a young man who's never known a loving father as the spiritual head of his household, and that young man has only one chance. It's black or white; there are no shades of gray. His one chance is to learn about our common Father and to feel *his* presence and *his* power. That's it. One chance. Or he's going to repeat the cycle in some way. Government programs and psychologists can work on his mind and his motivations. But the only way to really change that young man is in *his heart*, and only the Lord can do that."

"You've obviously seen this power," Hugh said. It was not a question, but a statement.

Wood gave a hearty laugh. "That power changed me from a two-bit hoodlum headed to an early death into someone so thirsty for knowledge that I ultimately earned a Ph.D. And I've been privileged to watch that same power change hundreds of other people: blacks, whites, men, women, addicts, corporate presidents, homosexuals, prostitutes—you name it, I've seen God do it."

Hugh's earnestness was obvious as he said, "Jennifer and I have heard about this power, Joe. We listened to Michael's talk on Easter Sunday, and we prayed for Christ to come into our lives. We've been trying to read the

Bible, and we've joined a church. But I can't say we've felt this power. I'm even beginning to question whether it's real."

"Oh, it's real. Better to say *he* is real. The Holy Spirit, the third person of the trinity of God. If you've really repented and surrendered your life to Jesus, the potential for that power is already inside you. But the Bible says if you're not feeling the power, you may be grieving the Spirit or quenching his presence in your life through your actions. Are you really trying to walk with him? Are there sins in your past or present that are keeping you from a relationship with God?"

Hugh felt a shiver as he replayed the evening at Guantanamo Bay in his mind. Joe continued, "God's power can work through *us*, but only when we yield to his Spirit and constantly submit to his will through prayer. Sometimes salvation and the infilling of God's Spirit happen simultaneously. But other times a believer has to begin his Christian walk, like your brother is doing, and the infilling of the Spirit comes through that process. Both are right. Both happen all the time. It's the same power, and it's just as real."

As the two couples considered Joe's words, Carrie smiled and looked at her in-laws. "And this is just our dinner. Wait till we get to Joe's teaching!"

After dinner everyone moved to the living room. The two couples sat on adjoining sofas, and Joe Wood faced them in an antique chair with several pages of notes spread out on the coffee table in front of him. Everyone had a Bible. Joe led with prayer.

Then he began, "We studied earlier how God established first the family, then the church, and finally government as the three foundations on which every society is built. Of course when you take out one or two of those foundations, the society, like a house, falls. But that's something we'll look at in a few weeks, after we get through the basics. For now we want to study the characteristics of a good and proper government, as he has directed in his Word.

"Turn first to Deuteronomy 17 in which Moses describes how kings, or leaders, are to conduct themselves. Now it's crucial to remember that Moses wrote this passage *four hundred years* before the Israelites ever even had a king! The Holy Spirit inspired him to give them specific instructions on a form of government that they would not even consider having for four hundred years. And look at what he told them:

> The king must not acquire great numbers of horses for himself...He must not take many wives, or his heart will be led astray. He must not accumulate large amounts of silver and gold.
>
> When he takes the throne of his kingdom, he is to write for himself on a scroll a copy of this law. It is to be with him, and he is to read it all the days of his life so that he may learn to revere the LORD his God and follow carefully all the words of this law and

these decrees and not consider himself better than his brothers and turn from the law to the right or to the left.

"God is basically saying that a ruler should not increase his own personal wealth, nor take pride in his power, nor become involved in a lot of emotional entanglements. But, and here's the key point, he should *himself* study God's laws so that he *hears* and *follows* God's will.

"And look what happens to David's wise son Solomon almost five hundred years later when he disobeys Moses' directions, in 1 Kings 11:

> He had seven hundred wives of royal birth and three hundred concubines.... His heart was not fully devoted to the LORD his God, as the heart of David his father had been...The LORD became angry with Solomon because his heart had turned away from the LORD.

"God takes the throne of Israel from Solomon's son. So we see that our choices *do* have the consequences which God has laid down, and also that God acts across generations to fulfill his purposes."

Hugh looked up from reading 1 Kings. "This is really interesting. I had no idea the Bible interacted like this across so many years and gave advice which seems to be so relevant today."

William nodded. "I guess it's hard to have God in our hearts when he's hardly known to our minds. And isn't it ironic that in our society, so full of all types of communication, there is almost never even the slightest communication about God? Everyone runs and hides at the merest mention of him, for fear of offending someone or of being sued. I mean God, the Creator of the universe, must really appreciate our bravery where he's concerned!"

Hugh looked at his older brother. "And you're doing studies like this several times a week?"

William nodded. "As you can see, Hugh, it's an incredible blessing for Carrie and me to have men like Joe and Michael teaching us."

"I'll say. Too bad you aren't taping it for the rest of us."

Jennifer added, "Maybe your teachers could put together a curriculum when you finish and call it 'What God has been teaching the president.'"

William smiled. "From my own reading, Jen, I imagine that just two generations ago your proposal would have seemed completely natural and probably accepted with great interest. But today the media would have a field day. All I'm trying to do is deepen my personal faith and learn what the founders of our nation took for granted: that every president and most citizens would simply always know these truths."

Jennifer suddenly turned to her husband. "Hugh, we forgot to tell

William and Carrie about that phone call from the network. That White House reporter, Leslie Sloane, wants to interview us next week, before Hugh leaves for the Mediterranean."

"That's right," Hugh said. "Do you have any idea why she wants to talk with us?"

William shook his head and smiled. "Leslie is putting together a program about our extended family. She's already interviewed Rebecca."

"If we do the interview next week," Hugh said, "should we mention your studies with Joe, Michael, and the other Bible scholars?"

William looked at Carrie and then at Joe. "We're not hiding this. We just haven't particularly broadcast it, either. We've still got a lot to learn. But I'm not sure the press would understand."

Carrie turned to Hugh and Jennifer. "Just speak the truth as the Lord leads you, but don't go out of your way to mention it. We're trying to study in peace, and I'm not sure we'd have much peace if the press started following our teachers around. But Ms. Sloane seems very nice. I'm sure you'll enjoy the experience."

"And now, Joe, back to you, if that's all right," William said.

"By all means," Hugh added. "This is fascinating."

"All right, then," Wood picked up his Bible again. "Let's look briefly at Isaiah 33:22, and you'll see where the founders got the concept for the three branches of our government."

RALEIGH   The Northside High School Wildcats defeated the South Park Patriots at Friday night's football game, so the dance afterward in the school gym was a victorious celebration. Matthew Thompson played tight end and caught the winning touchdown pass late in the fourth quarter. Thirty minutes later, after a shower, he was enjoying the dance with Sarah Prescott. Matthew and Sarah had begun dating in the middle of their junior year. Tall and athletically built, Matthew was also a good student. Although he did not attend Sarah's church, she knew he had gone to church regularly with his parents for most of his life.

After an hour of yelling to each other over the loud music, Matthew told Sarah at the end of a slow dance, "I'm starved. Let's go get a pizza."

Matthew drove them over to the Pizza Factory in a shopping center near their school, where they shared a medium pizza with everything, locally known as the Kitchen Sink.

The two major topics for discussion in their class late that September were college applications and the computer. Since Matthew wanted to be an engineer, he was applying to North Carolina State and Georgia Tech. Sarah, who was applying to the University of North Carolina at Chapel Hill with her cousin Katherine, obviously hoped that Matthew would remain nearby.

As they were finishing their pizza, Matthew said, "You really ought to check out that computer, Sarah. It's something else."

She looked down and blushed slightly. She managed a smile and said, "I heard you sort of liked it."

"It's really, like, unbelievable, to tell you the truth."

"Are you really going to take extra afternoon tutoring?" she asked, and they both laughed.

"No, but seriously, Sarah, you ought to try it when your section has the chance. I think it'll really get you in touch with your emotions."

She looked a little surprised. "I think I'm in pretty good touch with my emotions now, thanks."

He shrugged and took a bite from the last slice. "Maybe, but Ms. Bowers is explaining love to us and showing us how to express our feelings."

"Ms. Bowers is explaining love? In health class?"

"Yeah. It's really good. She's cool. You'll see, if you give it a chance."

Twenty minutes later they were parked in a dark cul-de-sac near Sarah's home.

Because she really liked Matthew, she found it perfectly natural to be alone with him and to share his deep and passionate kisses. After a few minutes, however, it was obvious that he was interested in more than kissing.

"Matthew, please, stop," she said, moving his hand.

"Oh, Sarah, I love you so much," he whispered, putting his hand on her cheek. "This is so right. So natural. We're supposed to express our feelings as they come."

"Matthew, I like you a lot. Maybe I even love you. But this isn't right. You know God says to wait."

"I'm not thinking too much about God right now," he said softly against her neck. "Besides, that was written for ancient people. This is today. Look at what we've got today that they never dreamed of—look at that awesome computer. Sarah, I've learned through that computer that love and sex are good and natural. And I love you so much. Please, let's share our love together, as God meant two humans to do."

"Matthew, don't make it any harder for me than it already is. I get turned on, too. But"—her voice cracked as she fought back tears—"please don't push me now. I feel like I'm under so much pressure from everyone about that stupid computer and about sex. And besides, it's almost twelve-thirty. So please, can we just go?"

He pulled back, and even in the dim light of the radio, he could see the strained emotions on her face. "Sure, okay, Sarah. I know it's difficult." He turned the key in the ignition, then looked at her and smiled, "But you really ought to look at that computer. I think it would really help you."

Straightening her skirt and avoiding his look, she whispered, "We'll see. But now I just want to go home."

WASHINGTON It was mid-Sunday afternoon, and William and Hugh were getting dressed in the same basement locker room where William had given his life to the Lord three months earlier. The two couples had finished the weekend with a doubles tennis match after church, and Hugh and Jennifer would be driving home to Norfolk shortly.

"Thanks, big brother, for a great weekend. I always try to do something special with Jen right before I leave on one of these deployments, but this trip to D.C. we'll both always remember. I can't believe your schedule. Thanks for the time you spent with us."

"Hey, you're defending the country. It's the least we can do for a sailor."

Hugh laughed, then said, "Seriously, thanks for letting us join you and Carrie for your Bible studies. Joe Wood is unbelievable, and Robert Ludwig's tying together all the events in the Book of Acts on Saturday morning was really interesting. You're one lucky guy to have teachers like that five or six times a week."

"I know, Hugh," William said, buttoning his shirt. "I often think about why I'm here, and how I got here, and all that's happened. It sort of blows my mind, to be honest."

"So what's the answer to all that? Has this teaching made a difference? Do you feel any different about anything?"

"That's really the great question, Hugh. I've got fifty years of one set of tapes playing inside me, programmed by Mom and Dad and college and law school and many years of experience. So far some of it squares with what the Bible says, but some of it doesn't. I do believe God's power can change anyone, particularly me. He already has in several ways. But sometimes it's tough to just throw out what has seemed logical for all that time—and particularly before I understand how it all fits together, which I must admit is starting to happen."

"I know. It's tough to change habits."

William nodded. "Particularly where so much is at stake. I'm beginning to see where some of my strongest beliefs may be dead wrong—the worst course for our country. And what's really helped me, besides the Bible and prayer and these courses, is the writings of the men who founded this country. They seemed to have it right, and I'm trying to figure out exactly what they believed. But if and when I change my beliefs and act on them, I could be affecting millions of people. So I've got to be *really* sure that anything I propose to change is truly God's will. Because the fallout could be very serious, and I have to know I'm right."

"I guess I hadn't really thought about that. But I see your point. I'm still dealing with your social experiment in the navy, remember. That certainly has affected a lot of people."

"That's one I've thought and prayed and studied about a lot. Hugh, I'm still trying to figure out what's right. I think I know, but before I say anything, even to you, I want to be very certain that I'm right. So stick with the situation for now and try to make the best of it, if you can."

Hugh finished tying his shoes and rose from the bench. "I am. It's all sort of mellowed, I guess. We don't think about it too much, except on Something Awareness Week. But I have to tell you, William, it just doesn't feel right, deep inside. There's this underlying tension—maybe a sexual tension, I don't know. I mean the homosexuals did great at Gitmo, and the women did, too, though I still worry about some of them having the simple physical strength they may need in a real emergency. But I'm told it's not politically correct to ask those sorts of basic questions."

The two men walked over to the windows and looked out at the beautiful afternoon with a touch of fall in the air. "Anyway," Hugh continued, "assuming all that's no problem, there's still the simple issue that we're different. Like those tapes inside us you were just talking about. Men, women, homosexuals, lesbians—there's just this tension on the ship that was never there before. And everyone is afraid of saying something for fear of offending someone else. When did everyone lose their sense of humor, by the way?"

"So what's your bottom line opinion on how it's working out with men and women on a combat ship?" William asked.

"As far as I can see, women are just as capable as men, except for physical strength, like I said. I think all the services changed their physical standards, especially for upper body strength, when women couldn't meet the old ones. Some people are asking if the old standards weren't important, why did we have them?

"But, again, the women on our ship are fine. Too fine, in some ways. I mean, William, frankly, I'm going to leave Jen on Friday and go spend six months, eighteen hours a day, with a young woman who works for me who's really attractive."

William turned toward his younger brother, real concern on his face, as if his forward-thinking policy was not supposed to cause basic problems like this. "I didn't know that."

"*Please* don't say anything to Carrie, or to Jen. It'll be all right, I think. But it isn't easy, to be honest. And then you've got the lesbians and homosexuals, and everyone's sort of skittish about what might happen with them after a few months."

"You know I still haven't made up my mind there, but Michael Tate showed me the many passages in the Bible about homosexual behavior, so I guess I'm being spoken to. Then Michael said something I found interesting about homosexuals."

"What's that? I could use some help in that department in the coming months."

"He said we have to hate the sin but love the sinner. We should never legislate in favor of immorality, but we also have to remember that all of us are equally sinners before God. Christ told the adulterous woman to sin no more, and he meant it; but he told her accusers that only a sinless person should stone her. Then Michael said something that really struck me: homosexuals are not the enemy—they're the victims. And that of course led me to the question: who exactly is the enemy, and what is he trying to do to us?"

"Does Michael mean evil? As in Satan?"

"I think so. We're going to study evil and spiritual warfare next week."

"So that's it, gentlemen," the president concluded at the next morning's early breakfast meeting in the Cabinet Room. "Have we accurately summarized your concerns with our programs?"

Warner Watts and Bill Phillips, the congressional leaders of the opposition party, exchanged glances, uncertain of what to say. The others around the table, Patricia Barton-North, Jerry Richardson, Ted Braxton, and Robert Valdez, waited with the president. Finally Senator Watts responded tentatively, "We'll of course have to study the whole presentation in more detail, but it does seem to capture the main points of our differences pretty accurately."

"Will you join me, then, to explain that to the American people?" the president asked for a second time.

"You mean the two of us, together, in prime-time television, presenting our different programs?" Watts asked.

"Yes. As quietly and as calmly as we can. You, of course, can make your own presentation package, and we'll work together beforehand to create a clear explanation of the differences, the costs, and the benefits. I won't attack you or your party personally, and I'd hope you'd do the same. The idea is to give our people a clear understanding of the choices and the trade-offs involved and then let them decide, either by communicating with us or, ultimately, by electing representatives who are clearly for one course or the other."

"Those are pretty high stakes," Phillips interjected, coming to the aid of his colleague.

"What do you mean?" William asked.

"Well, frankly, I'm not sure it'll work in the first place. I don't know if the average American can understand all of this, no matter how simple you make it. And I don't see how it can really be impartial—one side will inevitably be favored. And you're asking people to vote for a program by electing representatives who agree with them. That's putting all our jobs on the line for a domestic package. I'm not sure I'm prepared to do that. The side that loses will lose a lot of experienced faces on the Hill."

The words that Joe Wood had read from Deuteronomy flashed into William's mind: *and not consider himself better than his brothers.* "Let me see if I understand. Our programs are too complex to explain to the American people, who probably wouldn't understand, anyway, like we do." His pointed words were in sharp contrast to his quiet appearance. "And if they did understand, our own job security is more important than this legislation. Warner, is that what Bill just said?"

Senator Watts looked down at his hands on the table and then back at the president. "I think your wording is a little extreme, Mr. President, but that's close, and I think he's right. How can we be sure this approach will work? It might backfire and cause a disaster."

"Telling the truth in a calm and intelligent manner, trying to show all sides of an issue, so that people will truly understand and can make an informed decision, might backfire?" A note of exasperation crept into William's voice, despite his earlier resolve to remain calm. He noticed out of the corner of his eye that the vice president was quietly smiling.

"Yes," Phillips said. "You never know how things are really going to appear on television. One side might lose lots of votes because someone wears a clashing tie, appears to be nervous, or just doesn't come across well on TV. It's too important to leave to that sort of chance."

"Well, we'll tape it ahead of time. Or forget television, and we'll make a presentation to the press and let them ask questions. We'll hand out our charts and agree on what those should say beforehand. I just want to get the facts and choices out in a clear and understandable way."

"We're all for clarity," Watts added, "but I agree with Bill that it might not be possible in this case. However, we'll definitely think about it and give you a response within thirty days."

"Thirty days? Warner, I'd hoped we could make our presentations within two weeks—that's why we prepared all the information you see here. You need thirty days just to consider it?"

"Yes, I think we do. It's not as simple as you make it sound. There's a lot at stake. Bill brought up some important points. But we'll talk about it and let you know as soon as we can."

He knew he was blocked, but for some reason felt neither as bad nor as angry as he had in the past. William found himself smiling. "All right, that's fine. Take all the time you need. The Lord willing, we'll still be here. Now if you'll excuse us, we've got some other things to go over."

The two leaders from the opposite side of the aisle rose and shook hands with the president's advisors and with the vice president. "Thank you, Mr. President," Watts said, as they left. "We appreciate the opportunity to work with you."

After they left, Jerry Richardson angrily summarized with words William himself would have used only months before. "Isn't that great? We can't pass either their program or ours because no one has a majority; we can't explain something complex to people who are educated by our own system; and we can't risk either side gaining a majority because we're not certain who will win! Am I wrong, or is gridlock to be the constant American government status quo from now on?"

The vice president leaned forward and fixed her gaze on the president. "I *told* you this wouldn't work, and I'm glad they're going to torpedo it, though not for the same reasons. We've got *our* supporters and *our* program to look out for! Those are too important to chance to some television debate or election, for heaven's sake." She tapped the top of the table with her index finger. "We clearly know what's best for this country. We've done all the studies. We know we're right. We're in office now. We can't waste time or risk losing our chance just because people might vote against us. The majority of people don't have a clue! *We* do. Now in the name of all that we've worked for, stop fiddling around with these crazy ideas, and let's get back to playing hard ball and getting our programs passed. Now!"

William let her finish and noticed that Robert Valdez was again nodding slightly as she spoke. He realized that no one had talked to him during their first nine months in office like his own vice president had just done, but he was surprised to realize that he wasn't angry at all, with her or with their political opponents. It was as if he had a new peace; he didn't know exactly what they should do, but he knew that becoming angry over these issues would not help.

"Patricia, I respect your opinion on this, but I disagree completely. We saw what our first six months were like. It's occurred to me, sitting here today, that our nation is so divided into self-centered interest groups that we've lost the connecting threads that held us all together over our country's first two hundred years. I have to agree with Jerry. The only governmental action our myriad divisions will now allow is stalemate, because to take *any* action implies stepping in some small way on someone's sacredly defended turf. So gridlock is the natural result of our obstinate divisions; we here in Washington are just the closest to it, but it's caused by everyone's intransigence across the nation.

"So it seems to me, Patricia," the president continued, "that you can talk about 'hard ball' all you want, but it will never work, short of outright blackmail, which I won't allow. We're not just two political parties in gridlock. Every race, sex, ethnic group, generation, religion, city—almost every block—has its own interest group with a platform of wants and complaints imbedded in stone, just waiting for someone to violate them in some way, any way. Everyone is focused on 'me,' and the result is that there is very little 'we.' So nothing can change."

"Mr. President," Patricia Barton-North said, staring intently at him, *"you've* changed. You've lost the fight you used to have. What's happened to you? Oh, you still support the same programs, but your methods have changed completely. You're too philosophical. We've got a *war* to win, and we need you to be a strong leader for all that we believe in."

"And what *do* we believe in, Patricia?"

"Why, our programs, of course. Our platform. Progress. What we ran on. Our promises to our constituents. We can't let them down. We've got to fight."

"Patricia, you just proved better than I could exactly what Jerry and I have been saying. *Everyone* in the nation feels like that, only from different persuasions. To everyone it's a life or death struggle with no compromise, and every supposed transgression is inflamed by the trigger-happy press. Everyone's looking for someone else to blame, either in the courts or on television. Everyone is a victim. We all want a government program to fix our particular problems. I still think some programs can help, but no one looks beyond the programs, which gain a life of their own, to the fundamental principles. What if we're wrong on some of our details? Didn't we exaggerate our program needs slightly in the beginning to gain maneuvering room? But now even those exaggerations are cast in stone. We won't budge, and don't they do the same thing?"

Patricia crossed her arms and glared at William. "See, there you go again. I'm tired of arguing with a brick wall. You've got to lead us!"

There was a long pause as all eyes focused on the president of the United States. He finally replied in a calm and almost cheerful voice, "I will. I am. But I want to lead by the strength of our ideas, the correctness of our hearts, and our willingness to listen and to serve others. I want the American people to see those qualities in us, so they'll think we're worthy to be their leaders and choose to follow us."

The vice president rose to leave, frustration clearly on her face. "Oh come on. You've been at this twenty-five years. You know this isn't about the correctness of our hearts, whatever that means. It's about *power.* Pure and simple. Figuring ways to make people do what we know they should do for their own good. Please shake off whatever's got a hold of you and get back in the game. I'm sorry, but I've got another meeting to go to." She walked toward the door.

Robert Valdez rose as well. "I'm sorry, but I do, too."

William looked at both of them. "That's fine. Just remember that this is a team, and I'm both the coach and the quarterback. Rightly or wrongly, we're playing the game my way, and for now I'm convinced the old ways won't work. We're going to try this new approach, with or without the opposition on the program with us. The American people deserve better than they've had for the past thirty years, and we're going to raise the level from a shouting match to a debate."

The vice president stood with her hand on the door, her anger obvious. "All right, coach. But your game plan won't work."

The president, still seated, was amazed by his own calmness. From somewhere he found himself saying, "The old ways haven't worked, either. Have faith, Patricia. Anything is possible."

She looked at him with a strange expression, turned, and left, followed by the secretary of the treasury.

When they were gone, William surveyed the remaining two members of his team. They were obviously confounded by the unusual exchange. He smiled. "We've got a lot to do, but we've made a good start with what our team has already put together here. I want to go ahead with a televised presentation, with Warner's party or without it. If necessary, we'll make their argument for them. Anyway, let's try to be on the air in about three weeks. I'll leave you two to figure out the best timing. And, thanks. We're still on the same course as when we started, but I'm just tired of playing to the lowest common denominator. If we don't raise the level, who will?"

With that, William rose and left the Cabinet Room.

Jerry Richardson and Ted Braxton sat in silence for a few moments. Finally Ted said, "What's happened to the president? He's really trying something very different. And he didn't even raise his voice when Patricia blasted him—and her behavior was pretty inappropriate. She *is* right on one thing, though: he's a different person."

"I wonder what it is," Jerry said.

The Christian religion is the most important and one of the first things in which all children, under a free government, ought to be instructed.... No truth is more evident...than that the Christian religion must be the basis of any government intended to secure the rights and privileges of a free people.

NOAH WEBSTER

13

Tuesday, October 16
Three Weeks Later

RALEIGH Sarah Prescott had agonized for weeks over what to do. She had listened to her friends and her parents and prayed when she remembered to. The previous week their section had begun the human sexuality curriculum, and two days ago her friend Becky had spent her first turn with the virtual reality computer. Like Jessica, she reported that at first she had felt silly. But then she became involved in the experience and wound up really liking it. "You ought to try it. It's really amazing. In fact it was awesome," Becky had summarized that afternoon. "I can't wait till next time. You ought to go ahead, Sarah. It won't bite! And it really opened my eyes. Sex is kind of cool."

Sarah's agony had been increased by Becky's report, added to all the others, plus Matthew's continued praise for what he was experiencing on the computer. He told her it was preparing him for "real life."

After an almost sleepless night, Sarah finally made a decision. This Tuesday morning in mid-October she stood outside Ms. Bowers's office door and knocked, her stomach churning. Soon she was seated next to the health instructor's desk while her teacher finished grading an exam.

"Now, Sarah, what can I do for you?" she asked, marking the exam and moving it to a small stack on the edge of her desk.

Looking down at the notebook in her lap, Sarah haltingly said, "I...I'd like to go ahead and try one computer session. It sounds like it's okay, and I guess I can learn from it. So please schedule me for one with my section. And I'll decide about others after that. Is that all right"

Ms. Bowers smiled and said soothingly, "Of course, Sarah. I'm so glad you've made this decision. I'm sure it's the right thing to do. And you're correct—you will learn a lot. I'll arrange for a session later this week. By the way, what do your parents think?"

"They...I...they don't really know about my decision, though they told me it was mine to make. I just want to try it once, so I'll know what it's really like. Then I can make a better final decision. That seems like the most mature approach to me. So I'd just as soon not tell them until I try it and can tell them my final decision."

Ms. Bowers reached out and put her hand on Sarah's forearm. "Of course. That's fine. It'll be our secret until you finally decide. You're very courageous, and I respect the process you've been through. It seems mature and sensible to me. And, again, I know you'll learn a lot from the computer. It's really well done and doesn't cause any problems at all, while teaching you so much."

Sarah rose. "Thank you, Ms. Bowers. I hope so. I'm just glad to be done with this. It's been driving me crazy."

"I'm glad for you. I'll let you know your schedule during class this afternoon."

NEW YORK Ryan stood and smiled when Leslie walked into his office. By moving away from the door, they were able to share a kiss without others in the large bullpen area outside his office seeing them.

"I'm so glad to see you," he whispered, holding her.

"Me too. Last weekend was awful. Did you have to go to Brussels?"

"NATO accepting Russia as a full member was big news, and I needed to be there. But this weekend will be different, I promise."

They broke their hug and Ryan sat down behind his desk, while Leslie sat in a chair across from him. "Why don't you come down to Washington on Thursday to cover the president's talk and then just stay?" she asked. "Can't you be 'on assignment' on Friday night—in my apartment? Valerie can handle the broadcast that night by herself."

He smiled. "Maybe. We'll see. It sounds great. What should I cover on this assignment?"

"Me."

He laughed. "I'll try. They owe me a couple of days off. Listen, what's the president going to talk about?"

"Something about economics and their stalled domestic program, I think. I've never seen so much security around a speech—almost no one is talking. But one of the vice president's press aides told me it's going to be some sort of different approach than before. She was vague and didn't sound too keen. If it's so mysterious, you really need to come to Washington to help cover it."

"Okay. I get the message. Too bad you can't stay over tonight after the meetings. Anyway, how are your interviews with the president's family going?"

She shifted in her chair. "Fine. We've done all three siblings, and we've begun editing them into a piece that should play pretty well about his childhood. We've got lots of pictures of his parents, many with him as well, and I think the timing is perfect to create a lot of sympathetic feelings over their deaths. You can really see where William got a lot of his good ideas, particularly from his mother. We've got someone trying to run down as many letters and articles as we can—she wrote quite a few. She was apparently never wanting for an opinion!"

"They were nice people. I met them once. What a tragedy they were murdered."

"Yes, it was."

"What are the president's siblings like?" Ryan asked.

"One of his two sisters and his brother are normal enough. Sort of all-American, though a little diverse in their views."

"What do you mean?"

"Well, the younger sister, Rebecca, has been a nurse for so long she doesn't have many views outside her profession, which is fine. Her boyfriend, Bruce, has been through a lot, and he's really got his act together. He thinks a lot of the president, by the way. He figures William is the only hope for changing the country for the better. He said he and the president had shared several long talks on important issues, and the president is 'right on.'"

"Did you get that on tape?"

"Of course. I figure it'll help the president with the younger crowd—my age, you know," she said teasingly.

"Okay, okay." He raised his hand in mock surrender. "What about the other two?"

"The brother, interestingly enough, is on one of the ships with the crew experiments. He seems a bit conservative, actually. He wouldn't say much, maybe because they were leaving three days later for a deployment. But I get the feeling he's not crazy about that particular part of his brother's package. Anyway, he and his wife seem like a perfectly normal navy family."

"And the older sister?"

"Now there's the wacko. Mary, and her husband, Graham. If you can believe it, they're Christian fundamentalists!" She laughed. "Right in the president's own family. They tried to hide it, I think, at the first of the interview. But I could tell—they said things like 'we're blessed' and 'God willing.' Just like I used to hear at home all the time. So I asked them pointblank what they thought about the president's abortion policy, and of course it came out. So anti-women! I couldn't believe it. How could William and Mary have grown up in the same family, especially with good parents like they had?"

"It's hard to understand," Ryan agreed. "How will you handle them on the report?"

"Oh, I figure we'll put in something about them having a strong faith, just to pick up a little support in that dying corner of the universe, and then focus on their wholesome family and their good values. We'll use as little of their actual speaking as we can, though it may show inclusive tolerance for all sorts of views to mention in passing that they're Christians. But mostly I think we'll concentrate on the other two and on the president's childhood. It should be a good piece, and should really help him, frankly."

"Good. It sounds like he may need it. We've had some pretty interesting segments in the news about the men who're opposing the president's programs. Some of them are pretty bizarre old guys. One has had five wives; another had a state road built to his mountain home—seventeen miles at taxpayers' expense—when he was governor. Anyway, we should be making a pretty good platform of credibility for the president to restart his domestic program before the end of the year. I hope he's noticing."

"I think he is. At least his administration is. The vice president's press aide was very appreciative of those news stories. She said they might even have some more leads for us in the future."

"Great. It's wonderful what a free press can accomplish for the good of the people!"

GOLFE JUAN, FRANCE On Wednesday afternoon the USS *Fortson* anchored off the small French port of Golfe Juan, ten miles east of Cannes. There had been little rest for the crew since their departure from Norfolk. Other than a twenty-four hour stop to check into the Mediterranean command at a base near Cadiz, Spain, the ship had been at sea continuously.

Timing brought them to this part of the world just as Russia officially joined NATO. To commemorate the event, the *Fortson* and the other ships in the task group surrounding the aircraft carrier USS *Eisenhower* immediately launched into joint operations with a smaller Russian task group and their carrier the *Pushkin*. For the crew of the *Fortson*, who were just relearning close order formations with allied ships and planes, the challenge of operating with the Russians kept everyone in the operations and weapons departments on their toes twenty-four hours a day for ten days. Finally they were due some rest.

The task group had split up, each ship going to a different port to rest until they formed again on Monday afternoon south of Marseilles. The crew of Hugh's ship considered themselves lucky to draw Golfe Juan, even if they did have to anchor out and run small boats to the fleet landing, instead of tying up at a pier, which was usually possible at larger ports.

Hugh was tempted to go ashore, but he was so tired and had so much paperwork to catch up on that he decided to eat supper on board, work through the evening, and sample the south of France the next evening.

Although in northern Europe it could be quite cool by mid-October, along the Mediterranean coast the days were still warm, and there was only a slight chill once the sun went down. After dinner Hugh decided to walk outside to watch the beautiful October sunset, and he wound up on the helo deck near the stern of the ship, overlooking the fantail where their five-inch gun was mounted. Couples, both straight and gay, walked hand in hand around the helo deck and the fantail. When women had first been stationed on noncombatants, displays of public affection on board ship had not been allowed. But three months earlier an attorney for a gay couple on the USS *Pierce* had won that right when off-duty. It had been ruled a constitutional guarantee of freedom of speech, and so by reverse logic it had to be permissible for heterosexual couples as well. The result was that some had now nicknamed the *Fortson* the "Love Boat."

Hugh tried to ignore the couples, even those he knew well like Maggie Simpson from Teri's division and Electrician Chief Garnett Ellis, who were huddled in a tight embrace only twenty feet from him. Instead he thought about his and Jennifer's visit to the White House.

The sessions with Joe Wood and Robert Ludwig had been like a shot of adrenaline for their marriage, and he hoped that it would last. Jennifer had given him a special *Read Daily Thru the Bible*, which divided God's Word into 365 segments, complete with commentary and cross-references. He and Jennifer had decided to start reading with the calendar, so as he departed they found themselves beginning the New Testament. He'd already written her two letters about insights he'd gained from his reading, and he hoped she was equally as engrossed.

As for Teri, neither of them had mentioned the night at Guantanamo Bay again, and he had maintained a pleasant but professional relationship with her during the long operating hours of the past three weeks. He had decided that the temptation she represented would always be there, but he would try to do his part to keep it in the background. And he had begun praying every day for God's help.

"A quarter for your thoughts," Teri said, coming up beside him as the sun drew a beautiful pink tapestry in the west.

He looked to his left and returned her smile. Her hair was still damp from a recent shower. She smelled clean. "Hi," he said. "I thought it was a penny."

"Inflation. And I thought I'd make you an offer you couldn't refuse."

His smile broadened. "I see." He decided to be totally honest. "Well, I was just thinking about Jen and the kids and how much I miss them. It's almost easier when we go at full speed; there's less time to think. Stopping like this is necessary, but it's almost torture."

It was Teri's turn to say, "I see." She turned to face the sunset. "It really is beautiful out here. Looking at this it's hard to imagine we'll actually be here through the whole winter, until early April. Will we keep going at this pace? My girls are exhausted. Most are sleeping in tonight or relaxing in other ways." She nodded toward her friend, now kissing Chief Ellis and oblivious to everyone around them.

"Yes…well on my other deployments the heavy operating times have come in cycles; we've just started off at a very fast pace. It should let up a bit next week without the Russians."

As they continued to talk, they noticed a small group of eight enlisted men and one woman gathering on the fantail below them. Hugh was surprised to see that they all had Bibles. Although he and Teri could hear sounds, they were just a little too far away to make out the words. But it was soon apparent that Radioman First Class Ross Ewing was leading an evening Bible study for several of his shipmates.

Hugh and Teri continued to talk, and about five minutes later Seaman Raymond Tyson, the young sailor from the supply department who had suffered the name-calling from Wolf Higgins, walked up to the group below them and tentatively began talking with Ewing. Several minutes passed with what appeared to be quite a bit of discussion in the group. Finally Ewing nodded his head and smiled. Tyson joined the group, and one of the men shifted his seat on the deck so Tyson could look on in his Bible.

"Interesting," Hugh said. "Well, I've got a lot of forms and other exciting stuff to catch up on. I hate to leave this romantic spot, but duty calls."

Teri nodded. "You're forgiven. I'll match my paper pile with yours any day. The needs of the navy…see you in the morning. Good night."

He turned and walked away, glad that he'd mentioned his wife, whom he knew he loved more than ever, but nevertheless feeling a curious warmth in his chest and face. Meaning every word, he briefly closed his eyes and said, "Dear Lord, please give me strength."

WASHINGTON "So those, we believe, are the issues, benefits, costs, and choices before us." William was concluding his presentation on national television that Thursday evening. "We've tried to present them as clearly and as evenly as possible. We offer the American people our program as a solution to our nation's problems. We realize that implementing it will cost our nation, just as not implementing it will cost our nation.

"But beyond our program I urge you to examine your own values, to learn about the principles on which this nation was founded, and about the men and women who risked everything to breathe life into it. Then communicate those values to your representatives and to your president. And I urge you to vote—our next national election will be in just over a year. Vote for men and women who share your values and will implement them in Washington. Our nation is stuck in a legislative gridlock, as we've acknowledged tonight; the only sure outcome will be ever increasing debt with no real results. We need a clear direction here in Washington, and only you can give it. So write, call, and above all, vote. Thank you and good night."

An exterior shot of the White House appeared on the U.S. Network's feed to its stations around the country, and then TV viewers saw Ryan Denning in the Washington newsroom.

"Tonight we've seen a different sort of presidential speech, almost a classroom discussion on national economics and the choices before us, at least as President Harrison sees them. Leslie Sloane, our chief White House correspondent, is here tonight with two key congressional leaders, Trent Patterson of the president's party, and Bill Phillips of the opposition. Leslie…"

The camera cut to a set where the well-known newswoman and her two guests sat in three comfortable chairs. "Thank you, Ryan. Congressman Patterson, let's start with you. Did you have any idea that the president was going to take this approach to restarting your party's domestic program?"

"Not specifically until the briefing of leaders from both parties two days ago, when he laid out the same statistics and choices that the American people have seen tonight."

"What do you think?"

Congressman Patterson smiled. "I think he's sincere and means what he says. We're of course prepared to support this program one hundred percent, as we have in the past."

"But he seemed to imply that perhaps your party doesn't have all the answers, especially with economic predictions."

"Well, I think he actually said that no government or party can predict the future perfectly, and any economic model can be off, especially in a dynamic economy like ours. But frankly, I think we've got some pretty good models giving pretty good results."

"So you're more optimistic than the president is about the predictions of economic boom to follow the period of job training and housing starts?"

The congressman appeared to be uncomfortable. "Perhaps a little. But I think we'll all just have to wait and see. I do believe our party's jobs and housing programs are the right ones for the nation."

"Congressman Phillips, what was your reaction to the new approach proposed by the president?"

"Well, if he's sincere, like my good colleague believes him to be, I guess it will be refreshing."

"Do you doubt his sincerity?"

"I don't know. I hope I have no reason to. But we've heard these media inspired 'fresh starts' before. Then soon it's back to politics as usual."

"I must say, congressman, I don't believe I've ever heard a president take, let's see, eight minutes to give a detailed synopsis of what the opposition would say is wrong with his program, and to do it so genuinely. Have you?"

"No, not in such detail," Phillips agreed. "But his calling for the voters to elect representatives who agree with their values sounds a little like a power play over the heads of seated congressmen and congresswomen, which frankly his party is famous for. So we'll be watching to see if his actions speak louder than his words."

"Wait a minute, Bill," Trent Patterson said. "I don't agree with your statement that our party singlehandedly appeals to voters over the heads of Congress. Look at what *your* last president did every time he got into a little trouble—he went traipsing to the media to tell the people how awful Congress was. I heard William Harrison say he'll work with Congress."

"But did he mean it?" Bill Phillips replied. "And what will be the cost of finding out? How long will he work with us? We need time to prepare a response to tonight's introductory economics lecture."

"Of course he meant it," Patterson answered.

Phillips smiled silently in response.

Leslie Sloane tried to regain control of the interview by asking Congressman Phillips, "How do you feel the president did on representing your position as the opposition?"

"I haven't had time to assess that, Ms. Sloane. There's a lot at stake here for the American people, and we need time to analyze all the consequences of these various program proposals."

"But haven't you been doing that for over eight months already?"

"Of course. But the economy has changed from last January when this administration took office and first proposed its programs, and I thought I heard some slightly new things here tonight. So we'll analyze it, and hopefully we can work together, as the president has requested."

"Thank you gentlemen. That's the congressional reaction. Back to you, Ryan."

RALEIGH Two hours after the president's speech, Sarah Prescott was on her knees by her bed, fighting back tears. She was overwhelmed by the mixture of feelings she was experiencing. She felt dirty, elated, betrayed, let down, and excited. She had experienced the virtual reality computer for the first time that afternoon, and her emotions had been on a roller coaster ever since.

"O God, what am I supposed to do? I'm so sorry. I...I should have waited to be married. I feel so dirty. Please forgive me."

But as she was praying the images from the experience that afternoon exploded in her mind again and caused her to catch her breath. She fought and fought, but the thought still came: *It was fantastic, just like everyone said. I liked it. I liked it a lot!*

"O God, forgive me. Please forgive me. I know it's wrong. Please..." Tears ran down her cheeks. "I'm so bad. What will Mom and Dad think?"

Hey, that guy was like so cool. And so real. I had sex today—but I didn't! Isn't that awesome? And I can do it again next week. As much as I want. Whenever I want.

"I need your help, dear God. I've done a terrible thing. I've broken your law. I feel so dirty, and used. *Please help me!*"

But it's not really sex. I'm still a virgin! It's no big deal. I haven't done anything wrong. I'm learning about love and sex without hurting anyone. It'll make me a better wife for my husband when I do get married. And that guy was so awesome.

"Please, God, help me know what's right. Help me do the right thing. I'm really confused. I don't want to do something bad, but I don't want to miss something good, either. Please help me know, so I can tell my parents. In Jesus' name. Amen."

She felt better after praying. She got into bed to read. Ten minutes later, as she switched out her light, she thought *I wonder if we get to choose from the same guys in the next session?*

WASHINGTON William Harrison found himself once again unusually at peace, despite the issues swirling around him. His staff had put together a tape of all the major network reports following his national address. They would discuss them together in the morning, but now he and Carrie were sitting in their living room, finishing the final segment on the tape. With the last anchorperson's ten-second analysis fading out, William turned off the VCR. He turned to Carrie, whose hand he had been holding on the sofa.

He shook his head slightly and said, "Isn't it amazing, when you think about it. We tried to make a real break with the status quo, to signal a willingness to talk openly and to share ideas so that Congress and the people could decide the best course of action. And we kept our new approach under wraps until the last minute. Yet you'd think every politician they interviewed had practiced his or her response for a month! They all put up a smokescreen that basically said, 'No, let's keep everything like it is, doing nothing, but keeping us all in power, and maybe this Harrison guy will go away in three years.' Am I wrong, Carrie?"

"No, I think you pretty well summarized what we've just seen. But maybe after a day or two when they get your real package, they'll respond more positively."

The president frowned as he said, "I hope so, but don't count on it. They'll also have more time to think of reasons to continue waffling. I don't expect anyone to attack my idea head on. It's a little too logical for that. From what we've seen here, they—and I mean both parties—apparently just plan to chew around the edges until it disappears a month later in some final sound bite. And the gridlock will remain."

"It's funny, William. I think you're right, but you don't seem upset, like you used to get," Carrie offered, turning on the couch to face him and bringing her knees up under her.

"I guess you get so far down, there's no reason to keep screaming. If this approach winds up not working, Carrie, I really don't know what to do. Since we started in January I've tried party politics, persuasion, blackmail, and now, thank God for what he's done, honesty and logic. If none of those work, and we're still stuck, then I've run out of ideas. But you're right, I'm not angry. I feel like we've lost, but we haven't been defeated. I just wish I could do better for the nation. Our people deserve better. They need a leader like Washington or Lincoln, someone who can show them the way out of this debt-ridden bureaucratic mess. Get our nation back on a solid foundation. But instead they've got me."

Carrie squeezed his hand. "Weren't you the person who told me that our best leaders felt inadequate?"

"Do you have to remember everything I said?" William asked smiling and squeezing her hand in return. "You're right. Our founders did feel inadequate. Actually," he added, "pretty often."

"And what did they do when they felt that way?"

"My best guess is that they prayed. Fervently and often. They believed that God was their Ruler and that they should turn to him for guidance."

"Well, I know we've been praying together for a couple of months, ever since Michael suggested it. But our prayers have mostly been for our family and for general wisdom to follow God's will. Let's try being really specific. Let's pray for his guidance on your legislative program and on other issues. Maybe we should even ask others to pray for you. And perhaps you should pray in your office. Is there anyone else on the staff who would pray with you?"

"I don't know, but you're probably right, Carrie. It's like Robert Ludwig said the other night in our study. We ask Christ into our home easily enough, but then we leave him standing alone in the entrance hall, not expecting him to get involved in our bedrooms, kitchens, or closets. And we certainly don't extend the invitation to our offices! Then we suffer the consequences of underestimating his power. You're right. We should have been doing this already. Here, let's pray now, and tomorrow I'll start a list of issues on which I really need his guidance."

The president and first lady bowed their heads, then William silently slid to the floor on his knees, and Carrie followed him.

When they finished praying, William stood and felt a momentary chill. It occurred to him in a burst of silent understanding that perhaps God was no longer interested in America. *How awful that would be!* he thought again, a few minutes later, as they walked together to their bedroom. His body shook involuntarily. *Could that be possible?* Carrie gave him a questioning look. But the possibility that God would leave them to their own divided and godless desires was too awful for him to share. *Please, Lord, don't forsake us,* he silently prayed. *Please...* As they walked, he squeezed Carrie's hand, but he wasn't smiling.

ODESSA, UKRAINE It was just after noon in the Black Sea port of Odessa, where the *Bright Star* was tied up alongside a pier. Sadim Muhmood and the nuclear technician, Andrei Kolikov, were having lunch with the captain, Kalim Kutub, in his stateroom, as was their custom. Usually their meals were pleasant enough, but this day there was tension in the room.

"You said two days maximum. Already this is three," Sadim said to Kolikov, the man who had first approved the Ukrainian warhead when it was still half buried in its motherland's dark soil. Sadim's eyes revealed the anger his associates knew was always just below the surface. Now it threatened to boil over. "How much longer?"

Kolikov shrugged and replied sheepishly, "Things here do not always go as first advertised. More people had to be paid off. We rejected the first replacement part they brought because it was too old. We've sent them back to the original military source, and hopefully by tomorrow we can be on our way."

"It's too dangerous for us to stay here. There are still questions being asked about that agent's death in April. I've watched the same men every day walking along the pier and asking about our ship. Khalim"—the leader turned to the *Bright Star's* captain—"be sure to stress to your crew again that they are to talk to no one."

"Yes. I will. They know the rules. They were hand-picked for this mission."

"I know. But some of them are young and might slip up. So tell them to stay out of the bars and the brothels while we are stuck here."

"None of them would set foot in a bar, Sadim," Khalim objected. "But to tell them to forego their women?"

"Yes. Besides our immediate safety, which worries me, this is a holy mission, and the least they can do is keep themselves clean in this city of infidels. But I particularly want no talk, do you understand?"

"Yes, Sadim."

"And," Sadim added, rising to go, his lunch only half eaten, "we are leaving tomorrow afternoon at the latest. Andrei, if we have to, we'll leave you here in Odessa for a week to find the replacement part. Do you think your good comrades from the old days would like to find you here? Then we'd have to kill you."

Kolikov blanched. "We're supposed to have the right part in the morning, Sadim."

"We'd better. Our safety and success cannot be risked for such a slip-up. Get more reliable people. We have a timetable that *will* be met, and I will not tolerate dangerous delays like this."

As Sadim slammed the stateroom door, the Russian, who was a professed atheist, nevertheless prayed that the proper part would show up on time.

Of all the dispositions and habits which lead to political prosperity, religion and morality are indispensable supports. In vain would that man claim the tribute of patriotism, who should labor to subvert these great pillars of human happiness....The mere politician...ought to respect and to cherish them. A volume could not trace all their connections with private and public felicity. Let it simply be asked, Where is the security for property, for reputation, for life, if the sense of religious obligation desert?... And let us with caution indulge the supposition that morality can be maintained without religion. Whatever may be conceded to the influence of refined education on minds...reason and experience both forbid us to expect that national morality can prevail, in exclusion of religious principle.

GEORGE WASHINGTON
FAREWELL ADDRESS, SEPTEMBER 19, 1796

14

Wednesday, November 7
Three Weeks Later

RALEIGH "Hi, Sarah," Mary called from the den as her daughter closed the front door and started up the front stairs. "Don't forget the interview is on TV tonight. How was school?"

"Hi. Fine," Sarah replied as she continued up the stairs.

"Your midterm report card came today."

Sarah stopped. "How was it?"

"Good. Real good. But sometime I want to ask you about health."

"Okay." Sarah continued up the last two steps, walked down the hall-way, and quietly closed the door to her room. She had been dreading this day for the past several weeks. In fact, she had been checking the mailbox for days, hoping that she would be the first to open the envelope from the school, as if that would make a difference.

Just last week her mother had asked her whether she wanted them to file a formal protest with the school board when her mandatory failing grade in health arrived. Sarah had not actually lied to her mother, but she had dodged the discussion with a series of "Mms" and "I'll think about it." Now she assumed her mother knew she hadn't failed the course.

I'll just tell her the principal intervened on behalf of those who didn't want to use the computer, and that will be it. She'll be happy and never ask about it again. And I can go on to the eighth session, which everyone says is incredible.

But a mixture of guilt—she had never directly lied to her parents before on a major issue—and a creeping suspicion that her mother would probe more deeply and discover the truth, persuaded her that lying would not work. That left Sarah with telling the truth, which felt even worse. She threw her backpack on the floor and fell on her bed, anger, guilt, and frustration swirling inside her.

Sarah curled up into a fetal position. Her homework remained untouched in her backpack. She dreaded going downstairs to dinner, which would be ready in an hour. For an instant she felt she should pray for guidance, but she knew it would open a door to feelings of guilt, and she slammed it shut. Instead of praying, she reflected again on how dumb her parents were for wanting to deny her this experience. And the more she thought, the more angry she became.

ATLANTA Rebecca had arranged her schedule to get off early so she could fix dinner in time to watch the special program about the president's family that evening.

"Blue cheese or ranch?" she asked Bruce as she stood in front of the open refrigerator door and he cut open the baked potatoes. Moments later they were seated in the dining area of her high-rise apartment, the early darkness outside presaging the coming winter.

"I wonder if they'll use much of the tape they shot here," she thought out loud, looking around her small but tasteful apartment.

"Probably," Bruce smiled in reply. "I liked the shots of us at the gym. I think our friends were blown away when Leslie Sloane herself showed up to ask questions. Of course the downside is I hate for the whole nation to see what a good looking woman you are; you might get a better offer!"

"I doubt that will happen," she replied. "But if I start getting fan mail, we can answer it together. How's that?"

"Fair enough. Just let me be in charge of answering any letters that include pictures!"

"First we'd better see how this goes tonight..." There was a moment of silence as they each took a bite from their skinless broiled chicken. "Bruce, I want to tell you about something sort of weird that happened again at the hospital today. I left early, to get home for this program, and as I was walking out through emergency admitting there was another one of our Ob/Gyn charity mothers, almost full term, demanding to have an abortion. I guess I still feel strange whenever I see that—I know, you don't agree," she responded as he began to interrupt, "but the weird thing was that Harvey Thompson and Priscilla Sawyer were there again, on duty, ready to perform the abortion."

"What's strange about that?" Bruce asked.

"Well, I think that's the third or fourth time this fall I've come across a full-term abortion—and usually in the late afternoon, now that I think about it—when the two of them have been on duty together. Just their being on duty at the same time so much is a little unusual, but these abortions happening as well. It just seems odd. I don't know."

"I think you're imagining things. What could be the big deal, anyway?"

"I don't really know. I just thought it was strange."

"Well, abortion is abortion, and they're doctors. Sounds perfectly normal to me." Bruce took another bite of chicken.

Rebecca started to say how *un*normal it sounded to her, but with the show starting in less than an hour, she decided it was no time for an argument. "Anyway, if it happens again I'll really be curious..."

WASHINGTON William flew into Washington late that afternoon from a three-day visit to the West Coast. On his trip he had visited several housing projects in Los Angeles damaged by yet another earthquake the previous year, rebuilt and receiving their first residents; met with the new president of Mexico to symbolize the increased trade between the two countries, as all tariffs were scheduled to be removed on January first; and toured a navy and an air force base to commend the men and women in uniform who had been largely responsible for the tenuous peace in the Pacific, as Japan, China, fresh from swallowing prosperous Hong Kong, and the two Koreas vied for economic power, and each built up its military forces in reaction to threatening remarks from the other.

Sandra Van Huyck, his foreign policy advisor, and Lanier Parks, his secretary of state, were worried that a war might break out somewhere in the Pacific rim, and William had met secretly with U.S., Japanese, South Korean, and Australian military leaders to assess the threats and their combined capacity for action, given the United States' low level of military spending over the previous several years. One key question would be Russia's reaction to any sort of hostility in that area, and Parks would be flying to Moscow before Thanksgiving to meet with his counterpart to discuss the possibility of a joint peacekeeping role.

Carrie had stayed in Washington while William travelled, and he gave her a warm hug and a kiss as he entered the White House from the South Lawn helicopter pad. As he turned to head for a briefing on congressional reaction to their domestic initiative of three weeks before, Carrie said quietly,

"I asked Michael to expand our regular study tonight to watch the interview, since he knows your family. He may be bringing Elizabeth as well, and I thought we could all have dinner together in about two hours. Okay?"

"Sure. Fine. I'm glad he's coming. I've got something I want to share with him. See you in a little while."

That evening the Harrisons and Tates enjoyed a simple meal in the president's private quarters. Given William's just completed trip and Michael's international ties, the dinner discussion revolved around the situation in the Pacific. "So, particularly if Russia helps, I think we can head off outright war, though tensions will remain high in that area for years, and our forces are really spread thin," William concluded, as Carrie offered everyone refills of coffee.

"What about your domestic programs?" Elizabeth Tate asked. "We enjoyed your televised presentation several weeks ago—it was so refreshing!"

"Well, you two should know I'm completely at peace that we've done the right thing. I guess that's the Lord working in me, maybe, thanks to your teachings on courage, trust, and truth. But Congress apparently is not real excited. There are a few exceptions of course—genuine calls to work together from both sides of the aisle—but in general we now have gridlock on gridlock. Our program scares the other side, and they still haven't come up with an alternative. John Dempsey from our party apparently had a talk with a colleague from the other side who said they're in disarray because we've challenged them to propose a serious alternative, and they're so used to complaining that they don't know what to put forward because they know we might actually embrace some of it. So here we sit, fast frozen, going nowhere."

"I think it's time for the show," Carrie reminded them.

"All right, let's see what Leslie Sloane does with the rest of the family," William said, as they rose to move into the living room.

An hour later, as the credits rolled on the screen, William put down his coffee cup and turned in his chair. "Isn't it incredible how they can take reasonably normal, imperfect people, and make them seem either all good or all bad right before our eyes? Was that news or a campaign piece?"

"It was a *little* strong, dear," Carrie said, "especially about your parents. I had no idea your mother was so all-knowing. Do you think Leslie was just being nice because of what happened?"

"I don't know, but, pardon the comparison, you'd think I could walk on water after seeing that show and hearing what they had to say about me in my earlier years. To say I'm a little embarrassed is an understatement."

"They treated Mary and Graham kind of like misguided freaks who enjoyed the sympathy of everyone else in the family," Michael observed.

"Yes, that's the other thing. Here the Lord is at work in my life as never before, yet Mary is tagged as a far-out fundamentalist. What will Leslie do when she finds out that I now share Mary's belief in God and Christ, and am humbled by it?"

"When is that day going to be?" Michael asked.

"I'm not sure. Soon, I guess. I still feel like I'm putting together the pieces of a puzzle but can't see the whole picture, yet. I think I will, soon, though."

"It's good that you're taking this time 'in the wilderness,' so to speak, William, to study, to learn, to pray, and to deepen your faith," Michael said, "As we've already seen, that's biblical. Most of us do well to take a period on our own, learning his will for our lives. So you're right to do it. But at some point each of us must move out in faith. I doubt we ever know it 'all' before we act on God's will for us. That, too, is part of his plan for us, to trust him and to act on our faith in *his* ability, not ours."

"Well, I'm feeling better and bolder. So I guess it won't be long, particularly since you've said our study course should end around Christmas. But"—and William's mood seemed to change as he spoke— "there's something I've been agonizing about, and I want to share it with the three of you, to get your input."

"Please, go ahead," Michael replied.

William paused and locked his hands in front of him. "Late at night, and sometimes during the day, even when I'm praying, I get this chill. It's like an awful dread. And a voice—not someone else's. The sound is my own, but the words come from somewhere else—tells me that God is turning his back on us, as a nation, because of all we've done to anger and displease him. It's like he's leaving us, and I'm crying out for him to stay and give us one last chance. But he's gone…Michael, it's so real, and as his light disappears, this utter darkness moves in, and our nation is ripped apart by hatred and violence. Then the darkness completely engulfs us. It's happened so many times now. What do you think?"

The other three remained fixed in their chairs, observing the obvious anguish on William's face. Finally Michael spoke.

"It's always hard for one person to assess the thoughts of another, but I would say, regrettably, that what you've experienced could be the Lord speaking to you. Many of us have certainly preached for years from pulpits all across the nation that our society has been driving God from our children's hearts and replacing his Spirit with the worst forms of humanist, and even outright evil, motivations: lust, greed, envy, hate, you name it. Now those children are parents themselves, and the process is only worse. Yes, many of us have been sounding the warning for years and years. Maybe, just maybe, and I feel a chill, too, when I say it, he has finally given up on us and turned his back on our wickedness."

"What…what would it mean?" Carrie asked, almost in a whisper.

"Well, if we look at what he did when Israel repudiated him, the picture for us is pretty bleak. Violence, disease, division, the fall of governments. Ultimately foreign invasion and domination…"

"Why?" Carrie continued.

"The Bible is so clear. In the Old Testament, the focus appears to be on the chosen nation of Israel, and in one sense it certainly is. But over and over, as we've discussed, God in both Testaments is always searching *individual* hearts. Both the hearts of the people and the hearts of the leaders. Let's see, I think there's an example of God searching the heart in 1 Chronicles 28, where King David is quoted as saying,

> For the Lord searches every heart and understands every motive behind the thoughts. If you seek him, he will be found by you; but if you forsake him, he will reject you forever.

"Then in the New Testament, Jesus again addresses the heart of man, asking whether it longs for the Lord or is hardened against him by the world. And Paul and John address not nations, but churches, chastising them for turning their hearts from Christ. In all these cases, this turning from God, this hardening of the heart, results in punishment. It's that simple. It's not like we haven't been warned!"

"So you think William's terrible dream could be inspired by God?" Elizabeth asked.

"Yes."

William started to speak, then stopped. He looked down, then up again at Michael. "Were there ever cases in the Bible when God's anger was about to burst, and something happened to turn it aside? I guess I'm asking, is there anything we can do, if this vision is correct?"

"Yes, many cases. That's the incredible thing about God. He is so patient and wants no one to be lost. Yet ultimately even his patience runs out."

"What happened in those cases when he relented?"

"The people turned to him and accepted his ways again. They turned their hearts to him. And, by the way, there have been revivals like that in the Western world, in just the past few centuries, when great movements of God, usually kindled by laypeople, swept across entire nations, leaving behind changed hearts."

"Yes," William said, "I want to hear about those, too. But right now, please give us some examples from the Bible."

"There are so many. Look at Ninevah in the short Book of Jonah. Most people think the focus of the book is on the whale, but it's really on repentance. Jonah is sent by God to warn the people of that city to change their ways or be destroyed; the leaders and people listen to Jonah and are saved.

"Or look in 2 Kings 22 at what happened when Josiah, the young king of Israel, found God's Law, which had been lost in the temple ruins, read it for the first time, realized how they had been violating God's will, wept, tore his clothes, and led the nation back to a long period of following God's will and of worshiping him.

"Or earlier, in Joshua, at the end of that book. The people had been punished for forty years for worshiping a golden calf, instead of the true God who saved them from the Egyptians. After they then successfully took the Promised Land as their inheritance, Joshua called the entire nation together and told them what Moses had already made clear: they could serve other gods, and break God's will, which would lead again to his anger and to their ruin. Or they could serve God and his will, and the Promised Land would remain theirs forever. He gave them the choice—in fact, he had the whole nation vote."

"Vote?" William asked.

"Yes. Look at the end of the book. They voted to serve the Lord, and Joshua challenged them to keep their word. And in the New Testament there are so many examples you could almost say the whole text is really God's revealed Word about how to have victory over destruction by believing in his Son and receiving the blessing of eternal life."

"So the key is the individual heart," William said. "One man can't wish another man into God's kingdom. Each heart must turn on its own. But, particularly from what you mentioned in the Old Testament, it does appear that the rulers had something to do with it."

"Yes," Michael agreed. "It's interesting. It's as if the ruler of the nation set the right tone. The state of *his* heart was reflected in the laws and the practices of the people. He often had to fight with the entrenched leaders of the day who wanted a different path. But, again, it was the people's behavior that ultimately decided God's reward or punishment. Look at Moses, Israel's great leader; yet his people worshiped a golden calf. Then other leaders turned the nation around, like Josiah. There was an interesting interaction between the nation's leader and the people. God searched the hearts of the people, but without godly leaders who read and ruled according to God's law, the people didn't have much of a chance."

"It's funny," William said. "That sounds almost exactly like what Joe Wood told us last week about families. Without the parents—and he was really addressing fathers—reading and willing to teach God's laws for living, how can any family expect to survive today?"

"That's a good connection," Michael said. "Families and nations are a lot alike. Each has a leader. The individual members can flourish or wither. Each prospers with a biblical foundation for behavior. Each tempts disaster without the Lord."

"We've really had a heavy discussion tonight. And, hey, we haven't even started your lesson yet!"

Michael smiled. "It's late. I think we've actually already done quite a lesson. Here, let me write down those references for you, and a few more. And, William, about the vision you keep having: it sounds very real and very possible to me. I encourage you and Carrie to pray about it, as Elizabeth and I will do. Ask God to reveal more to you, if it's his will. Pray and study his Word, as you've been doing. Be open to his leading, and learn to live by faith. He says that if we will just seek his kingdom, he'll take care of all the other details in our lives. That's really pretty amazing, when you think about it, and gives me lots of comfort when everything seems crazy."

"Thanks, both of you, for coming tonight," William said. "I feel at the same time both overwhelmed by all that he is and also somehow strengthened by him as well. Yes, Carrie and I are praying more, and we'll continue. Now, can the four of us pray together?"

THE ADRIATIC SEA The U.S. Network interview with the Harrison family aired at two in the morning local time off the coast of what used to be Yugoslavia, and Hugh stayed up in order to watch it in the wardroom on the U.S. Armed Forces satellite link from the states.

As the show began, Teri Slocum opened the forward port door to the wardroom and quietly sat down next to Hugh; he had mentioned it to her at the start of their deployment, and she had noted it on her calendar. Since midnight rations had concluded two hours earlier, they were the only officers in the dimly lit space.

They talked quietly during the commercials, and at the end of the show, Hugh turned down the volume and said, "Boy, that was great seeing Jen and the kids, even if it was a little strange watching us being interviewed."

"You've really got a wonderful wife and beautiful children," Teri said, turning slightly toward him in the chair.

"Yes," Hugh replied, obviously moved by seeing them again, "God has blessed me with a wonderful family. I miss them a lot...and we've got five more months to go."

"Mmm. In the interview you didn't sound too much in favor of the new crew arrangement on the ship, though you were diplomatic enough not to say it outright."

"I guess it showed, huh?" Hugh said. "Well, that's the truth. I'm not. But I'm trying to roll with the punches and wait to see what happens."

Teri's eyes, close to his, reflected the light from the television, and Hugh, sitting close to her in the dimly lit space, suddenly felt very much at home sharing his thoughts with her. It was as if a chapter in their relationship was over; physical attraction was no longer the main driving force. It was still very much there, but now it was in the background. *Maybe it's because I've been praying,* Hugh thought. It was as if she were suddenly a really good friend. No, more like the attractive younger sister of his best friend—the tension was there, but it now acted to energize the periphery of a far deeper relationship, one which combined friendship and playfulness with respect, protection, and concern.

He looked into her eyes, and it was if she shared his understanding, their shift to a deeper, less sexual, but more profound relationship, in that single moment. They held each other's eyes as the understanding passed between them. Neither said a word, but they both felt it, and each eventually smiled.

"So, should I get off at the next port?" she asked demurely.

"What? And leave me with all your women to deal with!"

"Should we all get off?"

He hesitated, and his expression grew more serious. "Teri...yes and no. I've told you many times it's not about you or your division's capabilities or readiness. And the same goes for the homosexuals. They've shown that they're very capable. It's just, again, that we're different. There's tapes inside us—I'm a man, you're a woman. I react in a certain way to things you do, and vice versa, I guess. Frankly, and I know this is going to blow your mind, but since I've been reading the Bible, it seems to me that God—yes, God—created us for different roles. Not one better than the other. But, and don't go bonkers on me, I truly believe there are servant leadership roles for men, and servant leadership roles for women... So if you really want to know how I'm starting to feel, then here it is: I think you can handle a missile shoot just fine, no question; and I can probably nurture children. But the God who made us designed roles for us—they're pretty obvious if you just look at us— and we violate those roles at some real risk. It's not that it *can't* be done. The question is whether it *ought* to be done."

Despite the early hour and her fatigue, she listened attentively and thought for quite a while before she answered. "Hugh, this may blow *your* mind, but in my quietest heart of hearts, I probably agree with you, or at least with most of what you said. When I'm totally honest with myself, I have to admit that I'd like to marry a wonderful man and have a family and raise our children—just like it seems you and Jennifer are doing. It's just that...well, that right man hasn't come along, and I worry a lot whether he ever will. And while I'm waiting, another part of me is really intrigued by what we're doing here, now, serving the country and being the best I can be. So it's tough. Real tough.

"The part of me that's worried about not finding a husband pushes me to do more and to be more, in case I'm left completely out of the family thing. And yet I know the irony is that in that push, that rush for doing, and for total 'equality,' the process almost seems to make it harder to find a husband, which was the real goal in the first place. As a group we women may be scaring all the men off. So—and I know this is a pretty deep thought for three in the morning in the Adriatic Sea—it's, like, what seems rational for one woman, seeking to do everything I can, turns out to be irrational for all women as a group, because men either run the other way or forget how to be men. It's very, very frustrating. Almost all men have run, of course, except the few wonderful ones like you, I mean," she ended with a warm smile.

He looked at her but didn't say anything for a while. He was starting to feel the late hour. Finally he said, "You're right, of course. It *is* very difficult. I don't know what I'd do if I were a modern woman—how I'd cope. The problem seems to be that as we've focused so totally in our society on the individual and his or her rights, which is all we hear about, that we've created a brave new world in which the customs and habits that used to support individuals, in a collective sense, no longer work.

"So you and every other woman live with the real possibility that you won't ever find a husband; or even if you do, he'll divorce you and leave you with two kids. So you need to be an individual with skills and rights to protect yourself when he does. The 'triumph of the individual' appears ultimately to be a lot of miserable individual men, miserable individual women, and miserable individual children. What an irony! But the question for tomorrow, or maybe later this afternoon, my beautiful female philosopher, is how to solve this problem. Perhaps we can tackle that after three hours sleep."

They slowly rose together, and Hugh turned off the television.

"I enjoyed talking tonight," Teri said.

"Me, too. Shall we meet again tomorrow night?"

"It'll have to be on the bridge. I've got the midwatch as the JOOD."

"You junior officers have all the fun. Well, good night, Teri."

"Good night, Hugh."

RALEIGH "What happened tonight, Graham?" Mary asked, as they sat together in their den with the sound of Sarah slamming her bedroom door still reverbrating in their ears.

"We're finally unmasked on national television as misguided Christian fundamentalists threatening the White House, and we just lost our little girl. Otherwise, it's been a great evening," Graham answered from his chair at the end of the sofa.

Both of the Prescotts thought back on the two hours since supper. At the dinner table Mary had asked Sarah about her health grade, and neither parent had been prepared for the angry eruption from Sarah, reminding them that she was old enough to make her own decisions and that she'd decided to try the computer once and that it had been nothing to worry about. The rest of the meal had been tense, and once it was over she tried to go immediately to her room, but her father had asked her to tell them about her decision.

Mary and Graham were stunned to find that Sarah had participated seven times in the virtual reality sex education program and that she intended to finish the section. She refused to give them more details, dodging their few other questions.

The family had reassembled for the televised interview. At the end, when Mary tried again to ask Sarah how she felt about the sessions, Sarah stood up and, with tears filling her eyes, shouted, "I hate all this faith stuff! Look at us on TV—we look like idiots! What will the kids say tomorrow? Just when I was getting over all the computer garbage you stirred up, we're shown on TV as goody-goody Christians—too good for everybody else. Well, *I'm* not! I'm just a person." Now the tears really came, and Tim, wide-eyed, moved quietly to the door. "I don't *care* about all that church stuff! I just want to live my life and be normal, not crazy or wacko or holier than everybody else. *Yes,* I used the computer. You know what? It was great! So please, leave me alone about this. It's my life. Just leave me alone!"

And with those words Sarah ran upstairs and slammed her door, leaving her parents in stunned silence, until Mary asked Graham her question. Now she thought about his answer.

"Am I wrong, or is that the first time Sarah's screamed at us since she was three?" Mary asked.

"I think you're right. I guess we underestimated the power of temptation at her age, and the peer pressure."

Mary paused. "*Now* what do we do? It's as if she's experienced sex, but she hasn't. Good grief, Graham, think what she might have already experienced if they're past the seventh session. When do they do all that group and lesbian stuff? Do you realize in the past few weeks she may have had—or simulated—or I don't know which way to say it—all sorts of sex that neither of us, thank God, has ever known? What does that do to our relationship with *her?* That course is absolutely rotten, Graham! It's the secular/humanist ultimate individual experience, all in the name of 'learning'! And just to top it off, it inflames kids and ruins their relationships with their parents. Give the bad guys a perfect score!"

Graham tried to lighten the tension. "Now you sound like a Christian fundamentalist."

"The truth is the truth. You're right, but we simply believe what *most* people believed forty years ago, and now we're held up on television as extremists. Oh, Graham, Satan is gaining speed, destroying our nation, one family, school, and church at a time, and yet the press and the leadership are saying that *we're* the crazy ones. But, Graham, I really heard Sarah's pain. She must feel so left out. We've got to pray that God will send her some Christian friends who can support her faith—otherwise, I think she's going to have a very difficult few years. And so are we."

"We've got to pray about that and much more. Our family, William, our nation, that computer..." He shook his head, then looked at his wife. "Do you know what we need? We need help with our prayers. Why don't we get together with the other parents who share our beliefs and ask them to bring their pastors, so we can enlist a larger group of prayer partners?"

"Yes, and I'll mention it again at Moms in Prayer. I wonder if the national leadership of MIP knows anything about this computer. Maybe I'll give them a call."

"Good," Graham said. "But back to Sarah—Mary, we've got to walk a fine line with her. Our relationship is bent, but not broken—at least I hope not. But if we push her too hard, we may lose her for many, many years. On the other hand, we can't condone what she's doing either."

"She already knows how we feel. I think her explosion had been building, and there was probably some guilt fueling it."

"Let's hope so. If we keep loving her but don't give in on what we know is right, hopefully she'll come back to her faith and to us when this has run its course."

Mary thought for almost a minute in silence. "Yes, I think you're right. But how long may it take, Graham, and what will be the cost?"

Graham reflected on her words before answering. "I don't know. But you know what just struck me? I bet this is almost exactly what believing parents go through when a child announces that he or she is gay. The Father of Lies just has a new high-tech, addictive lie to use, and it's apparently working. Thank God that whatever lies he tries, we've got access to the one sufficient answer. Here, before we get too depressed, let's give all of this to the Lord. Let's pray."

Mary and Graham prayed out loud for several minutes together in their den, interceding for their daughter. At one point Sarah quietly opened her bedroom door and could tell from the lowered voices in the den below what her parents were doing. The battle inside her raged again: she wanted to scream for them to stop, yet she also wanted to scream for them to pray harder. She silently closed her door and fell on her bed, quietly sobbing.

We have no government armed with power capable of contending with human passions unbridled by morality and religion... Our Constitution was made only for a moral and religious people. It is wholly inadequate to the government of any other.

JOHN ADAMS

15

WASHINGTON It was mid-morning on the first bitterly cold day of the new winter. The sun was shining but the strong wind behind the cold front which had passed in the night made commuting unpleasant. As William sat behind his desk in the Oval Office, he was glad that his daily commute was by elevator. *But I guess we make up the miles in other ways—like a "quick trip" last week to Puget Sound for Thanksgiving with the kids. It was certainly good to see how the aerospace industry has shifted to peaceful projects. Wouldn't heads turn if I gave a speech on strong defense?* He couldn't resist a smile.

William finished going through the morning's key foreign communiques in anticipation of the meeting with Sandra Van Huyck, Jerry Richardson, Patricia Barton-North, and Lanier Parks on the secretary of state's mission to Moscow, where he had discussed the difficult situation in the Pacific. William thought briefly about the vice president. There had been no subsequent flare-ups since their confrontation over his new approach to their domestic policy. William knew that the détente in their relationship had been reinforced by the final passage of a pasted-together national budget, several months after it should have moved through Congress. Seven continuing resolutions had been required to permit the federal government to keep operating after the start of the new fiscal year in October, but William had held on to the hope that his new approach would encourage Congress to pass at least some parts of his domestic package.

He was wrong. Within days after his televised address, business as usual returned to Washington, and the final budget turned out to be the kind of watered-down compromise, accomplishing little and making no one happy, which Ted Braxton had predicted months before. So the legislative stalemate continued. But at least the nation's top two executives appeared to have declared a truce for the moment, since the budget battle was over for that year.

William's thoughts had just turned to what he should try to do differently in the following year when Barbara Morton's familiar knock signaled that the team had assembled for the briefing by Lanier Parks. The door to the Oval Office opened, and William greeted each of them in turn.

As they sat down in front of the fireplace, where a roaring fire provided some extra warmth against the sudden chill, William said, "We're closing in on the end of our first year. Before we hear from Lanier on the Russians, I just want to say we all know that we've taken our lumps on our domestic agenda this year. But in foreign policy I think we've presented a balanced approach. I appreciate your hard work, Sandy, and I hope you and Lanier can give us some initiatives for next year that will build on this year's accomplishments. During the next two weeks I'd like all of you to please have your teams put together some brainstorming ideas which we can look at before Christmas, so we can hit the ground running after the holidays and include many of your initiatives in the State of the Union address in January."

It was Barbara's longstanding custom to wait by the open door of the Oval Office until a meeting actually began, in case her boss or another participant had a last minute request. As the group settled in she was about to leave when Bob Horan took a half step into the office. Everyone seated around the coffee table looked in his direction.

Smiling, he said, "Hey, you folks, I've got some good news!"

Silence and blank stares greeted his announcement. Horan took a few steps into the office but remained by the door in deference to the imminent start of their meeting. "The Supreme Court just overturned the Utah state law against polygamy."

"What?" William asked.

"Yeah, it's great. You know, the case has been around for several years. That Mr. Nelson, a member of the Church of Latter Day Saints—a Mormon—sued the state, claiming his religion allowed for more than one wife, and he didn't want the state to prohibit the lifestyle he wanted. He lost in the local court and in the federal appeals court. But in a five to four decision, with our two appointees carrying the majority, the Supreme Court just overturned the law and ruled that polygamy can't be outlawed."

Everyone was shocked. William sat back in his chair, stunned. Jerry Richardson asked, "How? On what grounds?"

Obviously delighted, Horan explained, "We don't have the entire opinion yet, but apparently it's based on two key points. First, on the First Amendment's separation of church and state. The majority opinion agreed that the state should not interfere with Mr. Nelson's religious beliefs. And here's the best! The court said it was continuing its tradition of overturning laws based solely on the Bible. Apparently when the law was last tested in the late nineteenth century, the Supreme Court at that time cited the Bible and the Christian character of our nation—whatever that is—to rule in favor of it. But today the Court ruled that civil law cannot be based on religious law. They saw it as a simple argument between two religions and ruled that the state had no right to interfere. Isn't that great? Our two guys helped overturn an old biblical myth. With this opening, think of the other laws we can change!"

William listened to what Horan had to say, but said nothing himself, a look of disbelief on his face. It was the vice president who spoke first.

"You mean one man can now have more than one wife?" she asked.

"I guess so," the speechwriter answered. "And, although it's not strictly part of the ruling, I imagine one woman can have more than one husband. And maybe we gays with more than one partner will stop being hassled. To think this administration is already having such an important and long-lasting impact."

But the vice president obviously was not happy. "I don't think it's so great. The adolescent fantasy of every man is now legal? To have a harem? In America? You know men will take advantage of this far more than women, and because of past economic exploitation, men more than women have the means to do it. This is *terrible* for women! How could the Supreme Court do this? *Our* nominees voted for this?"

"Yes...hey, I thought you'd be happy. We've struck another blow for human reason against bigoted religious absolutes!"

"You mean another blow for male exploitation of women!"

Horan, flustered and obviously not expecting this reaction from the vice president, looked bewildered and turned to the president for help.

William Harrison still had not moved since the original announcement; he hardly seemed to have blinked. Still looking straight ahead, he asked in a quiet voice, "Patricia, why do you think men will take advantage of this more than women?"

The vice president opened her mouth to answer, then reconsidered. They could see she was thinking. "Because men are different from women. Women are just more loyal and monogamous by nature. It's obvious."

"Thanks. It's not really on the subject, but I thought I heard you imply for once that men and women are different, and I just wanted to be sure I had understood you correctly. On the real issue, it's incredible to me that our Supreme Court, which until just a few years ago deferred to the Bible as its ultimate authority on all our laws, now throws out any law that derives its precedents from that same document! Don't the justices know that virtually every law we have comes from the Bible? I guess it was ominous when the chief justice had the Ten Commandments erased from behind their chairs three summers ago because some lawyer was offended."

Now Bob Horan was really surprised. "You mean you think our laws ought to be founded on the *Bible?* Why, the Bible is anti-women and anti-gays. When did you suddenly get excited about that old book?"

William turned to face the younger man. "It's a long story, Bob; I'll be glad to share it with you sometime. But rather than argue what you just said, let me simply say you're wrong. The Bible is against sin, not against people. Ironically, Patricia and I have reached the same conclusion about this ruling: it's terrible for women. But, unlike her, I also think it's terrible for men, children, families, everyone. We unhitched ourselves from the Bible's moral absolutes a few years ago, not realizing where it would so quickly lead. Well, today we're starting to see the mess we've made."

"I just don't understand this place sometimes," Horan said under his breath, as he turned to leave. "I'm sorry to have interrupted you."

"No, thanks, Bob," the president managed to smile. "We needed to know. Now, I know this is very unusual, but," and he looked around at his foreign policy team, "Russia and the Pacific Rim will have to wait a little while. Barbara, can we reschedule this meeting for later this afternoon? Good. Now, if you'll excuse me, I've got to handle something else. I'm sorry, but we'll start again at five. Thanks."

The vice president left quickly, heading for her office and a telephone. The others filed out, talking among themselves about the latest news from the nation's highest court. Barbara Morton gave William a questioning look, and he said, "Give me about half an hour."

When everyone had left, he closed the door, walked to the middle of the Oval Office, dropped to his knees, and after a moment, for the first time in his life, fell forward, prostrate on his face before the Lord God Almighty.

O God, what have I done? he prayed. *What more will these Supreme Court nominees do to dishonor you? How can they say your law is not our one true source, when all of the nation's first lawmakers and judges looked primarily to the Bible for legal authority? O God, forgive me. Forgive us. Help us, dear God. We are cast completely adrift. And without your law to guide us, what will be our laws? Who will decide what's right and wrong? Will it change every few months? O God, how can a nation survive like that? I'm so sorry. Please forgive me, heavenly Father. I didn't know what I was doing. I see everything so differently now. Please help me and guide me to do the right thing for this nation and these people. Help me learn how to stop the destruction of families which so obviously hurts the very women and children who some scream need more rights...O God, please, please help us. Heal us, heavenly Father. Please heal our nation.*"

William stayed like that, on the floor of the Oval Office, for almost thirty minutes, humbling himself before his Creator, asking for forgiveness and guidance, deeply disturbed about the state of the nation.

ATLANTA   "Sally, hey, this is Eunice."

"Hi. How are you?" Sally Kramer answered.

"Okay. I guess. How are you?"

"Fine. Did you have a good Thanksgiving?"

"I guess. But I'm worried about Christmas," Eunice answered. "I want my kids to have a good Christmas, but..."

"It's expensive, isn't it?"

"Yeah. That's what I'm worried about... Listen, was that doctor serious about us maybe doing that again?"

"Yes. I'm working with two others—plus myself—and he asked about you the other day, how you're doing."

"Is he still offering the same five thousand dollars?"

"Yes. The same."

"Well, if I agreed now to do another one, soon, say after the first of the year, do you think he could advance me a little toward the thousand up front?"

"How much?"

"Oh, I was thinking maybe five hundred, just so I could get the kids something nice for Christmas. And some winter coats."

"Well, I doubt he'd do it for most women, but maybe I can talk him into it for you, since you've done so well in the past."

Eunice laughed. "Yeah, I can't do much, but I guess I can carry a baby!"

"Any problem getting pregnant?"

She laughed again. "No, not hardly."

"Well, I'll check with the doctor and call you back."

"I'd sure appreciate it, Sally, and so would my kids."

THE CENTRAL MEDITERRANEAN   The sunlight was fading in the area south of Italy where the *Fortson* was operating with the aircraft carrier *Eisenhower*, three other U.S. ships, an Italian cruiser, and two Russian guided-missile frigates.

The group was in its third day of joint operations, and to give the air wing a rest for maintenance, the surface warfare admiral assumed overall command that afternoon while the ships practiced tactical maneuvers under conditions of radio and radar silence. This meant that their close screening formations around the aircraft carrier were designated by signal flags or flashing lights alone. Each ship's bridge and signal bridge had to be alert to read the codes quickly and then execute the formation changes precisely on time. Clipping along at over twenty knots, only a thousand yards apart, the big gray ships appeared to maneuver in graceful formations like motorboats, but the turning diameter for even the smallest one was over eight hundred yards.

And the *Eisenhower*, at over ninety thousand tons and a thousand feet, was a huge structure blasting through the water at the center of the formation with little room for error.

The maneuvers had been going on all afternoon, giving the Russians plenty of practice with the formation codes of their new allies. Each captain had used the opportunity for his junior watch officers to observe and then to practice sending the screening ships to different locations around the carrier.

On the *Fortson* the regular afternoon split watch from 1600 to 1800 had assumed its duty on the bridge and in the combat information center on time, and the last of the extra maneuvering practitioners had departed the bridge by 1715 to grab an early supper before the watch changed again at 1800. The admiral on the carrier had designated the drills to continue until 1730, when the last of the winter sunlight would be gone, so the final maneuvers were being handled by Lt. Henry Early as officer of the deck and Lt. Teri Slocum as junior officer of the deck. Captain Robertson had been on the bridge all afternoon while his junior officers practiced, but he knew that Lt. Early was an experienced ship handler, and since he had several messages to answer, he left the bridge and descended one level to his cabin, confident that the next fifteen minutes would be uneventful. All the rest of the ship's officers were either on duty or eating supper in the wardroom.

Above Henry and Teri, on the starboard side of the exposed deck over the bridge, two missile fire control technicians were putting the finishing touches on their afternoon's work, taking advantage of the group's radar silence to perform some much needed maintenance on the coupler between the main computer and the number one fire control radar.

Fire Control Technician Petty Officer First Class Margaret "Maggie" Simpson, the tall, twenty-five-year-old strawberry-blond woman who had followed Teri Slocum in high school, was bent over the computer coupler. She was trying to push a heavy drawerful of electronic equipment back into its housing so that she could secure it and be done; but for some reason the drawer was sticking on its runners and wouldn't budge despite Maggie's considerable strength.

Watching her and trying to be helpful was Fire Control Technician Third Class Alice Pritchard, who had been learning from her friend and mentor all afternoon. This was their final job, but it had taken longer than expected because they had had to stop and seek refuge behind the radar itself whenever the ship's maneuvers brought them directly into the stiff wind so that the ship's speed made the wind across the deck almost fifty knots.

Alice Pritchard had grown up in a broken and unhappy home. Petite and weighing at most ninety pounds when soaking wet, she tended to be shy and withdrawn. She had joined the navy out of desperation two years earlier, right out of high school, after eating like a horse for a month to pass the minimum weight test. Unfortunately, her naval experience had been going nowhere fast when she met Maggie Simpson at a missile school and then was transferred with her to the *Fortson*. The older woman had taken the younger one under her wing, and immediately they had become fast friends, despite their differences in size, background, and personality.

This day was no exception, and Maggie had spent the afternoon showing Alice how to perform the precise maintenance required on the fire control equipment. But they were being pushed to finish by the fading sunlight and the dropping temperature. At that moment the ship was running exactly downwind, so they were working in an eerie calm. But the women knew the ship's course would change again soon, and Maggie swore out loud with her good-natured smile as she pushed again on the unmoving drawer.

One level down, on the bridge, Lt. Early was conning the ship from the starboard bridge wing, as the eight screening ships ran together in a tight circle, only a thousand yards separating each of them from the carrier. The *Fortson* occupied the two o'clock position in the circle. The signalman had just brought Early the decoded message to turn right and take a new position directly behind the carrier, once the maneuver was executed. Early showed the message to Teri Slocum and asked her to stay on the starboard wing, since they would be turning right, while he crossed to the port wing to watch for the execution signal from the carrier.

A minute later, when the execution flag dropped, Early saw it in his binoculars and shouted to the seaman holding the wheel, known as the helmsman, "Right standard rudder."

The young helmsman who had nervously but correctly performed the critical maneuvering drills for almost two hours now made a mistake. All afternoon the OOD himself had been the visual guard on the turning side; this time Teri Slocum was silently performing that duty on the right bridge wing. Although he repeated Early's command, "Right standard rudder, Aye, sir," the tired seaman unthinkingly turned the wheel toward Early's voice, to the left.

Henry, watching through his binoculars the carrier's huge shape off their port quarter, didn't pick up the direction of their own rudder movement for a few seconds, until Teri yelled, "That's *right* standard rudder!"

The helmsman, obviously flustered, looked quickly at Teri, then at the rudder indicator. He mistakenly turned the wheel even *more* to the left, then back to the right, and finally looked over to where Henry Early was standing, while the *Fortson* wound up on a course taking her directly in front of the carrier, its massive shape already looming large through the bridge windows.

In the next instant, twenty-four year old Henry Early had to make a decision. He realized that they had gone too far left to turn back. If they did so, they stood a good chance of being sliced in half in a matter of seconds. He made his decision.

"Increase your rudder to left full! Port shaft emergency back full! Sound the collision alarm!"

This time there were no mistakes. The rudder swung very slowly, it seemed, toward full left, and the engine room watch officer followed the command signaled to him from the bridge by instantly dumping high pressure steam into the reversing turbine on the port propeller. Meanwhile the mate of the watch pulled the handle for the collision alarm, sending a high pitched, wailing siren throughout the ship, punctuated by the mate's voice over the ship's announcing system yelling, "This is NOT a drill! This is NOT a drill! All hands prepare for a collision! This is NOT a drill!"

The *Fortson* had been steaming at over twenty knots. The combination of the full left rudder and the backing port propeller caused her to heel over severely to starboard, as Lt. Early prayed their tight turn would be enough to save them. One level below the bridge the captain's messages slid off his table, and those officers sitting on the starboard side of the wardroom table wound up with all the evening's dinners and drinks in their laps. Their television fell out of its recessed shelf and crashed to the deck, and the collision alarm sounded.

All hands rushed to shut and latch down the hatches and watertight doors belowdecks, while the captain did his best with the severely angled deck to reach the ladder leading to the bridge.

On the upper level, as the turn began, Maggie Simpson, who had been pushing against the drawer, suddenly found herself falling backward on the rapidly inclining deck. Involuntarily she held onto the equipment drawer's handles, but with the force of the turn she and the drawer slid down and back. The drawer jumped its track and came off in her hands just as the deck approached forty degrees, and she fell on her back. The force of the fall and the extra weight of the drawer propelled her down the incline toward the edge of the deck, and she started to yell as she realized she was about to slide under the guardrail.

Alice Pritchard had been standing by the drawer with nothing to hold on to, so she fell on top of Maggie's left side, adding to the propulsion and pinning Maggie's left hand, preventing her from grabbing the safety rail as she slid under it. But the rail almost knocked Alice unconscious. She managed to grab the rail with her right hand and caught a vertical stanchion with her right foot as she lunged for her friend, who was grasping back desperately for her. Most of the larger woman's body was already over the edge and starting to fall as the equipment drawer headed for the dark sea directly below them.

Their hands caught, their eyes locked, and Alice tried to pull Maggie back to the safety of the deck. But as the ship came around to the left, the relative wind went from calm to almost fifty knots, and her best friend became a very heavy pendulum, buffeted by the strong wind. Alice screamed and pulled, but she just didn't have the strength. Maggie was ripped from Alice's grip as she grasped wildly back to her friend, her mouth working, but no sound coming, and she fell into the cold Mediterranean Sea.

Alice screamed, then yelled, "Man Overboard!"

Teri Slocum had moved inside the bridge when the left turn began, and like everyone else she was watching the carrier, not the starboard side, as Maggie Simpson crashed behind her into the water. It was only on Alice's third desperate yell that Teri heard her over the noise of the collision alarm, and she rushed, almost falling, back to the starboard wing. She looked up and saw Alice holding on for life, pointing to a spot fast receding, and screaming.

Teri yelled to Henry Early, "Man Overboard!" just as the captain reached the bridge.

"CIC—mark the spot. Continue your turn."

As they all watched and held their breath, the aircraft carrier *Eisenhower* passed very, very closely down their starboard side, meaning that Petty Officer Simpson was somewhere in the dark, broiling sea between the two ships.

The instant the immediate danger from collision passed, Lt. Early turned to the task of trying to locate the spot where their crew member had just disappeared. But the delay to let the carrier pass, the dark, and the wind made it very difficult. With one eye on the captain, to see if he would take the conn, Early ordered the helmsman to continue all the way around to the course Early judged they had been passing through just before Teri yelled. As they approached that heading, he ordered, "Rudder amidships. All engines stop."

The man overboard detail had been called out, meaning that there were men stationed along all the railings, watching and listening. The signalmen traversed their signal lights across the dark water.

"Who is it? Do we know?" the captain asked Teri.

She was about to explain what she had seen when the chief boatswain's mate opened the door at the back of the bridge and half escorted, half carried Petty Officer Pritchard up to the two of them. Lt. Early conferred with CIC by telephone to check the probable location, and they all ignored for the moment the radio call from the admiral on the carrier.

Desperately trying not to sob, fighting back her tears, Alice Pritchard explained what had happened. "I...I had her," she concluded. "She was there. But...the wind...she was just too heavy. I...I'm so sorry. Oh, Lieutenant Slocum, I'm so sorry. Will they find her?"

"We'll stay here till dawn if we have to," Captain Robertson replied, trying to sound optimistic. But they all knew it was December, it was dark, and Maggie Simpson didn't have a life jacket.

RALEIGH Mary motioned for Cynthia Williams to come in and take a seat while she finished her telephone conversation.

"Okay, dear. Have a safe trip, and I know your speech will be great. God bless...Yes, goodbye."

She hung up and smiled across the desk at her friend.

"Thanks for letting me come by, Mary," Cynthia said.

"Hey, thank you for bringing lunch. We real estate magnates have a reputation for eating high off the hog, but on most days sandwiches are the reality. Everyone's scrambling to buy homes, it seems, before interest rates go up."

"Yes, so I've read," Cynthia said, passing Mary a deli sandwich and some chips. "Is Graham going somewhere?"

"He's the incoming president of his engineering association, and their annual convention starts tomorrow in San Francisco. He's been working on his speech for weeks—mostly about business ethics. Should be interesting. I told him to call tomorrow night, even if it's late."

Cynthia had been one of Mary's strongest prayer partners in Moms in Prayer over the years. She and her husband, Tom, had a son in Sarah's class, and an older boy away at college.

After they'd each taken a bite from their sandwiches, Cynthia opened her large purse. "I need to show you this. I couldn't describe it on the phone."

She pulled out a copy of *Pet Girl International.* "This is a little embarrassing, though not as bad as when I bought it yesterday." She tried to smile. Then her look turned serious as she hunted through the magazine for a page she had marked. "Here, look at this." She opened the slick journal and passed it across the desk to Mary. "Our son David phoned Tom from college—he's obviously heard about the virtual reality computer from his younger brother. Anyway, David told Tom to check out this ad."

Mary put down her sandwich and looked at an expensive two-page color advertisement near the front of the magazine. Besides the attractive couples and the provocative language describing the delights one could experience, there was a picture of a computer and terminals that looked exactly like the equipment that had been shown to them at the special PTA meeting in April. Called simply the "Sex Machine," the computer, special hook-ups, and software were being offered at an introductory price of only $1,995; first deliveries were expected in March. A toll-free number for credit card calls was provided, and one could receive a special certificate suitable for giving as a Christmas present while awaiting the arrival of the real thing.

After studying the ad Mary said, "This has to be the same equipment our kids are using."

"That's what we thought."

"I wonder how we could find out for sure?"

"Tom said to tell you that if you're game, the three of us can visit the BioTeam Company and ask them, face to face."

"I wonder what Principal Perkins will say about this wonderful educational device if it's being advertised like this."

"We don't know, Mary, but we thought you'd like to go with us."

"Count me in," Mary said. "I've been wanting to talk to those people for a few weeks now anyway. Can I show this to Graham?"

"Sure, just bring it with you when we go. I'll call BioTeam after lunch. Hopefully they'll see us soon."

ONBOARD USS *FORTSON* Twenty minutes had passed since the ship came to a stop at Henry Early's best estimate of where Maggie Simpson fell into the icy water. The captain had gone below to use the radio handset in his cabin to return the admiral's demand for an explanation of what had happened, but he left orders with Lt. Early to be recalled to the bridge if Maggie were spotted.

The other seven ships had proceeded on course, but with word of the man overboard, the carrier launched two helicopters with powerful searchlights to join in the effort to find the missing petty officer. Unfortunately, given all the circumstances and the lack of visual references in the open sea, Henry Early and Thomas Dobbs, who was overseeing the surface plot in CIC, knew that they could already be several hundred yards from her real point of impact; and with each passing minute they were being blown further downwind.

Hugh Harrison had walked several times between CIC and the bridge. Although he didn't have a direct role to play in this effort, he had spoken a few words of consolation to Lieutenants Early and Slocum for how well they had handled both emergencies. Hugh had just called down to sick bay to ask the ship's "doctor," a corpsman chief, for a sedative for Alice Pritchard, who was standing forlornly in the back corner of the bridge, when Electronics Chief Garnett Ellis suddenly burst through the door from CIC.

"Is it Maggie?" he asked loudly to no one in particular, looking wildly around the darkened, quiet bridge. "Is it Maggie?" he asked again, recognizing Hugh Harrison standing near Petty Officer Pritchard.

"Yes, chief, it is," Hugh replied.

"Awww," he wailed, closing his eyes. Turning and almost cowering over the seaman at the ship's wheel, his rage building, he yelled, "You! I heard how you screwed up the helm order and caused this mess! I'll knock your head off, you stupid little—"

Hugh moved toward the enraged man. "Wait a minute, chief, we don't know—"

"I *know* that the only woman I've ever really loved is probably dead right now, thanks to this son of a—" His eyes, adjusting to the dark, now saw Alice Pritchard, cowering in the corner. "And you! Some help I hear you were. Crying as usual, doing nothing. I don't know what Maggie ever saw in you. You're so unlike her. You—"

Heny yelled, "Chief Ellis, we're trying to find Petty Officer Simpson. You're not helping. I order you to leave this bridge."

The chief's exploding rage now burst and turned to tears. Those on the bridge who had been watching him turned away as the thirty-year-old chief stood in the middle of the bridge and wept.

The door opened again, and the captain and Doc came in together. The captain almost ran into Chief Ellis. Unaware of what had been happening, he asked, "Henry, any news?"

"No, sir. No change. We've ordered the helicopters to work upwind. Their rotors are so loud we couldn't hear a yell from the water if one came."

While Early spoke, Chief Ellis quietly slipped past the captain and left. Hugh whispered to Doc and showed him Alice Pritchard, who had now slumped to the deck, her arms wrapped around her, head bowed.

As Doc helped Alice stand up to leave, Hugh glanced over to see Teri, who was standing on the port bridge wing and desperately searching the dark sea for her leading petty officer, wipe tears from her eyes.

WASHINGTON AND NEW YORK   "So, what about this polygamy thing?" Leslie asked, the telephone balanced on her shoulder, as she used her computer to draft an outline of the president's response to the Supreme Court's ruling.

"Sounds great to me," Ryan replied. "I'm working up an application form now. I'm expecting a strong response. Should I send you one?"

"No way. I don't share. You want more than one wife, you'll have to start with someone else."

"Well, how about a ten-year exclusion clause? After ten years I can bring in a younger model, still keeping you around, of course. That's the nice thing about this—divorce won't be necessary. I can just bring in a relief pitcher from the bullpen and keep the team together."

"Bull is right! Can we get serious for a second and talk about this story?"

"I *was* serious."

"Okay...look, apparently there have already been twenty or so polygamous relationships—harems?—that have 'come out of the closet' today, just since this morning. We've got local news teams in Salt Lake City and Memphis running them down, so we should have video footage soon. Most of them seem to be one man and two or three women, but in one case there are apparently fifteen wives and twenty-six children!"

"Good heavens. What did the president say?"

"He released a statement through Chris White denouncing the ruling as anti-family, anti-children, and—get this—unbiblical!"

"That's a new one for him, isn't it?"

"Yeah. Maybe he's sticking up for his older sister, after the piece we did last month on her family's faith."

"Okay, Leslie, sounds like we'll have a lot to say tonight on this one. We're checking in Chicago now on what the National Real Estate Society thinks will happen to home designs and bedroom sizes as a result of this ruling. But, seriously, what do you think of it?"

"Well, it's kind of new and hard to take in. I really don't think I'd want to be part of it. But if it's equally available for men and women, and it's an alternative lifestyle that someone really wants, I don't see how I can be against it. If I opposed consensual polygamy, then I'd have to think again about a lot of gains we've already won, which I don't want to do. So I guess the president and I part ways on this issue."

"Yes. And I hear the vice president is upset, too. She disagrees with you—thinks it's anti-women. Listen, I've got to run. Keep your ears open for any more of these Bible references from Harrison. That's odd enough to be a little troubling, all on its own."

"Will do. Oh, and thanks for the wonderful weekend."

"Maybe we should buy a condo in Philadelphia."

"Naw. The hotels with room service are just fine, thank you. See you later."

WASHINGTON "I've got Senator Dempsey on the line," Barbara Morton said over the intercom to the president, who had asked her to return the earlier call from the senator from Ohio. They had not talked in private since his call to the White House back in June.

"John, how are you?" the president asked cordially, but still subdued because of the day's events.

"Fine for an old politician, Mr. President. Just fine."

"What can I do for you today?"

"Well, I was going to call you even before the ruling, but as soon as I read your statement, I picked up the phone."

"It's pretty bad. Think about almost any important subject, and this ruling will affect it. Negatively."

"I know, Mr. President. But what I had planned to call about anyway was to tell you that I've been watching closely, and I wanted to let you know that I must have been wrong about some of the things I said to you back in

June. You've played it straight, and I particularly admired your initiative to tell the voters the truth about your programs. Then I was really proud of what you said today. Most people may not have noticed, but I did. The subtle reference to the Bible. Something's different, or else I've lost my touch on judging people."

William was silent for a while as he thought back to their last long telephone conversation. "Different. Yes, John. And don't apologize for what you said—and did—back in June. Unfortunately, you were right on target then. But there *has* been a difference, one your father would have understood. It's simple, John. Not many people know. It's God. I gave up to Jesus, and I'm trying to let him influence my life now. But today hasn't been good. Those Supreme Court appointments we made back in March swung this vote, and I've been asking for God's forgiveness all day. I feel awful about it. Several of my decisions—not just these appointments—have turned out to have had terrible consequences. I'm really kind of down, to be honest. To think that I could have helped cause yet another blow to families..."

John Dempsey's voice was reassuring. "Mr. President, nothing is ever as good or as bad as it's first advertised to be. I share your faith. There must be some reason for all this, for you being in office. God is at work. Trust him."

"Oh, I do, for me and my family. But our nation worries me. It really worries me."

"Then let's pray about it now."

"On the phone?"

"Sure. I do it all the time. In fact, there's a group of us who get together this way...nobody knows."

"Well, okay. And I'd like to join that group, if you'll have me."

The President and the senator prayed out loud, interceding with their heavenly Father that he would forgive their nation's sins and heal their land.

RALEIGH AND WASHINGTON Sarah Prescott was lying on her bed that afternoon, doing her homework, trying to quell the feelings churning inside her after her experience with the virtual reality computer that day, when the phone rang next to her.

"Hello."

"Hey, it's me."

Sarah's face lit up and she adjusted a pillow behind her head. "Hi, Katherine. How are you?"

"Great. We've been so busy at school since Thanksgiving I haven't had a chance to call. Did you have a good time down there?"

"Yeah. The usual. Mom always fixes way too much, but it was really good. How was Seattle? Where did you stay?"

"On an island! Some industrialist built this awesome house on an island in Puget Sound years ago, and somehow we got to stay in it. We went out by boat, but Dad flew in to meetings in a helicopter."

"Cool...So what else is happening?"

"Not much. I'm surviving this year much better than last. The Secret Service has let up a little more. Mom and Dad are, I don't know, just different. They're getting along much better. They hold hands and stuff. It's stupid, but it's kind of cute. Anyway, I'm so nervous about college I can hardly stand it. Aren't the first rounds of early admissions due out next week?"

"Yeah, I'm nervous, too. I sure hope we both make it."

"Me, too. Anyway, are all of you coming up to Camp David for Christmas?" Katherine asked.

"Yes, I think so," Sarah said. "At least that's what Mom said yesterday. It's sure nice of Uncle William to have us back again."

"Hey, islands are okay, but I think we'd go crazy at Christmas without everybody. Mom and Dad still think Easter was like real special, so it should be great. I hope it snows."

"That would be great, wouldn't it?"

"So, how's Matthew?"

Sarah smiled. "Oh, he's fine. He's already heard that he got into State."

"And how's that computer thing?"

Sarah's smile faded. She paused before answering. "Well, it was really great at first. I mean I guess it was, like, very realistic—I mean *very*, Katherine. They say it was just like having real sex."

"Awesome...I guess."

"But for the last few times it's really gotten sort of weird. I don't know. It's just too wacko, and I guess I'm starting to question whether I should keep doing it."

"What do you mean?"

"Well...I'm embarrassed even to talk about this...but like today they programmed it for lesbian group sex."

"Gross!"

"I know. They have one third of the experiences either in homosexual or bisexual situations. They say it opens our understanding of alternatives to traditional roles and makes us more loving and caring of all types of people. But I think it's pretty stupid."

"Yeah, that sounds really dumb. What was it like?"

"Well...they always make it pleasant, if you can get past what's, like, happening. I just think it's all gone too far. Spending the night with Matthew would seem so normal and tame after all this."

"Have you done *that?*"

"No. But I've thought a lot about it. I know he loves me. And, well, this computer *has* opened up a whole world of new feelings and experiences...if it just weren't so creepy. I mean all those wires and stupid situations. Just quietly being loved by Matthew seems real nice—"

"Sarah, your parents would die! You told me yourself you want to stay a virgin until you get married."

"I know. But I was thinking like a little kid then. I know so much more now. You would, too, Katherine, I promise, if your school had one of these computers."

"Maybe, but I'm not sure it's the best thing to have, from what you're saying. Anyway, don't do anything dumb, and we'll talk about it at Christmas."

"I don't know. Matthew and I are really in love, and he makes me feel good. I'm not making any promises, but I'll see you at Christmas and tell you what happens."

"Seriously, Sarah, don't sleep with Matthew now. We're still in high school."

"So? We're seniors, aren't we? And soon we'll be in college. Everybody else is doing it. And our teacher, Ms. Bowers, has helped me understand lots of feelings I didn't know I had. It's not that big a deal, one way or the other. I really feel like I've already done it."

This time Katherine paused. "That computer has really changed you, Sarah. Look, I guess I don't know all that you know, but you're the one who's been telling me all these years that the Bible says to wait until marriage. Now *I'm* studying the Bible with Mom and Dad and agreeing with you, but meanwhile you've changed. What's the deal?"

"The deal is that Matthew and I love each other, and sex is a natural part of love, and God made both nature and love, so I think it's okay."

"Well, you're playing with fire. What about marriage?"

"Katherine, you and I probably won't be married to anybody for years and years. I don't know about you, but I've experienced almost real sex, and I'm not going to wait years and years. It's good. Really good."

"Sarah, every girl I know who's given in on this regrets it—sometimes the next day, the next week, or the next year, but *always* sometime. Always. I don't know, but they all say it, like, changes the relationship. The boys just start focusing on sex and expecting it. It becomes the main thing—"

"Listen, I know Matthew, and he's not like that. If we do it, we'll be just like adults. We can handle it. And I wouldn't be 'giving in'—I'm thinking about it a lot myself. So don't worry."

"I wish I could see you. Please wait till you come up here."

"Like I said, we'll see. Anyway, what else is going on?"

WASHINGTON The study topic for that evening was evangelism, and Joe Wood was explaining to William and Carrie that God simply wants each believer to move the unbelievers he or she knows one step closer to him.

"That clearly means you're not running around harvesting new Christians every day of the week. Hopefully you'll do so more than a few times in your life, but it'll be because someone else, maybe in a different place, maybe ten years earlier, planted seeds, and others watered those seeds over the years. Only God knows when a heart is ready to turn to him, but he's commanded us to plant, to water, to cut weeds, and then, when the time is right, to harvest. The main thing is to be faithful, to do those things he has commanded, and to be open to how he can use each of us in his process with different people, if we're sensitive and we let him."

"You mean Richard and Janet 'harvested' William," Carrie said, "after maybe Mary planted seeds and others watered with words and actions over the years."

"Exactly. Hey, William, you all right?"

William had been quiet and subdued during their entire session that evening. "Yes...actually, no. I'm sorry, Joe. I know this is one of the few things Jesus actually directs us to do... I *have* been listening. I guess I'm just really down about the Court ruling today."

"I understand. It's definitely not good. Not good. I've read that in societies with multiple wives all the women and children wind up competing for the father's attention and love. So unlike children growing up in a nuclear family where they know they can be loved unconditionally, instead, wives, their sons and daughters wind up in competition with each other, and there are winners and losers. It really sounds like just what we need—more kids worried about whether their fathers love them!"

"I don't see how the Supreme Court could be so stupid," William continued. "And of course I feel terrible because two of the key votes came from justices I nominated. Joe, I've personally screwed up this country!"

Carrie said, "By their reasoning, Joe, it seems now that the worst thing a law can have is a biblical origin. William's right. That's so stupid. From what William's read to me, virtually *all* our laws are based on the Bible. Yet the courts seem to pick the ones they want to discredit purely on that basis."

"It's simple." Joe smiled. "Once you unhitch our laws and our standards for behavior from God's rules, you're headed for unchartered water and disaster. Or probably so."

"Why do you say 'probably'? It seems pretty certain to me."

"Look, William, the nation's laws are clearly very important. You're right in saying that they should be based on God's laws, as they were in our nation for over two hundred years, counting the time before independence. But look. Why are these laws changing now? Because people's hearts have been changed for the worse. And changing all the laws back overnight, if that were even possible, wouldn't change people's hearts again. Men and women have to come, individually, to their Creator on their knees to get their hearts changed—I know that—and you know that. By God's grace we've experienced his power to change us.

"So as important as our laws are for setting an environment for right behavior and for controlling actions, don't fall into the trap of thinking that unless Washington does something, it won't be done. God is bigger than Washington! People's hearts get changed by what happens in their neighborhoods, their homes, their churches and their schools, and with their friends. Christ comes in and can eventually rule a nation, but he does so one heart at a time, usually by individual witnessing, over time, like we were just talking about. Not by an act of law.

"I understand your depression. It's bad, this ruling today. But adultery and abuse and abortion and robbery and murder go on to some extent with or without laws to the contrary. Yes, we should have the laws. Presumably there were less of these sins when we swiftly punished some of them and didn't lift others up as wonderful alternatives. But the sins won't stop completely until the hearts change. And that's a very local issue—so local that it's individual."

"Then how do I, as the president, affect people's hearts, Joe?" William asked.

"I think you have to search out that answer in prayer with God. The Bible says we *all* have talents. Some are teachers, some evangelists, some providers, some helpers. Most of us have several talents and can take different roles in different situations. I suggest you spend a lot of time on your knees asking God that question and then listen."

"Do you think I—we, Carrie and me—*can* affect hearts and change how people act?"

Joe smiled. "I've got no doubt. You're a fairly good orator. And you're in a reasonably high position! Once these classes end in two weeks, you'll have plenty of time. But whether you're just supposed to affect the hearts of your own children or of millions of people, I don't know. Both are important. Again, ask God. It's so important to do that. We've had a wonderful course here for, what, four months? Now you can put all you've learned to work. But you have to listen for God's will, and his timing. The only way to do that is by continuing to study his Word and to pray."

William reached for Carrie's hand. "Then if we're through with the lesson itself, let's start now. And, Joe, I can't tell you how many times in the last few months I've been led by Carrie, you, Michael, or someone back to the point about the importance of prayer. Do you think God's trying to tell me something?"

Joe's smile broadened. "I'd say he's got out his two-by-four, trying to get your attention."

William thought for a moment. "You're right. Here, let's kneel and ask for his will and his guidance in our lives."

So for the third time that day William prayed to his Father to lead him. "I just want to submit to your will, Holy God," he prayed from the bottom of his heart. "Please, Lord, lead me as your servant, and use me however you want. Show me your way."

ONBOARD USS *FORTSON* The ship searched for Petty Officer First Class Maggie Simpson until two hours past dawn the next morning. One of the Russian frigates returned during the night, and together they conducted a coordinated box search of the entire area. Finally, with the crew exhausted, Captain Robertson ordered the search stopped and instructed the navigator to set a course to rejoin the task group.

Two hours later, after showers but no sleep, the captain convened a meeting in his cabin with the executive officer, Electronics Chief Garnett Ellis; his division officer and department head, Thomas Dobbs; Maggie Simpson's division officer, Teri Slocum; and her department head, Hugh Harrison.

Everyone was clearly in a very somber mood as the captain began, "Chief Ellis, I've never really had to do this at sea before, because we've never had loved ones so close by, frankly. So forgive me if I stumble a bit, but I want to tell you how sorry I—we—are. Tell me, please, were you engaged?"

The chief had been examining the captain's tablecloth in detail, his arms folded across his chest. "Yes, two weeks ago."

"I'm so sorry."

Teri said, "I didn't know, Chief Ellis. Maggie didn't tell me. I'm really very sorry."

"She—we—were afraid how the navy might take to us getting married. I told her we'd have the right to share some sort of married housing, even on the ship." The captain and executive officer exchanged glances. "But she was afraid we might get separated or put off. And she loved her job. Then it *killed* her. But I told her we had a right to live together, after we were married. I figured if these guys"—he pointed to Thomas Dobbs and said with a bite to his voice, which the others tried to ignore—"can all live in a big commune, then the rest of us have some rights, too." Everyone glanced away. Then he added bitterly, "I'd almost talked her into asking you to marry us, sir."

The captain shifted in his chair. "I would have been honored, Chief Ellis. I've never had the pleasure of officiating at a wedding. Though I guess you may be right; it might become more common now."

"Well, now you get to do her funeral."

There was an awkward silence.

Finally the chief spoke again. "So, when does the inquiry start?"

"We're getting statements from everyone on the bridge, the watch officer in the main engine room, and Petty Officer Pritchard. Then I'll submit a report to the admiral."

"Then the inquiry starts?"

"No. That's the whole process. It was obviously an accident, but we have to record what happened and make recommendations for steps that could prevent a similar tragedy in the future."

"You mean the only woman I've ever loved is killed by acts of obvious negligence and stupidity, and you're just going to label it an accident and forget it?" the chief asked, his voice rising. "No way."

Everyone turned to the captain, to see how he would react to the chief's less-than-respectful language.

"Chief Ellis," the captain responded, his voice level despite his fatigue, "the navy has procedures for almost everything, including accidental death on a combat ship. This job that we have is inherently risky. On an average deployment an aircraft carrier will lose four people to some type of accident. It's awful, but we're handling weapons, fuel, and natural forces twenty-four hours a day. So I'll follow the procedure set out in naval regulations to investigate and report it."

"Maggie was just pushing on a drawer. How dangerous should that have been? If that helmsman had been properly trained and supervised, or if weapons department procedure called for a safety belt, Maggie would still be alive."

"Chief, I know you're upset. We all share your grief. All of us knew Petty Officer Simpson. But there was no negligence here. It was an accident. A tragic accident."

"I'll never believe that, and neither will my older brother, who's an attorney in Chicago. By the time we get back—maybe even before—I'll have him research everything he can to find out who's really to blame for Maggie's death, and we'll sue until we get real answers."

Richard Anglin leaned forward in his chair and said, "Chief, the captain has explained that it was an accident, a freak accident. And people don't sue the navy over a casualty at sea unless it involves intentional harm."

"You mean Maggie is killed and no one's to blame? No way. Someone's *got* to be responsible. And if you won't investigate, we will. My brother's a mean attorney. Most of the other attorneys in Chicago hate him, 'cause he never gives up. So don't sweep this too far under the carpet, or you may have to crawl in there yourself to pull it out."

Hugh couldn't believe the chief's impertinence and looked at the chief's department head, expecting him to say something. Tom Dobbs saw Hugh's look and said, "Chief, that's really out of line to talk to the captain and XO like that, no matter how tired you are, after we've spent over twelve hours looking for your fiancée."

The chief was unmoved. "Thanks a lot for nothing. And what would you know about this, anyway? Maggie was a woman, and one great *woman* at that. Now she's gone. And I promise you all, someone's going to pay for it."

The captain slowly rose, and Hugh felt he looked ten years older than the day before. "Chief Ellis, we're all very sorry, and obviously we're all very tired. Before any of us says something he or she might really regret, I suggest we break up for now. We'll follow the set procedure, as I've outlined. You're welcome to participate and to read the statements, so long as you don't interfere with the process. If, after all that, you still feel compelled to sue the navy or us or me, then I guess you'll know where to find us. Now, good morning."

The others rose with the captain, and they all filed out of his cabin, except Anglin, whom the captain asked to stay for some further discussions.

As the others headed for their staterooms or working spaces, Teri asked Hugh if she could stop in his room for a minute. Inside, she collapsed on his chair as he sat on the bunk built out from the wall.

"They didn't train us for much of this at Annapolis," she said, her voice fading from lack of sleep and the emotional drain.

"No, you're right. No one foresaw husbands and wives—or lovers—serving together on combat ships! Where does Ellis imagine we'd create married housing? Build condos on the upper decks? And for longer deployments we could turn one of the ammunition magazines into a nursery. I assume that having kids on board, as the 'right' of the parents, will be next."

Teri managed a smile. "Oh, I think he's just very, very hurt and looking for a target to blame right now." Then she turned serious again. "I was talking about death. They don't train us about death. Maggie was such a wonderful young woman and a friend. She had everything going for her. Everyone liked her—and obviously at least one man loved her. Now she's dead. And maybe I *am* to blame in some way. I mean, that radar is ours. Maybe there should have been more maintenance on those parts. And the helmsman; maybe I should have caught his mistake sooner. If I'd done either of those, Maggie might very well still be alive."

"Come on, Teri. Don't start down that path. You heard the captain. It was an accident. Pure and simple. We can't foresee everything. Only God can do that. And I guess for reasons we don't understand, it was his will for Maggie to die now. I can't explain it, but I know he's in charge. You're not to blame. Now we all need to grab some shut-eye before lunch." Hugh stretched out on his bunk and put his hands behind his head on the pillow.

Teri slowly stood up and turned to the door, putting her hand on the doorknob. "Thanks. I may be too tired to sleep. But I appreciate your thoughts. I'm going to check on Alice and the rest of my girls. Most of them are taking Maggie's death pretty hard. I don't think they've ever *really* considered how close we all might be to death here. Anyway, maybe I'll eat an early lunch and then try to lie down. Thanks again. See ya."

She turned around to nod good-bye but found that Hugh was already sound asleep. She nodded anyway, turned off the overhead light, and quietly shut his door behind her.

We are a religious people whose institutions presuppose a Supreme Being.

U.S. SUPREME COURT
ZORACH V. CLAUSON, 1952

16

Sunday, December 23
Three Weeks Later

WASHINGTON William awoke at just after four in the morning. His alarm was not set to go off for over two hours, yet he realized that he was fully awake. After five minutes he got up, put on his robe against the continuing chill, and walked over to the window to look out at the lights around the Washington Monument.

He wondered for a moment why he was awake. Was it because his family would gather again that afternoon, this time with Carrie's mother and sister as well, to spend Christmas at Camp David? Perhaps that was part of it. Was it more worry about the still unfound nuclear warhead, about which there had been no further news for months? Or from listening to his advisors during the past week while their teams presented their goals and plans for the new year, which sounded exactly like the old year? Perhaps. But for the past week he had also felt a new expectancy, an unusual coming together, as though a page in his life was turning. *No,* he thought, *not a page. More like one whole book closing, and another book opening.*

Their concentrated, formal course of study with Michael Tate, Joe Wood, Robert Ludwig, and several other gifted teachers had ended the previous week. *What a blessing that course was! To be discipled and taught by such godly men and women. Thank you, Lord,* he humbly prayed. William felt he now had almost an alternative advisory team—not people who understood laws and policies, but people who could serve as a collective moral rudder, enlightening him on God's Word whenever he asked. And through them he and Carrie had hosted several quiet dinners with a few economists, legal professors, educators, and business owners who shared their faith and tried to implement the Lord's will in their professions. *I didn't know such people even existed six months ago. Or at least I didn't know they were so sane and reasoned! Another incredible blessing.*

Six months...it was just about six months ago that I gave my life to Jesus Christ and his Holy Spirit started to work in me. William smiled. *What a six months! The best of my life. Why did I wait fifty years to find out these simple but powerful truths? God can do anything.*

William had been praying daily for those six months, but for the past three he and Carrie had focused on asking the Lord for his guidance. Over and over William had prayed regularly, sometimes several times a day, that his heart would be opened, that he would submit his will to God's, and that God would use him however he wanted. At times he wondered whether his prayers were heard, but Michael reminded him to be patient, that God had to prepare the heart before he could use the other talents given to each one of us. Michael assured him that if he continued to pray, to read the Bible, to worship, and to seek God's will, the Lord would always be faithful. So William had persevered.

Now, alone in the stillness of the dark morning, he felt led to pray again. He fell to his knees by the window, bowed his head, and started to pray. As he began praising God and asking for his guidance, it was suddenly as if his own words stopped and someone else began to speak. William still heard his own voice, but the control of what was being said was no longer his, as if someone had taken over the microphone in his mind.

A chill ran down William's spine, and he bowed his head further. Words were spoken that he had never before expressed, many in direct contradiction to what he had always believed. It was as if he were a spectator—no, a scribe—and the words were being written on his mind and etched on his heart.

William stayed on his knees for almost an hour. But it seemed to him like only a few minutes. Near the end of the time his initial chill was replaced by a growing warmth, as if his soul was filling with a new power, a new and different energy, which both surrounded his thoughts and were themselves the thoughts. His heart began to race.

After filling him with visions he had never before expressed, the pictures and thoughts began to recede. William was left limp, done in, but completely at peace. In fact, he felt filled with a new and almost inexplicable peace. When he realized that his thoughts were again his own, he lay prostrate on the floor, physically drained but spiritually filled. *Thank you, O God! I'm in awe of your power and your grace! You have in fact been faithful, more than I could ever imagine. O God, like Solomon, I pray for your wisdom. And no matter what happens, let me always remember that you alone are the source of my strength. Thank you, holy Father.*

Lying on the floor of the White House bedroom before dawn on that December morning, William Harrison, the president of the United States, for the first time knew exactly what God wanted him to do.

CAMP DAVID The family gathered at the White House, as they had at Easter. Lunch was followed by Christmas carols provided by a combined high school choir from around the Washington area. Then the extended family entered the presidential helicopters for the ride to the Maryland retreat, confident of beating the front that was predicted to bring precipitation—and maybe even some snow—that night.

Most of the guests had asked for their earlier accommodations again, though Carrie moved Jennifer and her three young children into the cabin near Laurel Lodge where the elder Harrisons had stayed in April. Jennifer hoped for a special phone call from Hugh on Christmas morning.

Rebecca's daughter Courtney and Robert's friend Sasha were the only other two Easter guests who were not in attendance; Courtney was visiting the home of her new boyfriend in St. Louis, and Sasha had purchased an inexpensive winter ticket to visit his parents in Kiev.

As William and Carrie walked hand in hand to Aspen Lodge, the president said, "It's really hard to take in all that's happened since we were last here with the family."

Carrie smiled. "It really is. That seems like a decade ago. Neither of us knew the Lord, your parents were still with us, we didn't know Michael Tate or Joe or Robert—it's truly incredible that it's only been eight months."

"And our domestic package still hasn't passed Congress," William laughed. "Some things change more slowly than others!"

"Yes, but from what you've told me about your experience this morning, it's maybe a good thing."

"You're right, Carrie. I realized the same thing at our final Treasury briefing just before lunch. I guess God protects us from ourselves sometimes, even when we don't know it, and we think he's wrong."

She looked up at him. "I want to hear more about what happened."

"You will. In fact, I want to discuss it with you in detail. Then I hope we can use some of the time here to think and to pray and to write."

"Sounds good to me," Carrie said, walking closer to him.

He put his arm around her and whispered in her ear, "I love you."

As they neared the steps of Aspen Lodge, Katherine bounded out, wearing a warm-up suit and carrying her tennis racket. "Sarah and I are going to start. Robert and Tim are coming over in a little while," she fired off as she sped by her parents.

"Isn't it a little chilly for tennis?" Carrie asked.

"Not really." Katherine turned and walked backward toward the courts. "And it's s'posed to *snow* tonight, so we thought we'd better play today."

"Have fun," Carrie responded. She turned to William as they started up the steps and said, "She seems so much happier. Won't it be great having the two of them together at school next year? They're like peas in a pod. I'm so glad they both got in."

"Yes. And I think Sarah will continue to be a good influence on Katherine," William concluded as they entered the lodge.

"So, what happened with you and Matthew?" Katherine asked, as the two girls did stretching exercises by the court.

Sarah smiled as she came up from touching her toes. "Oh, I accepted your cousinly advice. We didn't do *it*, but we've done about everything else. Matthew is so sweet. He's great—I don't just mean with sex, but he *is* great at that, too."

Katherine rotated her right arm and frowned. "You sound awfully serious. I don't mean to sound preachy or anything, but everything I've ever heard or read says to wait. I hope I've got the strength."

"Come on, Katherine. Believe me, it's not a battle. It's natural. Trust me. After what I've experienced on that computer, making love with an eighteen-year-old man will be so nice. I think we'll probably do it over New Year's." They unzipped their racket cases and moved out onto the court. "Matthew says we can get a motel room. Won't that be awesome?"

Katherine shook her head. "I don't know. Sounds sort of cheap to me. What do you think he'll want to do the next weekend? And the next?"

Sarah stopped bouncing the ball and said seriously to Katherine, "Look, he's not like that. We've got a mature relationship. I know what I'm doing, so please don't criticize what you don't understand. Okay?"

"Okay...truce. But you're the one who's always told me to wait. Then you get excited by a machine, now by Matthew. You're right. Maybe I don't understand. Here, let's play."

Although Mary had briefly seen Carrie and William in August when she drove Katherine back to Washington at the end of summer vacation, the two couples had not been together since Easter. They had decided during lunch at the White House that after unpacking, Graham and Mary would walk over to Aspen Lodge, where there was a roaring fire in the living room fireplace. The four of them pulled up comfortable chairs in front of the fire and talked about all that had happened since they were last at Camp David.

After about twenty minutes, Mary said, "William, did you have any idea that the polygamy ruling was coming?"

He frowned and shook his head. "No, big sister. And, believe me, I feel terrible about it."

Graham spoke. "In Raleigh, we've already had lots of multiple marriages. The city's insurers are threatening to send big bills, apparently because of increased benefits to so many more people, if employees pick up additional wives and children. And over in Chapel Hill a thirty-five-year-old aerobics instructor has three young husbands."

"We're making a further mockery of marriage and the family," William lamented. "After all that's happened the last forty years, is it any wonder no one understands God's intent for a permanent relationship between a man and a woman?"

"It's not just marriage, William," Mary said. "Do you remember that sex education computer we told you about? Well, Sarah decided to go ahead and experience it."

"Oh, Mary," Carrie said sympathetically.

Mary and Graham went on to explain all that had happened, including Mary's visit with the Williamses to BioTeam and to their high school principal. "We didn't expect BioTeam to deny that it was their product being advertised in *Pet Girl International*, since it looked identical to the computer at school, and they didn't. But what blew us away was that the principal, Lester Perkins, also knew about it."

"He *knew* that the school is using a device being sold as pornography?" Carrie asked, her eyes widening in surprise.

"Yes. Isn't that great? But Perkins told us that something's value depends on its 'situational context.' He said that some great literature could be considered to be erotic or to be promoting bigoted mores if taken out of context, and he preferred to view the computer's value within the context of the students' health class, where he was sure it was having a positive effect."

"What double-speak!" Carrie said. "In other words, 'We're happy to be teaching your children with pornography'!"

"Exactly. And then when I tried to tell him about the negative effect the class was having on Sarah and on our relationship at home, he told me that ours was an isolated example, probably caused by our 'overly religious lifestyle.' He said all the other parents seemed to be very happy."

"That sounds awful," William added. "Can't you get relief from the school board? At least this is *one* problem for which the federal government's not responsible."

"We tried," Graham said. "The school board is so much in favor of this machine that it's trying to raise funds to buy ten more. And, unfortunately, that's where the federal government *does* come in. BioTeam has apparently filed for a grant under a program pushed through Congress last year by Enlightened Parenthood and the U.S. Teachers Association to fight AIDS. There are tens of millions of dollars available for teaching programs that help prevent AIDS. If you can believe it, BioTeam is pushing this machine, which I'm sure promotes promiscuity, as an anti-AIDS program! They're even using *our* school as the model for their program. And they're asking for enough money to put one computer in every public high school in the nation!"

"Dear God, help us," Carrie said, almost involuntarily.

"I'm afraid you're right," Mary added. "Graham and I have had this awful feeling for months now that God is turning from us, that things are getting worse at an increasing rate. We've been praying fervently for national repentance and revival."

"Yes…yes…we've felt exactly the same way," Carrie said, then looked over at her husband. "William has really felt that burden. We've been praying, too. And maybe early this morning William may have heard at least the first words in answer to those prayers."

William nodded quietly, put two logs on the fire, and sat down again. He then explained what had happened when he had been awakened so early.

"Oh, William, it gives me chills," Mary said, as he concluded. "Do you think you can do it?"

"With God's help, we can do anything."

"Then let's pray, now," Graham said.

The Harrisons nodded. The couples stood up, held hands, and bowed their heads in what for William now seemed to be a completely natural act of acknowledging the real ruler of the nation.

The entire family assembled at Laurel Lodge an hour before dinner. There was a roaring fire, hot cider, and a tall Christmas tree which the younger members of the family decorated while the older members talked and gave advice on ornament placement.

Rebecca and Bruce, still flush from a long jog and recent showers, found their way to where the president and first lady were standing by the fireplace. Everyone smiled and shook hands. Bruce spoke first. "We didn't have much time at the White House earlier today, but I just want to tell you again, Mr. President, how much my family really appreciates your help with my mom's operation. She's doing great, and we're so thankful."

William appeared to be embarrassed but continued to smile. "I'm so glad she's okay, Bruce. And we were glad to help."

"If there's anything I can ever do for you, just let me know," Bruce continued. "I think you're the best thing that's happened to this nation in a long time, and if you decide to run again, I'd like to help your campaign in Atlanta. I just hope your legislative package finally passes next year—it was awful what Congress did to your initiatives."

"Sometimes what we think is terrible actually has a positive reason behind it. Anyway, I do hope we break the gridlock this year. Carrie, do you need some more cider? Rebecca? Here, let me get some, and then I want to hear about the hospital."

PARIS "Trent, so glad to see you again." Wafik extended his hand as Congressman Patterson came through the front door of the spacious villa located on the western side of Paris.

"The pleasure's all mine," responded the congressman. "I'm just sorry the fact-finding dinner at our embassy took so long. But to come over on the taxpayers' money, I've got to at least do a little of the taxpayers' business," he said, smiling. "Or seem to."

"Yes, I understand completely. You know we keep late hours here anyway. Please, come have a drink in the drawing room before you turn in."

Trent looked around the foyer. "Are...are they?..."

"Marie and Paulette? Yes, they're here. They were so excited to hear of your return. And since Francis is not along on this trip, I'm afraid they're both yours for the night. They're waiting for you upstairs."

Trent's eyes widened and his smile broadened. "Yes, well, let's have that drink...but we better keep it short. Jet lag and all." He winked.

Wafik nodded his understanding and showed the congressman into the drawing room, where Trent again apologetically went through his ritual with his anti-bugging device, which again missed Wafik's special computer.

Once they were seated before the fire with Trent cradling a large brandy snifter, Wafik spoke, "We noticed and appreciated your outspoken support for our people in your Congress."

Patterson swirled the brandy, then took a sip. "And I noticed and appreciated the money in the Swiss bank account," he said. "But, seriously, you were right. These are measures I now believe we should have been supporting all along. My conscience is clear that I'm doing the right thing."

"Well, I'm glad our arrangement could help in that understanding."

"Yes, absolutely. And you know, I was frankly astonished by how many of my colleagues agreed with my statements. Several of them, even from the other side of the aisle, went out of their way to tell me how much they appreciated my leadership and assured me of their support."

"It seems you may have touched upon a subject that has genuine support in your Congress."

"Yes, I think so," Patterson said and took another sip of brandy.

They continued to talk for ten more minutes, when Trent finished off his brandy, stood up and said, "I really appreciate your hospitality, my friend, especially at this time of the year. But I truly am a little tired, and I'd like to continue this in the morning."

Wafik rose and offered the brandy bottle. "Of course. Of course. Here, take some more brandy with you. Please, have a very good night."

A few minutes later, as Trent reached the top of the stairs, he wondered if the twins would notice how much younger he looked after a month of using Grecian Formula in his hair.

CAMP DAVID Carrie Harrison had again placed the extended family at small tables for their meals, and she and William were seated with Carrie's mother, Shelly Roberts, and her older sister, JoAnn, who had taken back her maiden name after her husband left her fifteen years earlier. Carrie's father had passed away five years before, but her mother was still very healthy and active. Also at the table were Jennifer—Katherine and Sarah had volunteered to give her a break from her kids during the meal—plus Rebecca and Bruce.

Before they sat down, William offered a blessing, and then the staff served the meal of oyster pie and roast pork for the adults, with hot dogs for the children.

After a few minutes of catching up, William said, "Jen, I heard about the death of the young sailor on the *Fortson* at a briefing. Has Hugh said anything to you about it in a call or a letter? Did he know her?"

"He apparently didn't know her real well, but she was in his department and pretty popular. He said it was a tough blow for everyone. They found out later that she had a fiancé on board. Hugh's been on ships where men have died, but he said that having a woman die really sort of subdued everyone. Actually I met the woman and her division officer. Hugh says she took it pretty hard, too. A real tragedy. The ship's in Barcelona for Christmas, by the way. I hope Hugh will call; thanks for telling us how to call through the White House switchboard."

"Oh, no problem," William said. "I hope I'll get to talk to him, too. I've always admired Hugh deeply for doing what I didn't do and serving in the navy. What happened on his ship was a real tragedy. We'll be praying for protection for all of them for the rest of the deployment." Bruce looked up at the second mention of prayer and seemed puzzled.

William continued, "Rebecca, I'm sorry I missed your update on the hospital. Anything new since we were together this spring?"

"Not really. Our internal data on the morning-after pill continues to show disasterous results, both in pregnancies and in a resurgence of AIDS. And this isn't exactly dinner conversation, so we can talk about it later, but, William, these full-term abortions are just awful." Bruce scowled at her but kept eating.

William looked hurt. "I know, Rebecca. I'm agonizing over them… over all abortions, really." Now Bruce turned to the president, not believing what he was hearing, as William continued, "I've been praying and reading on that subject. Frankly, we're close to a new policy."

"Which will be?" Bruce asked.

"Perhaps we'll come out against all abortions, Bruce."

"*What?*"

"We'll see. As Rebecca said, this isn't exactly dinner conversation. There've been some changes in my thinking on several issues, Bruce. We'll have a chance to talk about them while we're here. By the way, you certainly came off well on the TV interview."

Bruce was obviously embarrassed that Leslie Sloane had so prominently featured the only non-family member and his views on issues and on the president. He smiled sheepishly. "Yeah, well, you know those TV people do whatever they want. I had no idea they'd use so much of those interviews."

Rebecca looked at Bruce, raised an eyebrow, and said, "And didn't he look good in those gym shots?"

"Hey, give me a break. You didn't look so bad yourself."

"I've always wanted to know TV stars," Shelly Roberts quipped.

OVER THE ATLANTIC OCEAN OFF SOUTH CAROLINA   Later that evening the first-class cabin on Air Carib flight 557 from Washington to St. Thomas was abuzz with the presence of Ryan Denning and Leslie Sloane. Ryan had hopped the shuttle to Washington that afternoon, and now they had an entire week to relax together over the Christmas holidays.

As the steward removed their main course dishes then served them more wine, Leslie in particular felt she could finally unwind after a very difficult month. In addition to the continuing story on the polygamy ruling and the probing she had discretely been doing around the White House on the president's unusual use of a biblical reference, she was determined that at some point during the next week she would bring the future of their relationship to a head. She was too old, she felt, to become semi-permanently entangled with Ryan if marriage was not in the cards. But she would let that subject wait at least a day.

Leslie sipped her wine in the window seat. She leaned closer to him and said, "This was a great idea, Ryan. I hate not seeing my folks over Christmas, but I really need to get away."

He smiled at her and touched his glass to hers. "We both do—and I'm just so glad you could come."

A few moments of silence passed between them. Then she said, "You know, I've been following up on your question about the president, when he said that polygamy is 'unbiblical.' No one on the president's team seems to think anything of it, or at least if they do, they're not saying. But one of the vice president's staffers told me that she's really bent out of shape about what she calls the 'new president.' Apparently they had a real run-in a few months ago over his 'truth in domestic programs' thing, but they've mended their fences. Anyway, I didn't get very far, but I do feel there's something different about the president. It's hard to put my finger on.

"Oh, then I had our guys just sit and watch for two weeks who's going in and out of the White House at night and on weekends. Usually it's just been an assortment of friends, actors, politicians, and foreign dignitaries. But two weeks ago there were apparently three different ministers who visited the White House on separate occasions. One, a Michael somebody, came twice! They haven't been back since, and we don't know exactly who they were visiting—maybe the daughter, Katherine. But it's so unlike his first months in office. Anyway, that's what I've found out so far."

"Is there enough for a story?"

"Hard to say. I told Cindy to check out the three ministers while I'm away, to find out who they are and why they might have visited. I mean, it's really the president's business, of course, but I guess we have a right to know if he's holding nighttime services in the White House theater!"

Ryan laughed. "Or being advised on some issues by his sister's buddies. That's all we need! Another Christian in the White House!"

"Really, Ryan, that's a little far-fetched. William Harrison? It's very possible that he was just getting some advice on this polygamy issue. After all, the nation *is* split into all sorts of factions on that one. I hear the VP is really fit to be tied, ready to impeach their own Supreme Court justices! She claims the whole thing is a white male heterosexual trick to put women back in bondage."

"Good," Ryan said. "We haven't been blamed for anything really terrible for, let's see, about six months now, since the equal-but-separate riots at the end of the last school year died down. I was starting to forget how to feel guilty for all that we white males have done to everyone else."

"Oh, come on," Leslie said and gave him an affectionate punch on the shoulder. "Hey, I'm all for individual freedom. Whoever wants polygamy, it's fine with me. It's the ultimate 'do your own thing,' I guess. If we really stand for women's rights and abortion and gay rights, then we have to be for the right to consensual polygamy, it seems to me, and not get all hung up like the VP. Or again get worried about families like those right-wing wackos. I mean, kids may actually have *more* parents! Just don't expect me to participate, though."

"So you don't want to meet Beth and Jane in St. Thomas?"

She raised her glass as if to pour wine on his head, but he stopped her with a kiss.

ATLANTA Much later that night Eunice Porter let herself into her humble but immaculately kept apartment after finishing her waitressing job. She tiptoed in to check on her two sleeping children and said a prayer of thanks that her sister, who lived next door, could put them to bed every night so she could work at the restaurant.

After taking a shower and cleaning up their dinner dishes, she stole another look at each of the children in their beds, then knelt and prayed to God to protect them.

Finally, exhausted from the schedule she kept, she went to her closet and pulled out the boxes from the department store. She opened them and looked at the two beautiful, warm coats she had purchased with part of the $500 advance from Dr. Thompson. Taking out her bag of wrapping paper, she soon had each coat wrapped in colorful paper and placed beneath the small Christmas tree.

It was early on Christmas Eve morning as she turned out her light, knowing that her young children would awake in a few hours. Tired to the point of physical pain, but determined that her children would have a chance, she lay her head on the pillow. In the instant before she was asleep, she thought, *I guess I owe Dr. Thompson another baby—I'll have to get going on that right after Christmas.*

CAMP DAVID The Harrison family awoke on Monday, Christmas Eve morning, to a thin blanket of snow from the passing front. The young children ran and jumped and hollered on the way to breakfast, insisting they could build a snowman from the meager quantity of lingering beauty. And what adult would argue with their logic on the day before Christmas?

The fires in the lodges were stoked and kept blazing all through the cold day. The children played outside while the adults tended to last-minute holiday duties, read, talked, and napped. William and Carrie spent time with each branch of the family, but they also worked together for two hours in Aspen Lodge following his abbreviated national security briefing.

The one devotional service of their stay was planned for that evening, thirty minutes after supper, so that even the youngest child could attend. Reverend Robert Ludwig had agreed to lead the family celebration of Christ's birth, and thankfully the roads from Washington were clear for the minister and his wife, Nell, who arrived together late that afternoon.

William introduced the Ludwigs at the usual gathering before the meal, and everyone could sense the increasing anticipation in the air with each passing hour. After dinner the staff cleaned up and then rearranged the dining room seating area into a theater setting; the chapel was too cold to hold a service in during the winter. Thirty minutes later the entire family, joined by several members of the Camp David staff and Marine Guard, began following Robert Ludwig in "O Come All Ye Faithful"; it was again snowing outside.

After songs, prayers, and readings about Jesus' foretelling in Isaiah 53 and about his birth in Luke 1 and 2, Robert Ludwig asked everyone to be seated. "At this point it would be normal for me to give a homily or sermon, and I have a short one planned. But first there's someone here who wants to share with you his testimony about his faith. It's only appropriate as we celebrate the birth of Christ that we also celebrate the birth of a new Christian. So I'd like you all to listen for a few minutes to our host, President William Harrison."

William rose from his third-row seat next to Carrie and his two children and walked to the front near the Christmas tree. He turned to face the assembly and began, "I want to share with the people closest to me the great joy that has been building in this imperfect person since I gave up trying to run my life—I'd made a big mess of it in most ways—about six months ago and instead asked God's forgiveness and accepted his Son as my Lord and my Savior. It's been the best six months of my—our—life," he said, glancing at Carrie, "and I finally feel that I understand how God wants me to live my life, and also what he wants to do with my life at this time. It's an absolutely wonderful joy, and I want each of you to know how it happened, so you can listen for God's voice in your own life as well."

William then went on to describe his general shortcomings and frustrations—both before and after being elected—his reading about the faith of the Founding Fathers, Carrie's conversion at Easter, and finally his own submission with Richard Sullivan in June. It was obvious to everyone listening that something very real and very powerful had overtaken this most powerful of men, something that humbled him and also gave him great peace and confidence. Both qualities seemed to flow from him as he spoke.

Then he told them that he was still a very muddy glass of old water, but that he was doing his best to replace the mud with God's clean water, day by day, by reading, studying, and praying. He kept his testimony very personal. He could have been anyone, not the president of the United States.

As he spoke, he looked out over the listeners and saw smiles of encouragement from Mary, Graham, Carrie, and Katherine. Most of the others gave him a general look of interest or curiosity, as he shared with them the eternal truth he'd learned. And there was complete astonishment on the face of Bruce, and to a lesser extent Rebecca.

"So that's what God has done in my life, and I give him all the glory and all the praise for his kindness and goodness. Carrie and I plan to share our faith with a wider audience soon. In the meantime, I'd like to ask all of you to respect our wishes on this and let us choose the time and place to do that. But we couldn't let the celebration of our Savior's birth go by without sharing our personal joy—even amazement—that God would send his Son to save sinners like us. On this night, especially, we're reminded of his incredible love and his infinite patience. My last wish is that if God is speaking to your heart tonight, I urge you to listen carefully. Thank you."

William sat down again and received a squeeze of the hand and a broad smile, punctuated with a tear, from Carrie. Reverend Ludwig gave a short and joyful homily on Isaiah 53, recounting the life of the great prophet and the promise of Christ's coming 750 years before his birth. He then tied that earlier promise into the specific promise for each individual's salvation, using William's testimony as an example of how God works out his purposes in each person's life.

The young children began to shuffle and squirm as the service came to an end with "Joy to the World" and "Silent Night," sung with only the lights on the tree illuminating the lodge.

After the service the family stayed together for almost an hour, talking among themselves, after which those with small children began to leave. William and Carrie finally walked back to Aspen Lodge thirty minutes later. The second snowfall had been heavier than the first, and even though it wasn't deep, the snow was sparkingly beautiful.

As they walked, William asked, "I didn't see Rebecca or Bruce after the service. Did they disappear?"

"I'm afraid so, dear," Carrie answered. "As you were thanking Robert Ludwig, Bruce almost shot out the side door, pulling Rebecca with him."

"That's a shame. I know what I said must have been a shock to them, and I hope we get a chance to talk together about it. I wonder how I'll do trying to explain my faith one-on-one—sort of like the evangelism Joe was talking about. But at least I know *exactly* how they feel! God was so incredibly patient with my own pride and arrogance."

They walked on. As they started up the steps of the lodge, William said, "For a moment, as I looked out at the falling snow during the service, I thought of George Washington."

"Why?" Carrie asked, as he opened the door for her. They walked into the main room of the lodge and over by the fire.

"I think it's because after reading so many of his prayers, letters, and speeches, the man is beginning to come alive for me. I was thinking about how he led his army across the Delaware River and won a great victory over the Hessian mercenaries on this same night over two hundred years ago, and it must have been a night like this. Then I thought about the Continental Army, a year later, suffering such pain and losses during the winter at Valley Forge, again in cold snow.

"But what really struck me as I looked out the window was what a leader Washington must have been, to have caused men to follow him into battle on Christmas Eve, when they would want to do almost anything else; or to stay at Valley Forge, suffering, starving, cold, and dying. What a leader."

Carrie thought for a minute as she warmed her hands by the fire, then said, "William, I know not to compare you to George Washington. That's of course impossible. But if he were standing here tonight, I know, from what you've read to me already about his faith, that he'd credit those successes you've just mentioned to God, and he'd encourage you to seek God's help, as he did."

William put his arms around her and held her close. "I know, Carrie, I know," he said, looking past her to the snow outside. "That's what both scares me and exhilarates me. Washington was clearly led by God to do great things—I can't possibly fill those shoes, but our nation is in as perilous a state as anything Washington faced, though most people won't acknowledge it. But who will follow *me*? Who will even *listen* to me?"

Carrie smiled and looked up at her husband. "You can't fill those shoes, William, but God can. As you said tonight, trust him."

He held her close for a long moment before the fire. Finally he whispered, "Merry Christmas, Carrie. What an incredible gift that our Savior was born, as Michael says, in an unspeakable barn, to live and to die an unspeakable death, so we might spend eternity with God."

"Yes, William," Carrie said softly, returning his hug, "and how wonderful it is that this year we finally both opened the gift God meant for us to have all this time."

"You're right. What did I do before I accepted his gift? And I would never have known about it except for you. Thank you, Carrie." William bent down and kissed his wife. At that moment he was overcome by how God had woven together so many strands of his life, particularly Carrie's patient love, to bring him to this night and to their mutual recognition of what they had to do in just the next few weeks. As they ended their kiss and he again held her tight, feeling the joy of her body next to his and thinking about the wonder of it all, he could only say silently, *Thank you, Lord. O thank you dear Father. Please, give me your strength.*

A MEDITERRANEAN PORT Christmas was not a holiday where the *Bright Star* was docked, and in the late morning Sadim and the ship's captain were standing on the main deck between the number two and number three cargo holds, watching several workers from the shipyard weld the finishing touches on a large platform about four meters above the deck. When completed, the new addition would provide a firm platform separate from and aft of the bridge superstructure by about twenty meters, easily accessible by the ship's cranes.

"We seem to be a week or two ahead of the original schedule," the captain finally said, trying to engage his sometimes enigmatic passenger/leader in a conversation.

"Yes," Sadim replied, shielding his eyes from the bright winter sun as he examined the work above them. "At least in the ship's readiness. Hopefully our special gift will also be ready on time."

"But everything goes well below, does it not?"

"So it seems, by the grace of Allah. But there is still much to do in final preparation. Plus installing the listening and defensive devices. Much to do.

And we must be completely ready to sail into the Atlantic in early November to arrive at our destination on time."

"Yes. The American Thanksgiving is when? Late November?"

"The last Thursday. But we must be in place several days earlier. And sometimes there are storms at that time of year, as you know better than I. So we must remain hard at work. Much better to leave early than late."

"Much better," the captain agreed.

CAMP DAVID Christmas morning in the Maryland mountains dawned clear, bright, and cold. By common agreement everyone came to Laurel Lodge at eight to see what Santa Claus had left the younger members of the family, followed by breakfast and general gift opening. William could hardly remember a morning when he had been happier, and he expressed that joy openly to Carrie and to anyone else who would listen. Looking out at the clean snow shining gloriously in the sunshine, he felt as if he were finally on the first page of the second book of his life.

William and Carrie wanted to read through the several books and papers they brought to study over the weekend for their special project, but they knew they would have more time during the coming week, which William had been able to carve out for a working vacation. Michael Tate and Joe Wood had arranged for a group of special visitors at Camp David, starting Wednesday afternoon. But this day was a special day with the family, so they settled into chairs near the fire at Laurel Lodge to watch the children try out their new toys and to talk with the far-flung family, while the smell of roasting Christmas turkey began to fill the air.

William was helping his nephew, Hugh's son, Todd, replace a battery in a new portable computer game when Rebecca and Bruce entered the lodge and made their way from child to child, looking at their gifts. The phone rang on the table next to Carrie. She answered and smiled. "Yes, Hugh, Merry Christmas. Jenny and your family are right here."

Jennifer and her children moved into a small alcove near the kitchen door to take the call from Hugh in Barcelona. Rebecca, sipping some hot chocolate, came over to William and Carrie. "I told Courtney I'd call her about noon in St. Louis. I'm curious to hear what her boyfriend's family is like."

Carrie smiled from her chair. "Sounds serious."

"Maybe. Courtney's twenty-four. If it is serious, I just hope he's a good man. She's had her share of questionable ones. And not growing up with a father at home, she may not be the easiest woman for a man to live with."

"She'll be fine," Carrie said. "Courtney's very sensible."

"I know," Rebecca agreed. "But relationships always need more than sense. I hope she can give."

Bruce walked over, also carrying a mug of hot chocolate, clearly agitated about something. With only a glance toward the president and first lady, he said with haste in his voice, "Come on, Rebecca, I told Peter we'd help with the sled they found in the tool shed."

"Merry Christmas, Bruce," William said from his chair.

"Yeah. Thanks," he replied, looking away toward the door. "Come on, Rebecca."

"But it's so cold, and I—"

Rebecca's reply was interrupted by William. "Is something wrong, Bruce? It's Christmas morning, you know."

"Yeah, I know, Mr. President." He finally turned and looked at William, who was still sitting next to Carrie. "I don't mean to be rude," he said, his voice gaining strength as he spoke, "but, yeah, I guess something's wrong. I couldn't believe what you said last night.Do you have any idea how depressed you've made me? I…I believed in you—a lot of people believed in you." He paused, his distress obvious. "And now I find you've sold out to the bigoted junk your sister's been selling."

"How can we be bigoted, Bruce, by simply trusting God?" William asked in a calm voice.

"Religion. We elected you to move our nation forward based on sound programs of fairness and justice. Now I suddenly find"—his voice rose so much that Jennifer looked over from her phone call—"that you're a *Christian!*" He moved his hand through the air, a note of despair in his voice. "You've sold out! You won't move us forward—you're heading us back to the Dark Ages. Look at what's been done in the name of religion—war, inquisition, pogroms, overpopulation, Ireland, slavery, Yugoslavia, hate—I can't believe it! It's certainly a Merry, Merry Christmas for those of us who were naive enough to trust in you!" As he concluded with a note of derision in his voice, everyone else in the family was listening to him, except for Jennifer, who was trying to talk to her husband, her hand over one ear.

William paused before answering. He looked at Bruce, who was upset, hurt, and angry, then at Rebecca, who appeared startled and embarassed, then back at Bruce. Finally, William said, "Bruce, there's so much I want to say to you, and in most ways I feel inadequate. But let me touch a few points. First, I admit that in some extremes the Christian religion hasn't always been what God intended. But those are the exceptions. I'm really talking about *faith* in Jesus Christ, not organized religion, anyway. But in just those recent periods when Christianity has been strongly revived in men's hearts, look what has followed: universities, hospitals, schools, orphanages, child labor laws, the *abolition* of slavery, first in England, then America, the civil rights movement—not to mention the huge wave of brave men and women who founded the American colonies and then made the nation grow, one small community of church, school, and courthouse at a time. Of course no one ever hears about all this in school, so I don't blame you for not knowing about it.

"And, if you want to make an unbiased list of what various movements have brought in their wake, try the ones that were or are openly hostile to the God of Judaism and Christianity—Communism, Nazi-Socialism, and the more radical branches of Islam. How much suffering and how many *tens of millions* of dead bodies do these isms, based on forced acceptance, claim? At least Christianity is based on repentance and a voluntary personal choice, not on a gun held to the head.

"Anyway, I spoke last night about what God has done for Carrie and me as individual sinners. Yes, frankly, I'm very worried about our nation. And, yes, we'll change our approach to some issues and try to do what the Lord has long ago laid down as the way to live. But it won't be following anyone's specific religion, and it won't be the Dark Ages. In fact, God's way should free people from fear and hate—that's God's promise to us, if we follow his commandments."

"So you're suddenly going to start interpreting God's will for us? What are you, Mr. President, some kind of a prophet? Will we sit at your feet while you tell us God's truth? I can't wait!"

While Todd began speaking to his father on the telephone, the others who were standing or sitting nearby, including Rebecca and Mary, shifted uncomfortably. Bruce's attack seemed so rude and so out of place on this holiday morning.

William smiled. "No. I promise not to be a prophet, Bruce. But I do honestly believe that after a lot of prayer and reading, God has given us some ideas on what is wrong with our nation and on how to begin to approach these problems for healing with *real* solutions."

"See? You *do* think you've heard God's voice! This is insane! Rebecca, I've got to go outside. I can't stand it. Our president is suddenly listening to God, and we're in trouble."

William continued in a calm voice. "Bruce, it's not that I've heard some message that has me heading down a new course I've invented. What I've heard is just old truths, tried and tested over centuries, that we've unfortunately forgotten or ignored for the last forty or so years. I'm not proposing a new course, Bruce, but instead a return to a well-proven old course. And I'm still not exactly certain about any of the specifics. I'm still praying and reading and listening."

"The Dark Ages. Back to the Dark Ages. Anti-everything. A presidency based on myths and stories. I can't believe it. Come on, Rebecca. I'm going, whether you come or not. I need some fresh air. There's too much hot air in here."

Rebecca looked back and forth between the two men, torn between her brother and her boyfriend. "Okay, I'll come," she said to Bruce. Then she turned to her brother. "William, I'll be back. And I want to hear more."

William smiled at her and stood up. "Sure, little sister. We'll see you at

Christmas dinner—unless that wonderful smell of turkey is a myth."

Bruce turned and walked quickly to the door, not looking back. Rebecca followed him, but took time to say a few words to the children. Jennifer said good-bye to Hugh and came over to the fireplace where the rest of the family was still gathered. "What happened?" she asked. "I was trying to talk to Hugh and listen to you at the same time."

"How is he?" William asked.

"He's fine. He said to wish everyone a Merry Christmas. They visited a famous monastery yesterday, and he says they had a great turkey dinner... but what happened here?"

William remained standing, with Carrie, Mary, Graham, and their children nearby. He looked crestfallen. He folded his arms across his chest and looked at his wife. "I'm really great at sharing my faith, aren't I? I couldn't explain how my heart feels one-on-one, so how will I ever do it to the nation? And I'm particularly proud of my last barb—I'm sure Jesus would have done that. What's that Joe said? Meet people where they are? Instead, I ran them off."

Carrie moved close to her husband and took his arm. "I thought you did fine. And that last comment may stick with him. Who knows? Remember, Joe also said that each of us is to move another person just one step closer to God and not expect miracle conversions at our feet. And I dare say you've made Bruce think more about God in the last two days!"

"Yeah, but I don't want his thoughts to be negative."

"William," Mary said, "every time I share my faith I feel I've botched it. Later I can always think of things I *should* have said. But God says he'll give us the words that are right for that time and not to worry. I remember once when I heard someone else sharing his faith, and I was convinced he was doing a *terrible* job. But then I noticed the tears in the eyes of many of the people who were listening, and a lot of them decided to give their lives to God that day. So we just can't judge God's work with our own imperfect yardsticks."

"But Bruce seemed so negative and so angry," William continued.

"William, the Bible also says that until God lives in us, we won't understand spiritual things. What seems obvious to the believer is gibberish to the unbeliever. Wisdom follows faith. And faith by definition defies logic, or it wouldn't be faith. Bruce is like most people today. It takes role models who can tell you what living by faith is like to prepare you to accept God. The tragedy is that, unlike years ago, someone like Bruce sees almost none of those role models. Where would he? On television? At the movies? On the news? In school? In college? At a church he doesn't attend? So then when someone like you does come along, you're not the tenth or twentieth person with faith he's ever known or known about—you're the *first.* And everything in him says it can't be real because he has no spiritual frame of reference at all.

"God's been banned from all public discussion, political debate, courts, schools, entertainment, history books—for whatever convoluted reasons. So people like Bruce can't know his wisdom because they can't accept faith, and they can't accept faith because they don't know anyone who has ever lived by faith, either now or in history. An equal competition between God and secular thought isn't possible when by definition the secularists have excluded God from the stadium."

When Mary finished, William smiled broadly. "Wow, big sister. Have you ever thought about speechwriting? That was really right on."

Mary blushed, suddenly realizing that all the adults in the lodge had been listening to her. "Oh, I was just more or less quoting some things our pastor and Sunday school teacher have said recently. That's all. I didn't mean to get carried away."

"Unfortunately for our nation, you make a lot of sense," Carrie said.

"I do feel a little better," William said. "I'll keep planting and watering with Bruce when I can—and with Rebecca. Now, let's turn back to the reason for all of us getting together. Todd, here, show Uncle William how that computer game works."

The real object of the First Amendment was not to countenance, much less to advance, Mohammedanism, or Judaism, or infidelity, by prostrating Christianity, but to exclude all rivalry among Christian sects, and to prevent any national ecclesiastical establishment which would give to an hierarchy the exclusive patronage of the national government.

JUDGE JOSEPH STORY
NINETEENTH-CENTURY SUPREME COURT JUSTICE

17

Friday, January 11
Almost Three Weeks Later

NEW YORK "Either they're all lying, or they truly don't know, Ryan. And I'm still not sure there's anything to know," Leslie said, as she and Ryan Denning looked through the summaries of the visitors who had apparently come and gone to the White House in the evenings and on weekends for the preceding month. The small conference room table was covered with the remains of their lunch and the reports her team had pieced together by watching the gates and talking to members of the staff. "I'm not even sure what we're looking for."

Ryan removed his reading glasses and put down the one-page summary on Reverend Robert Ludwig, who had visited the presidential quarters at least twice during the month. There were similar studies on several economists, political scientists, journalists, and professors.

"This all seems pretty normal to me," she added. "A president needs advice, and these people are all in the advice business. Most are associated with think tanks or universities."

"Yes. But they're all either outright Christians or conservatives. Until today I wouldn't have classified William Harrison as either of those."

"Not all of them. Sally Roe is with the House of Hope school in the inner-city of D.C.—she's a firebrand," Leslie said, looking through the other papers.

"But her message is usually about self-sufficiency and against government programs. Everyone knows her message may be relevant for a tiny minority but will never help those who need it most."

Leslie pushed back from the table and sighed. "You're right, Ryan. These are not the same sort of people who were advising Harrison this time last year at the end of the transition. Or the sort of people on his own White House staff, for that matter."

"And you don't think his top advisors are even aware of these visits?" Ryan asked.

"No. From what I can tell, they're either working on the tensions in the Pacific, redoing the domestic legislative package, buttonholing Congressmen, or working on the president's State of the Union address. The White House is a pretty busy place right now, and I think most of them have never taken that much interest in what the Harrisons do at night in their private life, anyway."

"But is this private?" he asked again.

"A good question, Ryan. I don't know. Some of it may just be more advice on this polygamy thing. The VP has gone ballistic, as you know. Last night she apparently told a United Association of Women conference in New Haven that legalized polygamy is a plot against all women. It's really kind of funny to hear her talking in favor of families with only one husband and one wife at home—it's almost like she's jealous that men will have too much fun! So these are strange times, Ryan, and maybe the president is just trying to get a moral handle on some of this craziness before the Supreme Court rules on another issue and throws the nation for another loop."

"Moral handle I can accept. But then why only Christians? Why not Buddhists, Hindus, and Muslims? I tell you, Leslie, I can't believe it, but it looks like the president may be listening to Christians! And that scares me. The next thing you know, he may have kids believing in prayer and even praying in school—or come out against abortion."

"Come on, Ryan. Not William Harrison. No way."

"Well, let's continue to watch and to ask. You're right, we don't want to make more of this than it is. But on the other hand, if the president is being advised by some new shadow cabinet of Christians, we in the press have a duty to disclose it to the nation."

"Agreed," Leslie said, as she stood up. "I'll try to find out what the Secret Service knows, too. In the meantime, we've got those spots to tape, and then I have to catch the shuttle."

"Okay," he replied, rising. "But first let's warm up for the weekend."

She smiled but pushed away his advance. "Come on, sweetheart, you'll mess up my lipstick. And I haven't exactly heard an answer to the question I asked you over Christmas."

He held on to her hand and replied, "I know, but you will. Just let this divorce get a little further behind me. You know I love you, Leslie. I just can't think about marriage again right away. But soon!" he added, as she pulled her hand away and turned toward the door.

"Tick goes the biological clock, Ryan," she said, "and the wake-up alarm is about to go off."

"All right. All right. Give a guy a break. We'll talk about it again real soon."

"Real soon," she said, and opened the door.

THE ADRIATIC SEA Radioman Manny Figueroa ascended the ladder from the main deck to the landing just outside the admiral's cabin, a clipboard and a message form in his hand. Just as he knocked on the door, Seaman Joel Simpson suddenly descended the ladder from the landing between the bridge and CIC, where he had been waiting.

Before the cabin door opened, Simpson moved close to Figueroa and, in an agitated, derisive voice whispered, "A blank form, Manny? Did you forget the message for the lieutenant commander?"

Just then Thomas Dobbs opened the door and found both of the younger men in a quiet but intense argument.

"Hey, Mr. Dobbs asked me to bring him a blank form for a message. I'm just doing what he asked, and it's none of your business, anyway," Figueroa retorted, also in a whisper.

"Yeah? I used to bring him blank requisitions from the ship's store—I know all about it! And don't give me any bull, because I checked—you're not even on duty now."

Figueroa looked down, knowing he had been caught, but not wanting to admit it. "I'm doing what he told me!"

"Got a closet you need help coming out of, Manny?" Simpson's voice dripped with derision.

Dobbs, his lips pursed in anger, took the clipboard from Figueroa and stepped aside for the young radioman to come into his cabin. "Both of you keep it down if you know what's good for you. Joel, Figueroa is on official business. Just back off and leave him alone. I'll deal with you tomorrow."

Simpson moved toward the door to come in. "But you said we'd—"

The operations officer stopped him in the doorway with his hand. "I said tomorrow," and he closed the door and locked it, leaving Simpson alone in the passageway.

ATLANTA Rebecca Harrison answered her page at the nurses' station that afternoon and picked up the phone.

"Hello"

"Hey, it's me." She could tell from the tone of his voice that Bruce was depressed.

"What's wrong?"

"The doctor just called from Boston. Mom hasn't been feeling well and went in for a check-up. Apparently the tumor is back. He's afraid it's real bad."

"Oh, Bruce, I'm so sorry."

"Yeah..." He sighed. "I've booked a flight tonight. It's the same mess all over again. I...I..."

"What can I do?"

"Come up tomorrow—I imagine I'll be there for several days. I'd like you to meet her—and dad. I doubt your brother feels like bending the rules for another operation, after what I said to him at Camp David."

"Let's don't worry about that now. I'll call him if it turns out she needs it."

"I doubt I'll ever ask him for anything again. My blood boils whenever I think about the lie he's living."

"Bruce, William isn't living a lie. He's obviously just found, or renewed, his faith."

"Yeah? Well, the American people deserve to know who's controlling this nation now—a total *Christian!* You can't imagine how many times I've almost picked up the phone and called that Leslie Sloane. What would she say if she found out about him, after what they said about your sister?"

"Oh, Bruce. William said he wants to choose his own timing on that. Please don't violate his trust. He was very open with us. And I know he only wishes you the best—and your mom, too."

"We'll see. Anyway, I've got to go home and get packed. I'll call you in the morning when I know something."

"Okay. And I'll try to rearrange my schedule so I can come up. I...I'll pray for your mother."

"Wonderful. I don't think there's anyone up there listening, but pray if you want to."

Several miles away Eunice Porter put on her coat to leave for her waitress job—her children were at her sister's—and noticed that the light on her answering machine was flashing. *The phone must have rung while I was in the shower,* she thought as she pushed the play button.

"Hey, girl. It's Sally. Are you with the program yet? I'm gettin' some heat to get you coming along like me and the others, especially with your advance and all. So give me a call and let me know. See ya."

Eunice rewound the tape and left the apartment, locking the door behind her.

Yes...I'll 'get with the program.' I've just got to find the right guy. If it wasn't so much money I wouldn't put up with all this trouble."

RALEIGH Sarah Prescott's emotions were careening wildly that night as she snuggled next to Matthew while he drove her home in his father's car. She felt scared and confident, happy and sad, as though she had lost something important and wasn't quite sure yet the nature of what she'd found. While they were supposed to be at a dance, she and Matthew had instead spent the last four hours together in a motel room, and there was no longer anything technical about her loss of virginity.

"Mmm, that was wonderful," she said, knowing from soap operas and the computer she was supposed to say so, even though she really felt "it" wasn't all it was supposed to be. But she was completely honest when she added, "I love you so much, Matthew."

"I love you, too, Sarah," he said, putting his right arm around her and driving with his left hand.

They drove on, Sarah thinking about how wonderful it would be to be married to Matthew, imagining what sort of job he might have after college, and even trying to imagine the living room of their home. Meanwhile, Matthew was wondering when they could next spend time together at the motel.

"Listen, that was so good." Matthew said. "And we love each other so much. Let's don't break this special time together. Tomorrow night, instead of going to that movie, let's go to the motel again. Can we?"

Somewhere in a far corner of Sarah's mind a little warning bell went off, reminding her of something, but she ignored it. *We do love each other, and it was the first time for both of us. He's so sweet. I probably owe it to him for being so kind and gentle—not like that stupid computer thing. But we can't make a habit of this, it's not right. There's more to a relationship...*

"Yes. It *was* wonderful. Let's do it again tomorrow. But, Matthew, we can't do this all the time. I love you, but we can't just do this."

He pulled her closer as he drove, a smile on his face in the dark as he thought about the next night. "No, Sarah, of course not. But this weekend is special."

Five minutes later they arrived at Sarah's house, and Matthew walked her to the door, where he kissed her before she opened the door with her key and went inside.

There she found her father turning off the light in the den, where he had been reading and waiting up for her.

"Did you have a good time at the dance, dear?" Graham Prescott smiled.

"Uh, yes, Dad, it was great," she lied. *I've got to be more careful in the future.*

"Well, I'm glad you had a good time. Good night and God bless," he said and kissed her on the forehead.

Sarah walked upstairs, her stomach churning. Voices tried to assault her about what she had done, from sleeping with Matthew to lying to her father, but she pushed them all back. *What's done is done. I'm a woman now...and it* was *wonderful.* The last thought she silently repeated several times, trying to convince herself.

She showered, slipped into bed, and turned out the light. For the first time in a long time she didn't bother to say her prayers. She didn't think a lot about it, but it was still a conscious decision. What she had done, she felt, shouldn't end with a prayer of repentance because she hadn't done anything wrong. *What we did is okay. Ms. Bowers tells us that developing our own feelings is what's important at our age, and I feel great. I don't need to be forgiven because I haven't done anything wrong. And I plan to do it again, anyway. It's natural and logical, and we're in love. It's okay and I'm fine.* She repeated the last sentence in her mind until she finally fell asleep.

Upon my arrival in the United States, the religious aspect of the country was
the first thing that struck my attention; and the longer I stayed there, the more
did I perceive the great political consequences resulting from this state of things, to
which I was unaccustomed. In France I had almost always seen the spirit of religion
and the spirit of freedom pursuing courses diametrically opposed to each other; but
in America I found that they were intimately united, and that they
reigned in common over the same country.

ALEXIS DE TOCQUEVILLE

18

Sunday, January 27
Two Weeks Later

WASHINGTON It had been a long, hard weekend of work for the first family, punctuated only by meals and a church service. Robert flew in from Chapel Hill on Friday afternoon. On Saturday evening the Harrisons invited in guests for a "movie," but the guests were the five ministers who had taught them all fall, along with the advisors to whom they had been introduced through that process. They assembled in the White House theater, but instead of watching a movie they first listened to William, then offered their opinions on what he had to say.

After church on Sunday the family again worked together, with Robert and Katherine acting as proofreaders for the draft speech William had written with Carrie's help. While his children read, William made marks on a different text prepared by Bob Horan and Chris White of his White House staff.

By the time they sat down to dinner that evening, the four of them were satisfied that they had done all they could do and that the outcome was now in God's hands.

The next morning William met early in the Oval Office with his chief of staff, Jerry Richardson, as was their custom on Mondays.

As they sat together at his desk, William handed a notebook to his advisor and friend. "Here's the draft of the State of the Union speech that Bob and Chris put together with the team leaders. I made some notes on this copy. They should have time to make all the changes before the press needs it tomorrow afternoon."

"Thanks, Mr. President. We'll take care of it. Everything seems to be ready for tomorrow night."

"Good. I hope I'm not as nervous as last year."

"This will be your second one, Mr. President." Richardson smiled. "It should be old hat."

"We'll see."

"Can I ask you a question before we start the Mideast briefing?"

"Of course."

"Mr. President, if you don't mind me saying so, you seem different than you did a year ago. You're definitely calmer. But, I don't know, it's more than that, like you've been aloof these last few months. I don't mean publicly, but with us. I mean, last year you worried over every *i* and *t* in the State of the Union address; this year, you've just made some comments. And I'm still waiting for your approval and go-ahead on this year's domestic program. You've been listening, but so far you haven't given us much direction. Am I missing something?"

William paused, then said. "Jerry, remember when you told me last spring that your mother always advised you to pray before tackling something important?"

"Uh...yeah."

"Do you think she was right?"

Jerry shrugged. "I guess so. If it's really important, then it can't hurt to have God's help. I *do* believe in God—there just hasn't been much time to attend church the last thirty years."

"I know, Jerry, I know. Isn't that a shame? Anyway, would you mind if we prayed for our domestic program now?"

"Well, no, I guess not. That's fine."

So William bowed his head and prayed for God's continued guidance and help with the right programs and priorities for the nation.

When William finished, Jerry looked up and said, "Mr. President, I didn't know you could pray like that."

William smiled. "God's been teaching me a lot of things lately, Jerry. We all ought to listen to him more. And you need to find a way to get to church. Would you like to go with us next Sunday? Bring Diane."

"Uh, sounds good. Sure. We'll see."

"Jerry, about your question. I'm deeply aware of the need for leadership. Frankly, I've been seeking God's will for several months. But don't worry—I'm about to let you know our agenda for the coming year. In fact, I meant to ask you first thing this morning—please get as many of the top staff together as you can on Wednesday morning. I know it's short notice, but bring in all you can. We'll go over our agenda then and map out our specific plans."

Relieved, Richardson sat back. "Great. We're ready to go. It'll probably be another fight with Congress, but this year I think we'll start out much stronger."

"Mm," William said noncommittally as Richardson rose to let in the foreign policy briefing team. "Jerry." The chief of staff stopped and turned around. "Whatever happens this week, remember what your mother said, and remember this meeting."

A look of confusion crossed his face, but he nodded and said, "Sure. Of course."

RALEIGH Sarah Prescott sat on her bed that afternoon, surrounded by her books, but she couldn't concentrate on her homework. Her mind went back to Saturday night at the motel, after which she'd again lied, this time to her mother, about going to a movie.

Matthew had been coming to her church youth group on Sunday nights for several months. The previous evening the program had been on trans-generational faith—honoring your father and mother, so that you would later reap what you had sown with your own children. Sarah had felt sick, thinking about lies to her mom and dad, but Matthew had seemed unfazed.

She had been shocked when he suggested that they skip their usual pizza afterward and instead stop on the way to her house at a home under construction near hers. Matthew said he had two sleeping bags and a flash-light in the trunk of the car and that they could spend more than an hour together. She had said no, but his disappointment was so great that she had relented and finally agreed. She didn't want to upset him or lose his love.

So now she'd made love with Matthew—what, five times? And three times since Friday night—twice in an old motel with stained carpets and once in the cold and dark of an unfinished house. Somehow it wasn't what she had pictured—or seen on the virtual reality computer. But Matthew was so insistent. He told her last night that their love had reached a new level. But he'd also mentioned that maybe next weekend they could try a hotel downtown.

Somebody might see us! That's crazy! This…he…why is sex all we're doing now? It's okay, but is this all we're going to do? That's not what we said before. I…I don't know…but I'm sure he loves me a lot.

BOSTON At that same hour Bruce was sitting alone in the living room of the two-story home in which he had grown up in a working-class neighborhood of Boston. He had met with the doctors again that morning, and it had been good to have Rebecca there for a second weekend to ask the right questions.

Unfortunately, the answers had not been good. It appeared that the new, rapid growth of the tumor meant that his mother had less than six months to live; she could easily lose her motor skills or her memory or both at almost any time. Meanwhile, his father was still battling emphysema. At that moment he was upstairs in their bedroom on oxygen, his mother helping him.

Bruce had just returned from driving Rebecca to the airport. She hadn't even asked when he might return to Atlanta; both of them knew it could be quite a while.

His mother came downstairs and sat next to him. "He's sleeping now, Bruce. He said to tell you he hopes to be up and around and more help tomorrow. Since he's sleeping, I think I'll go to the store to pick up a few things for dinner. And, oh, I've really liked Rebecca these two weekends. She seems to be a good person. But, Bruce, isn't she a little old for you?"

"I don't know, Mom. I don't know much of anything right now. I like her a lot, but who knows? We'll see. Right now I'm more concerned about you and Dad."

"Our time is coming, Bruce, but God will take care of everything."

"Mother, God doesn't 'take care' of things. *People* take care of things. Just like you've taken care of Dad. I'm sick of hearing about God doing this and God doing that, like he's right here in this room!"

"You're young, dear. You'll see. Now I'm going to the store. I'll be back in thirty minutes to start dinner."

After she left, Bruce sat and thought some more about his family and how unfair their lot had been. Then he got up, found the phone book, and looked up the number for the U.S. Network affiliate's television station in Boston. When the operator answered, he asked, "Can you give me the number for your news bureau in Washington?"

ATLANTA Late that night Eunice lay alone in her bed, unable to sleep. Her emotions were on a roller coaster. She lay very still, hoping that by staying perfectly calm her heart would slow down and she'd feel better about herself.

Ben Candler had been a regular at the restaurant; he apparently had an office nearby. Sometimes he brought in guests, but often he ate alone at the wide bar. Many times he and Eunice had talked, and she had learned that he was divorced. Eunice thought that he was quite handsome, and on several occasions in the past months he had intimated about them getting together. She had always rebuffed him, claiming she was too tired after working so late, but tonight she had encouraged him, and the encouragement had paid off. Just before she left work, he returned to the restaurant, showered and clean shaven.

They had gone to one of the late-night spots for dessert and coffee. Then she suggested her apartment, to which he readily agreed. She had enjoyed being treated so nicely, and she began to think that perhaps this relationship might actually have a future beyond her duty to fulfill an obligation, which weighed heavily on her.

It had been after one in the morning when she unlocked the door to her apartment and suggested he fix himself a drink while she checked on her sleeping children who, as usual, had been cared for in the late afternoon and put to bed by Eunice's sister.

In almost no time Ben and Eunice were together in her bed, and she was again surprised by his gentleness. But then, an hour later, as he put on his clothes to leave, he asked her, "How much?"

At first she hadn't understood, but when he repeated the question with his wallet in his hand, she realized that he expected to pay her. The realization left her momentarily speechless. She didn't know whether to laugh, to refuse, or to be mad. Then she thought about her kids. She had no idea "how much." Finally she said, "Whatever you think."

He had put some money on her bureau and walked over to run his hand down her cheek. "I hope we can do this again sometime," he said.

"Yeah. Me, too," she had managed to smile.

He had left what—thirty minutes ago? She hadn't moved, except to curl into a fetal position. She didn't know how much money was on the bureau. When the door closed behind him, she felt a chill, and she had been cold ever since, despite the blanket.

Money going in and money going out. This might get to be a pretty good business. She tried to rationalize and laugh it off, but she couldn't manage it. The confusion and the chill wouldn't go away. *This isn't what God wants. This isn't right. But God wants me to provide for my two children, and I am. What's wrong with that? I don't do drugs. I work hard so they can eat and have a place to live. And I try to be their mother. No, you're no better than a whore, and mothers aren't supposed to kill their babies... But other little kids need the organs, the doctor said. It's better for them, but what about the baby we could have made tonight? How about his or her life? Is he just a thing?... O God!*

Eunice rolled over on her other side. Wiping tears from her eyes, she felt very, very alone. *O God, please help me! I guess I'm a hooker now. Please, God, help me and my kids. What am I supposed to do? It's so much money, and we need it bad. You know how much we need it. But please, God, don't let me do what I'm not supposed to. Please, God, help me. Please!*

It took Eunice another tormented hour to fall asleep, while inside her womb, cells were already dividing in the miracle of new life.

A MEDITERRANEAN PORT Sadim entered the captain's cabin on the *Bright Star* to have breakfast. Before sitting down with the captain and Kolikov, Sadim crossed the cabin and turned on the television. He changed the channels until he was satisfied that they could receive World News Network from their position in the shipyard.

"I'll try not to bother you," he said to the captain as he sat down at the table, "but I want to watch President Harrison's address live, tonight."

"Why?" the captain asked. "That will be about two in the morning when it starts."

"I know, but there are few predictable times when I know he will be on, and I always like to watch him. I learn something about him every time." *And we're sending him a little present in honor of his speech* he thought. "So tonight I will watch and listen to his second State of the Union Address, as they call it. If he even dares to have a third such address next year, after our visit, it will be interesting to compare them!"

The other two men seated at the table nodded approvingly.

WASHINGTON "We'll be going over to the Capitol at seven-thirty. You'll enter the House chamber a little after eight, when all the networks will begin their coverage," Chris White explained, while the president walked and he rolled from a luncheon with key congressional leaders in the cabinet room down the hall to the Oval Office.

"Just like last year." William smiled as he took a list of his afternoon appointments from Barbara. "And those guys at lunch sounded just like last year, too, didn't they?"

"Pretty much," White replied. "We'll make advance copies of your speech available in the press room starting at five this afternoon, on the usual basis that no one can quote from it or be specific with references until after you've given it."

"Fine. Sounds like we're ready to go. I know the speech pretty well, but I'll look at it again late this afternoon. Now I've got to meet with the Japanese foreign minister about their never-ending trade surplus. Is that it?"

"Yes. We're set. See you tonight at seven-thirty."

As William glanced through his messages he noticed one taken by one of the two receptionists who answered the private lines in the outer office. She had neatly typed on a White House message pad:

A gentleman called from The Council. He said to wish you a Happy New Year and to tell you that this is the year. He said he'd be watching your speech tonight. He said to be sure to tell you that their work is almost finished and that you'll definitely hear from them soon. He wished you good health. He didn't leave a return number but said you'd understand.

BOSTON AND WASHINGTON   "Hello."

"Is Bruce there?"

"Just a minute..."

"Hello."

"Bruce?"

"Yes."

"This is Leslie Sloane."

"Oh. Hi. How are you, Ms. Sloane?"

"I'm fine. And please, it's Leslie. I'm sorry we've had so much trouble getting together since yesterday, but with the president's speech in a few hours, it's kinda hectic here."

"I can imagine. Listen, that's why I'm calling."

"The president?"

"Yes. I think I've got some information you in particular might find interesting. But, like me, you'll also probably find it depressing."

Leslie sat down at her desk and took out her notepad. "What is it?"

"Can I tell you something as an anonymous tip, without your having to say who told you?"

"Yes, of course. But then, even more than usual, I'll have to check out whatever you tell me with other sources, since otherwise it's just hearsay or rumor."

"Oh, what I'm going to tell you is true, all right. And I don't think you'll have any trouble finding other sources to back me up, once you hear it."

"Well, we'll do it on that basis, then. An 'anonymous steer'—how's that?"

"Fine."

"So, what is it?"

"The president is a Christian."

Leslie was silent for a moment. "Well, I was raised as one, too."

"No, I mean a born-again, fundamentalist, bigoted white male Christian of the first order—just like the Prescotts."

"William Harrison?" Leslie sat up straighter in her chair. "That's a pretty strong accusation, Bruce. How do you know?"

"Because he told me, as well as everyone else at Camp David, on Christmas Eve. So there're lots of people, including the staff, who you can check with. But I promise you it's true."

"It would certainly explain a lot, particularly the activity this weekend..." Her voice trailed off.

"What?"

"Nothing. So, did he tell you anything more? How is his new faith going to affect his policies and programs?"

"That he wouldn't say. He was very cagey. You know how they are. He said he had to pray some more before he could be sure! Can you believe that? William Harrison!"

"I've covered him for several years, and I have to admit it's hard to imagine him as a born-again Christian fundamentalist."

"Well, get ready to believe it."

"Do you think he plans to announce it—or make reference to it—in tonight's speech?"

"I don't know. I wouldn't put it past him. Ms. Slo—uh, Leslie, he's going to try to undo so much that's important—I just know it. We've all believed in him, and now he's sold us out. You've got to unmask him for what he is and try to rally support for all the good things he originally stood for."

"If it's as you say, Bruce, I agree. We'll definitely check into it further. I don't know if we'll have time before tonight, but actually we've already been scratching the surface a bit. It's too bad we can't use your name. Then we could go with it right away, maybe even on tonight's news."

"No. No, you can't. He asked us not to tell, but I couldn't stand the silence any longer. So I'm telling you. But I don't want him to know that I'm doing this."

"I won't divulge my source. But we'll start checking around for others who will speak on the record. Anyway, thanks, Bruce."

"Thanks to you. And good luck."

As soon as she hung up, Leslie turned to her assistant who was passing outside the office door. "Has the courier arrived yet with the text of the president's speech? Please go find Ryan. He flew in to co-anchor with me tonight, and I think he's over in Al's office. Thanks."

WASHINGTON The first family had decided to have a light meal at six, then meet together again after the speech. After they finished eating, the four of them gathered in the living room of their private quarters and prayed for the Holy Spirit to be present in the House Chamber that evening. Then William went to their bedroom to change.

In the churches of the five ministers who had been teaching the Harrisons, prayer groups had been meeting and praying since Sunday after their worship services; now the five sanctuaries filled again as the congregations reassembled to pray for the president. In Raleigh, a large number of the Prescotts' friends met with them and their church's staff in their chapel to add their voices to the chorus being lifted up to heaven for protection and guidance that evening.

Michael Tate and the other four ministers walked as close as they could to the Capitol building, then fanned out around it, praying and interceding in Jesus' name against the forces of darkness that indwelt the whole area.

"I've checked the entire speech. There's nothing about God or Jesus or the Bible or anything," Leslie said, as she and Ryan sat with the evening news producer, and the clock ticked down to their news broadcast's sign on.

"Could this Bruce guy have been imagining things?" Ryan asked.

"Maybe. I don't know him that well. But he seemed perfectly rational when we interviewed him with the president's sister."

"And there's no other corroboration?" the producer asked.

Leslie tapped the table with the eraser of her pencil. "This just dropped on us late this afternoon. We're looking to find anyone who would have been at Camp David besides their family, but it'll take some time."

"Well, reading through his speech for tonight, which is plain vanilla political rhetoric from last year," Ryan summarized, looking at his two colleagues, "and with no one else saying anything, I don't think we can use this on the news. But keep looking for someone else, and if we can corroborate, maybe we can bring it in during our analysis after the speech. What a story, if it's real! And if it's true, we'll have a lot of work to do in the coming months. Now, that leaves the evening news intact, so let's go do it. We're on in ten minutes."

Ninety minutes later Leslie and Ryan moved across the U.S. Network's Washington studio to a set that had been especially prepared for political coverage, resplendent in red, white, and blue. The network planned to continue this design, with its colorful waves and subdued stars, throughout the upcoming campaigns for the House and Senate that November. With the regular news finished, they now carefully scanned the text of the president's speech, looking for any rare statement that could be considered controversial or newsworthy, then checking with the experts they would interview after the speech—four of their own reporters, two television political pundits, and a cabinet member from a previous administration.

Precisely at eight o'clock the light on the number one camera glowed red and the two anchorpersons, Leslie on the right and Ryan on the left, began their coverage of the State of the Union Address, with a huge screen showing the exterior of the Capitol building bathed in light behind them.

As all of the nation's major networks completed their top-of-the-hour commercials and switched live to the common feed from the Capitol, William Harrison stood with the House of Representatives' sergeant at arms just outside the historic chamber, smiling at the surrounding well-wishers and thinking of the incredible acts of bravery, cowardice, sacrifice, and selfishness that had taken place over the decades in those same halls and chambers, permanently affecting the farthest reaches of the world.

As he closed his eyes for a moment to offer his own silent prayer for guidance, strength, wisdom, and God's Spirit, it occurred to him that the whole world looked to the men and women who occupied this place and the surrounding buildings for truth and leadership in a world turning increasingly splintered, violent, dark, and hateful. He felt a sudden chill and opened his eyes just as the sergeant at arms opened the tall door and walked in to announce his arrival. *May this be for your glory alone, O Father. Not my words but yours be spoken. Amen.*

"The president has shaken hands with just about everyone along the central aisle," Leslie Sloane said, voicing over the picture of William Harrison as he walked into the hall, offering his personal greetings to the assembled political and judicial might of the nation and moving toward the steps leading up to the central podium. There he shook hands with the Speaker of the House and the vice president, who would be seated behind him during his speech. Behind all three of them was a large American flag hanging down the entire back wall. And throughout the seven minutes it took William to make his entrance and to be introduced by the Speaker, the applause had been almost continuous.

Smiling and looking physically fit and confident, his graying hair adding a distinguished touch, the president waved several times from the podium, but he also used those moments to locate Carrie and his children in the balcony. Husband and wife locked eyes for a moment, and her solid smile and nod gave him a boost he could feel. It overcame the nagging doubts that had crept up so quickly as he had walked down the aisle, surrounded by so much that was familiar, comfortable, and unchanging. As he reached the podium he had been tempted to open the text left on the lectern for him and ignore the different, more difficult road he knew God wanted. But with Carrie's spiritual support he again felt a chill, which this time visibly shook him. He grew serious, said a last silent prayer, and reached into his suit pocket for his text.

After several final waves of his hand, the chamber fell silent. William Harrison looked around at the most powerful assembly in the world and began.

"Ladies and gentlemen of the Senate, members of the House of Representatives, justices of the Supreme Court, members of the Cabinet, distinguished foreign guests, and citizens of our nation, it is our custom every year at this time for the president to give his assessment of the state of our historic union and to use this occasion to chart a course for the following year.

"In this age of media-defined reality, of image over substance, of positive projection for favorable instant polls, and of instant solutions to oversimplified problems, we are tonight going to try something different. We're going to travel a different, more traditional road not seen in this setting for many years—a road of truth over image, honest assessment over impossible promises, and long-term cures for long-term, complex problems. We are, in short, going to give you a *real* state of the union, focusing unfortunately on our problems, because they could shortly overwhelm us, but then also offering a specific program of workable but difficult solutions, and leaving the outcome where it always belongs—with you, the people.

"If you listen closely tonight, no matter what your political persuasion, you will undoubtedly find one or two subjects in this assessment not to your liking—you'll probably disagree with them. I can't help it. I believe with all my heart that what we are going to lay before you tonight is the absolute truth. I'm at peace that we must face these issues now, today, if our nation is going to survive, and I don't use that overworked term lightly. I mean it quite literally—if we are to survive much longer in this world as a nation of free people with free institutions blessed by the God who made us. You will have to decide, as will every American, whether the truth we lay before you tonight is worth accepting for our nation's sake, even when it is personally unpleasant or temporarily inconvenient. Please listen, wait, and see."

William could feel the silence in the chamber and noticed members of his audience looking questioningly at one another. His heart rate, already high, increased. Again he felt momentarily unsure. The thought crossed his mind to stop and to pick up the other text, to start over. But then suddenly he was at peace, ready to tell God's truth to the nation. As an affirmation to himself, he smiled briefly, picked up the text that had been left at the podium, and moved it to the side.

"Before we really start, let me apologize to those of you with an advance copy of the anticipated text of this speech. We won't be using it. And you can turn off the Teleprompter. Those words don't address the real state of our union. Listen carefully, and we'll tell you the truth here. Then we'll make copies available tonight for your review. I'm sorry for the inconvenience, but the road we are going to outline begins now."

"What's he doing?" Leslie asked Ryan, as they watched the monitors built into their desks.

"I think you can call off the people trying to find someone who was at

Camp David, Leslie. I don't think after tonight we'll need any third party corroborations of what has happened to him. We'll only need to find out *why.*"

As William began his speech the vice president and Speaker of the House were clearly visible on the nation's televisions. Patricia Barton-North looked down at her hands in her lap. But when William first mentioned God, she suddenly glared at the back of the chief executive's head.

The president continued. "We've got a lot to cover, but let's start with a brief recap of the state of our union today. I'm not going to spend a lot of time on these points because most of you living outside Washington already know these issues well, and you've just been waiting for someone here to voice them for you. Here goes:

"We are overcome by a sense of helplessness to deal with the crime and violence that invades our lives and our homes, making many of us prisoners in our own houses.

"We don't trust our leaders, and often for good reason. And good people are afraid to step forward to become leaders because their private lives will be ripped open by the press.

"Our families are being assaulted at every turn. In the name of 'rights' for women and children, we've instead created an impoverished class of women and children, sent tens of millions of unborn babies to their deaths, and unhitched millions of men from any sense of male responsibility to raise, protect, or train a family."

The vice president, visible behind the president whenever the television director chose a wide angle, twisted in her chair and looked off to her right, her arms folded tightly across her body.

"Our educational system, only two generations ago the pride of our nation, is a disaster.

"Selfishness, materialism, and 'me-first,' or at least 'my group first,' rule the nation. Our country was built on sacrifice, generosity, savings, delay of gratification, and building for the next generation's good. But today we are awash in the false 'truths' of instant everything, consume now, discourage savings, and forget the children. I'm ashamed to say that my generation is probably the first in all of recorded history that, by ignoring our education system, promoting abortion, and encouraging divorce has openly and consciously chosen its own immediate happiness and convenience over the well-being of the next generation, our own children.

"Think about it. We've pushed suffering on those least capable to cope or to understand—our children—so that we don't have to be bothered with some inconvenience, like figuring out how to stay married. And on top of that, we've saddled *them* with paying for the mess we've created by astronomically increasing the national debt, because we like to spend but haven't even got the guts to pay for our own extravagances! This is almost unforgivable and has to stop."

For the first time there was a smattering of applause from the audience, and even the Speaker of the House clapped briefly.

"Our welfare system, originally designed to help families with short-term needs, is now in many cases supporting the fifth or sixth generation of welfare dependency, promoting by its own inherent system the perpetuation of the problem. I said dependency, and I meant it. Our system promotes addiction, from one generation to the next, and destroys families.

"Our federal tax code, now stretching to several thousand pages of mis-guided social engineering, is incomprehensible. It's estimated that over *six billion* man hours every year are wasted in some part of the tax industry, making, enforcing, calculating, collecting, or escaping taxes. This entire industry—including the hours and hours we all spend trying to understand it—serves no productive purpose whatsoever; it's a huge drain on our econ-omy, as we pay people to send paper to other people, for no productive result.

"In the name of 'rights' and 'free speech,' we've legitimized all types of aberrant behavior: pornography, abortion, divorce, homosexual activity—yes, you heard me right—and now suicide and polygamy, most of which not only fly in the face of our own Judeo-Christian rules for correct living, but also violate the laws of almost every civilized society that has ever prospered on this earth. You don't have to be a rocket scientist—and thank God, because we aren't making many of them any more—to figure out that we violate these universal moral laws at great and immediate risk to us and, again, to our children and their children."

There was more applause, this time stronger and louder, though still clearly a minority in the chamber.

Leslie turned to Ryan and said, "He's lost his mind. Next he'll bring out clay tablets and show us the Ten Commandments! Where is he going with this?"

"I can't imagine."

"We could go on recounting these problems," the president continued, "but there's no need. As I said, most of you are dealing with one or more of these every day of your lives, and our purpose is not to further worry you, but to offer a real path for solutions. Unfortunately and tragically, what we've just reviewed is the state of our union today, and it can't be papered over with pleasant political rhetoric.

"We've talked about the visible problems, but they're just the logical and predictable results of the underlying cause, which we're now coming to. In order to fix something, you've got to know the cause of the trouble. So before offering solutions, we need to examine what got us to where we are.

"We're going to start with a very simple concept, one that really defines everything that is to follow. This concept is that we are standing today at the scene of a colossal collision of historic forces—a collision of two diametrically opposed worldviews which have been at war for a long time. If we understand these two opposing worldviews, then the details of everything else we'll discuss tonight will fit into place. Without this understanding, we'll endlessly debate secondary issues, which both political parties have done for three decades, missing the important points. So, please listen and begin now to decide which worldview is yours—that's the key to turning this nation around.

"The first worldview is the Judeo-Christian one on which this nation was founded. It begins with the belief that there is a God, that he created us, and that he has a purpose for each one of us. It's that simple. Do you believe that?"

William paused and looked around the chamber. There was only silence. Then he continued. "Since he created us, he's given us rules to live by which, if we follow them, will benefit us, both as individuals and as a society; and if we break them, will result in our harm. Moreover, God has chosen to reveal himself and his laws through the Bible, which represents his 'Creator's Manual' for us to read and to understand his will. Man in this worldview definitely has reason—he is created in the image of God. He is to be the master of the earth, which he needs his intelligence and reason to accomplish. But he uses these abilities within the moral framework provided by his Creator.

"This worldview also acknowledges that this world is only temporary, that there is more importantly an eternal world, and that what we do here influences what happens to us there. Finally, God has provided by his grace the only means for joining him in that eternal world through our individual belief in his Son, Jesus Christ, who voluntarily died on the cross, as a real historic fact, so that we have the opportunity to live with God forever."

As the president spoke, the vice-president, seated behind him, lowered her head and rubbed her forehead with her right hand. The camera panned around the hushed audience, some of whom were listening attentively as the president spoke. Others, however, had joined the vice-president in postures of obvious disagreement.

"The second worldview begins with the belief that man and woman are it. It believes either that there is no God, and we're all the result of some still-unexplained mistake, evolving on our own incredible strength from some unexplained but conveniently present ooze, or that there may be a God, but he simply made us and then left town, leaving us to our own devices. This worldview tells us that we're on our own and that we've got to improve and even perfect ourselves on our own. There are therefore no overriding rules or absolute values in this view—everything like that is to be determined by us and refined continuously by our so-called enlightened reason.

"We're to be fervently all-inclusive, and *everything* anyone might want to do is basically fine because it all starts from human reason. So what's *really* okay and not okay must be decided by the majority or, better yet, imposed by those who have somehow obtained more 'enlightenment' than the rest of us.

"Since mankind has evolved on its own in this view, we and what we do must be inherently good because it's 'human.' If an individual goofs up, it must just be because of poverty or educational deprivation or a bad neighborhood or bad parents or some other fixable mistake. If we could just fix those or get rid of outdated, constraining rules so that his behavior is redefined as acceptable—or perfect this person a bit further with one more government program to help him—then he'd be okay, too. And all of us could then work toward our ultimate goal—to be 'free,' to return to a state of pristine nature, where everything is wonderful and people are pleasant and prosperity pours out on everyone in a paradise of human enlightenment.

"Now those are the two opposing worldviews. One starts and ends with God. The other starts and ends with man. As a nation we've recently debated a lot of issues and programs, but the real question is very simple: which one of those views do you believe to be correct? They're mutually exclusive, meaning that they can't both be right. It's either one or the other. They lead to completely different conclusions and completely different activities for our government. And tonight I'm proposing that each one of us has to choose."

William paused again and looked around the House, stopping for a second to glance up at Carrie, who again gave him a nod.

Bruce, sitting with his mother in Boston, picked up the phone and called Atlanta. When Rebecca answered, he asked, "Are you watching this?"

"Yes. How are your parents?"

"Okay. Later. But how can your brother be saying all this? He's talking like we're living in the Middle Ages!"

"I don't know. It sounds pretty logical to me so far. Let's listen and I'll call you back when it's over."

"Fine. But I hope he doesn't go completely off the deep end."

William continued, "How have these two worldviews played themselves out over the last three centuries, to arrive at this point? Historians use the words 'the Reformation' and 'the Enlightenment' to describe their two separate beginnings. And we have early examples of the two distinct results in the American and French Revolutions.

"Despite recent myths to the contrary, which I'll address in a minute, America was founded as a Christian nation with the Christian faith as the foundation for its laws and morals. The colonies were essentially the completion on freer soil of the Christian Reformation begun in Europe, providing a new place and a new beginning for men and women seeking to submit their lives to God's will. We don't have time now, but if you read through the papers and the speeches of all the early leaders of the colonies and of our nation, as my wife, Carrie, and I have done over the past eight months, you'll be struck by how much virtually every one of them not only believed strongly and publicly in God, but also gave him all the credit for their free nation, their lives, and their new government.

"The American Revolution was a revolt by one set of governments against another—calling on God's authority in the Declaration of Independence to override laws which the colonists believed to be wrong and unjust. They never proposed doing away with rule by law, but proclaimed that the colonies had a responsibility to follow God's higher law for their citizens' lives, liberty, and pursuit of happiness. And throughout the long years of the Revolution and then during the creation of our nation, these same leaders constantly called upon God—publicly, in these chambers, in their speeches, and in their laws—for his guidance, his protection, and his forgiveness.

"Contrast that approach, clearly following the first worldview, with the French Revolution only a few years later. There the rallying cry was not for God's law, but for just the opposite—unchecked individual liberty and equality. The humanistic philosophers behind that movement believed that man was inherently good and government was always bad—and if they could get rid of oppressive government, first the king and then subsequent manifestations, then real 'freedom' could be obtained. As a symbol of their intent, the cross in Notre Dame Cathedral was replaced by a statue of Reason.

"The result was an orgy of death, destruction, and dictatorship that perfectly previewed later revolutions also begun by supposedly enlightened philosophers who believed in the second worldview. But these later revolutions in Russia, Germany, and elsewhere were all ultimately defeated, like the French Revolution, not by the promised blossoming of perfection, but by their own godless murdering strongmen: Napoleon, Stalin, Hitler. These killers filled the vacuums that are created every time we turn over the rule of society to some group that is going to 'perfect' us, because then the only arbiter of resources and power becomes the state. This is the ultimate irony of the second worldview: in its rush to embrace romantic individual freedom, it always degenerates into the loss of *real* freedom, either to a coercive state in a humane society or to a dictatorial state in a less tolerant one. But freedom is *always* lost to the government.

"And why not? In this view, since there is no God in control, then by default, who is? The state *must* be. And who is the state? The ones with the most power. Who loses? Those without power, such as the weak, the non-violent, and the 'unenlightened.' The natural state, which the second view seeks, turns out *not* to be a pristine and glorious paradise, which it never was anyway. What we have instead are the ugly rules of 'eat before you are eaten' and 'survival of the fittest.' *That's what nature has really always been.* And mankind always returns to it without God's laws to lift up his better ideals and to promise punishment for those who insist on doing wrong. Far from being constricting, a Christian society is actually freeing and uplifting. Without its influence, we are each someone else's meal. And we're already seeing that truth beginning to infect our own society today.

"Back to our worldviews. The overriding view of our own founders was the first, the one in which man only acts knowing that God is in control. It's not surprising that hardly anyone realizes this fact any more. For forty years if the word 'God' appeared in a text, that text couldn't be used in our schools. And because our nation's founders spoke so often with references to God, hardly anything they said could be taught to our own children! Isn't that absurd? Is it any wonder we've lost our way, when simply quoting a speech by our first president, George Washington, in which he gives thanks to God for delivering our nation, is somehow equated with establishing a state religion to which we all must belong?

"So, what, then, is the cause for our current unhappy state of the union? It's that we've slowly but certainly been led off the path of a nation founded on God's worldview and are instead fast becoming just another one of the many nations that have come and gone because they're founded on man's worldview. Look at history—what a miracle the founding of this nation was! How have we then been led astray?

"As recently as 1892, Supreme Court Justice David Brewer could write in an official court opinion, 'This is a religious people.' And he quoted an earlier opinion that stated, 'Christianity, general Christianity, is, and always has been, a part of the common law.' And it was. Then starting in about 1910 our universities began seriously embracing the teachings of men such as Freud, Nietzsche, Darwin, Marx, and others—all of whom proclaimed, like Rousseau before them, that man is the master and God is meaningless.

"By the 1930s many of the university faculties in this country accepted that worldview, and by the sixties, when my generation came of age, it was further embraced by the media and the nation's entire 'enlightened intelligentsia,' from students to, sadly, the Supreme Court, which at that time was made up of men almost exclusively from *political* rather than judicial backgrounds."

William looked down at all the Supreme Court justices seated just in front of him and noted a look of surprise on most of their faces. "While rightly correcting the aftermath of one great blemish on our Constitution—the institution of slavery—this court also went, without precedent, directly against 150 years of rulings and many judicial precedents to falsely proclaim, on its own, that our Constitution erected a 'wall of separation between church and state,' which was simply not true."

Several of the justices shifted in their seats, and the vice president, already red, was almost hugging herself in obvious anger.

"Since then, the eternal principles on which this nation was founded have been removed from almost every aspect of public life. Again, it's no wonder that people today don't realize what's happened, because this same spurious idea of separation and the ever present threat of a lawsuit keep us from even being exposed to the real founding principles of this country. And most people's obvious first reaction—believe me, I understand it—is to discredit the kind of statements like I've just made. But from the bottom of my heart I want you to know that I'm telling you the truth. The problem is that you can never be taught the real truth if by definition you can never be taught about God's role in our nation! Why, any day now I expect the Declaration of Independence to be proclaimed unconstitutional because it mentions God! Could the Constitution be unconstitutional as well? Only the justices in their enlightened wisdom know—and the rest of us will find out."

There was a smattering of laughter as the thought sank in of the Declaration of Independence and the Constitution being declared unconstitutional.

"This is wonderful," Graham Prescott whispered to his wife in the fourth row of the chapel in Raleigh. "I can't believe he's saying this to the nation."

"Yes, it is," Mary replied. "God bless him and give him strength."

"This is preposterous," Ryan Denning hissed under his breath in the press booth in Washington. "I can't believe he's saying this to the nation."

"Yes, it is," Leslie replied. "Where does he get this stuff?"

William continued, "Now there's one last connection that has to be made in the chain causing our problems, but this connection also starts us on the way to understanding the cure: the heart of the problem is the problem of the heart.

"Institutions, no matter how bad, don't directly make problems by robbing banks or committing murder or deserting children. People do. And people act like that because their hearts don't know or respond to God's leading or his law. And they don't know about him or his laws because he's been evicted from debate, discussion, school, the news, television, movies, history, government—everywhere other than churches themselves.

"But God's worldview is true seven days a week, not just on Sunday. God is still in control of our lives on Monday at the office, but you'd never know it. And if he's evicted from schools and not allowed in our offices, then it's no wonder he's also not in the housing projects or the streets or in the divorce courts or at the pornography stands or anywhere else in our society. We've shown him the door, and then we wonder why our society is falling apart. Every day in a hundred ways, no matter what we may say on Sunday, we proclaim the worldview that man is in charge and God doesn't matter. He's shown that he's very patient, but if we really want him to leave, he will. Ask the people of Russia or Germany or Cambodia or Rwanda what that's like, when he's gone.

"So the ultimate answer to our problem, Christian faith proclaims, is not an election or a parade or a speech or a new law, but a change of individual hearts—a national turning to him, one heart at a time. The ultimate solution against the man who has just pulled a trigger and killed someone is not more police to chase him or more prisons to incarcerate him, but a change of his heart so that *he doesn't pull the trigger in the first place.* That can only come from inside. But it gets inside from being taught, from seeing role models, from having fathers, mothers, and teachers who teach values and discipline. So while the ultimate solution is the individual heart, the first important step toward that solution is the creation of a society in which faith, God's laws, and his moral expectations can be seen and can flourish.

"That brings us to the question of what we *can* do as a nation, and for that answer we should look back to what the men and women who founded this nation believed they were creating. First, let's be clear on what they never intended: this is certainly not supposed to be a theocracy—a Christian Iran—where you have to be a card-carrying Christian to vote, or where the state can collect your tithe with a tax. That would be the worst thing that could happen, both for our nation and for Christianity. No, that's *not* what Americans ever meant by a 'Christian nation.'

"So what *was* their intent? After much listening to others, prayer, and the reading of their own words, I believe that while the founders never meant America to be a Christian theocracy, they did assume that our society and its leaders would always be set on a *foundation* of Christian morality and belief. In fact, they openly despaired of what this nation would be like without that foundation.

"The First Amendment to our Constitution guarantees the free exercise of religion—without restriction on where or when. It's the same amendment that guarantees freedom of the press, which everyone today accepts as meaning universal freedom for the press within government, schools, everywhere. Why should the press be freer to exercise its rights in our nation than religion is?

"This amendment simply prohibits Congress—not the states or schools or any other institution—from making a law respecting an establishment of religion. Notice the 'an'—it isn't talking about religion in general—in that case it would say 'the' establishment. It's referring to officially establishing any specific faith or sect, as had been the case in England, and was already the case in some of the states at that time.

"Because of a couple of Supreme Court rulings, made without judicial precedent, and threats of other suits, we have incorrectly focused on removing all discussions or manifestations of religion from government, schools, public buildings, and almost everywhere else. We've forgotten the free exercise part of the same First Amendment, unless someone tries to restrict the free exercise of the press, of course! And the result is that Christians and people of other faiths are afraid to speak or to proclaim their spiritual values in the public arena, with the negative result being that the foundation meant for our society—its Christian morality and ideals—is removed from consideration in any and all public debate. To say you are a Christian and want to discuss any topic today from the perspective of your faith is a sure ticket to being labeled a nut—just the opposite of what the founders envisioned. They believed our national leaders would debate and discuss issues, as I'm doing tonight, within the context of Christian ideals and of God's will for the nation.

"So I propose to offer us all a new path, which is really an old path, to begin restoring God's worldview to our national agenda and to our political debates. It's a path that, if followed, will begin to underpin us again with the biblical morality and laws we so desperately need, without creating a theocracy and without denying anyone of any other faith his or her absolute right to pursue that faith openly and freely.

"At the end of the Book of Joshua, after the Israelites have entered the Promised Land and initially subdued it, their leader, Joshua, calls the entire nation together in one place and reminds them that it is God who has provided their victories. He then has the entire nation vote together, at one time, whether they as a nation will serve God or not. They vote to serve the Lord, and their successes continue when they do.

"We are proposing tonight that it's time for this nation, this generation, to decide which worldview we believe. Is God in control, or is man in control? Is this government really a miracle among nations, founded by God, or just a fortuitous coincidence? Will we seek to be ruled by God's laws, or will we just create our own changing version of what's right and wrong as we go along? Will we, in short, serve the Lord, or not?

"If we vote to serve God again as the creator and protector of this nation, then it's time to examine all our national goals, priorities, programs, and laws to honestly ask whether they conform to the guidelines he wishes for us.

"If we vote that God is not worth serving, that man is in control, then our nation can continue on that chosen path. And we can then no longer consider it contradictory, for example, that the murderer of an unborn baby by abortion is paid, while the murderer of an unborn baby by gunshot is prosecuted. But if a majority of our nation votes for the second worldview, once and for all pushing God's presence in our nation aside, then I'm announcing tonight that I will at that time resign from this office, and the vice-president can assume my duties as the leader of this nation."

Patricia Barton-North, who had been sitting in almost every possible position during William's address, was at that moment slumped forward, looking like she was napping. But at William's announcement of his possible resignation, her head popped up, and the television captured a serene but confident look, as if she had just found a reason for enduring the president's speech.

William continued, "Now we can't all come together in one place and vote as the Israelites did in Joshua's day. And we all need time to consider the implications of what I've said tonight and what this vote will mean for ourselves, our families, and our future. I hope most of you will want to study as my wife and I have, and even pray about your decision. I hope there will be a true and honest national debate that will last longer than a ten second sound bite.

"So this is what I'm asking you to do. Will you serve the Lord? If you will, then I ask you to vote in the congressional election this November for men and women who openly and clearly hold the worldview that God is in control and that they are serving him. You may have to do some real studying of candidates. You may have to ask hard questions. I don't care which party they're from, or even if they're from a party. They can be current members up for reelection or new candidates. I don't care whether they're liberal or conservative. I don't care whether they're black, white, male, or female— just people who try every day to submit their lives to God.

"If you, the American people, will elect a House of Representatives and a third of the Senate according to those criteria, then I promise strong leadership to break all gridlock, to examine *all* programs and laws in light of their adherence to biblical principles, and to work with Congress to produce a completely fresh program that will truly turn this nation around.

"I not only urge all of you to vote next November, but I urge many of you to prayerfully consider whether you should run for office, to use your talents in a way that will honor God."

There were some murmurs in the House as the elected officials realized that the president was openly advocating that many of them not return next year.

Richard and Janet Sullivan were sitting with their son Tommy in their den, watching Richard's old law school classmate. "Isn't God's power amazing?" Richard asked, the note of astonishment obvious in his voice. "To think that William hardly knew the Lord in June, and now he's challenging our nation to return to God's healing ways! I can't believe what God can do."

"Our youth group leader says," Tommy replied, "that if you can explain it, then it can't be God!"

"Finally, when I say a completely fresh program, I mean it. One that will reestablish biblical principles in our nation, that will tell the world it *does* make a difference in America that it was the Ten Commandments which until recently were on the wall of our Supreme Court, not Hammurabi's Code. That it *does* make a difference that our coins say 'In God We Trust,' not 'In Buddha We Trust.' That it *does* make a difference that our public buildings abound in quotes from the Bible, not the Koran. We need a program which will ground us again on God's principles and which will unlock the creative spirit God has put within all of us.

"I'll address some of those possible programs in a minute. But first I want to reiterate to those who are not Christians that I am *not* talking about creating a theocracy. Though this nation has always been predominantly Christian, it has, with rare exception, always encouraged all faiths and will continue to do so. As one conservative Jewish writer has said, people of his faith should pray for Christianity remaining the dominant religion in America because of the protection and tolerance it has traditionally provided.

"In fact, Christianity by definition can't be coercive—each individual is a 'prospect' until the moment he dies—a 'prospect' with a choice to accept Christ. The Christian can't demand your faith from the barrel of a gun—he can only plant seeds and let God himself work on your heart. So no one should fear that by electing people who believe in God's rule that he or she will give up any freedoms. In fact, just the opposite. I welcome other faiths in the public debate. Christianity can hold its own in that arena, and one's faith can be sharpened when debate occurs. The tragedy is that for more than a generation no one has been able to discuss faith in public—*any faith*—and that has got to change.

"Now, finally, what are some possible programs and policies that this new Congress of men and women seeking God's will might consider, if you, the American people, elect to serve the Lord?

"We'll soon publish a short paper on each of these, and there'll be more suggested between now and November fifth, I'm sure. So tonight, because of the hour and because you've been so patient, I'll only touch on some highlights—but we want you to see that we mean real and productive change."

"This ought to be good," Ryan said. "Everyone take notes—they're all we'll have for our discussion afterwards."

"I still can't believe this," Leslie added, picking up a sharp pencil and turning the page on her pad.

"First, we'll propose a step that will instantly reinvigorate the country, remove a huge drag on the economy, and even do much to right the wrong mentioned by Jesus in Luke 11, 'And you experts in the law, woe to you, because you load people down with burdens they can hardly carry, and you yourselves will not lift one finger to help them.'

"We'll propose to this new Congress to do away completely with our nine billion annual pages of IRS forms and instructions and replace them with a simple flat tax, pegged at eighteen percent of income.

"There'll be no deductions or exceptions. There willl be a gross income floor of about twenty-five thousand dollars per couple plus six thousand dollars per child below which no tax will be owed. But after that, there will be a straight eighteen percent payable on all types of earned income, corporate and individual. We'll raise the same amount of tax we do today, but we can disband almost all of the IRS, plus most tax attorneys, some accountants, advisors—the whole tax industry."

For the first time since early in his speech, there was general applause in the chambers.

"Second, welfare reform and families. We'll propose a negative income tax so that a family earning less than a set amount will simply receive quarterly a check for the difference. People will decide for themselves how to spend it, and the system won't discriminate against those families with a man residing there. Most of those employed by the welfare departments in each state can then find other jobs."

There was more applause, slightly louder and longer.

"Third, affirmative action. I'm going to express out loud what many of us feel. Our founders made a terrible and tragic mistake in condoning slavery. We need to help right that wrong, but then move on. For seven years and only seven years, anyone from a minority who feels that he or she has been discriminated against because of race or national origin will be able to apply for an outright grant for education, either to high school, college, and/or technical school, to assist him or her to attend. We'll do everything we can as a nation to level the playing field and to make up for any possible past discrimination.

"But America is about equality of opportunity, about using one's God-given talents to be and to do as much as one can. We've been sidetracked by the humanist worldview into trying to insure equality of *outcomes*, which is simply impossible. It winds up dragging everyone down, especially the minorities, into mediocrity, instead of lifting us all up to excellence. We'll invest seven good years and all the money it takes in righting those wrongs—but that will be the end. After seven years, unless one can prove specific, unlawful discrimination, there will be no more singling out for anything—good or bad—because of one's race. We are all equal in the sight of God, and we'll all live by that law."

William paused, but there was only a smattering of applause for this untested idea.

"Fourth, the poor. Jesus said they'd always be with us, and he mandated that we take care of the fatherless. Well, tragically, today we have a whole lot of poor and fatherless people, and we have to take care of them. But not the government. The government is the worst possible choice to teach individuals who need help anything about skills, working, values, or habits. Only in extreme cases of neglect, mental illness, and helplessness should the government intervene. Otherwise, this is the job for families and churches. First, the extended family of the people in trouble. Second, other families.

"We will propose that families who want to help others can register as clusters of two or three families together, and they will be matched up by private agencies with individuals and families who are of low income and who similarly register that they need help. By spreading the task—or opportunity—to help one family with the combined resources of two or three families, the financial burden will be light. But the primary benefit is that people can actually learn from one another. The only tax deduction in the whole flat tax plan will be granted to families who help others in this way, and only for four years on a decreasing scale, since the goal is to help lift the targeted individual or family into a productive status as quickly as possible. But people will again be helping people, face to face and family to family."

The applause was the loudest so far. From somewhere came a shout of "Amen," which produced a welcome round of laughter and helped relieve the tension from William's hard-hitting speech.

"Fifth, education. We'll propose that the same mix of public and private educational funding that has been used successfully in our colleges for years be moved to the elementary and high school levels in the form of a combination of public grants, vouchers, corporate endowments, and private gifts, all centered on *choice* by parents of where they want their children to attend school. Maybe something else will work in twenty years, but for now we've got to shake up our largely failing system and put responsibility back in the classroom by giving parents a real and viable choice."

He turned and looked directly at the Supreme Court justices. "Sixth, we'll pass a constitutional amendment, if necessary, on Religious Foundations and Freedom, to send the message that our laws are to be interpreted, whenever they are vague or unclear, from an historical and biblical perspective, and that the free exercise of religion, both individual and corporate, is just as important as the prohibition against establishing an official national religion. That means the free exercise of religion by students in our schools, in our government utterances about law and morality, in our courts, and in all public areas. And, again, though this is predominantly a nation of Christian heritage, that means the free exercise of other religions as well. Today our children only get to see the 'no prayer' option in school—and look what it's done for us. God has been expelled, with disastrous results. Better that they be able to pray, if they want, and to see others doing the same, including those from other religions, than to deny, as we have, the free exercise of that right to everyone except atheists."

William almost didn't pause and was surprised by the strength and the length of the solid applause that followed this proposal.

When the applause died down, he paused and again surveyed the silent chamber. "There will be much more to do if and when we have the opportunity to work together with the men and women of such a Congress next year, but for now our last proposal concerns laws on individual behavior and morality. I know that a year ago I advocated laws cut clearly from a belief in the humanist worldview. But I'm standing here tonight admitting to you that I was wrong. It *does* matter what types of behavior we lift up as the standards for our society. Simply stated, once we depart from God's laws, where do we stop? Our only safe harbor is provided by him. And the consequences of violating those laws are already obvious for all to see in our society, primarily in our embattled families and in the waves of violence.

"So we will propose laws and rules—or encourage the states to do so where more appropriate—against abortion, polygamy, homosexual activity, assisted suicide—those activities God's higher authority says are wrong and for which there are societal consequences when disobeyed. We cannot say we believe in a God-centered worldview if we ignore how he has instructed us to behave.

"Now everything we have proposed in this list of programs must wait until you decide, at the election in November, because we will not impose godly rules on a nation that denies that God is important. If you acknowledge his authority and elect such a Congress, then we will push for the fine-tuning of laws and programs similar to these. But in one case I can't wait. That is abortion. Last year I signed an executive order allowing full-term abortions in the federal health care system, which was a terrible mistake, and for which I have asked God's forgiveness many times. Tomorrow I will rescind that order, returning to the previous situation of first trimester abortions only. And then we will start doing everything we can within the existing laws to discourage *all* abortions. The deaths of so many innocent babies simply cannot be ignored until November. But in all other cases, we'll leave every law and program in place, while we campaign for and with those who share God's worldview on these and other issues.

"So tonight we've asked this nation's most fundamental and important question: whom will we serve, God or man? As you've seen, from the answer to that *one question* inevitably flows the answers to *many* issues that have frustrated and bothered us for years. The key is to answer the first question first. The rest then follows.

"So, my friends, that is the *real* state of our union. We have a terrible, fundamental identity crisis about who we are. That's why our legislation is deadlocked, not able to go in any one direction.

"I'm proposing that we solve that crisis with our vote, just as the Israelites did. I'm asking you to vote in November to follow the Lord, as our forefathers did, by electing men and women not just of good humanist character, but who have God's view of the world in their hearts and a willingness to turn this nation around in their minds.

"Now again, I'm not naive enough to tell you that electing good people or changing our institutions will directly make everything wonderful in our country. In order for our problems to be reduced, we as individuals must return one by one to God's worldview and learn to submit ourselves to his teaching. That's how our nation will fundamentally change, one heart at a time. But we can start that process and make it more possible for our hearts to hear the truth by taking the step I've proposed tonight. It's crucial. It's fundamental. And I'm convinced that God, who has blessed us and protected us beyond all measure, is watching and waiting to see what we'll do in nine months. Will we turn back to him and allow him to heal us? Or will we turn away from him once and for all, and suffer the consequences?

"Please think, pray, and read about what you have heard tonight. This will be the most important election this nation has held since before the Civil War. Carrie and I stand ready to help all those men and women who share our faith and a God-centered worldview, who want to run for office themselves or who want to assist others. And we'll debate anyone who has a different opinion. But our nation's future is not up to me—it's truly now up to you, the voters."

Again William paused. A peace seemed to descend on him as he slowly surveyed the chamber and concluded, "I've reminded you about the vote Joshua called for among the Israelites. Well, with total humility, I want to conclude tonight as Joshua did, thirty-five hundred years ago. Carrie and I pray that each of you, each family, will make the important commitment we've outlined here. But whether you do or not, our own way is clear. I'm going to read now from the last chapter of Joshua's book:

> Now fear the LORD and serve him with all faithfulness...serve the LORD. But if serving the LORD seems undesirable to you, then choose for yourselves this day whom you will serve.... But as for me and my household, we will serve the LORD.

BOOK THREE

The Bible, the Word of God, has made a unique contribution in shaping
the United States as a distinctive and blessed nation.... Deeply held convictions
springing from the Holy Scriptures led to the early settlement of our Nation....
Biblical teaching inspired concepts of civil government that are contained in our
Declaration of Independence and the Constitution of the United States.

UNITED STATES CONGRESS PUBLIC LAW 97-280
96 STAT. 1211
OCTOBER 4, 1982

19

Immediately After The Address

When William ended his State of the Union address there was strong applause and even some shouts of praise. But it was not like the previous year, or most years before. It was not an orchestrated hoopla, but a serious response to a speech that even William's detractors knew had taken immense courage to deliver and that managed to touch most of those present despite its difficult content and its call for a different kind of Congress.

There were nevertheless some obvious dissenters. While two Supreme Court justices stood with most of the elected officials and clapped, three stood without clapping, and four remained silently seated.

After acknowledging the response, William turned and shook hands with the Speaker of the House. When he glanced over at the vice president, she leaned down toward him, not offering her hand, and smiling only for the cameras she knew were on them, said in a low voice, "What a crock! You should be ashamed. I'd say you're finished, you self-righteous idiot. What a waste!"

"Patricia, before you write off what I said, you ought to read—"

"Give me a break, William," she interrupted, leaning back but still smiling. "I don't care about your distorted version of history. I just care about *now.* What happened a couple of hundred years ago isn't important. See you." And she turned and stepped down from the podium.

William turned and made his way back through the still applauding body of the chamber, shaking hands and smiling politely, but overall looking subdued. He glanced up briefly and got a thumbs-up from a beaming

Carrie, while Robert and Katherine applauded next to her.

With the network picture still focused on William, Leslie and Ryan looked at each other off-camera. Ryan shook his head in disbelief and began his voice-over, "And so there you have one of the most unexpected and unorthodox State of the Union addresses ever delivered, I would venture to say. Leslie…"

"It would certainly get my vote in that category, Ryan. And speaking of a vote, wasn't that an extraordinary challenge the president made, to draw the line in the sand in January for the elections in November?"

"Yes. But even more than those political overtones, I'm frankly amazed by the whole content—really the point of view of the speech. Here's a man we've all known to be forthright in his political preferences, suddenly changing drastically and hitting the nation with an entirely new agenda—no, a whole new way of thinking—one year into his administration. I wonder if the American people will feel short-changed by the sudden flip-flop of the man they thought they had elected as their president?"

At that moment William exited the House chamber, and the red camera light in the studio came on.

"That could well be, Ryan," Leslie said, looking at him, then into the camera lens. "You know, here at the U.S. Network we recently heard from a well-placed source that William Harrison had undergone a total Christian conversion, and we were checking on it when this happened. Obviously the president has been through quite a transformation, and I guess some might even question his ability to govern."

"That thought certainly entered my mind, Leslie," Ryan answered, the camera angle shifting to show a floodlit picture of the White House behind the respected newscaster. "Some will wonder whether he can correctly maintain the constitutional separation of church and state, now that he's been through this extreme conversion."

Leslie smiled. "Remember, Ryan, he now says that wall of separation has never existed!"

"Yes, that was incredible, wasn't it?" Ryan said, "Let's get an expert opinion. Tom Hankins has reported on constitutional issues for the U.S. Network for ten years, and he's here with us tonight. Tom," Ryan said, looking to his left, "what do you make of the president's speech, particularly the part about how the founders never meant there to be a wall of separation between church and state?"

The camera came on in front of the network reporter seated just to the right of the two anchorpersons. He gave a small smile and shook his head a bit. "Ryan, Leslie, I've obviously never heard anything quite like it. Nobody has. I'm afraid that whatever the authors of the Constitution may have meant, the president is bucking a Supreme Court that has clearly stated for at least the past fifty years that the document means what the court interprets it to mean, like it or not. And now he's saying, in essence, that they've been wrong in at least several key areas, and he's calling them on it. It should really be interesting, during this time period leading up to the election. But as for the 'wall of separation between church and state,' he's right that only the words 'of' and 'and' appear in the First Amendment. None of the rest of them is even there."

"Really?" Leslie asked, and it was obvious that her question was genuine.

"The term never appears in the Constitution or the amendments. It comes from a letter written years later by Thomas Jefferson, who wasn't even in the country when the Constitution was drafted or adopted—he was our ambassador to France at the time. And, frankly, Jefferson probably meant the prohibition he described in that later letter to go only one way—the state not interfering with the church. He did lots of things—just one of them was proposing federal funds to teach religion to Native Americans—that would indicate he felt the church ought to have a pretty strong influence on the state."

"Um, I see," Ryan smiled. "Thanks, Tom. As we've said, the president has drawn a line in the sand where the election, and really also where the Supreme Court, are concerned, flying in the face of almost fifty years of rulings by our nation's highest judicial body. We'll come back to you, Tom, but now…"

BOSTON AND ATLANTA "I don't know, Bruce," Rebecca said, clicking off the post-election analysis from her sofa. "I really have to say that I lean more toward the first worldview, that God *is* in charge."

"*You do?* Come on, Rebecca, don't you flip out on me, too! When was the last time some god spoke to you?"

Rebecca was silent for a moment. Then she said, "I guess never, Bruce. I know it sounds odd, coming from me. I was struck when William said that both worldviews can't be true—either God matters, and then he matters for everything, or else he doesn't matter for anything. But I've been dodging that truth and basically believing whatever I wanted from either view when it suited me, which I guess is really a form of deception. I can understand what William's saying—you can't really have it both ways, and you have to choose."

"And what you're saying is that you'd choose the first worldview?" he asked.

"Tonight? I have to think about it more, Bruce, but if I had to choose now, I guess I would, because it's the one with God and with hope, and I couldn't be a nurse if I didn't believe in God and in hope."

"You can believe in people."

"I do, Bruce. But there has to be more. If that's all there is, then like William said, right and wrong can change all the time. What's murder one year might be someone's 'ultimate solution' the next. No, William's right to make us choose, and I guess I'd have to choose God."

"I can't believe this! First Mary, then Jennifer, then William, now you. Do you all have some irrational disease? Don't leave me, Rebecca, not now. I need you."

"I didn't say I was leaving you, Bruce. Where did you get that idea?"

"I don't know. I guess I just can't imagine living with someone who believes in what William was talking about—it's crazy!"

"Then that would be you leaving me, wouldn't it?"

There was silence over the phone line.

"Anyway," she continued, "it's been a long night, and I know you're very tired from all you're going through. Let's talk again tomorrow. And I hope you come home soon."

She could feel his tired smile across the miles. "Thanks. I hope I come home soon, too. And I *am* tired. I love you, and I'll call you tomorrow."

A MEDITERRANEAN PORT At the end of the speech, while William was still leaving the House chamber, Sadim stood up from his seat, turned off the television, and shook Kolikov in his chair. The captain dozed on his bunk, his responsibilities as their host not able to overcome his fatigue.

Agitated, Sadim shook his associate again and, when the Russian was awake, asked him, "Kolikov, can we be ready by late October, a month early?"

"Why?" his colleague asked, still a bit groggy.

"Never mind. Just answer me. Can we finish all our work and depart in time to be there in early November?"

"Well, we'd have to push, but yes, barring some unforeseen problem, that should be possible, if we had to."

Sadim stood up straight again in the darkened cabin, his own fatigue wiped away by the news he'd heard tonight. "Good. Very good." He allowed himself a small smile. "Then make it so."

WASHINGTON As the presidential motorcade pulled away from the Capitol for the short ride back to the White House, William sat back in the seat, Carrie beside him, their hands clasped together. Robert and Katherine sat across from their parents.

"What a great speech, Dad," Robert said. "How do you feel?"

"Exhausted, I guess." William smiled and squeezed Carrie's hand. "But also exhilarated and at peace. How did it seem from where you sat, Carrie?"

"Fine, just fine. I was so proud of you. You told the truth, whatever else happens. Finally, someone told the truth. Thank you. And I'm sure many, many people in our nation thank you."

"But will a majority agree with us?"

"We'll see. There's almost ten months left for the nation to read and to consider, dear. That's longer than you've had!"

"But they won't have the teachers we had," William said.

"Maybe you could arrange that, Dad," Katherine interjected.

"Maybe we can. But for now let's thank God for allowing our family to be used for his purpose tonight. Katherine, why don't you start?"

As the limousine made its way behind its escort, the Harrison family bowed their heads and prayed fervently, lifting up heartfelt thanksgiving, praise, and requests for protection—interceding for the future of the nation.

The next morning while it was still dark William was tying his tie in front of his mirror in their bedroom, when Carrie came in, still in her bathrobe, holding three newspapers.

"Looks like we've sent most of the press into orbit," she said, laughing. "Including last night's newscasts and this morning's newspapers, there's everything from you've got your facts wrong to you've lost your mind and should be impeached for incompetence."

"I guess I expected that, at least from the folks in New York and Washington. Maybe in other places they'll be more sympathetic. But we knew there'd be division. How could there not be? For all the people like the Prescotts and Sullivans who called last night, I'm sure there are at least an equal number who share the views of those editorials." He turned to her as he finished his tie, then slipped on his coat. "You know what worries me now?"

"What?"

"All the people I see every day whom I've been around a long time. Most of them hardly ever say anything to me. Like Barbara's typist, or the Secret Service detail. I've got knots in my stomach—I know it's crazy, but I do—because I've just completely bared my soul to everyone, live and in color, and now I don't know if those people, when I see them today, will be thinking that I'm right, wrong, or crazy. Will they be silently laughing at me? And then there's our meeting of the inner team at nine. What will they say? Will some of them quit?"

"Maybe so. But that's one of the reasons why you felt led to do it this way, so everyone would hear your convictions at the same time. I suspect you'll hear both the best and the worst today, as God or otherwise moves people to respond to your words and to your challenge. But we know you spoke the truth, and that this nation needs to return to a godly foundation for its laws. So I guess you'll just have to be content with being God's instrument to bring the division Jesus talked about. You told people to choose, so we can't really be surprised when they do."

William gave Carrrie a hug. "Thanks, honey, I needed that! I love you so much. But please pray. I know we did the right thing, but I suspect the next few days are going to be a little tough as we all try to figure out what God has planned next."

"Of course. I'll do just what the Bible says," she said, looking up and returning his hug, "I'll pray constantly and worry not at all—or at least not very much!"

On the way to the West Wing for his early morning security briefing, William was pleased to receive three very positive "Great speech last night, Mr. President" greetings and two neutral stares from the staff. He caught himself fixing on people's eyes, like a child looking for approval, and smiled. Outside the Oval Office, Barbara Morton was already waiting, and she walked toward him, beaming, when he came near.

"Mr. President—William, since no one else is here—I just want you to know how proud my husband and I were last night. What a speech! I cried for joy because we've been praying for you and your family every day for all these years, and God really answered our prayers last night! Thank you for having the courage to tell the truth."

Overwhelmed, William stopped and reached for her hand. "Barbara, I had no idea. Why didn't you tell me about your faith before?"

"I did once, years ago, but you probably don't remember. You shrugged it off and told me God was too busy to worry about one lawyer. I think it was when you were seeing that other attorney in Charlotte. I hated what you were doing to your family and to yourself, and I almost quit. But my husband and I prayed about it, and the Lord seemed to be telling us to stay with you and to pray for you. So that's what we've been doing, every morning and evening for seventeen years. And now, finally, our prayers have been answered! Isn't God wonderful?"

William was speechless. He thought his affair had been a well-disguised secret all these years, yet Barbara had known about it and had been praying for him! "Thank God, Barbara, for you and your husband. You've been praying every day?"

She nodded and squeezed his hand. He started to search for words again, but she stopped him, tears forming in her eyes. "You don't need to say anything, William. God has blessed us all by the mercy and love he's shown you. Just continue to pray for others who don't know him. Always remember, William, they're not the enemy—they're the victims of the real enemy."

He tried to remember where he'd heard that phrase before, but his mind was too full of her revelation. Finally he just said, "Yes, thank you, Barbara. And God bless you." She squeezed his hand one last time, and he opened the door to his office.

Ninety minutes later at a little before nine, as William was reading another generally negative article about his unexpected speech, Jerry Richardson knocked and opened the door. William smiled and waved for him to come in. The president stood behind his desk, waiting to hear the other man's response.

Richardson walked all the way over to the desk before saying anything. Then he put out his right hand and smiled, "That was one incredible speech, Mr. President. How did you do it, all on your own? All the way home from the Capitol I kept thinking about what you said about choice and how much courage it took to say it the way you did. And alone in the car I decided that you and my mother couldn't both be wrong! When I got home, my wife was agitated—both our mothers had called to say they'd waited years to hear a politician speak the truth about this nation and about race relations, and they'd finally heard it last night!

"I called my mother back, and she told me again that the only hope to heal racial prejudices in this nation is the Spirit of God, who transcends races and can bind all of us together through our common faith. She told me I'd better work my posterior off for you, so here I am at fifty-four, reupping for another enlistment in what I imagine may be a slightly different army, if you'll have me."

William returned his smile and his strong handshake. For the third time in that short morning he was overwhelmed by what he was hearing from others. *Maybe that's one way God speaks to us, when we listen.*

"Jerry, of course. I need your help now more than ever. So far the team is kind of small—you, Barbara, Carrie, my kids, and me. Oh, and the Lord! So maybe it's not so small after all."

"There'll be more, many more. But I'm afraid we've also got some unhappy folks as well who feel you've gone off the deep end, or have suddenly become a Christian bigot."

William motioned his chief of staff to take the chair at the end of the desk, and they both sat down. "Yes, the vice president gave me an earful while we were still on the podium last night, and I assume Bob Horan will be upset. Who else?"

"Robert Valdez called me at home last night to ask whether our meeting this morning was still on, since you were now doing your own thing and probably being advised by the Pope—his words. I told him yes on the meeting, but I don't think he's too pleased. Chris Wright caught me on the car phone this morning. He was miffed that he'd worked so hard with Bob on a speech you didn't use, but his was more a passing temper tantrum."

"Yes, I owe them an apology. But it was the only way."

"I understand. And I think he will, too. I have no idea about Ted, Sandy, or Lanier. We'll find out in a few minutes, I guess."

"Well, let's take a second to ask his presence in what we're about to do, and in this whole day."

"Yes, please."

And they bowed their heads at the president's desk.

RALEIGH In the crowded central hall of their high school early that Wednesday morning, Matthew caught up with Sarah between assembly and first period. "Hey, how are ya?" he said, leaning down a bit as they walked along.

"Good." She smiled up at him. "Tough trig test coming up, though."

"Yeah. Definitely a bummer. Listen"—he leaned further and lowered his voice—"I got us a reservation at the Regent Hotel for Saturday night. We can check in that afternoon and stay till your curfew. It'll be awesome."

"Matthew, I'm not going to spend all day and night Saturday at the Regent Hotel with you," she said, obviously annoyed.

"Why not? We talked about it! It'll be just like we were married, and we blew into town for a weekend. We'll have room service and everything. It'll be great!"

Just like we were married, only we aren't! We're in high school! "Matthew, if I have to explain why I'm not going to spend all day in a downtown hotel where anyone might see us, then we must be very different people. The answer is no!"

They arrived outside Sarah's math class. Matthew was clearly disappointed. "Well, what if I get reservations for us at a hotel on the other side of town, where no one would ever know us?"

"I've got to take my test. Matthew, just don't get *any* reservations, okay? We'll talk about it later. See you at lunch." And she left him standing in the hall.

BOSTON AND WASHINGTON Leslie sat at her desk and dialed a number in Boston. When there was an answer, she said, "Bruce, good morning, it's Leslie Sloane."

"Oh, uh, hi."

"Did I wake you?"

"Uh, no. I was awake. Just a late night. How are you?"

"Fine. Listen, we really appreciate your tip about the president. It was obviously right on."

"Yeah, but I guess after that speech you don't need any more back-ups, right? It's pretty obvious how he's shafted us!"

"Yes. If I had time I'd be even more angry and depressed, since I believed in him and did so much to help him. What a knife in the back! But now we need you even more. We're putting together a full report for the news, then a one-hour special tonight on what's happened to him. We need your input on what he said and did at Camp David."

"You mean at Christmas?"

"Yeah. When he told everyone that he's a Christian."

"You want me to tell you now, on the phone?"

"I'd like to know the highlights now, but we really hope you can get downtown to our affiliate station in Boston. Then you, Ryan, and I will do a video conference, which we'll tape and use tonight. You're bound to have the best perspective of anyone on this."

"You and Ryan Denning together?"

"And you. On prime-time television tonight."

"He'd know that I was the one who said those things, then."

"Who?"

"The president."

"Yes. Of course. But it's your chance to say whatever you want about all this. Mainly we want your eyewitness report on exactly what happened. We'll probably be the only network with that kind of insight, if you'll help us. We're also trying to track down some of the ministers and other people who've been secretly advising him all this time. We see it as a kind of plot by religious zealots to influence our government at the highest level."

"Rebecca would not be pleased."

"I guess it's a matter of your principles, Bruce, and of courage."

There was a long pause. Leslie held her breath and kept silent. Finally Bruce said, "What time should I go to the station?"

She smiled. "A little after eleven. They'll do the make-up and stuff, and we'll start the interview about eleven-thirty, if that's all right with you."

"That's fine. But let me ask you something: Could I just describe what happened, like an eyewitness? I can give you some insights, and you can ask questions, but you do the editorializing. Okay? That way I hope I can keep Rebecca, if she understands."

"That's acceptable, and I'm sure she will. Ryan and I will see you in a couple of hours. Thanks. Now, can you just give me a few key quotes from what he said to you during that service on Christmas Eve?"

"Sure."

WASHINGTON Right at nine Barbara knocked on the door to the Oval Office. William nodded, and the inner circle of advisors filed in to join the president and his chief of staff, led by the vice president. As William rose to join them by the fireplace, where there was already a roaring fire, he noticed that all of his closest team members had made the meeting, and they all seemed serious and somber. He said a silent prayer for strength as his stomach knotted. Then he walked over to join them.

"Please, everyone, take a seat," he began. They positioned themselves around the coffee table, with Press Secretary Chris Wright in his wheelchair at the opposite end from the president. The vice president sat a half-chair length back from the rest, closest to the door and the farthest from William.

"I'm glad everyone could be here. I know that last night I probably threw a curve ball for some, if not all of you. Bob and Chris, I have to apologize to both of you for all the work you put in on the speech I didn't give. It's excellent, and I did take notes. I assure you that parts of it will be used again shortly."

William looked around the room at his advisors, then said, "You've all known me for quite a while, and we've been through a lot together. There's no reason to repeat what I said last night, except to say that I deeply believe that every word I spoke is the truth. I didn't come by those beliefs lightly or quickly—Carrie and I have been studying with some pretty exceptional men and women, reading the works and letters of the men who conceived this nation, and debating with another group of advisors who approach issues with the biblical worldview I described in my speech—a group I hope you'll meet very shortly.

"I'd be pleased to describe in detail to any or all of you how the deepening of our Christian faith and our acknowledging of God's worldview came to happen, and what it's meant to us personally. But this morning I realize we've got to focus on our work and on where we go from here.

"I was quite serious last night in describing the need for change and for a new foundation for Congress and the nation. I was also serious about the need for the nation to choose one course or the other, with or without God's influence. I want our team to fill in all the details of the outline I began in the speech—to define what a modern secular government founded on God's principles will be like, if that's what the people choose in November. It will be a very busy time, first of studying, then of talking and debating, finally of writing and persuading. But we won't implement anything unless and until our people want this course for our nation."

"Except on abortion," Bob Horan, the speechwriter, interrupted.

"Except on abortion," the president agreed but added nothing.

William paused and looked around the circle again. Most of the looks were blank, but he couldn't see Patricia Barton-North, who was partially hidden behind Robert Valdez. Then he continued. "I already know the vice president doesn't think much of this new course—she told me so last night. And I appreciate that some or all of you may agree with her. Jerry was kind enough to come in early and to offer his complete support. I would ask each of you to choose, as I described, just because I think we'll be trying to implement at least some policies that may be impossible for someone who doesn't start with the biblical worldview to accept. And I frankly need coherent, well-thought-out advice, not more gridlock.

"But I realize that making that decision may take some time. This is quite a change in some ways. So if you're prepared to join us, then we want you. If you're willing to try and to make a decision say, in about a month, then your help is needed. But if you know this is not your way, then it's probably time to part now. After last night you can't embarrass me by resigning—I'm beyond that," he said and smiled. "That's all I'd prepared to say today, so now I'm ready to listen."

Bob Horan's face had grown redder as the president spoke. He said, "I think I've got a right to go first. How could you say what you did about gay people, after all we've been through and all you've done to lift us up?"

William paused again and looked directly at his old friend. "From a personal point of view that was one of my toughest decisions, Bob, but no less correct. And ironically that decision began months and months ago, when I first saw what a pro-homosexual national policy was doing in areas I hadn't even really considered. You see, in my private moments, even before I became a Christian, I asked myself whether I would want either of my children to adopt your lifestyle. And the answer came back loud and clear, for a number of reasons, no. Then I had to look at what we've been doing to the armed forces, movies, churches, the Boy Scouts and Girl Scouts, adoptions—all those areas and many more have become flashpoints for an agenda that promotes a lifestyle I wouldn't want for my own kids.

"Then when I became a Christian, besides the biblical teaching, which is clearly opposed to homosexual activity—not the individual, but the act— I was even more impressed with what I've come to understand as tough love, what Jesus meant when he said to love your neighbor *as yourself*. It's not mush or sympathy: it's love, wanting exactly the same for you that I'd want for me. So I started asking this question in many areas: Would I want to be on welfare? Would I want to be an unwed mother or father? Would I want to be a wife in a polygamous marriage? Would I want to be a homosexual? And if the answer was no, then tough love means I've got to do what I can to help others—particularly when we're talking about government policies—not to suffer those consequences either.

"My efforts won't be perfect. Some will fall through the cracks. But it's really the height of conceit and of condemning others—not loving them— to promote and encourage situations for them that I would not stand for myself or for my family. So that logic will pervade much of what we design for the nation over the next nine months: is any particular program what I would want for myself or my children in that situation? If not, then there's going to have to be a really strong reason to go along with it anyway—because my inclination will be to discard it.

"And so that's how I come back to you, Bob, and the other homosexuals I know. I have to say that what you're doing I believe is wrong, and our government and other opinion-setters in our society shouldn't promote that lifestyle. What you do yourself is of course between you and God, but our government shouldn't encourage it any more than we should encourage adultery, prostitution, polygamy, or any of the other behaviors that are arguably just 'lifestyles,' but nevertheless strike at the biblical foundation of our society, the family."

Bob Horan rose from his chair and said, "You're wrong about me and other homosexuals. We can't help the way we are, and you're going to discriminate against us again. You're as bad as any Christian bigot I've ever met, and I assure you that if I'm burning in hell someday, you'll be there, too." He then began moving toward the door.

William replied, "I hear you, Bob, and understand that you believe it. But I've recently met several men who used to say the same things and now, by God's power, have been saved from what you're going through. I'd really like you to meet and talk with them."

Horan reached the door and looked back. "Save it. I've heard it all before, William. And I don't care. I *like* being gay. I like kissing my big handsome lover—does that make you squirm, William? You're just a wimpy little hypocrite, hiding behind some crazy revelation from Moses, and the voters will see you for what you are and crush you in November. Then you'll have to follow through and resign! I'm just sorry I have to waste the next nine months waiting for your destruction. You can count me off your team—in fact, you can put me down as your *enemy*. In words that I'm sure are found somewhere in your mythical Bible, stuff it!" And he walked out, slamming the door.

Jerry Richardson looked at his boss and said, "We're all having to make tough decisions. You made yours, and Bob made his." Turning back to the group, he asked, "Who else has an opinion?"

"I'm inclined to believe you and to stay with you," Chris White said from his wheelchair. "But I'd like to see and consider a little more. So put me in the category of watching what happens over the next few weeks."

"Thanks, Chris. We can really use your talents," William said.

"I'm in that category, too," said Secretary of State Lanier Parks. "I think you're probably right on most counts, but it's been a long while since I've thought about them. I'd appreciate knowing some specific books you'd suggest on the two worldviews. Last night after your speech I even read some of the Book of Joshua—it's been a long time."

Abruptly, the vice president stood and said, "Before this becomes a holy roller service, I'm repeating that I think you're just all wrong, William. The second worldview is obviously correct. If there's really a God, how could he or she allow all the murder and violence and mess in this world? That's no god I want to worship. We're on our own, William, and you're leading people back to syrupy but disastrous myths. We've got to believe in ourselves and in no one else—particularly not in some unseen and uncaring God.

"So count me off the team. I'm not going to quit my job, for obvious reasons. You've made this change, not me. So you can take the heat and the disaster. My staff is already hard at work distancing me from all of this nonsense as fast as they can. Call me when there's some official function we have to do together, William. Otherwise I guess as of this morning we're officially 'divorced,' and I'll be in my office at the Capitol doing my best to be ready to be president when you resign in November. Those of you who find out that this is all smoke and mirrors and want to get back to real work are welcome to join us. Good luck, William. You'll need it."

As she turned to leave, Robert Valdez rose. "She's right, William. You're off the charts. I'm joining Patricia right now, to help her get ready. I hope the rest of you will come with us."

The two of them walked out of the Oval Office without looking back.

William looked down and said quietly, "There goes the nucleus for the secular humanist government in exile, across the Mall, waiting. This really will be an interesting nine months."

"I'll see a few more cards on this side of the Mall," Foreign Policy Advisor Sandra Van Huyck said with a smile, and everyone was surprised by her gambling metaphor. Looking around she explained. "My dad was a deacon in our church who lived in mortal fear that the preacher would stop by on a Thursday night when he and his buddies were always playing poker in our basement. So I'm actually a good Baptist who can quote the Bible and figure the odds on drawing to a straight."

"Thank you, Sandy. We may need both of those talents, along with your foreign policy skills, before it's over. I hope you're here permanently."

"We'll see. This is all pretty new. But I'm game to see what happens next."

All eyes now turned to Ted Braxton, the President's oldest friend among his advisors, who had not yet said a word.

He acknowledged the looks and then said, "I decided last night that I'm staying, but it's not because I had some conversion on the road or saw a bright light. I'm staying because of the courage it took you to say and do what you did, which struck me hard, and because of thirty-five years of friendship.

"Now this morning you've talked about us having to make a choice. Well, I may not be able to do that in a month, or ever. I may never be a

Christian like you are, William. Maybe I will, but maybe not. And I differ with you on one thing. I think you may need some folks on this team who aren't committed as much as you, but who can still share most of your vision—for balance and perspective.

"And I do promise one hundred percent loyalty. If I can't go along with something, I'll tell you. Until then, I'm totally on the team, and I won't be talking to anyone about anything out of school. So I'm still here if you want me, ready to help you try and fix this old country, not so much because I believe in God, William, but because I believe in you."

William was moved by his old friend's words and his confidence. He reached out and shook Ted's hand. "Agreed. And I'm sure you're right. Just tell me you won't fight what you see God do, and if it looks like he's doing good things, you'll also consider joining that team as well."

"Deal," Ted said.

Everyone sat back, and William exhaled. "Well, now that we've decided who's still here, I want to get us together with the men and women who were the real brains behind last night's speech. You have much more practical government experience than they do, but they bring the perspective I think is so important if we're truly going to do God's work, and not just be noisy, ineffective politicians for another year or more.

"I've asked them, and I'm asking you, to come for lunch tomorrow, and we'll begin integrating these two groups into one team under Jerry's leadership. And since Lanier asked, let me give all of you a couple of titles that you might find interesting about how God has intervened in the life of this country right from the beginning.

"Jerry, you and Chris should draft statements about the resignations of Bob and Robert. I'm sure the vice president will be saying plenty on her own, and we need to get something out pretty quickly. We'll consider over the next week how we want to reorganize the Cabinet. The press will be trying to get quotes out of all of us, and we'll be questioned on all sides. But remember that many others have been waiting and praying, like Jerry's mother, for someone to have the courage to say what we're saying.

"We've got to defend daily against a bunker mentality. It's not us against them. Let's be wise in dealing with everyone but keep God's joy in our hearts, remembering that he's in charge and that he's using us. We've got a huge mission, but in just the last hour we've already doubled the size of his team. If we keep that up every hour for nine months, we really will turn this country around!"

As the president started to rise, Jerry touched his knee. "Mr. President, you and I started together this morning with a prayer. Let's end with one as well."

"You're right, Jerry. Why don't you start, and anyone else who wishes to, please join in."

THE MEDITERRANEAN The group of officers involved with the ship's investigation and recommendations on the twin incidents of the near collision
and the death of Petty Officer Simpson were concluding their final meeting
in the captain's cabin.

"If everyone is in agreement on the final draft," said Captain Robertson,
"we'll type it and forward it to the admiral. He may then decide that a further investigation is required, which I imagine would occur at our next port
call. All right? My thanks to each of you."

The officers rose to leave, and a few moments later in the passageway
the operations officer stopped the weapons officer.

"I guess you're pretty happy with your brother's speech last night. Did
you have anything to do with his attack on homosexuals?" asked Dobbs.

Hugh turned around in the narrow confines of the passage and faced his
fellow department head. "Not directly, Thomas. And I haven't even read
what he said—just the news summary on the ship's broadcast. But you and
I both know how I feel on the subject, though I've really done my best to
give credit where it's due."

"Thanks for your condescending hypocrisy."

"Hypocrisy?"

"Yes. You've got a double standard on the issue of gays and women. I've
seen how you look at and nuzzle up to Lieutenant Slocum. It wouldn't surprise me if there weren't some late-night footsteps in forward officers
country!"

Hugh, enraged by the accusation, as well as the guilt of the near-truth,
moved closer to Dobbs, who didn't budge. "Listen, Thomas, my conscience
is clear on that one. First, Teri's a great woman, but we haven't done *anything*,
understand. And, to set your record straight, if I can use that word with you,
I've told her pretty much the same thing that I just tried to tell you—the
issue for me is not whether women or homosexuals are *capable* of performing most all naval operations. The issue is all the other stuff that apparently
goes with it, like this conversation, and all the people walking around on the
fantail every night holding hands and whatever, and Chief Ellis's lawsuit, and
everyone hot and bothered in some way. *That's* the very simple reason why
I don't think you or Teri ought to be here, because it distracts all of us from
what we're supposed to be doing. And I can argue that point before we ever
get into what the Bible says about your activities or the role of women. So
you and I differ, but I certainly didn't write William's speech, and I'm not
using a double standard, except to say that unlike you, Teri can't change
being a woman."

"The Bible. Your whole family is full of Christian bigots who hate people
for what they are."

"Thomas, I don't know that much yet about Christianity—my brother
and sister would probably doubt whether I'm even a Christian. But I know

that both of them, if I can use them as Christians, focus on what people *do*, not on who they *are*. They're as far from bigots as you can get, in my book, so just back off with all your politically correct double-speak. Okay?"

"We'll see who's speaking double in November, when your brother resigns and is out on the street, and those who really care about the future of this country and progress are in power again."

Hugh turned and started to walk away, then stopped. "All right, Thomas, that's fine by me. Just calm down some before then, or you'll blow a gasket. At times you're a pretty decent guy, but you make it really hard to get past the scarlet 'H' on your chest!"

RALEIGH As the U.S. Network special report on what had happened to the president came to an end, Graham Prescott clicked off the television in their den and turned in his chair to Mary and their children. "It's hard to believe that in twenty-four hours my emotions could go from so high to so low," he said.

"All that footage from our previous interviews, cut and edited to make it look like William is just a puppet of his older sister's mind control," Mary agreed in disgust.

"So now you're a 'high priestess,' huh Mom?" Tim kidded his mother. "And why was Rebecca's boyfriend on so much?"

"I'm not sure," Mary replied. She turned to her husband. "You know, Graham, Bruce really just repeated much of what William said at Christmas. But it was the *way* he said it, like he was describing someone catching a terminal disease—a tragedy he had to recount to the world. I wonder if Rebecca agrees with him?"

"I don't know. At least your parents came out of it okay. And they didn't say too much about Hugh or Jennifer," Graham volunteered.

"Yes, I was interested to discover that Mom was the last sane Harrison. The family's apparently gone downhill ever since, at least according to Leslie Sloane and Ryan Denning."

"Boy, after what the vice president said," Tim got up to finish his homework, "do you think Uncle William will ever let her back in the White House?"

"I think he has to," Mary said. "After all, she *is* the vice president of the country. But you're right, she wasn't too kind. And she twisted what's happened this last year to make it seem like the legislative stalemate was because of William's weak leadership and because he spent too much time reading the Bible, which really makes me angry."

Sarah, who had said virtually nothing all night, stood up and, her voice slightly raised, blurted out, "Angry? What about me? Does anyone care how

I feel? I don't even want to go to school tomorrow! We looked like idiots! It's one thing to believe in Jesus—but it's another to use it to try to change the government. No one will even speak to Tim and me, I bet—our parents are Christian reactionaries! Why can't you just leave something alone for once!" and Sarah stormed out of the den.

Mary looked at Graham. "What did we do? We don't call ourselves reactionaries—that's what *they* said."

Graham tried to smile as Tim followed his sister up the stairs. "I guess there's not much difference in Sarah's mind. The television has spoken, and we're the bad guys."

"But that should be an honor—"

"Mary, maybe for you, or us. But Sarah's still seventeen, and frankly she hasn't seemed very happy for weeks now. Have you noticed how short she's been with everyone? So this maybe just set her off. I think she probably needs a little extra time and understanding right now."

Mary paused and thought for a moment. "I guess you're right—she has been on edge. Hopefully she'll cool off, and tomorrow I'll speak with her again."

Upstairs Sarah was sitting on her bed, trying to study, but almost overwhelmed by all the emotions swirling within her, from Matthew's insistence to her mother's outspokenness to her own guilt over giving in to him and criticizing her. Next to her bed the phone rang.

"Hey, it's me."

"Oh, hi Katherine."

"You don't sound very happy to hear me."

Sarah paused, trying to fight back tears which had suddenly filled her eyes. "Well, because of your dad and my mom, I'm now a freak in a freakish family of 'Christian reactionaries' trying to like subvert our government from within the president's mind. And I'm so mortified I may be sick at home for the rest of the school year, but other than that, everything is fine."

"Oh, come on, cousin. It's not that bad!"

"Yes it is, here in the real world. You can at least live in the White House, where no one will bother you. But I have to deal with kids who think my mom's a witch or something."

"No way. You should have heard some of the kids at my school today," Katherine answered. "I'm sure they were just repeating what their parents said, but I got some pretty weird stares, laughs, and comments. But I guess I expect it a little bit—the Bible says to expect it, if you're doing God's work."

Sarah exploded. "The Bible says! The Bible says! I think if I hear that one more time I'll scream!" It was all she could do to keep from hanging up on Katherine.

"But that's what *you* used to say. Now I believe you were right. The Bible *does* have good stuff, Sarah. This is me, cousin. You should chill out a little."

Sarah let out a long sigh. "I…I'm sorry, Katherine. It's just this whole week has been so crazy. I'm just not prepared to like be crucified tomorrow for what my parents do."

"You'll survive. Just don't let them get under your skin. Anyway, how'd you like Dad's speech?"

"Oh, it was okay. I guess I really did admire him for saying all that. Was he nervous? I'd have been scared to death!"

"Yeah, I think he was pretty nervous. But we all helped him write it, and we prayed a lot before he went to the Capitol."

"You helped?"

"And Robert. He came home for it."

"Cool."

"Yeah. Listen, how's Matthew?"

Sarah paused. She wasn't sure she wanted to talk about Matthew right then. "He's…uh, fine. Fine."

There was something about Sarah's voice. A bolt hit Katherine. "Sarah, did you sleep with him?"

Sarah thought about lying but realized she wouldn't get away with it. She lowered her voice. "Uh…yeah. I guess it's been eight or nine times."

"*Eight or nine times?*"

"Yeah."

"Good heavens. What was it like?"

"I don't know—like that computer, only much better. Matthew and I really love each other."

"Love?"

"Yes. He's wonderful to me. He's like told me how much he loves me every day this week."

"I'll bet he has. And what have you two got planned this weekend?"

"He wants to spend Saturday in a hotel, but I told him no."

"Finally! Sarah, this is crazy. Remember what I said about my friends saying sex takes over? And you said no way. Well? And how are you going to feel if your future husband someday asks you about all this?"

"Maybe Matthew will be my husband."

"Probably he won't. You told me it would be years and years before we're married."

"Well…maybe it's not perfect. But I've done it. *We've* done it. So that's that. I've been thinking: do you know anything about getting birth control pills?"

"Sarah, no. You've got to stop now, no matter that you've done it. Stop, and tell Matthew you've both got to stop."

Sarah laughed. "And never see the bo—man I love ever again?"

"Maybe. If that's his decision. Who cares? It's you, Sarah, I'm worried about. Listen, our youth group leader said last Sunday that you can always tell the difference between lust and love because lust takes and love gives. It sounds to me like you're in love and Matthew is in lust."

"Look, just lay off him, okay? Whatever we've done I wanted it myself, too. And what do you know about it anyway? How's your love life been lately?"

"You're right, Sarah, on that one. Score one for you. But someday the right man will come along. You're right that it probably won't be real soon. But I pray I'll still be able to say I *haven't* done what you've done, that I saved that experience to share first and only with him."

"Wonderful. Have you thought about writing romance novels? And what am I supposed to do, even if I wanted to? I've done it!"

"The Bi—I mean, I think God is always ready for us to start over again with a clean page, if we ask to be forgiven."

"Well, that's fine, but I don't really feel any need to be forgiven. We're just doing what everyone else is doing, and not *everyone* can go to hell!"

"Um, I don't remember any restrictions on its size." Katherine had to smile, despite the serious nature of their discussion. "Look, we're not supposed to do what God says not to do. It's that simple. I know you'll regret it."

"And I feel just fine, so get off my case, okay? Matthew and I will do whatever we think is right. God must have created love in the first place, and we love each other. So just cool it."

"Okay, cousin, I'll cool it."

"And don't you dare say anything to your mom or dad," Sarah added.

"I won't, though we all ought to be praying for you."

"Pray for the homeless people in Yugoslavia, Katherine. I'm telling you, Matthew and I know what we're doing."

"Fine. But I'm still going to pray for you."

"If you want."

"I do. I've got a bunch of homework left after that stupid show. I'll call again in a few days."

"Okay. Talk to you soon."

"Sarah, I... Never mind. See ya."

ATLANTA AND BOSTON That night Rebecca called Bruce. He barely had said hello when she asked, "Bruce, how could you be there on that show after all that William did for you and your family?" She was clearly upset.

"Hey, I tried to call you this afternoon to tell you about the interview, but they said I'd have to leave a message because you were teaching a class, and I didn't want to do that."

"You haven't answered my question."

"Well, I didn't do anything, really. I just told them what happened at

Christmas—just facts. What's wrong with that?" His tone was defensive.

"But William asked everyone there not to say anything," Rebecca protested.

"Hey, I waited until after he'd told the whole world. It really wasn't news by that time."

"What he said at Camp David was—it was personal. How did they know to call you, anyway, especially there in Boston?"

"I guess they just got lucky. That's what reporters are paid for. That Sloane woman tracked me down from our interview together."

"Well, you sure helped make my brother look bad."

"Hey, I didn't know how they were going to put all those shots together. I just told the truth about what actually happened. What's wrong with that?"

Rebecca calmed down a bit and thought for a moment. "I guess I feel like I'm responsible for bringing someone into the privacy of our family at Christmas who now has told the whole world all about William's private thoughts. So I'm upset with you and upset with me, wondering what William and the others think of me—and you."

"I frankly don't care what he thinks of me any more," Bruce said, and knew he'd made a mistake as soon as the words left his lips.

Her anger returning, Rebecca said, "That's obvious, Bruce. But I do. He's my brother! Look, I hope your mother is better, and I don't wish you any problems. But I've got to think about all this, including our relationship. I'm too upset now to talk. So I'll call you tomorrow."

She hung up the phone before he even had a chance to say good-bye.

Had the people, during the Revolution, had a suspicion of any attempt to war
against Christianity, that Revolution would have been strangled in its cradle.
At the time of the adoption of the Constitution and the amendments, the
universal sentiment was that Christianity should be encouraged, not any
one sect [denomination]. Any attempt to level and discard all religion would
have been viewed with universal indignation.

HOUSE JUDICIARY COMMITTEE REPORT
MARCH 27, 1854

20

Friday, February 1
Three Days Later

ATLANTA Late that Friday morning Eunice Porter and Sally Kramer entered
the office borrowed by Dr. Harvey Thompson for meetings such as theirs.
He rose and offered them the chairs in front of the desk.

"How are you both today?" he asked, smiling.

"I guess we're fine," Sally offered. "But we wanted to meet with you after
what the president did the other day. I'm starting to show already, and
Eunice may be pregnant, too, so we wanted to find out what you're going to
do."

The doctor's smile broadened and he placed his elbows on his friend's
desk. "I don't think we ought to do anything but just keep going as we've
already agreed."

"But I heard some of the other girls at work saying the president has
signed some law or something making full-term abortions illegal again,"
Eunice emphasized. "I sure don't want to be pregnant if we can't do the same
thing this time as last time."

"An executive order—he signed an executive order dealing with those
hospitals and clinics taking federal funds, the same sort of thing he did a year
ago to make it legal in the first place. But look, ladies, let's not panic, especially since in both your cases we've already advanced money to you, which
you'll owe us if we don't go ahead." He raised his hand as they both began
to interrupt.

"Look, this can't last. There are already several lawsuits about to be filed to overturn his latest order, since so many women are being denied their rights arbitrarily, and a coalition is forming to work with Congress to pass new laws if the courts or the state legislatures don't move forward fast enough. Listen, you're in good shape. Think about our other clients who are in their seventh or eighth month. We're looking fast for solutions. So for now, just cool it and wait for us to get it fixed."

"But what if none of that works? Eunice and I don't want to wind up with more kids!" said Sally.

"If all else fails, you'll still be taken care of. Maybe we can't do the procedure here in the main hospital like before. Maybe not even in Atlanta. But I've got friends in other places, like New York, where things are not quite as tight. So worst case, we'll send you up there and take care of our business."

"Who buys the ticket and pays for all that?" Eunice asked.

"If it comes to it, we will, of course," Dr. Thompson answered.

The two women looked at each other. "Well, I guess it's all right, then, at least for now," Sally answered. "But we need to know what's going on. I certainly don't want any kids."

"I'll give you a call whenever anything happens with either the courts or the Congress. Don't worry. Just because the president has lost his mind doesn't mean everyone else has to suffer. Trust the courts to do the right thing, like they always have."

"Well, thanks," Eunice said, standing up. "I'll let Sally know if I'm pregnant, which I should know real soon. She can pass on any news you've got. Oh, thanks again for that advance. It made my kids' Christmas real special."

"Think nothing of it," Dr. Thompson said, showing them toward the door, "We always like to help when we can, especially where children are concerned."

WASHINGTON Leslie was again stationed at her familiar spot on the White House lawn, waiting for Ryan to switch live to her as part of the lead segment on that Friday's evening news. Her network had kept up its steady coverage and inquiry into the changes in the president and his administration since the State of the Union address, including its scoop of the rest of the media with Bruce Tinsley's eyewitness account of the president's testimony at Camp David a month before. Like the rest of the Washington press corps, Leslie was having to move fast, as politicians of all types either embraced the president's message, denounced it, or waited to see which way the wind was blowing back home. In her earpiece she heard the director's ten-second warning, and then she was on, live, broadcasting into millions of homes.

"That's right, Ryan," she said, answering the anchorman's lead question, "it *is* quiet now. But that wasn't the case several hours ago, as these pictures will show."

With those words the studio started her taped piece from earlier in the day showing Leslie standing in LaFayette Park across Pennsylvania Avenue from the White House, the street completely blocked with demonstrators and the police standing shoulder to shoulder with their backs to the White House fence. She had to yell above the noise of the honking horns and the bullhorns behind her. Clearly visible were signs reading "Abort this President" and "Holy Unfit."

"Today's demonstration, which started at noon, is the largest yet since they began on Wednesday, the day after the president's speech. Behind me are groups from Act Out! and Women for Abortion. The organizers claim that tomorrow there will be even larger crowds, with buses coming from several major cities. Meanwhile, the vice president continues to distance herself from what some are calling the president's radical break with our nation's tradition of separation of church and state, and many congresspeople are being asked to choose a worldview, not just by the president, but by their own constituents."

The tape cut to what appeared to be a law library, but it was really a set used by members of Congress for television interviews. Leslie was sitting at a round table with Trenton Patterson and Warner Watts. The piece began with Congressman Patterson speaking. "Those of us in the president's party in particular are seeking clarifications on exactly what he meant and what he intends in several key areas before making our final decisions, Leslie."

"How could his message have been any clearer, Congressman Patterson? Have you, for example, chosen one worldview or the other, as he requested?"

The congressman smiled. "Well, that's just the sort of thing I mean. Were those just good words for a speech, or did he really mean that? Obviously I *want* to support him, once he clarifies a few things. But the White House is so busy right now, with all the changes, that it's hard to get straight answers on questions like that."

"Thank you. Senator Watts, what about you? Have you made a choice yet?"

Again a smile. "No, Leslie, not hardly. And that's very personal, anyway."

"I agree, Senator. What about your party's assessment of the president's proposals?"

"Well, parts of it sounded good, but other aspects were very troubling. For example, if we really adopted his novel flat tax idea, think how many good people it would put out of work—accountants, attorneys, government workers. Why, it might trigger a recession all on its own!"

The cameras then showed Leslie live, standing in front of the lighted White House, bundled up in a long coat against the winter chill. "Ryan, we'll have more of that interview with Congressman Patterson and Senator

Watts on *NewsLine* tonight after the late local news. But here are two last points. In the interview Congressman Patterson made the interesting point that this November's bi-election will really be like a four year presidential election, since afterward apparently either William Harrison or Patricia Barton-North will be the president, depending on how the vote goes. And we understand from the organizers of today's protests that they're planning a huge demonstration and march on Washington for Easter weekend. We'll bring you more on that as it develops."

"Leslie," Ryan's head appeared in the top right-hand corner of the screen, "we've heard that the president has quickly assembled some Christian replacements for the members of his Cabinet who have resigned, and that these still mostly unknown people had lunch yesterday with those members who've decided to stay."

"That's right, Ryan, except that this Christian group has actually been together for quite a while. We understand it's made up of the preachers, economists, and writers who clandestinely helped the president with Tuesday night's address. We're still trying to track down exactly who they are. Chris White, the White House press secretary, did find time in all of the confusion today to tell us that the president should be announcing these new names early next week."

"All right, Leslie, thanks for that report. You've certainly got your hands full with all the changes in Washington these days."

As Leslie removed her earpiece and handed her microphone to her sound man, she thought, *It's sure nice of you to volunteer to come down to Washington for the weekend to help me sort through it all!*

That evening the Harrisons shared a meal with Michael and Elizabeth Tate, Jerry and Diane Richardson, and Bradley and Susan Fullerton. Around the dinner table they talked about the blending of the president's two advisory teams. William was delighted that Bradley Fullerton and Larry Thomas had agreed to take leaves of absence in order to work full-time at the White House, along with eight second-level personnel recommended by their mentors the previous fall. And he was still hoping that Michael Tate would join them as well, at least until the November elections.

"Well, I think we got off to a good start yesterday afternoon," Jerry said, "and we should hit the ground running by Monday with the moves being completed this weekend. Larry should arrive from the West Coast on Tuesday."

"What do you think, Jerry," Michael asked, "from your corporate background: will this fusion work?"

The chief of staff considered for a moment. "Of course I haven't known the new group very long, but everyone on both teams seems truly committed to making it work. I think most of us from the old team have thought about what William said in his speech, and we agree that this may be the one last chance to turn the nation around, back to its foundations, whether one describes those in faith terms or not. So, yes, I think it will."

Fullerton, who for ten years had headed the Christian Economic Research Institute after twenty years in government and academia, said, "No one's ever tried anything like this, that I know of. We've got to keep the current government running in place, if you will, until the nation votes in November. But we've also got to formulate policy recommendations that will be attractive first to potential believing candidates, and then to all voters. And the recommendations have to be detailed enough to convince the public and the press that we know what we're doing, but not so complete that we preclude real congressional input after the elections. And we need to do all that as quickly as possible, so we can overcome the largely negative stories now circulating and begin to build our case. But other than that, the next few months will probably be boring!"

Everyone smiled. Diane Richardson said, "It sounds like there's a lot to do. Is it really possible to accomplish it all?"

Fullerton continued, "The good news is that many of us have been complaining, if you will, for years; and through that process we've developed a set of biblically based policy recommendations across the entire legislative agenda—not just in economics—which have been debated and fine tuned among a fairly wide group, and they're almost ready to go. And the great news is that the first version of William Harrison's administration scared most of us so much that we worked twice as hard in the last twelve months, not realizing that God had a purpose for all that work."

Now everyone laughed. William raised his hand. "I'm guilty—but I'm glad to know there was even a purpose for my misplaced policies."

"Thank God there's always a purpose," Michael added.

"And you need to add yours to the team," William said. "How could you pass up the chance to work with so many witty and well meaning people?"

Michael smiled and nodded in the president's direction. "I'm still praying about it. When I hear the answer, you'll be the next to know."

"What would Michael do?" Elizabeth asked.

"I'll answer that," Jerry said. "I'd like to have his organizational experience as the deputy chief of staff, helping to coordinate all that we've got to accomplish. We can divide up the tasks so as not to get in each other's way. And of course his expertise and contacts in so many foreign countries will be of immense help. Finally, I hope he can enlarge the course he designed for the president to reach a wider group, maybe even a mass audience, in preparation for November."

"Remember when we talked about that possibility back in September?" Carrie asked William. "Now what seemed impossible may actually happen."

"That's God's way," Michael said. "Elizabeth and I will talk together and pray, and I'll let you know soon."

"Good," William added. "We really need your help. I knew in my mind that this wouldn't be easy, but even I wasn't ready for the attacks this week. And not just from the obvious groups. Even the 'religious right'—some of them have apparently questioned my new faith, saying that if I were really a believer, I would go ahead and change everything I could now, without a national vote, and that I would fire the whole Cabinet, as well as the vice president! As if I could. I just hope there's a majority of people out there who believe not only in God and his sovereignty but also in our Constitution, in between the very vocal extremists on each side who have filled the press since Tuesday night."

"They're out there," Susan Fullerton offered. "At least I believe they are, going about their business and raising their families and not getting involved in more than their schools and churches and Little Leagues. But they're what this country is all about. They *are* this country. They've *got* to be there. And we've just got to get them involved again in this nation's political process, before it's too late."

"There's our new speechwriter to replace Bob," William said to Jerry.

Susan blushed. Her husband added, "And she's the best one I know. Susan's been writing my speeches for years."

"Then if you're available and you two don't mind working together, you're hired," Jerry said.

Susan thought for a moment. "Only if Michael joins us."

"That's what I like, a team player who can apply pressure to her teammates." William laughed. "What about it, Michael?"

"We'll see. We'll see. You must realize that there are some parts of the world where what this team is trying to do will not be taken too kindly. And to have an ordained minister in the Cabinet might add insult to injury."

"You pray, my friend," William said, "and we'll let God decide. I think we can take the heat around the world, if it's God's will. What would an unhappy government do, anyway? Launch missiles over our new policy of trying to honor God?"

Everyone except Michael Tate smiled. "No, probably not," he said. "But, seriously, there are strong feelings in many places not only against our government but also against our God, particularly our reliance on the work of his Son for our salvation. By putting the two more closely together, we may make some people very unhappy. Maybe not governments, but very possibly some militant extremists."

William had only focused on their new course as a matter of domestic policy. For the first time since he began his Christian walk, he considered that his decision to follow God might have an impact outside the country. Could it affect whoever was threatening to use the Ukrainian nuclear warhead? For a moment he stopped breathing. Carrie, the only one at the table who knew about the bomb, obviously thought the same thing, for her eyes met his, and he could see the anxiety in them.

The others stopped talking, noticing a change in him. Then William said quietly to his guests, "I guess, since we're all going to be working together now, there's something I need to tell you about."

PARIS As America went to bed that night, Sadim awoke after only a few hours' sleep in yet another Paris hotel, this one notable for its lack of notability, on the southwest side of the city. He had begun his circuitous trip late Wednesday after signaling Wafik that an unexpected meeting was necessary; and he'd arrived in the City of Light on Friday evening. After changing hotels twice he finally felt safe enough to give in to the fatigue that swept over him.

But with the morning he was up, praying and exercising in his room. The dining area in his hotel was too small for them to meet safely, so at nine Sadim joined his colleague at a bustling neighborhood café that served delicious croissants.

"Ah, my friend." Wafik smiled as Sadim approached from the front door and joined him at a corner table. "What a pleasure to see you here so unexpectedly."

"Yes. Allah be praised. Thank you for arranging all things on such short notice. I'm afraid we must change some of our strategy to use the great gift we have been given."

"Let us order, first. I assume you could use some coffee," Wafik said, his smile contrasting with the seriousness in his eyes. "And then please tell me this news."

After they ordered, Sadim leaned forward and asked, "Do you have all the tapes of the congressmen?"

"Yes, of course."

"How many are there?"

"Twenty-one. Twelve representatives and nine senators."

"And they are all clearly heard to be taking money?"

"Oh, yes. Some even boast about it!"

"Good. Did you see President Harrison's address on Wednesday morning?"

"No, it came on too late. But I've seen clips since, and I read the entire text after your call."

"Excellent. It's hard to imagine how anything he could have done could have played more precisely into our hands. It must be a great gift from Allah, wrapped in Harrison's own religious blasphemies."

Wafik held up his hand to stop the conversation while the waiter served coffee and croissants. After the waiter left, Wafik said, "Please explain what you mean."

"Gladly," Sadim replied, first taking a sip from the steaming cup.

Twenty minutes later he concluded with, "And so that is why you must move back to America within the month. You are the only one of us with the experience and sensitivity to report accurately on the activity before this election and to guide our final moves. And of course you must also continue to instruct our twenty-one congressional friends on their new foreign policy initiatives, so they will be ready to do our bidding on the election as well, encouraged by your tapes when necessary, in case any of them begin to waiver."

Wafik reflected for a moment on what he had heard and then nodded. "Yes, you are right. It is a great gift. We will have to be ready a few weeks earlier than originally planned, but it's worth it. I will propose this change to the Council, and assuming that it meets with the approval we both expect, I'll move back to the Georgetown apartment by the end of the month."

"Good, then I will return to the south after we finish here this morning," Sadim concluded.

"So little time in Paris after such a long journey?"

"Unfortunately yes, my friend. If we are to meet the new schedule, there can be no slip-ups, so I must be there. But obviously our work is being blessed."

"Obviously." Wafik nodded in reply.

No free government now exists in the world unless where Christianity is acknowledged, and is the religion of the country.... Its foundations are broad and strong, and deep.... It is the purest system of morality, the firmest auxiliary, and only stable support of all human laws.

SUPREME COURT OF PENNSYLVANIA
UPDEGRAPH V. THE COMMONWEALTH, 1824

21

Saturday, March 2
One Month Later

HARTFORD, CONNECTICUT William awoke early, alone in a hotel room, just over a month after his State of the Union address. He was on his first regional swing out of Washington to speak on behalf of their new course. After a fund-raising breakfast followed by television interviews that morning, he was scheduled to speak at a large rally in the center of town at noon, then go on to Boston.

As he was drying off after his shower, he thought, *I hope it's a large rally. New England is tough for us. Despite strong Christian roots around here, where are the believers? Our polls show that people are still personally religious. But unless the churches get behind this rally today, it could look terrible...Just what we need. More negative press.*

He shaved and dressed, thinking about Carrie, who was doing her own tour of eastern Virginia that weekend. He hoped that all was going well with her. *What a joy it is to be friends again. What a fool I was.*

But as he took his tie off the hanger, the emotional heaviness that had been building in his heart for days seemed to gain a physical weight. He had tried to be strong, too, but the crescendo of one attack after another on their plan—which now contained twenty very specific and, he felt, excellent points for the nation to rally around on schools, taxes, prayer, abortion, welfare, defense, the national debt—had begun to wear him down, and he found himself questioning what he was doing.

I haven't really prayed in days. I've missed my quiet time with God because of our schedule. Well, this morning we'll just have to be a little late.

William walked over and took the phone off the hook, then knelt in front of a chair in the living room part of the suite.

O Father…Dear God…I praise you for always driving me back to your strength, even when it takes some pain to get my attention. Thank you for all your blessings, and your love for this nation, this people, and her institutions. Thank you Father for all the people who have been encouraged and have rallied because of this challenge—help me Father to focus on your agenda rather than the media's agenda. Your timing rather than theirs. Jesus' ultimate victory rather than Satan's temporary boasts.

He went on to praise God and to seek his will. Within a few minutes the heaviness on his heart began to lift as he unburdened his doubts and his fears. As he continued to pray he once again began to lose control of his words, just as he had the morning in the White House back in December, and he heard his own voice saying quietly, *One at a time. One person at a time. One at a time.*

For several minutes this experience continued, then the words began to lose their intensity. Eventually he was able to pray again, and he continued to do so for another ten minutes.

Then he rose, finished dressing, and departed for their breakfast reception, not worried any longer about the size of their rallies. He knew that the count in November was the only tally that mattered.

RALEIGH Graham had taken his son Tim for their haircuts late that morning, and Mary was sitting at their breakfast room table addressing invitations to a fund-raiser for a good friend of theirs who had just announced his candidacy for Congress, citing William's challenge as the "wake up call" that led to his decision. As Mary finished the first bundle, Sarah, dressed in jeans and a light sweater against the day's still chilly weather, walked in and placed an overnight bag and party dress on the free end of the table.

"Matthew will be here in a minute," she explained, turning to the refrigerator for some water.

Mary had been praying for her daughter and their relationship since the night of the news special a month earlier. While Sarah had obviously survived any immediate jabs from her peers, Mary worried that their relationship was worse than it had ever been. There was a distance, a coldness between them that had never existed before. Now that Sarah's health class had moved beyond the computer section, Mary assumed that the network show and normal growing pains were the problems, unaware that another, bigger change had occurred in Sarah's life at almost the same time. Unknown to Mary, Sarah's embarrassment over her uncle and her parents had driven her even more heavily into the arms of her boyfriend. Mary had decided the week before to back off and to just be herself, rather than push her daughter, hoping that this passive approach would salvage their ability to communicate before Sarah left for college in the fall.

Mary looked up over the tops of her glasses. "I hope you all have a good time at the baseball game, and please remind Matthew to drive safely. What time is the dance over?"

Sarah swirled the ice in her cup. "Midnight."

"And the game will go on too long for you to come home and change?"

"It could. It's the first away game of the season, and Matthew wants to stay after our game and scout the teams in the second game, who we play next week. He says it helps him when he's pitching. So then we'll have to hurry to dinner and the dance."

"And where will you be changing?"

"At Amanda's. She lives over that way." She and Matthew actually had no intention of staying for the second game or of even attending the dance, except that they might drop in for the last thirty minutes after spending six hours alone together.

"Well, tell Matthew good luck. Oh, Cynthia Williams called about these invitations before you woke up and mentioned that she and Tom were driving downtown last night and saw you and Matthew, she thought, near the Royal Suites Hotel."

Sarah turned away to look out the kitchen window. "She, uh, had to be mistaken. Matthew and I were at the movie, like I told you. Oh, here he is. Bye!"

She quickly scooped up her things, waved in the direction of her mother, and went out the door to the turn around.

As she left, Mary said to herself, "That's what I told Cynthia—she must have been mistaken."

WASHINGTON Michael Tate had accepted William's invitation to join their new team one week after their dinner. His commitment was only through the election, but he was enjoying the opportunity to work with so many intelligent and committed people for what they prayed would be a real turning point for the nation.

This Saturday morning he and Joe Wood were in Michael's new office in the White House. They were discussing the committee that the African-American pastor hoped to establish from contributions. It would print literature and distribute it across the nation, summarizing the writings of the founders about God's important continuing role in the life of America.

The phone on Michael's desk rang, and he answered it.

"Reverend Tate, hello, this is Janet Sullivan."

Michael thought for a moment and then remembered the name. "Oh, yes, hello, Mrs. Sullivan. How are you, and how can I help you?"

"Well, I'm sorry we haven't met yet, but I know from Carrie how you discipled William, and I want to thank you."

He smiled. "And I know from Carrie how you and your husband brought William to the Lord's feet last summer."

This time she paused. "Only as the end of a long process begun by others."

"I know. Thank God. Now, what can I do for you on this beautiful Saturday morning? By the way, Joe Wood is here with me, so I'd like to put us together on the speaker phone." He pushed the speaker button and replaced the receiver. "Go ahead, Mrs. Sullivan."

"Hello, Reverend Wood, as well. I read that William is travelling, and I hoped that you could either give me a phone number for him or at least take a message."

"As much as they're moving around, I think the message will be easier, unless it's an emergency," Michael answered.

"No. And after you hear the message, we may need to talk, anyway. The message is that after a lot of prayer and fasting, I've decided to run for Congress."

"What? That's great! I know both William and Carrie will be thrilled. How did you decide?"

"Well, actually I told my husband, Richard, on the night of William's speech that he should run, as William challenged. He didn't immediately say no, but after a week of praying he said that not he but I should enter the race. He felt that my background in communications would help me in the race, and, if I'm elected, in Congress as well. I then prayed and thought and talked to our children and friends, and last night we decided together to make the jump. So we're on the team, at least until November! We're ready to help, and of course we need help ourselves."

"That's wonderful. Welcome. I guess you more than most new candidates know what's ahead of you. God bless you, and thank you," Joe Wood said.

"No, thank all of you. And, yes, I've seen lots of campaigns. We pray that ours can be somewhat different, though we're ready for the tough work. But what sort of help can you give us?"

"First things first. Which party do you plan to run from?" Michael asked.

Janet almost laughed. "That's the really funny thing. We've never been supporters of William's party."

Michael smiled as well. "That's no problem. At least half of the candidates who've identified with us are in the same position. And it *is* interesting, since the traditional parties don't know exactly what to do. It's almost like the Civil War. Both parties' leadership is so divided by all that's happening that they're talking about just splitting the campaign funds for this fall down the middle and giving half to those who support the president and half to those who don't. It's really pretty bizarre, but you should at least get a little money that way. Otherwise I'm afraid it's the usual old method of personal, local fund-raising."

"I see," Janet said. "What about other kinds of help?"

"We're still working on that, but for now we've got a nice presentation of the twenty key points which we hope all the candidates who identify with God's worldview will support. We'd like to begin our work next January with this road map of what to tackle first. While most of the brainpower for that piece is right here, we of course had it printed by contributions, not at government expense. The same is true of everything associated with the election, as opposed to current government policy.

"Other than that, we've set up a bureau to coordinate speakers and good ideas that seem to work, and Joe and I are brainstorming over a couple of other things. But by and large these elections will be run and paid for locally. Oh, most important! We'll add your name to our national prayer list, which is being lifted up by prayer warriors all across the nation, every hour of the day. So far we think we have over four thousand voices from that same number of churches, *every hour*, and growing!"

"Praise God," Janet whispered.

"Yes," Joe added. "Praise *him*, not any man or woman."

"Certainly the president will want to come out and speak for you," Michael added. "I'll let him know tonight when we talk."

"Thank you. And I guess we'd better get to work raising money for all that expensive TV time," Janet concluded.

"First, let's start you off by praying together," Joe suggested. And they did.

ATLANTA Bruce had stayed in Boston an additional two weeks, making preliminary arrangements as best he could for his parents. He returned to Atlanta in the middle of February. While still in Boston he'd had long days and nights to think about his future and to plan. Since returning he'd been especially nice to Rebecca, but the tension caused by his appearance on the U.S. Network was still there, although the two of them had only referred to it in passing.

Saturday afternoon was cool but sunny, just perfect for a jog on one of the long nature trails by the Chattahoochee River. They had just finished a five-mile run and were cooling off by walking in the crisp sunshine. After a long period of silence, Bruce turned to Rebecca and said, "Look, I'm sorry about that show last month. They called and I did it. You know I don't agree with your brother's new ideas, but I was careful just to say what happened and not to give my opinion. So will I ever be forgiven, and will our relationship ever be the same again?"

Rebecca listened and considered well before answering; she knew this could be an important conversation with a man in whom she'd now invested more than a year of her life. "Bruce, William's beliefs were just so personal...and you seemed so condescending, treating his beliefs like he had been brainwashed, like you knew the truth and he'd missed it. *That's* what upset me the most—besides the shock of you just being there—the tone, the derision for someone who had done so much for you."

Now it was Bruce's turn to be silent for a while. "I guess you're right, but if it makes any difference, the tone was unconscious, not intentional, I guess because I *do* feel that way about his new ideas. But you're right, he did help my mother, though it now looks like the operation only postponed the problem. Anyway, I think people need to trust in themselves and their government, not in some invisible, magical God."

They walked along in silence. Rebecca decided not to argue with him about God—they'd been over this ground before, and her own growing belief in God was so ill formed and nebulous that he always found some way to discredit it.

Finally, hearing no argument, Bruce mustered the courage to say what had been on his mind for two weeks. "Turning closer to home, to us, Rebecca, I had a lot of time to think while I was in Boston. I now know that I love you very much, and that I want to spend my life with you. So I'm asking you if you'll marry me."

She stopped walking and looked up at him, shading the sun from her eyes with her left hand. She just looked at him, without saying anything, seeming to concentrate on his eyes, as if she were looking at him for the first time. After a while he smiled and took her right hand, but still she said nothing.

"Come on, Rebecca, I've never known you to be speechless. What do you say? Will you marry me?"

"I...I truly don't know, Bruce. I'll think about it very seriously, but right this second I don't know."

Bruce was momentarily confused. "Uh, well, how long will you have to think? What do you have to think about?"

"I don't know, we'll see. Hopefully not long. Maybe later tonight. Maybe tomorrow. I'll think, and let you know."

He turned and started walking again. "Okay. But I hope you'll say yes, and real soon."

"We'll see, Bruce. We'll see." And they walked on in silence.

PALMA DE MALLORCA When the *Fortson* arrived in Palma on Friday all of the slips at the deep water pier were taken, so the ship had to anchor out and run small boats to the landing for the crew's liberty. Hugh had stayed onboard that night, but Teri had mentioned to him on Saturday morning that it was her birthday, and he decided that they could both use a break from what was now five months of deployment.

Hugh had just been reading in his daily Bible sessions about Paul's teaching on fleeing from temptation, and he'd even smiled that afternoon while shaving, thinking about it. He really didn't consider going out with Teri to be a temptation any more—he knew he wouldn't actually do anything.

But he hadn't counted on the electricity between them that evening, as they danced at a restaurant near the harbor. Maybe it was that the end of the deployment was actually in sight. Maybe it was a reaction to the hard work and danger. Or maybe it was just being away from home for so long. Whatever it was, he felt the tug of her presence, so close, as they danced slowly together. He held her close and smelled the fragrance of her hair. The tension between them was almost as strong as it had been that night at Guantanamo Bay.

Once again, as he felt his throat go dry and his heart begin to race, he thought of Saint Paul, only this time he didn't smile. *How do I get myself into these situations? Why didn't we just bake a cake in the wardroom? Please Lord, just get me out of this safely, and I promise to run the other way from now on!*

Teri seemed to sense his thoughts. She pulled back as they continued to dance slowly, her face only inches from his. She looked into his eyes as she whispered with a slight smile, "I know, Hugh, this is tough. I'm sorry to get us into these situations. I guess you know that I could love you very much... I also know that you're taken. Jennifer is a wonderful wife and mother—I just got here too late. I only hope someday I'll find a man like you. Please forgive me—this has been a wonderful birthday present. Thank you."

Hugh felt torn. He almost leaned over and kissed her, but caught himself and felt disgusted by his own thoughts. He stopped dancing but kept hold of her hand, took a very deep breath, and said. "Teri, Teri. Look, this is about to do me in. You're great. You're beyond great, but I can't do this. Come on, Lieutenant, let's head home."

"Is that an order?"

"I guess so." He smiled.

"My place or yours?"

"Uncle Sam's."

Thirty minutes later they were huddled with twenty sailors in one of the ship's small boats for the cold and sometimes choppy run out to the *Fortson*. As Teri snuggled close to him, Hugh thought how easy it would be to go astray without the help of a moral compass, even one as crude as his still was.

And he said a short prayer of thanks.

During the evening the wind and tide had changed, swinging the ship almost completely around at its anchorage. The starboard midships ladder from which they had departed that afternoon was taking a beating in the increasing wind, so the deck crew rigged a temporary ladder in the protected lee off the ship's port quarter. The small boat stood off the ship for five minutes, circling, while the crew finished their work on the fantail. Once alongside, naval courtesy called for the senior officers to depart first, so Hugh and Teri were the first two to come onboard by that path all night.

As they made their way into the port passageway leading forward, they couldn't miss the loud cheers, whistles, and claps coming from behind the closed door to the machinist mates' quarters. They were about to pass on when the content of the loud comments and exclamations caused them to stop. They looked at each other for a moment, listening. Then with a quick rap on the door, Hugh opened it, found the compartment to be dark but packed with men, and flipped on the overhead light.

Followed by Teri he entered the space, which had bunks on both sides and 'n open area at the far end. The bunks were full of sailors who had been cheering but now were grimacing as the lights flicked on. The floor in the open space was covered with blankets, and the area had been illuminated by flashlights held by several sailors on the top bunks. There on the blankets two of the ship's female Admin personnel had obviously been putting on a show for the assembled men. Teri looked past Hugh, saw what had been going on, whispered "Gross!" and left.

Hugh looked around and was shocked to see three of the ship's junior officers on the top bunks, one holding a flashlight.

"Ensign Malone, what's going on here?" he asked, the anger obvious in his voice. He noticed some of the sailors starting to leave, and before Malone could answer, he barked, "Pearlman! Everybody stays."

Clearly embarrassed, Ensign Malone looked at the senior officer, shrugged, and tried to smile. "Sir, gee, I guess it's been a long trip, and, well, some of the guys got together and put some money in a pot and asked around the ship's office if anyone wanted to make some money, and that's all. No one was going to do anything."

"This isn't *doing* something? How much money?"

Malone hesitated. "I think about two thousand dollars—a hundred dollars a man."

Hugh was stunned. "A thousand dollars for each of them?"

Malone nodded.

"I see." Hugh turned and offered a hand to the two sailors on the floor, who by now had wrapped blankets around themselves. "I'll escort you to your berthing space. Malone, I want you and Burton here to get everyone's name who's in this room."

Malone hung his head. "I think we've already got that, sir. We had to pay up front and get on the list to get in."

"Wonderful. Then everyone turn in—no one leave the ship until further instructions, and I'll take the list to the XO and see what he wants to do about it. Come on, ladies, after you."

WASHINGTON That Sunday morning's *Meet the Nation* featured another coup for Leslie Sloane: a live interview with the vice president, the first in-depth, one-on-one interview she'd granted since the night of January 29, and Leslie was proud to have won it. The two women were seated in comfortable chairs in the vice president's enlarged office in the Executive Office Building, which some in Washington were now calling the Far West Wing of the White House, since the vice president was beginning to issue policy statements of her own, and sounding more presidential every day.

"Ms. Vice President," Leslie began, "let's start with the State of the Union address. Did you have any idea what was going to happen beforehand?"

Patricia Barton-North smiled like a schoolteacher and sat just a little taller in her chair. "None, Leslie. We'd had some general indications that not everything was right with the president for a month or two beforehand, but nothing that prepared us for what happened that night."

"What kinds of indications?"

"Well, that whole program of trying to tell everyone's side of a debate, for example, which just confused people, seemed awfully presumptuous to many of us."

"Did you try to warn him about your concerns?"

"Yes, of course. But unfortunately, he wouldn't listen to good advice. We had no idea, you know, that he was spending hours every day reading the Bible and being taught all sorts of stuff by people no one even knew were in the White House. It's no wonder he lost his attention so quickly!"

"I see. And immediately after the president's speech, what did you do?" Leslie asked.

"It's ironic. I came right back to this office that night. Right here. And I made a list of good, intelligent people, men and women from all races and backgrounds, whom I believed this nation could count on at this time of crisis, and I began calling them."

"That night?" Leslie was obviously impressed by her take-charge initiative.

"Yes, that very night, and again on Wednesday, after our meeting in the White House. I wanted to get the message out that not everyone in Washington had lost their minds, that there was still a stable and sound executive branch, waiting to get back to real work."

"Tell us about the Wednesday morning meeting with President Harrison."

The vice president shifted in her chair and straightened her dress. She looked as if she were describing a meeting with a delinquent child. "Leslie, I can only say it was bizarre. And I repeat what I've said so often: I have nothing against the president. This is a human tragedy. He told us the same things he'd said Tuesday night, that we should each choose one worldview or the other—you know how he calls them 'God's' and 'man's'—and that unless you chose his version of God's, you were out of the administration! Can you imagine that? In this day and age, telling someone what she or he has to believe, or be fired!"

Leslie slightly shook her head. "That does sound unusual. What did you do?"

"I stood my ground. I told him that what he was doing was wrong, that the American people wouldn't stand for religious tests—they're unconstitutional, by the way—and that if he persisted, I'd have to leave his team, but remain on in my official capacity, of course, awaiting what I think will be the obvious decision of the voters in November. I just hate that our country has to be paralyzed for yet another year because of what's happened to someone who was once such a great leader."

"Have you read his Twenty Points? What do you think of his program?"

"Yes. I think his program is a tragedy—a dangerous, tragic disaster being foisted on the American public."

"How?"

"Leslie, everybody knows that God doesn't drop what he's doing and worry about every little problem we've got. I mean, should I pray for guidance on my grocery list? Those were all myths, which man's—and woman's—reason has triumphed over during the long centuries since the Dark Ages. Now William wants us to return to them, giving people some kind of cruel false hope that if they'll just believe in God, everything will be fine. It won't be. We'll still have all the same problems. We've got to use our own rational minds to solve our problems, even to choose between what's right and wrong. We've been doing a pretty good job of it since the founding fathers erected the wall of separation between church and state, and I'm not about to let him and his inexperienced pals destroy this great nation because of their misguided and dangerous faith!"

Leslie took a deep breath. "If you believe we should be able to choose what's right based on each individual's rights, then why are you opposed to consensual polygamy?"

The vice president leaned back, obviously surprised by the question. Then she said, "That's completely different, Leslie. That's not right versus wrong. That's exploitation! Men exploiting women, setting up a system of sexual subjugation to fulfill their own misguided sex drives. Using women, pure and simple."

"But some women seem to prefer it. Shouldn't they be allowed to live that way if they want, as their individual freedom?"

"No, because even though they don't know it, or won't admit it, they're being exploited, and we can't allow that as a role model for our children. Those women are simply wrong, and anyone who thinks it through will agree with me, I'm sure."

"Thank you, Ms. Vice President. We have to take a short commercial break, but when we return I want to ask you about your plans for the upcoming People's March on Washington on Easter Saturday, and for the election in general. This is *Meet the Nation*, and I'm Leslie Sloane. We'll be right back."

AT SEA OFF PALMA Captain's Mast is one form of American justice that is still swift and tailored to the offense. The captain of a U.S. Navy ship is both judge and jury for minor infractions, though his decisions can be appealed.

After leaving port that Sunday afternoon, the *Fortson's* department heads and executive officer were assembled around the big table in the captain's cabin. Seated at one end of the table, Captain Robertson began, "We've got Captain's Mast scheduled for sixteen-thirty in the wardroom, but Lieutenant. Commander Dobbs wanted to meet with the XO and me beforehand. Since so many of our people were involved last night from so many divisions, I thought we all ought to get together. Thomas, you've got the floor."

"Thank you, sir. I simply want to be sure that these two young women will be treated as the victims they really are in this incident and not charged with any type of violation."

The captain seemed genuinely confused. "Just a minute, Thomas. Are you aware of what they were doing?"

"Yes sir, of course. I've spoken with them, with Hugh, and with Ensign Malone. I know *what* they were doing, and I know *why*, which is what I want us to focus on."

"You've lost me," the captain said and obviously meant it.

"Sorry," the operations officer smiled. "Let me explain. In the first place, what two off-duty sailors want to do together is their business and should not be subject to punishment, or else it's a violation of their individual rights. I'm sure that's not the first time those two sailors have engaged in a legitimate and natural act of love, nor do I doubt that there are others on the ship of all sexual preferences who have their own personal love lives. So I believe you would be wrong even to charge them for something so personal.

"Second, these young sailors were obviously used and exploited by those older and senior to them for their own lurid purposes, and rather than being charged, they should be allowed to bring charges against those who forced them to display themselves in this way."

Hugh, sitting on the opposite side of the table from Thomas Dobbs, thought, *Is this a capital ship of the United States Navy or Alice in Wonderland?*

The captain, more confused than ever, said, "Thomas, I think we'll hear in a few minutes that three young seaman thought this idea up and offered to pay them. The women are both third-class petty officers, and they accepted the proposal. This episode may be a lot of regrettable things, but how is it exploitation?"

"Sir, officers were present! Clearly this was sexual harassment of the most basic and sordid type. I'm sure they felt if they didn't go through with it, there could be negative repercussions on their careers."

"Thomas, Ensign Malone is a twenty-two-year-old Iowa farmboy who's been in the navy six months. Do you really think he intimidated them?"

"Sir, he and the other two ensigns *are* officers, nonetheless, and there were four chiefs in attendance old enough to be their fathers. That's harassment and a violation of their rights."

The captain seemed flabbergasted. "I'm not sticking up for the men—I intend to throw the book at them. But without the two women, nothing would have happened! And did I hear you correctly a minute ago that you believe there's nothing wrong with everyone having sex on this ship whenever they want to?"

Dobbs smiled and looked directly at the captain. "So long as they're off-duty and not affecting anyone else, what right does the navy have to interfere?"

The captain was obviously flustered. "I...you mean...why, because it's wrong! We're not supposed to be like cats and dogs, Thomas. The law and for that matter the Bible say not to commit adultery, fornication, or sodomy. How can we run this ship if everyone is sleeping with everyone else or worrying about who's sleeping with whom? Not to mention pregnancy and deadly disease. There are good reasons for all those old regulations, Thomas, and we shouldn't change them willy-nilly. We'll regret that very much."

"You see!" Dobbs retorted, as though he'd caught the captain in a lie. "Now you're quoting the Bible, too. Forget about what it says, or even Navy Regulations, if they're based on the Bible. The Supreme Court has ruled that our collective rational minds establish what's right and wrong—not some religious myths. And despite what President Harrison said in his last address, the Supreme Court is still very much the ultimate law of this land, not him, thank goodness, *or* the Bible."

Hugh squirmed in his chair as Dobbs concluded, "So if two consenting adults want to play cards or dance or make love off-duty, the navy has no reason and no right to stop them. And if you try to do so here, I'm sure there'll be an appeal, and you'll have a lot to explain on this deployment, from obvious sexual discrimination and harassment to the death of a hard-working woman sailor."

The other officers couldn't believe Dobbs's final remarks and expected the captain to blast him. Captain Robertson opened his mouth as if to do so, but then stopped and sank back in his chair. There was a prolonged and embarrassing silence.

Finally the captain spoke, looking down at his fingers resting on the edge of the table. "I joined the navy almost thirty years ago to help defend our country, Thomas. I can tell you every detail of the Battle of Trafalgar, the workings of a high-pressure steam boiler, or the flight characteristics of a standard missile. But I don't understand social experimentation on navy ships, and I don't understand violating well-proven laws, whether they originally came from God or just from men wiser than us." He looked up at the operations officer. "I stand by my warning that we violate those laws at our own considerable risk. But it's probably time for me to retire and leave all this to you younger types. Come on"—he unexpectedly stood up, and the others quickly rose as well—"it's time for Captain's Mast. I hope I get some insight into what to do about this mess in the next few minutes." And he walked past all of his officers, picked up his hat, and headed for the wardroom.

Without saying a word, the others left as well, leaving Thomas Dobbs alone with his victory.

ATLANTA The weather in Atlanta that Sunday changed back quickly to a cold winter rain, meaning that Bruce and Rebecca could not jog, but instead worked out that afternoon in the gym. On returning to her apartment, it was obvious that Bruce was agitated, and finally, as they drank orange juice in her kitchen, he asked, "Well, have you decided, yet? I can't stand not knowing."

Rebecca looked down at her juice glass and pursed her lips. Then she looked back at him. "Bruce, I…if I have to decide right now, then I must say no, at least for now." He put down his glass and turned away from her toward the window. She continued, "I obviously care for you very much. We've been together a long time and helped each other through a lot. But between your problems—you may have to go back to Boston any minute, God forbid—and my own doubts, I'm not ready to commit the rest of my life to our relationship. I may next week, after things calm down a bit, but right now I'm just not sure."

"It was that TV program wasn't it?" he asked bitterly, turning back to her.

"That…may be some of it. I still don't understand why you did it. But it's also, as crazy as this sounds, worldviews, just like my brother said. I just don't know if I can live with someone who is so hostile to God."

"And what are you, now, suddenly a born-again believer?" he asked derisively.

"No, Bruce, I'm not. Not yet, at least. But I'm thinking. Everything that's happened this year has made me think. But it's comments like you just made that make me worry about whether or not we could make it if we got married. You're...you're so on the edge all the time."

"Oh, give me a break. Now you're a psychological specialist!"

It was her turn to look away, a note of sorrow on her face. "Bruce, I just don't know. I need some time to work through this."

"Well, I'll save you the agony. I think a year is long enough. If you don't love me now, when will you? And you know what, your brother really *is* a jerk. He seems real cool at first, but inside he's a jerk. He didn't really want to help my mom in the beginning—you're the one who made him. And now he's a flipped-out Christian. So I don't think I could stand being in a family with him, anyway. You keep him, and I'll keep believing in myself. I can't seem to find anyone else to trust in! At any rate, I'm out of here." He finished his juice, walked over, and set the empty glass on the counter.

"You're leaving?" she asked. "Now? In the rain?"

"You got it. Just give me ten minutes to pack and you can pretend you never knew me. Then you can have lots of quiet prayer time without me to bother you. Good luck with William, Mary, and their myths."

While Rebecca stayed by the window and looked out at the rainy afternoon, Bruce packed. Her heart was heavy, and she found herself fighting back tears. But she knew they were tears of both loss and relief. Without either of them saying another word, he left.

The foundations of our society and our government rest so much on the teachings of the Bible that it would be difficult to support them if faith in these teachings would cease to be practically universal in our country.

CALVIN COOLIDGE

22

WASHINGTON Ryan Denning awoke on the Saturday before Easter in Leslie Sloane's bed and looked over at her while she slept. They had abandoned any attempt at outward propriety, since virtually everyone in the media knew of their relationship, and they now regularly stayed at each other's apartments in Washington and New York.

She had continued her pressure for marriage and had given him another ultimatum only a week before. As he looked at her that morning, he considered again that they would, in fact, make a good match. *Maybe tonight after the march I'll propose. That'll surprise her.*

An hour later they shared a simple breakfast, which he fixed because it took her longer to get ready.

"We'll be in position on Pennsylvania Avenue for the parade by ten-thirty," she reviewed out loud as they sipped their coffee. "Then I'll join you in the booth near the Capitol for the speeches."

"It's great that all the major networks are giving the march live coverage. Hopefully we'll derail the president's plans before they ever really get started," he said.

"Yes. I hear the vice president is treating her speech like the kick-off to her campaign for the presidency. With the parties dividing and the possibility of a new president, this certainly is a strange year!"

Ryan smiled and there was a moment of silence. "Speaking of strange, Leslie, you know there are going to be some 'strange' groups in this People's March on Washington today. I hope your director and crew know not to show them."

"I know. We've heard that every group from the Gay Paratroopers to Women Who Love Trees will be in attendance, many with floats. It's a shame these tiny minorities get so much attention. They divert people from the issue of running our nation on rational human values, which is the real purpose for the march."

"Well, just use your commercial breaks and background discussions judiciously, and the folks in the rest of the country don't even have to know that those groups exist. I think the speakers at noon will be great, though. When it's over, let's have dinner at a really nice place tonight and celebrate what I hope will be the beginning of the end for Pope William Harrison's crazy ideas."

She rose and put her dishes in the sink. "You're on. Now I've got to run."

RALEIGH At about eleven-thirty that morning Mary and Graham were in their den with Tom and Cynthia Williams, the television turned down low with the People's March on Washington in the background. Cynthia had called Mary and asked to come over to discuss something with her. She was just making her key point.

"And so there are at least ten families who want to work together to lobby in Congress against the BioTeam federal education grant for the computer—many of our kids will join us—and we hope that you'll not only join us, but consider becoming a spokeswoman for us, given your recent notoriety and the president's challenge to the nation."

Mary turned to Graham sitting next to her on the sofa and then back to Cynthia. "I doubt you want my kind of notoriety! The media has painted our whole family as Neanderthals. And I'm not sure I have the time for another battle we'll probably lose, anyway."

"Not so on both counts," Cynthia countered. "We believe this grant is far from a sure thing, especially when we show the videos in open session and disclose the tie-in with *Pet Girl International.* And we think you'd be a great spokesperson. Not everyone believes what's being said in the media. And with your brother's challenge this year—" Cynthia was about to tie the two campaigns together when the front door opened and Sarah, without more than a muffled grunt from the hallway, stormed upstairs to her room and closed the door.

Graham looked at Mary. "Weren't she and Matthew supposed to be building a house downtown as a school service project all day?"

"Yes, I thought so," Mary replied, frowning. "Give her a few minutes, and I'll go check."

WASHINGTON The first family had planned to spend Easter weekend in the Orlando area attending several large rallies with Florida congressional and senatatorial candidates. These included two incumbents who had embraced their Twenty Points. They hoped to attend a huge Easter morning service at an Orlando community church. But the march on Washington had forced them to change their plans. Some advisors had suggested that William should go on to Florida, but he had disagreed, arguing that he needed to stay in the kitchen when the heat was turned up and not run from the city just because those who opposed God's worldview came to march.

In fact, in conjunction with several local churches, there were prayer teams all along the parade route, silently invoking God's help. William and his key advisors were in the Oval Office, from where they could not see the parade directly. But they watched the first half of the march on television while they reviewed drafts of a colorful thirty-page booklet they hoped Joe Wood's committee would soon print. It expanded in plain but inspiring detail all the key ideas in William's State of the Union address. The booklet included important quotes from the Bible and the Founding Fathers; an exposition on the real intent of the First Amendment from the perspective of the debates surrounding its passage; explanations of the two opposing worldviews and the implications of each one for government actions; and finally, the intended benefits of the Twenty Points.

As the march schedule moved toward noon and the speeches at the Capitol, William, Jerry Richardson, and the others working in the White House stopped their discussion and offered a short prayer, interceding for those who denied his existence and praying for him not to turn his face from their nation, despite the vocal public displays against him.

RALEIGH Mary left the others watching television and went upstairs. She knocked on Sarah's door. When there was no answer the second time, she opened the door and found Sarah sitting on the edge of her bed, her feet resting on the sideboard, her arms around her legs and her chin on her knees. She did not even look up when her mother opened the door.

"May I come in?" Mary asked. When there was still no response she closed the door behind her, walked over, and sat down next to her daughter. Sarah did not acknowledge her presence.

After a few minutes of sitting silently together, Mary finally began, "Sarah, if—"

Without looking toward her mother, Sarah interrupted her, speaking with her head still resting on her knees. "Mother, you might as well know...I'm not a virgin any more. I haven't been for three months. I slept with Matthew right after New Year's. It seemed so much more natural than that stupid computer machine, and it was. Then almost immediately, just like you and everyone else told me, sex changed our relationship, then ruined

it. I'm home now because I finally put my foot down and refused to go to a
hotel with him when we were supposed to be building a house. He kept
pressuring me, but I said no. He told me that sharing our love was more
mature than building a house for poor people, and I told him he was wrong.
I guess he'd made big plans, thinking I'd go along, because he got pretty mad,
and here I am. I wish I could cry, but I'm just too mad. Mad at me, mad at
him, and mad at that machine. I feel like it blinded me and robbed me of
so much. I can't cry right now, but I want you to know that you were right,
and I'm very, very sorry." Still, she stared at the wall.

Mary was silent. When Sarah had said she'd slept with Matthew, it was
as though a knife pierced Mary's heart, and she lost her breath at the same
instant. But as her daughter continued, although Mary's anguish didn't
decrease, it was mixed with concern for her daughter's well being and then
with admiration for her decision. As Sarah finished, Mary wanted to hold
her for all she'd been through, punish her for being so stupid, and praise her
for being so brave.

As these emotions moved through Mary, Sarah finally turned her head
to look at her mother, and their eyes met. They looked at each other for several heartbeats, then finally Sarah's eyes grew moist. She turned her head
away, but Mary slid over close to her and put her arm around her.
"Sarah…I…I was so worried about that machine, but then I…I'm sorry…I
should have been more forceful in opposing it. I'm so…"

Sarah sat up and looked at her mother. "Mom, you did all you could. I
was just stupid. You told me exactly what would happen. Katherine told me.
Our youth advisors at church told me. I heard. I just didn't want to believe
you. And I can't blame that machine completely. *I'm* the one who did it. Oh,
Mom, I just wish"—and now the tears started in earnest—"I just wish I
hadn't been so dumb. I've messed up big time, and I'm so sorry. I wish I
could take it back. I'm sorry. I know I did it, but I feel like that machine and
Ms. Bowers lied to us—they only told us half the story. Mom, am I right to
feel like that?"

Mary hugged Sarah to her when she started to cry. "Oh, Sarah, I don't
know right now. I'm sorry for you, but proud of you, too, for understanding what has happened and for standing firm, finally, with Matthew. That
took a lot of courage, and I'm so glad you found it within you to do it." She
pulled back and looked Sarah in the eye again. "And whether we hate that
machine and Ms. Bowers or not, we sure ought to try to keep other kids
from going through what you've gone through, don't you think?"

Sarah wiped her eyes with the back of her hand. "Yes."

"Well, maybe some good can come out of this mess," Mary tried to
smile.

"I hope so, Mom, because I don't feel very good right now."

Twenty minutes later Mary descended the stairs, wiping her eyes with a tissue, and rejoined Graham and the Williamses in the den. Mary walked over to the sofa and sat down. "Cynthia, I think you've just found two new recruits for your team."

WASHINGTON   Leslie climbed the stairs to the temporary platform from which the U.S. Network planned to cover the speeches that day. She reflected on some of the strange groups she had seen in that morning's march. They had, for the most part, been edited into television oblivion. But she had seen them, nevertheless, up close and personal. And a small hairline crack appeared in her otherwise solid support of everything "inclusive" and progressive. *Do those people represent the world I'd want my children to grow up in?* she found herself thinking, and then admitting how bizarre and unlike her that thought was. As she reached the top she saw Ryan smiling at her, so she suppressed the thought and sank into her chair.

"Good job on the parade," Ryan said. "Warner Watts is the first speaker from the podium."

Senator Watts had been leaning toward opposing the transformed president when the vice president called him and indicated that his name was under strong consideration for a Cabinet post in her new administration, to be formed in November after Harrison resigned. Although he and the vice president had not seen eye to eye on many domestic issues, he felt that he might be able to bring a voice of reason into her camp as the elder statesman. Therefore, he decided that coming out against the lame-duck president was a no-lose proposition for him.

So Senator Watts was the first speaker at the podium on the day before Easter, and his central theme was that even though he was a fiscal conservative, he believed the president had no right to require that anyone proclaim a Christian worldview in order to be elected to Congress. He never mentioned that William had only suggested it for the voters' consideration.

After Watts came a congressman, an actress, a talk show host, and an elder statesman, all restating in one way or another that the government had worked fine, thank you, for a long time, that the nation was not nearly as bad off as William had portrayed, and that the American people should not be fooled by snake-oil Christianity of the type being offered by William Harrison. "True Christians should recoil," the statesman proclaimed, "at the presumptuousness of this man to try to think for them!"

Between the speeches, Leslie and Ryan's commentary was marginally neutral, but they only talked about those who were opposed to the president, and only in glowing terms.

Forty minutes after Watts began the speeches, Leslie announced on camera, "And now, just before the vice president herself addresses this huge crowd on the Mall, estimated by some to be as many as half a million people, the other guests on the platform will be introduced."

The master of ceremonies, a superstar Hollywood actor, introduced the leaders of several organizations opposed to the president's new course. "And now one final guest. Ladies and gentlemen, here is someone special, someone who saw what happened to the president first-hand. Bruce Tinsley was Rebecca Harrison's close friend for over a year. In fact, they were considering marriage when he, due to his own conscience, had to end their relationship after the woman he loved seemed to embrace the ideas of her brother, the president. He is with us today at a very difficult time—Bruce buried his mother on Tuesday after a long illness—so please welcome Bruce Tinsley."

Bruce stepped forward and acknowledged the applause with a wave to the crowd.

For William and all the members of his family watching the events in their homes, Bruce's presence on the stage was unexpected and particularly devastating because it was so personal. The president hardly heard the introduction of his former running mate, Patricia Barton-North, who referred to him throughout her speech as "poor William."

The thrust of her speech was that William had created a historic crossroads, and it was time to vote, as William had asked, for a worldview; but one had to vote for a worldview that represented the future, not the distant past.

Except for her personal references to William, her speech was not so much an attack on him—she didn't need to after the six preceding speakers—as it was a recounting of all that she was prepared to do in her administration to insure that good things happened to people in need, from welfare grants to mass transportation to disease research to women's rights. "And we won't have to wait for miracles," she concluded. "We'll roll up our sleeves and tackle these issues in the finest American tradition of cooperation, hard work, and logical, rational thinking. In my administration, human dignity won't take second place to any ancient myth or superstition. In November, please support women and men who share your needs and goals, not those who think they're somehow better than you because God supposedly talks to them. While they're wringing their hands over ancient rituals, we'll solve your problems. Count on it! Vote for common sense in November. Thank you."

No one in the Oval Office had spoken while Patricia gave her speech. As she finished, the president was slumped in his chair like someone who had been dealt a knock-out blow. He knew he had to get up and say something positive to his team, but he felt too stunned to move. *How did what we're doing get so far off track? They twist everything, and they sound right! I'd believe them, if I didn't know they're lying. The Father of Lies is winning. Somehow we have to get the real word out, but with most of the media opposed to us, how will we ever do it? If we really are going to win this battle one heart at a time, we've got a lot of hearts to go, and I'm not sure we can possibly touch so many in so little time. How will we do it? I don't think we possibly can.*

For the first time William felt the tinge of panic creeping around the edges of his awareness. *What have I started? With all these leaders arrayed against us, and their arguments so believable, we obviously can't finish this. And then the country will be* worse *off than when we started, and I will have dishonored God! Is this just all some ego trip on my part? Is God really interested in this? Have I led all these people astray?*

His team remained seated in the Oval Office around the television as Ryan Denning wrapped up the day's successful events. The silence among them was growing ominous. William felt they had already lost, and he could tell that the others, even Michael Tate and Jerry Richardson, shared that opinion.

He closed his eyes and said a brief prayer for strength, then stood up and turned off the television. From somewhere an image came into his mind as he turned around and addressed the men and women who, other than his family, were closest to him.

"If we had eyes that could see spiritual beings, I imagine that Washington is right now almost totally dark with Satan's powers and demons. They must be reveling in what has been said and done here today. They must feel that they've already defeated us...and I have to confess that I've let them convince me that they're right!"

He looked around the room and could tell from the diverted eyes and shifts in chairs that he was not alone. "And they *are* right, if we keep relying on our own abilities and resources. Ladies and gentlemen, *we* can't defeat them. I felt a minute ago that we ought to give up. But I'm convinced that that's what the enemy wants us to believe. Well, we're not going to, only because his power is so much greater than theirs. As Paul writes, we've got to call on him, because in our own strength we'll always lose—that's the history of this nation for the last forty years. We didn't start down this road to honor our own wit or brilliance, but to honor God, whatever happens in November. And we can start that process right now by honoring him with our *trust,* that no matter how dark it seems right this minute, in God we trust. That's the whole point of what we're about—we don't know what the next seven months hold for us, but we know who holds the next seven months!

"I want us to pray right now, and pray as Brewster must have done on the *Mayflower,* and Washington at Valley Forge, and Lincoln all through the Civil War, that God will use our impending, predictable defeat so that the unexpected victory will then be his, and his alone! Please join me in surrendering completely to him, but not to the enemy."

Everyone in the room slid to their knees, and William began their prayers by resubmitting their lives and their efforts to God's will and to God's guidance. Then Michael Tate prayed for their protection and for boldness in proclaiming what they knew to be the truth. All the other members of the team joined in lifting prayers from the White House to God's throne room, and they stayed on their knees for over an hour, humbly beseeching their Creator to use their weakness to create a victory that the whole nation would acknowledge as God's, and God's alone.

As the most powerful men and women on earth finally admitted their total lack of power and gave their futures completely to him, God's Holy Spirit was at last released to begin his work in the land.

OFF THE SOUTHERN COAST OF SPAIN As the crew of the USS *Fortson* prepared to leave the Mediterranean through the Straits of Gibraltar, Hugh Harrison was in his stateroom finishing up his paperwork so that he would be free for their last anti-submarine exercise off Iceland on the way back to Norfolk.

That Saturday evening he reread the final report on the death of Petty Officer Simpson, with the conclusion of accidental death affirmed by the admiral. But he had also watched the day before in Barcelona as Chief Ellis had sent a copy of the report to his attorney brother in Chicago, still promising to anyone who would listen that someone had to "pay" for his fiancée's death.

Now Hugh had to write an objective fitness report for young Ensign Malone. He sat with the blank form in front of him for over thirty minutes, searching for the words that would fulfill the requirements of the Captain's Mast but not destroy the well-meaning young man's career before it started. This task brought back memories of the afternoon a month earlier when the senior officers had assembled in the wardroom for the Captain's Mast after the incident with the lesbians' show. Hugh would never forget how distracted Captain Robertson appeared that day, clearly worrying about lawsuits from Chief Ellis on the one hand and a gay rights attorney on the other.

After all the testimony the captain had punished everyone involved, but the degree of punishment in Hugh's mind didn't square with the reality of what had occurred. The three seaman who were the ringleaders were each demoted one rank and fined a thousand dollars. The three officers, including Malone, were each fined two thousand dollars, restricted to the ship until Norfolk, and a letter of reprimand was to be placed in each of their service records. All the other participants were fined five hundred dollars. But the two lesbians were given a verbal warning not to participate in such activities in public again, and fined a hundred dollars. Hugh would never forget the smile on Dobbs' face when these last punishments were announced.

So he had been sitting, trying to write something sounding like a reprimand, as ordered, but that also somehow communicated that young men away from home for six months will behave exactly like young men away from home for six months. *And any lawyer who doesn't agree should stop going to the local nude review in his hometown,* Hugh thought. But words he could write just wouldn't come, at least not words he could make a part of the official record.

There was a knock on his stateroom door.

"Come in."

The door opened and in came Radioman First Class Ross Ewing and Seaman Raymond Tyson, hats in hands. Except for receiving radio messages from Ewing and watching the incident between Tyson and Wolf Higgins months before, Hugh had had almost nothing to do with these men, who were both members of other departments.

Ewing, the older of the two, spoke first. "Mr. Harrison, I know this is a little unusual, but Seaman Tyson has a problem, and he's tried to handle it like his chief told him, but he's still got it, and we both thought maybe you could give us some advice."

Hugh motioned for them to come in. In the cramped quarters of his small stateroom there were only two chairs, so the younger men stood, and Hugh shifted around to face them. "Why me, Ewing?"

The senior petty officer smiled. "I'm not sure, sir. It's just that when you hear the problem, well—you've always seemed like a fair and reasonable person, and we're not looking for you to do anything necessarily, just give us some advice."

"Okay. Shoot. What's the problem, Tyson?"

"Sir, you know I came onboard with the homosexuals in the supply department. Two weeks ago, after reading the Bible with our study group for five months and praying daily, I asked Jesus to come into my life and to save me from what I now know is a lie and an abomination to God. And, sir, praise God, he has! I don't want that lifestyle any more, and I know that God has saved me from it. I can't tell you what joy and peace I've found. I know I've got a lot to work through and a lot of problems ahead, and he has to work in me every day, but I'm *free.*"

"That's wonderful, Tyson. I'm very happy for you. But that sounds like a...a blessing, not a problem."

"Oh, it is, sir. It is. But here's the problem. I'm trying not to be pulled back into that lifestyle. But when I went to Chief Osborne to ask to be moved out of the homosexual berthing area—I just can't live there any longer, sir!—he told me to see Lieutenant Commander Dobbs. And when I went to see him, he blew up at me and told me that homosexuality is not a choice and that I'd always be a homosexual, and I should just live where I'd been assigned and be quiet. He particularly didn't like it when I told him that

Jesus had set me free from the lie that I know has engulfed him, too.

"But that was ten days ago, sir, and I'm still living in that place and, sir, the things they do—I don't want to go back ever again. I'm trying not to fall back into that life, but living there makes it almost impossible for me to resist. Please, sir. I want to break away. I've asked God to help me fight it. But I can't live there. And Lieutenant Commander Dobbs says I *have* to. Can you *please* help me get away from them?"

Hugh thought for a few moments. Having just barely resisted a strong temptation himself, he understood exactly what young Seaman Tyson was saying. *What a situation for Dobbs, to have one of his homosexuals go against everything he's been preaching and choose not to be a homosexual any more! And what should the captain do? Will Dobbs threaten to sue to keep Tyson a homosexual?* Hugh almost smiled at the thought, but realized that for Tyson this was nothing to smile about. *And what about the social engineers in Washington who never considered that homosexual activity might be a choice?*

Hugh rocked forward in his chair. "Of course, Tyson, I'll try to help. Neither Lieutenant Commander Dobbs nor I am the last word on where people berth on the ship. But the best thing for you, and I might recommend it if you agree, is for you to get off in Lisbon and start over at another duty station, without the baggage you'll take with you, one way or the other, anywhere on the *Fortson.*"

Tyson looked at Ewing and then back at Hugh. "Yes sir, that might be best, as much as I'd hate to lose Ross and the others in the Bible study. But I understand what you're saying. A completely clean start in a new place is probably best for me."

"Well, I don't think there's any real precedence or procedure for this, but I'll talk to the XO in the morning, and we'll try to work something out."

"Thank you, sir," they both said, and left.

ACROSS THE NATION   Morris Mason was William's age and had been a pastor in a mainline Christian denomination in Sacramento for twenty-five years. His decision to attend seminary had been primarily based on his desire to help other people and only secondarily to escape the Vietnam War draft. He had joined with friends and radical professors at the seminary in questioning whether Jesus Christ had in fact physically risen from the dead, whether the Bible was really infallible, and whether any doctrine really mattered, so long as one genuinely tried to be a good person, and taught others to be good.

But years of belittling other pastors who clearly harbored no such doubts about their own faith had recently given way to a questioning of his own assumptions; and when in late January the president had issued his national challenge, both his parishioners and he had wanted to know which world-view was right.

That Saturday he had watched the entire People's March on Washington and listened to all the speeches. He was troubled. Was there really no God? Was man alone to make it on his own? Were the few parishioners who had reported miracles of healing and of changed lives over the years just deluded? Most importantly, was his life a lie? Was the altar to which he prayed every week empty, in which case why did he continue? Or if it really was filled with the presence of the God who made everything, then how could he deny that God had also made the Bible, or had supernaturally given mankind's sins to his Son? He realized on that Saturday afternoon that he finally had to choose one way or the other. *Both could not be true.*

Reverend Mason told his wife that he had some work to do and went down to their basement. But he actually went to be alone and to pray. Three hours later a different Morris Mason came up the stairs, his eyes red and wet. He walked slowly to his study, found his already neatly typed Easter sermon, tore it up into small pieces, and sat down to write a completely different Easter message to his parish.

Peggy Bowden and her husband, Martin, had attended church with Janet and Richard Sullivan for five years. Janet had asked Peggy to use her many civic connections to serve on her fund-raising committee and to help her go door to door in her precinct. As Janet had said, "Even if they don't vote for us, the information we leave behind may get them thinking about the Lord."

Peggy owed Janet a response, since her candidacy was to be announced officially on Tuesday. Peggy was sitting alone at her desk that Saturday afternoon; the kids were off at college, and Martin was playing golf. She had a piece of stationery out, along with her checkbook; she intended to write a pleasant note to Janet declining to work on the campaign because of time pressures, but enclosing a small check.

As she picked up her pen, she for some reason visualized herself and Janet calling on her neighbors, door to door, telling them that God not only exists, but holds their eternal futures in his hands. Peggy had prayed for her neighbors for years, and she'd prayed for the courage to witness to them. Now it was suddenly crystal clear to her, in a moment of total clarity, that the call to work with Janet's campaign was the answer to that long-standing prayer. She smiled and wished that Martin were home. It was simply obvious that she would have to cancel some other commitments, at least through November. Never had she experienced anything spiritual which was so certain!

Feeling a joy for the Lord she realized had been lost for the past few years, she wrote a note to Janet accepting the post on her campaign committee and included a check which was ten times larger than she had originally intended.

Bob McEver and his son were having a late lunch with Bob's divisional supervisor, Ralph Pendergrast and his son, at a local Milwaukee fast food restaurant; the two boys were on the same Little League team, and they'd just won a close game. The boys were at one booth with some teammates and the two men were at another booth across from them.

"I guess Congress isn't going to act on reinstating the investment tax credit this year, after President Harrison's shake-up two months ago," Bob ventured, knowing that a new ITC could significantly boost their production of large air conditioning compressors.

Ralph nodded and looked disgusted. "I don't think *anything's* going to happen until the Reverend President gets over all this religion stuff and gets back to running the country."

It had become a fashionable joke at the office to refer to William Harrison as the "Reverend President," and his State of the Union speech had been an easy target for the cynical crowd in the coffee room. Bob McEver had been raised in a Christian family, had lost his faith for a decade, but had then seen his rediscovered relationship with a personal Savior heal and save his marriage. He had felt the power of God change him, but he had never told anyone outside their family about his experience.

For a month he had quietly smiled at the jokes about the president, but inside he'd known that William Harrison was exactly right, and he'd prayed for the courage to speak up. Now he found himself saying to his older and more experienced supervisor, "Ralph, I know this may be hard for you to believe, but I kind of agree with the president. I think the best thing he can do right now to run the country is stick to his 'religion stuff,' because that's the only hope for our boys here. Without it, I don't think they'll have much of a country, ITC or not."

Ralph Pendergrast was shocked. He asked incredulously, "You mean you believe, like the president, that God is working around the clock, and we should be praying to him about every little thing that happens?"

Bob waited and then said. "Ralph, look at those two little boys. Do they look like mistakes or chance happenings to you? Did you hold your son when he was born? I remember thinking what a miracle Jeb was. *Only* God could have made him. And if God made Jeb, then where do you draw the line to say where God doesn't get involved? You see, I know that God has healed my relationship with Cheryl—Ralph, I was a gonner, I was out the door. And two days later he simply changed me, and that means Jeb will have his father around—think what that means for him. So God's done all that for me—he can do and does do anything; so yes, we ought to pray, constantly, and William Harrison is right on target."

Ralph Pendergrast had always respected the younger man's intelligence and hard work. Now he was amazed to see the sincerity on his face. "You're really serious, aren't you?"

"Yes, I am. Because I've felt God's power myself."

"And God runs everything in your life?"

"Think about it, Ralph. What's the alternative? Coincidence? Chaos? A part-time God? And if he does run it all, then we better get ourselves and our nation right with him, and that's why I support the president."

Ralph paused for a moment, thinking. "You say God healed your marriage?...Frankly, Jane and I have been...no, it's too crazy to think about."

Bob began to tell Ralph how to have a restored relationship with God through belief in his Son as the best foundation for relationships with others, particularly one's spouse. Because they didn't have time to finish that afternoon, Ralph asked Bob to have lunch on Monday to continue their discussion. For his part, Bob was amazed at how easy it was to share his faith with someone else for the first time.

We are not to attribute this prohibition of a national religious establishment [in the First Amendment] to an indifference to religion in general, and especially to Christianity, which none could hold in more reverence than the framers of the Constitution.... Probably, at the time of the adoption of the Constitution, and of the Amendments to it...the general, if not the universal, sentiment in America was, that Christianity ought to receive encouragement from the State.

JUSTICE JOSEPH STORY
U.S. SUPREME COURT, 1833

23

Thursday, May 23
Three Weeks Later

ATLANTA "Eunice, are you back again so soon?" Rebecca asked, then realized her remark had been neither tactful nor professional.

In for prenatal care on the National Health Plan, Eunice Porter had hoped that the president's sister had moved to some other ward or department, but here she was.

Rebecca closed the door and walked to the examining table. Eunice answered, "Yes, I guess so."

"Well, I'm glad to see you. How are your children?"

They spoke for a few minutes, waiting for the doctor, but the conversation was almost a monologue. Rebecca was sensitive enough not to ask the question of how someone who'd had a full-term abortion in August could be back again almost four-months pregnant in May.

When the exam was over, Rebecca went downstairs for a late morning cup of coffee. Something more than the rapidity of Eunice's pregnancies was bothering her, but she couldn't figure out what it was. As she stood in the short line at the coffee shop, she glanced over to the central elevator bank and saw Eunice and an even more pregnant Sally Kramer walking toward the exit. As she watched them gesturing and arguing, it struck her that they weren't talking like the many pregnant women she regularly saw, but like businesswomen discussing a deal. She knew she had to be wrong, but there was something about these women that seemed bizarre, and she made a mental note to try to figure out why.

RALEIGH   Mary and Sarah Prescott, with Cynthia Williams and her son Tony, had gathered for a meeting at Northside High School with Principal Lawrence Perkins and health teacher Jean Bowers.

"Thank you for seeing us," Mary said, as they all sat down around the small conference table in the principal's office. For five minutes they conversed amicably about the upcoming graduation exercise.

Then Mary said, "We're two of about twenty families who are very concerned about the virtual reality computer and its effect on our children. With the school year about to end, we want to ask you not to use it again next year and not to help BioTeam in any way to secure a government grant to put these in more schools."

Jean Bowers smiled politely. "Mrs. Prescott, I talked with Sarah myself before she made her own informed decision, and I think she acted in a very mature and responsible manner."

Sarah, sitting next to her mother, obviously felt strongly about what her teacher had just said but was not used to interacting with adults in this way. Stuttering a little she responded, "But—but, Ms. Bowers, you told us about how much we'd learn about sex. You didn't tell us what that would *do* to us."

"What do you mean 'do' to you, Sarah?" the teacher asked.

"I mean, like making us want to have sex, and feeling kind of stupid if we didn't—and then encouraging us…you know, like to lose our virginity and all. I feel terrible about it."

Ms. Bowers smiled and looked around at everyone else in the room, then back at Sarah. "Come on, Sarah, ours is a health class, not a psychology or morality class. We're mandated by the state to teach sex education, and we can't be responsible for what you do with that knowledge or how you *feel* about yourself, for goodness sake!"

"But this machine," Cynthia Williams argued, "goes way beyond some sort of simple knowledge. It becomes experience itself. Then the kids want more."

Still smiling, the teacher replied, "Well, that's sort of the way sex is for some people, Mrs. Williams. I can't help it if Sarah is one of those who likes sex"—Mary gasped loudly—"but our job, again, is to teach your children about sex, and I think this machine and our curriculum do a better job than has ever been possible before."

Mary couldn't stand it any longer. She was enraged. "Ms. Bowers, this machine, under the respectable name of education, steals our children's chance to learn about sex where God intended them to, in a loving marriage relationship. Instead it lowers sex to a mechanical but still quite intoxicating set of stimuli, which are separated from the reality that people are normally attached to them. Your concept attacks our children, reducing their chances for happy marriages, and it attacks families, disconnecting love and commitment from physical intimacy. And because it attacks families, it attacks our society, which doesn't need any more forces—especially masquerading under the name of education—encouraging young people to have sex—and therefore babies or disease—whenever they feel like it."

Jean Bowers looked at Mary as if she'd just discovered the key to the woman's long-standing insanity. "I suppose next you'll give us your brother's two worldviews. Since when does God have anything to do with health class in a public high school? Forty years ago the Supreme Court ruled that God and education shouldn't be mixed—it's unconstitutional!"

"Ms. Bowers, I agree that the public schools are no place to become a Baptist or a Lutheran. But the discussion of those two worldviews is actually very applicable here. As William said months ago, here we are arguing over details and missing the real point. To answer as simply as I can what you just asked, it was God who *created* what you are *teaching*, and since he made it, he also made some pretty explicit rules about it. And his words are therefore relevant to your health class because you're teaching the kids to go ahead and have sex without also teaching them the rules he laid down. And the *consequences* for violating them, which Sarah, Tony, and our families are now suffering with."

"Oh, come on, Mrs. Prescott," Lawrence Perkins said, "aren't you being a little dramatic?"

"No. As a matter of fact I haven't even touched on the emotional pain we've been through—and Sarah and Tony will go through in the future. I think I've been rather clinical!"

"Well," the health teacher responded in obvious disgust, "you're coming on like some sort of old-fashioned preacher. Get with it. Kids today don't have time to deal with all that. They're thrown into the real, tough world at an early age, and it's our job to help them learn how to cope with it."

"I'd say you're the one doing the throwing," Tony said quietly.

Everyone turned to look at the young man for a moment. Then Jean Bowers looked back at Mary. "Whatever you think, you're a very small minority. We have letters from other parents telling us how much they like this program and what good it's done for their kids."

"Well, we have a survey, conducted personally by Tony and Sarah," Cynthia said, "of virtually all the seniors in their class. It may not be terribly scientific, but it includes a tabulation of how many have been sexually active, and unfortunately it's virtually one hundred percent"

Jean Bowers leaned back. "Most kids their age are sexually active. That's no big deal."

"It's funny," Mary said. "That's one of the lies that people like you have been putting out for years, trying to create a self-fulfilling prophecy, I guess. We're waiting for the exact national statistics from the Family Institute for Research, but the average for kids in schools like ours is way below 'everybody.' Sadly, for Northside High, thanks to your course, it really is almost everyone."

"So what?" the teacher responded defiantly. "Again, what these young people do with their advanced knowledge is up to them; our job is to give them that knowledge. We can even prove scientifically the progress these young people made as they went through this course."

"How?" Cynthia asked.

"We kept excellent records of each student's experiences on the computer, and we've charted them for increased levels of complexity, tolerance, and creativity. Every student in the class exceeded our initial expectations, and we plan to make this study available to BioTeam for their grant application."

Ms. Bowers looked around the room as if she had won the argument, but the others seated with her, including Principal Perkins, were trying to understand what they had just heard.

"What do you mean when you say that you kept 'excellent records' on each student?" Mary finally asked for all of them.

"Why," Ms. Bowers looked at Perkins for support, "we videotaped the computer side of the interaction, what the student wanted to see and feel, for each session, along with a reading of pulse rate from the gloves. We can then go back and reconstruct the student's experience, and grade it in the major areas."

"Wait a minute," Sarah said, sitting up straighter. "You mean you have a tape of every session I had with that thing and can play what I saw and felt on a TV for others to see?"

The teacher smiled nervously. "Well, yes, I guess you could say that. We've used these tapes for scientific research, of course." She looked again at the principal, who was frowning. "We would never disclose the specific individual involved on any report."

The reality of what she was describing began to sink in. "And when you say 'we,' who exactly is that?" Cynthia asked.

"Why, Ed Cheatham, my fiancé. We're writing our doctoral thesis on this research. It's very interesting."

"I bet it is!" Cynthia said. "Mr. Perkins, whatever else comes from this meeting, I want any tapes from Tony's sessions destroyed today, with witnesses and without copies being made!"

"But what about our research?" Jean Bowers pleaded, her disdain giving way to anger. "We've worked hard. You have no right!"

"No," Mary said, standing, "*you* have no right. Destroy Sarah's, too, and today. With witnesses. Perhaps other parents who supposedly wrote so highly about the program will want to come by and review what little Johnny is thinking, but I find it both frightening and disgusting! I think you've got our message. And we finally understand your full agenda. Please, please don't do this again next year."

"You don't understand," the teacher replied, also standing and obviously angry. "We're opening up an expanded world of thought and experience for these teenagers, which will make them better adults. We may even expand the program to the eleventh grade."

"And you don't understand," Mary concluded, picking up her pocketbook, "that this program is a lie straight from hell."

WASHINGTON After the initial shock of the president's late January message had passed, the nation's capital settled into a predictable routine, though a much different routine from any previous spring in memory. The gridlock of the last twenty years remained, though this political season the reason for the stalemate was out in the open, as was the solution. The gridlock this year centered on people—whom to elect in November—rather than on legislation. If the president was right, legislation would follow in January and flow quickly. It was a time of choices, as the president had challenged every citizen. There was a growing expectation on both sides of the debate that by the end of the year the gridlock would be broken, with one path or the other finally chosen for the nation.

And in the meantime, government from the White House to the courthouse took a collective breather and concentrated on dusting off postponed projects and on how to work more efficiently. The primary exception was foreign policy. While the rest of the world was curious about America's upcoming choice, it did not stop or wait. The administration still had to make decisions on dealing with the continuing violence and death in former Yugoslavia and in several parts of Africa; in both areas traditional government had all but disappeared, leaving force as the only arbiter of grudges.

The president had just returned from a G-8 summit conference in Berlin, where he had urged greater European intervention with America in finding international solutions. He had suggested to his politely smiling counterparts that there would be no real long-term solutions in these or any other troubled areas of the world without God's involvement. And he had quietly reminded them about the impending bomb threat to America and asked for their governments' redoubled help in finding the terrorists quickly.

That Thursday William Harrison was meeting in the Oval Office with

Jerry Richardson, Michael Tate, Larry Thomas, and Susan Fullerton for an update on the political situation. As they settled into their chairs, William asked, "So, how are we doing at the end of our fourth month?"

"Mixed," Larry Thomas volunteered. "Some of the good news is that we now have at least one candidate who has embraced our Twenty Points in every single congressional district, and all of the Senate races. Thirty percent of them are incumbents. So we have someone running in every local election, and our coordinating committee is making the rounds, meeting all of them and sharing ideas we hope will get them elected."

"Of course the committee isn't taking sides," Susan added, "where there's more than one of our people running in the same race. We want local constituents to make that decision."

"What's the previous party affiliation count?" the president asked.

"It's really amazing—about one-third each: us, them, and independent," Jerry answered. "And our polls indicate that nobody much cares this year. Whatever else we've done, we've made people focus on the worldview issue, not the political party."

"Maybe when it's over we'll witness one of those rare generational shifts, when political parties realign," Larry said.

"Another positive development," Michael Tate said, "is that we're beginning to hear reports from the field—small towns, inner cities, and suburban neighborhoods—where individuals are calling in and saying that they've 'converted' a new volunteer. And some churches are volunteering to go door to door with the booklet Joe Wood's committee has published—it's really a good piece, by the way."

"And so the bad news?" the president asked.

Jerry sighed. "The bad news is that for the last month all the polls—ours, theirs, everyone's—have shown that the divisions have remained virtually unchanged, despite the opposition's big name entertainment blitz and our grass roots organizing. Which means about twenty-five percent believe in God and will vote overwhelmingly for our candidates, twenty-five percent just as strongly reject any faith in him, and fifty percent express a belief in God but have heard so often about the 'separation of church and state' that they can't imagine voting for anyone or anything based on their faith. As if what they believe only matters on another planet."

"And the tragedy, of course," William finished the thought, "is that if that hesitation remains through November, then their inaction is as good as a vote for the other side. They'll reject our challenge to choose, but in the process they'll choose just as decisively by default."

Everyone was silent for a minute. Then William continued. "If any of those decisive fifty percent are going to vote for our candidates, then their hearts have to be changed. And to change their hearts is going to take preparation. What about the Jewish vote?"

"The polls among Jewish voters are running closer to fifty-fifty, as is the opinion of their leadership," Larry replied. "Many have strongly endorsed us for the obvious reasons, but many others have denounced us as hate mongers."

"But several of the candidates we're supporting are Jewish," William said. "Clearly a devout Jew has a godly worldview."

"We know," Michael said. "And we're reaching out, one-on-one, trying to get past the stereotypes in the press."

"Well," William asked, turning to Susan, "where are we focusing for the next ninety days?"

"Our main efforts for the summer are our speakers bureau, our fund-raising for TV spots in the fall, the distribution of the Twenty Points booklet, and the Fourth of July Day of Fasting and Prayer. Hopefully those efforts, plus the ongoing news interviews, will prepare people for the message from their local candidates."

William leaned back in his chair. "I'm fine with this right now. You're doing a great job, all of you. If we keep praying, keep ourselves focused on him, ignore the personal attacks on us, and always bring the issues back to the worldview, which includes God as Lord, then whatever else needs to be done, he'll do. As we read so many times in the Bible, if we'll just do the simple things he asks, then he'll always do as he's promised."

Jerry smiled. "I know what you're saying is true, but it's so hard for us Type-A personalities to just trust God."

William returned his smile. "I know. But while we're asking others to believe in him for the first time, we've also got to walk our talk and spend more time on our knees than on setting goals in our pocket calendars. That's what faith is."

ATLANTA   Six weeks after Bruce left, Rebecca spent a long weekend in Washington with her brother and sister-in-law, and she asked their forgiveness for Bruce's too-personal attack on their family. William assured her that he knew she was not to blame and that he expected such attacks, so she shouldn't worry any more about it.

By the end of their time together Rebecca was convinced that William meant it, and she was also convicted by the tremendous peace and strength she saw in the two of them and in Katherine. She left Washington not as a practicing Christian believer, but as someone who had reaffirmed her belief in God and who was open to hearing more. She decided that in November she would have to vote for candidates who believed in the biblical worldview; it was the only one that made sense to her.

On returning to Atlanta she'd taken three days to write a long letter to Bruce, outlining beliefs that had been difficult for her to define earlier, but which she wanted him to understand. During the intervening weeks she'd become more and more sensitive to what people around her were saying about the election. She understood those who denigrated the biblical worldview, like her trainer at the gym, a young woman in her early twenties she'd known for six months. So after two weeks of hesitation, that Thursday afternoon as they finished their session at the club, Rebecca asked, "What do you think's going to happen after the election in November?"

The woman's puzzled look encouraged Rebecca to continue, and the ensuing conversation lasted almost an hour. As they left that night, Rebecca hoped that she had at least planted a seed.

WASHINGTON Since Ryan had proposed to her, Leslie's life had seemed to have more purpose. She knew where she was going. They'd decided it would be impossible to schedule the wedding before the election, given their responsibilities, so they tentatively chose the Saturday after Thanksgiving as the date.

That sunny May afternoon she was working in her office, preparing for the nightly news, in which she planned to spotlight a speech by the vice president on the need for pluralistic diversity in education. There was a knock at her open door.

She looked up to see a young man dressed in an immaculate blue suit whom she knew to be one of their assistant directors—he had often been on remote locations with her, most recently at the People's March on Washington—but she had forgotten his name.

"Ms. Sloane, hi, I'm Porter Doran. Do you have a minute?"

Leslie smiled but knew her time was tight. "Yes, Porter, but I've got this piece to write for tonight. What can I do for you?"

The young man came in, obviously feeling out of place one-on-one with a national personality. He hesitantly took a chair in front of her desk.

"Ms. Sloane, I, uh, guess this isn't so easy for me, but I've been wanting to ask you ever since the march, whether you've ever felt the power of God in your life?"

Oh, no! she thought *What is this all about?* "Uh, no, Porter, I don't guess I have, and I don't expect I ever will, since I don't really believe too much in God."

"Well, I have, and I wanted you to know about it. You know those groups during the march that we kept panning away from all the time, the 'strange' ones?"

"Yes."

"Three years ago I would have been in one of those groups, half-naked, doing those things."

"You, Porter? That's hard to believe."

"Yes, ma'am, I know. And that's what I want to tell you about."

Thirty minutes later Leslie had been challenged to imagine that there might be a spiritual side to life just as real as the physical side because this intelligent young man had described experiences that appeared to be unexplainable in any other way. But everything in her mind fought it.

As he rose to leave, he said, "I know you've got a lot to do. But is there anything in your life that I can pray for?"

Leslie was taken aback. No one had ever asked her that question before. She waited a moment and then replied, "Uh, why I guess, Porter, you could pray for my upcoming marriage to Ryan Denning, and also that we do a professional job in our reporting of the election."

Porter took out a piece of paper from his pocket and wrote down her two prayer requests. "Okay, I'll be praying for those. And would you mind telling me when God answers either one, so I can cross it off?"

She smiled. "Sure. Sure Porter, I'll let you know."

NORFOLK After returning from the Mediterranean deployment the crew of the *Fortson* spent almost a month in a stand-down status, allowing for extra leave and a chance for the crew to catch up with their families. Hugh had been ecstatic to see Jennifer and the children waiting at the pier, and he had done his best to be sensitive to her as she adjusted to having her husband in the house again.

Enough time had now passed that they were back to normal, and Hugh had caught up on events, both personal and public, which had happened in his absence. He was intrigued to see how seriously the nation appeared to be taking his brother's challenge, and their church had even laid out a grid of their neighborhood, hoping to insure that every house heard first-hand about the need for a God-believing Congress in Washington.

Jennifer had spent some of her free time in his absence reading the Bible and being discipled by an older woman who led a small women's study group on their street. Hugh was impressed with his wife's growing knowledge of Scripture and her commitment to the Lord. And she had in turn encouraged him to reach out to those in his own special workplace, which was what brought him to be standing outside the door to Captain Robertson's cabin that afternoon. He knocked.

"Come in. Oh, hi, Hugh. What a coincidence. I'm just reading a letter from Seaman Tyson. He says he's really happy in Newport, and he appreciates our help in having him moved. And he says to tell you that so far God has continued to watch over him."

Hugh entered the cabin and stood by the captain's desk. "That's great, sir. I hope he continues to do well."

"Yes. But he may have to come back in about six weeks and testify."

"Why, sir?"

"Well, the XO and I were called to the admiral's office this morning, and it looks like we're going to have some sort of human rights inquiry on the *Fortson.*"

Hugh looked surprised. "Why?"

The captain motioned for Hugh to have a seat. "Well, it seems the experts running our experiment with women, gays, and lesbians became concerned when they found out that we'd had one tragic death, a lawsuit pending, a homosexual 'expulsion'—that's what they call Tyson—and disciplinary action for the lesbian show. Apparently they're questioning our abilities as officers, and so they're sending a team to investigate the ship's senior officers—which includes you—for our 'fitness' to serve in the navy."

"You mean they're questioning decades of service, when *they're* the ones who created this situation for which none of us was trained or prepared?"

"That doesn't seem to matter, Hugh; at least not to some of them. The admiral has promised his full support, and we'll just have to pray that whoever they send is fair and just. Hopefully they'll understand that none of us could have foreseen those events. But, to tell you the truth, Hugh, it is a bit discouraging."

Hugh could tell his captain was actually feeling the implied lack of confidence much more than he'd expressed.

"Sir, it's funny, but that's sort of why I came to see you. I don't mean to be presumptuous, but I noticed that this stuff sort of gets you down sometimes, and I just wanted to encourage you in general, and also urge you to vote in November for candidates who'll work with my brother to change some of this."

The captain smiled. "Thanks, Hugh. We all need encouragement sometimes. I'm embarrassed to tell you, but I don't think I've voted in over twenty years. Trudy and I have moved around so much to different duty stations— and it's such a pain to vote by absentee ballot. So I haven't thought much about it."

Hugh spent several minutes explaining why he thought the upcoming election would be so important and how he felt God's hand starting to work in his own life.

As he finished he asked for and received a commitment from the captain to register—both he and Trudy—and to vote in the election for candidates who shared the president's worldview.

"Captain, is there anything I can pray about for you?" Hugh asked.

"No one's ever asked me that before… I guess besides the obvious of praying that this inquisi—I mean inquiry will go well, I'd ask you to pray for Trudy. She's going in for some tests tomorrow, and we're hoping that it's not cancer."

"Yes, sir. Absolutely. Let me write those down, and please let me know about her. Anything else?"

THE BLACK SEA   Despite the clear night and ample moonlight, the captain of the *Bright Star* was using the ship's surface search radar to assist in threading through the heavy traffic of small boats as they departed the Bosporus. Sadim stood on the darkened bridge, reflecting on how greatly they appeared to be blessed in their endeavors. Kolikov assured him that they had made up the necessary time and would be able to leave the Mediterranean by mid-October at the latest.

They were on their way for what should be their last visit to the Ukrainian port of Odessa. It would also be their largest and most complex pick-up of equipment since they'd transferred the bomb itself on board. The passive sonar array and electronic warfare antenna were supposed to be crated to look like farm machinery. *We should have no problems,* Sadim thought, *unless some official insists on being more nosy than smart.* And that possibility concerned Sadim, since they had so few options for escape when tied to the pier in a port that was, at best, neutral to their cause. He believed that enough bribes had been paid to insure a smooth loading and no problems. But Sadim did not expect to get much sleep for the next few days.

*The Congress...desirous...to have people of all ranks and degrees duly impressed with
a solemn sense of God's superintending providence, and of their duty, devoutly to
rely...on his aid and direction...Do earnestly recommend...a day of humiliation, fasting, and prayer; that we may, with united hearts, confess and bewail our manifold sins
and transgressions, and, by a sincere repentance and amendment of life...and, through
the merits and mediation of Jesus Christ, obtain his pardon and forgiveness.*

CONTINENTAL CONGRESS
MAY 16, 1776

24

Tuesday, July 2
Six Weeks Later

ATLANTA As Rebecca drove to work that morning she thought about the
billboards along the interstate and the banners on cheap hotels (and on one
or two pricey ones) that had been erected since the Supreme Court had ruled
in early June that states and cities could regulate prostitution but not prohibit it. The justices had decided in a six to three opinion that prostitution
was simply a personal service business and the state could not deny the rights
of those who wanted to participate in this occupation. Almost overnight
there was wholesale advertising, and just this week she'd seen the first television spot on the six o'clock news extolling the virtues of a particular brothel.

Some in the media had asked whether this ruling was a delayed but
pointed reaction to the president's verbal attack on the Court in his State of
the Union address.

But all of the justices retained their customary reticence. The ruling
cited a long list of recent precedents in which actions previously considered
unlawful by way of prohibition in the Bible were ruled now to be quite
appropriate. The Court went out of its way to state that from this point on
it would look with displeasure on any law whose only foundation was its
biblical precedent. "We have moved beyond ancient texts as our tools for
deciding what is right and wrong between consenting adults, when there is
no victim," the justices in their wisdom had proclaimed.

No victim? Rebecca thought again as she rode the hospital elevator to her floor. *What about the girls lured into lives of degradation, violence, and disease by the promise of quick money? What about boys for whom sex is just another trip, like going to the grocery store for food? What about families, torn apart by a husband's infidelity? What about AIDS? Drugs? Where are the ultra-feminists on this one? I hope at least some of those women and their friends are on their knees, searching for answers this morning, while I have to deal with the pregnancy and the disease they've helped to create by their "rationality."*

Rebecca had to smile to herself as she prepared for her first patient. *It's amazing. I would never have been thinking like this a year ago. I guess brother William has had more of an effect on me than I sometimes realize.*

She checked at the central nurses' station on her floor and then looked down the list of women who were already signed in that morning. Eunice Porter and Sally Kramer. *Here they are again. I meant to check on their records. And there are all those other women who keep showing up pregnant and then just disappearing.*

She walked down the hall, stopped at Room 317, opened the door and smiled. "Hello Eunice. How are you this morning?"

"Fine," she said, but looked away.

"Let's see. You're about five months now. Is everything all right?"

"Yes. Fine."

Rebecca was present while the doctor examined Eunice. Afterward, as Rebecca was about to leave the room, her curiosity led her to ask, "Eunice, it's probably none of my business, but I'm sort of curious. Haven't you and Ms. Kramer gotten pregnant now twice together? And didn't both of you have almost full-term abortions? Is that by coincidence?"

Eunice looked down. "I guess so. And I don't guess it's any of your business anyway." She got off the examining table and walked into the curtained-off dressing area.

"Well, I'm sorry," Rebecca said, standing outside the curtain. "It's just that I'm in the business of healing and protecting life, not ending it. I assume you won't be aborting this one."

"We'll see," was the noncommittal response.

"What? It's against the law again to abort a baby as far along as yours. Why are you even thinking that?"

"Uh. I'm not. I didn't understand. I know about that law."

Rebecca was silent. When Eunice came out of the dressing area, Rebecca felt led to say, "If I can arrange it, right now, would you like to see the baby—maybe even tell if it's a boy or a girl?"

"How?" Eunice buttoned the last button on her maternity top.

"With ultrasound. Come on, I bet we can squeeze you in, and I'll be there with you. It doesn't hurt at all, and I think you'll see things you never believed possible."

Eunice was hesitant, but Rebecca's enthusiasm was infectious. "Well, okay, I guess so, if you think it'll be okay."

"Sure. Come on with me, and we'll set it up."

Rebecca took Eunice gently by the arm and led her down the hall. Forty-five minutes later, Eunice, with Rebecca holding her hand, had seen the little boy inside her womb. And for the first time in five months she found herself calling him a baby, not a fetus.

RALEIGH Sarah walked into the Prescotts' breakfast room late that morning and sliced two bagels in half. She and Katherine, who was visiting again that summer, had worked the evening shift at the sandwich shop the night before.

"Mom, we heard last night that Denise Farris is pregnant."

Mary looked up from writing her Fourth of July dinner grocery list. "Oh, no. I'm so sorry. Can we talk to her about adoption?"

"I think she's probably going to consider it. I haven't talked to her personally yet. Maybe Katherine and I can go see her this afternoon. But I guess this will cut into her starting at Yale this fall!"

"Probably. But hopefully she could get a deferral."

"I hope so."

"Sarah, isn't this, what, eight girls in your class who we know are pregnant?"

"Uh, let's see…yes, eight."

"What a shame."

"Mom, I know that but for the grace of God there go I…"

"Yes, sweetheart. I thank him every day and pray for those who haven't been so blessed."

Katherine came into the kitchen, still looking a little bleary from sleep. "Hi. Were you talking about Denise?"

Sarah answered, "Yes. Mom, when is that hearing on the computer grant? Will I get to speak before we start at UNC?"

"They're apparently still gathering applications for the grants, but BioTeam is bringing pressure through our local congressman to be heard quickly. I think there's going to be a regional competition in August and then perhaps a final national interview this fall."

"Can you have the data ready on your senior class by August?" Katherine asked.

"Yes," Sarah answered. "It's not too scientific, I guess, but it's real. Not everyone would answer the questions, of course, but I'm sure most of the pregnant girls will testify, at least at the regional level."

Katherine spread strawberry preserves on her bagel. "I hope that's as far as BioTeam goes, from what you've told me."

"Don't count on it," Mary answered.

NORFOLK The executive officer and department heads had assembled in the wardroom that morning at eleven, and a few minutes later they rose to their feet as Captain Robertson escorted Rear Admiral Robert Waldrin in to start their meeting.

"Please be seated," the admiral said and took his place at the head of the wardroom table, the captain and executive officer on each side of him.

"I'll get right to the point. You of course know that a committee from the navy's Human Rights Commission has been here for a week investigating all aspects of the experiment in which you have participated for over a year, particularly the events that were tragic or unusual, such as the death of a female petty officer and a live sex show viewed by junior officers. You also know that some have questioned the circumstances of those events and even suggested that the officers and chiefs on the *Fortson* are either incompetent or bigoted or both.

"As I've just briefed Captain Robertson, you'll be pleased to know that the committee, after extensive interviews with individuals from every group and minority on the ship, has tentatively ruled that these events were either accidents or isolated incidents and that there is no reason for any action or reprimands. In fact, in most cases the leadership on the ship appears to be all that could be expected under these sometimes difficult circumstances. After seeing the progress made on the *Fortson,* the commission approved six more ships for this manning configuration in January, even before the final report is in, and many of you will have the opportunity to transfer to those ships, if you want.

"I used the word tentative because the one recommendation we will be implementing is for the Human Rights Commission to study the situation on board firsthand for an additional six months. For that reason, normal transfers and rotation of personnel will be frozen until the end of the year, so that the same individuals can continue to interact; and two members of the commission will be assigned to the ship for that same period. The *Fortson* will be assigned to various training exercises along the East Coast, then enter the shipyard at the end of the year to begin the decommissioning process. I guess she's finally going to retire after many exemplary years of service to her country. That's it, and I appreciate the time many of you put into helping the committee with its work. Are there any questions?"

There was silence among the officers. Hugh Harrison, knowing he should keep quiet, nevertheless could not help asking what he assumed many of them were thinking. "Sir, will these two commission members also be members of the 'mind police,' taking notes on how we react to situations and what we think?"

Out of the corner of his eye Hugh could see Thomas Dobbs take a deep breath and fold his arms across his chest. Admiral Waldrin looked at Hugh for a long moment before answering. "Even if I sympathized with your question and allowed for its partial validity, I prefer to think that these persons will be on board to learn from the great work you've been doing. Isn't that better?"

Hugh knew he had been skillfully rebuffed and that this was no time or place to pick a fight with the admiral. He simply answered, "Yes, sir."

"We obviously appreciate the hard work and assistance of the admiral and his staff in this effort," the captain said. "Admiral Waldrin, all the officers and crew on the *Fortson* will continue to give this situation our best efforts, and hopefully we'll have a final report for all concerned with this experiment by the end of the year."

The admiral nodded, rose, and departed with the captain. The meeting was over.

WASHINGTON The next day the president finished a round of speeches in the Midwest supporting the local congressional candidates who embraced a biblical view of life. He spent a full day with Senator John Dempsey. His plane returned to Washington that evening, and he arrived back at the White House about ten. An hour later he and Carrie were in bed together, and he was trying to read from his notebook of documents written by the Founding Fathers. However, he was having trouble concentrating.

He put his notebook on the bedside table and turned to Carrie. "I'm looking forward to reading the Declaration of Independence aloud at the Fourth of July celebration tomorrow, but I'm concerned how the nation will accept our proclamation on making it the first national Day of Fasting and Prayer in a century. The polls show we're still stuck—some improvement, but only about thirty percent will vote with us in November. Almost fifty percent are still undecided or leaning against us. We have no idea what they'll think about fasting and praying."

Carrie smiled. "To quote a president I know, 'It doesn't matter what others do; it only matters that we seek God's will and follow it.' "

William sighed. "You're right, as usual. I just hope that some communities actually do as we've suggested and use the Fourth to pray and fast, delaying their festivities until the evening."

"Now, William, you already know that tens of thousands of them are doing just that, and the networks have even begrudgingly had to report it. So listen to your own advice and trust God."

He smiled, leaned over, and kissed her. "I'm sorry. Thank God for you, Carrie."

She set down her book and put her arms around him. "You *do* need to study the Declaration some more, I know. But I bet the founding fathers didn't *just* write all the time. Otherwise there wouldn't have been any founding mothers or founding children!"

"I see...more valid historical commentary! Are you suggesting that this president needs to tend to the home fires a bit more?"

"Something like that," she said, pulling him closer. "It's good for your constitution."

In May William had issued the official proclamation that this year's Fourth of July would be the first Day of Fasting and Prayer in decades. Many people and communities ignored it, either from principle or claiming that their plans had already been made. But many organizations, cities, towns, and individuals decided to heed the president's call. Those included quite a few who said they were still undecided about November but understood the need for a change in the nation and were willing to try prayer and fasting. So most of the holiday's cookouts and celebrations were moved to the evening, and churches were open across the land for people to pray.

The main event of the day was to be a national hour of submission and prayer scheduled for noon. A platform had been constructed near the base of the Washington Monument. The president planned to walk over from the White House about eleven-thirty and at midday read aloud the Declaration of Independence, originally proclaimed on July 4, 1776. There would then follow several prayers from the platform, but all the Washington-based events were to be concluded by twelve-thirty at the latest, because the emphasis was on the united prayer at similar gatherings at courthouses and state capitols across the nation, where after a brief local word or two, men and women of faith were to pray silently, interceding for the country and the country's leaders.

The networks were planning to cover the events in Washington just as they had covered the opposition's march at Easter, but network personnel were wondering what they would do during thirty or more minutes of silent prayer. It wouldn't appear to make a very interesting visual. Ryan, who had again flown down to Washington, Leslie, and their directors at U.S. Network had decided simply to show the silent prayers from Washington and the fifteen other cities and towns from which they expected local feeds, believing that the sheer boredom would turn viewers to other programs, yet fulfilling their responsibility for "equal time."

Since there was no parade planned and no speeches other than the president's reading and a few prayers, Ryan would anchor the broadcast in their Washington studio, and Leslie would report from near the Washington Monument atop one of their mobile units, which had been outfitted with a platform for just such events. She was in position by ten-thirty and chatted with Ryan on their internal intercom about their plans for the afternoon.

Across the nation that morning special services were held in tens of thousands of churches and synagogues. The emphasis in each was on prayer, intercessory prayer for the nation. Most congregations had made a point to reach out and to invite, by going door to door, everyone in the neighborhoods around them. And because the president himself had proclaimed this to be a national day of fasting and prayer, many people responded who normally would not have attended a church.

At a church in Nashville, veterans were invited to stand and to pray out loud. At a church in Boise, the members read from the pulpit the Articles of Confederation and prayed between each reading. In many older churches research was done and prayers that had been offered for the nation in those very churches in the eighteenth and nineteenth centuries were prayed again.

All across the land, people who had been called by God's name repented, asked his forgiveness for turning from his ways, and humbly asked for renewal and revival, one heart at a time, as the nation considered its course in November. Though the prayers were many and deeply sincere, the numbers of those praying were still a distinct minority of the nation. But no one was counting that day.

Though these services were carried by many local television stations, the national networks ignored them, concentrating on Washington. The U.S. Network's van had threaded its way through a huge number of people early that morning, many of whom had camped or arrived before dawn, to take its assigned place near the Washington Monument. Leslie stood next to their large van parked in the bright sunlight near the monument and talked with her crew. She was aware that a great number of people were now walking toward their position from all sides of the Mall. There was no parade or demonstration. The coordinating committee had simply asked all those who could to assemble near the monument, and those who lived too far away were asked to do the same at their state capitols and county courthouses.

By eleven-thirty the Mall was completely full of people standing quietly; Leslie could see that some were already praying, many kneeling in the grass. She climbed up to their platform and looked out across the scene. She was astounded to see that the numbers spilled back all the way to the Capitol and to the Lincoln Memorial and that there were even people standing in every side street leading to the Mall. Without anyone telling her, Leslie knew that this was the largest number of people ever assembled in Washington for a single event. She was stunned; and she was amazed by how quiet the huge crowd was. It was simply eerie, and she felt a chill. The word "reverent" came to her mind.

Twenty minutes before noon the president appeared, walking through the crowd with a contingent of Secret Service personnel toward the podium on the platform erected for this event. As he reached the monument, the U.S. Network's coverage began, and Ryan Denning led from their studio, showing the crowd in Washington from a blimp overhead. They then cut to similar gatherings at state capitols in Providence, Columbus, Atlanta, Austin, Helena, and Sacramento. He was impressed by the numbers but reported the gatherings in a dry manner, as if he were reading from an encyclopedia on state capitals.

For Leslie, in the midst of so many people, it was impossible to remain aloof. When Ryan cut to her, he was not prepared for the excitement and enthusiasm in her voice.

"Ryan, it's hard to describe the scene here," she began. The camera panned around from her position, showing the hundreds of thousands of people all around them. "I'm here in the middle of what must be the largest crowd ever assembled in this city, yet I'm almost having to whisper, it's so quiet! People are already praying silently"—the camera focused in on several groups kneeling around their position—"and I guess I've never felt anything like this before, to be honest."

"Felt?" Ryan asked from the studio, "What do you mean?"

"Yes. It's difficult to explain, Ryan, but there's a feeling here, a...a power, almost. I've never been in the midst of a million people quietly praying, and to tell you the truth, I can definitely feel something stirring."

The camera cut back to the studio and Ryan smiled on camera, "Thanks for the report, Leslie. We'll switch live to Sacramento after this commercial break."

Once they were temporarily off the air, Ryan spoke to Leslie through her earpiece. "Leslie, what's the matter with you? You were supposed to find some wildly praying crazies—even the ones who talked about crucifying themselves during this hour. You sound like you want to join them!"

"I'm sorry, Ryan. The crazies aren't here, or at least we don't see them. There are just a lot of seemingly nice people standing, kneeling, and praying. Some around us are crying, and the president hasn't even read anything yet. I really can't describe it, but there's a powerful feeling here."

"Well, try to keep your enthusiasm under control. Remember, that's William Harrison up there—the man who thinks that women ought to be barefoot and pregnant and that abortion is a sin!"

"Okay. You're right. Thanks."

Right at noon William made his way to the microphone at the podium. "Thank you all for coming today, this anniversary of our Declaration of Independence from England and of our Declaration of Dependence on God. We're here for one single task, to intercede in prayer for our nation and for our nation's leaders at every level, from local communities to state capitals to Washington. This is not a time for speeches, but for prayer. So I now want to read the document our forefathers wrote as the result of daily prayer in Philadelphia over two hundred years ago. It's our prayer today that these truths will be reborn in our nation—that men will say decades from now that this generation turned back to the Lord."

William began to read, "'When in the Course of human events, it becomes necessary for one people...'"

Leslie was watching him on their monitor, which provided a close-up picture, but her eye was drawn to the west over the Lincoln Memorial, where from nowhere there appeared a speck of a dark storm cloud in the otherwise brilliant blue sky.

"'The separate and equal station to which the Laws of Nature and of Nature's God entitles them...'"

Leslie focused back on the president.

"'We hold these truths to be self-evident, that all men are created equal, that they are endowed by their Creator with certain unalienable Rights, that among these are Life, Liberty and the pursuit of Happiness. That to secure these rights...'"

Leslie was drawn back to the dark cloud, which in just a few moments had grown tremendously and now covered at least a third of the sky, though the sun still beat down brilliantly. Nevertheless, she could see others in the crowd around her turning to look at the dark mass that seemed to grow more menacing with each minute.

The president read on, and as he did so the cloud blocked out the sun. The wind began to pick up. He held his papers tightly and glanced up at one point, but despite the wind he read on, his voice seeming to grow stronger.

To Leslie and the more than one million people gathered around the president, it was obvious that a dangerous storm was approaching. As William began the last paragraph, the first crack of lightning flashed between the clouds, and the resulting thunder drowned him out for a moment. Leslie realized that there was no protection for all these people and that there was nowhere they could go. She feared a stampede as the wind picked up even more, and again a burst of nearby lightning lit the almost black sky. But no one in the crowd moved.

"'And for support of this Declaration, with a firm reliance on the protection of Divine Providence, we mutually pledge to each other our Lives, our Fortunes, and our sacred Honor.'" William concluded the reading and then continued, almost yelling over the roar of the wind, "Friends, we have nowhere we can go. We're here. We came here to pray. Whatever now happens, we've got to trust in God and pray for his protection of us and of our nation. Please, pray with me."

Leslie was astounded. As the flags around the monument almost came off their poles in the wind and she had to grasp the rail atop the van to keep from falling over, more than a million people calmly went to their knees, many with outstretched hands, and listened as the president began to pray.

"Dear heavenly Father, the creator of everyone and everything, we come before you today to affirm that you are the true founder of this nation, that it is your will we should seek, your laws we should uphold. We repent and—"

There was a tremendous lightning strike at the top of the Washington Monument, and instantly a clap of thunder so loud that Leslie ducked and screamed involuntarily. Then the rain burst in driving torrents, pushed almost horizontal by the wind.

The power went out on the podium and in the van. The sky was so dark that it seemed like night. A million people were instantly soaking wet, trapped outside in a lightning storm like no one had ever seen.

As she clutched the rail, Leslie found herself falling to her knees because she couldn't stand up. Her cameraman was lying on the roof next to her, trying to protect his camera.

Again a lightning bolt hit close by, setting a tree on fire, and then the hail came. Leslie screamed as the hail pummeled her body. She bowed her head and turned her back, but the hail wouldn't stop. She began to cry. She felt the vibration that meant the men in the van had started their portable generator. She cried out, "O God, please help us." Not even the cameraman next to her could hear her plea in the roar of the wind and the hail. But her cry came through to millions of households across the nation as the returning power allowed her to be seen in the lens of the downed camera, just as she sobbed her prayer.

Ryan was appalled at the only scene they had—Leslie drenched, kneeling, covering her head, and crying. Then power somehow was restored to the pool camera opposite the podium, and they had a picture of the president and the others on the platform, kneeling and praying in the rain and the hail.

Unbelievable, Ryan thought. As if in answer to his thought, the technician on the pool camera managed to swing his camera around, and there for the whole nation to see in the rain and the dark and the hail and the lightning were a million or more people, kneeling together on the Mall. No one was running; no one was even moving. They were all praying.

From the safety of their downtown studio, Ryan said over the pictures, "Ladies and gentlemen, obviously we're all hoping that the president and the others gathered on the Mall will be protected. We'll come back to Washington in a moment, but now let's quickly move to Providence and John Sherry."

The scene shifted to the area around the courthouse at the Rhode Island capital, which was filled with people on their knees, praying in silence under a bright blue sky with a strong wind blowing. "Yes, Ryan, we're here in Providence," anchorman John Sherry came on live, "where, out of an otherwise beautiful sky, a very strong wind just began to blow. But, as you can see, the gusts have not diminished the fervor of the people gathered here today. They listened to the president read the Declaration of Independence, then the governor prayed and invited everyone to, in his words, 'seek God's face for our nation.'"

"Thanks, John, now let's check in on Chuck Shields in Austin."

"Hi, Ryan," the anchorman answered from just inside the edge of a tarp which was shaking wildly. "The crowd here in Austin is tremendous, and they're silently praying now. Some were standing a moment ago, but they're all on their knees now. A strong wind began blowing just as the governor finished his prayer. It was eerie, Ryan. It's been raining all morning, but in just the last few minutes the clouds have disappeared and this wind has begun blowing."

Ryan went on for brief reports from Atlanta and Sacramento, where he was surprised to find throngs of people praying, clear skies, and a strong wind. But not the menacing wind of the storm raging in Washington, which they were still monitoring during their reports from around the nation. Finally he couldn't stand it any longer and during a commercial break asked the director to check. The answer came back: there were brilliant blue skies and a strong wind in *every* one of the fifteen capitals and county seats they were monitoring, and in every case the skies had cleared and the wind had started just after noon. And in every case the people were still there, praying.

Ryan couldn't believe it but decided that they would say nothing about it—coincidences did happen. More importantly, he needed to check with Leslie. The hail appeared to have stopped, but it was still dark and raining. While a report came in from Boise, Ryan spoke to Leslie over the intercom. With the noise now reduced, Leslie could hear Ryan in her earpiece, though she didn't realize that the camera was trained on her. The picture could be seen in the studio, but it was not then being broadcast.

"Yes...yes...Ryan, I'm here."

"We've got two cameras working. One's up there on you, and the other is somehow up and running on the president. Whoever's manning that one ought to get a medal."

"On me?" They could see her look around, still shielding her face from the rain, until she saw the camera on the roof, her cameraman still trying to protect it. "Oh. Ryan, you wouldn't believe what's happened." She struggled to stand up. As she did, she looked out from the van for the first time since she fell and gasped, "Ryan, I can see at least two trees smoldering, and I don't know if anyone's been hurt. But, Ryan, these people are *all* still here, and they're *still praying!*" She started to cry again. "It was so awful, I—"

"Leslie, get a hold of yourself," Ryan said over the intercom. "Wipe your face as best you can and stop crying. We've got to come back to you there in Washington in just a minute, or people will start to worry. Now everything's all right—you'll be fine. We've got a team checking on damage, and once the wind dies down we'll get the blimp back in position. Just give us a positive, heads-up report, will you? You'll be a hero."

"Yes, yes. I will," she replied into her microphone. As the rain slackened, her cameraman stood up again and put the camera on his shoulder. Leslie wiped her face and looked out. People were standing in the wet grass and in the mud, lifting their hands, and *smiling* while they prayed!

"We're going back now to Leslie Sloane in Washington," Ryan voiced over a picture of the president still praying on his knees. "Leslie, that was some storm. Are you all right?"

The cameraman on the van focused on a very wet Leslie Sloane on top of the van, the presidential platform behind her. "Yes, Ryan, we're all fine here, though I'm not sure about other spots on the Mall. Ryan, you won't believe how this storm came up; I hope we've got it on tape. I *felt* it coming, just like I felt these people praying. Ryan, I don't know anything about spiritual warfare—that's what the president's sister called it in our interview with her—but I feel like either this storm was one of the century's greatest coincidences, or we've just lived through a real spiritual battle."

"Great, Leslie. We're glad you're okay. We'll check with you again in a little while, but right now we've got a live update on the Independence Day Golf Classic."

In towns and cities across the nation, believers and others drawn by concern for America's future knelt in prayer through much of that afternoon. And in many churches, July Fourth was the kick-off day for their congregations to pray around the clock, seven days a week, until the elections scheduled for Tuesday, November 5.

It yet remains a problem to be solved in human affairs, whether any free government
can be permanent, where the public worship of God, and the support of religion,
constitute no part of the policy or duty of the state in any assignable shape.

JUSTICE JOSEPH STORY
U.S. SUPREME COURT, 1833

25

Monday, September 16
Two Months Later

ATLANTA Eunice Porter answered the phone in her apartment late in the morning. It was Sally Kramer, and her voice was excited as she relayed her news. "I've got my train ticket for New York, and Dr. Thompson says your date is all set for the very beginning of November. He wants to wait as close to your due date as possible."

"Oh. Okay," Eunice said, her voice showing no emotion.

"You don't sound too excited, girl," Sally said. "Doesn't five thousand bucks mean much to you these days?"

"Yeah, sure. But I just hate going all the way to New York on a train, especially so close to my due date. I thought he said they'd get it worked out to do it here."

"He did. But he says while the courts and the attorneys are all fighting over the law, the president's executive order, or whatever it is, stands. So we have to go to this clinic up there run by a friend of his."

"Well, I don't much like it. I wish I weren't doing this."

"What? Hey, you're the one who needed the money last Christmas. Remember?"

"Yeah, I remember. I don't know. I guess I'm just thinking some about this baby and all."

"That isn't a baby till it's born. It's a *fetus!*"

"Well, it sure kicks like a baby."

"Come on, girl. This is the best thing we've ever found. Don't mess it up for us. Do I have to go up there with you?"

"No, I don't guess you do. I'll be okay."

"Fine. Now wish me luck. I'll call you just before I leave."

Rebecca was finishing her review of the night shift's paperwork when there was a knock on the door to her office at the back of the nurses' station. A young man was standing there with several sheets of computer paper.

"Hi, Alex. What's up?" Rebecca asked.

"I finally got around to running those inquiries you asked for six weeks ago before the family went on vacation and our department changed offices. Sorry it took me so long."

"Oh, thanks. Did you find out anything?"

"Well, it's pretty weird, actually."

"How so?"

"You remember you asked me to check on Ms. Porter and Ms. Kramer and the other full-term abortions during the year when they were legal, to see if there were any unusual circumstances?"

"Yes, sure," Rebecca replied.

"Well, the most unusual thing is that Dr. Thompson and/or Dr. Sawyer were the doctors on *all* of them. In fact, Dr. Thompson only missed one, and his partner happened to be there."

"That does seem strange," Rebecca agreed, taking the printout from the young computer whiz. "Let's see, twenty-four full-term abortions in that year, and Harvey Thompson happened to be on duty for all but one of them. And look, they all seem to have taken place in the early evening hours. What are the odds of that being a coincidence?"

"I don't bet," he said, "but they've got to be slim."

"Hmm. Well, thanks, Alex... Look, can you sort of poke around with your computer and see if there's anything else going on in these dates and times that's odd? I mean, maybe Dr. Thompson just always signs up for this shift, time after time, and these women for some reason all decide in the afternoon that they want to abort their children. Please check, if you can, Dr. Thompson's other duty days. All right?"

"I'll try. It may take a while because they're just getting all our equipment hooked up again, but I'll take a look."

"Thanks, Alex. I don't really know what we're looking for, but if it's there, I know you'll find it!"

VIRGINIA BEACH Hugh and Jennifer were sitting at their dining room table. The children had finished supper and were watching television before bedtime.

"Tomorrow night we're starting our Bible study," Jennifer said, "in Romans. I'm sorry you're going to miss some of the sessions."

"Me, too," Hugh said, sipping his coffee. Jennifer had joined one of their church's small groups while Hugh had been deployed; they met weekly just two streets over, and Hugh had enjoyed getting to know the small group of believers. He particularly liked the host couple who led the Bible study. "I guess we'll be gone on these training operations and 'Show the Flag' trips several times between now and Christmas. We're supposed to make visits to Boston, New York, Charleston, and Port Everglades."

"Well, I hate for you to be gone, but at least we had almost the whole summer together, and going for ten days at a time is sure better than for six months."

"Yeah. I really should have been transferred to some shore billet by now, but rotations are still frozen until the end of the naval Human Rights Commission study."

"How's that going?" she asked, rising to get the key lime pie she had made for dessert.

"Oh, just wonderful," he exaggerated. "Some days I think the captain wishes the committee back in June had just decided we were all bigots and chopped off our heads on the spot!"

She laughed from in front of the refrigerator. "What do you mean?"

"I mean, as hard as he's tried—we've all tried—to bend over backward to be fair to everyone concerned in this new environment, we still don't know if we're getting nailed for enforcing regulations or which ones still apply or who can sleep with whom and when. I mean, it's just crazy. These two commission members just roam around the ship all day, watching and listening and taking notes on their clipboards. We *have* to let them into any conversation on anything at any time. One of our men asked me quite seriously yesterday if I thought their sleeping compartment was bugged!

"They're now talking about permitting officer and senior chief couples to live together on board—if they're married. A lawyer argued that otherwise the navy would "discriminate" against marriage. Isn't that quaint? Living together in staterooms. I guess soon we'll be needing cruise directors and nurseries."

Jennifer set the pie on the table. "Oh, come on, it's not that bad, is it? Who did you say are the representatives from the commission who are riding the ship?"

"We've got an Hispanic lesbian and a young white guy who graduated from Annapolis in June. To think that Captain Robertson's last months of command at sea are lived out in mortal fear of what those two might write about something one of his four hundred crewpeople might say or do! It's truly insane. I sure hope William gets the right people into office in November, so maybe he can undo all this politically correct mind control before we no longer have a navy—or an army or an air force, for that matter."

"I guess you're right, dear," Jennifer said. "Unfortunately I don't think it looks too good for November, from what I read. But like William keeps saying, we've got to pray."

"I do, Jen, I do. I just hope we make it."

CHAPEL HILL Katherine and Sarah had enrolled three weeks earlier as freshmen and roommates at the university, and they were living at the suggestion of the Secret Service in one of the smaller women's dorms, where one agent at a time could watch the patterns of those coming and going without too much trouble. So far they were enjoying both college life and rooming together, and their shared, renewed values had already helped them get through one fairly traumatic double date with two aggressive juniors.

Just before classes started, Sarah had traveled with her mother to Atlanta to testify in the regional hearings for the anti-AIDS federal grant for which BioTeam had applied. Despite their testimony, and that of three other students who shared Sarah's disgust with the device, the virtual reality computer had won the endorsement of the regional committee on the twisted logic—Mary felt—that while the computer had its admitted drawbacks in the areas exposed by the teenagers, it nevertheless had proven to be completely effective in stopping AIDS.

When the announcement had been made, Mary had wanted to scream from the back of the auditorium, "Yes, no AIDS cases this year, but surely the increased sexual activity leads to greater overall risk!" But she had restrained herself, knowing that they had one more chance to derail the juggernaut for this machine. And that was the purpose of Mary's phone call this Monday night.

She and Sarah first caught up on the few things that had happened since Sunday afternoon, when the two cousins had driven back to school from nearby Raleigh. Then Mary said, "Sarah, I got a call today. The final hearing on the federal grant for BioTeam is being held in New York, of all places. Anyway, it's set up for the morning of Monday, November fourth. The BioTeam hearing is at eleven. I hope you can arrange your classes so that we can fly up on Sunday, testify, and be home by late Monday."

"I think I can, Mom. And listen, since Katherine didn't get to go to Atlanta, do you think she could come with us to New York?"

"Well, if William and Carrie and the Secret Service say it's okay, it might not hurt to have the president's daughter sitting with us in our corner when we testify. I'll leave it up to the two of you. Just let me know how many hotel rooms we need."

"Great! We'll ask and let you know."

"And, Sarah, we've really got to pray and do all we can to discredit this awful thing. The PTA approved the use of the BioTeam machine at Northside High in the second half of junior year."

"That's awful, Mom."

"I know, dear. I know."

"Mom?"

"Yes?"

"I know I've said this before, but it really means so much to me that you and Dad forgave me for being so stupid—about the machine and Matthew, I mean."

"Honey, your father and I were not exactly saints in our younger days, unfortunately, and of course we forgave you. I know Katherine's glad to have you back, so to speak. And it's really between you and God, anyway. He's the one who wipes our slates clean. But you know that."

Mary could tell Sarah was smiling. "I know, Mom. And I've prayed, and I know I'm forgiven. But it's still special that you've forgiven me, too."

"All right, honey. We love you. You and Katherine get a good night's sleep."

WASHINGTON Leslie could not remember ever being angry with Ryan, not really angry. *But this evening might qualify,* she thought as she waited for the videotape to rewind.

She had covered Joe Wood's speech that afternoon to the Black Educators' Leadership Forum for the network and had been unexpectedly impressed with the courageous and seemingly logical things the street preacher, corporate board member, and White House advisor had told his mostly African-American audience.

But after the luncheon she had also covered the vice president's much anticipated Second Emancipation Proclamation, at which Patricia Barton-North held a press conference to announce that after she became president in November she would introduce to *her* Congress in January a broad set of reforms that would proclaim freedom and protection for all types of behavior and lifestyles which were matters of individual choice. Specifically, she would ask for federal legislation to legalize *and protect* in every state an individual's right to express homosexual love, to perform any and all art, to take soft drugs, to receive full-term abortions, even to practice polygamy and prostitution, the vice president having apparently decided it was better to mend her fences with all her progressive friends, so that she could be the "president for all the people."

Since Leslie had interviewed the vice president earlier and was their White House reporter, the news directors in New York had decided to let her cover the Second Emancipation Proclamation on the evening news as a major story, and Ryan would mention Joe Wood's speech in the other news about the upcoming election. So Leslie had uploaded the entire video of the pastor's speech to New York, keeping a copy for herself, as usual. And Ryan had, as expected, covered the talk in their newscast, which had ended twenty minutes earlier.

It was her copy of Joe Wood's speech Leslie now wanted to see again in its entirety, so she sat alone in one of their small studios with a pad and pencil while the video began. She fast forwarded through the introduction at the hotel podium and the applause. Then she settled in to listen to the pastor speak again.

He wasted no time after his few introductory remarks. He blasted the leadership of the nation, black and white, of both political parties, for the previous forty years and for what they had done to black families, to black men, and to black children.

"I'm so tired of hearing about black leaders. What would most of them do if black people *really* made it? We wanted civil rights, and we turned to the federal government to guarantee what the Declaration of Independence says about *all* men being created equal by God. But then we made a mistake—we looked to that same government to guarantee *outcomes*—and it has. Oh, Lord forgive us, it has! Black leaders and white leaders 'guaranteed' everyone into a federal plantation system that emasculates our men, turns our women into degraded baby machines, and then enslaves our children with more of the same programs.

"My friends, this is a majority white nation. You got that? We can't change that, and it'll hurt more than help to pretend ourselves into little groups and call ourselves 'equal but separate.' Where are we going to "separate" to? Instead we can keep our own culture while living successfully in this society. Look at the Italians and Ukrainians and Irish in America—they have as much or as little of their culture as they want while still living in the American mainstream. And unlike them"—he smiled from the podium— "there's no chance that we'll be lost in that mainstream!

"I know our ancestors didn't ask to come here to be slaves, but before you get too racially righteous, remember that black chiefs in Africa were the ones who sold their own people into slavery and pocketed the first cash for their souls. Look around today. Look at the death and violence in Bosnia, Rwanda, Ireland, Somalia, and you'll see the perverse good news that greed and hate and sin—yes, sin—are not a white condition or a black condition or a brown condition—they're *the human* condition, and they always will be without God in our lives!

"As I said, this is a majority white nation. It is, or was, also a Christian nation. And I'm here to tell you today that as imperfect as this nation is, it's the best place I know of to live. And the white people I know and work with genuinely want the best for my family and me, just like I do for them, because we don't see black or white, we see children of God—and it's *that* truth that made this nation different for blacks. When people genuinely have Jesus in their hearts, they transcend their *many* human differences—which are all too easy to see!—and focus instead on the spirit of God in whose image *all* of us were created.

"Folks have been slaves on this earth for thousands of years. But it was the power of God working through mainly *white* people who *freed* us in this nation! Where else has that ever happened? Thousands and thousands of whites who worked tirelessly from pulpits and podiums from the time the first slave arrived here through Abraham Lincoln and the bloodiest war in our history, right up to the men in power who listened to Martin Luther King Jr. and *were changed in their hearts!* Now who changes hearts? Not politicians. Not commentators. Not rioters. *God* changes hearts!

"We're the inheritors of the greatest setting free since the Hebrews left Egypt—except that in our case the Pharaoh's heart *did* change—but just like the Israelites, we've forgotten the God who freed us. We've trusted in a false god, the golden calf of the government, and forsaken the God who really saved us. Government programs never have and never will make us prosperous. Education, yes. Equal rights, yes. But programs that pay a woman more money for more children when there's no husband at home are only bound to make the plantation and its degradation larger and larger. Where are the black leaders who are willing to stand up and say that? And then help get rid of these programs, to replace them with what has always worked in the past—people and families helping people and families.

"Ladies and gentlemen, we don't need black leaders. We don't need white leaders. We need *God-fearing leaders* of both races! Men and women who first acknowledge God's sovereignty in this nation and in their lives. Where do we start? How about 'Love your neighbor as yourself.' If *you* wouldn't want to be on welfare, then why propose it for someone else? How about 'Husbands, love your wives…as your own bodies' and 'Fathers, do not exasperate your children; instead, bring them up in the training and instruction of the Lord.' Does that mean to do everything we can to keep families together? Do you realize that ninety-five percent of black families with a mother and father living together with high school educations are above the poverty line? You don't have to be a black rocket scientist to figure out what works! How about 'look after widows and orphans in their distress.' We've created a whole lot of literal and figurative widows and orphans, and *we*— not the government—better start looking after them, or the consequences for all of us will be disastrous.

"*We* can do *all* of that—we've got the blueprint. I've just quoted you a few short lines from it. The real wealth in this nation is one that's virtually untapped: the wealth of people's hearts. *And hearts only come in one color.*

"Let me make it real simple. To make black people prosperous, we must do two things: encourage education and family formation for those who haven't been sucked into the government plantation, and family-to-family emergency help for those who have. And that's what we'll to do if you elect a group to Congress in November who first fear the Lord and are willing to accept that he knew the answers long before we invented social engineers.

"Friends, there *is* hope! Everyone in this room is a living example of how good this country can be to all of us. Rather than whining and pointing fingers at the white people who mostly want to help us, I ask you to pick up a ballot in November and help us tear down the walls of the plantation that still has so many of our brothers and sisters enslaved. It won't be easy, but ladies and gentlemen, listen: *there is no other way.*"

Leslie watched the end of the tape as the predominantly black audience sat in silence. Then there was a smattering of applause that led quickly to a tumult, and most of the listeners rose to their feet as Joe Wood sat and acknowledged their applause with a single wave of his hand.

Next Leslie took out her tape and inserted a copy made from their nightly newscast only a little while before. She fast forwarded through several segments, including her own story on the vice president, until she came to Ryan Denning on the screen with a still picture of Joe Wood behind him.

"In other political news today," Ryan led off, "the president's second highest ranking black advisor, the Reverend Joe Wood, addressed a meeting of black educators in Washington. In his speech, Reverend Wood accused whites of creating governmental plantations for blacks but went on to say that blacks should nevertheless put their trust in God and whites—that black leaders are no longer needed."

There followed quick excerpts from the address, run together, showing Joe Wood saying, "White leaders 'guaranteed' everyone into a federal plantation system that emasculates our men, turns our women into degraded baby machines, and then enslaves our children... My friends, this is a majority white nation... Trust God... We don't need black leaders."

The camera came back to Ryan Denning, who looked very serious and said, "We understand that the president and Jerry Richardson are trying to obtain a copy of Reverend Wood's address. Now, for more on the upcoming election, here is John Sherry in Portland with the president of Keep America Strong—No Church in Government."

Leslie was even more angry than when she first heard his report. After writing a final sentence, she put in a call to New York. Two minutes later she reached Ryan, who was apparently about to leave the studio.

"Hi, Leslie. How'd we do tonight?"

"Awful," Leslie replied. "How could you so blatantly misrepresent what Joe Wood said today?"

"Misrepresent? Come on, Leslie. We used his own words, and everything I said was one hundred percent true."

"But you quoted little pieces of sentences and put everything in the wrong context to make him look bad to both whites and blacks."

"Hey, he said what he said," Ryan replied.

"But he *didn't* say it how you reported it. You were grossly unfair and inaccurate!"

"Leslie, that was Joe Wood up there. The president's chief Uncle Tom who wants to put black people back in chains with religious garbage—

singing spirituals while they hoe cotton."

"Come on, Ryan. I was there, and that's *not* what he said or even implied. In fact, he said just the opposite!"

"Leslie, have you forgotten that this is a war we're in? That's one of the president's generals, and in war you do what you can to take out generals. We've got to discredit him, and if we can do it with his own words, then so much the better."

"But you—we—lied tonight!"

"So what? Not really. And the goal of dumping these wackos certainly justifies a little creative editing."

"I don't know, Ryan."

"Hey, *I* know. It's important. And here you and I are fighting, when we're supposed to be married in just over two months. You know, I'll be glad when this election is over. You really haven't been the same since back on the Fourth of July. That storm must have really affected you."

Leslie was silent for a moment. "Yes. It did. Ryan, I think I felt the *real* war that day, and I've been trying to figure it out ever since."

"Come on, Les…"

"No, really. And I wish you'd told me about all those other cities before last week. Ryan, don't you see it's impossible for that to have just 'happened'? I checked yesterday with the National Weather Service record office. The wind in each of those cities was blowing from a slightly different direction! It's like God was saying 'I know there's a battle raging in Washington, but I want to show everyone that I'm still in charge, and I can make a strong wind blow in fifteen cities from clear skies, all at the same moment, from any direction I want, so don't lose sight of the *real* power.' But we missed the miracle. It happened right before our eyes, and we missed it!"

"Leslie, that was just a coincidence and nothing more."

"Sure, Ryan. I think it was more like *really* creative editing!" And she hung up.

When you become entitled to exercise the right of voting for public officers, let it be impressed on your mind that God commands you to choose for rulers just men who will rule in the fear of God. The preservation of a republican government depends on the faithful discharge of this duty; if the citizens neglect their duty and place unprincipled men in office, the government will soon be corrupted.... If a republican government fails...it must be because the citizens neglect the divine commands, and elect bad men to make and administer the laws.

NOAH WEBSTER

26

WASHINGTON William Harrison had just finished the strategy session with his key advisors for the last two weeks before the election, including the plans for the final rallies on the weekend of November 2, and was seeing them out the door of the Oval Office. Waiting outside for his scheduled appointment was Senator John Dempsey.

"Hello, John." William offered his hand and a smile of genuine affection.

"Hello, Mr. President," came the older man's reply, as they went in and shut the door.

"Let's sit together by the fireplace. What can I do today for the senior senator from Ohio?" The president sat down in a wingback chair, as did the senator.

"Well, I want to thank you again for campaigning with us a month ago," Dempsey began. "I don't want to get ahead of myself, but the polls show that I've got about a seven-point lead, and I'm grateful to you."

"I'm flattered you consider my involvement an asset. In some districts my presence at a campaign rally is considered the kiss of death." William laughed, but both men knew his assessment was accurate.

"I hear from around the state that most of the congressional races are within a few points of being dead even. What does the picture look like nationally?" Dempsey asked.

"We've pulled up a bit. I think there's been a tremendous amount of one-on-one persuasion. It's starting to show, as people really consider the implication of voting against a biblical view of the world. Our biggest problem right now seems to be that many, many people, when confronted with the choice, still want to sidestep it. Unlike the Israelites before Joshua, our voters can do that just by not voting at all."

"And, Mr. President, despite all you've done, I still hear people say that they believe strongly in God but they don't want to drag him into politics or national government."

"Which is just a vote for the other side," the president said.

"If you can't beat 'em, confuse 'em."

"I guess that's been Satan's motto since day one."

"Yes, you're right. But hey, I had a more specific reason to ask to see you today," Senator Dempsey said, reaching into his coat pocket. He took out three audio cassettes and an envelope, which he held out to the president.

"Here. Take these. I told you I'd give them to you on the last day either of us is in public office. Well, today isn't that day, but you're not the same man I talked to then, either. I've seen enough to know that only the Holy Spirit could do in you what's obviously been done, and I don't want these tapes hanging around where they might cause some embarrassment. That's the affidavit plus the original tape and the only two copies I ever made."

William slowly took the tapes and the envelope. "John, thank you. And thank you for being tough with an unbelieving president who was about to do some very stupid things, and would have, if you hadn't brought him up short with these."

"We all can change, William. Thank God that he can do that. And I hope you destroy all of those before the sun sets today."

"You can count on it. And God *is* amazing, isn't he? Think how far we've come in less than two years. The interesting thing is, if I had known and believed then, before our election, what I know and believe now, I probably would never have run for office."

"God's timing is perfect, William."

ATLANTA Eunice Porter answered the knock at the door of her apartment. It was Sally Kramer. She opened the door and stepped back. "Come on in."

"Thanks," Sally said as she took off her light coat. She sat down on the couch and opened her shoulder bag. "Here, I've got your train tickets. You go up on Saturday evening, November 2. You arrive on Sunday and they do it on Monday. I just did the same thing, and it's a piece of cake."

Eunice sat down beside Sally and took the tickets. "Thanks. I've got a question, though. Will they pay for me to have someone stay here with the kids at night if I'm gone that long?"

"I don't know, but I'll ask. I think they should, since it's so far for you to go. Or I can stay with them when your sister's not here."

"And where is this place?"

"It's the Burroughs Clinic, located on 110th Street. The people are real nice. They'll put you up in a hotel nearby. I tell you, there's nothing to it. I came back the next day with my money."

Just then the phone rang on the table next to the couch, and Eunice answered it.

"Hello, Eunice, this is Rebecca Harrison. Listen, I'd like to see you if I could."

"I'm not scheduled for another appointment for a week."

"Well, can I come see you there?"

"I...uh, I don't think so. Can't you just tell me what you want to talk about?"

"Well, I'd rather see you in person. But, Eunice, I think I've figured out, with the help of our computer guy, that last year when you had your abortion, the organs of that baby were transferred out of here and maybe sold. Is that true?"

Nervous because Sally was sitting with her, Eunice stalled. "Why do you say that?"

"Well, my friend started looking at all the records—I asked him to—and he finally hit upon a pattern of you or other women coming in for an abortion, all done by the same doctor, and then a completely different medical record appearing later the same night indicating that a transfer of organs was made with the permission of another mother, due to an accidental death. But none of those records check out in the details of the deaths. The mothers have turned out to be fictitious, as far as we can tell, and each one happened the same evening as one of these abortions. Now I realize those abortions were legal then, but selling the body parts was and is illegal, to prevent unscrupulous doctors from creating baby-parts factories from aborted babies. Is that what you were doing, Eunice?"

"I, uh, I don't...no, not really. At least I don't know. Listen, I gotta go, and I don't think it's really any of your business, anyway, my personal life."

"I'm sorry, Eunice, but if that's what was going on, it very much *is* my business. And, if it's true, now that these abortions are again illegal, I think I understand why you want a baby of your own so soon."

"Please, just leave it alone."

"I wish I could, but that's not possible. I'm going to dig a bit deeper and see what turns up. If you ever want to talk to me, I think you've got my numbers, don't you?"

"Yeah, somewhere. But I won't. Please, just forget it."

"I'll call you back if I learn something new. Call me anytime. Goodbye."

Eunice hung up. Sally had taken an interest in the call and now looked questioningly at her friend. "Who was that?"

"That nurse, Ms. Harrison. You know. She said she's figured out about the abortions last year and is going to keep digging into it further. You heard me tell her to drop it, but I don't think she will."

"I'd better tell Dr. Thompson."

"Yeah. Maybe he can stop her or something. At least she doesn't think it's still going on, with the law changed. She thinks I want *this* baby because of that abortion." Eunice looked down at her extended abdomen and ran her hand over it. Just then the baby kicked, and she felt the same cold chill that had racked her with every single kick since she'd seen the boy on the ultrasound. She closed her eyes, trying not to feel the emotional pain and wishing she didn't owe the doctor five hundred dollars or need five thousand.

"Okay, well I'd better go and give him a call. I think you're all set. You should have your money in about two weeks." She stood up and put on her coat. "Call me if you have any questions. All right?"

"Yeah, sure. I'll call. And let me know about them paying for a sitter. I try to be a responsible mother."

OFF NORFOLK The *Fortson* had spent the previous weekend on recruiting detail in Boston, and the ship had then operated with a Canadian squadron for three days before returning to her home port that Friday afternoon. As they neared the sea buoy, Teri Slocum found Hugh Harrison in the combat information center behind the bridge.

"Here are the reports the shipyard needs to prepare for the removal of the fire control radars in January, and these are some personnel evaluations for your review," she said, handing the stack of paper to her department head.

"We should be able to see land," Hugh said, glancing at the surface search radar. "If you've got a minute, let's go outside."

"Sure," she answered, and they walked out through the bridge to the port bridge wing, where it was sunny and protected from the wind. Teri leaned against the captain's chair, letting the fresh air revive her. "I had the midwatch this morning, I can use a little sunshine right now."

"Good," Hugh responded, glancing through the papers she had given him. "I hate to see this ship made into scrap. But the radars on the new ones can nail a fly at over a hundred miles. Are you going to transfer to one?"

Teri smiled. "Well, frankly, no. I think after more than eighteen months on board, including one deployment, I'm ready for a change. Shore duty doesn't look too bad now."

Hugh paused, thinking of the decisions he had made as a junior officer when he was about Teri's age. He lowered the papers to his side and looked out at the Virginia coast. "Now that you've actually been stationed on a combat ship, do you think you'll stay in?" he asked.

She thought for a moment and then looked over at him, shielding the sun from her eyes with her hand. "You know, I've thought a lot about it, and to be very truthful, the answer is probably no."

Hugh turned toward her. "Why not?"

"I guess for all the same reasons that a lot of guys don't stay in—the long periods at sea. The pay. The difficulty in starting, or keeping, a family. The navy is definitely not easy. I can't imagine how a married man does it, much less a married woman."

"It's definitely not easy. But where else could we be doing what we're doing? And have so much fun with such wonderful people!"

"You know, Hugh, I used to think exactly that, too. But you want to hear something really ironic? I don't think *that* navy is going to exist much longer. The final irony is in all the navy's had to go through to make it compatible for us women and gays and lesbians, all this worry about who said what and why and who thinks what—all that stuff—it's changed the navy from what it must have been before all this started."

Hugh began to speak, but she raised her hand. "I know, I know—I'm one of the women who wanted in, and now it sounds like I'm griping. Well, I guess in a way I am—not at you, Hugh, or most of the men in this outfit. It's just that I never realized what we'd all have to go through in order to make this change—not just us—I mean what the navy itself would have to go through. Hugh, man or woman, I don't want to be on a ship where someone is checking on the correctness of your thoughts; and no one can tell jokes; and a hug is either an invitation to instant sex or sexual harassment; and nobody knows which is which without a referee. I mean, it's just crazy! This isn't the navy I wanted to be in, and I realize—how much I realize!— that it's partly my fault, mine and others like me. It's a mess, Hugh. I don't know what to do, and sometimes I feel terrible about it."

Hugh looked out at sea and then back at Teri. "Boy, ask a simple question..." He grinned. Then his expression grew serious. "You're probably going to think this is a dumb response, but hear me out. Trust the Lord on this one. And vote next month for Sandra Clayton. She's the one from our district who I think has her head on straight and can help William straighten this stuff out. We certainly can't! We're supposed to get in from that recruiting weekend in New York by Tuesday morning, so we should have plenty of time to vote."

"I hope and pray it's that easy, Hugh. I know you pray a lot. Maybe sometime I could come to your church with you and Jennifer."

"Sure. Come this Sunday. We'd love to have you."

"I'll think about it. And I probably will vote for Sandra Clayton. I think the country could use a good dose of her common sense."

"I know the navy certainly could."

THE STRAITS OF GIBRALTAR While the *Fortson* made her way into Norfolk, the *Bright Star* was just leaving the Mediterranean Sea on a beautiful and full-moon October evening. As the freighter broke out of her home for the previous three years and headed out into the Atlantic, Sadim and Kolikov joined the captain on the bridge, the excitement evident among every member of the hand-picked and well-trained crew.

"Ten days and we're in America," Kolikov stated more to himself than to either of his companions, the dim red lights from the gyrocompass repeater reflecting in his face.

"With holy work to do," Sadim quietly reminded him.

"Yes, of course," Kolikov replied, though they knew the Russian did not share their faith and had worked with Sadim for these years because of steady deposits into his bank account in Switzerland, not because of religious fervor or need for revenge.

"We seem to have been blessed," Sadim continued, "and your work appears to have gone well. We have installed the best equipment and trained long hours. The result is now out of our hands."

There was silence among the three of them for several minutes as the *Bright Star* left Gibraltar behind and plowed westward with its deadly cargo.

"Tell me, Sadim," Kolikov finally asked. "Why did we have to hurry to gain these weeks?"

Sadim smiled in the dark. "Because of the gift President Harrison gave us with his special challenge for the American elections. You see, our original plan to appear at their Thanksgiving holiday and to demand our rights, including the return of the land Israel stole from us, was good. But now we can bargain for those *plus* the election of a Congress that will be truly sympathetic to our needs, because it will not be dominated by either Christians or Jews! We will get rid of Harrison, gain our demands, and elect people who neither know nor revere their Bible. It's truly a gift for us!

"And the best thing is that while they could theoretically double-cross us on the other demands, even with our deadly threat, they can neither postpone nor undo their election. Once someone is elected, even under strained circumstances, he will remain elected. So in the long run we should gain even more tangible results from the people we help to elect."

"I see," Kolikov replied. "Yes, I see. You are right. And it does sound like it will work well."

"We shall see," Sadim said quietly. "We shall see."

27

Friday, November 1
Two Weeks Later

EAST OF NEW YORK The *Bright Star* arrived early at the designated coordinates and loitered for two days until rendezvousing with its much smaller back-up ship, the *New Dawn*, an ocean-going yacht outfitted with two sleek small boats and a helicopter. The two ships ran alongside each other for over an hour, passing messages by low-power, coded radio. Once their discussions were finished, Sadim waved to his old friend and counterpart on the smaller ship, knowing they would be together to celebrate their victory by the following Tuesday night.

As the ships opened up a more comfortable distance between them and turned toward their target, Sadim reflected on the news passed to them from Wafik. He would be in New York City by that afternoon and in position to observe the harbor from an office he had rented for just this purpose the previous month. Although the election polls were narrowing, the consensus still seemed to be that an anti-Christian majority would be elected, which made Sadim even more certain that their special "nudge" would insure that result. But the best news from Wafik that morning was that President Harrison himself would be in New York that Monday morning for a final rally, a gift Sadim considered to be a divine signal of blessing from heaven.

He will turn and run like the coward that he and his Christian blasphemers are! And then the victory for us will be all the greater!

The most important weekend of Sadim's life, the culmination of all he had dreamed of and worked for over the past twenty years, was beginning very well indeed.

ATLANTA Rebecca felt a little intimidated, but her anger kept her going. She had been sitting alone in her car in the staff parking garage attached to Peachtree North Hospital. It was very early, but she'd already been there thirty minutes. She hoped, as she waited across from Harvey Thompson's assigned space, that it would not take too long.

A few minutes later Dr. Thompson swung his European touring car into his space and opened the driver's door. Rebecca quietly did the same. He picked up a briefcase from the back seat and then closed the door. Rebecca walked across the concrete deck toward him.

"Dr. Thompson?"

He looked up quickly and frowned, then tried to smile. "Oh. Hello, Ms. Harrison...I, uh, understand you've been trying to call me."

She reached him, and they stood together next to his car. "Yes. For two weeks. I'm glad to know that you at least got the messages, even if you didn't return my calls."

He smiled again. "Sorry. I was on vacation until Wednesday, then yesterday was crazy. This is a little strange, here. What can I do for you that's so important we have to meet in the parking garage?"

"You can tell me about Eunice Porter and Sally Kramer and what I think was a business to abort full-term babies and then sell their vital organs to out-of-state recipients."

Rebecca watched his face, but no surprise registered. "Those are pretty strong statements, Nurse Harrison. What makes you think that of me?"

She told him about her record-check with Alex and then about his finding the coincidences with the organ transplant entries on the same days.

"I'm afraid you've jumped to some pretty wild conclusions based on nothing more than coincidence. You should be careful what you say about people, particularly professionals with reputations."

"That's why I've been trying to see you all this time to find out if you have any explanation first before I start checking with the individuals involved."

"I see. Well, you know those abortions were completely legal at the time and will be again soon, if either we win our case next month or your brother is defeated on Tuesday as we all expect him to be."

"Selling body parts from abortions of any term was and is against the law," Rebecca said firmly.

"So you plan to be a good detective and uncover a nefarious ring of baby killers? You should stick to nursing."

"I will. But I've been around babies all my life, and it's been bad enough to see them killed for convenience—killing them for money just might get me real angry."

"I see." He turned and started walking toward the elevator lobby. Rebecca followed. He continued, "And what about the other babies who might have been tremendously helped—even had their lives saved—by such a hypothetical transplant? Don't they need some protection under the law? Does your joy for them equal your anger for the others?"

"I guess I'm happy for them in one sense, but I'm upset at doctors who would break the law and play God for profit."

"If this ever actually happened, as you allege."

"Yes."

They reached the elevators. He pushed the button and turned to face her. "Ms. Harrison, let me suggest that no one, particularly a district attorney, is going to care one bit about something—even if it ever really happened—that between the courts and the election on Tuesday should be completely legal by the time you could get around to saying anything about it. Both full-term abortion and the donating of critical organs from abortions to those in verified need are in the vice president's platform. I think it's a foregone conclusion that your brother will not be our president much longer. So I suggest you just let this rest. Detective work is sometimes dangerous business, and even if you turn out to be brilliant at it, no one will care. Now, I've got several early operations waiting, so if you'll excuse me..."

He walked into the elevator, turned and smiled silently at her while the doors closed.

WASHINGTON "I hate to be away from you for these days, Carrie," William said as he buttoned his shirt that morning in their dressing room. "But if we were to lose on Tuesday by a slim margin, I'd feel terrible that we didn't give it all we had at the end, especially with Patricia's rally at the Jefferson Memorial."

"I know. And two of us can be in twice as many places."

"It's wonderful of you to do this, Carrie."

"Hey, I've kinda gotten used to living here. I'm not ready to leave after only two years. And think what will be possible when a godly Congress is elected!"

"I like your enthusiasm, dear," William said, giving her a hug. "I'm leaving in a minute—I'll grab breakfast on the plane. We start in Dallas and work around the coast all weekend at dinners and rallies. I'll get to New York on Sunday night, and we'll have the last big rally in Central Park at noon, when you're in Chicago. Then we'll collapse back here together Monday night."

"You know Katherine will be in New York at the same time with Mary and Sarah, attending that hearing on the sex education computer. Too bad you can't get together."

"Now that she's escaped most of the Secret Service hassles at college, I'm sure the last thing she wants is to see me in New York! No, let's just let her be a private citizen with her aunt."

"You're probably right. Well, God bless you, William. It's been a wonderful joy since June a year ago, whatever happens on Tuesday."

He enfolded her in his arms again. "You're right, Carrie. And what a miracle you are. None of this would have happened without your prayers and your help." He kissed her, then let her go. "See you Monday night."

As she watched him go she felt an odd uneasiness. It settled over her like a dark cloud, and she found herself trembling. Quickly she knelt by their bed, giving her family once again to the Lord for his protection.

NEW YORK The *Fortson* steamed into New York harbor that morning and moved up the Hudson River to a berth at the Forty-sixth Street pier next to the ships of the USS *Intrepid* Museum. As was now their standard routine for these recruiting weekends, the crew secured all the electronic gear and put away anything that might easily walk off with a visitor. At noon, with all the ship's systems turned off, two-thirds of the crew went on liberty in the Big Apple, while the other third prepared to open key parts of the cruiser to visitors starting at two that afternoon. The ship would be open all day Saturday and Sunday. They were scheduled to depart Monday at eleven for the trip back to Norfolk.

Early that afternoon Wafik arrived in New York on the shuttle from Washington. He took a taxi to Two World Trade Center at the Battery, where he had leased an office wrapping around the southwest corner of the ninety-eighth floor, giving him a commanding view of the entire harbor. Since he had paid in advance, no one questioned why the office had been vacant for the first month. Now Wafik carried a designer duffel bag that contained food, a camp chair, sleeping bag, lap-top computer, three cellular phones, binoculars, a walkie-talkie, and more.

He set up his command post and surveyed the harbor and rivers below. He was pleased to confirm that he could see everything that moved from the mouth of the Hudson River on the west around the harbor and up a portion of the east side. And he was particularly pleased that the only ship tied up at the docks at the Governor's Island Coast Guard Station, just off the tip of the Battery, was an unarmed buoy tender.

But as strategically placed as the office was for watching the harbor, it was not possible to see very far up the Hudson River, because One World Trade Center, located just to the northwest, blocked the view in that direction; the pier at Forty-sixth Street was completely out of Wafik's sight.

ATLANTA Despite her many other duties, Rebecca thought all day about what Dr. Thompson had said to her that morning. She alternated between agreeing with him that her investigation would prove fruitless and feeling outrage that he would harvest unborn children.

She finally decided late that afternoon that she had to know more. She called Eunice Porter's home number but got an answering machine and decided not to leave a message. There was the same result at Sally Kramer's home, the only other woman she felt she knew well enough to call with so little to go on. As she left for the gym, she resolved to keep trying all weekend until she reached one of them.

NEW YORK On Saturday morning the *Bright Star* and the *New Dawn* parted about fifty miles offshore, and the larger ship continued toward New York harbor with its nearly three-quarter megaton, Soviet-built nuclear warhead. The cabin cruiser slowed and followed the same course an hour later at a reduced speed.

In the early afternoon the freighter's captain radioed the harbor pilots' office; the ship was expected. The customary paperwork had been filed a week earlier by an agent acting at the request of a shell corporation in Cyprus, set up years before by Wafik. A harbor pilot was dispatched to meet the ship and guide it to an anchorage, instead of a pier, which the captain had requested in order to perform some repairs on the steering motors. A coded fax received by Sadim in the *Bright Star's* command center, one level below the bridge, confirmed from Wafik that everything in the harbor appeared to be normal.

An hour later the New York harbor pilot arrived on the bridge, and the captain nonchalantly mentioned that if there was a choice, this being their first and probably only stop in the famous American port, the crew would like an anchorage as close to the bright lights at the end of Manhattan as possible, while they remained on board and made their repairs. The pilot was an obliging man. Soon, after navigating the lower harbor and the Narrows, they dropped anchor at a location just south of Governor's Island in upper New York Harbor, off the southeastern tip of the nation's most expensive real estate.

ATLANTA Rebecca called both Eunice and Sally all during the morning between running errands. By early afternoon she was frustrated by the lack of an answer. She told herself that Eunice or her sister had to be home at supper time to cook for her children, and she decided that she would head over to the address she had copied down on Friday and wait, as she had done for

Harvey Thompson, if there was still no answer by five.

When the call from her car at that hour produced no results and a check with the hospital confirmed that Eunice was not in the maternity ward, Rebecca shook her head and turned toward the street where Eunice's family lived.

On arriving she knocked at the door of the townhouse apartment. When there was no answer she returned to her car to wait. *Detective work seems to include a lot of sitting,* she thought. *But there's no way I'm going to stay here past dark.*

She didn't have to wait nearly that long. Soon in the rearview mirror she saw Sally Kramer walking up the sidewalk with two small children who were about the ages of Eunice's kids. As the three of them neared the steps to the townhouse, Rebecca left her car and walked over to them.

"Hello, Ms. Kramer," Rebecca said with a smile.

Sally, who had been fumbling with the unfamiliar keys, hadn't noticed her approach and was clearly surprised. So much so that she dropped the set of keys. "Oh, hello. Shoot. Uh, hi, Ms. Harrison. What are...why are you here?"

"I've been trying to find you or Eunice all day. Are these her children? They're precious!"

"Mommy's gone to Newark!" the older child blurted out before Sally could silence him.

"Newark?" Rebecca said, bending down and smiling, but glancing up at Sally as well. "What's in Newark?"

"The State of Liberty!" he said, and stood still with his hand raised like the famous statue in New York harbor.

"Oh, New York. Your mother's gone to New York?"

They both smiled and nodded.

Rebecca stood up and looked at Sally, who was quickly trying to put the right key in the lock to get away from their inquisitor. "How could she fly to New York? She's nine months pregnant."

"Mommy took the train. We waved bye-bye!"

Rebecca bent down again and smiled. "Really? Great! Where is your Mommy going in New York?"

"To the hosbitil."

"The hospital?" Rebecca repeated, suddenly concerned. "Why?"

As Sally finally opened the door, the little boy said, "I don't know."

Rebecca stood in the way as Sally opened the door and tried to maneuver the children inside. "Sally, why is Eunice going to a hospital in New York? And—where's *your* baby?"

"Do you have a baby?" Eunice's boy asked.

"No, I don't have no baby!"

Sally pushed the boy inside and reached for his little sister.

"Sally, what happened to your baby?"

"Nothing. Now go on, Ms. Harrison. I've got these kids to tend to, and it's getting late."

"Sally, what happened? Did you have an abortion?"

The way Sally stared at her, Rebecca knew the answer.

"And Eunice. She's gone to New York to get an abortion?"

Sally's eyes spoke all Rebecca needed to know.

"For Doctor Thompson?"

As if in a daze, Sally nodded her head almost imperceptibly.

"Where?"

This time there was no response at all. Sally started to close the screen door, but Rebecca held it with her hand.

"Where?"

Rebecca could just barely hear the whispered answer, "The Burroughs Clinic. Now please, go."

Sally pulled the children inside and closed the door. Rebecca turned and bounded down the steps. On the way to her apartment she called and made airline reservations.

NEW YORK   Sunday morning Wafik awoke at seven and immediately scanned the harbor and its approaches as he had done almost continuously during the previous day and every two hours at night. Everything appeared to be normal at this slowest point in the weekly cycle of commerce. He pushed a button on his laptop and faxed a coded message of "all clear" to the ship by transceiver.

Then he focused in on the *Bright Star* and could clearly make out the crew erecting, aft of the bridge, the prefit parts of the tower superstructure onto which the bomb would be lifted. Kolikov had told the Council that the device would have its greatest destructive impact if it was placed outside the freighter's hull and as high above the water line as comfortably possible.

From the ship's anchored position Wafik was able to estimate, using his map of the city and the briefing Kolikov had given them two years earlier, that the bomb would virtually vaporize everything surrounding the harbor, knock great chunks out of buildings as far north as Twenty-fourth Street, and cause death and massive destruction from intense heat and hurricane force winds to anything unprotected just south of Central Park. A similar fate awaited Brooklyn, Queens, and near-in New Jersey, parts of which were actually closer to the anchorage than Manhattan. The lingering effects of the radiation from the cloud and the harbor water would doom many more, depending on which way the wind and the currents happened to be moving when Sadim detonated the bomb. Wafik smiled.

Rebecca had stopped by the hospital for a few things that Sunday morning and then caught a flight from Atlanta that arrived at LaGuardia Airport right on schedule. As she stood by the baggage carousel she was surprised to see her older sister Mary and her two nieces, Sarah and Katherine, waiting by the next carousel, along with two men whom she knew must be Secret Service agents.

They were as surprised as Rebecca, and after their initial greetings, Mary asked Rebecca why she was in New York. "It's a long story, which I'll tell you on the way into the city. You want to share a taxi?"

"The Secret Service makes us take a limousine with Katherine here," Mary said, smiling. Rebecca curtsied to Katherine as if she were royalty.

"Come with us, Aunt Rebecca." Katherine laughed. "I try to dump them, but they won't leave. I promise this is *all* we have to put up with."

"Hey, I never turn down a limo ride!" Rebecca said.

"Do you have a place to stay?" Mary asked.

"Not yet. This all happened so fast. I figured I'd just wing it and find something when I got here."

"Well, come stay with us at the Trenton on the Battery. It's also where we have to testify tomorrow. We reserved a suite, and there's plenty of room for one more member of the family."

"Yes, please Aunt Rebecca," Sarah added.

"Thanks," Rebecca said. "The Battery's a bit of a trek from where I need to go, but I'd love to join you."

"And Dad's going to be staying at the Park Empire off of Central Park tonight for the rally at noon tomorrow," Katherine said. "But we'll have to miss most of it because our testimony is scheduled for eleven."

Mary saw their bags and pointed them out to a Secret Service agent, who retrieved them. "You know, I talked to Hugh last weekend, and I think his ship is supposed to be in New York now on some kind of recruiting trip or something. I wonder where they'll be?"

"In the water," Sarah laughed.

Mary pretended to put her bag down on her daughter's toe. "I'll never know how I managed to get such a brilliant daughter." Then she said, as they moved toward the exit, "Isn't it funny that all four of us are together in New York at the same time?"

On the drive to Manhattan, Rebecca explained her reason for coming to New York, and her family was shocked and concerned for Eunice and her baby. At Rebecca's request the limousine and the car following it detoured to the address for the Burroughs Clinic, which Rebecca had discovered from a directory in her office. The mid-size building was located in the middle of a block on East 110th Street, just northeast of Central Park. Her directory had mentioned that the building had been a small hospital for the neighborhood in earlier times, converted fifteen years ago to doctors' offices specializing in Ob/Gyn and family practice.

Rebecca asked the driver to slow down as she looked for and found a small coffee shop across the street from the clinic. Though it was closed on Sunday, the sign said that Harry's Diner opened at seven on Monday morning, and Rebecca planned to be sitting there with a good view of the front door of the clinic.

In the early evening, covered by the large number of pleasure craft in the water that Sunday, two small boats from the *New Dawn* made their first run in from the large yacht, which was holding its position in international waters just outside the twelve-mile limit. As darkness fell they took approximately half the crew from the *Bright Star* out to the safety of the second vessel.

Sadim watched the boats depart. Then he turned again toward the towering Manhattan skyline as thousands of lights came on, seeming so close that he could reach out and touch them. But the beauty only fanned the flame of hatred in Sadim's heart. *These blasphemous people have lived in abundance while my people have died daily in putrid camps! Allah demands justice! He shall have it on Tuesday! How different this place will look in forty-eight hours! Revenge for injustice is coming, you lovers of Israel!*

William arrived in New York late that evening from a dinner and speech in Philadelphia, transported by helicopters that landed at the southern end of Central Park. The president and Jerry Richardson were surrounded by Secret Service agents and New York City police as they walked the short distance through the park to the Park Empire Hotel. The small group in the press pool traveling with them dispersed to other nearby hotels. Leslie Sloane took a taxi to Ryan Denning's apartment.

He opened the door and gave her a big smile. "Boy, am I glad to see you."

Leslie walked in with her overnight bag after giving him a quick hello peck on the cheek. "I'm glad to be here, but I'm really exhausted."

"I'll bet. The president's been on a whirlwind. Would you like a glass of wine?"

"Sure. And let me change clothes."

An hour later, after a light dinner, the two sat together in his living room. Ever since their confrontation over Joe Wood's speech six weeks earlier, their relationship had not been the same. They'd gone through the motions and even joked about the conversation. But it was obvious to both of them that Leslie in particular wasn't happy. Ryan broached the subject that was on both their minds.

"Have you talked to your mother this week about the wedding?"

Leslie swirled her third glass of wine and thought for a moment. "Ryan, I think I want to postpone the wedding until after the first of the year. This campaign coverage has really drained me, and Christmas is coming up. I just can't think about all I have to do right now. Would you mind?"

Ryan had expected worse. "Well, no, I guess not. I just want us to be married and living together as soon as we can. But mainly I want you to be happy. So it's fine. We just need to let everyone know. When were you thinking about?"

"I'm not sure. Maybe in late January."

"Fine. We can make some calls tomorrow. Are you all right?"

"Yeah, I'm fine. Just tired. I'll be okay." She smiled.

They spoke together for another thirty minutes, the tension between them reduced. But the other shoe dropped for Ryan when Leslie, at her insistence, spent the night alone on the couch in his living room.

William and Jerry were up in the living room of the president's suite late that night reviewing the schedule for their final day of campaigning when the telephone rang. Jerry answered it. He listened and then hung up with a "Thanks, Brad."

Jerry turned to William and said with a grin, "That was Bradley Fullerton in Washington. They just got the results from the weekend's instant poll, and for the first time we're neck and neck—dead even! Isn't that great?"

William smiled, sat back, and rubbed his tired eyes. "All those people... all those people going one-on-one with their neighbors and co-workers. That's what's doing it, Jerry. Not us."

"I know, and God knows, but at least we've helped provide some direction and vision," Jerry answered.

"'Where there is no vision, the people perish,'" William quoted.

"What?"

"Oh, I was just agreeing with you. It's out of Proverbs."

"Sounds accurate to me. You were wonderful today at giving vision. And tomorrow across the street is the last act."

William smiled again. "Thank God. Then it's up to the people to vote, just like Joshua asked his people...Jerry, do you think we'll win?"

The chief of staff thought for a moment. "It depends on the turnout. I'd like to think our people outnumber the rest, but if they don't turn out and vote, we'll lose."

"We can't lose, Jerry. *We can't.* The consequences for our nation and our children are just too awful."

"So we'll give it one more push tomorrow, then turn it over to God."

"That's right, Jerry. That's right."

The Church must take right ground in regard to politics.... The time has come that Christians must vote for honest men, and take consistent ground in politics or the Lord will curse them.... God cannot sustain this free and blessed country, which we love and pray for, unless the Church will take right ground. Politics are a part of religion in such a country as this, and Christians must do their duty to the country as a part of their duty to God.

CHARLES FINNEY
NINETEENTH CENTURY MINISTER AND LAWYER

28

Monday, November 4
The Next Day

NEW YORK HARBOR The remaining crew of the *Bright Star* was up early that morning, long before sunrise. They opened the main cargo hold and, following Kolikov's directions, used the ship's cranes to slowly raise the nuclear device to its final resting place on a platform twenty feet above the deck.

While the aft crane was used to unfold the helicopter landing platform on the stern, Kolikov and two assistants carefully checked again all the connections to the bomb, including the heavy power cord to the special generators that would create the necessary electrical surge. After everything checked out visually, Kolikov moved to the command center one level below the bridge and rechecked every system, including their special defensive sensors, by computer.

When every system checked perfectly he confirmed that fact to the bridge, where Sadim was watching the two fast boats from the *New Dawn* approach from the south. Forty minutes later the boats departed with the remainder of the crew, leaving only Sadim, Kolikov, the captain, and the chief engineer on board. Sadim carried a device just a little larger than a shoebox with which, once the generators were powered up, the bomb could be detonated instantly. He only had to push two buttons simultaneously. As the sun arched above the skyline, the Council's complex plan was fully operational, and Sadim faxed their status to Wafik by coded message. Then he thanked Allah for allowing him to give his life, if necessary, for their righteous cause.

MANHATTAN Rebecca rose early that morning and, without waking Mary or her nieces, dressed and caught a taxi for the long ride uptown. Just as Harry's Diner opened she walked in and took a table right by the front window. She ordered the first of what she imagined would be many cups of coffee and began her vigil across from the front door of the Burroughs Clinic.

At eight the crew of the Fortson raised the colors and began counting down the final three hours of their now very familiar getting underway checklist.

William rose that morning in the Park Empire Hotel and immediately knelt next to his bed.

Mary and the two cousins rose at that hour and dressed in fashionable but conservative suits for their testimony later that morning before the AIDS Education Selection Panel, scheduled to meet in the Grand Ballroom of the Trenton Hotel. When all three women were ready, they took the elevator down to the main hotel restaurant for breakfast.

As nine o'clock approached, Rebecca was worried that something had gone wrong, that she had the wrong place or that Eunice had used a back entrance. An hour earlier she had switched to decaf, and she actually found herself praying that God would help her.

Just before nine her prayer was answered. She looked up from her mug to see a very pregnant Eunice Porter walking slowly down the sidewalk toward the front door of the clinic. Rebecca quickly handed the waitress, with whom she had become well acquainted, a ten-dollar bill and told her she hoped to be right back.

Eunice was looking at the brownstone building in the bright morning sun and didn't see Rebecca approaching from across the now busy street.

Almost next to her as she reached the steps of the clinic, Rebecca said, "Eunice. How are you?"

Eunice turned and shielded her eyes with her hands. Her face revealed the surprise at seeing Rebecca Harrison at the Burroughs Clinic on 110th Street in New York. "What?...Why?...What are you doing here?"

Rebecca smiled. "I came for you and for your baby."

Eunice frowned. "I...well, I'm here 'cause I have to be...to take care of business that I can't do in Atlanta any more. So, if you'll excuse me, I'm sorry you came all this way."

Rebecca moved slightly between Eunice and the steps. "Eunice, I know all about Dr. Thompson and the abortions and him paying you. Please, just come across the street to the diner and have a cup of coffee with me, and let's talk for a minute about your options."

"But my appointment's at nine and I'm not supposed to drink anything."

Taking her arm gently, Rebecca said, "Oh, you can be a few minutes late. Come on, we won't be long. You can have some water. I've come a long way just to spend ten minutes with you. Please."

"All right, but just for a few minutes. I don't have much time." She patted her stomach, as Rebecca began walking with her to a crossing.

William was giving his usual speech that morning at the breakfast fundraiser at the Park Empire Hotel. Leslie noted from the back of the room that this morning he seemed to be filled with unusual energy and made his points about the nation's biblical foundations really well. *Or maybe I'm just finally ready to hear him.* That thought surprised her so much that she almost spilled the coffee she was sipping. She visibly shook her head and frowned. *I've just been listening to him too long!*

As Hugh and Teri met in the passageway outside the wardroom, Hugh said, "The captain asked me to remind you not to turn on any of your radars until we're well into the lower harbor. He doesn't want any network television shows fried by our presence!"

Teri smiled. "Aye, aye, sir."

Eunice and Rebecca had been sitting for almost twenty minutes in Harry's Diner. Rebecca told Eunice enough to convince her that she really did know all about the baby harvesting process led by Dr. Thompson, so Eunice went ahead and filled in the details from her own experience. As she did so she watched the genuine grief spread across the nurse's face, further troubling her.

As Eunice finished, including how she had asked for and received a cash down payment on this baby and how degraded she had felt when the unsuspecting father had also paid her, Rebecca reached across the table for her hand and said, "Eunice, you don't have to kill this baby."

"I...it's just a fetus."

Rebecca noted the pleading in the other woman's voice. She retrieved her purse and pulled out the ultrasound photo they had made months earlier. She handed it to Eunice. "I stopped by the hospital yesterday morning and got it for you. That was months ago, Eunice, and look how your baby has grown now! He's been growing and maturing inside you. He wants to live, not die. Don't kill him, Eunice. You're his mother."

Eunice lowered her head and looked at the picture. She was silent for a minute. Rebecca noticed the tears forming in the other woman's eyes. "But what about the money I owe them, including the train fare and hotel?" Eunice asked. "It must be close to a thousand dollars. And how can I possibly raise another child in my situation?"

Rebecca reached for her hand again. "I'm not sure, Eunice, but I *am* sure this baby is supposed to live, not die today. I'll help you with the thousand dollars, and I know people who want to adopt children, if you can't keep him. I'm not thinking much beyond this moment right now, but I *know* there are answers, right answers. And his death is not the right one."

Eunice looked up. "You'll help me? You'll talk to Dr. Thompson?"

Rebecca smiled. "You *bet* I will! I've got quite a lot to say to him, as a matter of fact. And I imagine that when I get through, not only will you not owe him any money, but he might be making a contribution to your medical bills. A substantial contribution!"

There was the beginning of a smile through the tears. "You really think I don't have to do this? Isn't it a contract or something?"

"Eunice, in the first place, what he's asked you to do is simply illegal. But far beyond that, it's immoral. You're that child's mother, his life-giver, not his executioner. Don't worry at all about Dr. Thompson. I'll handle him. You worry about your son." And she pointed again to the photo on the table.

Eunice was silent for a minute. Then she said decisively, "Well, if you'll help me, I'll do it. I'll have this son. And then you'll help me figure out what to do?"

Rebecca could hardly contain her joy. She felt like jumping up and clapping. "Yes, Eunice. I won't leave you. I promise. And we'll sort out his future once we get back to Atlanta and he decides to join us!"

Now Eunice was smiling broadly. She reached across with her other hand to hold Rebecca's between hers. "Thank you. Thank you, Ms. Harrison. I know this is right. Thank you and thank God."

"Yes, thank God."

"What do we do now?"

"Well, it's almost nine-thirty. Let's walk back to your hotel, pack your bags, and find out when the next train leaves for Atlanta. I'll call the Burroughs Clinic and tell them you won't be coming in. Then we'll head downtown for my bag and the train station."

"Oh, thank you again, Ms. Harrison. My hotel is just there at the corner."

"Please, call me Rebecca. If I'm going to be this boy's honorary god-mother, we ought to be on a first-name basis!"

"Yes. Thanks." The two women rose and left to walk the short half block to Eunice's hotel.

Precisely at nine-thirty Sadim keyed a computer connected to one of the transceivers in the command center of the *Bright Star,* and an instant later Wafik received a short encrypted fax in his high-rise observation post. The message from Sadim said to begin the operation.

Wafik smiled, gave a prayer of thanks, and touched several keys on his powerful laptop. A few moments later six other computers in remote loca-tions around the country began sending a steady stream of identical faxes to all the nation's television networks, wire services, the White House, the New York police, twenty key metropolitan newspapers, and the fax machines in the Pentagon. The message appeared virtually simultaneously in all these places and read:

> Greetings from the Council for the Liberation of Palestine, and all praise be to Allah. This message is to inform the government and people of the United States, the imperialist gangster nation which has propped up its puppet, Israel, for far too long, that on this day steps are being taken to right the wrongs done in the land of Palestine.
>
> There is a ship anchored in New York harbor which has on its deck a nuclear bomb with a yield of approximately six-tenths of a megaton. The ship is the *Bright Star,* and a red dye is being released around it to confirm its location. All authorities and individuals are warned not to come near the ship, nor to take any action which could even appear to be hostile, as any such activity will result in both retaliatory action and the possible instant detonation of the bomb without further warning.
>
> For our tormentors in the Pentagon and White House, the device is a Soviet-built weapon which was liberated from the Perzomaisk region of Ukraine several years ago and modified for our use by Soviet-trained technicians. The serial number on the bomb is A672-393-811T. We invite your verification of the records in Moscow. The *Bright Star* has been modified to provide the power necessary for detonation, and at this moment the bomb can be triggered manually by our mission leader, who is on the ship in the harbor, or automatically in case of attack. Six photos will follow this message showing close-ups of the device and of our modifications.

Within one hour *all* air traffic must cease overhead, including high-altitude commercial flights. All helicopter flights will cease in the harbor area south of 14th Street. Do not try to attack this ship. It has been fitted with the most advanced countermeasures in the world's arsenals today. In addition to sophisticated air search and surface search radar, there is passive sonar for detecting even the slightest underwater activity. Electronic equipment is scanning all military and police radio, radar, and telephone frequencies. In addition, we have visual observers in the area who are monitoring the entire harbor. Any attempt to approach or attack the *Bright Star* will produce an enormous tragedy for which we will not be responsible.

This device will not be detonated if the government and the people of the United States do the following to correct their unbalanced, prejudiced, and illegal approach to the people of Palestine:

1. The President will cause the government of Israel to release all political and so-called terrorist prisoners and transport them safely to the border with Syria by noon tomorrow. A specific list of the prisoners to be released will be sent to the White House and to the Israeli prime minister.

2. The government of the United States will abandon its opposition to the United Nations' resolutions calling for the return of all lands taken by Israel since 1967, and the U.S. government will cause the Israeli government to begin its withdrawal from these lands by noon tomorrow.

3. The people of the United States will repudiate the attempt by Christian fundamentalists to take over their government, which we would consider openly hostile to the interests of the Palestinian people. They will instead elect members to the House and Senate in tomorrow's election who are sensitive to the plight of the Palestinian people and reject a government built on the blasphemy of the Christian faith, which contradicts the teachings of the one true prophet and has criminally aided the Israeli oppressors in destroying our homelands.

We consider that the West, led by the United States, has been in a state of war with the Palestinian people for over forty years. Directly and through your agents the Israelis, the U.S. has caused untold death, destruction, and misery among our people. Tomorrow will either move our two peoples on a path towards peace and reconciliation, or else it will be a moment of supreme revenge for all the terrible injustices your nation has inflicted on us.

What happens tomorrow—peace or unspeakable destruction—is in the hands of your President, your leaders, and your people.

The choice is yours. There is no one among us to contact. No one to negotiate with, because these demands are not negotiable. If our requests are not met, then shortly after the election tomorrow night lower Manhattan and the surrounding areas will no longer exist. If the demands are met, then our peoples can build a bridge of peace together. We will be waiting to learn of your decision.

The Council

The producer and director for the *News at Noon* capsule were in the U.S. Network's headquarters on Fifty-sixth Street when the fax came in. The director called their local New York affiliate and asked the location of the station's traffic helicopter. He gave the station manager a summary of the fax and asked for his help.

Five minutes later Ryan Denning came into the newsroom to begin his workday, and the producer quickly apprised him of the situation. Then the phone rang, and the director answered it. He turned pale and put down the receiver. "There's a freighter anchored just where the fax says with a big crate sitting on a tower above the deck and dark red dye in the water all around it."

During the next fifteen minutes several of the recipients of the fax used various means to verify the existence of the freighter. The Pentagon staff quickly confirmed to Vince Harley that the serial number and pictures matched the warhead the Russians had been unable to account for in their joint destruction program with the Ukrainians.

Ryan and the director waited until 9:50 and, when the Pentagon and White House would neither confirm nor deny the accuracy of the bomb's serial number, they interrupted the network's morning talk show with a live news bulletin, read on the air by Ryan, carefully prefacing the report with the caveat that nothing in the communication had been independently verified. Within a few minutes all of the major networks had broadcast similar reports, promising to interrupt their regular programming when and if more was learned. As Ryan finished his brief report, which then replayed as a crawl at the bottom of the screen, he could hear the wail of sirens beginning on all sides of the city, and he suddenly wondered if Leslie was still with the president.

Vince Harley directed the duty officer at the national security desk in the Pentagon to alert the president. A message was sent via the top-secret White House network to the military aide carrying a communications device in the president's traveling entourage. This aide was standing with a Secret Service agent in an alcove of the hall outside the small ballroom in the hotel where the president was finishing his fund-raising breakfast, and when the special briefcase he was holding started to hum, he actually jumped. It was the first time in his eighteen months on this duty that this had happened.

He opened the case and found the micro printer inside discharging a fax with the following message:

> Flash. Top Secret. 1446Z: Castle believes there is a 60% chance that the previously threatened nuclear device under terrorist control is located on a ship in New York harbor. Verification is underway. See attached message received 1431Z. Suggest Eagle depart earliest possible time and return to House.

The printer then began to provide a copy of the original message from the Council.

The military aide was astonished and told the nearest Secret Service agent that he had to speak immediately to the president. Neither man had ever been in this position, but the agent cracked open the door to the ballroom and noticed that Jerry Richardson was standing nearby. He went in and explained that a flash message had just been received for the president. In less than a minute the chief of staff, message in hand, was approaching the podium, just as sirens started to wail outside.

"Excuse me, Mr. President," he said from a few feet away. "I'm sorry to interrupt, but something has come up that needs your attention."

The president turned to the audience of supporters who had given generously to the work of their election committee and smiled. "Well, it seems the government never rests. I have to go, but we were about to wrap up anyway. Thank you all from the bottom of our hearts, and may God bless each of you."

William waved as the audience stood and applauded. He, Jerry, and several Secret Service agents went out a side door that led to the service elevator.

"What is it?" he asked.

"The bomb we've gotten the threats about may now be here in New York harbor under the trigger finger of Arab terrorists," Jerry Richardson said. "The Pentagon received this message twenty minutes ago." He handed it to the president as the small group, plus the military aide, entered the elevator for the ride up to the president's suite. "The Pentagon wants us to leave New York immediately."

"Finally." William almost whispered. "And today of all days!"

William read the messages again as they exited and walked to the door of his suite. Only he and Jerry Richardson went inside.

When the door was closed the president walked over to the window and looked out on Central Park. He could see the platform erected for the noon rally at the edge of a huge grass field, as well as the three presidential helicopters. Silently he prayed, *Dear God, give me your strength, wisdom, and discernment.*

William turned and said, "Jerry, we don't know yet that it's for real. But if it is in fact the real thing, is the commander in chief supposed to leave a battle just because it's dangerous? There are about ten million people in this city, and most of them don't have helicopters. If this turns out to be for real, then my place is here."

"William, come on. This isn't a battle! These could be fanatics who'll trigger the bomb no matter what we do. You've got to get out so that, God forbid, you can help with whatever comes next. Please get your things and let's go back to Washington as fast as we can, in case this *is* for real."

"You go, Jerry. I'm staying. I'm not saying forever, but at least for now, I'm staying. So have those communications people patch in some phone lines from the Situation Room in the White House—better use regular telephones with encryption if they're monitoring the military frequencies. Of course this may blow over in a little while and we can get on with our rally."

Just then there was a knock at the door. Jerry opened it and an aide entered and saluted quickly. "Sir, this just arrived." He handed William a single sheet of paper. William read it and passed it to his chief of staff. It read, "Photos check with earlier ones and appear to be real. All dates and details appear to check. Modifications are those that would be made for a static blast. Castle upgrades the probability of a real threat to 90%."

Jerry lowered the paper, his mouth turning dry. William took off his suit coat. He said calmly, "Jerry, either leave now or get to work on those communications lines. Have our helicopters leave soon but remain on standby not too far away—they may not be safe there in Central Park when word of this breaks. Tell them to wait long enough to take anyone on our team who wants to go—and that includes you. Whoever stays, tell the hotel we need this floor. I'm going into the bedroom to call Carrie. If you're back here in twenty minutes, I'll assume you're going to stay till the end. Oh, and I guess the rules require us to get the vice president on the horn and send her to the Situation Room. Ask Vince Harley to leave someone good in charge at the Pentagon and get him over to the Situation Room, too, with a direct line to here and also back to Castle. Got it?"

Jerry Richardson had jotted a few cryptic notes as William spoke. Then he looked up and nodded his head. "Yes, sir." And he was gone.

Within half an hour news of the nuclear bomb on the ship spread through the city and around the nation. In New York, everyone on Manhattan Island wanted to leave, or at least move uptown, at the same instant. Sirens could be heard in all parts of the city as the police tried to get to the tip of the Battery to cordon off the area and to do as much as they could to promote an orderly evacuation. But the streets, already crowded with incoming traffic on Monday morning, came to a near standstill as motorists, taxis, and buses tried to turn around and find the shortest escape routes across the choke points of the relatively few bridges and tunnels from the island. And equal pandemonium in neighboring Brooklyn, Queens, and Jersey City made the evacuation of Manhattan itself all the more difficult.

CHICAGO The phone in Carrie's hotel room on the lake shore rang just as her senior Secret Service agent was beginning to brief her on the situation in New York.

"Excuse me," she said and walked into her bedroom.

"Hello."

"Carrie, it's me," William said.

She was filled with relief at the sound of his voice. "Oh, William, I'm so glad. What's going on? Are you still in New York?"

"Yes. It may be interesting here before long. Palestinian extremists have finally emerged as the owners of the bomb we've worried about for so long. They aren't real happy with our policies and want us to change—plus they don't want Christians elected tomorrow."

"Oh, William. And they've got the bomb?"

"Apparently."

"What will you do?" she asked, pacing back and forth as far as the phone cord would stretch.

"We'll be talking with the Pentagon shortly. They should have the Situation Room in the White House up in about twenty minutes. They've been war gaming this problem ever since that first fax arrived, so hopefully they've got a solution. In the meantime, pray. And if they don't cancel your rally in Chicago, please ask everyone there to pray as well—tell them you've talked to me and we asked them to pray. Then please get back to Washington as soon as you can. Listen, where are Katherine, Mary, and Sarah?"

"They're staying at the Trenton, I think it is." The location suddenly dawned on her. "Right on the Battery!"

"We'll send the Secret Service to get them."

"William, Rebecca's there, too."

"*Rebecca?*"

"Yes, I talked to Katherine last night. They ran into her at the airport. She's trying to stop someone from having an abortion up there. Oh, and Hugh's there, too, on his ship."

"The *Fortson* is in New York now?"

"Yes, I think so."

"What timing. My family is all here within range of a nuclear bomb!"

"You've all got to leave."

William was silent for a moment. "Carrie, yes. Pray for us. I'll do everything I can to get the women on helicopters. But Hugh is on a ship—maybe they can help somehow. And I...well, I'm not sure I can leave."

She closed her eyes and sat down on the bed. "William..." was all she could whisper.

He filled the silence. "We'll see. We're taking each minute as it comes. I'll talk to you again. We need your prayers. Then get back to the White House, and I'll see you there."

"Yes...Oh, William, I love you."

"Carrie, I love you more than you'll ever know. Now I've got to go. God bless you, dear."

"God bless you, William."

Mary, Katherine, and Sarah had returned upstairs after their breakfast to prepare for their testimony, scheduled for eleven. As they sat and read their notes, Mary said, "I know New York is a big city, but I've never heard so many sirens!" Then there was a knock on their door.

Standing outside was Secret Service Agent Tyler Blevins, one of the team assigned to Katherine. He was calm but insistent. "Mrs. Prescott," he said, as he entered their living room, "we've just received word that there's a nuclear bomb on a ship just there off the Battery." He pointed in the general direction. "I've been ordered to get you to Central Park, from which the presidential helicopters are going to leave in an hour. We've ordered a limousine for you, so please put whatever valuables you have in your purses—leave the rest for now—and let's go downstairs."

Sarah said, "Is the hearing canceled?"

Blevins smiled. "For the time being it is. But when this all gets straightened out, I'm sure it'll be rescheduled. Now please, let's hurry."

"Do we have time to change into our jeans?" Katherine asked.

"If you really hurry," Blevins said, noticing their conservative suits and high heels. "I'll wait outside. But they've pulled the other agents up to Central Park, so I'm the only one with you now, and we're supposed to be in the park in fifty-five minutes. Please, let's roll." He turned and left as another message came across his earpiece.

The young ensign standing watch on the quarter-deck of the *Fortson* was the first on board to hear the news, when one of the longshoremen on the pier yelled it up to him, as sirens wailed past the head of the pier. He phoned both the captain and the executive officer. Two minutes later several officers were watching a news report on the wardroom television when Captain Robertson came through the door.

"Richard," he said, addressing the executive officer, "we've just received a Flash Aim High message to stay where we are and to shut down everything that could give away our identity as a United States Navy ship. Thomas," Captain Robertson turned to the operations officer, "pull the plug on every radio transmitter and search radar, even the surface search, to be sure no one turns them on by accident. Hugh, the same goes for all your fire control radars. I want this pier cleared of civilian personnel and an armed patrol posted at the end. Mount our machine guns at the railings and don't let anyone or anything come near us, from the pier or from the river. Until someone tells us otherwise, we're handling this just like a war. Prepare to be underway on five minutes notice, and we'll shift into port and starboard watches."

"If we're shut down, how will we communicate?" Dobbs asked.

"We can still receive the satellite broadcast," the captain answered, "and I imagine within an hour there'll probably be live TV coverage from the harbor. If we need to talk to somebody, they've given us two phone numbers at the Pentagon."

"You mean we use a pay phone on the pier to report?" Dobbs asked.

"You got it," the captain replied. "And in fact, that's a good thought. Put two of your radiomen at the pay phones now and call these numbers. When they get through, tell them not to hang up. We'll keep an open line back to Castle. Now, everyone, let's move, and be quick about it."

While Eunice packed, Rebecca phoned Amtrak and booked two seats on the evening train to Atlanta. As Eunice put her final things in the suitcase, the sirens and the noise outside the hotel finally caused Rebecca to turn on the television. There on virtually every station was a slightly out-of-focus picture of a ship surrounded by water that appeared to be blood red. They listened with growing concern to the newscaster while the picture of the ship bobbed up and down, indicating it was being viewed through a powerful tele-photo lens.

After ten minutes of watching the news, Rebecca and Eunice knew almost as much as the generals in the Pentagon.

"What should we do?" Eunice asked.

"I guess do our best to get to the train station. Hopefully trains will still be running. Or maybe they'll have extra trains."

Eunice looked at her suitcase. "Think we'll get a cab?"

"I don't know. Maybe you'd better take out some—"

Rebecca never finished her sentence, because just then Eunice's water broke.

HARRISBURG The news from New York began to pierce the calm and quiet of this day before a national election, when all of the country's congressmen and a third of the senators were home fighting the most unusual campaign anyone had ever seen.

About a third of the incumbents running for reelection had declared themselves to be supporters of the biblical worldview, including Congressman Trent Patterson. But his delayed announcement led many to wonder if his decision had been based more on reading the direction of the wind in his home district than on any personal sense of commitment to God.

At any rate, he and William had continued to support each other, and he had just arrived at his office after a breakfast fund raiser when his secretary told him that there was trouble in New York. Trent went into his office, hung his coat behind the door, and turned on the television. He watched for a few minutes. Then his private phone rang.

He left the television on and walked around his desk to answer the ring.

"Hello, Congressman."

"You? Why are you calling me here?"

"Because it's where you are, and I want to talk to you," Wafik said.

"Where are you?"

"It doesn't matter." In fact, Wafik was in his observation post in the World Trade Center, watching the harbor with binoculars as he spoke. He was using a relay through a radio transceiver and a seemingly out-of-order pay telephone booth to make tracing difficult.

"What do you want?"

"Please, a little more patience. Have you heard of the demands of the group with the bomb in New York harbor?"

"Yes. They just played them on television."

"Good. We want you to support them. Quickly and vocally."

"What? Hey, are you behind this...this bomb threat?"

"It doesn't matter whether we are or we aren't. The demands seem reasonable to us, and we want one of our key friends in Congress to support them, starting now, to help build a groundswell."

"But that's almost treason! And I've been supporting the president's candidates. I can't switch now."

"Yes, we noticed your lapse a few months ago. But you did continue to support our initiatives, so we let it go. Now, however, there's no time for that luxury. Both our nations need you to be a peacemaker, to help heal wounds." Then he said more sternly, "We want you to cancel your appointments and fly back to Washington now, call a press conference, and say that it's in the best interest of the United States to agree to these demands. Call other congressmen and encourage them to do the same. Start with the ones who have supported your views on the Israeli withdrawal. Do whatever you have to do to erode the president's position and to build credibility for the Palestinian alternative. I'm sure others will then rally to you."

"But that's impossible! There's a bomb threatening ten million people. I can't undermine the president at a time like this. He's my friend, and he's in New York himself!"

"Please listen very carefully," Wafik said, and pressed a button.

At first Patterson couldn't make out what he was hearing, but then he recognized his own voice in the drawing room at Wafik's villa outside Paris, laughing and thanking Wafik for the cash. As he listened, his breathing grew labored, and he sat down.

"How?" he whispered.

"Good technology, don't you agree?"

There was silence. "You want me to sell out my country, and you're prepared to ruin me if I don't."

"That's very harsh, my friend. Let's just say we want you to continue the enlightened leadership you've provided for the past several months where a more rational policy toward our people is concerned. That's all. And it's good for your nation, as well."

There was a long silence. Finally Wafik asked, "Are you still there?"

"All right...God help me. But no more, Wafik. This is it!"

"Of course," Wafik replied. "If this goes well and the right people are elected tomorrow, we won't need any more of these, shall we say, extra incentives. You'll be off the hook, as you say."

"I should hope so." And the congressman hung up. He turned to the open door of his office and said, "Cheryl, I have to go back to Washington to help deal with this thing in New York. Please book the next flight and then call all of today's appointments and tell them what's happened."

His secretary came to the door, obviously concerned. "Yes, sir. Was that the president on the phone?"

Trent stopped loading his briefcase. "No, not the president," he said, feeling a sudden hollowness in his chest.

"Well, good luck."

"Thanks. I'll probably need it."

WASHINGTON Thirty minutes later the vice president and the chairman of the Joint Chiefs arrived in the Situation Room in the basement of the White House. Patricia Barton-North was in the city for a rally planned that afternoon on the steps of the Jefferson Memorial, supporting those candidates who opposed the president's Twenty Points. The secretary of state, Lanier Parks, whom she had not seen face to face for several months, had called her in her Capitol office a little before ten, just as the news was starting to break, and asked her to join them in the White House to chair their deliberations until William could return.

Also present were Sandra Van Huyck, Ted Braxton, Michael Tate, and several of Vince Harley's aides, including an air force general and a navy admiral. Patched in by speaker phone were the President and Jerry Richardson from the Park Empire Hotel in New York.

Once they were all seated around the conference table, William spoke over the speaker phone, which had been placed in the center of the table. "Is there anything new, Vince, from your folks?"

The general leaned forward toward the device, "Only that we've again confirmed the serial numbers and photos with Moscow. Unfortunately, this one is the real thing. We're getting men in position all around the harbor to watch everything that happens, using high-powered videos. We should have live pictures in a few minutes. And we've scrambled the Delta Force, who are on their way east from San Diego in case we decide to take the ship by force."

"What do you hear from here?" William asked no one in particular.

Ted Braxton spoke up. "It's pretty bad and may be getting worse. The police have tried to secure the Battery, but, if you can believe this, there are people standing wall to wall, looking toward the *Bright Star*. The streets are a sea of jammed cars and people. It's almost impossible to move. The subway is no better. There are reports that already three people have died because they were accidentally pushed off platforms in front of trains. What can you see from your room?"

Jerry Richardson answered. "It's difficult to tell, because so much of what we see is Central Park. But people on foot have clogged every street we can see. It looks like everyone's given up on cars and is trying to walk as far from the Battery as possible. I suspect that helicopters are going to become pretty valuable and may be targets for those who want to move faster than their feet will allow. Our helicopters haven't been touched, and we've got New York police helping the Secret Service guard them. We'll be sending them off in a few minutes, as soon as the president's daughter arrives."

"Vince," the president asked, "got any quick ideas on how to deal with the *Bright Star?*"

"We've obviously got people working on it. We're looking for plans of the ship and studying every offensive possibility. Our Delta Force teams are trained to take a ship at anchor, but it sounds like these folks may have some pretty sophisticated countermeasures on board—a cut above the usual terrorist threat. We'll be studying close-ups of their deck and antennas, looking for clues of what they've got on there.

"We could probably fly a smart bomb down the stack from twenty thousand feet, but we'd have to fly overhead and then illuminate it with a laser, and we don't know whether they've got something that'll detonate the bomb if we shine a laser on them."

"If we could blow up the ship, what would happen to the bomb?" William asked.

"It almost certainly wouldn't detonate—it takes a particular blast sequence to do that. But you'd have radioactive fallout from the nuclear material all over the harbor and directly downwind. It'd be a mess, but not nearly as bad as a detonation. The best would be to destroy the man or the equipment controlling the bomb, without damaging the device itself. But that probably means putting men on board, and we just don't know if whoever's on the ship would have time to trigger it before we could stop him. Or maybe it's on some type of automatic trigger. We just don't know."

"And so, General Harley," the vice president said, "you really don't know what to do or how to do it. Is that right?"

The Chairman of the Joint Chiefs was obviously stung. "Ma'am, we've been at this just a little less than an hour. I gave the president a quick assessment. We should have several detailed contingency plans for your consideration in about two hours, at the outside."

Patricia Barton-North leaned back, frowning. Then she leaned forward again. "William, when are you coming back?"

There was a pause. "I'm not sure. There are a lot of innocent people here, including members of my family. Maybe, when we see how things are going, I'll try to come back tonight. I just don't know."

The vice president continued, "Let me play devil's advocate. Why don't we just give them what they want? The first two items concerning Israel are reasonable, anyway. And you know your candidates are not going to win the election tomorrow, so just give in now, sparing New York City. Why shouldn't we? Why kill more Americans in one instant than the Jews lost in the entire Holocaust? They'll understand."

No one spoke. Finally from the speakerphone William's voice came through. "Patricia, I almost feel that if I have to explain it, I... But I'll try. Once you give in to this kind of terrorism, it never stops. No matter what the demands are today, what might they be next time? But we can't give away Israel's security—the Golan Heights are part of the land the terrorists want. And as for the election, I won't give in for the same reason, no matter what I may feel personally, pro or con, about our candidates' chances. What happens the next time? Who threatens what to get their way at the next election? Patricia, that would be the end of our democracy."

"Come on William, this is *New York* we're talking about. This will be the end of *millions* of people. We can patch up all that other stuff after it's over. It won't be the end of the world. I say we do as they ask, get rid of this awful threat, and go on about our business."

"With you as president," Jerry Richardson added.

"That has nothing to do with it! I'm thinking about our nation and the lives of millions of people, including yours and the president's, I might add."

"That's enough," the president said. "No more talk about giving in. I don't want anyone killed or made to suffer. We didn't start this. But we can't give in to their demands or our nation—and Israel—will be finished."

"So you're not going to grant their first two requests?" she asked.

"Lanier and Sandy can talk to the Israeli Prime Minister to see if there's something we can do short of capitulating—some compromise that will make the terrorists happy. I'm not crazy. I don't want people to die."

"I see," she said. "And if the American voters tomorrow were by some chance to elect your candidates, it will cost us millions of dead?"

"Patricia, you make it sound like the bomb is my idea," the president said. "Some insane people have done this, not us. If we give in, millions more will be threatened in the Middle East. God expects us to do what's right and to trust him. We don't always know his purposes, but the quickest way to insure failure is to take a shortcut around his principles. We'll do the right thing—we won't give in to threats of violence, no matter how grave—and we'll keep trusting him, just as the leaders of this nation have done for well over two hundred years."

The vice president stood up. "Don't bring God into everything, William! It's stupid! We're talking people's *lives* here, not a tent revival! It's clear to me that our *only* hope to save New York is for *our* candidates to win tomorrow, and for us to promise now at least to consider the other two requests. I don't have time to attend any more unproductive meetings like this—I've got to spend every second insuring that sane people are elected tomorrow. William, get out of there as soon as you can, and we'll save New York at the ballot box for you! Then you can retire and write a book about how God just barely missed his chance to intervene. This, William, is the sound of the vice president leaving." She walked out and closed the door.

"She's gone," Ted Braxton said.

"It's just as well," came William's voice from New York. "This is no time for a divided house. If anyone else thinks we ought to give in or throw the election, you ought to leave now too. This isn't going to get any easier in the next few hours. We're going to be guided throughout these two days by what we know is *right*, not by what seems temporarily expedient. It's right to resist this attempt to dictate to us. It's right to hold the election. We'll do the very best we can to defuse the threat, but in the end, it really is up to God. Anyone who doesn't believe that won't last long on this team. Now, Vince, let's reconvene when your contingency plans are ready, or when anything else important comes up. Ted, think about TV—some kind of statement. We'll get you an update from up here as soon as we can."

NEW YORK   Mary Prescott waited outside the Trenton Hotel with Agent Blevins, Sarah, and Katherine for almost fifteen minutes. It was painfully clear that no limousine could make it to them, since the same cars were stopped in front of their hotel for their entire wait, and no traffic was moving at all.

"How far is it to the Park Empire Hotel?" Mary asked.

"At least eighty blocks—over four miles," Blevins answered.

Looking at the girls, she said, "Well, I don't think we're ever going to get there at this rate. I think we'd better walk. Maybe taxis are moving further uptown. Let's head in that direction."

"I think that's all we can do," Blevins agreed, wishing he'd worn different shoes and cursing the high rise buildings that made it almost impossible for his low-powered transceiver to reach anyone.

It had taken Rebecca almost ten minutes to calm Eunice down after her water broke. She lay on the bed and kept repeating, "O God, what are we gonna do now?"

Rebecca knew that reasoning with a woman in Eunice's condition was not always easy, but she also knew that they had to move out quickly, before her labor began in earnest.

"Eunice, please, let's go. The clinic is just down the street. I'm sure they'll help us. They must have good equipment. Let's go." On the fifth try, Rebecca coaxed Eunice up, and they moved slowly down the elevator and out onto the sidewalk, where there was utter pandemonium. People were running in all directions. Or they were trying to run, but the sidewalks were so crowded it was difficult. A huge man carrying a suitcase ran right into Rebecca and knocked her down. She got up quickly to keep from being trampled, and she thanked God that he hadn't hit her friend.

The two women finally made it to the door of the clinic, but it was locked. Rebecca rang the bell. No answer. Eunice grabbed her stomach and started to moan—her first contraction. Rebecca swore. She stepped back, then looked up and down the block.

"Eunice, stay here. I think this place must have a back door. I'm going to try to get in. I'll be back."

Eunice could only nod in her pain. Rebecca shoved her way along with the crowd until she reached the end of the block. She turned north and quickly walked a half block, where she found the entrance to a dark and narrow service alley which served the backs of the buildings on the two main streets.

Rebecca looked down the alley toward the back of the clinic on the left, and was relieved to see that the area appeared to be deserted. Saying a prayer, she cautiously entered the alley and then ran to the back door to the clinic. She knocked twice, but there was no answer. The glass panels of the back door were wired for a burglar alarm, but Rebecca decided that having the police come in the next few minutes would be a great improvement, so she picked up an old brick from a trash pile and threw it through the glass pane closest to the door handle, which immediately set off a loud siren. She tried to ignore the piercing sound and, her heart racing, she reached inside to unbolt the door.

Once inside, she closed the door and ran through the empty and dark ground floor, finding her way to the front door, which she opened into bright sunlight. Eunice was sitting on the steps, clutching her stomach, and Rebecca helped her stand up and walk inside. She locked the front door and asked Eunice to stay in the waiting area while she made a quick search of the building with the siren still blaring loudly all around them. The ground floor and second floor contained typical doctors' offices and examining rooms, but on the third floor she found a well-equipped operating room. *Where the abortions are performed,* she thought.

When she returned to the small elevator, her curiosity made her press the button for the one remaining floor above her. There she was immediately struck by the smell of dust and disuse. Cobwebs were everywhere. She glanced down the hall and decided that these had been overnight rooms for patients back when the facility was more of a functioning community hospital.

Rebecca returned to the ground floor and helped Eunice to stand. "You and the baby are going to be fine. There's a great operating room upstairs. I've never done a delivery in New York, but it can't be much different than in Atlanta."

Eunice appreciated her attempt at humor, but she was in too much pain to respond. As they entered the elevator, Eunice said, "I just hope he's not delivered today only to die tomorrow! And I wish that siren would—"

As if it heard her, the siren stopped, apparently connected to a timer. The silence was eerie. Then the elevator door opened, and Rebecca showed Eunice to the operating room. "Come on. Let's take one problem at a time. Right now we're going to use this abortion clinic to bring your son into the world. With that kind of start, he ought to be something else when he grows up!"

Leslie Sloane and her camera and sound men made it to the U.S. Network's headquarters building from the Park Empire Hotel in thirty minutes, stopping at several points to take footage of the huge crowds on the streets and of the completely frozen traffic.

When she arrived at the newsroom on the thirty-sixth floor, Ryan jumped up and gave her a long and genuine hug. "Hey, we've been so worried about you. Are you all right?"

Leslie collapsed into a chair in the news director's office and gladly accepted the soft drink Ryan offered.

"Yes, I'm fine. But it's crazy out there. We got some pretty good footage, if you can use it. What's the latest?"

"The mayor and police chief are of course urging everyone to stay calm—no problem!—and to evacuate at least the lower half of Manhattan, plus all of Brooklyn, Staten Island, and Jersey City. But the reality is that everyone's trying to leave who's within fifty miles of the city, and all the roads are completely jammed for as far out as anyone can check. They're trying to get some sort of emergency vehicles in to evacuate the hospitals and the elderly, but I can't imagine that there's much of a chance of that."

"It's a mess," Leslie agreed.

"Where's the president?" Ryan asked.

"When I left the Park Empire, I think he was still there. Probably by now they've left in the helicopters."

"No, they're still in Central Park."

"Really?" Leslie sat up and put down her drink. "Do you think he's *staying?*"

"I don't know. I can't imagine. Of course the rally's been canceled, but apparently the vice president's going to go ahead with hers at the Jefferson Memorial in Washington at three. In fact—" he walked over to the window as he spoke—"they want me to take one of our helicopters off the roof to Philly and then catch the Metroliner to Washington to cover it. Actually, I was just leaving when you came in. Washington is your beat, Leslie, do you want to take it?"

She thought for a minute. "The president is my beat, Ryan. If there's a chance he might stay, I'd like to try to interview him, then catch a helicopter out tonight. Will there be others going?"

"I think so," he said, still looking out the window.

She stood up. "Okay, then. I'll get my guys and head back to the Park Empire. Do you think we could get a walkie-talkie or something?"

"I'm sure they can fit you with an earpiece and transceiver for your purse. We'll see Dave."

"No, you go on. I'll take care of it." While she spoke, he moved over to her. "Ryan, you need to get to Washington. I'll be along, hopefully tonight."

He held her. "Please, Leslie. Don't do anything stupid—or heroic! Just get your interview and get back here. I'll tell Phil to be sure there's a space saved for you in a chopper."

She smiled up at him. "Sure, Ryan. Now we'd both better get going."

He picked up his briefcase and headed for the elevator, and she went to find their technician.

Sadim was prepared for the first challenge to come from some daredevil individual boater or pilot—Wafik had warned him. Ninety minutes into their operation, at about eleven, a private speed boat began criss-crossing the harbor near the *Bright Star,* with each pass coming closer to the ship.

Sadim waited in the command center until the boat was easily in range, then took over manual fire control of the high-powered Gatling gun point-defense cannon mounted on the bow. Instead of aiming right for the craft, as the computer would have done, Sadim's aim led the boat by about fifty yards and, on its sixth pass, he opened fire.

The driver and his female passenger were close enough to hear and see the firing of the cannon and the shell bursts hitting the water in front of them. She screamed, he turned the boat away, and they quickly beat a retreat up the Hudson River. But one piece of the *Bright Star's* defense had been uncovered and captured on video and photographs from around the harbor. And the two New York police officers who had volunteered for the mission were given the rest of the day off. Except there was nowhere for them to go.

William and his chief of staff hung up from talking again to the Situation Room. Vince Harley had emphasized that they were still examining photographs of the *Bright Star,* but for the moment there were no plans that could guarantee either a taking of the ship or its destruction without some chance of detection, and therefore some chance of nuclear detonation. Absent some new plan, the general said that their task now was to work up the probabilities, based on previous incidents, of which scenario had the greatest chance for success without triggering the device.

He did confirm that the antenna array indicated air and surface search radars and that the stack had been modified and encased to reduce its heat signature. In addition, there were two fast-repeating point-defense Gatling guns for destruction of incoming missiles, as well as matchbox launchers on the port and starboard sides, which the photo reconnaissance experts believed to contain surface-to-air missiles.

After the conversation William stood, took a deep breath, and walked over to the window. He could see the three helicopters in the large field and the small contingent from the New York SWAT team that was helping the

Secret Service guard them. A crowd had gathered around the perimeter, and William was concerned for the safety of the crews. He rubbed his hands on his temples and thought, *I wonder where Mary, Katherine, and Sarah are? They should have been here long ago. And Rebecca, where is she? And what are we missing? What else should we be doing?*

The three women and agent Blevins were about halfway to the Park Empire Hotel, walking along Fifth Avenue near Thirtieth Street. Although the going was slow, at least most of the foot traffic was headed uptown with them, and they were definitely moving faster than the taxis and cars which had all but stopped.

The earlier gridlock had caused many motorists to leave their cars in desperation and join the pedestrians. The large number of abandoned vehicles in all the streets meant that it would be almost impossible to restore any sort of traffic flow for several days. And several days they did not have.

The four of them rested under an awning at a large electronics store with televisions and video equipment in the window. This store, like most others, was closed, but the TVs were still running behind the large, electronically guarded display windows. The screens showed a map of New York with arcs drawn outward from the position of the ship. Although they could not hear the audio, they could read the labels on the arcs. Sarah looked for a street sign and then said, "Hey, we're safe here. The buildings here won't be melted—just all the glass blown out and some structural damage, plus lots of heat and radiation! Piece of cake...I say we stop here and have a picnic."

The others smiled as they turned to walk on. Mary said, "Onward, Christian soldiers! No picnics until we get to Central Park."

They had not walked twenty yards when there was a huge crash behind them. They spun around and Tyler Blevins drew his automatic pistol from his shoulder holster. Someone in the crowd behind them was clearing away the jagged edges of the remaining glass in the window of the appliance store. A moment later, ignoring the loud siren, the crowd surged inside.

Blevins shoved his gun back into the holster and said in disgust beneath his breath, "Alternative shopping." Then to his charges, "Come on, we'd better make tracks. The longer this goes on, the more unruly this crowd may become, and we've still got a long way to go."

As much as the conditions on the street would allow, there was a new urgency in their steps as they headed uptown.

"Push, push, Eunice," Rebecca urged, as the mother screamed and the baby's head exited the birth canal.

"Push again!"

A moment later a new life entered the world, and Rebecca laughed, exhausted with Eunice, as she lay the baby on his mother's stomach. Eunice smiled through her tears and reached for him; Rebecca cut the umbilical chord. He started to cry, and Eunice pulled him to her.

"Okay, Eunice, let's push the placenta out and get you cleaned up so we can get your son to a safer climate."

The new mother hadn't stopped smiling. "Thank you, Ms. Harri— Rebecca. He's so handsome, don't you think? O God, please don't let anything happen to him!"

Just then the burglar alarm went off again.

Many of the *Fortson's* officers were watching on the wardroom television as events unfolded down the Hudson River from their position. Helicopters over Manhattan showed the massive exodus of pedestrians struggling to move uptown and over the bridges to...to where? Off Manhattan it was like a flood of refugees arriving in a land that had been deserted. The overhead cameras also caught the violence spreading from the looters in lower Manhattan to the well-heeled refugees who wanted food from locked suburban grocery stores.

The executive officer looked over at Hugh after a scene showed people at gunpoint taking over an old ferry boat and forcing the crew to take them up the Hudson River. "Let's double the armed guard at the head of the pier, as well as the roving patrol on the pier and the ship. We might have as much threat right now from panicked citizens looking for a way out as we do from terrorists."

"Yes, sir," Hugh said, and left to find the young officer in charge of the ship's few service weapons, normally kept under lock and key.

When he returned, Teri waved him over to the television, where everyone was watching a civilian freighter making its way down river toward the *Bright Star*, ignoring the New York Police boats in front of it.

The announcer was saying over the picture, "The captain of this freighter is either completely oblivious to the events of the day and to everything around him, or else he's determined to get out of New York at any cost to himself and to millions of others."

Viewers all over the world stopped and watched as the network helicopters, hanging back over Manhattan, broadcast a clear picture of the freighter headed on a course that would bring it within a few hundred yards of the *Bright Star*.

Teri, standing next to Hugh, grasped his arm and held it tightly as the freighter kept on its course, and the small boats and helicopters dropped back and retreated, as if they were afraid of what was to come.

"O God, please don't let us all die. Not now. Not like this," Hugh heard Teri whisper. A knot formed in his stomach and grew tighter as Teri's grip on his arm increased.

Suddenly from the port midsection of the *Bright Star* there erupted a flash of light, and a missile shot from its matchbox launcher directly in front of the freighter but did not home onto it.

As if awakened from a trance, the freighter instantly turned to port, away from the *Bright Star*, and opened distance between them.

"That was close," Lieutenant Early said.

"That was a warning, just like with the speedboat," Hugh said. "He could have taken out that freighter if he'd wanted to. Whoever's driving that tramp freighter is very lucky."

"Aren't we all," Teri added, realizing that she was still squeezing Hugh's arm.

As Rebecca cleaned up and Eunice tried to nurse her son, they heard the sounds of breaking glass and of cabinets being ripped open on the ground floor.

"Drugs," Rebecca whispered. "They're looking for drugs, and I imagine they'll be coming up here real soon."

Eunice's eyes widened, and she looked down at her baby. "What are we going to do?"

"I'm not sure, but one thing *is* sure—you're going to have to move, and I know that won't be easy."

By early afternoon the press corps at the White House was clambering to know more about the president's location and what he was doing to solve the crisis. Lanier Parks, Chris White, and Ted Braxton gave a news conference at two in which they retold what everyone could see on their televisions and confirmed that the president was still in New York, still very much the commander in chief, and reviewing the option list his advisors had prepared. They would not confirm his exact location but did say that he had no intention of leaving the city. And they called for calm, law, and order.

Unfortunately the crowds north of Grand Central Station had not heard the White House advice. On several occasions Mary and her group had been forced to detour several blocks due to mobs looting stores. Once they'd hidden behind cars in an alley when a noisy gang of young toughs had come marching down the street, screaming obscenities and ripping purses from women. Blevins had pulled his gun out as they crouched, and Mary had feared for their lives.

But they had survived that moment and were only about ten blocks south of the perimeter, which Blevins understood from his radio the New York Police had established around the buildings for three blocks immediately south of Central Park, and extending from Eighth Avenue on the west to Fifth Avenue on the east, including among others the Park Empire Hotel.

As they crossed Forty-fifth Street with a sea of people moving north, one young man in a group loitering in the cross street suddenly said, "Hey, that's the president's daughter."

"No way," one of his friends exclaimed, throwing down his cigarette.

But the first one had started moving, and the other three followed him into the flow on Fifth Avenue. "Yes, it is! Hey, she's gotta be a ticket outa here!"

"Or a great time till we all go!" another called, laughing.

Blevins sensed the rushing forms behind them before he heard the shouts. He turned his head and yelled to Mary and the girls, "Go!" With that he spun around and blocked the lead pursuer, who was not expecting his maneuver. The two of them tumbled into the three others immediately behind.

Mary looked back, almost stopped, but then pushed the girls to run as fast as they could, given the crowd around them.

Blevins twisted and landed on his knees. As he rose, he reached into his jacket toward his holster, but a knife in the small of his back sent him back to his knees, and he fell forward onto the sidewalk, where he was soon trampled.

In their room at the Park Empire Hotel, William was being briefed by the mayor, who was using a large map of the city spread out on a table to show how they hoped to speed up the flow off the island, as well as what the city would look like if the bomb were actually detonated.

The mayor had been in touch with various officials at City Hall as well as the media. "Within the hour we'll be broadcasting instructions for anyone who is trapped in the city to begin stockpiling drinking water now—that will be a major concern for days, maybe longer, after the blast. I've been told everyone who survives will need to stay inside for several days. If it's detonated tomorrow after the election results, we'll have an extra mess on our hands for emergency personnel due to the darkness. If it's raining, the radioactivity won't spread as far, but there'll be strong concentrations and hot spots caused by the run-off."

"And the outright destruction?" Jerry asked.

"Interestingly enough, the experts concur that it won't be total devastation of the entire city. In addition to Brooklyn and Jersey City, on Manhattan itself vaporization will only really happen to the Battery. But there'll be massive destruction up to about Thirty-fourth Street, mainly from the heat and the winds, which will instantly exceed hurricane force. Up here at the park, given all the buildings in between, most of these structures and their inhabitants should actually survive, though radiation poisoning could be severe for anyone exposed outside."

"Sounds really promising!" Jerry said sarcastically.

"Hey, this isn't my idea," the mayor retorted.

"I'm sorry. I know. I guess this is getting to all of us a bit."

"As well it should," the president added.

Just then there was the sound of four gunshots in rapid succession in the park. The three men stood up and walked over to the window. As they did, they heard the jet engines on the three presidential helicopters starting to engage. Looking down, they could see the bodies of several policemen lying on the ground by the copters, and people boarding the craft, while other armed men kept the rest of the crowd back at gunpoint.

We should never have left them there so long, William thought. As they watched, the rotors spun up, and the gunmen jumped on board. The first two lifted off without incident, but the crowd surged toward the last one, which was not as quick to ascend. As it did, people grabbed its skids, hoping to be lifted to safety.

The three men in the hotel watched in horror as a gunman leaned out and at point-blank range shot a woman holding onto a skid. But the weight of all the people was too much for lift-off, and the copter peeled to the right. The main rotor sliced through the crowd and then hit the ground. The helicopter tumbled and exploded, killing many more all around it in a fireball of death. But the other two helicopters flew off to the north.

"God help us!" William exclaimed. "We should have sent them on, with or without Mary and the girls. It's my fault."

"How terrible," the mayor whispered.

"I have a feeling we're going to be right here to test those experts' theories about these buildings in person," Jerry said.

"I never really intended to leave," William said, turning from the terrible scene outside. Visibly shaken, he continued, "I may not be the best president we ever had, but I *am* the president. I'm not running. And I'm not doubting God's sovereignty. Jerry, get those guys in the White House on the phone, and let's hear their plans to get rid of the madmen on that ship. Then we have to go outside and be seen!"

Rebecca quickly looked in several closets before she found what she was seeking: a fold-up wheelchair. *Thank you!* she thought as she opened it and helped Eunice slide into it. Looking around, she picked up two knives, some towels, their purses, and a plastic bottle of water.

For the first few minutes after the alarm went off there had been a lot of noise downstairs. But they had heard nothing now for more than five minutes. *Have they gone?* Rebecca hated to use the elevator; she knew the noise would attract attention, but she didn't know how else to get Eunice to the top floor. So she decided to chance it, and she rolled Eunice over to the elevator door and was about to press the up button when the elevator started running! *Oh no! This is it!* she realized. Holding a knife in her right hand, she moved toward the elevator doors, ready to lunge at whoever was inside.

But the elevator stopped at the second floor. They heard the doors open just below them, and several people exited. She immediately pushed the up button, hoping that it might seem like a normal exercise for the elevator. But she heard men cursing, and as soon as the doors opened she quietly rolled Eunice into the cab and then held her breath as she waited for the doors to close. Thank God, it went up!

They arrived at the fourth floor. Rebecca rolled her friend and the baby down to the last room on the right and was going to close the door when she noticed the wheel tracks in the dust, leading right to them. She deposited Eunice and her son on the floor, then took the wheelchair and the towel and quickly created false tracks into additional rooms, wiping sections of the floor with the towel, hoping that there would be no patterns to follow. Then she retreated to the last room, where she sat down in the corner with Eunice and the baby, hoping that the newborn would not cry at the wrong time.

WASHINGTON The rally featuring the vice president had never been seen by its organizers as a large event. It was instead timed for maximum exposure on the network news on the last night before the election. And the Jefferson Memorial had been chosen because a smaller crowd could fill it. But the unexpected events of the day had given more importance to the rally, and it would be broadcast live by all the major networks, especially because no one had seen the president since that morning.

Ryan Denning arrived just as the first speaker approached the platform and began lambasting the president and his "God Squaders" for most of the ills of the nation, including the ship now threatening New York. Two more speakers followed in that vein, urging the people to elect "rational" members to Congress, men and women not "brainwashed" by biblical myths and religious rituals.

Then the master of ceremonies, a well-known Hollywood star, said, "Before we hear from the vice president, we've got an important announcement to be made by a very important Washington leader, Congressman Trenton Patterson."

To the sound of much applause the Pennsylvanian began his remarks by reminding the audience that he had previously supported the president's Twenty Points. "But I'm here today to tell you loud and clear that I was wrong. And our president is wrong to push these preposterous 'solutions' on our nation. They won't work. They'll hurt good working people. Please don't elect any candidate who has draped himself in the president's Twenty Points—they're like the emperor's new clothes. There's nothing there! Vote for rational leaders who can solve our country's ills, including this mess in New York harbor, by logic and reason, not by faith and ancient superstition!"

He continued for five more minutes and then sat down to a huge ovation. A minute later, after a brief introduction, Patricia Barton-North continued the attack.

"Thank you, Congressman Patterson for that outspoken endorsement. I know that it took great courage to give it, and we certainly hope that you win big tomorrow.

"You know, we assembled here at the Jefferson Memorial to symbolize for the nation that not all of the Founding Fathers were Christians. Our nation has always had a pluralistic approach, Jefferson being one of the first and best who shrugged off belief in Christianity. We want to keep that separation alive today."

The vice president continued her prepared attacks on the president's ideas. But as she neared the end of her talk, she added, "Now the events of this day give us all a real and definable choice tomorrow. Although I was in the White House Situation Room just a few hours ago, considering responses to the requests made by the Council to Liberate Palestine, I now want to make clear that I do not agree with the belligerent path that I believe our president is set to follow, risking the lives of millions of people in New York City. I say, let the people of Palestine and the people of New York City live!" There was much applause.

"The requests broadcast by the freedom fighters on that ship are really quite reasonable and should have been implemented years ago. There is simply no excuse or reason for massive destruction and loss of life over these simple issues.

"So, to you, the voters of America, I urge you to vote tomorrow for candidates opposed to the president's destructive beliefs and in favor of peace and reason.

"And to those in control of the *Bright Star*, I say that not all of us are crazy, nor do we wish you or your people ill. If the president does not meet your first two demands tomorrow, don't despair. When the election is over and we've won, we'll insure that those requests are met in full, or Israel will receive no more American aid. It *is* time, as Trent Patterson has expressed so well, for a rational, balanced approach to the Palestinian issue, as well as a rational approach to our own government.

"Ladies and gentlemen, voters of America, I submit to you that the future of this nation, and certainly of several million people in New York, is clearly in your hands tomorrow. Vote for a rational future. Vote for us!"

NEW YORK The president didn't hear the speeches in Washington. He had a frustrating briefing from Vince Harley in the Situation Room in which no new solutions were offered, but the arrival of the Delta Force at Fort Dix in New Jersey was confirmed. Afterward he said to Jerry and the mayor, "Come on, we've been cooped up in here all day. Let's go outside and see what's happening."

"But it's virtually a jungle on the street," the mayor warned.

"Don't we have a restricted zone for a few blocks around the hotel?" he asked.

"Yes, but I'm not sure how solid it is."

"Grab your coat and let's go see. Jerry, tell the Secret Service we're going down."

Rebecca and Eunice held their breath as they heard the elevator door on the fourth floor open. For the last ten minutes they'd listened to what sounded like the operating rooms being ransacked below. Now Rebecca slowly rose and walked toward the door, knife in hand, and she prayed that the baby would stay asleep in Eunice's arms.

It sounded as if two or three men had exited the elevator. "What's this?" Rebecca heard one ask. "Old storerooms?"

There was the sound of a door opening. "No, they look like bedrooms. Must have been hospital rooms. There's a bed in this one."

"Nothing in these two," a voice said from down the hall.

"Well, I got the bed tonight," the first one said.

"We'll see."

Rebecca breathed again as she heard the elevator doors open and the men leaving their floor.

Leslie and her crew were sitting in the Park Empire Hotel lobby, waiting. When the helicopter had crashed, all the other journalists who had been hoping for a glimpse of the president rushed out and across into Central Park. But Leslie had instructed her team to wait. Finally their patience paid off when the elevator doors opened and the president, his chief of staff, and the mayor of New York walked out with several Secret Service agents. The latter seemed much more nervous than usual.

"Mr. President!" Leslie waved from across the lobby as her video man hurried to start his camera. William turned at the familiar voice and acknowledged her. She walked quickly over to him as the camera began to roll.

"Mr. President, what will your response be to the demands from the ship?"

"It never works to give in to terrorists, Ms. Sloane."

"Then you won't propose to them any sort of compromise?"

"Israel is a sovereign state, and they can make concessions, if they wish. Lanier Parks in Washington has been in touch with them, and if they decide to do anything, I'm sure you'll know. As for the election tomorrow, I think you, of all people, know where we stand. As corny as it may sound to some people, I said it in January: we're trying to serve the Lord, and throwing the election isn't what I think he has in mind."

"Even if it means the destruction of New York?"

"As terrible as that would be, think of what the next round, the next threat might be. Think of the almost certain deaths in Israel and Palestine if those lands are just suddenly vacated by Israel. Unfortunately, it's not a 'New York or nothing' question, Leslie. It's 'New York now or something worse later.'"

"I see." She lowered her microphone. "Mr. President, is there any chance that we could do a more in-depth interview with you on these issues in time for the news tonight?"

He thought for a moment. "Yes. In fact, I'd like to make a short address from the hotel. Can you set that up? We're going to check the situation outside now, but we can do the interview when I come back. You're welcome to come with us now, if you like."

"Great! Yes, we can do it. Let's go, guys."

Leslie and her small crew followed the men out onto the street, which was not as crowded as the areas just to the south because the police had limited access to workers and residents. But most residents were fleeing anyway, many carrying small suitcases or backpacks. And over in Central Park they could still see the smoke and hear the sirens around the burning helicopter.

The president could see the concern, fear, and near panic on the faces of passersby near the hotel. He stopped a few to talk; most shook his hand, asked him to hurry up and solve the problem, and left to continue their flight. He walked east, accompanied by the mayor, Jerry Richardson, and a large group of Secret Service agents. And Leslie's crew captured it all on video, as the only television team aware of his presence on the street.

They rounded the corner of the Avenue of the Americas and headed south, still stopping to talk, to listen, and to encourage. Some individuals smiled and encouraged him; most asked him to bomb the ship; one angry young man told him to quit the presidency and join the priesthood.

Looking at the blocks and blocks of office buildings, stores, and apartments, William was reminded of the horrible devastation in Oklahoma City in 1995. *That was just one building,* he realized, stopping short. *This would be that same kind of destruction for miles and miles! O God, help us.*

As they were turning around to retrace their steps, they suddenly heard a frantic girl's voice shouting, "Daddy! Daddy!"

William turned and saw two policemen half leading, half carrying Katherine and Sarah up the street toward them. The two girls were disheveled, their clothing ripped, and they both were crying. He ran to Katherine and embraced her. "Oh, Daddy," she cried. "It was so awful. These men chased us. I don't know what happened to Aunt Mary. And the Secret Service agent, he…he…"

William hugged her and stroked her hair. Then he reached out and hugged his niece to him as well. "It'll be all right. You're here now, and we'll find Mary. It'll be okay."

He hugged both girls a moment longer. Then he turned to Sarah. "Where did you last see your mother?"

She pointed downtown. "About four or five blocks that way, on the other side of the police line. Some men were chasing us, and we don't know what happened." She started to sob again.

"Okay." Turning to the mayor, he asked, "Can you send some men that way, past the lines, looking for my older sister, Mary?"

"Sure. I think I know what she looks like," the mayor answered. "What does she have on?"

"Dark blue pants, a white turtleneck, and a navy jacket," Katherine answered.

While the mayor left to talk to the police, the president walked back toward the front door of the Park Empire Hotel, one arm around each girl.

In the lobby, Leslie scribbled a note and gave a video cassette to her sound man. "Here, run this over to the newsroom with this note. Then get back as soon as you can with more cassettes—better yet, try to commandeer a live mini-cam set-up, if one's available. I'll call ahead for you. We'll do our best to work the sound till you get back, and we've got one tape left. Tell the director we're about to do an exclusive address with the president!"

WASHINGTON Carrie had returned from Chicago and watched a tape of the vice president's rally. She was so upset she could hardly speak. She spent the next thirty minutes praying. Then she called Graham, Jennifer, and Courtney. With each of them she also prayed.

Downstairs in the Situation Room the president's advisors and the best minds in counterterrorism at the Pentagon had not been able to come up with a foolproof plan. Any form of smart weapon attack meant some type of electronic targeting, and no human assault could happen instantly. So far a simultaneous attack by four remotely launched cruise missiles skimming the surface of the water, with a last second final targeting by laser seemed the most workable idea. But with the *Bright Star*'s sophisticated radars, even that scenario carried substantial risk.

In a moment of frustration and anger, Vince Harley slammed his fist on the massive table and exclaimed, "There *has* to be a better way!"

After the rally, Congressman Trent Patterson rode to the Capitol with the vice president. As they parted, she invited him to have dinner with her and her advisors that evening, which he accepted. He then walked into his own office to find only a skeleton crew remaining because of the election, but he could tell that they were not happy with his unexpected defection from the president's slate. He walked into his private office and closed the door, the events of the last few hours weighing heavily on his heart.

NEW YORK The live mini-cam equipment and crew arrived within thirty minutes, and the police and Secret Service escorted them upstairs to where Leslie had prepared an impromptu set at a desk in a living room in one of the empty suites. They set up the small dish in the window, and within a few minutes the equipment was ready.

As Leslie walked down the hall to the president's room, the elevator at the far end opened. Cut and bruised the president's older sister emerged. Leslie was embarrassed by what her earlier program on the president's family had said about Mary, and she stopped. But Mary recognized her, and the smile on her face seemed genuine. Mary called out, "Ms. Sloane—so glad to see you!" and she began limping toward the newscaster.

The sound of her voice traveled inside. A door opened and Sarah rushed out to hug her mother. Leslie stood in the hallway as Mary was reunited with her brother and niece as well. As Mary hugged William, Leslie heard her say, "Oh, William, I don't think that wonderful Secret Service agent made it. I think they stabbed him. It was awful."

After more hugs, William turned and saw Leslie. "Here, Mary, you remember Leslie Sloane? She did the special on our family."

"Yes, we were just starting to say hello when Sarah came out. Hello, Ms. Sloane," Mary smiled.

Leslie advanced and shook the hand that was offered to her. "Hello, Mrs. Prescott. You look like you've been through a lot. I'm glad you're okay."

"Me, too."

"Listen," William said, "I've got to go with Leslie to do this television broadcast. Come with us, Mary, or rest, and I'll be back when we're finished."

Five minutes later the president was seated behind the desk in the living room of the hotel suite. The lighting was low but adequate. Just before he began, Leslie said, "Mr. President, we're feeding this live to all the other networks—take as much time as you want. And good luck."

"Thanks Leslie. Thanks a lot."

The video man started a countdown from five, and a moment later they were on the air.

"Good afternoon. I'm speaking to you from New York City, where this day's events are certainly well known to all of you. I want to take this opportunity to give you our assessment of the situation and to ask for your help. I'm doing this without benefit of notes or lengthy preparation, so please bear with me in this moment of testing for our nation.

"First, let me say clearly and categorically that we as a nation simply cannot give in to terrorists, no matter what the price, because the next price will be even worse. Consultations with our Israeli allies may produce some concessions on their part, but those will not be demanded or even requested by us. Israel must make her own defense choices absent our pressure. We will honor the decisions of Israel's leaders.

"Second, we will not concede tomorrow's election. I'll speak more on that in a moment, but we can't alter our election process because a particular group wants a particular outcome. If we start down that road, I'm convinced that within a few years democracy as we know it will be finished in America—the strongest will simply rule by force and by threat. No, we have to hold up the institution of democratic elections against all attacks. Otherwise, there is no democracy.

"Third, I'm in New York and will stay here. Whatever happens to New York will happen to me. I say that not because I'm brave or want to die. I say it because our nation is being attacked, I'm the president, and I need to be where the battle is. In fact, several of my family members are here now as well. While I hope to find a way for them to leave, I will stay and see this situation through to its conclusion. That's my job.

"I think that's all I want to say about the threat here. If possible, I'd like you to look beyond this situation and focus on tomorrow's election. There have been dark chapters in America's history when we chose what was expedient over what was right, always with disastrous results. Our treatment of Native Americans and the enforced slavery of African-Americans come immediately to mind. Then there have been other chapters in our history when we chose what was right over what seemed expedient, always resulting in blessings for us and our descendants. Our own Revolutionary War, the emancipation of the slaves, our standing up to Nazism and to Communism—all seemed virtually hopeless at times, and many people in those

times urged our leaders to compromise and to give in. But by sticking to
what was right, instead of what was easy, God blessed us in millions of ways.

"We can't begin to know all his blessings, but his hand has clearly moved
among us at times of crisis. It happened right here in August 1776 when
Washington impossibly saved eight thousand troops by moving them from
Brooklyn to Manhattan under the eyes of the British, who couldn't see them
because of a sudden fog that disappeared as soon as the last men were safely
on the other side. And it happened again at Gettysburg, Midway, and Nor-
mandy. God's intervention is obvious to anyone who considers what
happened when decisive 'coincidences' occurred. And the lack of his intervention in our nation is now just as obvious to each one of us, as we read the
newspaper or consider the latest day's news.

"You've heard the arguments from both sides in tomorrow's election.
You've read the position papers. The choice could not be clearer. And it is
yours alone. I urge you now to join with me in doing what is right, not what
is easy. Vote tomorrow for men and women who will turn this nation back
to the God who, through ordinary men and women like us, founded this
nation as a light upon the hill.

"The road ahead from tomorrow is not precisely clear. We believe our
Twenty Points will be a good start to placing this nation back in the care of
the One who made us and who expects much from us. Again, we have to
change this nation one heart at a time if we are truly to change. I urge you
to spend time on your knees tonight, as we will be doing, praying of course
for this situation here in New York, but praying also for this nation and for
your individual part in its future.

"Please, tonight, ask God to come into your heart through the wonderful, powerful presence of his Son living within you. And then tomorrow ask
God to come back into the heart of our nation, by electing men and women
who rightly fear God more than any terrorists.

"Thank you. Pray for us. Vote for our nation. May God bless each of
you and your families. Good-bye."

At the end of the president's speech, Leslie found herself wanting to clap,
tears streaming down her face.

Sadim sat with the ship's captain in the command center beneath the bridge.
While monitoring all of their threat evaluators, they'd managed to watch
both the vice president's rally and the president's speech.

"That blasphemous infidel!" Sadim exclaimed as the president's talk
ended. "He should have run!"

The captain turned down the volume on the television. "Well, one way
or the other he'll be finished tomorrow."

"Yes," Sadim agreed, and looked carefully at the monitors giving complete coverage around *Bright Star*. "And praise Allah for the vice president. She understands our needs—we can work with her. By tomorrow night she should be president. Now all three demands depend on the vote of these people, and despite what that fool told them, they *will* vote for reason, not faith. They know that reason will save New York City. Faith will destroy it!"

"Any news?" Hugh asked the executive officer at dinner in the wardroom that night.

"No. But the phone line is open. By the way, I thought your brother's speech was good, Hugh. I'm sorry we're all here dealing with this, but I'm proud to be serving under him, and I never thought I'd say that when he started."

"Thank you, sir. He *has* changed quite a bit."

"Sir," Ensign Malone asked, "whatever happens, will we need the whole crew? I mean, couldn't some people be let go, to give them a chance to escape? We could run small boats over to New Jersey."

"The captain and I have discussed it, and in the morning, depending on what happens, we may try to clear something like that with the Pentagon."

Thirty minutes later the set in the room at the Park Empire Hotel had been taken down, but Leslie and her two-man crew were still on the floor. She knocked on the door to the president's suite and then opened it. The president was standing with Jerry Richardson next to the map of the city, and he signaled her to come in.

"Mr. President, I just wanted to...I just...well, I think I've been wrong about you and about a lot of things for a long time....maybe ever since college, actually. But I do remember what my parents taught me about God and about Jesus, and I just...I just wanted to say whatever happens tomorrow, thanks. Thanks for having more courage than any man I know."

"You're exaggerating, Leslie," William said, giving her a warm smile. "But thanks."

"And I also want you to know that I called our office and they'll be glad to fly your family out on one of our helicopters—I've asked for them to be on the one at nine tonight. And if you need to fly military helicopters in after it's dark to airlift people out, you're welcome to use the helipad on the roof of our building. It's just inside the perimeter, and we've got armed guards watching it." She was referring to reports that on several buildings intruders had hidden on the roofs, waiting to commandeer helicopters at gunpoint.

"Thank you, Leslie. I'm sure we'll take you up on that flight for the two girls. Mary wants to try to find Rebecca in the morning, if she hasn't turned up by then. Mary says they drove by some clinic where she was headed this morning. Anyway, we'll also pass your offer to the Pentagon—it could be a big help. By the way, when are you leaving?"

"That's the last thing. The guys and I would like to stay, if it's all right with you. Sort of document all this, in case, in case..."

William smiled. "You're welcome to stay with us, Leslie, but it will be very dangerous, and it isn't a media event. I'm not sure how much will really happen, anyway. And I can't have the media, even someone as good as you, in on our meetings. If you can stand waiting down the hall, we'll try to let you know what's going on and include you whenever possible. But this may be hazardous to your health, big time."

"We want to take our chances."

"Fine. Let me go get Mary and the girls. I'm sure they'll be relieved."

The room in which Rebecca, Eunice, and her baby hid was now completely dark except for the light from nearby neon signs outside the one window; these still flashed advertisements despite the threat of devastation. They had hoped their tormentors would take the drugs and leave, but the sounds below of partying and destruction had ebbed and flowed with the hours. Rebecca and Eunice sipped their water and talked—whispered—about many things, from their very different backgrounds to their children. And Eunice nursed her baby when he cried.

"If it's ever quiet for a few hours, we'll try to leave," Rebecca said. "And listen, you ought to practice walking some. I can't push you the whole way."

"Just exactly where are we going?"

"Mary said that William was at the Park Empire Hotel at Central Park. I doubt he's still there, but I figure we'll head in that direction, if we ever get out of here, and hope to find a cop. I wonder what's going on out there?"

It was a difficult night for every person left in New York, whether they were still trying to leave or not. Few people slept. The same was true in Washington and across the nation. Tens of millions responded to the president's request and prayed—some for hours.

WASHINGTON Carrie planned to stay up all night praying. The phone rang a little after eleven. It was Katherine on the other end, safe in Philadelphia. The Secret Service had dispatched a limousine to meet them when the initial call about the plan came through, and she expected to be home to the White House in the early morning hours.

"I'm sure I'll be up, honey," Carrie said. Then she began what would be several hours of praying, reading the Bible, and talking to her family and friends by phone. She hoped William would call, but she also hoped he would get some rest.

Trent Patterson tried to sleep, but couldn't. The vice president's dinner had been pleasant enough. Few specific programs had been discussed, other than a complete review of relations in the Middle East, the second emancipation of the human spirit, and legislation to protect the rights of children, with certain minimum enforceable behavior standards for parenting.

But it wasn't the specifics that distressed Trent. It was the unspoken but very real presumption by the people seated around the dinner table that they would soon be in power and that they were far better equipped to manage and to make decisions for the nation than anyone else. They seemed to know what was right for everyone and for every family, and they were not hesitant to express it.

And besides this problem with the vice president and her staff, Trent had a problem with himself. He knew he was a traitor.

All of us who were engaged in the struggle must have observed frequent instances of a superintending providence in our favor.... And have we now forgotten that powerful Friend? or do we imagine we no longer need his assistance?

BENJAMIN FRANKLIN
THE CONSTITUTIONAL CONVENTION, JUNE 28, 1787

29

Tuesday, November 5
The Next Morning

NEW YORK Sadim dozed in his chair at the console, but the captain was awake next to him. They had divided the watch in the command center between them, in case there was an attack. Both of these men, and the chief engineer, would consider it an honor to die if Sadim or the computer detonated the bomb under the threat of an attack.

But not so Kolikov. He, too, tossed and turned. These last days on the ship with the bomb ready to detonate had been a condition of his employment five years earlier. He'd known they were coming, but he had never imagined the excruciating tension he would feel. He was almost sick with worry. He hoped the Americans would not be foolish enough to attack, for he had no doubt that Sadim would detonate the bomb without a moment's hesitation. His only consolation was his Swiss bank account, which he knew would take care of his wife and two children. But he nevertheless wanted to grow old with his grandchildren, and knowing he was only several feet from an armed nuclear bomb didn't help him relax.

William tried to sleep, but couldn't. He regularly checked with the Situation Room, twice with the Israeli prime minister, and twice with Carrie. He also called Jennifer when Carrie told him Hugh had never called; William said nothing about the *Fortson's* presence in New York but encouraged his sister-in-law not to worry.

With Carrie he talked for almost an hour about the days when the kids had been young and they had scraped by on his small salary, remembering old times together that he had all but forgotten. They had even laughed once or twice. But behind it all was the knowledge that this might be his last night on earth—that they might never be together again in this world. Carrie tried to be upbeat, but once or twice she found tears in her eyes as they spoke. As they hung up at a little before three, she said, "William, I love you. And I'm so proud of you. May God watch over you."

Hugh was also turning in his bunk, wishing that he could call Jennifer, knowing that she was worried. He looked at his clock. It read 3:10. There was a knock at his door.

"Come in."

"Hugh, it's me," Teri said.

He sat up in the bunk and turned on the light. He was fully clothed, except that his shirt was unbuttoned. "What's up?" he asked, rubbing his eyes.

She came in and shut his door. "I think I may have figured something out."

"What do you mean?"

"A way to attack the *Bright Star* without triggering a detonation. At least not right at first. To give us time to destroy the command and control mechanisms, or maybe the bomb, too, before they retaliate."

"How?" Hugh asked, suddenly awake.

They talked for fifteen minutes. When Teri finished and he added a few suggestions of his own, he splashed water on his face, dried off with a towel, and said, "Come on."

"Where to?" she asked.

"The captain needs to hear this."

The measured breathing told Rebecca that Eunice was asleep, propped next to her in the corner of the room, her baby in her arms, resting on her lap. Rebecca had been listening and thinking for over an hour. Now she rose to her knees, crawled to the middle of the room, and bowed her head.

Dear God, I imagine you don't like it when someone only prays to you when she's in trouble. I know it seems like that now. And I guess it is. But I mean for it to be more than that. I really do. I've done nothing but mess up for years now— mainly I just haven't thought about you at all. I've tried to do everything myself, ignoring your rules and...you. I'm sorry. I'm so sorry. I see now—William has really helped me see—what a self-centered person I've been. I've looked at his life, and Carrie's, and seen their happiness. O God, I want that kind of life. I want your Son in my life. Please, God, take me in the mess I'm in and change me. Forgive me for what I've done and make me over. Rebirth me, as new as this little boy here. Help me to learn your ways. Help me to keep your rules. Please, God, bless us and help us here. And bless William and the nation today.

Forty minutes later the captain and executive officer had heard enough to authorize Teri to begin the modifications that would have to be made, since time would be running short if her plan was approved.

"I'll go down on the pier myself and talk to the Pentagon," Captain Robertson said, taking a long sip from his coffee. "Hugh, what do you think?"

"I have no idea what they're considering in Washington, sir, but I really think this has a decent chance."

"I do, too. That's why I want you to try to get to your brother and tell him about it. I think it'll carry more weight coming face to face from you."

"Do you want me to go now? The Park Empire Hotel isn't that far. I should be able to jog it in less than thirty minutes."

"No, wait until it starts to get light, then take four or five men in civilian clothes armed with .45s with you. Get back here as fast as you can— after you call Jennifer from the hotel." He smiled. "But be careful what you say to her!"

"Yes, sir." Despite the early hour and complete lack of sleep, Hugh suddenly felt much better.

"And Hugh, ask her to call Trudy."

Rebecca looked out and could notice the first traces of gray in the early morning sky. She was very tired, but she prayed again, then shook Eunice. It had been quiet in the clinic for almost three hours. At least one of the men had come to their floor and apparently gone to bed just down the hall.

"It's time to go," she whispered.

Both women had slept in their coats. Eunice sat up, then stood while Rebecca held the baby in one arm and helped her with the other. She took a few steps toward the door and then sat in the wheelchair, and Rebecca placed the baby, wrapped in towels, in her arms.

Rebecca opened the door as quietly as she could and slowly pushed Eunice down the hall. The baby started to squirm, and Eunice reached to nurse him.

From the elevator they could look into the open door of the bedroom, and there a huge man, face up on the bed, was snoring. Rebecca said her third prayer in as many minutes and pressed the down button. Luckily the cab was there at the landing, but just the sound of the doors opening was deafening in the silence of the early morning.

Without looking back she rolled Eunice on, pushed the button for G, and turned around before the doors closed to see the man starting to roll over.

In the elevator itself, which was as noisy as an amplified train crash, the baby started to cry, and he wasn't interested in nursing. Rebecca and Eunice had no idea what would be waiting at the bottom. They held their breath.

When the doors opened and the baby's cries moved out into the larger area, Rebecca looked in the near darkness and saw one man sprawled in the hall toward the rear and another lying in the hall between them and the front door, with perhaps just enough room for the wheelchair to pass.

Rebecca maneuvered the wheelchair out of the elevator and started down the hall toward the front. The baby continued to cry. As they passed the man in the hall, he appeared to wake up. He propped himself on one elbow, and Rebecca said, "Excuse me."

He grunted a reply from his daze, but let them pass.

Rebecca, her heart in her throat, quickly unbolted the front door, and as it opened the burglar alarm siren went off again. "Eunice, you'll have to walk down the steps. I'll push the wheelchair. Hurry!" Rebecca bounced the wheelchair down the stairs then ran back up for the baby. Eunice followed, holding onto the railing with both hands. At the bottom, with shouts of "Hey!" coming loudly from inside, Eunice sat down in the chair again, holding her baby tightly, and Rebecca started pushing them down the sidewalk as fast as she could go.

At about the same moment Hugh and five men dressed in civilian warm-ups left the head of the pier and jogged north and east in the graying dawn.

Twenty-five minutes later he showed his ID and a letter from Captain Robertson at the police line, and shortly thereafter Hugh was in the elevator on the way up to the president's floor.

The two brothers embraced in the living room, which had become the New York version of the Situation Room. "Thanks for coming to see us in New York, little brother," William chuckled. "You didn't have to come all this way."

"Just glad to be of service to the family," Hugh replied.

After a few minutes of catching up on the twenty-one hours since Wafik's message had come over fax machines across the nation, they sat down at a table with a map of the harbor.

"Vince Harley told me you'd probably be coming. Your captain briefed him on the plan, and they're studying it. He said you'd give me the details."

"Teri Slocum—you've heard me speak of her—came up with this idea a few hours ago. She reasoned that whether by automatic control or by manual override, the terrorists would only detonate the bomb if they felt they were actually under attack. They might fire defensive weapons at a perceived threat—they've already done that twice—but the bomb would go off only if the end seemed upon them. So she figures the key is to get close enough in a situation that leaves doubt in their minds—or in their computer's mind—and then attack in a way that doesn't forewarn them—doesn't alert them with electronic lock-ons or laser targeting. And what started her thinking all this was seeing the missile they fired in front of that freighter yesterday. It was an AirFox."

"What's so special about that."

"An AirFox would be no good against a slow-moving ship, especially one up close. It's programmed for air defense only, and the warhead probably only becomes active after more than a mile of flight. If they only have Air-Fox missiles, they probably had no choice but to fire at nothing specific, in front of that freighter, to make it look like a warning. Teri doubts they could have hit it if they'd wanted to. And now that I've thought about it, I agree.

"They've got those deadly point-defense Gatling guns, but they're programmed primarily for incoming missiles. In short, they seem to be ready for anything and everything high-tech, but if Teri is right, John Paul Jones could slowly come alongside in an old man-of-war and blast 'em!"

"Have we got any old man-of-wars handy in New York?" the president asked.

"We just might," his younger brother replied.

Rebecca pushed Eunice and her baby a full five blocks without stopping before she paused to catch her breath at the upper end of Central Park, which they could see in the approaching dawn was filled with people, some lying, some standing. They were both exhausted but ecstatic.

"I guess I know why I've been training at that gym all these years!" Rebecca gasped, holding her hands over her head. She was sweating from the exertion, and she unbuttoned her jacket. "I think we could place in the Olympic mother-and-child-in-a-wheelchair sprint, don't you?"

"Definitely. You did great, especially considering that you're wearing a dress and flats!" Eunice said from the chair.

"Well, after what you did yesterday, I couldn't let you down today. We're quite a team!"

As Rebecca grasped the handles again, four young men came diagonally across Fifth Avenue toward them.

"Uh-oh," Eunice whispered, "looks like more trouble."

The unshaven toughs surrounded them in the increasing light, and one of them pulled a revolver out of his jacket.

"Let's have your money. Now."

Rebecca looked at them and then down at her passengers. Many people walked past, but no one stopped or seemed to be interested, as if this were now a common occurrence. "We don't have any money. I guess we left our purses at the place we were staying."

"No money, huh? You, get up."

Eunice slowly rose, clutching her son to her. The leader had expected to find a purse wedged behind her. Seeing none, he grew angry. "No money! We ought to kill you, but you'll probably die today anyway. Here, give me that chair!"

Speechless, Rebecca and Eunice watched as the leader took the wheel-chair under his command, and the four of them sauntered back across the street, laughing. Halfway across he sat in the chair and had one of his friends push him to the sidewalk.

When they had disappeared around the corner, Eunice looked at Rebecca in despair. Rebecca smiled. "Here, give him to me. We've only got about fifty blocks to go. If we can't find a ride and have to walk all the way, we should make it by Friday!"

WASHINGTON It was now seven-thirty, and Ryan Denning had been able to catch a few hours sleep before taking his chair again in the election set which also doubled as their nation-in-crisis set. He was midway through his recap of the few developments during the night and the first election poll openings in New Hampshire, when the director spoke in his earpiece and announced that they had a special guest appearance coming up after the next commercial.

Two minutes later Trent Patterson joined Ryan on the set, and an impromptu interview began. Patterson was immaculately dressed in a blue suit and red tie, clean shaven, and gave no indication that he hadn't slept at all.

"Congressman Patterson, welcome to this special election day edition of *This Morning*. We're always glad to see you, and we wish you well in today's election."

Trent smiled. "Thank you, Ryan, but frankly I hope I'm only elected long enough to resign."

"What?"

"Ryan, for the last day—no, really the last year—I've been living a lie. A lie to my constituents and a lie to the American people. I accepted a huge bribe from certain Mideast militants—I believe the same ones who now have the ship threatening us in New York harbor—and I've voted how they wanted me to vote on Mideast questions. I suspect I know some other congressmen on the same payroll."

As Ryan listened in disbelief and they skipped two commercial breaks, Trent Patterson outlined in specific detail how and why he had changed his vote on the Mideast. He described the meetings with Wafik in Paris on the taxpayers' tab. And he finished with a description of Wafik's call the day before, his demand that Patterson change his support for the president, and Patterson's reluctant agreement to do so.

"I did that because I was scared. But I'm not scared any more. I'm ashamed, but not scared. My speech yesterday at the Jefferson Memorial was nothing but lies motivated by cash and fear. If William Harrison can face our enemies in New York, trusting in God, the least I can do is support him and his program here in Washington.

"Ladies and gentlemen of my district, vote for me today to keep my opponent out, and I'll resign in January. I'm a disgrace to your trust. But William Harrison and his Twenty Points are what this nation needs. As I depart public life and face whatever punishment awaits me, please make my ordeal of the last year count for something, and elect the president's slate today at the polls. What he said last night is correct. None of us knows what today holds. But he's right in saying that God holds today. Thank you, Ryan, and good-bye."

Without saying another word, Patterson rose and left the studio.

NEW YORK   Hugh called Jennifer after talking with William—it was the most difficult call of his life. He knew he very well might never see her again on earth. And he had to hurry as well, because they needed him on the ship. They shared their love for each other, and he said he'd see her in a few days. "Kiss the kids for me," he concluded, his heart almost breaking, and hung up.

Then he told William good-bye with the same sense of finality.

"Keep working on the details of your plan, and if the Pentagon approves it, they'll let you know on the open line," William said. "Thanks for everything, Hugh. I'm sorry you're here, but I'm also real glad you're here. Please pray as often as you have time."

And with a final embrace, the two brothers parted.

William had made arrangements the night before for five Secret Service agents to accompany Mary as she tried to find Rebecca. They decided to walk the length of Central Park—about fifty blocks—to 110th Street. After a quick breakfast Mary kissed William good-bye and promised to be back, or to check in by radio, no later than noon. Because the clinic was located on the east side, they first walked over to Lexington Avenue before turning north. They had no way of knowing that Rebecca and Eunice were walking south at a terribly slow pace, against the flow of everyone else that morning, on Fifth Avenue.

ACROSS THE NATION It was an election day like no other in memory. Many workplaces didn't even bother to open, and most people on the job spent their time in front of televisions or radios. The live picture of the *Bright Star* taken from a high-rise building continued to dominate the coverage on every channel, though for at least the morning Congressman Patterson's confession drew a lot of coverage and comment.

And all across America people voted. Election officials reported from every city and town that the turnout was much heavier than usual. Reporters who stopped people on the street to get their opinions found that the voters were maddeningly balanced. No one could predict the outcome. As the morning went on, tension mounted across the nation. There were calls for William Harrison to resign immediately. Churches held prayer vigils and services for national repentance. The voting continued and continued to be heavy. Whatever else President Harrison had done with his challenge, he had drawn a line in the sand and encouraged Americans to choose—to serve the Lord or to serve man. And apparently motivated as well by the terrorists in New York, Americans were responding. But no one knew how they were voting.

NEW YORK Late in the morning, after a long and moving phone conversation with Trent Patterson, William again took to the street with Jerry Richardson and the Secret Service. This time they walked directly to the edge of the police perimeter and noticed far fewer people on the street, though it was still moderately crowded with people and a few cars heading north away from the Battery. No one could know whether the majority of people had actually left Manhattan or had resigned themselves to stay or were trapped. The mayor had set a five o'clock deadline for emergency personnel and vehicles to attempt to evacuate the elderly and the injured. After that time all city personnel were to assemble inside the police perimeter just south of Central Park. They would then be assigned to designated spaces in the interiors of buildings that faced north, and emergency vehicles would be parked in underground car parks.

At that same hour all subways would be stopped, and any citizens still left in Manhattan would be encouraged to seek shelter for the night in the subway stations and along the tunnels.

"The maddening thing," William said to Jerry as they walked, with Leslie's crew following and taping—but with her agreement that nothing would be broadcast without the president's permission—"is that we don't know exactly when they might do something.

"I mean, on the chance that the vice president might win and the terrorists' demands be met, should we risk attacking them and perhaps destroying New York in what will in hindsight seem like a tragically desperate move on our part?

"But if we win, when will they blow up the city? Immediately? While they're still on board? After they've escaped? At three tomorrow morning? And what constitutes us winning, in their minds? A network prediction? A certified ballot? This is really going to be difficult, Jerry, particularly if the Pentagon approves one of the attack plans. When should we initiate it?"

His chief advisor and friend walked on in silence, then spoke. "I don't know, William. I don't think we can give too much weight to what *might* happen. For all we know, they might blow us up at 12:01 today because the first two demands aren't met on time. Or they might blow us up no matter what else happens. I think we've got to wait until one of the attack plans is as ready as it's going to be, then move. Hindsight can prove anything. We've got to deal with what's here, now. And that means take them out when and if we can."

William reflected for a moment. "That makes sense, Jerry. Thanks. I guess we'll wait to hear from the Pentagon."

Hugh arrived back at the ship and reported to the captain on his meeting with the president. Then he found Teri in the missile fire control area of the combat information center.

"How's it going?"

"Slow but okay. It's the first time any of us have done this. Want to hear something ironic?" she asked.

"Sure."

"Well, first, our Harpoon anti-ship missile won't work because it's fixed at a forty-five degree angle—it would fire right over the freighter. So our only hope is a standard anti-aircraft missile in surface mode, fired from the swivel launcher; we're one of the last two or three ships in the navy to even have it. And then the missile modification we're doing has only been possible for about a year. It was one of the last changes MisWepsCom developed before your brother de-funded them out of existence after he took office."

"Timing is everything."

"Right. The missile gunners mates are down in the magazine making the changes necessary in the hardware, and we're about done with the software programming. I figure we'll rig maybe four missiles to detonate on impact at short range—I doubt we'll have time to fire many more. And of course we'll have no way to test these. We'll find out if we're doing this right when and if they work, and not before."

"But the manual says you will have overridden the arming delay, and changed the detonator to impact only."

"That's what it says," she answered.

"So we'll have four missiles that are really just glorified cannonballs?"

"You got it. No radar. No laser. No infrared. No guidance. No minimum flight distance. Just 'It hits, it explodes; it misses, it doesn't.' Pretty simple."

"And no one knows it's coming until it leaves the rail," he added. "Are the guys making similar mods to the five-inch gun and the Gatling guns?"

"Yes. I think we'll be ready here in about three more hours. Lieutenant Commander Dobbs has the signalmen rigging the lights on the stack and the stern."

"Fine. Call me if I can help. The captain wants the department heads in the wardroom. I'll give him your time estimate to pass on to the Pentagon."

"There, that's it!" Mary pointed to the Burroughs Clinic from down the block. It had taken them much longer than expected to reach 110th Street. Once the sun came up, the crowds came out again. A strange phenomenon seemed to be occurring. Those who lived above the middle of Central Park had been frightened on the first day and had fled as best they could off the island. But to those who lived or worked near the Battery, this same area seemed relatively safe, after watching the television simulations of the expected blast, and they'd already come a long way. Many from lower Manhattan decided they'd walked far enough and simply stopped, either in the park, in the street, or in other people's shops or apartments, whatever they could find. So the police-imposed low density of the restricted area around the Park Empire Hotel changed into streets full of people, starting from about Eighty-second Street north.

The television and radio were urging all citizens left on Manhattan to move indoors and to stay there for several days. The sea of people outdoors in Central Park and on the streets began trying to move inside the surrounding buildings. Individual acts of kindness, where stranger helped stranger, were matched by acts of violence, where those outside forced their way inside.

As Mary and the five agents reached the front door of the clinic, they noticed it was ajar.

"Phil, Gary—go around and see if there's a back door and report," the chief agent said.

"Nothing seems to be going on," came the reply over the chief's transceiver two minutes later.

"Somebody probably broke in for the drugs. They may still be in there."

"Well, let's go, two in front, two in back, weapons drawn. And let's not shoot each other!" said the chief. "Phil, you stay here with Mrs. Prescott. Why don't you wait over by that diner?"

A few minutes later an agent signaled from the front door for Mary and Phil to come across the street. In the main hall Mary saw three unshaven men sitting on the floor, their hands in cuffs. "They say they haven't seen anyone," said the chief, "but I'm not sure they know what planet they're on right now. Our guys are searching the place."

Exiting the elevator, one of the agents said, "Here's a suitcase and two purses. They were in an operating room upstairs. They were opened and things thrown around. And there were some bloody rags in the trash."

"Let me see," Mary said. The man handed her the shoulder bags. "Oh, dear God. Yes, that's Rebecca's purse. And the other one says Eunice Porter, the woman she was supposed to meet."

"Okay, guys," the chief said, kicking one man's foot, "you want to tell us what happened?"

"Hey, I told you already. We been here since...since yesterday, I think. But I swear we hadn't seen nobody. We found that stuff and just looked for money. What's the big deal?"

"The big deal is that we don't believe you, and we're going to get the police here to take you in. Phil, can you get them on your radio?"

"I'll try. They're pretty busy and may not respond."

"Hey," the most awake one on the floor said, "I think I seen two women leave this morning—like in a wheelchair! One pushin'—one sittin'—with a baby! Yeah! I thought it was a dream, but that stupid alarm went off. We had to rip out the wires. The baby was screamin', too. I swear!"

"What time?" Mary asked, suddenly realizing he was telling the truth.

"Gee, I don't know. Early. It was just gray outside. I swear."

"Which way did they go?"

"Come on, lady. I barely remember them being here."

"Okay. Okay. I bet they're headed for the Park Empire. Can you leave one man here, and let's go south again, looking for them?"

"Sure, I guess so," the chief replied. "Two women with a wheelchair headed south against everyone else shouldn't be too hard to spot."

"If we get the right avenue. Let's split up and go down Fifth, Madison, Park, and Lexington."

"Only if we stop at every cross street and check-in with one another. I'm not going to lose any of you. And, Mrs. Prescott, I'd like you to come with me."

"All right, but let's go. It's getting late."

WASHINGTON Ryan spoke to Leslie over her earpiece just before they were to begin the noon news recap of the situation in New York, followed by a report from polling places around the nation.

"Hey, this is one fine piece of reporting you've done, Leslie," he said. "What a scoop to be right there in the hotel with the president."

"Yes," Leslie spoke into her lapel microphone. "We've got some footage that'll make one heck of a documentary. I just hope I get to put it together."

"You will. You can easily make the one o'clock helicopter. They're going to stop at three—mayor's orders. There have been two awful crashes because of people holding onto skids again. He's afraid that as security personnel leave the city, copters will really become sitting targets, even on roofs."

Leslie said in a low voice, "I'm not leaving, Ryan."

"What?"

"I'm not leaving."

"Yes, you are!"

She laughed.

"Come on, Leslie. I love you. You've got to leave right after this piece."

"No, my assignment is the president, and he's here. I'll be fine, Ryan. And if I'm not, I'll at least be doing what I want to be doing. Ryan, if we do come through okay, I want to talk with you about...I don't know. Our marriage and other things."

"But, Leslie—" The floor director was giving him the five-second countdown, so he had to break off and quickly read his first cue on the monitor. "While events remain about the same in New York—we'll have a live report in a moment from Leslie Sloane with the president—the vice president here in Washington has been reacting to Congressman Trent Patterson's confession this morning and predicting victory for her candidates. John Sherry reports from the vice president's office in the Capitol."

The scene shifted to the vice president walking toward a podium. Sherry's voice said, "Ryan, this was the scene thirty minutes ago here at the Capitol."

The tape showed the vice president reaching the podium and beginning to speak. "Ladies and gentlemen, I'm pleased to let you know that voters, and particularly our supporters, are turning out in record numbers. Our own exit polls show that our candidates are leading by a decisive two to one margin across the board, in big cities and in small towns. We're very encouraged and ask our supporters to continue their great job of getting out the vote. This country's future is too important to leave to brainwashed fundamentalists!

"I'm also pleased to announce that we're prepared to make our Cabinet nominations tomorrow, once William Harrison resigns. This administration will not miss a beat in providing the best possible solutions for the nation's problems.

"And one of our first orders of business will be to accelerate the implementation of the requests made by the freedom fighters on the ship in New York harbor. This message is addressed to them: it's almost noon, but please don't despair. Tomorrow we will move quickly to meet your requests.

"And this message is for the American people: only this administration will save New York!

"Let me comment briefly on Congressman Patterson's personal tragedy. We are so sorry he felt led to take a bribe, after serving so many fine years in the House. We have not considered his selfish use of us yesterday for his own gain as a personal attack, because of the enormous pressure he created for himself. We consider his efforts to discredit us in this way to be a sad tragedy, and we know the American people both agree with us and also wish him well in confronting a possible jail sentence. To the people of his district in Pennsylvania, I say elect Claude Rabun. There's no point in returning a criminal to office.

"Thank you, and we'll see all of you tonight at one of the big victory parties!"

Then Ryan Denning was on camera. "Thank you, John. And now a live report from Leslie Sloane with the president in New York."

The camera in front of Leslie came on. "Ryan, while others have been posturing for the future, the president has been here in New York at ground zero, talking with his key advisors both here and in Washington, trying to figure out the best response to this grave threat. He has displayed a personal courage that has been rare in recent memory among top officials. We have a tape of a briefing from this morning."

But when the scene changed, it was to a dog food commercial.

Sorry Leslie, Ryan thought, *but you're out of control!*

NEW YORK At two that afternoon the officers assembled in the wardroom at the captain's request. As he entered, the executive officer said, "Attention on deck!" and everyone stood.

"Seats, please. I've just spoken to the Pentagon. They want us to be prepared to attack at approximately three hours after sundown, or about 2030. They haven't said go, but they want us fully prepared to leave the pier by 2000.

"We'll have to navigate at night with only our small civilian radar and arrive within a few feet of our intended position to have any hope of being effective with the one chance we'll have.

"There's a reasonable probability that we'll fail, meaning that for a split second we'll have enough light to navigate with no problem! Even if we succeed in stopping the detonation, but we hit the bomb itself, there will be radioactive chunks flying everywhere, and we'll be right next to them. There's also a reasonable chance that we'll be attacked by missile or Gatling gun, and we won't be able to defend ourselves because we'd give away our true identity.

"But even with all that, I'm told that our plan has the best chance for surprise of all the plans they've come up with so far, and surprise is the key factor. So I imagine we'll be going."

The captain let his last statement sink in before proceeding. "Each department will meet immediately to go over your specific duties tonight. Department heads report to me with a status report at 1600 and every thirty minutes thereafter.

"One last thing. Not everyone will be needed for this mission. There's no point in risking more lives than necessary. Some key divisions will need a higher percentage than others. I'd like department heads and division officers to submit a manning requirement to the XO after your meetings. All nonessential personnel will be left here on the pier. For security reasons no one may depart the ship until then; but those people will have a much better chance of surviving up here at the pier than down in the harbor.

"Any questions?"

"Leave me, Rebecca," Eunice said, as they sat on the steps of an apartment house on Fifth Avenue. "Take the baby and go. I'll catch up."

Rebecca smiled. "No. I said I wouldn't leave you, and I won't. Look, we've only got about ten more blocks to go."

Their progress had been painfully slow because it was so difficult for Eunice to walk, and she had to rest and nurse the baby, whom Rebecca carried most of the time. And they were bucking the flow of nearly everyone else still on the streets.

"We'll make it. Rest another minute, then we'll go."

As she spoke, one of the Secret Service agents, looking for two women and a wheelchair, walked past but didn't give a second thought to the two women sitting on the steps of what he believed to be their apartment building.

It was after three when Mary and the other agents met again at the Park Empire Hotel. For the previous thirty minutes they had noticed a marked thinning of people on the streets, as everyone made preparation for shelter during the coming night. There even seemed to be fewer policemen near the hotel. No one could really blame them. They were human, too, many with families. It was easy to go somewhere on an assignment and just not bother to return.

"We must have missed her," Mary exclaimed. "I know she's here! She's not upstairs?"

"No, we checked on the radio. What do we do now?"

"You guys go on to whatever else you have to do. I'm going to take one last walk up Fifth Avenue, next to the park."

"I'll come with you," the young agent named Phil volunteered.

Upstairs the president and everyone on his floor were preparing to leave.

"We're set up and ready to communicate from the large ballroom one floor below ground, with no windows," Jerry Richardson said to William. "The Situation Room is patched in and working. We've got a television for every network. By the way, the hotel has been stockpiling water, and a portion of the auxiliary kitchen has been cleaned and made ready as an emergency hospital, if necessary. There're plenty of tables and sinks. And we've got three doctors in the hotel standing by."

"Well I guess we're coming down to it," William said. "But this isn't exactly how I pictured watching the election returns when I launched this journey back in January."

Mary and Phil had only gone two blocks when Mary suddenly screamed and started to run. Rebecca looked up from the curb at the corner and yelled back. Her older sister almost knocked her over with her embrace.

"Oh, Rebecca, Rebecca, we've been so worried about you."

"Me, too. About you." She hugged back. "Here, Mary, meet Eunice Porter, and her son, who is a mighty healthy young man."

Mary turned and kissed Eunice, then peeled back the towels to reveal the naked little boy. "Hey, it's getting cool. We need to get him inside."

"I've been keeping him under my coat," Eunice said. Obviously weak, she sat down on the curb. "You go on. I'll be there," she said.

"No way," Rebecca said. "We've come this far, we'll finish together. Mary, take the boy ahead so he'll get warm. Then come back. We're almost—"

Phil stopped her. "If one of you ladies can do a fireman's chair with me, we can carry Ms. Porter, and we'll all arrive together."

"You're on," Mary said. "Let's go!"

As the sun began to set, Sadim was feeling very satisfied, convinced that he had helped create a huge change in the history of his people by forcing the election of a government in America that would agree to their demands or suffer the consequences. He expected that the next day he would negotiate safe passage for the *Bright Star* out to sea—no, all the way back to the Mediterranean, with a U.S. Navy escort!—after concluding the other two items on his agenda with the new American president.

Still, it was a shame that William Harrison would escape with his life. At least he would be leaving in total disgrace.

As originally planned, the jet helicopter from the *New Dawn* would be joining them after dark following a sea-top flight and a flash of their recognition code, but it appeared to Sadim they might not need the escape ship after all.

The Harrisons held a joyous reunion in the lower ballroom of the Park Empire Hotel. William hugged Rebecca, who introduced everyone to Eunice and her son. Leslie and her crew recorded their arrival on tape. Rebecca recounted for them how Eunice had chosen not to have the abortion.

After they listened to Rebecca's story, William said, "I'm glad you're here, Rebecca and Eunice, but I'm sorry as well. All helicopter traffic has been stopped, and with the police pulling into shelters at this hour, it's really not safe to be on the street at all—as you know! So I'm afraid there's now no escape for any of us. We're here for whatever comes."

"That's all right, William," Rebecca said. "This is a whole lot better than where we've just been. And I never miss family reunions."

Despite the gravity of the situation, everyone laughed, momentarily lightening the tension.

"It is amazing, isn't it," Mary said, "how we're all four here in New York on this election night. Think from where we've all had to come to be here together."

William felt a chill. Everyone was silent. Finally he said, "Now that we're all found and everything's been said that can be said, and polls in the East close in two hours, I think we need to thank God for his goodness, and pray that whatever happens tonight, he won't turn his face from this land."

There were murmurs of agreement all around. "Jerry, let's turn down all these televisions. In fact, turn them off for now. Check with Vince and tell him to go with what he thinks is right. He knows those details better than we do, and we've approved all three of their best plans. Then let's gather here for the last two hours of voting in the East and pray."

Five minutes later William, Mary, Rebecca, Jerry, Eunice, Leslie, her two crewmen, a secretary, twelve military aides, and several of the Secret Service agents all knelt in the ballroom and prayed together.

At seven many members of the *Fortson's* crew began descending the ladder from the quarter-deck to the pier. Hugh was on his way to check the five-inch gun mount on the stern, and he walked through the quarter-deck area just as many couples—heterosexuals, homosexuals, and lesbians—were kissing and saying good-bye. Many were crying. Hugh looked at who was going and who was staying and realized that in most cases the more senior member of each couple was in essence ordering the junior one to leave for more safety. *I wonder how this would work in a ship's fire? Or a collision? Too many awful decisions have to be made in an emergency. How can we have people in love with each other running around on a navy ship?*

Fifteen minutes later the captain and the executive officer descended the now empty ladder to the pier, summoned by a messenger. The ensign on the open line handed the receiver to Captain Robertson.

"Captain, can you hear us? This is Vince Harley and Secretary of State Lanier Parks. Do you recognize our voices?"

"Yes, sirs, I do."

"We're going to say the same thing to your XO in just a minute, so there's two-man recognition on both ends. If you're ready, go ahead with the operation as planned, and may God bless you and your crew."

"Aye, aye, sir." He handed the phone to his second in command.

Thirty seconds later the two men bounded up the ladder, and the *Fortson* prepared to get underway.

At the same time the group in the ballroom stopped praying and turned on the televisions, giving prominence to Leslie's U.S. Network. After watching for over thirty minutes, William stepped over to one of the tables and called Carrie at the White House.

"Hello, dear. We found Rebecca, and she's with us now. How are you and Katherine?"

"We're fine. She and Sarah enjoyed the helicopter ride. I'm glad about Rebecca, although I'd be happier if you were all safely out of New York."

Before William could respond, Jerry came over to him. "You aren't going to believe this, but based on their exit polls and first returns, U.S. Network is projecting that we'll take a majority of the House seats in New York State!"

"Really?" William asked.

"Yes, and now they're saying the same thing about Pennsylvania and maybe even Massachusetts."

"What? Carrie, I'll call you back. Are you watching this? Okay, I'll call you right back."

At the central television William heard Ryan Denning saying, "Our exit polls show that Trent Patterson's confession on our program this morning played a significant part in what we're now predicting will be the president's stunning victory in Pennsylvania."

William found it hard to believe, but then heard himself thinking, *Don't be amazed by God!*

A few miles away in the harbor, Sadim saw the same news and was appalled. *That stupid, cowardly Trent Patterson. Wafik should never have used him!* He looked at the television monitoring their stern and was glad to see the sleek helicopter that had recently landed. *Maybe we will need it after all.*

Slowly, without a tugboat to help, the *Fortson* edged away from the pier, leaving behind about a fourth of her crew, many of whom waved good-bye in the night, some crying. The captain conned the ship from the starboard bridge wing as they backed out of their slip. Soon they were inching out into the Hudson River, the only vessel moving in the harbor, but still unseen either by Wafik or by Sadim's radar.

The crew had rigged special lighting to fool a visual observer. This night the *Fortson* had a new bright light on the nose and a single range light on the stack, plus white lights rigged all around the stern. With the rest of the ship darkened, the *Fortson* had the appearance of a much larger freighter.

Five minutes later the captain turned the bow downriver, and the *Fortson* started her slow journey toward the harbor and the *Bright Star.*

At that same moment Sadim saw on two different networks that Florida and Maine were projected to go to the president's candidates. So far only two states appeared to be safe for the vice president, and each by only one congressman! Sadim's disbelief slowly turned to anger. *If the American people repudiate our demands, then they'll get what they deserve!* He was appalled by a report from a small town in Massachusetts, where they'd started ringing the bells in one church and the idea had spread to all the other churches in the area. Now, almost the entire state was ringing with church bells.

In the ballroom below ground level, Mary watched, holding William's hand, as their home state of North Carolina was projected to be squarely in the president's corner at a little after eight. Tears formed in her eyes as a reporter tried to talk live from outside St. Stephen's Church in Raleigh, where she had been the first member of their family to meet the Lord all those years before. The reporter was talking loudly because the famous bells of St. Stephen's had joined what was now confirmed to be tens of thousands of churches all across the country, ringing in joy and defiance for what was beginning to look like an astounding victory for those who put their trust in the Lord.

Sadim's anger turned to rage ten minutes later when the key states of Ohio and Illinois were predicted to have majority delegations with a biblical worldview. He called the captain's cabin on the telephone and simply said, "We're going. Fax to Wafik."

Just then his surface alert console lit up, and he quickly looked at the radar screen to see a large blip coming out from behind the building clutter well up the Hudson River, five miles away. The computerized evaluator analyzed the contact's size, slow speed, and the signature of its surface search radar and printed out "Freighter."

Sadim was not satisfied. As their own helicopter's blades began turning on the stern and Sadim pulled the detonator box closer to him, he typed on the computer for faxing to Wafik, "What is that ship in the river?"

Wafik had received the first message from the captain, and his heart had begun to race. He put the few things he needed in his bag and was about to leave the office, having seen the helicopter take off through his binoculars, when the second message came in. He put the bag down and walked to the windows, looked out but could see nothing in the lower portion of the Hudson River visible from his location. He wrote "Nothing moving here" on his laptop, pushed the fax button, picked up his bag, and left.

He climbed the several flights of emergency stairs to the roof of the World Trade Center as he had practiced a month before, opened the top door with a key supplied by a maintenance man Wafik had befriended with cash several weeks earlier, and let his eyes adjust to the dark. He appeared to be alone.

A minute later the jet helicopter appeared from the harbor below and was soon in its landing approach to the raised helipad at the center of the roof. As it came in, Wafik started to climb the stairs from the roof to the pad, but three men with guns suddenly materialized from the shadows, heading for the stairs themselves.

Wafik dropped to his knees and fired his automatic machine pistol. He took out all three men in one long burst, just as the craft touched down. He replaced the clip and looked quickly around, then sprinted up the stairs for the copter, threw in his bag, and settled quickly into one of the five seats in the rear. In another second they were off again, departing just above the three bodies sprawled on the roof.

The news in the ballroom grew even better. William had called Carrie again and was actually talking to Katherine when Tennessee and Kentucky went in their column. Then came news that Janet Sullivan would be a member of the new Congress in January.

Ryan Denning was saying with a clear note of disbelief in his voice, "Without a sharp difference in the West it now looks like the president's candidates could win a landslide victory in the House and also control the Senate, turning politics in this country completely around."

"Isn't it wonderful, Daddy?" Katherine asked over the phone.

"Yes, yes, it is. But you know what? I stand in awe of all the individual decisions it took to do this. Isn't God just incredible?"

"Yes, he is, Daddy. He is. He's certainly been good to us."

The helicopter returned to the *Bright Star* with Wafik, and Sadim took one last look around the command center. He then inserted a key into the primary console and switched the defense setting to automatic and the detonate setting to automatic/remote. The bomb would now be triggered automatically in the case of a direct threat, or he could do it by radio with his hand-held detonator from up to twenty miles away.

Sadim turned to the captain, who had joined him in the command center. "Let's go. On the flight to the *New Dawn*, take a good look at New York. We'll be the last few to see it!"

The *Fortson* continued her slow and methodical advance, trying to look very much like a freighter and not at all like a warship. The captain was still conning the ship himself on the bridge. Thomas Dobbs was in charge of the combat information center, which for the moment had only a surface plot feeding from the civilian radar into the navy computer, but he still suggested course corrections to the bridge to bring their starboard side right alongside the port side of the *Bright Star* at a range of only three hundred feet.

"Range three miles," Dobbs relayed over the intercom.

Hugh and Teri sat side by side at the missile console, both of their fingers required on the two triggers to fire the missiles when the time came. With Dobbs's announcement, Hugh glanced to the right, and Teri looked his way. Their eyes met and locked. Then, without saying a word, they turned back to their console.

Kolikov had been nervous before, but this was the worst time of all. They were still on the ship, but he knew the bomb could be set off by the computer thinking they were under attack. He knew there was a two-second delay built into that part of its threat evaluation so that no single piece of erroneous data could detonate it, but he also knew that computers could make mistakes. So he hurried to get into the back of the helicopter, and he hoped that Sadim would not linger.

For his part Sadim stood by the helicopter and took one last look at the ship moving in the dark night toward them. It certainly looked like a freighter. *And,* he thought, *whatever it is, it will be vaporized before it can do us any harm.*

He then handed their portable television to Wafik and crawled into the copter. He sat down and put the detonator between his feet, then flashed a thumb's-up to the pilot. They began to lift off, much to the relief of Kolikov.

"Mary, Rebecca, everybody." William motioned for everyone to gather around. "This is wonderful news tonight, so far. We give God all the thanks and all the glory. But I'm afraid with each new victory for our team, we're coming closer to a nuclear detonation in the harbor. So let's pray again, please, giving thanks for the changed hearts and the courage of our voters and praying for protection for this city."

Again they gathered around, this time holding hands, and prayed.

As the helicopter lifted off the *Bright Star,* Captain Robertson called out, "We've got an unfriendly helicopter departing the target. Henry, track him visually as long as you can. Feed the information to CIC. Thomas, be ready to find this guy quick when we bring up the radars. Hugh, are all the weapons systems ready?"

"Yes, sir," Hugh replied over the intercom.

"Very well," said the captain. "Bring the first two missiles out onto the rails."

Teri pushed several buttons on her console in CIC, and massive hydraulics in the front half of the ship engaged, opening huge blast doors and quickly running two of the especially modified missiles out onto the launcher. Once the missiles were in place, the launcher turned to the right and took up the slight angle of elevation that they had calculated from rough estimates should point them at the upper superstructure of the *Bright Star,* where everyone assumed the command and control equipment was located.

Simultaneously a round was loaded into the five-inch gun on the stern, and the starboard Gatling gun was placed on manual.

The *Fortson* was now only about three hundred yards off the port quarter of the *Bright Star* and closing quickly.

On the *Bright Star* the threat computer recognized the presence of a surface target closing on its search radar, but the target did not yet present any specific threat. The software called for retaliation at one hundred yards, however, threat or not. And of course instant detonation of the bomb in the face of any hostile action.

The helicopter rapidly opened up the range as it headed out to sea for its rendezvous with the *New Dawn*. Six miles. Eight miles. Kolikov felt better and better, and for the first time in two days allowed himself just a small thought about all his money.

On the television balanced on Sadim's lap, Ryan Denning was saying, "And so, ladies and gentlemen, based on the results that are already in, on our own extensive exit polls, and on the preliminary returns in the western states, the U.S. Network is now prepared to state that William Harrison has won his majority for Congress in what can only be called a stunning and frankly surprising landslide victory!"

The faces of the men in the helicopter were grim as Sadim reached down to pick up the detonator.

In the ballroom of the Park Empire Hotel there was hugging and crying. Mary and Rebecca embraced William as all three gave thanks to God. Leslie cheered and hugged Eunice so tightly that she almost crushed the new baby, who a few minutes before had been named William.

In Washington, Carrie, Katherine, and Sarah embraced.

All across America, tens of thousands of church bells pealed continuously.

The bow of the *Fortson* was just about to break the invisible one-hundred-yard envelope around the *Bright Star*. Captain Robertson was getting a feel for the range. He had never targeted missiles manually before, and to hit the superstructure with blind missiles was going to take some real seat-of-the-pants guessing and a lot of luck.

"All systems ready!" he said.

In the back of the helicopter, now fifteen miles away, Sadim grasped the detonator in his fingers and started to bring it up to his lap. "Say good-bye to New York, my friends." He smiled.

The *Fortson* entered the exclusion envelope. The computer evaluator on the *Bright Star* still registered no terminal threat—there was no radar lock-on, no laser illumination. So the computer did not detonate the bomb. But the *Fortson* had come too close. There was no presence of an air threat; Teri had been right in deducing that the ship only had anti-air missiles. But the Gatling guns were called into action. After the mandatory two-second delay to determine if the threat remained constant, the stern Gatling gun suddenly opened fire on the *Fortson* and raked the ship's starboard side from bow to midships.

The Fortson, like an old man-o-war, could not return fire until her batteries were alongside. The first raking by the Gatling gun luckily was at an elevation which was well below the bridge but right at the level of the main deck. It did significant damage, but the ship's weapons systems were still intact.

Sadim lowered the detonator into his lap and prepared to push the two buttons. Unseen by anyone, a mighty wind came out of heaven and moved across the face of the earth.

The Gatling gun waited its mandatory two seconds and recycled to fire another pass, this time aimed slightly higher. As the warship drew almost amidships, the gun raked the Fortson again, and this time a round damaged the starboard missile on the launcher and put rounds through the captain's cabin and Hugh Harrison's stateroom. Fortunately they were both at their duty stations one level above.

Just before the detonator settled into Sadim's lap, the helicopter was violently shaken by a strong wind, which the pilot had no way to anticipate. The copter was thrown from side to side, and the detonator rolled out of Sadim's lap and onto the floor. Sadim cursed and reached for the detonator again as the shaking died down.

Three lights went out on the console over Teri's head. "We've lost the number one missile," she reported over the intercom.

The Gatling gun swung back, waited, and then began its third run at a higher angle, which would devastate the bridge and CIC.

Just then Captain Robertson yelled "Fire!" Teri and Hugh pulled their triggers simultaneously, and like a broadside of old, the one undamaged missile, the five-inch gun, and their own Gatling gun opened fire blindly at point- blank range.

The five-inch shell only nicked the stern, but it was enough to detonate, destroying the *Bright Star's* Gatling gun as it was starting to fire again.

The computer on board now realized it had been attacked and started the two-second clock to detonate the nuclear bomb.

The single missile from the *Fortson* had been fired a split second too late; it was going to pass just in front of the freighter's superstructure without exploding. But the same strong wind that had battered the helicopter blew across the harbor as well and turned the *Bright Star* ever so slightly at anchor, exposing another few inches of the port superstructure to the missile's blind path. The warhead just grazed the exposed corner and exploded in a tremendous ball of fire, blinding everyone on the *Fortson.*

The automatic detonator clock in the control console, located against the wall of the superstructure where the missile exploded, disintegrated at a count of 1.75 seconds. The onboard receiver for Sadim's remote manual detonator was demolished a half second before his signal arrived.

The *Fortson* sailed on. Crouched and rubbing his eyes, the captain yelled, "Light off your radars. Find that helicopter and take it out!"

The massive air search radar above them began rotating while Teri pushed buttons to reload the one undamaged launcher rail with an antiaircraft missile. Hugh realized he was breathing again.

Ten seconds later Thomas Dobbs reported, "Contact identified, bearing one-six-five, range one-two miles."

Teri linked her fire control radars to the air search information. One of the powerful radars swiveled around and sent a pencil beam of energy out to illuminate the target. "Locked on!" she announced.

"Confirmed!" Hugh said.

"Fire!" called the captain.

There was another fireball from a second missile leaving the launcher.

As Sadim pressed the buttons on the detonator, they all looked away, out to sea, expecting a brilliant flash to turn night into searing day. But there was no flash. Sadim cursed again and turned to look back toward New York. There he could see a small illumination, like a fire, about where the *Bright Star* should be.

As he pushed the detonator buttons again and tried to figure out what he was seeing, there came another flash. But this time a bright star appeared to lift up and begin a quick journey in their direction. Instantly he knew what it was.

"Incoming missile!" he screamed.

The pilot immediately dove the helicopter toward the ocean and tried to run out to sea. But the fire control radar on the *Fortson* remained locked on, and Sadim watched in horror as the missile drew ever closer, homing on the reflected radiation bouncing off the helicopter's fuselage.

Kolikov screamed and tried to open the cabin door.

There was a tremendous explosion over the ocean, and the helicopter was no more.

The *Fortson* turned to starboard and circled the *Bright Star*, trying to assess the damage and the condition of the bomb. Looking through the big eyes, a signalman reported that he could see the bomb still resting on its tower, unharmed. But there were fires burning in the superstructure. Captain Robertson told Radio to send the precoded signals that meant: Best possible results. Command and control damaged. Bomb appears intact. Send fireboats. No radioactivity detected. Mission accomplished.

Within thirty seconds the message from the *Fortson* was relayed from the Situation Room to the ballroom in New York. Everyone clapped and cheered. Everyone except William and his sister Mary. They were standing together near the speaker phone when the message arrived. Silently they joined hands. William looked over at her and saw the same tears, the same peace, and the same joy he had first seen forty years ago in the pew at St. Stephen's Church.

"It's going to be all right," he whispered.

"I know," she said, tears streaming down her face.

"Not just here. I mean America," he explained.

"Yes, yes, I know," she said. Turning to face him, she smiled through her tears. "Thank God."

William offered her his handkerchief.

"If at any time I announce that a nation or kingdom is to be uprooted, torn down and destroyed, and if that nation I warned repents of its evil, then I will relent and not inflict on it the disaster I had planned. And if at another time I announce that a nation or kingdom is to be built up and planted, and if it does evil in my sight and does not obey me, then I will reconsider the good I had intended to do for it."

JEREMIAH 18:7-10

Afterword

My wife encouraged me for quite a while to write a book "about the government." Like most who consider that God made us and we do well to listen to his instructions, she and I share an increasing sense of frustration and pending disaster as our government in all three of its branches seems to jettison one proven biblical principle after the other. And we, like others, ask, "Why?"

Her advice was well taken, but how to approach the government in a work of fiction? I decided to write about a hypothetical administration several years from now, in which the events in the future are the direct results of seeds that are being sown today. After a short historic introduction, the perspective of the book shifts, as you know, to "just over the horizon," to the world we are creating for ourselves in only a few years if we don't mend our ways.

Having chosen that approach, I was then faced with two challenges. The first, sadly, was that as I wrote, trying to describe actions that our government will take in the future but that still seem far-fetched today, the challenge was to keep the fiction ahead of today's headlines! Over the past two years, as I would imagine some absurd situation or government action, reality kept catching up with me almost faster than I could write.

I must therefore issue an apology to the reader if some of the subjects and scenes in this book were neither pleasant nor godly. But I truly believe that they either represent our nation today or will all too soon. I tried to keep these situations to a minimum, while still communicating the tragic course on which I believe we are now set. Unless we recognize what we are doing to ourselves in all its reality, we cannot hope to be saved from it. I tried to use nonoffensive language to describe these situations, but I apologize if the concepts described still offended. Be aware that they offend me as well; but like a wound that needs to be cleaned to stop the infection, sometimes situations such as the ones described herein have to be brought out into the open and confronted in order to be healed.

The second challenge was much more positive. It involved rediscovering what the founding fathers really meant for this nation to be, and particularly the important role they saw for the Christian faith in our country. That challenge led me to study some of their original works and to read many excellent contemporary nonfiction books on this subject, which go to the heart of our problems today.

Most of these books are listed below. I am indebted to these authors for refining and polishing the many facets of the current debate on the proper role of faith in our government. Many, many of the statements by the fictional characters in this book began as concepts I first read about in these nonfiction works. It would be presumptuous of me to imply that these authors in any way approve of what you have read here; they have not. But hopefully on many issues this book can serve as a fictional complement to their works of nonfiction.

I am particularly indebted to David Barton and Gary DeMar. Both of these men and their staffs have spent untold hours over many years researching, documenting, and cataloging the original writings of our founding fathers, and both of them have written extensively on these subjects. Each one pointed me in fruitful directions on important but subtle distinctions. Most of the quotations from historic figures found in this book I read first in Barton's and DeMar's works. I highly recommend all of their books, and each man publishes a periodic newsletter.

I hope God both challenged and blessed you as you read this book, as he did me in writing it. My family hopes that your family will be blessed in considering anew the true foundations of this country, as well as the actions we must take as a nation in order to put our house in order.

If you are interested in reading more on this subject, I suggest the following books, all of which were helpful to me in considering the proper balance between faith and government, and the key role of Christianity in our American history. Most but not all of these are Christian in their worldview, but all will challenge you to a deeper understanding of the miracle we call America.

Barton, David. *The Myth of Separation*. Aledo, Tex.: WallBuilder Press, 1992.

Bauer, Gary L. *Our Journey Home*. Dallas: Word Publishing, 1992.

Bennett, William J. *The De-Valuing of America*. Colorado Springs: Focus on the Family Publishing, 1992.

Colson, Charles W., with Ellen Santilli Vaughn. *The Body*. Dallas: Word Publishing, 1992.

Colson, Charles W., with Nancy R. Pearcey. *A Dance With Deception*. Dallas: Word Publishing, 1993.

Colson, Charles W., with Ellen Santilli Vaughn. *Kingdoms in Conflict*. William Morrow/Zondervan Publishing House, 1987.

DeMar, Gary. *America's Christian History*. Atlanta: American Vision, Inc., 1993.

DeMar, Gary. *You've Heard It Said*. Brentwood, Tenn.: Wolgemuth & Hyatt, 1991.

Federer, William J. *America's God and Country.* Coppell, Tex.: FAME Publishing, Inc., 1994.

Grant, George. *The Family Under Siege.* Minneapolis: Bethany House, 1994.

Grant, George and Peter J. Leithart. *In Defense of Greatness.* Fort Lauderdale: Coral Ridge Ministries, 1990.

Guinness, Os. *The American Hour.* New York: The Free Press, 1993.

Knott, Paul D. *Remaking America: The Values Revolution.* Denver: Colorado Family Services, 1993.

Leithart, Peter J. *The Kingdom and the Power.* Phillipsburg, N.J.: Presbyterian and Reformed Publishing Company, 1993.

Lutzer, Erwin W. *Where Do We Go From Here?* Chicago: Moody Press, 1993.

Marshall, Peter, and David Manuel. *The Light and the Glory.* Tarrytown, N. Y.: Fleming H. Revell Company, 1977.